D0467204

A Love Story

Julie Anne Peters

A Love Story

DISCARD

Alfred A. Knopf
New York

Library of Congress Cataloging-in-Publication Data
Peters, Julie Anne.
Rage: a love story / Julie Anne Peters. — 1st ed.
p. cm.
Summary: At the end of high school, Johanna finally begins dating the girl she has loved from afar, but Reeve is as much trouble as she claims to be as she and her twin brother damage Johanna's self-esteem, friendships, and already precarious relationship with her sister.
ISBN 978-0-375-85209-1 (trade) — ISBN 978-0-375-95209-8 (lib. bdg.) —
ISBN 978-0-375-89358-2 (e-book)
[1. Family problems—Fiction. 2. Lesbians—Fiction. 3. Homosexuality—Fiction. 4. Sisters—Fiction. 5. Dating violence—Fiction. 6. Child abuse—Fiction. 7. Orphans—Fiction.] I. Title.
PZ7.P44158Rag 2009
[Fic]—dc22
2008033500

Printed in the United States of America

September 2009

10 9 8 7 6 5 4 3 2 1

First Edition

To Alyson Lacoste, who asked me to write this book
and I said, "No. Absolutely not."
Alyson is a very persuasive young woman.

RAGE

A Love Story

Joyland: Take 1

I'm wearing ultra-lowrider camo pants that barely cover my crack and if she looks she'll see the strap of my thong. This filmy beige crop top where, if I get a chill, my nipples will be my most outstanding feature. My hair looks sexy hanging in my eyes. My walk is killer. She can't not notice me.

I enter her field of vision, she does a slow double take, then stops talking with her clique, the LBDs, mid-sentence. Her eyes scrape me, skim me. Scratch and burn me. I feel her drink me in and salivate. I don't look. Not yet, not yet. My eyes shift slightly. ZAP. ZING. She's hooked. I smile her in.

She's mine.

. . .

Joyland: Take 2

Same sexy me. She detaches from the LesBo Dykes, or Les Beau
Dykes, and follows me to the parking lot. She gets in her car, stays
close to mine, runs a yellow light. She tracks me to the bank of the
river, to the edge of Fallon Falls. We park and get out. I step on the
slippery rocks, arms extended, balancing across the rushing water. I
spring to the shore, knowing she's on my scent. Around the side of
the boulder, I duck into a cave and wait. The smell of burnt sugar
tickles my nose. I hear her. She enters and steps in front of me—
reaches out a hand, both hands, and moves into me, slides her arms
around my waist, my bare skin, where nerve endings spark and
snap. There's no time to blink or moisten my lips.

"Hi. I'm Johanna."

She kisses me long and hard, awakens the ache of longing
inside me. Her lips are metal, then melon. Finally, finally she
lets me go. I gasp for breath and she smiles, a one-sided, sliver-

moon smile, and says, "Now that we have the introductions out of the way . . ."

. . .

"Johanna, dear?"

I jerk to the present.

"Mrs. Arcaro has passed," Jeannette says.

I missed it, the last breath of her life. A pang of guilt for daydreaming at this critical time stabs at my heart, but I chase it away. I give Mrs. Arcaro's frail hand a gentle squeeze and lay it on the sheet. I feel Mom smiling down on me from heaven.

As I'm leaving Memorial Hospice, I feel uplifted. I meant something to someone. Even if Mrs. Arcaro was a stranger, I'm the one who was there for her at the end.

I'm the one who stayed.

Chapter 1

I locate the room on the first floor where Mrs. Goins asked me to meet her. She was desperate, she said. So many seniors on the verge of not graduating, she said. Would I please tutor this one? A special one who needs special help with the senior project, she said.

I guess I'm meant to feel special, but I have my own stuff to finish—like that damn Film Studies class Novak talked me into.

I peek in. The classroom's empty. Did I get the room wrong? I've been losing whole blocks of time lately, spacing constantly. Where does life go when it's lost to you?

My backpack slips off my shoulder and a note falls out of the front pocket.

"I'm dropping Film Studies," Novak wrote.

An old note from the beginning of term. At the time I thought: Thanks. Abandon me, like everyone else has.

I hear Mrs. Goins coming before I see her. She's . . . rustling? Maybe her thighs are rubbing together or something. Since the first of the year, she's put on, like, twenty pounds. A lot of people call her Meaty Loins.

I would never do that.

The person behind Meaty Loins materializes.

"Johanna, this is Robbie Inouye. Robbie, Johanna Lynch."

Oh my God. Kill me now.

Robbie Inouye scares the hell out of me. He might be retarded, or challenged, or whatever terminology you use to dance around the truth. He's definitely messed. His eyes aren't symmetrical, or could it be his head's on crooked? The corners of his mouth are always caked with dried-up spittle and he lumbers, drags his feet like Frankenstein. He's not big. I'm five eight and he's shorter than me, but he *seems* huge.

Once upon a time, slow-moving Robbie would get jostled in the hall. I'd see people cut in front of him, making him stumble. Then came last November, right before Thanksgiving. I remember because Novak had been dumped by her boyfriend, Dante—again—and it was taking longer than usual to stanch the internal bleeding. We were in the restroom by the cafeteria. I got her past the point of slitting her wrists by reassuring her that she was an idiot for staying with him. "If I wasn't so fucking irresistible," she hiccuped, swiping at her nose, "I wouldn't attract vermin." "Exactly," I replied. I was late; I couldn't stay to hold her hand. "I'm better off without the asshole." "Too true." I had a midterm in trig and I'd blown the last quiz.

"Thank you, sweetie." Novak hugged me. "What would I do without you?" She held me so hard I couldn't breathe.

So I'm charging out of the restroom, dodging bodies and wedging through the mob of people exiting the cafeteria. Late bell rings and my class is two flights up. Then I hear this cry, more of a keen or wail. I look over and see a blur of skin, bone, and loose spittle, bared teeth. It's Robbie.

Someone had taken the instrument case he carries around. A guy was swinging it over his head and Robbie was lying on the floor like he'd been jumped. His books and papers had spilled down the stairs and one of his shoes was off.

Without warning, he rose up like Atlantis emerging from the sea, like Goliath in a rage, fists flailing, screeching and bellowing so loud my ears squinched. The guy with the case passed it to another guy, then a girl, a guy, the girl again. Robbie went crazy. He started swinging in all directions, clawing to get that case. He let out this high-pitched hawk screech, along with foam and spit, then busted the girl right in the chops with his fist. I felt the impact as she screamed and dropped the case.

The first guy made the mistake of retaliating for his girlfriend, hooking Robbie's neck from behind. Robbie whirled and smacked the guy's head into a brick wall.

I heard—*felt*—the crunch of bone.

I don't know why I did it, but the case was only about two feet away and I bent to retrieve it. Robbie grabbed the case and swung it up. The corner smacked me in the chin and slammed me into the stair rail.

His face came inches from my face, then his eyes rolled back into his head and he hauled off and whacked me on the shoulder. I crashed, tumbling down the stairs, feeling verte-brae crush.

My shoulder was dislocated. This was before my sister, Tessa, moved back home, so Novak took me to the Urgent Care Center.

The guy Robbie clobbered had a concussion, and his girl a fat lip, but none of us pressed charges. Unhappily ever af-ter, Robbie plodded the halls and people steered clear. Espe-cially me.

"Robbie, why don't you find a seat?" Mrs. Goins says.

Franken Psycho's case brushes my leg and I jump back.

Before I can get a squeak out, Mrs. Goins lowers her voice and goes, "Thank you for doing this, Johanna. He needs to graduate."

So do I. "Mrs. Goins, my work schedule changed. I just found out today, and now I have to go in at two. Um, every day, I think." My eyes shift to Robbie and I see he's helped himself to the teacher's desk and is rolling in the office chair. He pulls open the top drawer and removes a stapler.

Mrs. Goins looks at me over her granny glasses. "I thought I could count on you."

My face flares. She sponsored the Youth Service Club when I was in it, before Mom got sick. . . .

"You're the first person I thought of." The pleading in her eyes. Or is it desperation?

"I—I guess I can change my schedule back."

She rests her hand on my forearm. "Thank you, Johanna."

"Get out of my chair, Robbie," Mrs. Goins orders him. He's stapled together a bunched-up wad of his t-shirt, and as he yanks it apart, staples ping the window.

She motions him to a desk up front and he grabs his battered brown instrument case. It's the size of a trombone or saxophone.

"Robbie, Johanna is going to get you through the senior project so you can graduate with your class. She'll be tutoring you. Do you know what 'tutor' means? It means—"

"I know what it means," Robbie says in this sluggish monotone. Robotically, his head rotates, and his eyes fix on me.

A streak of phantom pain shoots through my arm. *Please don't hurt me.*

"He has the essay to finish. I'm not sure he's even started it. Robbie," she carps at him, "have you even started writing the essay?"

He doesn't answer.

Chill. Don't piss him off. She removes a sheet of paper from her messenger bag and waves it at me. Robbie extends his legs in front of him so I have to step over them. He raises them enough to make me half trip.

Asstard. Wait, I feel bad calling a retard an asstard. Wait, not really.

Is that a smirk on his face?

Mrs. Goins glances at her watch. "I have a student conference in five minutes, so I'll leave you to it. He needs to have the essay finished and handed in to the English department by next Friday." As she bustles by, she adds, "Robbie, do this one last assignment and you're out of here. Cooperate with Johanna."

I skim over the sheet. Oh yeah. I'm familiar with it. Name. Date. In no less than a thousand words, describe your best moment and your worst moment in high school and what each taught you about yourself.

We found out what the senior project would be last September at our first senior assembly. They told us we had to have it in by April first to graduate. It's already May.

"Cooperate with Johanna," Robbie says.

"What?" When I glance up over the sheet at him, he eyes me warily. I move behind the teacher's desk to put something solid between us. "Did you bring any paper?"

His arms fling out to the side and I lurch back, jamming into the whiteboard tray. Ow.

He smiles vacantly.

What's with this guy? I flop into the rolling chair and it almost tips over. He sniggers. "Do you have anything to write with?" I ask.

"Cooperate with Johanna," he says.

I tug open the top drawer of the desk and find a green mechanical pencil. There are sheets of white copy paper in a lower drawer, so I remove a few and click out a length of lead on the pencil.

Robbie watches me the whole time, mesmerized. I get up and hand him the paper and pencil. He holds the pencil up to his nose and sniffs. He does the same with the paper.

Weird.

Can he read? Well, hopefully, since he's a senior in high school. But half the jocks can't read. *Bad Johanna. Shouldn't stereotype.* Robbie has probably been mainstreamed, or whatever you call it.

I read to Robbie, "In no less than a thousand words, describe your best moment and—"

"Your worst moment of high school and what each taught you about yourself," he drones.

I give him the xeroxed copy of the senior project. *Can he write?*

"Johanna, Johanna, Johanna," he deadpans. He straightens in the desk and prints a series of words across the page. I peer over to see what he's writing.

He covers it up. Not before I catch a glimpse of my name. He's spelled it "Joe Hana." He wrote something bigger at the bottom of the page.

He lifts his arm so I can see. Two words: FUCK YOU.

Tutoring session over. I snatch my backpack off the desk and head for the door.

"Hey!"

I don't stop.

"Hey," he calls louder. The desk creaks.

"What?" I whirl.

He blinks fast. "I didn't mean you." His eyes bounce around for a second, then focus on something behind me.

I pivot. All the blood rushes to my face. My head and brain and ears explode.

It's her.

How long has she been standing there?

"What are you doing?" she asks.

I open my mouth to speak, to say the first words I've ever spoken to Reeve Hartt. Then realize she isn't talking to me.

Robbie says, "Cooperate with Johanna."

Reeve's eyes flash on my face for a second. It's fleeting, but I think she actually notices I'm here.

"We have to go, Robbie," she murmurs, and takes off. Not far. She stops and waits. I could reach out and touch her. I could take her hand. . . .

Robbie scrabbles to stand and snags his case. He trundles over to me at the door and I step aside to let him pass. He thrusts out the paper and pencil.

"Later, dude," he says. His arm clips my shoulder, and that phantom pain flares through me.

Reeve takes off with Robbie tramping behind her. At the end of the hall, at the intersection, he says something to her and she spins around and slugs him in the chest.

I flinch and squeal. Reeve shoots a dark look my way.

I leap back into the classroom as my heart gallops in my chest.

So close. I clench my pack to me and try to catch my breath.

What's their connection? I wonder. She knows him. They can't be together. Please. Robbie's retarded. Reeve's gay.

And mine.

But only in Joyland.

So far.

Chapter 2

I know I locked the door before I left for school. I'm positive.

Novak's sitting at the table, her laptop open and papers spread out. "Hope you don't mind. Tessa let me in."

It's still strange to have Tessa back. Sort of like old times, but not.

Novak doesn't even glance up as I sling my backpack to the floor and go, "You won't *believe* what I have to do—"

She sticks up an index finger, like, Hang on. She keys rapid-fire.

How long has she been here? Her knitting is strung from the divan to the coffee table. She glances over her shoulder, gets up fast, and gathers the yarn and needles, shoving them into her bag.

"What are you making?" I ask.

"A chastity belt."

"Better use steel wool."

"Oh, caw. It's actually something for the baby."

She returns to the laptop and I sprawl out lengthwise on the divan. I dig in the cushions for the TV remote and punch the power button.

Novak says, "Wait. I can't write with that on."

I remote it off. I twist my head to watch her, her arching back, her long hair streaming down over her shoulders, all silk and shine. A catch in my stomach makes me ache and I turn away.

Maybe once, I wanted her.

"How was hell?" she asks, still keying.

"You'd know if you showed up occasionally."

"I'm almost done. I just have this one paper to finish and I'm out of there."

I can't stop looking at her. The ache slithers up between my—

No. Stop it. You're just lonely.

"I brought your mail up," Novak says. She motions with her chin to a stack on the counter. I get up and sift through it. No college acceptances. Credit card apps and magazine subscriptions, all of them for Tessa or Martin.

Novak's reading over what she wrote. She looks up and air-smooches me. I stick out my tongue in a gag. We have this running game where she pretends she's into me and I fend off her disgusting advances.

It was always fun—until Dante.

"Mind if I turn on the TV now?"

She holds up a hand, then lowers it. Permission.

This low divan is the only piece of furniture I bought for myself. Tessa took the sofa bed when she moved out of the apartment to go to college in Minnesota. She brought back a husband.

I surf around, hit a movie in Spanish. A scene where these two are doing it under the sheets and moaning. It catches Novak's attention and she says to me, "Horndog."

"Speak for yourself."

"I am."

She resumes proofing.

Me and Reeve. God, she looked hot today. The outfit I'd conjured up in Joyland is the kind of thing Reeve wears. Lowriders and transparent tops, miles of exposed skin. I'd never even go without a bra. Once I wore a thong to school and felt uncomfortable all day, like rope was riding up my butt. I was scared everyone could tell by the way I walked.

The guy flings off the sheets and says something in Spanish. The señorita is *muy bonita.* She has on this filmy negligee. Thick mascara and eyeliner. I just love the way Reeve does her eyes. Some days she paints on eye shadow with stripes and patterns, like animal prints or abstract art. I choose my seat in the cafeteria so I can consume her at lunch. She has these wide anime eyes.

I've figured out that her moods are all in her eye art. If she's happy, there are pastel skies and rolling waves. Anger is jagged storms, big black slashes. One day she drew a teardrop below each eye and glued a blue jewel inside.

Is it hot in here, or what? I caterpillar back far enough to reach the doorknob and crack open the door. Below, in the main house, I hear the sliding door to the patio roll open and closed. Hurried footsteps. A car door slams and the engine starts. "What was Tessa doing home?" I ask Novak.

"Hmm? Oh, she says she was really nauseated today. You know."

I found out about my possibly future niece or nephew when I was down in the garage doing laundry. Martin came in with an armload of towels and said, "You can congratulate me now."

"For what?" I said. "Being dorky?"

He dumped the load on my head. "I assume Tessa told you."

"That you're a dork?" I said, digging out. "Nope. Figured it out all by myself."

"We're preggers." His smile lit up the night.

"Cool. Congrats," I said. I almost added, I hope it takes this time. God. I almost said that.

Novak comes over and lifts my legs to slide in under. A tingle spreads through my belly. "What are you doing?" she asks.

"Watching air circulate."

Novak sighs. "I swear, I'm going to hook you up."

I cast her a lethal glare. "It'll be your last act on Earth." The one time, the only time, she fixed me up was with this shaved and pierced feminazi chick who ranted all night about taking down the patriarchy and reclaiming her uterus.

Novak's quiet.

"What?"

"Can I ask Dante over?"

"Now?"

She hunches her shoulders to her ears.

Fuck-fest time. I need to get out of here anyway. "Keep it down, okay? Tessa will be on my case for running a whore-house."

Novak smiles. "I can take care of Tessa." She pulls out a crochet hook and slits it across her throat.

When we were younger, Tessa tried to teach me how to knit and crochet too, but I'm a spaz. I couldn't even cast on, or whatever it's called.

I push to my feet and Novak adds, "Thanks. Oh, by the way, you might be getting a call from Amanda Montero."

"Why?"

"I told her about your place."

"Told her what?"

"Well . . . she'll pay you."

It takes me a minute. "I'm not pimping my apartment. Novak—"

"Okay. I just thought you'd want to earn a little extra cash."

"I don't." Not like that. I head for my room.

"You could watch. At this rate, it's the only action you'll ever get. Just kidding," she calls. "Not really."

I say under my breath, "Fuck you."

"You know you want to."

I close my bedroom door. It's so hard being gay—I don't care what anybody says. Being gay and a virgin is just stupid and wrong. When I told Novak I was a lesbian, she was, like, "So, what's your point?" We were fifteen, just starting high school. Mom hadn't been diagnosed yet, and Tessa was gone. I came out to Novak the same year Tessa lost her first baby.

Why am I thinking this? There's no connection.

I wade through the piles on my floor for a clean shirt.

This is Tessa's second pregnancy.

I change into my skinny jeans and slip on checkered Converses. In the living room, Novak is lying on the divan, her arm flung across her eyes.

"Don't smoke, okay? Tell Dante that." Last time it reeked of pot in here for a week. Like living inside a bong.

"Love you, Johanna Banana. You juicy fruit." Novak lifts her arm and kiss-kisses me.

I should tell her, Game over.

I snag my backpack and keys, figure I'll hang at the mall for a while. No, not the mall. I'll go to the hospice. The stack of mail is still on the counter, so I scoop it up.

The apartment steps are wood and warped; they sag with the slightest pressure. Mom and Dad had big plans for fixing up the apartment over the garage. Then life had different plans, like them dying.

I draw open the patio door and slip inside the main house. The shades are drawn; it's dark and chilly, and the paint fumes make me cough. Martin keeps the thermostat at Polar. Tessa's painting the living room purple. Excuse me—aubergine. *Should she be painting when she's pregnant?*

I set the mail on the table and spot the slim stack Tessa's collecting for me. My car insurance. Bank statement. A twenty-dollar bill.

I keep telling her she doesn't need to give me money. I leave it. I drop the mail into my pack and head out. A flash of red ribbon in the trash can by the counter catches my eye and I fish it out.

It's the loop of the ribbon that was tied to the cast of my

handprint. A piece of the cast—my right pinkie—is now a shard. I dig out a bigger chunk, the palm and thumb. On the counter, I puzzle all the pieces back together. I made this in kindergarten. I can still feel the cold, squishy mush of the plaster of paris between my fingers. That cast has been hanging on the wall in our dining room forever.

Tessa comes back into my life just when I'm over her bailing. And she trashes my handprint. I run my index finger across the tiny fingers, the smooth palm, and this lump rises in my throat. It's just a handprint.

I made it for Mother's Day.

I sweep the plaster pieces over the edge of the counter into the trash. As soon as I can afford my own place, I'm gone. *You hear that, Tessa? Me. I'll be the one who leaves.*

Chapter 3

Robbie shuffles in ten minutes after the last bell, looking like he has no idea where he is, who he is, what he is. I know the feeling.

I wonder if people like him can remember stuff.

People like him. *God, I'm so mean.*

He crosses the room and stands at the desk. This bubble of spit clings to his lower lip and I want to clue him, lick my lip where the spit is so he'll wipe it off or suck it in.

"Do you want to sit down?" I ask.

He spins a full circle and spirals into a desk. Wow, that was kind of . . . balletic? Except for his case smashing into the desk beside him. The thud pongs around the room and lands in my chest.

From his pants pocket he withdraws a wad of string and shakes it out. He starts threading it through his fingers.

This is *so* not getting the essay written. I get up and hand him his paper and pencil. I brought lined paper and a regular pencil. A pen too.

He winds the string around and through his fingers.

"Hey!"

He jerks aware, untangles the string and lowers it to his lap. I set the essay on the desk.

"Your best moment," he says, staring at the paper and writing utensils.

"Right. Start over."

He glances up. "No. Yours."

"What do you mean?" *If he's going to be belligerent or something . . .*

"I mean," he says slowly and deliberately, "what was your best moment?"

"I lied on my essay."

He cracks a grin. "What did you write?"

I think back. "I wrote about this time I studied really hard and got one hundred percent in AP Physics. I can't even spell AP."

The grin widens.

"See, it doesn't matter what you write. Just not . . . my name. Or 'fuck you.' I have to hand this in to Mrs. Goins."

"Meaty Loins," Robbie says.

I suppress a smile.

"In no less than a thousand words," he adds.

"Right."

He peers down at the paper and scrunches his forehead. I return to the desk. I can feel him staring at me. He doesn't actually ever make eye contact; more like fixes on my mouth.

"What's your best moment?" he asks.

Didn't we just have this conversation?

Robbie says, "Don't lie."

Brain freeze. Seriously. I can't think of anything.

Robbie waits and waits. My mind seizes. Finally a thought breaks free, but the only words that form are "I don't think I've had a best moment."

He nods once. "Me neither. I have a worst moment," he says. "I have a whole bunch of worst moments."

"Good. I mean, not good. That you have bad stuff in your life. Start with the worst. Pick one of those."

He centers the paper on the desk, turning and twisting until the corners are equidistant and squared, for God's sake, then takes a year to decide—pencil or pen? Pencil or pen? Pen! I watch him write his name in the upper-right-hand corner. He has nice handwriting for a guy. Is that sexist? Martin's writing is completely illegible, which I only know because he wrote me a note once: "You're going to be an aunt! I'm calling you Auntie Mojo."

That was the first time, right after Tessa moved home.

Robbie scratches his scalp behind his ear. "How do you spell 'murder'?"

"What?"

He writes something.

"Who got murdered?"

Robbie raises his head a fraction of an inch. "My mother. I killed her."

The back of my head smacks the whiteboard as the chair slips. It must bruise my brain, because when I come to, I'm sidestepping out the door, telling Robbie, "I forgot something in my locker. I mean, my car. I mean, I'll be right back."

I bolt. My projectile body smashes into another moving object and the collision sends us both flying.

"What the hell?" Hands press against my shoulders. "What the hell!"

Oh my God. My mind and muscles engage. I've knocked over Reeve. I'm . . . on top of her.

I clamber off. My voice catches somewhere between my stomach and throat. *I touched Reeve Hartt, full body contact.*

I jump to my feet and hold a hand out to her. "Sorry."

She twists away and pushes to her feet.

"Really," I say. "It's . . . it's him. He's . . ." My eyes dart back into the room, where Robbie is still sitting, hunched over, writing. "He says he killed his mother."

"What?" Reeve's face contorts. She leans forward to peer into the room and for an instant I think she'll rush me, storm in, maybe bump me, ignite me. Her feet stay planted. "He's a head case," she says. "Did you think he was serious?"

I open my mouth. Suck up air.

All these years. All my imagined scenes and stimulations. The almost dreamlike quality of her, her skin all milky translucence. The rise of her breasts over the low-cut string camisole. My attention wavers. We lie together, on the hallway floor. She gazes into my eyes.

I swallow hard. "He wrote it," I say, "on his senior essay."

Reeve's eyes slit. "Butt nugget!" she calls into the room. "Get your dumb ass out here."

Her eyes meet mine again and hold. She seems to ratchet down a notch. Or I do? I smile. And hiccup.

Robbie's essay flaps in front of my face. "It's not done," he says. "A thousand words is ten times ten times ten."

I take it from him and skim the three sheets he's filled, front and back. He wrote a lot. A sentence fragment jumps out at me: ". . . cut up her body into bit size peeces and ate it."

Oh my God. He is a psycho.

Reeve says, "You told her you killed our mother?"

I look from him to her. *Our?*

A grin sneaks across Robbie's face but is snatched away when Reeve grabs his shirt, balls a fist, and punches him in the face. Hard. I feel the floor tilt.

"He's a liar," Reeve says to me. "Don't believe anything he tells you." She's twisting his shirt in her fist, choking him. "What else did you say, you dickwad? If you said anything about me . . ."

"He didn't." I reach over and press down on Reeve's wrist. "He didn't say anything about you."

She stares at my hand on her arm. "Why'd you do that?" She jerks away.

"I . . ." But she's not talking to me. Her eyes have resettled beyond me, on Robbie.

He recites, "Cooperate with Johanna."

Reeve backs up a step. "Time to fly." She pivots and charges down the hall, the frayed hem of her jeans sweeping the floor. Robbie lingers, like he wants to say something else. I want to ask if he's okay. Reeve turns and screeches, "Shut up, Robbie!"

Bling's is packed with tweeners. I swear they get younger and meaner every day. If I say, "Can I help you?" they give me this look, like, *Pleez. You? You suck.* My job at the mall is, basically, trolling for shoplifters. I clock in and immediately spy a clique of streaky blondes who are all dressed in coordinating outfits, trying on bracelets and fingering necklaces, removing earrings off the rack as they spin it. To cause distraction. So obvious. One of them drops two cards of gold hoops into her purse.

I mosey over. "Can I help you?"

She lunges toward the aisle. I block it. Frantically, she scans for her buds, who've scattered. *Nice.*

Adjusting the earring cards on the table, I lower my voice and say, "You won't get out the door. Everything is marked with an antitheft code. The alarm will go off and you'll get busted."

Her lower lip quivers.

I add, "When I look away, you're going to put the earrings back."

I retreat a step and hear her purse unsnap.

They aren't always so dumb. I mean, *come on.* Who'd pay to code six million pieces of junk jewelry? I catch her in my peripheral vision, skittering out the door.

I can't wait to go to college so I never have to work again. The biggest sale I ever rang up was $16.12. I wish I could spend all my spare time at the hospice, but volunteer work won't pay for tuition.

The mall closes at ten, and Shondri, my boss, says she'll clear the register and do the deposit. On my way past the food court, the smell of Chinese makes my stomach grumble. Dinner was a snarfed bag of chips.

But I know one place where there's always food—and socially redeeming work.

* * *

The hospice never closes. When Mom was here, I sat with her all night, every night, until the end. "Hi, Johanna," Jeannette greets me from the front desk. "You're here late."

"Couldn't sleep," I fib.

She's eating a burrito the size of a blimp. My eyes must glom on to it, because she says, "There's plenty in the kitchen." Jeannette dabs her mouth with a napkin. "Miguel's donated tonight."

Local restaurants are always bringing leftovers to the hospice. It's sort of weird to think about—there's never a food shortage for people who mostly can't eat.

I wander through the empty cafeteria to the kitchen, where one of the nurses is chowing down a chimichanga while reading a paperback. He glances up and smiles. "Johanna, right?"

Yikes. I don't remember his name. "Hey . . . you," I say lamely. The badge on his scrubs is covered by a jean jacket. He's either coming in or going out.

A tray of taquitos warms on the stove behind him, and as I lift up the foil, his cell rings. "Babe," he speaks into it. "Where are you?" He gets up and leaves with his chimichanga.

Solo mío. I find a plate and help myself. Jeannette wanders in. "I'm sorry about Mrs. Arcaro," she says. "I know you were close."

I nod and swallow. Mrs. Arcaro came to the hospice during the time Mom was here. I could've cared for Mom at home until the end, but Tessa decided I wasn't capable. Even though I'd been doing it by myself the whole time she was sick.

"Frank's been agitated all day." Jeannette pours herself a cup of coffee. "Maybe you could drop in and see him?"

"Sure," I say. Frank's this grizzled old guy about ninety years old who has dementia and diabetes and I don't know what all. He doesn't have any family, or at least no one who cares enough to visit. Too many people die alone in this world.

On my way to the ward, I stuff the rest of my taquito into my mouth. Frank's laid out in bed, masturbating.

Ew. "Frank?" I say softly. "It's Johanna."

He rubs his wanker. It's dark and wrinkled. "Frank?"

Nothing is really happening. No hardening of the, you know, arteries. For privacy, I pull his blanket over his lap. His eyes are far away and he has a quirky smile on his face.

It makes me smile inside.

Go for it, Frank.

Chapter 4

Joyland: Take 3

We're in this amazing bed, naked, spinning around and around—because the bed is round. Reeve is kissing me and I'm all over her, running my hands through the hair on her head and between her legs. She's soft and firm and arching into me.

She says, "Johanna. I love you. I want you."

"I want you too," I say. "I want you bad."

The bed spins and spins. We spin harder and faster, out of control. She screams, "Don't stop!"

"I won't. I promise."

She expels a breath like she's emptying her lungs or cleansing her soul. I breathe her in and out. I run a red silk scarf over her flat belly and around her breasts and in between them. She unties the red ribbon in my hair to unleash my ponytail and my hair splashes like a waterfall over her face. She holds it back and I kiss her. I kiss her so soft and gentle it's mist and fog. It's spray. The beating of my *heart is constant and steady, sharp as knuckles on wood and metal and pounding on wood and pounding, pounding. . . .*

. . .

Knocking? Someone is knocking.

What time is it?

I hold myself for one last surge, then stagger out of bed to answer the door.

Dante looms behind Novak, grinning like the fool he is. "Hey ya, Joho," he says.

I hate that he uses Novak's nickname for me.

"Hi, sweetie." Novak kisses me on the cheek. "We came to say hi. Hi." *She's high.* She slides past me into the apartment and I consider shutting the door in Dante's face. He's tall and thin, with razed hair and a shadow beard. His clothes are always the same—tight black tee and loose jeans that creep down his butt. One eyebrow is pierced.

I loathe this jerk for all the hurt he's laid on my friend. But she loves him. I have to honor that stupid fact.

"What time is it?" I check my watch. 7:46—p.m. I vaguely remember deciding I'd skip Film Studies to sleep in.

Dante tramps to the refrigerator and yanks it open, removes a can of Fresca. My Fresca. He pops the top and slugs it down.

Novak rests her head on my shoulder. "I love you, Johanna Banana," she says.

"Give me a minute," I tell her. "I'll bail."

"You don't have to." Novak snuggles in tighter. She's too close and I'm too needy.

I'm also hot and sticky. I beat a path to my bedroom to

change from my drawstrings into jeans, wishing, not for the first time, that my bedroom door had a lock. Novak knows it's off-limits, but I don't trust Dante.

When I emerge into the living room, Dante has Novak's shirt up around her neck and her bra unlatched. I snatch a hoodie off the divan and yank the door shut behind me.

The door whooshes open. Novak says, "Johanna," breathing hard. She wrestles her shirt down over her boobs and hands me something. "You can borrow it," she says.

They're keys to her Crossfire. "You're kidding."

She smiles weakly. "What would I do without you?"

"Get a hotel?" I say.

She blows me a kiss and shuts the door.

I sit in the Crossfire for two or three minutes, swooning, scared to crank the ignition. Plus, I don't know where to go. The hospice? The tweenie town mall? What a waste of a hot car.

Slowly, carefully, I shift into first and inch away from the curb. I drive around the neighborhood, getting used to the gears, the feel of the clutch and brake. The Crossfire was Novak's eighteenth-birthday present from her parents. My parents didn't quite make it to mine. The interior is white leather, no backseat. Too cramped for sex. But there's an MP3 player, GPS, OnStar.

Mickey D's is all lit up, a queue of cars at the drive-thru, honking and flashing their lights. Someone moons out the top of a convertible.

I idle at a red light, accidentally gunning the engine. A guy hollers, "Novak, you cunt! Suck my bone!"

I auto the window down and flip him the bird. Guys are so . . . typical.

An idea springs loose and I zip into the far-left lane, gunning for the Interstate.

I only know about Rainbow Alley from a flyer in film class. The Gay/Straight Alliance was hyping this horror-movie night at Rainbow Alley. I was too gutless to join the GSA, mostly because I knew Reeve was in it. Reeve and the other LBDs. Those girls, their tribal unity, intimidate me. Reeve doesn't just scare me. She terrifies me. It gets worse every day, this smoldering want, my crushing need. I think I've been in love with Reeve Hartt since the first time I saw her.

Why can't I just approach her, talk to her? The ache I feel every time I see her. It's killing me.

In downtown Denver, I drive past 1050 Broadway three times. No neon pink triangles or flashing rainbow flags. But there is an actual alley behind the building, so I veer into it.

Suddenly, the night opens up like Narnia. Lights glow, music blares.

Two people come racing down the alley, one squealing, the other chasing her with a pump water gun. They run in front of me and the guy with the gun thunks on the hood of the Crossfire.

"Hey!"

"Sorry." He holds the water gun over his head and sticks his face in my open window. "Tight wheels."

"Thanks."

He streaks off again.

I take a deep breath. Okay, I can do this. Now or never? Now. Cars and SUVs hog the cramped parking lot. The back door to the two-story building is propped open with a chair, and voices and music float out. On the fire escape stairs, a couple of girls are cuddling and kissing.

Can I do this?

Yes! Dammit.

I lick my dry lips. *Will I see her?*

The door to the Crossfire opens and my legs swing out. The girl from the chase-down says, "Bitchin' car." Her shirt's soaked.

"Thanks," I say. "It's not mine."

Her eyes waffle. "You jacked it?"

I stare at her nipples. "It's a friend's."

She eyes the interior over my shoulder. "Bitchin' friend. Introduce me."

I laugh, and so does she. She's a boy dyke, or whatever, with a shaved head and hairy legs. Not really my type, but what *is* my type? I have only one: Reeve Hartt.

"You here for the karaoke?" she asks.

"Um . . . I guess."

"Starts soon. I'm Tiffany." She extends her hand. "T."

"Johanna," I say, shaking it. She holds my hand longer than a simple greeting requires. Testing, feeling out the possibilities.

I loosen my grip.

T sighs and says, "Come if you're coming."

Am I? The lock on the car door clicks. I guess I'm coming.

The kissers on the stairs part to let us through. They nod at Tiffany and check me out. What do they see?

Tall girl, broad shoulders, average weight, longish, straight hair, tight jeans, sleeveless shirt. Converses. God, I should've dressed more sexy. I should've put on makeup.

T slows at the top of the stairs and leans against the door to let me pass. She checks me out the whole way. My eyes avoid hers as they soak up the scene.

A rectangular room, painted all different colors, a mural on the far wall. I can read the letters: PRIDE. There are two long couches and armchairs, people lounging. A girl sitting on a boy's lap. A guy fiddling with a microphone in the center of the room puts his mouth to it and says, "Pick up. Shut up." People begin to claim folding chairs and scrape them around to sit closer to the karaoke machine.

T touches my back. "See you," she says, and takes off.

People are talking and laughing, flipping through the karaoke notebooks. Reeve materializes out of the mural. She's playing pool with two other girls behind a beaded curtain.

She bends over to line up her shot and I can see clear down her halter. One of the girls with her I know from school. Brittny? Britt? She and Reeve were together last year, then they weren't.

Someone nudges me and I gulp a can of air.

"In or out?"

A kinetic surge draws me in, toward her. I stall under a string of twinkling lights.

I can't see if Reeve makes her shot. Her eye makeup tonight is dark and heavy. She's intense. Guarded.

Britt saws her cue stick back and forth over her hand

three, four times, and strikes the white ball. It smacks one of the striped balls, sending it careering into a side hole. Britt whoops.

Reeve's expression doesn't alter, even when she glances up and catches my eye. Or does it?

Does she recognize me? She circles the table, her back to me, and lines up her next shot.

Joyland: Take 4

She turns slowly toward me. Her eyes, they drink me up. She closes the distance between us and asks, her voice low and sultry, "Do you play?"

I smile. "I never have," I say.

She knows the truth when she hears it. "Do you want to learn?"

My smile widens. "I do."

I sweat and shiver at the same time. She doesn't speak, but the vibes between us are fingernails on a chalkboard, increasing their pressure and volume until my ears whine and my teeth hurt.

She leads me to the table. Hands me her cue stick and slides around behind me. All eyes in the room are on her—us. All the girls want her, and some of the guys too. She takes me in her arms and I drop the stick on the floor.

34

She laughs. So do I. I retrieve the stick. She sets it on the table.

Her lips start out hard as molded plastic, then turn soft as padded felt.

She runs her hands up under my shirt and the twinkling lights explode.

. . .

"Excuse me." A guy touches my arm. "I have to use the john."

I step aside to let him pass.

The karaoke blares and I'm swarmed; I lose sight of Reeve. As the crowd clears, I see her kissing a nameless girl. The girl has no face, no arms or legs or physical presence. No meaning to me.

A sharp edge gouges my arm.

"You want the book?" a guy asks. The black three-ring binder. The karaoke songbook.

"No, thanks."

Everything's tilting, listing in place. I refocus.

Where is she?

I scan, but don't see her. Maybe what I saw was a . . . projection? The person she was kissing was me, the girl I want to be.

The cue sticks are on the table, as if her game was interrupted. There, at the top of the stairs leading to the exit, I catch a glimpse of her ice blue halter.

A mob of people cram the doorway, all coming in for karaoke. I murmur, "Excuse me. Excuse me. Sorry," as I maneuver my way through. "Ow!" a girl yelps when I step on her foot.

"Sorry." I wince.

She smiles. "That's okay. Hi."

Reeve is bounding down the stairs, the other two girls ahead of her. She leaps from the bottom step, throws back her head, and cries, "Yee-ow-eeee!" at the top of her lungs. She smacks each of the girls on the back, sending Britt stumbling forward into an SUV and the other girl tripping. Reeve dances in a circle.

Britt hollers, "Reeve, dammit! That hurt."

Reeve laughs and laughs.

I stand on the landing, at the railing, breathing in her laughter. She slows near an SUV and pounds on the hood, as if she's beating out excess energy.

Britt goes, "What is your problem?"

Reeve says, "You."

The other girl, who isn't anyone, who isn't even there, unlocks the car door. Reeve dances over to her and grabs a clump of her hair. She yanks the girl's head back, gazes down into her face, and kisses her. I black out.

When I come to, Reeve is staring at me.

"Butt brain!" she yells. "Move ass."

Robbie emerges from under the stairs. He ambles to the car. Tossing his case over the seat to Reeve, he squishes into the back with her.

As the car pulls away, Reeve's head pops up through the moon roof. She cups both hands around her mouth and calls, "Cooperate with Johanna!"

OMG. She knows my name!

Chapter 5

The apartment door is hanging wide open. I barrel up the stairs and stop. There's a tall, shadowy figure in the kitchen, behind the refrigerator door.

Retreat? Go downstairs? Call 911? Scream? The guy leans back. It's Dante, buck naked. He shuts the refrigerator door and says, "Joho." He hitches his chin at me, then guzzles the beer. My apartment reeks. He burps. "Whassup?"

"Where's Novak?"

He notices he's dangling all over and steps behind the counter. Novak appears in the hallway, also naked, tossing her hair over one side of her head with her arm.

She's illuminated by light filtering through the hall from the bathroom. Her eyes meet mine, but I can't hold them. She has smaller breasts than I imagined, probably because she always wears push-up bras. Her hair is reddish blond . . .

down there. She drops her arms and straightens her back, like she doesn't mind me looking, like she's *inviting* me to look.

Dante skitters past Novak, covering his privates, clipping her arm and spinning her sideways.

"You were in my room," I say.

Novak crosses her arms over her breasts.

Fuck, I mime. My glare reams her out.

"Hang on." She backs up and disappears into the room—*my* room—behind Dante. I fling my pack on the divan. *Damn. Damn her!*

In a moment Dante comes out dressed, Novak cowering behind him. "Later, Joho," he says to me.

"Don't ever call me that."

He saunters past, taking his sweet time. I plant my feet and stare at Novak.

She bites her lip, nears me, shoulders hunched. "I'll buy you new sheets?" she offers.

God! I clench my jaw and turn away. Novak stops me, her hand extended.

"What?"

"My keys?"

I dig them out of my pocket and smack them into her palm. She goes, "Johanna, you just don't understand. You've never been in love."

"You just shut up. And leave."

She looks stung.

She's hurt? How dare she invade my bedroom? The place where Reeve and I . . . Where Reeve and I . . .

What? There is no Reeve and I. But one day . . . there might . . . *Will.*

"Johanna . . . I'm sorry."

She made my bed, which makes it worse. I never make my bed. Bundling the sheets in my arms, I storm downstairs to the garage, stuff the sheets in the washer, and dump a heap of Cheer on top. It's jammed wall to wall in here. Mostly Mom-and-Dad things. Tessa said I should go through them and I said she should.

As the washer fills, I flip over a full laundry basket and plop on top, elbows on knees, staring into the abyss. My face drops to my arms, then hands, and I feel it. The longing.

I miss Mom so much. Dad had Parkinson's and died of complications when I was twelve, but he was never all that present in my life. Mom and Dad met late in life and didn't start having kids until they were ancient. After Dad died, Mom sank into this deep depression. No one could lift it. Certainly not me. She just deteriorated, then she got sick and I got stuck.

No. Not for one moment do I regret a single second I got with Mom. The service club, chorus, all my extracurricular activities, time I might've spent with friends—I don't feel I sacrificed anything to make Mom's life easier at the end.

Don't think about it, Johanna.

Think about how hot Reeve looked tonight. In that faded baby blue halter with her destroyed jeans that sit so low they expose her sharp hip bones and smooth belly. She's so small, tiny. Lately she seems even leaner. I bet I could get one hand around her upper arm. I'd like to take both of them and pull her into me. Kiss her, meld her lips to mine. Her lips aren't small. They're her most distinguishing feature. Lush. Her eyes and her legs, her hips, waist, breasts. She has bigger breasts than Novak, I bet. Reeve tests the limits of the school dress code, for sure. She always wears these revealing tops with plunging V's, or string camis to show off her breasts. Why not? They're . . . scrumptious. She doesn't need a damn push-up bra.

That's Reeve, always flaunting it and proud to show it off.

Wish she'd flaunt it at me.

"Johanna?"

My elbows buckle and I wobble to my feet.

Tessa pushes her bangs back and a shock of hair sticks up in front. "Why are you doing laundry at this hour?"

"Did it wake you up? I'm sorry."

"Nah, I was up."

She still has her name badge on from work. She shakes off her fatigue, or whatever, and says, "If you get the urge . . ." Her arm sweeps across the ocean of laundry at our feet.

"I'm not feeling it," I say.

She cracks a smile. It's the most genuine exchange we've had since she moved home. Since Mom asked her to come back to handle all the financial affairs. Even though I could've done it. Tessa had been starting grad school; she flew home every other weekend, then flew back to be with Martin. I could've quit school and easily gotten my GED. I *told* Mom that.

Tessa and I stand for a long minute looking at each other, then it gets weird and we both look down.

"Martin has solemnly promised to go through all his boxes. He's such a pack rat. He won't throw anything away that has sentimental value."

"Good thing you don't have that problem."

Tessa gives me a funny look.

My eyes stray to her belly. There's maybe a bulge?

Why'd you leave Colorado? I want to ask. Why'd you have to go all the way to Minnesota? Didn't you get my letter? I want to ask. The last one, the important one? Does Martin hold you at night and tell you he loves you? Does his skin feel warm and does he make love to you when you want him? Is he there for you when you need him? The way you weren't there for me? And still aren't?

Tessa yawns, then does this thing with her jaw where she shifts it left and right until it pops.

It's always annoyed me.

She says, "Don't stay up too late."

I want to say, Talk to me. Will you please just talk to me about the letter?

Seniors have off-campus privileges and most drive to Pizza Hut or Mickey D's, but Reeve always stays in for lunch. She sits with the LBDs.

She stays, so I stay. There are separate blocks of designated tables, like ethnic neighborhoods. The gays and lesbians don't even associate much, since gay guys eat with their straight girlfriends.

When Novak's here, we sit with the stoners and skaters, like today. She sets a tuna fish sandwich from the machine in front of me and slides in across on the bench. "I owe you so much," she says. "You're my BFF forever."

"Redundant," I say. I sit so I can see Reeve. So I can bore my eyes into her soul and hope she feels me.

Novak rips open a bag of Doritos between us. "Dante says thanks, by the way, for use of the hospitality suite."

My gaze wavers long enough to fire a flare at Novak. I take a bite of sandwich. Reeve's spearing green beans onto a fork. There's a girl between her and Britt, some other nameless and faceless lesbian, jabbering away, telling a joke or something. Everyone laughs. Except Reeve. She bites each end of bean off the fork and chews, then holds the rest between her teeth.

I concentrate hard: Look up, Reeve. Look at me. See me. Feel the purity of my love for you.

". . . next Friday. And maybe Saturday too?"

Reeve raises her head a fraction of an inch and I think, Here!

Novak kicks my leg, diverting my attention.

"Are you listening to me?" She shakes the Doritos bag in my face. "Eat."

I remove a chip. Reeve returns to stabbing beans.

"So, do you mind?"

Reeve stands with her tray and I almost shoot up in reflex. "Mind what?"

"Letting us use your place both nights? Note how I'm asking you in advance?"

Reeve dumps the remaining contents of her lunch into the garbage, stacks her tray on top, and takes off. Where does she go? It's the same routine every day.

"Earth to Lesbo."

I turn on Novak. "Don't fuck Dante in my bed. Stay out of my room, I'm warning you. Don't bring beer or pot to the apartment, and be gone when I get home."

Novak flinches. Then she bats her eyelashes and salutes. "Yes, sir. Could you post the rules, sir? I'm a little slow, sir."

She must feel my rising simmer, because she reaches across the table and runs her fingers under my jaw. "Johanna, whatever you want."

I falter. I want it bad. Then I remember this is Novak.

Robbie doesn't show after school. I wait forty minutes, sitting at Mrs. Goins' desk, facing the door, watching the hall. Forty-two. Forty-three minutes.

He's not coming. Neither is she. A curtain of despair draws closed inside me.

Chapter 6

The veg girl's mother is leaving the hospice as I walk in. I shouldn't call her that. Carrie—that's the girl's name. I've only seen her once, when I was delivering flowers to the private ward and her mother was carting in luggage.

Carrie was in a car accident. She was speeding, joyriding after a party, and the other three people in the car died. Carrie lived, if you want to call it that. Her family decided to take her off life support, hoping for the best—the best being that she'd pass quietly and quickly.

It's been five months. People stopped coming by after the first month. Now the only person who visits regularly is the mother.

She complains about everything. Carrie's room, her bed, the linens, the room temperature, the level of attention Carrie gets. Nothing the hospice workers do is enough. I think at the end of life, enough is enough.

Jeannette's on the phone and I don't want to stand around being useless. There's harp music streaming out of one of the private rooms and it pulls me down the hallway.

Carrie's door is cracked, so I stick my head in and see she's covered to her chin, her sheets tucked in so tight she couldn't budge an inch if she did regain consciousness. Which she won't.

I slip in and sit in the chair beside her bed. Her face is like molded wax. Her hair has been curled and makeup applied. Her mother can't even let her die in a natural state.

Carrie's head is bent at a stiff angle and I relax her chin. Better. Her lips look dry. I open her bedside table to find her lip gloss. She has one kind, a favorite flavor, I'm guessing. Strawberry mango. I squirt a dab on my index finger and smooth it across her lips.

She doesn't move, doesn't react, doesn't alter her breathing. "I'm here," I say softly, pressing on her shoulder. "You're not alone."

Mom always said I was such a comfort to her—when she was still verbal. It's how I know what I'm doing here matters.

Carrie has her own bed linens and down comforter. I remove her hand from under it, loosen the sheets, and crook her elbow so her arm will rest comfortably while I hold her hand. Her fingers are cool. I rub them. She wears a class ring, engraved gold with a garnet. I run a thumb over the loose ring. Carrie is shrinking.

Her cheeks are caving in. She's beautiful, though. Even now.

Joyland: Take 5

She eases open my bedroom door and slices through the darkness. Opaline edges outline the contours of her body. I can't see her face, but I know it's her.

"Johanna," she whispers in the night.

"Reeve," I whisper back.

"Do you want me?" she asks.

"You have to ask?" A finger of electricity tickles the back of my neck. She doesn't move, but her eyes fix on me, weld my soul to hers. She says, "How much?"

I can't express in real numbers the depth of my desire for her. "Reeve," I say. "The universe and beyond."

She laughs a little. There's a hint of nasty in that laugh. In a sexy, smoldering way.

"Come here," I say. She notices that I'm naked on the bed. "Please?"

"Show me the money."

"It's all here."

She rushes in and flings herself across me, making me squeal and clasp my arms around her back. She starts kissing me on the cheek and eyes and nose. Her face is poised inches from mine. "Made you beg." She grins.

Made you mine, I think.

• • •

Mrs. Goins stops me in the hall on my way to class. "How's Robbie's essay coming?" she asks.

"He's working on the second part. About the worst thing." I know it's not cool to rat him out, but my motives are ulterior. "He didn't show up yesterday."

Mrs. Goins' eyes narrow. "I'll make sure he gets there today. If you've gotten him to write anything, you're a miracle worker. Thanks again, Johanna." She smiles. Something in that smile reminds me of Mom. Then it's gone.

She pats my arm. "It'll all be over soon."

I don't need it all to be over; I need it all to begin.

An impulsive, instinctive need to know compels me to follow Mrs. Goins into the staff room. "Can I ask you something, Mrs. Goins?"

Her head swivels.

"About Robbie."

She surveys the area and her eyes light on an empty table. "Over here." She motions me to follow.

There's a teacher at the Xerox machine. He says, "Morning, Paige. Counting down."

"Fourteen days," she says.

A knot of panic clenches my chest. Fourteen days. I'm running out of time.

Mrs. Goins says to me, "I'm retiring."

"You are?" I sound shocked. I guess I am. I thought teachers kept going and going until they died at their desks grading papers.

"What is it you want to know, Johanna?"

I wait for the other teacher to collect his copies and leave. "What's wrong with him?"

"Wrong?" Mrs. Goins pours herself a cup of coffee. "He has a slight deficiency, if that's what you mean."

Slight?

"Although it's puzzling," she says, dumping in about a pound of creamer. "He isn't mentally challenged, according to his IQ test. He's been termed a 'highly functional autistic.'"

Termed? Were we all "termed"?

Mrs. Goins adds, "I'm not really at liberty to discuss his case."

Like you just did? The bell rings and I jump.

"Do you need a hall pass?" Mrs. Goins asks.

I shake my head no.

As I race up the stairs to class, I think, Robbie's a case. What does that make Reeve?

Fourteen more days. No time to waste.

Robbie's head is down and he's writing away, hunched over his paper. He brought his own paper and pen and finger string and the instrument case, of course. It's perched precariously on the edge of the desk beside him. As I pass, I reach out to balance it. Robbie clenches my wrist.

His hold is insistent but gentle. He lets me go.

"What's in it?" I ask.

"M16," he replies.

"Is that a saxophone?"

"Cruise missile," he says. "Set to detonate on impact. The slightest movement and . . . KABOOM."

I flinch.

He shoves the case under the desk beside him.

It unnerves me, the way his eyes suddenly retract and die.

He resumes scribbling. He's not that bad-looking. From this angle, I mean, if he shaved or got a decent haircut. He has a round chin with a divot in it, same as Reeve. Her face is more chiseled, though. Her dimple is only noticeable to someone who notices her every amazing detail. Robbie has dark patches of stubble on his chin, down his neck. If you squint and blur his features, like Impressionist art or something, he's kind of cute.

His eyes, though. Empty holes. No emotion behind them. Is that the autism?

I slide my pack on top of the teacher's desk and sit in the chair. "What are you writing?" I ask.

He doesn't hear? Or the distance between us is so vast my words don't reach him, or his brain, his highly functional autistic—

She's here. I feel her.

I get up and glide in her direction. She's close.

Six, five, four feet away. There's a moment when my curtain seems too heavy to lift, or part. What's on the other side?

Fear?

Anticipation?

No.

Need. Desire. My arms extend, press against the curtain and . . .

She's sitting on the floor in the hall, huddling against the brick wall, her knees to her chest, head buried. She's clutching her legs so tight her arms lock. She's . . . shivering?

"Reeve?"

She jerks her head up and scrambles to her feet. We stand for a moment, face to face.

Close enough to notice her dimple. A solid wall of fire combusts between us. Does she feel it?

"Is Hell Boy ready?" It takes a moment to absorb her words, the fact that she's talking to me. When she cranes her neck to peer into the room, her head is an inch away from my arm. "Come on, we're going to miss the last bus!" she calls to him.

Robbie's pen lifts. His thought seems to suspend in midair, then evaporate.

Reeve steps away from me.

I step toward her.

Her head shakes from side to side as she keeps moving back.

Robbie barrels out the door, nearly knocking me over.

They're gone.

I rock on my heels and grind my palms into my eye sockets. Time bleeds away behind my eyes. Fourteen days left. All the time wasted. As I trudge back into the room to grab my pack, an object snags my attention. His case.

He forgot his case.

But if it *is* a bomb . . .

Stupid. It's *not* a bomb.

But if it's motion-activated . . .

I pull it out from under the desk and pray for the end to be quick.

A city bus crunches to the curb and they get on. I note the bus number, then sprint to my car.

The bus veers onto I-70 and exits at Vasquez, heading into Commerce City. Two stops to let people off, then Reeve and Robbie descend. I tail as inconspicuously as possible, ducking down every time I see Reeve look over her shoulder. Which she does a lot. She and Robbie turn up a gravel driveway and I swerve across the street to park.

What if they're just cutting through a yard? As I'm checking my side-view mirror to merge back into the street, I see Reeve through a picture window. This is her house. I twist off the ignition.

The yard is fenced with chain-link, sections of it sagging or bent to the ground. It's really just dirt and weeds. The houses here are old, crumbling, with flat gravel roofs.

Her yard is littered with trash. A garbage bag has burst open and spewed its contents across the yard and into the neighbor's.

I lock my door and sit for a while, psyched—I know where she lives.

One corner of her porch is caved in, like someone took a sledgehammer to the concrete. Upstairs there's black paper covering a window. Her room?

A van rumbles up the narrow street and takes a wide arc, almost ramming me. It squeals around me into the driveway. A guy jumps out and screams, "You *whore*! Don't you ever fucking run out on me again! I'll kill you!"

I cower down inside my car. He storms around the front of the van and wrenches open the passenger door. "Get out, cunt."

He reaches in and drags this lady out *by the hair*. As she flails her arms to detach the guy's hands from her head, he throws her down face-first in the driveway.

Oh God, oh God.

"Get up."

She struggles to her knees.

"Get the fuck up." He kicks her.

What should I *do*?

The woman curls into a fetal position.

The guy's hair is slicked back and his piercing black eyes cut so deep they hurt. I know this because he's looking right at me. When did I open my door and get out?

The guy knees the woman right in the face. I gasp as her head flies back and blood spurts from her mouth or nose. *Call 911! I don't have a phone.* The maniac is starting toward me!

I launch back into my car. As I switch over the ignition, he stops, pivots, and saunters back.

I turn the car off and slide down into the seat. I should . . . get out! Help that lady! Call the cops!

I can't. I'm paralyzed.

Reeve comes out, yells, "What'd you do to her?"

I sit up straight. The guy's disappeared.

Reeve bends to the woman and lifts her up. The front door

of the house crashes open and the guy appears on the rickety porch. He's guzzling a longneck beer, peering down the street at me. Salutes me with the bottle.

I shrink in my skin.

Reeve balances the woman on her hip. "Bastard!" she screeches at the man.

The beer bottle corkscrews through the air, narrowly missing Reeve's head, but hitting the lady square in the back. She lurches.

"Stop!" Reeve yells.

Now. My eyes graze the corner of Robbie's case on the seat, and I reach for it, then catch a glimpse of Robbie near the van. He scans the lady and Reeve says something to him.

Robbie smashes over a section of chain-link fence.

Reeve screams, "Robbie, no!"

He rushes the guy.

"No!" Reeve cries. "Robbie, no!" She shoves the woman against the van and charges after Robbie, who slams the guy down on the cement and starts to strangle him. Reeve jumps on Robbie's back, pounding and screeching.

Now I'm bolting from the car and racing to the porch. Reeve is trying to pry one of Robbie's hands off the guy's neck. I take the other.

Her eyes lock on mine.

The guy chokes and coughs. Robbie's so strong. I snake my arm around his neck and yank back. That loosens his grip enough for Reeve to lodge between them and push Robbie off.

Up close the guy's face is greasy, pockmarked. He clamps on to Reeve's arm and she fists him in the face. "Don't touch me," she says. "Don't you fucking touch me."

I have Robbie cuffed by his arms in back, but I know I'm not really holding him. He's wheezing.

The guy crawls to the edge of the porch and over the side. He says to Reeve, "Just ask your mother if she was using."

Reeve snarls, "If she is, I know who set her up." She looks at me. Her eyes become veiled and she curses under her breath.

Robbie twists out of my grasp and clomps toward the driveway.

The guy retrieves his beer, throws back his shoulders, and grins at me. "Bull dyke to the rescue."

Reeve just fixes on me and this fleeting expression crosses her eyes. Pain? Anger? She flings open the front door and disappears.

Leaving me outside alone. With *him*. His grin widens.

My brain informs my feet to move! I back down the walk, then turn and run. A shudder shakes my whole entire body.

He isn't coming after me, thank God.

That look on Reeve's face haunts me all the way home. It went beyond horror and humiliation. I shouldn't have interfered. But I had to.

I'd do anything for her.

Chapter 7

Joyland: Take 6

Snow sifts through the branches of our wild juniper, catching on needles and frosting berries. It's the middle of summer and the snow brings a welcome relief from the heat. We can have snow in our summer, anytime we want it. She's lying next to me on a towel, catching snowflakes on her tongue. A fluffy crystal lands on the tip and she curls her tongue at me. With my lips, I accept the offering.

A wind kicks up and blows so hard it yanks the branches. One breaks away and slams down on Reeve. I'm strong; I hike the branch and launch it. She's unhurt, smiling up at me.

Her eyes are blue-black, glittering diamonds of winter summer solstice. She snaps her fingers and casts a spell on me. We're in a snow globe, glitter raining down on us and sticking to our silver skin. She looks at me and says, "You saved me."

I say, "I always will."

• • •

Joyland dissolves and all that remains is flat terrain. I want to fall asleep so I can dream. But it's late, time for school.

The senior lot is full, so I park across the street. A van careers in front of me, backs up, and rams my bumper. Glass shatters.

Robbie surges out the passenger side and checks the damage.

"Your headlight's broke," he says as I leap out. To Reeve he goes, "You broke her headlight."

Reeve strolls off toward school.

"It's . . . okay. It was already broken," I call to her.

She crosses the street.

"Reeve!" I shout. She doesn't stop.

Robbie says, "You should get that fixed."

"Yeah, thanks." I reach in the car for my backpack. When I straighten, Robbie's in my face.

"She's sorry."

I gaze after Reeve. "I can see that."

He turns and hustles after her.

Damn. I should've given Robbie his case. He got me all rattled with his care and concern about my headlight.

Reeve isn't in the cafeteria with the LBDs. Where is she?

I buy a croissant sandwich from the machine and head out to my car. The van is gone. Chunks of busted headlamp remain. Message received, Reeve. Thanks.

I'd parked so the morning sun beat directly on my windshield and now the interior is stuffy and, oh, about two hundred degrees. I crank down both windows to catch a cross breeze, then lie with my head on the passenger door armrest, legs extended out the driver's side window.

Last spring Novak wanted me to fly to California with her to check out UCLA and UC Berkeley. At that time I'd been so consumed with Mom dying, I hadn't had time or energy to even think about college. Novak and I always talked about going to the same college, rooming together—before Dante.

When Tessa was in college, I wrote to her religiously once a week. She wrote back, but more sporadically. After Mom got sick, while she was on morphine and sleeping a lot, to pass the time I'd write this one letter to Tessa over and over. In my mind I'd see her read it and call me immediately. I got the letter, she'd say. I'm coming home. You don't have to, I'd counter, but she'd already be on the plane. Eventually I finished it. Sent it. And nothing. Most of the drafts are still in my spiral under the bed, along with the love letters I've never given to Reeve.

Letters from Joyland. Love, Johanna.

On the way to class, I make a pit stop.

She's in the restroom, refreshing her makeup, drawing heavy black liner over and under her eye. My stomach jams up my throat.

This is stupid. We've been through something. We need to talk about it.

"Hey, do you have any gum or breath mints?" I ask.

Her eyes fix on mine in the mirror, then away.

I move toward the sink and she steps back, like I'm contaminated. "I didn't brush my teeth this morning and the sandwich I ate for lunch was, like, pure onions." *Shut up, Johanna.* I twist on the spigot and thrust my hands under freezing cold water. Did I just tell her I didn't brush my teeth?

She looks like she either wants to say something, or kill me. I turn off the water. The paper towels are behind her and my hands are dripping.

She leans aside.

"Thanks," I say. I can't believe how controlled my voice sounds. "God, I need some gum."

"I don't have any gum," she says. "What were you doing at my house?"

I rip off a square of towel. "Robbie left his cruise missile and I came over to give it back to him."

"His what?"

"Whatever he carries in that case."

"He told you it was a cruise missile?"

"An M16 or something. A motion-detector bomb."

A slight smile cricks her lips. "And you believed that?"

"No. But what *is* in there?"

She ignores the question and turns to leave.

"Look, about what happened at your house—"

A trio of girls bursts through the door, giggling, shattering the fragile connection we're establishing. They jam into a stall and light a cigarette. It gets hot and crowded.

"Where is Robbie's bomb?" Reeve turns back.

"In my car."

Time passes. Babies are born. Old people die.

Reeve says, "Well?"

"Well what?"

She blows out an irritated breath. "Can we go get it?"

"Oh, sure." *We*. She said *we*. My feet move.

Reeve floats beside me and I feel huge, monstrous next to her. Uplifted and weighty both. I hold the outside door open for her.

We don't speak all the way to my car. All the things I can think of to say are weak. Or crucial.

Reeve stands aside while I get the case. As I hand it to her, she says, "Thanks," and our fingers touch. Nerve endings spark.

She turns away. Then turns back. "What you saw yesterday? You didn't see it."

"Okay," I say.

Her gaze drifts down the street.

"I did, though," I say.

She shakes her head.

I have the strongest urge to reach out and touch her. Just . . . touch.

She flinches, as if I had. She says, "No." I let her get away. For the last time.

Robbie bounds into the room a few seconds after me. Doesn't say hi or hello or no or "cooperate with Johanna." Slides into his desk, pulls out sheets of crumpled paper, and starts to write.

I want to ask, How's it going? Though I now know his life sucks on a very serious level.

He has his case with him, I notice. "Um, let me know if you need help, okay?"

Scritch-scratch of pen on paper.

I pull out my checkbook and thumb through the register.

Some fool has entered amounts with no notations of where she spent the money. At the end I wrote in a negative number. What is that? My bank balance? Last month I was overdrawn by more than a hundred dollars, and this month my car insurance is due.

I'm calculating how much I'll make if I work at Bling's every night, all weekend, all summer, every day for the rest of my life when I hear, "Aren't you done yet?"

My head shoots up. Reeve's resting a shoulder on the doorframe, her arms crossed.

"Hi." God. My voice is three octaves higher than usual. I clear my throat. "What time is it?" I check my watch. It's flashing 12:00. Cheap Bling's watch.

She saunters into the room and glances up at the big clock over the door. "Twenty after."

Oh yeah.

Her eyes shift to me. "What is he writing?"

"His memoir. Expect a call from Jerry Springer any day."

Reeve casts me a death look.

Shit! "I'm kidding. It's just the essay. The senior project."

Sometime during the day she had finished her makeup. Mood: murderous. "He won't have any trouble finding a worst moment," she says. "Choosing one, maybe."

"Really," Robbie mumbles.

"What's your *best* moment, asstard?" Reeve asks him.

Robbie stops writing and raises his chin. He doesn't look at Reeve. Or me.

Reeve says, "I bet I know."

Robbie gazes up at her and this powerful emotion passes between them—love or hate or what? It's a communion.

Reeve moves her lips. Robbie shakes his head. She motions with her chin and Robbie stands, cramming his papers into his back pocket.

"Wait." I almost knock his case out of his hand. Reeve has stopped right outside the door; impaled herself against the brick wall, looking like she's bracing for an attack. "What were you doing?" she asks.

"What?"

She rolls her eyes. "You ask that a lot. What? When? Who? You should develop better listening skills."

"Better what?" I smile.

She smirks. "While rat boy was working, what were you doing?"

"You mean, balancing my checkbook?"

"You have money?"

"No. That's the problem."

She holds my eyes. "You have a job?"

"Yeah. At Bling's. In the mall?"

"Career minded." She nods. "I like that in a girl."

"You do?"

Reeve opens her mouth like she wants to say something, like she's *aching* to say it. I know the feeling.

Robbie emerges and she grabs him, tugging him along after her. At the hall intersection, she slows and twists her head around. Robbie keeps going. Reeve reaches in her pocket and tosses me something, which I snag one-handed.

It's a pack of Orbit.

Chapter 8

I'm feeling energized, euphoric. After an evening at the hospice. After making contact with Reeve. I take the stairs to the apartment two at a time and see there's a note pushpinned to my door: "We need to talk. Come see me if you get home by 9."

Tessa's handwriting is tiny and cramped. My watch face is blank now. Inside, the clock on the cable box reads 9:48. Oops, too late.

I strip and climb into bed.

Sleep eludes me. I taste peppermint from the gum, all of which I chewed. *Reeve.* How she actually remembered and got me gum. The meaning in her eyes, the understanding between us, her gravitational pull toward me. She wore that short stretchy vest that ties under her breasts, over a skimpy tank. She doesn't own a lot of outfits, but she can wear that one every day for me. Her hair is black on top with that blond underlayer. How does she achieve the two-tone effect? Does someone do it for her? Britt maybe. Britt's hair is always highlighted or streaked.

No. I won't associate Reeve with Britt. Or anyone. Only peppermint. I can chew on that all night.

Heaven forbid Tessa should go to bed one minute after nine. She couldn't say, Come talk to me. Anytime.

I roll over and curl into myself. That letter, the one I never should've sent, it changed things between Tessa and me. I don't think . . . she loves me . . . anymore.

She used to call and say, "Do you want me to move back? Because I will. Just say the word." I'd always tell her, "No, everything's fine. Mom can still get around." Even when Mom couldn't, I didn't want Tessa to have to quit college. Tessa would say, "You're so strong. I don't know if I could handle it day after day." She meant watching Mom die.

I'm not strong, Tessa. It's just, some things in life, you have no choice.

I throw off my tangled sheet and pad out for a glass of milk or something. When I open the carton, the odor staggers me backward.

My stomach heaves as I pour the curdled gunk down the sink.

I have to get out of here, go somewhere. Back to the hospice. I throw on jeans and a hoodie. The misty air is heavy with the smell of burning wood. Who's up at this hour building a fire? Reeve and I would, if we lived together. We'd lie in front of the fireplace and make love all night.

Halfway to my car, I stop in the dewy grass. I'm barefoot.

Can you be wide awake and unconscious?

Martin and Tessa are both home, their cars parked side by side in the driveway. I slide open the patio door as quietly as possible. The lights are out, and dark shapes moving in the living room freeze me in my tracks. Martin steps behind Tessa, their silhouettes converging. He holds her around the middle, his hands spread across her tummy. Tessa's hands come to rest over his.

Martin says, "Hmm. Yes, I'm definitely seeing blue. Blue dots. Blue measles. We should name him Spot."

Tessa bops her head off Martin's chest. "Do you really hate the name Martin? We could go with Marty. Or Martina."

Martin says, "Let's stick with Spot." He asks, "When are you going in for your next ultrasound?"

She doesn't answer.

"We're twelve weeks now." Martin smoothes her bangs back from her forehead. "Right?"

The quiet wraps around them. Their last baby died at twelve weeks.

This is my cue to leave. I step back—on a squeaky floorboard. Their heads swivel in unison.

"Mojo?"

"Hey, guys." I wave weakly.

Martin lets go of Tessa but slides his hand into hers and raises it to his lips. "Word up, homie?" he says to me as he kisses her knuckles.

"I got your note," I say to Tessa.

"Oh, right. Don't let your car insurance expire."

"That's it? Gee, thanks for the sisterly advice." I head for the refrigerator.

Tessa follows me. "I mean it, Johanna. I won't let you drive without insurance."

Their milk is fresh. I drink right out of the carton because I know it galls her.

Tessa's cell phone rings in her bag. She fishes it out as Martin sneaks up behind me. He goes to tip up the carton in my face and I twist away. He did that once and I got a milk bath. I chased him out the front door into the street and pounded him good. Martin asks, "What are you doing up at the witching hour, Mojo?"

"Casting a spell on my evil bro-in-law." I wiggle voodoo fingers at him.

Martin smacks his cheeks and ovals his mouth in horror. It cracks me up. He's wearing this t-shirt that says: INTERNET ATE MY BRAIN.

"Geek," I say as I pass him.

"Gangsta." He yanks on my hoodie.

Tessa rushes out of the dining room into the living room. "I just put in a twelve-hour shift," she says into her cell. "Can't you find someone else?"

I say to Martin, "Spot, huh?"

His whole face crinkles in a grin.

I add, "For a middle name, how about Ted?"

Martin bursts into laughter.

My future niece or nephew: Spot Ted Däg. Yeah, I'm *good*.

I'm about to leave when Tessa sweeps back in. She lifts her carryall off the counter and tells Martin, "I have to go back."

"You just got off," he says.

"We're short-staffed. One of the new interns fell and broke

her ankle and Cody has strep. People are lined up around the building."

Martin cocks his head.

"Well, I'm sorry," Tessa says.

"No, it's okay."

God, he's understanding. I'd probably say, How about some me time? Some home time? Tessa works in a free clinic downtown as a nurse-practitioner.

Martin says, "Your jacket's pretty bloody."

Tessa scans the front of her lab coat. "Shit. We had a bleeder today." She drops her carryall and charges through the living room to the bedroom.

Martin expels a long breath. He turns to me. "Spotted Däg goes, 'Woof.'"

"Arf," I say.

Joyland: Take 7

We race across the granite path, tossing off our shoes and shirts. I'm chasing Reeve to Fallon Falls. She's agile and her small, angular body fits between the crevices as she slithers through the rocks to the river.

I'm laughing, my hair whipped by the stiff wind, and I'm breathless from chasing her and being this close to catching her.

"Reeve!" I call. "Wait up."

"Hurry. The show is starting."

Firecrackers from nowhere dazzle the sky. It's night and the falls reflect the blue and red and gold, streaks of rainbow water cascading over the edge.

Reeve ducks behind the falls, then splits the water, lifting her arms to take the power of the river. She cries out, "Ahweeeeeeeeee. Johanna, come and get me."

I'm close, a hand touch away.

Then the water sucks her up and she vanishes.

• • •

By Thursday all seniors are supposed to have reconciled their student fees and fines and cleaned out their lockers. We were advised a month ago to pick up our graduation announcements. The list of graduating seniors is posted on the wall at the guidance center and we have to check the spelling of our names for our diplomas.

I stay home and think off to Reeve.

The ringing phone jolts me aware. Still tingling all over, I straggle out of bed, but I don't get there in time. Novak leaves a message: "Johanna, where are you? I thought we were going to the senior picnic."

That was today? I squint at the clock on the TV. 4:38, p.m.?

"Hey, lesbo. I miss you. Call me as soon as you get this. And, Dante and I are still planning to use your place tonight, right? Okay? Call me. You didn't miss anything at the picnic. You had to bring your own meat, so I took Dante. Caw."

Did Reeve go to the picnic?

I'm starving. If I go grocery shopping, I'll have to write a bad check. I'm not scheduled to work until Saturday, but I call Bling's on a whim. Shondri says, "I got tonight covered."

Figures.

She adds, "That new girl just quit on me, though, so I'll need someone tomorrow night. Maybe all weekend."

"Put me down," I tell her. Yay. I get to eat.

Shondri says, "Is that more than thirty hours? I can't pay you overtime."

"I don't care. I need the work."

"We have to keep it under thirty hours, but plan to be here by four tomorrow and stay till closing."

"You got it."

She hangs on. What?

"You're the most reliable kid I've ever known." Shondri disconnects.

Wow. First of all, I'm not a kid. Second, what's wrong with me that I stay and no one else does?

Novak falls into my arms at the door. "So wasted," she slurs. Her breath exceeds the legal limit. Behind her, Dante smirks.

Detaching from Novak, I grab my bag off the chair and mumble, "Have fun." I want to add, Don't foul my sheets.

Dante says, "You don't have to leave."

"What?"

Novak teeters a moment, then flops onto the divan.

Dante raises an eyebrow.

What is he suggesting?

My eyes fix on Novak. She didn't. She wouldn't tell him. Dante doesn't know I'm a lesbian. But that smirk on his face . . .

Ew. Ickiness crawls under my skin.

I stomp out the door and down the stairs. Novak, how could you? I trusted you. And how could you sink so low? This one service project we did as juniors was going around to sixth- and seventh-grade girls, talking to them about the pressures they'll face in high school, the perils of dating. Our group would do role-plays to show girls how to get out of risky situations. Novak was better at it than me, since she'd had experience. Her closing line was always, "No means no. Respect yourself. Protect yourself. Just. Say. No."

In real life, how many times has Novak actually said no to guys, about anything?

All the way to Rainbow Alley, I think about it—her. Novak's been dating since she was twelve; hard dating by middle school. I don't know how many times she's asked me to buy her pregnancy kits.

I'm still shuddering and feeling sort of tainted when I turn into the alley. Does he want, like, a three-way?

Do people actually do that?

Maybe they do.

I'm only looking for a one-way—a one-on-one way.

Fewer cars are parked in the lot, and no kissers or smokers occupy the fire escape. I take the metal stairs two at a time and hit the landing. Posters collage the door—an ad for an indie-band fest, a poetry slam. Music and voices seep into the night from inside. I pull the door open and step in. A bunch of people are sprawled on rugs and pillows in front of the TV—movie night? Robbie's there, sitting on his case on the floor. If he's here . . .

My heart pounds.

She's lounging on a long couch, flipping through a zine. She doesn't see me come in—or does she? She drops the zine on the floor and scoots to curl up against the armrest, hugging her knees.

Nameless girl sits down beside her. She says something to Reeve, smiles and laughs, and nudges Reeve a little on the shoulder. Reeve lashes out an arm, clubbing the girl in the face.

Geez. What'd the girl say to her? Because Reeve definitely said NO.

The girl staggers to her feet and starts to cry. Reeve unfolds herself, springs upright, and embraces the girl. She places her hands on either side of the girl's face and kisses her.

I don't see that. It's not real.

Reeve's *mine*. She's saving herself, her *best* self, for me.

I exit the way I came in, clomping down the stairs, tracing the route to my car. A roar in my ears drowns the static and I take off.

My head hurts. My heart hurts. She's everything, everyone I want and need.

Why do I continue to allow myself to believe we're a possibility?

Blindly, I drive into the school parking lot. I don't hear the other car drive in, or the door open, or the footsteps. I don't see it coming. My passenger door swings open and a guy climbs in beside me.

I have the presence of mind to scream.

Chapter 9

The night swallows me whole as I fling my door open and am submerged in darkness. An SUV swerves into the lot and almost hits me. Brakes squeal. Or is that me, screaming? Headlights flood the interior of my Tercel and the guy gets out. He limps away.

Reeve springs from the SUV. "Who was that?"

I crush her in a hug. "God, if you hadn't come . . ." My arms tighten around her.

She goes stiff and I loosen my grip.

"Who was it?" she says again.

"I don't know. Some guy. He just got in my car."

She searches my face. "I didn't do anything with her," she says.

"What?"

"She's not my girlfriend."

I'm shaken, confused. "I'm sorry." I reach for her. "I mean, I'm glad."

Her lips part and a shallow breath escapes. I'm still hyperventilating, so I draw in a deep breath and exhale hard.

Reeve is here. Close like this, she seems fragile, like a dragonfly.

"What are you doing here?" I ask.

Her eyes flit around the parking lot. "Saving your ass from getting raped?"

"Yeah," I say. "Thank you."

We stand for a moment, looking at each other, into each other. Reeve saw my pain; she saw me run out, ran after me.

She says, "Did you know you were screaming?"

"Was I?"

"I'm deaf, aren't I?"

I grin. She smiles.

She adds, "Why did you come here?"

I check out the lot. "I don't know. It seemed like a safe place to go?"

She just looks at me. "You're kind of weird, aren't you?"

"Possibly."

She tilts her head. "That's a total turn-on for me."

All the blood rushes to my face. Thank God it's dark.

Her eyelids droop. They're painted silver and gold tonight, dazzling and reflective in the moonlight. This night, and that moon, and Reeve.

"Do you have any Orbit?" she asks.

"Will you go out with me?" The words just belch from my brain.

She blinks. "Now?"

"No. I mean, sometime."

"Why not now? Are you hungry?"

"Always."

"You have a cell? We'll call for pizza. Have it delivered here."

My eyebrows arch. "To the parking lot?"

"Hey, it's where you go," she says.

God, she's here, joking around with me. Flirting? I hate to admit I can't afford a cell. "I have a better idea. Let's go get a pizza."

She doesn't say yes or no. It's a stupid idea. "Or—"

"You drive," she says.

The closest pizza place I know is Montoni's, three blocks from the school in this melting pot–ish neighborhood— Italian, Middle Eastern, Vietnamese. Our service club used to meet here.

"I've seen this place," Reeve says as we pull to the curb. "I've never eaten here."

"I have. It's good." I reach for the door handle and Reeve clenches my arm. "I want this to be the first," she says. "For both of us."

First what? Date? Orgasm?

"What about there?" Reeve points. "Have you eaten there?"

My eyes follow her finger across the street to the Ishtar Café and Hookah. "No."

She takes off and I'm sucked into the wake of her comet tail.

The inside of the café is smoky, amber lamps diffusing the haze. There's no hostess or wait staff in sight. Reeve chooses a booth by the lotto machine.

A waiter appears out of nowhere and drops off two menus. He says, "You want hookah?"

Reeve and I look at each other. "Sure," we say together.

The waiter leaves.

Reeve picks up her menu and studies it for a moment. She catches me staring.

"What do you see?" she asks, lowering the menu.

The urge is strong, but I don't jump the table between us. "Two eyes, a mouth, a nose." Real poetic, Johanna. God, I'm freaking out here. I'm with Reeve Hartt on a date.

She smiles. A smile so tender and sad, I want to go to her, hold her, caress her face, kiss her lips, her eyes, nose, throat.

She resumes scanning the menu.

Something stops me from asking the same question of her. No doubt she sees a pathetic, desperate, freaking-out freak. The waiter sets a brass-and-glass urn or vase or goblet thing on the table and sprinkles these round, flat charcoals into a bowl. He lights the charcoal and says, "Shisha?"

Reeve and I go, "What?"

I giggle hysterically. She levels a stare at me.

The waiter says, "Eighteen?" pointing to me, then Reeve.

"Yeah. Do you need ID?" I ask.

He waves me off. "What flavor you like? Apple, melon, mint, cherry, banana, mix fruit . . ." He rattles off a dozen more.

Reeve looks at me and I shrug. We both say, "Cherry."

I smile into my chest. She lets out a small laugh.

He opens a wooden box and selects a square package. To-bacco, I guess. We both watch intently as he fills bowls and assembles the hookah urn. Snaking out from either side are long, skinny hoses covered in braided cord.

The waiter picks up one pipe and mimes what we're supposed to do. He hands me the hose, while Reeve takes the other. The waiter vanishes.

Reeve says, "It's like a bong."

There are mouthpieces at the ends of the pipes and Reeve inserts hers into her mouth. I copy. I suck a little and nothing happens.

I've smoked before with Novak. Not from a bong.

Reeve's eyes rest on me. "Are you getting anything?"

"Dizzy."

She cricks a lip. "Any smoke?"

"No. Are you?"

She shakes her head.

We must not be sucking hard enough, I figure. I try again and water bubbles in the clear globe of the urn. Smoke fills a chamber, and a second later I feel it on my tongue. A bite. It tastes like bark. Or burnt candy.

Reeve's eyes widen.

Oh wow. This is nice.

I inhale and the smoke tickles my throat. It isn't harsh, like cigarettes. Cool, I think. Warm. My muscles and bones and shoulders relax. Reeve closes her lids and inhales.

Her eyes are beautiful tonight. She looks like an angel. Or a water nymph. Provocative pastel eyes. She removes her mouthpiece and smiles.

That smile is total surrender.

"Oh, baby," she says. "So fly."

I'm soaring, all right. Is this legal?

The waiter comes to take our order and we both quickly scan the menu again. I don't know what most of this stuff is. Hummus, I've heard of. Reeve says to the waiter, "Number nine?"

I close my menu. "Same." The waiter leaves.

Reeve picks up her pipe. "Nine's my lucky number."

"Yeah? I'll remember that." We both inhale. Breathing out my last knot of nervousness, I ask, "Why?"

Reeve holds the cherry smoke in her lungs, then expresses a long, visible stream of breath. "That's how many girls I've fucked."

The shock registers only slightly, in my conscious brain. I suck in on the hookah extra hard, filling my chest cavity.

Reeve lowers her pipe. "What do you see now?"

Defiance? Daring? For a moment, though, she lets down her guard. "Two eyes, a nose, a mouth."

Reeve looks away.

"I see nine girls who didn't know what hit them."

A smile curls her lips. "You got that right."

I wave my pipe in the air. "Hookah!" I say.

She laughs, this silky, serpentine laugh that ribbons down my throat.

The waiter sets two football-sized plates in front of us filled with skewered meat and rice and globs of purplish goo. He uncovers a basket of pita bread.

Reeve sets her pipe beside her plate. "I hope you're paying," she says. "I don't have any money."

"I asked *you* out, didn't I?"

She spreads her napkin in her lap. "Thanks," she says. "Seriously."

"Hey, you saved my life. It's the least I can do."

She picks up her skewer of meat and sniffs, then nibbles the tip.

The meat is both chewy and tender. I'm not sure if you're supposed to just eat it off the stick, but that's how Reeve's doing it, so I do too. It's good.

We eat in silence for a minute, testing everything. Reeve says, "So what are the best and worst moments you've had in high school and how has each changed your life?" She dips her skewered meat into the purply gunk. "For extra credit, who gives a shit?"

"Really." Not me. Not now.

Reeve says, "Since you're having difficulty nailing it, I'll go first. Best moment? The day my dad left. Worst moment? The day my dad left."

I feel my forehead furrow.

"He's not the biggest asshole in the world." She lifts her pipe. Her hand is trembling a little when she adds, "There's always someone worse. At the time, you can't imagine who . . ."

We've spiraled into this deep discussion without warning. The urge to reach across and take her hand is overpowering, but my reflexes are slow and my arm won't move.

"Do you have one?" she asks. "Let me rephrase that. Is there an asshole in your life?" She blows out smoke.

My first thought is Dante, but he's *not* in my life. Then the door opens and a guy staggers in. His rheumy eyes graze the booths and glue on me. My stomach lurches. It's the guy who got in my car.

"You don't have to answer," Reeve says.

"No, I . . ." He slumps onto a barstool, turning his back to me.

I refocus on Reeve. "My dad is dead. When he was alive, he wasn't an asshole."

Reeve concentrates on my face. "How'd he die?"

"Parkinson's. Pneumonia, actually. He was older."

Reeve asks, "Well, is your mom a bitch at least?"

My eyes fall. "She's dead too. I live alone."

"How?"

"Cancer. She was—"

"How do you live alone?"

I look up. What does she mean? Like, how do I manage?

"Never mind," she says. "I'm sorry. I have to go."

"What?"

She's scooting out of the booth.

"Reeve—"

"I left Robbie all alone."

"Reeve!" I throw down my skewer. Scrambling to move, I snag my bag and slide out of the booth.

I have to dodge a drunk woman who stumbles off her barstool, then stop at the door because . . . we haven't paid.

I don't have any cash on me, and my checkbook's at home.

Reeve slips out as a man and woman come in. I insert myself between them to follow her. The guilt will gnaw at me later. I can come by tomorrow and pay. I will. But now—

She vanishes in the night. The sidewalk is empty, the street deserted. "Reeve!"

Her slim figure zips between parked cars across the street and I dash after her. The sharp night air is sobering.

My legs are longer and she isn't running very fast, so I catch her and spin her around. She shoves me. She pushes me so hard I fall on the asphalt, crunching my tailbone.

"Don't," she says. "Don't come any closer." Her voice sounds threatening. "I mean it."

I push to my feet, slowly. "Reeve, I . . ."

She backs up a step, then turns and flees. Over her shoulder, she yells, "Don't follow me!"

My heart screams, Go after her! Don't let her go! But my head rules. It always has.

I drag to my car and sit inside, stunned. My butt hurts. What just happened? What did I say, or do?

And what's that on my windshield? I open the door and get out to remove the paper from under my wiper blade. A fifty-dollar ticket for a busted headlight.

Fuck. Can I just catch *one* break?

Chapter 10

My brain won't stop remixing the scene from last night. Rewriting the ending: Reeve falls in love with me; Reeve comes home with me.

Reeve running from me—that doesn't play in Joyland.

I need mind-numbing activity. Today is senior ditch day, so school won't work. I decide to clean the apartment. It's the first time I've swept under the refrigerator. Entire ecosystems are destroyed.

The phone rings, but I don't get there in time. I haven't bothered to brush my hair or teeth yet, and I'm still wearing the oversized t-shirt I wore to bed. Do I stink? Maybe that's what scared Reeve away. I strip in the bathroom, and as I reach to crank on the shower, the phone rings again. I sprint to the living room to pick up.

"How does a lesbo spend senior ditch day?"

"Scouring the shit from her life?"

Novak is quiet. Then she sniffles.

I didn't mean her. "Novak, I—"

"Everything's fucked," she says. "Can I come over?"

"I have to be at work at four." Kind of cold, I think. But I'm not feeling all toasty warm toward her, not after last night.

"I won't stay long."

I don't say anything.

"Please?"

I realize I ran out here naked and now I'm all goose pimply. "Yeah, okay. Sure."

Novak's father is an international investment banker. The drive from Countryside Commons, where she lives, is fifteen minutes if you book it.

I take a quick shower and put my tee back on. In the kitchen I've removed everything from the cabinets. What was I thinking?

Was I thinking my life is an empty cupboard? Restock it. There's a can of cream of celery soup that must be left over from when Tessa lived up here in high school. After Tessa left and Mom got sick, I pretty much did all the grocery shopping. Mom would make a list. Until she was forced to leave her own home, she was making grocery lists. A knock sounds on the door.

"It's open!" I yell.

I'm restacking Tessa's Corelle plates as the door whooshes open. "You don't lock your door either?"

I spin around.

"I bring gum." She holds up a pack of Orbit.

My heart does a backflip.

Reeve takes in the chaos and coughs. "Sorry." She fans her face.

Lysol fumes. "I'll open the windows." I rush past Reeve to crack the front window.

"So this is your crib," she says, looking around.

"What?"

She slugs my shoulder. "I'm going to smack you every time you say that."

"Say what?" I smile and she balls a fist.

"Is this how you get high on ditch day?" she asks, dropping the gum on the divan. "Sniffing Scrubbing Bubbles?"

"Yeah, I'm a huffer. Actually, this is the first time I've ever cleaned this place."

Her face lights up. "And I get to share?"

I exaggerate a grin. "Epic."

She smiles back. That warm, tender smile I melt under.

She has on shorts and a faded pink crop top. Her hair's ruffled and loose and her high cheekbones glow with sparkles of glitter.

I haven't even combed my hair. "You could've come earlier," I say, sweeping my mess of tangles over my head. "To share in the first scouring of Terrifying Toilet Bowl."

"Oh snap," she says.

I measure the distance between us, allowing it to close in. Mentally I spin a web around us. No escape this time. She isn't struggling to free herself, just standing here surveying her territory.

I take a step toward her. This is my territory.

"I came to see how you live alone."

Another step.

She tenses, then propels herself across the living room to the dining room, which is the same room, though it suddenly seems larger.

"How did you even know where I lived?" I perch on the arm of the divan. Give her space, I think. The door is close enough that I can block it if she bolts.

Reeve turns and looks at me. Her eyes scan my front and settle on my thighs.

My naked thighs. I realize I don't have anything on under the shirt, which has ridden up. Can she see? Do I want her to?

"How do you afford this?" she asks.

I shrug. "I'm an heiress, sort of."

Her eyes bounce around. "Is there a john?"

"Yeah. He's in the bedroom. You came at a bad time."

She sees I'm joking and grins.

God, I love her smile. I point. "It's down the hall."

Reeve heads that way. My heart is in my throat. Reeve is here, in my apartment. "Wow, you have two bedrooms?" she calls.

I move to the end of the short hall, where it splits into two rooms. "No," I say. "Only one." The other room is a storage closet.

She peers into the cramped closet that's packed with junk. Tessa's sewing machine and skeins of yarn, her dolls and stuffed animals. Maybe that's why this apartment never felt like mine. Too much of Tessa left behind.

"It's a walk-in closet. If you *could* walk in."

Reeve snaps, "You don't know what a closet is." She charges me, bumps me backward, and shuts herself in the bathroom.

I've said the wrong thing—again?

My skin sizzles where she touched me. Water runs in the sink, and I think, Touch everything, leave fingerprints.

Thunks on the stairs draw my attention and Novak suddenly bursts in. "Johanna." She literally throws herself at me.

I remove her arms from around me and flatten them to her sides. Her face disintegrates.

"What?" I say, even though I know what. Make that who.

Novak bites her lip and twists her hair over her shoulder. Her hair is thick and luxurious, the kind of hair you see in shampoo commercials. "I'm sorry about last night," she says. "I didn't know Dante was going to do that." She tries to hold my eyes but can't. "Okay, we talked about it."

My jaw drops.

"You wouldn't have been forced to do anything you didn't want to. You could always say no. And you did." She shrugs one shoulder.

"Yeah. I guess I respect myself."

Novak swallows hard. "It wasn't my idea. We were talking about you and I told Dante you were a lesbian and he thought that was cool. He asked if I'd be willing to do it with you so he could watch."

"You *did* tell him."

I don't know what shocks me more. That she betrayed my confidence about my sexuality or that she agreed to the plan.

"Hey," she adds, "you should be flattered. Guys want you. Girls want you. You don't even have to choose. You know I'd sleep with you, even without Dante."

Our eyes meet and lock.

Novak's intense gaze breaks off and her eyes shift over my shoulder. "You didn't mention you had company," she says flatly.

Reeve is standing in the hallway. How long has she been there? She ducks around Novak and beelines for the open door.

"No!"

She's past me. I race out the door and down the stairs to catch her. "You don't have to go, Reeve. Don't go."

She slows and turns. Her eyes have lost their luminescence. They lift up to the landing, where Novak is slumped in the doorway, separating her split ends.

Reeve heads toward the van that's parked at the curb. I'm not going to let her get away.

Crushing grass in my bare feet, I step into a patch of goathead thorns and yelp. I hop on one foot, trying to brush off the burs as I make my way to the end of the yard, where I stub my toe on the broken sidewalk. "Reeve. Reeve!"

The van door slams shut.

I lunge for the handle. "It's only Novak," I tell her.

Reeve starts the engine. Exhaust coughs out the tailpipe and I have to raise my voice to be heard. "She's just a friend." The window's open an inch, so I know Reeve can hear me. "Please. Whatever you heard . . ."

Reeve meets my eyes. Hers are dark, and deadly.

"Can I call you?" I ask.

A flicker, a trace of uncertainty flashes across her face. She shifts into gear. I press my forehead against the metal trim over the window and ask, "Will you call me? Please?"

She doesn't jam her foot on the gas.

"Do you have something to write with?" I say. "I'll give you my number."

Reeve checks the rearview mirror and drives off.

I storm past Novak on the landing and fling myself onto the divan. A bur is embedded in my foot and I pull my ankle up chest high to dig it out. "Thanks. Your timing sucks."

Novak doesn't say anything.

I glance up to see her checking out my privates. I spin away and stretch my shirt down over my knees.

"Reeve Hartt?" Novak comes over and perches beside me. "You have to be kidding. She's such a skank."

I whirl on her. "Shut up."

Novak flinches. "God. Are you sleeping together?"

The bur pops out, and I throw it at Novak. "That's none of your business." I stand. "That's all you know, isn't it? Not every relationship is only about sex."

Novak says, "I love Dante." She picks up the pack of Orbit beside her. "I'd do anything for him."

Yeah, like betray your best friend. I snatch the gum out of her hand.

She sits back and makes herself comfortable. "Can I live with you?"

I glare over my shoulder. "No." *Hell, no.*

"Mom kicked me out."

"Wh-what?" My voice falters.

She drops her head, finds the pricker on the cushion and rolls it between her fingers. "She says I can stay until graduation, then I'm out. She says she knew what was going on all these years. She's always known."

She can't know *all* of it.

"It'll only be for the summer." Novak bends forward, sets the bur on the table, then presses her hands between her thighs. "Please?"

She can't be serious. "Why don't you live with Dante?"

"I can't."

"Why not?"

"His mother hates me." Her head twists to face me. "Every time I come over, she looks at me like I'm a blight on her darling baby's butt. She doesn't even say hello to me."

"Get a place together," I say. "He works. You could work." She's never had to work in her life. Dante works construction part-time, which has to be good money.

Novak sits up and arches her back, raking fingers through her hair. "We want to save our money for the future."

"So you figure you can live here for free? Move in and leech off me?"

She casts me a withering look. "Did I say I wouldn't pay you? Did I say anything about living here for free? I fully intend to pay you rent."

Sure. It's getting warm, so I cross the room to put distance between us.

"Johanna. Please."

No, I think. Don't do this. "What about Dante? You know he'll end up staying here too."

"He'll contribute his share."

Like hell. The three of us living together? "No way. It won't work, Novak. I'm sorry." I head down the hallway.

The divan creaks and I feel her rush up behind me. "Okay," she says. "It's okay. I understand. This won't affect our friendship."

She gives me a hug from behind and my breath catches.

Novak says softly, "Because I am your friend, I have to tell you." She comes around in front of me. Lacing her fingers with mine, she presses down. She's so close I can smell her sweet breath. "Don't get involved with Reeve Hartt. I mean it, Johanna. You'll be in over your head."

Joyland: Take 8

We walk along the sandy beach. We're barefoot. We step on glass. Back up.

We mount horses and ride. We ride bareback. We canter along the shore. We've both chosen enormous Thoroughbreds. Lacquer black. Only Reeve is willow white. Her legs hang free and her slender thighs press against the horse's flanks. She laughs, high and light, her happiness dispersing in a spray of seawater caught by the wind. Extending her arms to either side as far as she can reach, she spreads her fingers like wings.

I ride up beside her and touch her wing tips to mine. We close in, steeple our hands. In silent communion, we interlock fingers and press our palms together.

Slowing to a steady lope, we ride in mirrored strides. Our horses bump rumps and snigger, nuzzling like lovers.

We telepath our thoughts and feelings.

Reeve: Let's ride to the rocks.

Me: You're on.

I jam my heels into Black Beauty's flanks and the horse spurts ahead. Behind me, Reeve whoops a war cry. She gallops past and heads straight for the water.

Danger. "Wait, Reeve." My head drops and my thighs clench hold. I grip my horse's mane and urge her on. "Catch them. Catch Reeve. Don't lose her in the waves. Don't let her drown."

Reeve cries again. She's under.

Reeve!

I call to her, "Hold on, baby. I'm coming."

The last thing I see is a spray of black foam.

• • •

Chapter 11

Saturday, on my way to work, I stop by the Ishtar Café. No one even remembers we were there. Did I dream it? But I can still taste cherry tobacco at the back of my throat, so I leave money for our unpaid bill.

Eight hours at Bling's, then to the hospice. Carrie's mom is throwing a fit about the cleaning people moving Carrie's pictures so they can dust. She'll do the cleaning and dusting, she says, and she doesn't want that male nurse anywhere near her daughter.

Bitch. Sad bitch.

On the way to Frank's room, I have to pass the room Mom was in. I'm usually okay, but today my knees feel wobbly and my throat constricts. I wish I would've told Mom about me, about who I really am; wish she could've seen me with a girlfriend, being happy. She loved Dad so much. I want love like she had with Dad, like Tessa has with Martin. Why can't I have that? I can, and will.

I sit with Frank, watching professional poker on cable. His eyes are open, but he doesn't see, or doesn't comprehend. He falls asleep around midnight.

There's a manila envelope shoved under my door at home, sealed with tape, no writing on the front. I unclasp it. Five twenty-dollar bills. LATE NOTICE screaming out in big red letters on my car insurance.

Tessa has attached a sticky note: "We need to talk."

Where were you when I needed to hear from my sister so much it almost killed me? Answer that, Tessa Marie Däg.

Robbie shuffles around the bend in the hallway as I watch from the classroom door. He's alone.

"Johanna, Johanna, Johanna," he goes. "I am here to cooperate."

"Where's Reeve?"

He edges past me into the room, not answering. Locating his seat, he drops his pack, positions his case precisely in the middle of the desktop beside him, and sits with his hands folded in his lap.

I linger at the door, hoping, praying, she might be a step behind, riding through the fog on a horse.

The only fog is in my brain.

"Where's your essay?" I ask Robbie, tossing my pack onto the teacher's desk.

He cocks his head. "You don't have it?"

Do I? I dig through my pack. So much crap in here, I can't find anything. I dump the contents onto the desk.

"Just kidding." Robbie whips the pages out of his back pocket. He grins.

Hilarious.

His pages are folded lengthwise and he runs his jagged thumbnail down the crease, then makes a major production out of smoothing the pages over the desk.

"Do you need a pen?"

He produces a pencil from his shirt pocket and, touching his tongue to the sharpened lead, says, "Let us begin."

I study him as he writes. And writes. He has Reeve's intensity of purpose—is that autism?

The clock over the door ticks. Twenty more minutes of babysitting. Wish I had an iPod or cell. Maybe I could find something to read, or clean out my pack.

I feel impatient, restless.

"Can I see what you've written?" I engage Robbie. I get up and walk over to him; extend a hand.

He stops writing and lifts his head. His eyes blip around the room. I sit at the desk beside his, wiggling my fingers.

He drops his arms and slumps. I have to reach over and get the essay.

"March 12," he wrote. "I was born." Brilliant.

"May 23 I kill my mother.

"May 24 Ikilled myfather. May 25Ikilledherfather."

I glance sideways at Robbie. He says, "The plot thickens."

I set the first page aside and begin page two.

When he locked the closet me and Reeve hid in there and he found us. dark is no cover. Reeve says don't say anything she told him no don't. but he didn't lissen .evry night Reeve made me go in and we shut the door and waited in the dark and it was dark and cold and ther were bugs and roches skorpions and spiders in the dark and he'd come and say wer'e playing hide and seek kids and Reeve woud whisper don't say anything don't cry he won't find us in the dark. but he always did. He took me first and Reeve begged him, No take me. In the dark I heard her.The dark is no cover. she didn't cry or scream I screamed. that once. and Ihit him. and after that he took me first.

I force my eyes from the page, my heart hammering in my chest. I look at Robbie. He's staring into his lap, playing with his string.

God, if this is true . . .

darkdarkdarkdarkdarkdark . . . covercovercovercover

The rest of this page is filled with that. Then there's a third page.

I cot my mom shooting up and she says get out. I told Reeve she didn't believe me. I get the needle and Ishow Reeve and she takes it.She tells me forget it and stay out of moms way.She keeps the needle. I find it and I smell it smells like viniger. We hide in the closet. Evrynight we

hide in the closet he finds us. We disappear we cover oursells with all the cloths it's hot and suffcating dark. darkdarkdarkdark we covercover. Reeve says does he hurt you? I say no She says he hurts me. He burns me with his cigarette. He burns me too but I don't tell Reeve.

I shut my eyes, but the next line has already wormed its way in.

Reeve cuts. She doesn't know I know . . .

My stomach hurts. I can't—

I fold the pages together, hoping the words will fester, pop, ooze down the crease and off the page.

I turn to Robbie. "How much of this is true?"

He says, "Negative zero."

Is he lying? I lied on my essay. Everyone lies.

God. I can't turn this in to Mrs. Goins. She'd have social services or whatever all over them. But what if she should? Or what if it's a bunch of bullshit?

Does Reeve cut? I've never seen scars, but I never get past what shows—her face and breasts and legs and eyes. Especially her eyes.

"Where's Reeve?" I ask Robbie again, swinging out of the desk. "Is she coming for you?"

"She doesn't come for guys." He exaggerates a grin. "Do you want me to keep writing?"

"You know what?" I round the teacher's desk. "I think this is enough. Maybe tomorrow we can start on the best moment."

"We?" Robbie asks.

I have cramps. Head and stomach cramps. "You," I say. "I meant I'd be here for you."

He stands and scrapes his case across the desktop, then saunters to the door. He says, "I'm going to meet her now. If you want to come."

She sits cross-legged on the grassy knoll in front of the school, gazing up at the sky. Twisting her head slightly as Robbie tromps down the hill, me behind him. When she sees me, she springs to her feet.

"Hi," I say.

She looks the way I feel: dismantled. We lock eyes. Robbie plops on his case on the grass.

Reeve mumbles, "I need to get Robbie home by four."

"No, you don't," Robbie says.

Reeve fists his temple.

I wince. Does she have to hit him so hard?

She peers up the street. "There's our bus."

"I'll give you a ride home," I say.

A look of horror streaks through Reeve's eyes. "I don't want you coming to my house. Ever. Again."

"Okay. Then I'll drop you at the corner."

She levels me with her stare.

Reeve, please, my eyes plead. *Let me help you, be with you.* "Later, then?" I say. "Can we meet somewhere?"

Her eyes lose focus. "Not tonight. I can't tonight."

"Sometime? Anytime."

A long moment passes. I hear the bus grinding to a stop

and she goes, "You don't want this. You don't need me in your life."

I take a step closer to her. In a lowered voice, I say, "Yes. I do."

She can't help but look. Her breath seeps out between her lips.

A hand touches my arm and I flinch. Robbie says, "You know what I want? A grilled cheese sandwich."

Reeve and I go, "Shut up." This makes us laugh.

Reeve hugs his head to her and answers, "Okay."

Okay? To meeting me? Or to the sandwich? The bus door opens and we all tear down the hill. Robbie gets on, then Reeve. I watch through the filmed, scratchy windows as they take seats together near the middle.

The bus pulls out. Reeve turns to look out the window at me. Her eyes hold the longing I feel.

Blaring music in the background amplifies Novak's rant. "If she thinks I care that she's kicking me out, she's delusional. I just can't believe Dad's on her side this time."

She's talking fast and loud. Where is she? I can hear voices and laughter behind her.

"Johanna, are you there?" she screeches.

"Where are you?"

"It's like child abuse, you know? Neglect. They're throwing me out on the street."

Except you're not a child, I want to say. And they've given you everything.

Novak says, "She won't even let me use the pool."

"Well, fuck," I say.

"I *know*. Bitch. I was going to invite you guys over for a party. You could stay the weekend, like you used to. Except instead of sleeping with me, you'd be fucking Reeve Hartt." She coughs a short laugh. "And I'd watch."

"I'm hanging up."

"Come on, Johanna. I didn't mean that," she says in a rush.

The last time I stayed over at her house was Thanksgiving. Tessa and Martin had flown to Minnesota to be with his family, and even though Martin had asked me to come, I knew he was only being nice. But Tessa could've insisted.

We spent the whole weekend at Novak's in the greenhouse getting wasted. Then she and Dante had a fight. She wanted to ask him for Thanksgiving dinner, but her mother said not now, not ever.

"I love you, Johanna Banana," Novak says softly, then hangs up.

Novak. She drives me crazy. But I don't know what I would've done without her, especially this last year.

"What would you do if you knew someone who was in an abusive situation?" I ask Jeannette. We're sitting at the crafts table, molding Play-Doh with Mrs. and Mr. Mockrie. They have Alzheimer's, which I think is kind of sweet, both of them losing their minds together.

"Who?" Jeannette asks. "Who's in an abusive relationship?"

"Someone. A friend. It's a family situation."

Mr. Mockrie rolls a fat snake.

Jeannette stops pounding her Doh and looks hard at me. "Is this someone I know?"

"No." I see what she's getting at. "It's not me. It's a friend of mine."

Mr. Mockrie grunts and I help him dig off another glob of blue Doh to mold. Jeannette moistens her lips. "How old's this friend?"

"Seventeen. Eighteen."

She says, "You know this for sure? That there's abuse?"

"I know. But, I mean, I don't have it on film."

The buzzer sounds up front and Jeannette scrambles. "If that's Evelyn . . ." Her jaw sets. Evelyn is Carrie's mother. "Don't get involved." Jeannette scrapes back her chair and stands.

"What?"

She smashes her Doh back into the container. "You don't want to get involved in someone else's family business. Believe me."

What I believe is I want to be so deeply involved in Reeve's business there's no way out.

Chapter 12

A message on the closed door reads: NO CLASS TODAY. PICK UP YOUR REPORTS IN MY BOX. I don't care about the Film Studies report, except for everyone else in class seeing my grade.

My grade is 73. I spent at least an hour thinking about narrative structure and "how non-narrative short film applies the structure in the way documentaries don't." The note under my grade says, "You didn't credibly prove your point." Did I have one?

I stuff my report folder into my pack and head for my locker. As I round the bend, I'm obliterated by Reeve, slamming me up against the wall and saying, "Is this a good time for you?"

Her hand is splayed on my breastbone and I wonder if she can feel my heart exploding. "Absolutely," I say.

She hitches her head to the left, then takes off. My lungs empty as I peel off the wall and follow her.

We pass the band rooms, the practice studios and recording lab, and zip into a zigzagging hall. I've never even been in the new Arts wing of the building before. "Down here," Reeve says over her shoulder. She wrenches open a steel door marked B2 and holds it for me.

My eyes adjust to the red emergency light glowing halfway down the wall where more stairs descend.

When the door slams, Reeve pinches my arm.

Ow. "What is this place?" I ask as she brushes by, hip-checking me into the railing.

"Robbie calls it the pit of Acheron," Reeve says.

God, she's fast; I have to run to keep up. She has on this really short skirt and platforms, the pink crop top. Such a beautiful blur.

"Robbie found this place, like, the first week of school and we've been coming here." Reeve's voice echoes. "Nobody knows."

A burst of excitement jets up my spine.

Reeve flips on a light switch and an underworld labyrinth illuminates. Fluorescent bulbs flicker and buzz; metal glints. Tubes and aluminum boxes and vertical poles; horizontal vents snake and maze across a mile of concrete flooring. It's the school's heating and cooling system.

"Here!" Reeve calls. Her voice bounces. She ducks behind a floor-to-ceiling steel column, and when I circle it, she's gone.

"Over here." Reverberation. I twist.

"No, this way."

I spin around.

She laughs.

"Reeve."

I hear her plats clopping.

"Back here."

I suck at hide-and-seek.

Between two coffin-like units I come out at a drainage pit. Reeve jumps off a pipe and lands behind me.

I yelp.

She clasps her hands around my waist and turns me around.

Don't let go. I grab her hands and hold them there. We hook eyes.

"Come. This way." She breaks free and we navigate through a sea of aluminum poles, boxes, vents. At the farthest end is a door. "It was locked," Reeve says, "but Robbie fixed that."

He fixed it by bashing in the door until it splintered and the latch broke loose.

Reeve palms the door open and steps inside. She curls her index finger at me. As I move up next to her, her finger touches the tip of my chin. I think she might pull me in and kiss me, but instead she flips on the light.

I squint at the sudden brightness.

There's a short sofa, like a loveseat, with the foam popping out. A couple of plastic tubs shoved together for a table. Reeve's eye-shadow kits and eyeliner pencils, mascara, brushes, paintbrushes in all different widths and textures, glitter and beads and sequins.

Reeve says, "It's awesome, isn't it?"

With her here, yeah. But basically it's a pit.

She takes my hand and twirls me around under her arm. I have to duck to make it. She pushes me onto the loveseat, then hovers over me. "You're the only one I've ever brought here," she says.

Thank you, God or whoever.

She lowers herself to sit next to me. "I don't bring my girls down here."

"So . . . I'm your first?"

A smile tugs her lips. "You wish." Her head angles up at me and we hold eyes so long it almost becomes a contest.

I blink first.

"What did you want to talk about?" she asks.

I hate to break the communion, or whatever this is. "Robbie."

She drops her eyes. "What about him?"

I want her focus back on me—us. "I just need to ask you . . . to show you . . ." My backpack traveled with me through the labyrinth, it's such an appendage. I fish out the spiral with Robbie's essay in it and pass the folded pages to Reeve.

"I'm sorry you got stuck with him," she says, taking the essay. "He needs to graduate."

"No, it's all right. He's . . ."

Her eyes slit.

"Funny," I finish.

"In the head," she mutters. She shifts on the loveseat to pull one leg underneath her. "He almost died when he was a baby."

"Really?"

"No, I'm lying. You can't believe a word I say." Her one plat clunks to the floor and she pulls off the other. The pages rustle in her lap. She reads aloud: "'May 23 I kill my mother. May 24 I killed my father.'"

Reeve stops. "Nice."

"That's only the beginning." I remove the first sheet.

She reads the second page to herself, and the third. Her eyes dance across and down the pages and she doesn't breathe. She bends at the waist and her hair falls across her face so I can't see her reaction. When she gets to the end, she says, "You should correct his spelling and punctuation."

"What?"

"He has an IQ of a hundred and sixty, you know."

"Really?"

She clicks her tongue, like, Yes, you should know. What do I know about autism?

Reeve rereads something. As she does, she plucks eyelashes out of her eyelid. I notice then how almost all the eyelashes on her right eye are missing.

"Is any of it true?" I ask.

"It's Robbie's interpretation," she says.

"What's your interpretation?" What did she write in her essay? "Is he . . . Are you . . . ?" God. How to ask this? "Are you guys being molested?"

Reeve laughs.

My face flushes.

"I'm sorry." She claps a hand over her mouth. "It's just . . ." She laughs silently behind her hand.

She's laughing at me. My eyes skim up and down her arm, any square of exposed skin I can see. What do cutting scars look like? I just blurt it out: "Do you cut?"

She stops laughing. Releasing the leg from underneath her, she arches away from me and says, "Johanna, you can't begin to understand."

Is she right? Because I *don't* understand any of it. My own tragedies are so . . . ordinary.

"Don't ever ask me questions you can't handle the answers to." She stares down at Robbie's essay.

She thinks I'm naïve. Which, okay, maybe I am.

I reach over and place my hand on her leg. "I want to know you."

She sucks in a breath, like my touch burned her, or my words did. I remove my hand and she exhales. "All that stuff happened in the past," she says. "It's shit from Robbie's childhood. Nice childhood, huh?"

It was yours too, I think. "So," I say, "it's over?"

Reeve pushes to her feet and the essay sails to the floor. "The asshole's gone. He's been gone for years." She drops to her knees by her makeup, picks up a tube of mascara, and unscrews it.

"But who's that guy at your house?"

"What guy?" She opens a lighted mirror.

"That guy who beat up your mom."

She slaps the mirror down. "Is that all you wanted to talk about? My crappy home life?"

"No."

"What else?"

The tension crackles. "Us."

She shakes her head. "There is no *us*."

"Not yet," I say. "But I want there to be."

The atoms between us charge and split. Reeve says slowly, "Can't you hear? Did I not point it all out? You can't handle me."

"You don't know what I can handle."

"Fine," she says.

"Reeve." In one breath, I let out the life I've been holding in. "I want you. I don't care what baggage you bring. I've—I've got stuff too."

This shakes her visibly. She pushes to her feet and heads for the door. I shoulder my pack. "Don't forget Robbie's memoir." She points to the floor and I stoop to reassemble the strewn pages.

"He's supposed to write about high school, isn't he? Make him start over."

"Okay," I say. We'll start at the beginning. You and me, Reeve. Let's begin.

"Will you toss me my shoes?"

I do better than that. I gather the pair of plats and kneel in front of her to slip them onto her feet. I clasp her right ankle and her toes curl under. I run my index finger across the bridge of each toe.

She closes her eyes and opens her mouth.

I rise to face her and the light extinguishes. She says, "Forget it."

"No." I take her hand. "I know what I want, Reeve." Enough wasted time. "I know what I can handle."

Chapter 13

"Johanna, there you are." Tessa sits up in one of the lawn chairs out back, crocheting a square of pink and purple yarn. Her yarn bag overflows with similar squares, like she's making quilt blocks. I check out her stomach to see if there's a change. "Come over here," she says.

I almost say, You come here. I know what she's going to ask.

"Your graduation"—Tessa continues to work—"is on May twenty-third, right?"

"Um, yeah."

"Do you want a party?"

"A what?"

"If you want, we can plan a graduation party."

We, as in you and me? Or you and Martin? "That's okay," I say. "Novak's having one." Novak's mom is planning this extravagant celebration. Now that Novak's being evicted, though, are the party plans canceled?

"So, you could have one too," Tessa says.

Who would I invite? Novak'll be busy that day. Reeve? Would Reeve come to my party?

Tessa glances up, shielding her eyes from the sun. My eyes laser into her belly. I think the bulge looks bigger, which is a relief. The miscarriage happened right before she flew home to talk to Mom about "making arrangements." I never got to tell her how excited I was about becoming an aunt, getting a niece or nephew. I love babies.

Thank God I didn't say anything then. It was like Tessa was avoiding me, anyway. Novak had brought over a knitting project she said wasn't turning out right and she needed Tessa's help. They were in the dining room when I came out of Mom's bedroom. Tessa was bawling her eyes out. Novak said to me, "She lost the baby."

Novak hugged Tessa. I went over to be with her too, but Tessa got up fast and left. I ended up consoling Novak.

Tessa shoves her crocheting in her bag and stands. "We're coming to your graduation."

"You don't have to," I say.

"We want to." She starts past me.

I scrape my foot in the dirt. "I don't even know if I'm going. Hardly anyone goes." That's probably not true. Everyone is talking about announcements and rings and the slogans they're painting on their caps. Novak complained about the limited number of tickets she got for family members because all her aunts and uncles and cousins are flying in.

Tessa snipes, "Well, let me know, okay? I already put in for the day off. And so did Martin."

I snarl behind her back, "Oh, you'll be the first to know." Believe me, I'll send you a *personal* announcement.

Reeve says, "Hi." It stops me in my tracks. She adds, "I thought I'd find you here." She's seated at the teacher's desk.

She was looking for me?

"He's starting over. He needs supervision, discipline." Reeve stiff-fingers Robbie at his desk. "Get to work, wanker."

Robbie goes, "I only cooperate with Johanna."

I say, "Then get to work, wanker."

Reeve smiles at me.

God, wipe me off the floor.

She orders him, "Use proper English and punctuation. Don't be lazy."

Robbie thumbs his nose at her, then lowers his head and begins scribbling on a clean sheet of paper. Reeve gets up and comes toward me. She's wispy. I expect her to rise like a balloon with a string. Then I'd reach up and pull her down.

She clenches my upper arms in both her hands and pushes me out the door. Without taking her eyes off me, she says, "Keep working, Robbie. We'll be back." She steers me across the hallway and keeps going until I hit the wall. "What have you done to me?" she asks.

"What do you mean?"

"I can't stop thinking about you."

My heart thumps.

"You bewitched me," she says. "You did some kind of juju

spell." Her eyelids glimmer in iridescent pinks and blues, a se-
quin on each tear duct. She can't. Stop thinking. About me?

"It's mind control," I say. "You will succumb."

She pooches her lips. "I'm so mean to you."

My tailbone still hurts and I found a bruise where she
pinched me. "No, you're not."

"Yes, I am." She drops her hands and steps back. "I don't
want to be."

"I know."

"No, you don't." She looks off to the left. "It means I like
you." The trace of a smile on her lips. "Isn't that stupid? It's
so wrong."

"No, it's not."

She shakes her head.

"The liking me part. That's right."

"There's this party at Amanda Montero's. Do you want to
go? You'll be risking your life if you say yes."

"Yes," I say.

"I mean it." Her face and voice are serious. "I'm not a nice
person."

I look into her very soul. All I see is beauty.

Reeve says, "Don't say I didn't warn you."

Robbie fills the doorframe and announces, "I'm done." He
walks up to me and thrusts his papers in my face.

"Watch it." Reeve jabs him in the gut. "You almost hit her."

I absently scan the papers and think, It's nowhere near
long enough. "When's Amanda's party?" I ask.

"Friday night." Reeve clubs Robbie on the arm and he
steps back, out of our space. I automatically think, Don't
hurt him.

"You want me to pick you up?" I ask.

"No. God, no. I'll come and get you."

This is happening, right? It isn't a hallucination, or a mental stimulation. "When?"

Reeve pushes Robbie toward the exit. "Like, nine o'clock?"

Wait. "I have to work Friday."

"Then forget it."

"Only till ten. Or ten-thirty."

"Can I come to the party?" Robbie asks.

Reeve stops and slugs him on the arm. "Don't be a moron."

His expression doesn't change, but something does. Reeve's eyes soften. She blinks up at me and says, "Can he come? We could put him on a leash and tie him to a tree."

Okay, this is weird. A date with both of them? "Um, sure," I say.

Reeve smiles at me, apology and tenderness and sexiness in that smile. She goes, "Did I forget to mention, you go out with me, you get benefits?"

Benefits? Or burdens? Never mind, I think. I'll take any piece of Reeve Hartt I can get.

The three of us head outside, where the bus is slowing at the light. "Let me give you a ride," I tell Reeve. "I'll drop you at the corner or something."

"No."

Robbie says, "You can drive me."

"Shut up." She kicks him. "Okay. But leave us off at the 7-Eleven. And promise you won't go to my house—ever again."

"I promise."

Her arm grazes mine, igniting a skin fire. A car length into the parking lot, Reeve skids to a halt and Robbie plows into her.

There's someone in my car. Leaning out the passenger window, Novak flicks an ash off the end of her cigarette.

Reeve says, "On second thought."

I catch her arm.

She twists out reflexively and shoves Robbie backward.

"Wait." I grab her arm again.

She chops my hand down.

Ow. That hurt.

Reeve's face pales. She hustles away with Robbie in tow.

"It's fine," I call. "Reeve—"

"Just forget it," she barks over her shoulder. "Forget it."

"Was that Reeve?" Novak has her shoes off and her feet up on my dashboard. "Who was the guy with her?" she says.

My eyes stray back to Reeve and Robbie, loping to catch the bus. "Her brother."

"Flatliner is her brother? God, Johanna." Novak flicks her ash. "You sure know how to pick 'em."

I snap, "What does that mean?"

Novak sits up straight. "Reeve Hartt's a cold, hard bitch. And you're too good for her."

I get in and crank the ignition. "Who the hell are you to be giving me advice about who I should date?"

Novak's head lolls back. "You're right. I'm sorry. I just can't believe you like her." She tosses her still-lit butt out the window. "Does she like you?"

"I know it must seem impossible to you."

Novak casts me that withering look. "You're taking everything I say wrong." As I back out of the space, she tells me, "I'm moving in with Dante. I have no choice. His mom says I can sleep in the basement with the cockroaches."

If that's supposed to make me feel guilty . . .

"It'll be cool," Novak adds quickly, forcing a smile. "There's a futon down there, and a TV. Mold and mice to keep me company."

Dante'll sneak down. It won't be that bad.

"Could you do me a favor?" she asks. "Drive me home? Not my home. To my parents' house."

"Where's your car?" I slow at the intersection.

"Dante has it. He totaled his on Sunday."

"What?" I turn to Novak. "Is he all right?"

"Yeah. Oh yeah." She clutches a knee to her chest. "He fell asleep and jumped the median, then hit a retaining wall. He walked away. The wall didn't."

"Geez," I say.

"So I gave him my car."

"You *gave* it to him?"

"Loaned it. Whatever. What's mine is his."

I hope she doesn't tell her parents that. "I'm glad he wasn't hurt." I guess.

She opens her purse and lights up another cigarette. There's something she isn't telling me.

"What?" I say.

She billows a cloud of smoke from her open mouth. A sneaky grin creeps across her lips. "So, lonely lesbo has a fuck buddy."

I hit the speed bump hard. Damn. Straight.

Soon.

Chapter 14

Reeve isn't in school the rest of the week and I don't see Robbie either. I don't even know if we're going to the party or not. Why didn't I get her phone number? How did we leave it? Did she really ask me?

There's no wall clock in Bling's. I rearrange the watch display over and over to check the time. 9:58. 9:59—she's here.

She picks up a digital watch and tries it on. "Pretend you don't know me," she says.

My stomach somersaults. She wanders over to the hair scrunchies as a horde of girls surges in, dispersing in pairs. Robbie's in a corner playing with his string.

I check the time. Ten exactly.

Shondri has a line at the register. The store is small and cramped with this many people in it. Now Reeve is trying on shades.

I slip between bodies down the main aisle, attempting to look inconspicuous. Forcing myself not to scream, Everybody out!

Reeve catches my eye and smiles. I can't wait for these stragglers. Behind the counter, I press the button for the metal grate to lower.

"What are you doing?" Shondri asks.

"It's closing time."

"Johanna, we have customers."

"But I have to leave. I have curfew and, uh . . . I'm grounded." I've never been grounded in my life.

Shondri's eyes slit. "You mighta told me that."

I hunch my shoulders. "Sorry."

Reeve disappears behind a rack of earrings, then materializes on the other side. She mimes, Don't stare.

"Go on," Shondri says. "I'll close."

"Are you sure?"

"Do I got a choice?"

I rush to the storeroom for my bag and when I come back, Reeve and Robbie are gone. I skid out into the mall and see Robbie at the photo booth. "Hey!" I call. "Where's—"

Hands cover my eyes. "Trick or treat," she says.

"Definitely treat."

She's in front of me. "Ready?"

I've been ready forever.

"Where's your car?" she asks.

"This way." I start for the northwest entrance, by Target.

"Butt crack!" Reeve calls. She takes my hand, just like that. Like it's the most natural thing in the world.

My eyes drift down to her wrist, to the watch.

She forgot. She'll notice later and go, Shit. She'll return it to Bling's.

So there's no problem. And if she really wants it, I'll buy it for her.

Amanda Montero lives in Glenarm Canyon, in one of those cozy cabins that cost a million dollars. It's weird how geography dictates status. The poor neighborhoods, the ghettos, are built on a floodplain. The middle class is mesa. The upper crust, geographically speaking, claims the summit.

Why would Amanda Montero want to use my apartment? Her house is a four-star resort. There are signs and arrows directing people to the party out back, in case the strobes and blasting bass aren't enough. We, Reeve and I, and, oh yeah, my other date, Robbie, make our way up the driveway.

Reeve looks amazing tonight. She's wearing this straight, full-length skirt with buckles and grommets that's made out of nylon, like a backpack. Not new. Everything she owns is vintage cool. I have on my black pants and white shirt from work. So glam.

People glom together on the patio in cliques. Three or four girls in bikinis lounge at the pool. *Brr.* It's chilly in the mountains at night.

The pool is shaped like a scalloped oyster. A waterfall splashes down fake boulders, making me think of Fallon Falls. If we'd kept going up Terra Haute Road, we'd have come to Fallon Falls. Maybe I'll take Reeve there later? Throw Robbie off the cliff?

"I didn't know it was a pool party," I say to Reeve. The

only parties I've ever been to were at Novak's, where I immediately gravitated to the greenhouse.

"It's whatever," Reeve says. "You know."

One of the bikini chicks leaps to her feet and bounds over to us. Her boobs jiggle. "Oh, you are so leaving," she says to Reeve.

Reeve goes, "I was invited."

"By who?"

"Britt."

Amanda's eyes narrow. I survey the area but don't see Britt.

"You fucked my little sister," Amanda says.

Reeve goes, "Only 'cause she wanted it."

"You lying bitch."

My eyes dart back to the pool. One of the girls is Nameless, from Rainbow Alley. Is that Amanda's sister?

Amanda says, "She's *not* a dyke."

"Okay. You'd know."

Reeve and Amanda have a stare-down.

Amanda blinks over to me. "You can't bring him here."

Reeve says, "He's staying."

Robbie, she means. Why is she looking at me?

Robbie drones, "Fooood," and elevates his arms like Frankenstein, goose-stepping toward the wet bar. There are bowls of chips and coolers of drinks.

Reeve calls at his back, "Wander off into the hills where no one can find you!" Her fingers intertwine with mine and she says, "This is Johanna."

I say to Amanda, "We've met."

"We have?" Her eyes scorch me. "Do you go to our school?"

We've both gone to Jefferson High for four years.

Amanda points at me. "We had yearbook together last year. Right?"

"I don't think so," I say. "I'm pre-med."

Two guys sneak up behind Amanda, one pressing a finger to his lips. He grabs her arms while the other guy snags her ankles. They swoop her into the air and she squeals.

My hand absorbs the rapture of Reeve's fingers woven through mine. She has a tight grip.

She gazes up at me. "Are you really pre-med?"

"Do we even have that?"

She laughs. I smile back. Her attention wavers over to Robbie, who is standing at the bar shoving chips into his mouth by the fistful. "He is so bent," she says. "What am I going to do with him?"

"How come you're responsible for him?" I ask. "Can't he—"

"You wouldn't understand," Reeve snaps. She releases my hand and stalks off toward the pool. I stumble blindly behind.

She stops suddenly and turns to me. "Are you sorry you came with me yet?"

"Not at all."

"I guess you heard. My lucky number's ten."

I laugh. Not the reaction she expects, I guess. Somewhere in the back of my mind, at the instinctive level, I know I should be jealous. Am I?

Reeve's eyes graze the ground and she swings her right hand close to my body. Her wrist winds under my wrist and she tickles the tips of my fingers with hers. Tingles of desire radiate through my body.

Reeve says in a low whisper, "Let's go somewhere."

Fallon Falls.

She hooks her fingertips under mine and leads me to the pool. The party's gearing up.

"Reeve? Reeve!"

She slows.

"Hey."

It's Britt. Her eyes flit to our linked hands.

Reeve says, "This is Johanna," clenching my hand tighter.

"I know," Britt says. She has these blue-gray eyes like a snow cat's. They stare at me intently. What? Is she trying to telepath a message, like, Lay off? I telepath back, Reeve might've been yours once, but your number's up.

"You could've told Amanda you invited me." Reeve's voice is cold.

Britt's mouth drops. "I did. Melia's been telling everyone—"

"I know what Melia's saying. She should shut up. We have to go." Reeve tugs me ahead.

I turn to see Britt drilling me with eye daggers. It feels . . . satisfying.

She's negative zero.

We cross the pool deck and round the faux waterfall. Behind us, I hear someone screech, "Nooo . . . !" Then a splash. People shout and laugh.

Reeve seems to know her way around here. She creaks open an iron gate to a cobbled path leading down an incline. It's only wide enough for the two of us, so our arms press together. Around a rock ledge past a hidden alcove is a hanging garden.

Reeve says, "Do you want to sit or stand?"

For what? There's a patio set, an arched trellis with a spray of climbing roses. Reeve follows my eyes to it, then leads me that way and we duck under a spiny branch.

The roses are red. The archway is dark.

Reeve lets go of my hand and straightens to her full height. She's wearing her plats, and she's only, like, three or four inches shorter than me. Her eyes are subtle, brown eye shadow, white mascara, natural lip gloss.

"I don't know you at all," she says.

Oh, Reeve. I know you.

She adds softly, "But I want to."

With both hands spread, she touches her fingertips to mine. We stand a long moment with our hands out, wing tips pressing. Our palms never touch. As if on cue, our fists come together.

Reeve says, "Do you kiss on the first date?"

I let out a nervous laugh. "I don't know. This *is* my first date." Feminazi doesn't count.

She widens her eyes.

"Except for the hookah."

Her eyes go black. "That didn't happen. We weren't ready."

You mean you weren't.

Reeve smiles tenderly. A sensuous smile that stirs the night.

"Do you?" I ask. "Kiss on the first date?"

"I do," she says, sounding serious. "I definitely do."

I lick my lips. My mouth is dry and I swallow dust. Reeve angles her chin up and closes her eyes. I think, If I close my eyes, I'll miss. I'll kiss her forehead, or her nose, or . . .

Reeve pushes down our fisted hands and rises up to meet me. In sync, we come together.

Her lips part slightly and so do mine.

Velvet night against my mouth, her lips are moist and warm. She opens her mouth and I do too, then she twists her lips, her lip gloss a lubricant. She sucks my upper lip between her teeth and holds while I tremble with the Earth.

My hands unclasp from hers and wrap around her, pulling her into me. Her hand slides up under my hair and her rigid fingers drive down the base of my skull.

It's hard to breathe, hard to stand. My hands move to her lower back, to bare skin where her shirt has ridden up. I flatten my palms against her and crush her to me.

A little "Oh" escapes from my mouth. Reeve makes a sound, a long "huhhh." The tips of our tongues curl and touch and tickle.

Reeve's head jolts back. "God," she says. "I'm going to come."

I'm shaking so hard, I think I might die. "Is that bad?"

Reeve fingers my cheek, the back of my neck. I lean into her, covering her hand with mine, taking it and kissing it.

My eyes close. This is Joyland. My alternate universe I never dare inhabit. Until now.

It's real. I'm finally alive.

My eyes open slowly.

"Wow," she says.

"Yeah."

"That wasn't your first kiss."

"It was."

She arches her eyebrows and her eyes glisten. I can kiss! I'm a good kisser.

She touches my lips with the tip of her index finger and I kiss her fingertips. "You're my first everything," I say.

Her face changes. For a moment I think she might cry, and if she does, the depth of my desire will burst apart with her. She takes a step back, away from me. "We better go see what Robbie's up to."

"Reeve." I clench her arm and she reacts with a jerk.

Licking my lips, I lean into her. My arms enclose her, but she twists out, pressing her hand against my hip. She says, "Let's not get carried away."

Too late. I'm flying. I thought she wanted me.

She adds in a quiet voice, "I want you to savor your first time, okay? There's only one first time. Don't lose it."

I won't. I'll never let her go.

Chapter 15

Robbie could be one of those idiot savants, I think, like in *Rain Man*. I read through the last part of his essay, as much as I can decipher. His spelling and punctuation suck, but the content is moving. And disturbing, of course.

My best momen was when I kill everyone. Not Reeve. I learnd if you elimnnate the sourc of diseeze the symptms go away. but you always have the sicness inside you.

Does Reeve feel that way? Does she think she's got a sickness? I hope not.

I open the door to leave for work and trip over a box on the landing. Taped to it is a note: "Enjoy these. ♥ U."

Novak's loopy writing. I bring the box inside and set it on

the coffee table. Inside is a DVD player. She must really be moving out. A couple of DVDs are stuck in the side.

One is *Fantasia*. The other is—

Porn. Under the player are three more DVDs. They're all porn.

Girls on girls! Are these Novak's? I might watch . . . *one*. Now I wish I didn't have to go to work.

I surveil the entrance my entire shift, assuming, hoping, Reeve will appear. Certain she'll come by and return the watch.

Shondri says, "I'm giving you a promotion." She hands me my paycheck. "Assistant manager."

"You're kidding." I stare at the check stub. Ten cents more per hour.

"Don't let it go to your head."

That makes me laugh. Still, I've never been promoted. All I can think is, I want to tell Reeve!

How does Reeve spend her off time? She has girlfriends. Britt, others. I've seen her holding hands or nuzzling with them at lunch. I always imagine they're me and then I take that scene to Joyland.

This one time I caught Reeve in a passionate kiss with Britt. I came in early for a make-up test or something and they were outside on the quad before school. Britt was moaning and breathing hard, then she went, "Ow!

"You bit me!" Britt said.

"Did I?"

"I'm bleeding. You did that on purpose," Britt whimpered. "Why'd you do that? I never did anything to you."

Reeve said, "You asked for it."

Britt crumpled to the ground and started to cry.

Reeve would never make me cry. She *couldn't*.

I didn't see Britt for a while after that, and I'm pretty sure they broke up soon after.

God, this is driving me crazy. Why doesn't she come in?

Closing time and still no sign of her.

I'll drop by her place. I know I promised, but . . .

As I turn onto 68th Street, the house comes into view. At night, the trash and tires and abandoned furniture look like a haunted junkyard. I pull to the curb across the street and park.

The streetlamp nearest me has been shot out and the pole tagged. This whole ghetto street scene creeps me out. I spot a dim light on inside her house.

The front door suddenly crashes open, scaring the bejeezus out of me. Reeve storms out. "I told you, no!" she yells back inside. "I won't do it. I'm not doing it anymore."

A woman's voice rises in a screech, "I'll die! You know I need it."

That guy shadows the doorway, bracing himself with both hands in the doorframe.

Reeve shouts, "You go buy her shit! You fucking got her hooked again."

"Watch your language, young lady."

Reeve spits at him.

He laughs and fades into the background.

The woman—Reeve's mom?—staggers out, grabs Reeve by the arm, and wobbles. She's, like, completely anorexic. She's wearing saggy stretch pants and a bra.

Reeve catches her in a fall. "I won't buy for you, Mom," she says. "I won't do it."

Her mother's reply is faintly audible. "Fuck you."

"Fuck you! Your life is fucked."

Her hand flies out and slaps Reeve's face hard enough to snap Reeve's head back. Geez. Her own mother.

"Bitch," Reeve goes. Then louder, "Junkie bitch!"

The woman hauls off to slap her again, but this time Reeve blocks her wrist, pushes her mother in through the door.

I can't just sit here. Can I?

Reeve appears again. The guy follows with a thin brown cigarette dangling from his mouth. Reeve hops down off the porch, straight toward me, and the guy comes after her. "Where do you think you're going? Hey, dyke!"

"Cram it."

From inside, Reeve's mom yells, "You have my permission to do what you need to do, Anthony!"

Reeve pulls up short.

The guy approaches her from behind, cups her shoulder, and she knocks his hand off. He bends down to kiss her neck, but she whirls and kicks him in the balls.

Good.

He doubles over, then screams, "You fucking cunt! You cunt-licking—" He hits her with his fist square to her jaw.

Reeve crumples to the ground. My Reeve.

My fingers grab the door handle and I charge out. Reeve rises up and kicks him again, but I can see him lunge for her head. I yank him off her from behind. He's about my height, greasy, stinking of booze and b.o. He has tattoos up and down his arms and shoulders.

"Who the fuck are you?" He wrenches away from me. His eyes have no pupils.

"Johanna," I answer. My voice is surprisingly calm.

"Oh yeah. The dyke's bull dyke."

Reeve aims to kick him again, but he catches her ankle, twists her leg.

"Stop it!" I push him off and kneel to her. "Reeve."

He launches onto the porch muttering, "Fucking freaks," and vanishes inside.

I hold her face, fingering her chin with my thumbs where blood is dribbling and her lip is swelling. I wrap my arms around her. "It's okay. I'm here."

She thrusts up both arms. "What are you *doing* here?"

My mouth opens.

"Don't ever come here." She shoves me backward, onto my butt. "Go home," she says, scrabbling away from me. "Go back where you came from."

"Reeve . . ."

She rises to her feet and storms off.

I stand and stumble toward the street. *Don't leave her here!* my brain screams. *She'll die!*

"You don't know me."

I turn. "What?"

She's out of breath. "You never will. I don't ever want to see your ugly face in mine again. You disgust me."

She's traumatized; she doesn't mean what she's saying. "I can help you. I'll phone someone. The cops or—or social services."

"Don't do anything!" she shouts in my face. "Just get out of my life!"

I plant my feet, or try to. "There are people who can help, Reeve. Who want to, if you'll let them."

"Like you? Is this the way you help?"

A car alarm blares and diverts our attention momentarily. I take her hand and say, "I love you."

Her face shatters into a million pieces.

She jerks back her arm. "Don't."

"Too late." I open my hand to her.

She slaps it down. "Just go away." She sprints for the driveway before I can think what else to do.

I stall for a second at the gate. *Stay. Go.*

Reeve, I want you. I need you. I need to get you out of here. I concentrate so hard, she has to hear.

I feel her calling out. Her fear and longing and total sense of hopelessness. The guy's silhouette swoops across the window like some bird of prey and my blood runs cold.

Chapter 16

My film notes jumble into hieroglyphics—useless to study for my final. The way she lives. The violence, the brutality in her life.

How long has she been taking it? Forever? Her father, her mother, this guy. How many assholes have come and gone in her life? I knew people were terrorized. Child abuse. Spousal abuse. I've never actually known anyone who lived it.

God, Reeve. You're so strong.

I push my notes away and lay my head on the table. I will it to be different for her. Please, God, if there is a God, hear me. Help her. Show me how to help her. I need to take her away from there, shelter her and care for her and show her real love.

I hardly ever cry. When my mom died, when Tessa left, I cried. That time I got lost walking home from Fallon Falls and no one came to find me. I was scared. I'd taken a different trail through the trees and it didn't lead me to the road. I climbed and climbed, thinking I'd come out at the top of the mountain or someone would come looking for me. No one did. I had to find my own way.

I'm not crying now. I'm . . . seething. Yes, I'm angry at life, at God. *Think, Johanna.* I need a strategy. Power. I can find a way.

I prowl the parking lot, the quad, the cafeteria, first floor, second floor, Arts wing, B2. The door's locked. She doesn't have a locker—or if she does, I've never seen her use it. You have to pay for a locker. You have to bring your own lock.

The halls are filling and among the surface swell, a recognizable head of hair bobs by. "Robbie!" I race to catch up with him as he veers into the media center. When I touch his back, he freezes.

"Robbie, it's me."

He turns slowly. His face is blank, impassive. Where is he?

"It's Johanna."

"I am here to cooperate," he says like a machine.

"Whatever. Do you know where Reeve is? Is she in the pit?"

He stares at my mouth.

"Downstairs," I say. "The pit of Acheron."

He smirks.

"Is she?"

He stands there with that stupid smirk on his face, so I reach up and slap him. Not hard.

His eyes go dead.

"God. Oh God. Sorry. I'm sorry, Robbie."

He looks at me. "Medic," he says.

I slit-eye him. "Just tell me where she is, *please*."

"Here."

I peer around him. There are computers and books and TVs in the media center, and people, but I don't see her.

Robbie says, "Did you turn in my senior project?"

Shit. "No. I'll do it today." I was thinking I wouldn't turn it in yet. I wasn't sure it'd be acceptable to Mrs. Goins. I was thinking I'd rewrite it.

"I have to graduate," Robbie says. He reaches out a hand and my first impulse is to brace for an attack, but he only places it on my shoulder. Then, with his other hand, he touches my face, my cheek. It's . . . creepy.

He clamps a hand around my neck.

My life flashes before me.

Robbie deadpans, "Turn it in."

The bell rings for class and he heads into the media center.

Okay, he's kidding. He has a morbid sense of humor. I feel my neck to make sure my trachea is intact.

A batch of curled memos and announcements, a couple of sealed business envelopes fill Mrs. Goins' mail slot. I stuff in Robbie's essay. I should've thought to put the pages in a report cover. Wait, I have one.

My Film Studies report. I remove it. I search the mailroom for a blank sheet of paper and find a stack in the trash from the Xerox. On a clean side, I make a cover page.

Senior Project
My Best and Worst Moments of High School
and What They Taught Me
by
Robbie Inouye

I wonder again why his name is different from Reeve's. I re-arrange his three sheets to put the good stuff first. The part about killing his mother is at the end. My hope is that whoever reads and evaluates the essays never gets beyond page one.

The maze of vents and pipes echoes and knocks and winds in-terminably through the school's underbelly. I take a wrong turn and lose my bearings. Water gurgles through a pipe.

B2 was unlocked when I tried it again, so I'm pretty sure she's down here. The pit looms ahead. The door's been re-placed, along with a padlock. Oh no. Someone discovered them. "Hello?" I call.

Nothing. The door's locked. I rest my forehead on the frame and say, "Please, if you're in there. Let me in." *Let me in, Reeve.*

I don't know how long I stand there; stand in silence.

When I get upstairs, people are herding into the gym for a morning assembly. I forgot about it. The cops have hauled in a wrecked car from an accident that happened earlier this year. It's scrap metal. A mother talks about how her son finally died after being in a coma for six weeks and I think of Carrie. She should just die. Dying would free her and let her mom move on.

Would dying be better than living in a hell on Earth?

Reeve's not at the assembly, not at lunch, not in Mrs. Goins' room last period. It's wishful thinking; the project's over.

If she thinks I'm giving up, she doesn't know me. She does not know Johanna Lynch.

Carrie's mother rails at Jeannette, shouting so loud she's waking the dead—but not the comatose. Carrie has a new bedsore. Jeannette strides past me into the foyer, looking harried.

I sign in and check the status chart. Oh my God. Frank has passed. Sweet old Frank. Rest in peace, Frankie-wanker.

Carrie's mother hangs over my shoulder. "You are to make a note on my daughter's chart to call me if *anything* changes. I mean, *anything*."

"Okay."

She whirls on Jeannette, who's come up behind her. "Someone used Carrie's lip gloss. I want you to find out who and fire them."

"Evelyn . . ."

She pivots and slams out the front door.

I widen my eyes at Jeannette.

Her shoulders sag. Blowing out a long breath, she says to me, "I've been thinking about what you asked. Your friend in the abusive situation?"

I nod.

"I was wrong. I wasn't thinking clearly. If it was me, or one of my children, I'd want someone to care."

I care.

"Make the call."

Make the call. Make the call. The mantra burrows into my brain. If I make the call, what will happen? Take 1: The cops show up. They restrain that guy, Anthony. They drag him from the house and lock him up. Take 2: As the cops are leaving, they see what a waste case the mother is. They take her too. Reeve and Robbie have to move. I never see Reeve again.

It's selfish, I know, but there has to be a way to help without losing her.

My final in Film Studies is an essay question on Unit Five. "Name three films that serve as examples of film as institution and explain how each reinforces and/or resists cultural paradigms and values."

Why can't we just watch *Dumb and Dumber*?

I b.s. a brilliant answer.

My last final of high school—you'd think I'd be happier to have it over with. I feel emptied. Reeve is right. Firsts are better. Firsts are filled with mystery and expectation; firsts are beginnings.

At my locker, a body crunches into me and smothers me in a hug. "We're graduating. Can you believe it?"

Novak clenches my arms and holds me away from her. Then she pulls me to her and kisses me on the lips.

I wrench out of her grasp so hard I hit my head on the locker door. "Why'd you do that?"

She laughs. "Chill, lesbo. I'm just happy." She opens her arms to embrace me again, but I stiff-arm her away. "Go kiss your fabulous boyfriend," I say.

I take off running.

"Johanna!"

The memory of Reeve's lips on mine, my first kiss. The memory I need to sustain me until the next time. Novak. She ruined it.

"Hold up, Banana."

I charge down the hall, desperately needing to get away from it, from her, from all of it. High school, loss, grief.

I race around the corner and plow into Mrs. Goins. She drops an armful of folders. I stoop to help her pick them up.

"I received Robbie's project," she says. "I assume you put it in my box?"

My breath is coming out in great gulping heaves, but I manage a nod. I'm on the verge of tears.

"Are you okay?" she asks, peering over her glasses as we stand.

I swallow hard.

She asks, "Did you read his essay?"

I shrug, hoping that'll be enough response.

"It's . . . unsettling," she says.

"But it's done, right?"

She shifts the load in her arms. "I suppose. We talked about it this morning at the staff meeting."

"So he'll graduate, right?"

She hesitates.

"You said if he wrote the essay, he'd graduate. He *has* to graduate."

"Oh, he will."

Thank God.

"Johanna, do you know if any of what he wrote is true?"

Make the call. Make the call. "We didn't discuss it. I got it done for you, okay?"

My feet carry me to the staircase and down the steps. Get away, escape. B2.

The padlock is mangled. As my fingers curl around the doorknob to the pit, a nuclear reaction bubbles the blood in my veins.

She's here.

Chapter 17

I open the door slowly so I don't freak her out. A conversation halts mid-sentence.

She glances up from the loveseat, where she sits cross-legged, eating a burger. "Oh snap, it's Johanna of Arc," she says.

Robbie's on the floor, a few feet away from Reeve. He sits up fast and slams his instrument case shut.

I step into the room.

Reeve says, "Who let the dogs in?" and Robbie goes, "Who who?" like a routine they've rehearsed.

I ease the door shut behind me.

Reeve watches Robbie remove his string from his pocket and begin threading it through his fingers. A crumpled Mickey D's wrapper lies beside him.

"Stay out of his way," Reeve says. "I mean it, Robbie. Don't mess with him."

I've intruded again. I always feel that way when she and Robbie are together.

She bites off a nibble of burger. "You don't give up." Reeve meets my eyes.

"Not on you."

Her chewing slows and she lowers the hamburger to her lap.

I'm about to say, Reeve, talk to me, but Robbie blurts, "I'll kill him. I'll kill both of them."

Reeve snarls, "Drop it, Robbie."

He sulks.

I wish he'd go. I want to be alone with her. Robbie winds the string around his index finger so tight it balloons the tip purple. "Robbie," I say. "You're graduating. I talked to Mrs. Goins."

His head whips up and he grins so wide I see all his teeth.

Reeve says, "You can hang your diploma on the wall. Oh, wait. You don't have a wall."

Robbie ignores her, unwinding his string.

Reeve pushes to her feet, hands the rest of the burger to Robbie, and ruffles his hair. "Go do that somewhere else, gradu-asstard." To me she says, "What do you want?"

She knows what I want.

Robbie snarfs the burger in one bite, then scrunches the length of string in a wad and jams it into his pocket. He stands, grabbing his case.

"What time is it?" he says at the door.

I look at Reeve.

She says, "How should I know?"

My eyes fall to her bare wrist.

He exits. Reeve moves behind me and kicks the door shut. "I—"

She reaches up and presses a finger to my lips. "You cannot fall in love with me," she says.

Our eyes hold. I clasp her wrist gently and kiss the fleshy part of her finger. "I already am."

She pulls her hand away. "You don't even know me."

"I know you kiss on the first date."

She blows out an irritated breath and flops down on the loveseat. She doesn't look at me. I smile. *Look at me.*

"I don't care about knowing you," I say. "I mean, I do, but it won't change the way I feel about you." *I've been in love with you since the day I was born, or reborn.*

She buries her head in her knees.

I approach her slowly, lowering myself onto the cushion. "You have to get out of there, Reeve. That house. Those people."

"Anthony's my dad's half brother. My uncle." She twists to face me. "He might be more."

What does that mean? I start to ask, but she throws me this defiant look, so I drop it. "You can't be in that house," I say. "It isn't safe."

"I live there. What am I supposed to do? Run? Been there. Done that."

"I could make a call."

She sits up straight. "Don't. Please." Her eyes plead. "They've been called. Everyone's been called. The cops get called regularly for yet another"—she air-quotes—"'domestic disturbance.'"

I'm confused, or ignorant. "Then why doesn't somebody do something?"

"Like what? Arrest us?"

"Not you. Him."

"You think it's about him?" Reeve shakes her head. "Johanna, Johanna, Johanna."

Don't mock me, I think.

She pushes to her feet and I reach out to her. "I just want to help you. Tell me what to do."

"Nothing," she says. "It's too late. There's nothing you can do. The damage is done."

Damage can be undone. No one's died. "There has to be a way."

"Nope." She perches on the edge of one of the plastic tubs, extending her legs and flexing her toes. Her feet smell a little, but so what?

I scoot over to sit directly across from her, taking both her hands away from her feet and pressing them between my hands.

She studies our hands together. Mine are so much bigger than hers.

"Come live with me," I say.

Reeve throws back her head and laughs.

"What? I'm serious."

"Girl, you move fast."

Her arms retract, but I hold on.

She adds, "One kiss and you love me and want me to move in with you. Have you set a date for the wedding?"

"May twenty-third," I say.

She smiles and shakes her head.

"What?"

"You're something. But I'm not sure what." She angles her head to peer sideways up at me.

A streak of fire ignites my lower belly. I want to kiss her so bad.

Gently, I pull her toward me. She rises off her butt, then I do. We stand in unison. I slide my arms around her waist and she doesn't resist, so I nuzzle her neck and see her skin prickle. Is she cold? Excited?

I moisten my lips. I raise her chin and she closes her eyes.

Sparks fire off every nerve ending from my lips to my face, to my ears, head, neck, toes. The kiss is explosive.

I pull us onto the loveseat. I stretch out the length of it, drawing her close to me, still kissing. We lie together and kiss. Somewhere in that universe of time, I whisper, "I love you, Reeve Hartt."

She responds by kissing me harder and longer and deeper. She loves me too. She's just afraid.

All the way home, the feel of her mouth on mine is so visceral I almost come. When we had to break it up, Reeve looked as dreamy and lovesick as I felt.

There are four voice mails on my phone at home. Reeve, I pray. Please be Reeve.

Three calls from Novak. Three desperate messages: "Johanna, call me. Please."

The phone rings as I'm stripping off my underwear and bra to drop into bed. I let it ring, then think, It might be Reeve.

I get up to answer.

"Hey, caught you."

Shit.

"Are you going to hang up on me?" she asks.

I exhale exhaustion and weariness and need.

"I know I was wrong," she says, "to kiss you in public. I should've waited until we were alone. And naked. Don't hang up!"

Please. I can't hear this.

"Where'd you go today?" she asks. "You, like, blended into the woodwork. Not that you would. I mean, you stand out. Oh, forget it. The reason I called is this list my mother wants me to make for my graduation party. She's still going through with it, like she's a martyr or something. She doesn't want to pay the caterer's cancellation fee, that's the only reason."

I can't care about her life anymore.

"So the list. You and Dante. I told her you and Dante. That's not good enough. It's never good enough with her."

Novak has lots of friends. Why is she bothering me with this?

"Johanna?" She hesitates. "You are coming, aren't you?"

Reeve's hair is coarse and tangled. A little dandruffy. I wish she'd let me shampoo her hair. I'd massage her scalp and . . .

"You can bring Reeve," Novak says, channeling my thoughts. "Hey, I'll put her on the list. Do you know her address?"

I close my eyes and resume our make-out session in the pit.

"Johanna?"

I think I gave her a hickey.

"You are coming. Aren't you?"

Definitely coming.

A knock sounds on the door. "There's someone here," I say to Novak. "I have to go."

"Wait! I need to tell you something else."

I set down the phone.

I fumble with the deadbolt and chain, finally unlatching the locks and yanking open the door.

"Well, I'm glad to see you're taking precautions," she says, shoving my shoulder. She smiles and flips her student ID at me. "This is an unscheduled inspection of the premises," she says. She pockets the ID. "I understand you're harboring a fugitive. Or will be."

My heart leaps. Will I?

Reeve swerves around me and enters the apartment. She surveys the room. When her eyes catch mine, they cling. See—neither of us can let loose of the other. Is she really moving in?

"Johanna. JoHAAANNA." Novak's voice.

I roll my eyes at Reeve. "Just a sec." I trip over the box Novak left and almost take a header. "I have to go," I tell Novak.

"Who is it?" she asks.

Reeve's watching me.

"I have to go." I don't wait for Novak to hang up.

"I hate her," Reeve says.

"Who?"

"Novak. Your *friend?*" She makes it sound like it's more than it is.

"Why do you hate her?"

"She uses you." Reeve checks out the kitchen, the hallway. "She's a rich bitch. They're all the same."

"She has her good points." Why am I defending Novak to Reeve?

"I can't stay." Reeve backs toward the door.

I grab her. It happens so fast; she reacts by slamming into

the wall and extending her arms to fend me off like I'm going to hurt her.

"No, Reeve—" I hold up my hands.

She shrinks into herself.

"Stay. Just for a while."

"I can't. I snuck out. If Anthony sees I took the van . . ." Her eyes dilate like a trapped animal's.

"Come tomorrow, then," I say. "I'll pick you up somewhere. I'll make you dinner."

She waffles her eyes. "You cook?"

"If you want to call it that. I cook, I clean, I'm the perfect housewife."

Reeve smiles a little. "You're the perfect everything," she says. "That's your problem."

"No, I'm the perfect nothing."

The space between us narrows. I lean in to kiss her and she doesn't back away. She doesn't come to me either.

I let her decide, yes or no.

She glances to the left.

In that split second before, though, I see desire. I feel want.

I say, "No pressure, okay? When you're ready."

Please be ready. Be ready soon.

Chapter 18

The midday sun slants through the window and I shoot upright in bed. What will I make Reeve for dinner? Beyond nuking a frozen entrée or cutting open a bag of salad, I can assemble a sandwich.

No one's home downstairs in the main house. Martin's laptop is open and Tessa's crocheting is sitting on the table. "Guys?" I call, even though I can't feel a heartbeat in the house.

I move through the living room to the bedrooms. As I pass the bathroom, a change in heat and humidity shifts my focus. I backtrack. The shower door is open and a wet towel is heaped on the mat.

"Tessa?" The showerhead drips.

The door to their bedroom is open. The bed is made, shams aligned, closet doors shut tight. "Martin?"

They got hungry; they're at the store. Martin's the cook in the house, so maybe he ran out of broccoli or butter or whole grain bread.

I return to the dining room. It must've been a last-minute decision for Martin to leave his laptop on. The screen saver hasn't kicked in and I look at what he was working on. Some list of names.

There are cookbooks galore that Martin brought with him from Minnesota. I select a skinny one: *Quick Mexican Dishes*. I flip through it and the pictures make me hungry. There aren't too many ingredients. Tortillas. Cheese. I can handle Mexican. As I turn to leave, I spy a book on the top shelf and grab it. *Making Love to Food: A Guide to Sexual Cooking*.

Oh, baby. Forget the fajitas.

I have to grocery-shop. Damn. I haven't deposited my check. The cash for my car insurance is still in my bag.

Except, it isn't. I dump the bag and can't find the envelope. I check all the usual places—pockets, drawers, divan cushions.

I had it, I know I did. Martin keeps a stash of cash in a cookie jar, which I only know about because one day these band geeks came to the door selling candy and Martin was making dumplings or something; his hands were covered with flour. He said, "Mojo, would you buy ten candy bars from these guys? There's money in the loaded potato."

That's what he calls the cookie jar. Martin won't mind. I'll replace the money as soon as I get paid.

I leave Martin an IOU: "I unloaded 40 from the potato. Pay U back. J."

Writing out a grocery list makes me think of Mom, and I don't want to. I want—need—to be happy.

On my way home from Safeway I think about calling Reeve to make sure she's coming. I mean, she never said yes. We didn't set a definite time.

Stupid. What if I'm going to all this trouble and she doesn't think I'm serious? She'll have to learn that about me—I'm always serious about her.

As I'm slicing a mushroom from cap to stem, the way the book shows, the phone rings. It startles me and I cut my finger. "Hello?" I answer, sucking the blood.

"It's me," she says.

My pulse races. "What time are you coming?"

"Did I say I was?"

All the blood drains out of me.

"Kidding. I'm calling to ask what time you want me."

I'm really bleeding. "Any time." I stanch the bleeding with pressure from my thumb. "Come now if you want."

There are voices in the background, yelling, a TV blasting. Reeve's voice lowers. "Can Robbie come too?"

He wasn't exactly in the plan.

"Never mind," she says. "Forget it."

"No, it's okay." I shouldn't have hesitated. "It's fine. Of course he can come." Snuff the candles, fade out of Joyland.

"Are you positive?"

That I want *her* here? "Yeah. Positive." I hope I sound enthusiastic. "I'll need to make more food."

"No shit. He eats like a pig."

Great.

In a low, sultry hiss, Reeve goes, "Thankssss."

I say, "Hurry."

I run downstairs to unload another twenty from the potato.

Along with a jumbo can of refried beans and grated Mexican cheese, I splurge and buy a set of six dinner plates. Something nicer than Tessa's Corelle ware. The mushroom and puff pastry dish with marinated asparagus will have to wait. It was a recipe for two, anyway.

When Reeve shows up, she's alone.

"Where's—"

"He isn't coming." She cups her hand on the doorknob over mine and closes the door. "He's asleep."

If that's autism, THANK YOU. Reeve's hair is up in a clip and her neck is exposed and so are the top of her breasts. I feel light-headed and horny.

Inches away, she breathes in my hair and we empty our lungs at the same time. Her eyes skim me up and down and come to rest on my chest.

I couldn't decide what to wear. Jeans. Duh. I couldn't pick a top. The sexiest thing I have is this chiffon negligee Novak gave me when she cleaned out her closet before Christmas. I was only trying on the negligee to dream, to imagine what could be.

Reeve's eyes rise to my neck, then skid down my arm. I reach across my front and slide the spaghetti strap back over my shoulder. I should've put on a bra, at least.

Reeve is wearing a bra. It's visible through her black, see-through blouse. Her jeans are cut so low and fit so tight I don't even have to imagine every mound and curve of her.

She can't seem to take her eyes off my chest.

"Um, I wasn't quite done getting dressed."

She lifts her eyes to mine. "You look done to me."

I laugh. God, I sound like a goat. Reeve fingers my chin, draws it to her, and kisses me.

She curls a hand behind my neck and kisses me harder.

My knees buckle and Reeve catches me collapsing. She laughs. So do I.

"What are we having to eat?" She trickles a hand down my arm as she moves past me into the living room. "I'm starving." She dumps her purse off on the coffee table.

"I was going to make this puff pastry thing. Before Robbie . . ."

She whirls on me.

"Quesadillas," I say.

"I love Mexican food."

What if she hated it? I didn't even think . . . My strap slips off again and I slide it up.

"What can I do to help?" Reeve rubs her hands together.

All the plates and silverware are out. My hair is still wet from the shower. Did I even comb it?

No, I had to try on this sexy nightie.

"I'll set the table," Reeve says. "You finish . . . whatever." Her eyes glom on to my chest again.

As I travel past her toward the back, we touch hands. If it's going to be just the two of us, I'm not ready. I want to put on makeup and do my hair.

Ten minutes later I come out to find the table set and the salad on. Reeve found the candles I bought and is dripping wax into Novak's ashtray. "I couldn't find your candleholders," she says, swirling the wax carefully in a circle.

"Because I don't have any?"

She places the lit candle in the center and ignites the other off its wick. "There." Her fingers spread apart. "Perfect."

The table looks beautiful.

"Drink before dinner?" she asks. She twists around and grips a bottle of wine by the neck.

"Where'd you get that?" I ask.

"I never come empty-handed," she answers.

I lift a water glass off the table and hold it out.

Reeve uncrinkles the foil seal. "Do you have a corkscrew?"

"I don't know. What does one look like?"

"Like a corkscrew?" She cocks her head.

She's so funny. "Martin probably has one," I say.

"Who's Martin?"

"Bro-in-law. Be right back." I set down my glass.

She follows me to the door. And out.

"It's just downstairs," I say.

"I'll come with you."

I don't know why I feel strange taking her into the house. Novak goes in and out like she owns the place.

"Who lives here?" Reeve asks as I roll open the sliding door.

"My sister, Tessa, and her husband, Martin."

"You never told me you had a sister."

Our time together hasn't been wasted with inconsequential chatter. "Family," I intone. "You know." I flip on the kitchen light. In the dining room the same scene as before, except that Martin's laptop has powered down.

"Weird," I think aloud.

"What?" Reeve scans the area.

"Looks like they went somewhere suddenly. Like, just picked up and left." I haven't put on shoes and Reeve must've kicked hers off upstairs. Her toenail polish is dark blue.

"Did you used to live here?" she asks. She does a three-sixty in the dining room.

"Yeah. When Tessa moved back, I moved out." In the kitchen, I tug open the utensil drawer and scavenge around for a corkscrew.

Reeve says, "Do you hate your sister?" She fixes on me.

"I don't . . . hate her."

"You don't . . . love her." Reeve widens her eyes.

"We just don't . . . connect. Not like you and Robbie." I find what looks like a corkscrew and say, "Let's go."

Reeve says, "You want him? You take him."

I don't really want to talk about sisters or brothers or anything family. Reeve ventures deeper into the living room.

She's gazing at the ceiling, the walls, the windows, seeming to absorb all the architectural details. A swirling plaster ceiling and crown molding. Aubergine. Hate the color.

"This is nice," Reeve says. "You have a nice family."

I shrug. "They're okay. Can we go?"

"A nice house and a nice family." Her voice sounds odd. "And you're nice. Too nice for me."

My blood chills. "Reeve, I'm not that nice, but I am that hungry. Why don't we eat now?"

Reeve rushes by me, muttering, "I'm out of here."

She tries to close the sliding door in my face, but I stick my arm through the opening and get crushed. I suppress the wail of pain. "You can't go."

She flies up the stairs. I chase her to the top and into the apartment. "We haven't even had dinner."

She snatches her purse off the coffee table. "Later. Never."

I have to stop her, hold her, make her stay. I grab her wrist and she wheels around. Her arm swings back and a fist comes right at me, knuckles smashing into my cheek and knocking me off balance. I see her mouth drop and her hand unclench. This high-pitched sound escapes from her throat.

"Why . . . ?"

The door slams. Vertigo hits me and my legs give out. I'm down. Pain shoots up my face and eye socket. My fingers come away from my cheek wet, smeared with blood. It's my blood.

I take off after her. I don't make it to the bottom of the stairs before I fall and crunch to Earth. "Reeve, wait . . . please." My voice sounds far away.

Acid burn of tears. Every nerve ending hurts.

A car swerves into the driveway, headlights flashing off my face, and I burrow my head in my arms.

The thunk of a door. "Johanna."

I'm still on my hands and knees, shielding my eyes; an urgent voice in my head mingles with bewilderment. I push to my feet, or I'm helped. "Johanna." Martin's soft voice in my ear. "I'm sorry."

His hair is disheveled and his eyes are bloodshot. He rakes a hand through his hair and says, "Tessa lost the baby."

Chapter 19

No reason, Martin said. She was working, not even standing up. She was helping a woman fill out a Medicare form when she started to bleed. She'd lost a lot of blood by the time Martin got there.

The image of it cleaves my brain like a chasm to understanding. Tessa sitting there, feeling the wet. Knowing what it is.

"She's staying in the hospital overnight for observation," Martin added. "Nothing serious."

Nothing serious. Except her baby died.

The candles melt down to gooey gnomes. I blow them out, then sit at the table in the dark, thinking. Trying not to think.

The left side of my face throbs and I get up to look in the mirror. Dried blood is caked on my cheek and eyebrow. My hair towel from earlier in the evening is on the floor, still damp. I pick it up and dab at the wound.

The gash isn't deep, nothing serious. I haven't lost any-thing. *Reeve?*

Don't think about it.

My left eye is swelling.

I lie in bed but can't sleep, so I get up over and over again to look at myself. The longer I look, the more I morph. The image of me, Johanna Lynch, my external reflection. My in-jury merges with the way I see myself.

Then I focus and remember what's important. My sister's in the hospital. Reeve got away.

I wait in the living room for Martin and Tessa. I hear the door open and Martin say, "We'll try again."

"No," Tessa whispers hoarsely. "I can't keep doing this. I can't have this on my conscience."

"What, honey?" Martin sets her carryall on the table.

I stand at the sofa.

"You're creating life," he says.

Tessa bursts into tears.

I should leave. This is between them.

Tessa takes off for the bedroom. She sees me but doesn't stop. I want to run to her, hug her, tell her how sorry I am. Martin casts a shadow over me. Clenching my arms, he says, "Johanna. My God. What happened to you?"

Instinctively, I cover the side of my face. "I fell down the stairs."

His eyebrows arch. "Do you need anything?"

"I'm fine." My eye is swollen shut, but it doesn't hurt. "How is she?" I stare after Tessa.

Martin drops his head to his chest.

"Sorry, stupid question. Does she need to talk or anything?"

"She needs to rest. Doctor's orders." He clamps a hand on my shoulder, sort of steering me out. "I'm sure she'll let you know when she's ready to talk."

No, she won't. She hates me.

As I'm studying my face in the mirror up close and personal, the phone rings. Reeve, calling to apologize?

"Hey, lesbo. You're alive."

I slump into a chair at the table, where the candle gnomes have hardened.

"I'm moving today," Novak says. "I have gobs of stuff for you. Clothes, books, shoes if they fit. I cleaned out my closet. . . . You're probably really busy, huh? I thought I'd drop these things by. . . ."

I feel alive. For the first time.

"Are you busy?"

Tessa's baby is dead and I'm alive.

"Johanna? I don't blame you for not speaking to me. I'm sorry. For anything and everything I ever did to you, I'm sorry."

A smile curls my lips and I lift my head. Actually, I'm happy. How can I be happy?

Novak says, "I need you."

That engages my brain. "What do you need now?" I snap.

She hesitates. "I have all this stuff for you, but I can't fit it in my car. I thought maybe I'd drop some off, then you could follow me back with your car and we could load up the rest."

My face is a tie-dye of blue green purple black yellow amber tan. Sort of cool.

"If I don't get everything out of here, I'm afraid Mom will sell it or give it to the Goodwill. Dante has to work—"

"Tessa lost the baby."

"What?" Novak gasps. "When?"

"She just had another miscarriage."

"Oh my God," Novak says. "Johanna. My God. Poor Tessa."

"I know," I say. "I need to be here."

"Of course you do. I'm so sorry. Tell Tessa I'm sorry. Martin too." Novak inhales audibly. "Oh my God," she says in an exhale. "Is there anything I can do?"

I press the wound to see if it changes color. "You have to move. You're busy."

"I'm not too busy to—"

"I have to go be with Tessa."

Novak says, "Call me later. You know, if you want to talk." She adds, "How's it going with Reeve?"

I hang up.

Joyland: Take 9

I open the gate and walk up the crumbling sidewalk. I ring the door-
bell and Anthony answers.

"Is Reeve here?" I say.

He ogles me. "Who nailed you, bitch?"

"You did, asshole." It might as well have been your fist, I think.
It should've been your face.

Reeve comes to the door and the guy explodes in gaseous fumes.
"Johanna. My love." She takes me in her arms. "I'm sorry. I'm
sorry, I'm sorry, I'm sorry." She kisses my eye and my cheek and
my lips. "I love you so much. Forgive me."

"You know I do."

"I need you. I need you, I need you, I need you."

"I know."

"I love you, I love—"

156

I press a finger to her lips. She doesn't have to say it. I know it. I've always known.

"Come away with me," I tell her.

We float to the car and drive off. We drive off the edge of the world.

. . .

Eye shadow I have. Three shades of brown. Neutral lip gloss. No foundation or whatever it's called. I brush on sparkly cheek highlighter, which must be Novak's. It only enhances the cut and the mass of swollen flesh over my cheekbone.

I should probably stay home until I heal. *When will that be?*

I am fascinated with my face, a need for people to see me, stare at me. Look at me.

Why hasn't Reeve called? She doesn't need to apologize; it wasn't her fault. Not really. I was so sure Reeve would stop by, the way she does without warning, that I called in sick for work last night. "The flu," I told Shondri. I faked a cough.

"I'm real sorry," Shondri said.

"I'll be in tomorrow for sure."

"Don't come in if you're sick. I can handle it."

"No," I promised her. "I'll be there."

I check myself out in the rearview mirror as I'm driving to school. I look tough.

Mrs. Goins is the first to say anything. "Johanna." She stops me in the hall. "My gosh. What happened to your eye?"

"I fell."

She frowns.

"It was an accident."

"My gosh," she says again. She keeps staring at me.

Now I feel too visible. "I'm late."

"Maybe you should see the nurse."

"I'm fine." I scuttle off down the hall, sensing her eyes on me. Now everyone is looking. People turn their heads.

Novak is camped out at my locker. Why does she have to come to school today of all days? She scrambles to her feet when she sees me. "Oh my God." She covers her mouth with her hands. "What the fuck?"

"I fell." I nudge her out of the way to open my locker.

"You fell?"

"I tripped on the stairs." I yank my lock and swing the door open.

"You klutz. When?"

She's standing too close.

I step back. "Friday or Saturday. I forget."

Novak's eyes fuse to my face. "Are you all right?"

"Yeah. Why wouldn't I be?"

She can't stop looking.

Go away, I think. You're not the one I need to see. My locker is empty. Classes are over. Why am I here?

I guess I'm hoping Reeve still has finals.

"Johanna." Novak opens her arms to me.

No! "I told you. I'm fine."

Chapter 20

The media center is empty. I take that back. One person hunches over a PC, clicking away like a time bomb. As if on cue, she glances up, watches me as I wander toward the silent reading area and over to the beanbag chairs.

I drop into one and shut my eyes. I mentally call Reeve: *Are you here? I need to see you, touch you, tell you it's okay. I need to—*

I feel a presence and open my eyes. "What?" I ask Britt.

Tentatively, she lowers herself into the beanbag next to mine. She leans forward.

"What?" I say again.

"She did it to me too."

"Did what?"

"Marked me."

I make a face. Ow. "What are you talking about?"

"You know."

No, I don't. Marked her. How?

"She's mean," Britt says. "She's got this ugly place inside her and you never know what'll open it and set her off. She'll keep doing this to you."

"You're jealous. You had her; you let her go."

Britt just sits there, staring. Then glancing away like she can't look.

I push to my feet and sling my pack over my shoulder. I need to find Reeve.

The second I step out into the quad, a hand shoots out to clamp my wrist and I'm yanked backward so hard my shoulder pops.

His case clubs my leg. "Let go, Robbie."

He holds firm.

"You're hurting me."

His hand loosens. He looks crushed. "I just wanted you to come," he says.

"Come where?"

His eyes meld to my swollen cheek.

"I fell. Is Reeve in the pit?"

He doesn't answer. He turns and walks off.

If Robbie's here . . .

B2 is open. Robbie hits the light and illuminates the underworld. He doesn't check to see if I'm behind him, but it's like he knows I am. Like he can smell me.

When he opens the door to the pit, Reeve jumps up from the floor. A human shield, Robbie, blocks my entrance, and her exit. He pushes Reeve onto the loveseat.

"See?" he says, yanking my wrist to pull me in. "I told you."

Reeve meets my eyes and swallows hard.

"You did that to her," Robbie says accusingly.

"I know what I did." Reeve's eyes never leave me as she gets up, gazes into my eyes, moves toward me.

"Reeve . . ."

"Don't." She jabs my shoulder with the base of her hand.

"I know you didn't mean it."

"Yeah?" she mutters. "What if I did?"

Robbie says, "She didn't mean it. She loves you."

I blink over at him. He's fixed on Reeve. She turns away. Did she tell him that? I say to Robbie, to Reeve, "I love her too."

Robbie steps around me, out the door. Out of our space.

We lie together on the loveseat, touching each other's faces and eyes and lips. Tracing contours and lines and shapes. Reeve keeps kissing my eye.

She doesn't say she's sorry, but she doesn't need to.

I tell her about Tessa, the baby, how and when it happened. The first baby too. Reeve listens as she touches my forehead, my eyebrow; she kisses my eye. I tell her I understand about her hitting me. She can't help it.

She watches my lips as I talk. She says, "You're so stupid."

"What?"

"To love me."

"You love me too."

"I'll hurt you. I'll continue to hurt you. Ask Britt. Ask everyone."

"You can't hurt me," I tell her. Fuck Britt. And Melia. Fuck numbers one through . . . whatever.

"This doesn't hurt?" She presses a finger to my cut. Involuntarily, I flinch.

"See? You don't believe in reality? Physical evidence?"

"I believe in truth."

She runs a fingertip across my eyelashes. Her eyelashes are scant, both eyes now. "We didn't even eat first," she says.

"I *know*," I say. "Come over later."

"You didn't drink the wine, did you?"

I click my tongue. "No. I saved it. I knew you'd be back."

"Oh, you knew." A smile tugs her lips. "You know me so well."

I kiss her nose, her eye. "Plus, you forgot your shoes."

"Tell me about it. I drove home barefoot and stepped on broken glass in my driveway."

I get up to check out her feet. "Are you hurt?"

She pushes me back down. She rolls on top and kisses me hard.

Time dissolves.

"Do you have my shoes?" she asks, coming up for air.

"I'm holding them for ransom."

She gazes at me, into me. She slithers her fingers down the length of my arm. "Are you okay?"

"Yes," I say. "More than okay."

"I should have forced Robbie to come. He would've protected you."

We kiss again. Time washes away.

Robbie bursts in and says, "School's out." His case clunks on the floor.

Reeve and I both stagger to our feet, then giggle as we

steady each other. I glance over at Robbie, expecting him to smile, to be happy for us.

He looks . . . brain-dead.

As we wind through the labyrinth, one sentence circulates in my brain: Robbie would've protected you.

I've been physically hurt by two people in my life. Reeve, which doesn't count because it isn't her fault. And Robbie, when he dislocated my shoulder.

It wasn't his fault either, but there's a difference. Given time and love, Reeve could learn to control her rage. She has the capacity, I know.

I'm not so sure about Robbie.

"What's his name?" Jeannette plumps the pillow while I hold up Carrie's head. Her eyes are partially open but unresponsive.

Because only guys smack girls around?

"It was an accident," I tell her.

She motions for me to set Carrie down. As I do, a breath leaks out from between her lips and Jeannette and I both freeze.

But it's only a reflex.

Jeannette smoothes Carrie's silk comforter across her chest and shoulders. "It's always an accident, Johanna. Oldest excuse in the book."

This conversation is over. "I'll sit with her for a while."

"Don't touch anything. Evelyn has a photographic memory."

Jeannette's gaze penetrates me, like she can see into my core. "I'm fine," I tell her. My core is solid.

Joyland: Take 10

I feed her my last bite of chocolate mousse and she closes her eyes in ecstasy. "Rapture," she breathes. As I slide the spoon slowly out of her mouth, I place my lips against hers and taste.

Butter and cream. I lick the inside of her mouth and around her tongue. We kiss across the smoldering candle. Without detaching our lips, she comes around the table and slides onto my lap.

She clasps my face in her hands and kisses me hard, bends my head back on my neck. I think my neck will snap. Come with me, Reeve, I think. I can't die without you.

She slips my spaghetti straps over my shoulders, runs her hands down my bare arms, and presses her lips to my neck.

My arms curl around her waist. Bare, naked skin, soft and velvety. Baby fuzz. Her cami is silk, slick, and cool. My hands journey up underneath and I feel her ribs, her spine, her bra. I trace *both hands around her sides to the front. I locate the snap. As her breasts spring free, she says, "Kiss it."*

. . .

"What are you doing here?"

I jump.

Evelyn says, "Do you have permission to be in here?"

"I, uh . . ."

She reaches across Carrie and yanks her hand out of mine. Tucking Carrie's arm under the covers, she says, "Who are you? I've seen you here."

"Johanna," I answer, standing. "I volunteer at the hospice."

"As what?"

That's a good question. "I was just keeping Carrie company."

"She doesn't need company." Her mom adjusts her head on the pillow and adds, "In case you didn't notice, she's asleep. She needs to rest."

She needs to die, I think.

"Please leave."

Not a problem.

In the public ward, Mrs. and Mr. Mockrie have their beds rolled together. So sweet. They're both sleeping. Quietly, I pull a chair up and sit, drinking in their peace.

Joyland: Take 11

She says, "Will you marry me?"

"Yes." I don't hesitate.

Her luminous smile radiates sun and moon and stars. She is my galaxy, my gravity, the center of my being.

We decide to wear white, to symbolize the purity of our love. We buy matching wedding gowns, strapless and snug at the waist, flowing, milky rivers of white satin to the floor. Our veils are lace. Through the snowflake pattern, we gaze into each other's eyes.

At the last minute, in the bedroom getting dressed, we decide to walk down the aisle barefoot. She slips a garter up my leg and pauses, moving both her hands around my left thigh. She falls to her knees. She lifts my dress and kisses me, there, between my legs. It tingles. She crooks her finger and I look. She's left a lipstick print on my thong.

"Mark me," she says.

• • •

"Aggie? Where are you?" Mr. Mockrie struggles to sit up.

"She's right here." I take his hand in mine.

Tears bubble in his eyes and I pat his shoulder. "She's here, Mr. Mockrie. She'll always be with you."

Chapter 21

I stop at Taco Bell on my way home from the hospice, then remember I have quesadilla ingredients for an army. When the
cashier at Taco Bell stares at me, I just smile. Let her think
what she wants. My black eye, it's like . . . a badge of honor, or
proof I'm alive.

Reeve left two messages on my voice mail. "Hi. It's me. I
hate leaving messages."

Two: "Don't call me here. I don't want that bastard trash
talking to you. I think I can get out later, like eleven? Will you
light a candle for me?"

"A cathedral full of candles, Reeve."

I wrench on the shower and step in. My face pulses as
hot water expands every pore. I close my eyes and Fallon
Falls appears. I'm standing under the plunging cascade of
water, my face and body pounded by the force of unhar-

nessed energy. Reeve comes into view. Reeve disappears. Physically and emotionally drained, I'm too tired to even get to Joyland.

A dusty box of tea lights is left over from Tessa's days in the apartment. I light one for each window, then all the others for the planks of every step. When I switch off the inside lights, it looks totally romantic. I sit hugging my knees on the landing, waiting for Reeve.

I hear her first. She says, "Don't disappear. Let me know when it's time to leave."

"It's time to leave."

Robbie came?

At the bottom of the stairs, they stop. "Hi," I say, standing. "You made it."

Reeve doesn't say anything. Robbie goes, "Are we having a séance?"

Reeve backhands him in the chest.

"Come on up," I say.

Robbie asks, "Do you have rat traps? Are there spiders?"

"He's afraid of creepy crawlies," Reeve says. "He's a wuss."

"No rats," I tell him. "No roaches or spiders."

Reeve has to shove him up the stairs. He peers cautiously into the apartment, sniffs the air, and puckers his nose.

"Scrubbing Bubbles," I tell him. I smile at Reeve.

She pushes him in and Robbie goes, "Graup," or something. "You live here?"

Reeve says, "Look out for the bat."

He covers his head.

Reeve cricks a grin at me. She snakes a hand behind my head and pulls me in to kiss her.

A light-year later Reeve yells, "Don't go in there!"

I jerk around to see Robbie in the hall.

"That's Johanna's private space. You have no right." Reeve takes off after him.

"Don't worry about it." Shutting the apartment door behind me, I call, "Go ahead and look around. You guys want something to drink?"

Robbie stumbles back into the living room, his jaw slack. "You live here?" he says again.

Reeve shoves him a little. "Shut up. You sound like a tard."

"Could I move in?" he asks.

I look from Robbie to Reeve. "Anytime."

Reeve says, "Don't give him ideas." She retrieves an object from her bag. "I didn't have anything to wrap it with," she says, handing it to me.

It's heavy. "You didn't have to get me anything."

She looks into my eyes. "Yeah," she says. "I did."

Oh, Reeve.

"Open it."

The box is long and black, with a silver emblem. Pretty. I set it on the coffee table and lift off the top.

"Oh my God," I gasp.

"They're sterling silver," Reeve says.

Two candlesticks, a matched set.

"Oh my God," I say again. "Where did you . . . ?"

I don't finish. These had to cost, like, a hundred dollars. Where would Reeve get . . . She takes my face in her hands and kisses me.

"I'm dying of starvation," Robbie says. He finds the bowl of chips I planned to set out, along with the jar of salsa. *Don't think about where she got the money.*

Robbie sinks to the low divan, his knees hitting his chin.

As I'm replacing the candlesticks in the box, Robbie says, "Can we watch these movies?"

"What . . . ?" Shit. The DVDs.

Reeve says, "Go ahead. Put them out."

"What?" Oh, the candlesticks. "I don't have any long candles." I hurry over and snatch the DVD Robbie plucked up off the floor. His eyes glint.

Reeve says, "Damn. I should've bought candles. I knew I should have bought candles." She fists her leg, hard.

"It's okay." I scramble to gather all the DVDs and toss them into the coat closet. "Next time."

Reeve says, "Johanna?"

I turn. She's come up behind me with a glass of wine.

Robbie says, "Where's mine?"

"You don't drink," she informs him.

"Yes, I do."

"No, you don't." She sips, then spits it back into her glass. "I forgot." She raises her glass and chinks mine. "To firsts," she says.

"Firsts," I repeat. We drink together.

Robbie sprawls the length of the divan, looking pissed.

"He's on meds," Reeve says.

"No, I'm not. But you should be," Robbie growls.

Reeve lowers her glass and glares at him. Then her face softens. She walks over and hands him her glass of wine. "Okay. But don't get wasted. I may need you to drive home."

He drives?

Reeve returns to the kitchen for another glass, while Robbie gulps his wine, dribbling it down his shirt. He doesn't even notice.

"Shove over." Reeve throws his ankles off the end of the divan and Robbie flails to sit up. She flops down next to him. "Cheers." She raises her glass.

I sit on the coffee table across from her. "Cheers." We all clink.

The wine smells spicy and tastes like . . . cranberries? I'm not really a connoisseur.

Reeve eyes me over her glass. God, why did she bring him? I want to attack her.

I stand and say, "I'll start dinner."

"Let me help." Reeve bounces to her feet.

She shadows me to the kitchen, tickling the back of my neck, saying, "He'll pass out after one glass. Plus, his brain shuts down at ten."

"How can you tell?" I ask.

She thumps my back, playfully. I open the refrigerator to retrieve all the ingredients, but Reeve nudges me out of the way. "I'll get everything." She kisses me first and I melt.

The TV comes on at some point and there's heavy breathing and moaning. I glance over and go, "Crap." I missed a DVD, or he found them. I hustle across the room and wrench the remote out of Robbie's hand. "We're not watching TV."

He pouts.

"How's your sister?" Reeve asks from the kitchen, where she's sawing a tomato with a dull knife.

"I don't know," I say. "I haven't seen her." I haven't talked to her, haven't run into her. She hasn't come up to have a conversation with me.

"Tell her I'm sorry about the baby," Reeve says.

"I will. If I talk to her." Where'd I leave my wine?

Reeve opens the refrigerator and pulls open the vegetable crisper. She says, "I can't stop thinking about how it would be to lose a baby. I mean, if you really wanted it. Not like an abortion, where you choose. Mom tried to abort us."

"What?"

"Where's the cheese? You have cheese, don't you?"

"Um, yeah. In the door." I'm stunned. "How do you know?"

"About the abortion? She told us."

God.

"It was too late by the time she went in to have us aborted. She's so stupid. Do you want kids?" Reeve asks.

I take a gulp of wine. No. Yes. I don't know. I say, "I'm an avowed lesbian."

Reeve laughs. "Yeah. I used to think I was bi, for about an hour." She yanks open a silverware drawer and withdraws the meat cleaver. "Do you want this chopped or shredded?" She poises the knife over the head of lettuce.

"Whatever," I say.

Reeve adds, "I told you me and Robbie are twins, didn't I?"

My double take is classic. "How?"

She screws up her face. "The sperm meets the egg. . . ."

"I mean, you have different last names." I mean, he's autistic.

"Not to mention how much we look alike." She chops lettuce, while my brain scrambles to catch up. She says, "My mom's a whore. She turns tricks for money."

I don't get the connection. I sit in a chair at the table, wine in hand, watching Reeve butchering that head of lettuce.

"She was sleeping with so many dicks, there's no telling who our father is."

Unbelievable. Twins.

"I sort of look like my dad, or at least the guy Mom says is my dad. She was sleeping with Anthony too, so she gave him credit for Robbie." She exaggerates a smile.

Is that even legal? I want to ask her about the autism, but instead I say, "Do you want kids?"

"Oh yeah. Ten at least."

I can't tell if she's serious.

"I did it once with a guy," she says, looking up and meeting my eyes. "Does that disgust you? You being so avowed and all."

I stick out my tongue at her and her eyes gleam.

"Did it count?" I ask.

Her eyes go blank. Ripping the tortilla package open with her teeth, she spits out the corner and says, "What's Robbie doing?"

I swivel my head. His glass of wine is empty, clutched in one hand on his chest while the other arm hangs limply to the floor. "Zoning. Sleeping."

"I had to bring him," she says in a lowered voice. "I'm sorry." She searches a couple of cupboards for something.

"What do you need?" I ask.

"Cookie sheets. An aluminum tray. Whatever we're going to broil these on."

"Under the stove." I get up to show her.

She bends to the oven drawer and clangs pans around, then withdraws a blackened cookie sheet I've never used. I watch her assemble the quesadillas like she's done it every day of her life.

"Do I just put it on broil?" Reeve asks, studying the oven dial.

"The oven doesn't work."

She spins around.

"We'll have to nuke them."

Reeve just looks at me. "You might've told me that before I put them on a cookie sheet."

My face flares. "Sorry. You can use plates."

Reeve goes, "Then I'll have to do them one at a time."

"Yeah."

"And they won't be crispy."

"No."

She lets out a short breath.

She had a plan and I screwed it up. I suck as a girlfriend.

The quesadillas cook fast, anyway. Reeve hands the plates to me and I transport them to the table. The lettuce and tomatoes add a gourmet touch. "They look awesome," I tell her.

"They would've been better broiled."

"I know. I'm sorry."

Reeve goes over and shoves Robbie awake. As he stumbles to the table, I pull over a step stool so he can use my chair.

"No." Reeve pushes me off roughly. "He can sit on the stool." Is she still mad about the oven?

Robbie and I switch. He's groggy and I feel the same way, though my stupor is probably from the wine. Reeve refills my glass and hers. She pours Robbie a little. "To our first meal together." She raises her glass and clinks mine. She clinks Robbie's.

Robbie says, "To DVD porn."

Reeve ignores him. "To Johanna," she says. "My first avowed lesbian."

I crack up. Really? We drink.

"To Reeve," I toast. "My first . . . everything."

Robbie swipes his nose with the back of his hand, coughs, and a loogie flies out of his mouth and onto my quesadilla.

Reeve looks at my plate, then up at me. She bursts into laughter.

Her laughter makes me laugh.

She says, "He's an asstard, but what can I do?"

Chapter 22

Joyland: Take 12

Reeve strikes the last chord and holds it while the crushing roar of the crowd detonates eardrums. She throws her head forward, bending at the waist, flinging her arms out to the side and letting her guitar swing free on the strap. As she unfolds, the people scream their adoration. She nods to Robbie beside her.

He blows a discordant riff on his saxophone and the notes trickle into space.

I push the button to engage the hydraulic lift.

A square of stage shifts where Reeve is standing. Smoothly, it descends. Roaring cheers echo down into the chamber where I wait.

When Reeve hits the bottom, I'm there to meet her. She removes the guitar over her head and I say, "You were awe—"

She pulls me to her and kisses me hard, rough. Her tongue jams into my mouth. I catch my breath and inhale her. She's hot. She's thirsty. She digs her mouth and teeth into me and my flesh smears her sweat. Our knees buckle as we kneel together, kissing, tonguing, groping every inch of bare, slick skin.

Strobe lights flash above us. Raw, shooting streaks of blue and green and red. They ripple over our bodies. The noise is a drug.

I feel the jolt, the surge. Motors whir and we're rising. We're high, higher, Reeve's mouth is on mine, her body stretched out, legs extended. We're naked, horizontal, and exposed. I'm vaguely aware of the motion up up up, then off. We're on the stage.

The audience is manic. We're making love in front of a hundred thousand cheering people. We do it. We give them a show.

The sky glitters with stars and moons. Robbie blips a sparkling riff, then disappears. It's only me and Reeve, one star. We are the night.

. . .

Light streams through my miniblinds and I bolt upright. I check the time: 9:36. I forgot to set the alarm.

Wait.

There's no school today. I fall back down. School is over. I blow out relief and bliss.

I survived high school. Is there a club for high school survivors? A special-color ribbon? I really don't think I'll be looking back with fondness ten or fifty years from now. No medals or trophies or awards of distinction. My best moment has come at the end, when I finally connected with her.

I saved the best for last.

Novak calls as I'm reheating Reeve's leftover quesadilla for breakfast. Last night, Reeve and I had only started kissing and getting into each other when Robbie announced, "It's time to go." Reeve pushed me away so fast, it was like a car bomb exploded in her brain.

"We're going to pick up our caps and gowns today, right?" Novak says.

"No," I answer automatically. "I'm going with Reeve and Robbie."

Where did that come from? We didn't discuss graduation.

Novak doesn't speak for a minute. "So, do you hate me now?"

I suppress a weary sigh. "No."

"I didn't know what I was doing, okay? I was temporarily blinded by lust or insanity. Make that overwhelming guilt."

"About what?" I ask.

"All those times I had someone and you didn't."

A claw rips my gut. "So it was a pity kiss? Wow, thanks."

Novak huffs a breath.

"I have to go," I say.

"Johanna, wait. God!" she cries. "Mom hired this party planner and a decorator and a live band for my grad bash."

A live band? Just like in my sex dream. Hey, am I prophetic?

"Won't she be surprised when, like, two people show up?" Novak laughs.

I chew off a hunk of quesadilla and zone. If Reeve deposited DNA on her tortilla, we are officially exchanging body fluids.

"I sent Reeve and Robbie an invitation. Do you think they'll RSVP?"

I swallow my bite. "How'd you find her address?"

"I have my ways. Mooahaha."

"What ways?" I don't want Novak talking to Reeve—ever.

"Student directory? Duh." Novak rambles on and I'm gone. We both still had most of our clothes on, on the bed. Reeve kept her eyes closed when we kissed. I tried, but my natural instinct is to open my eyes, to see her.

"How's Tessa?"

That brings me back. "I don't know. Fine, I guess." Martin hasn't been up to report on her status. She certainly hasn't reached out.

Novak blurts, "Couldn't I come live with you? Just for the summer?"

Before I can reply, she adds, "I'm sorry. It's just . . . I hate it here. I'm lonely. Dante's never home."

Imagine Reeve living here with me. We'd spend every moment together, in Joyland, where we'd ride along the beach and dash under waterfalls.

"Okay, thanks for listening," Novak says. "I'll let you go. I didn't mean to make this your problem."

"Novak—"

"I love you, Banana," she says, and the line goes dead.

Please, Novak. Please get out of my head. And elsewhere.

What am I going to do today? I call Reeve.

Her mother answers. "Who is this?" She sounds drunk.

"Johanna. A friend of Reeve's," I say.

"What kina friend?"

I think I hear Reeve's voice in the background. "A friend from school." Her mother goes, "It's a frien' a yours. Since when do you have frien's?"

A guy laughs.

Reeve's voice: "Give me that, bitch." There's muffled scuffling and Reeve comes on. "Yeah?"

"Hi. It's me."

She says, "What are you doing?" Kind of mad.

"Calling you?"

"That was a good idea, wasn't it?"

My stomach plunges. Reeve doesn't say anything else.

"Are you busy today?" I ask. "Do you want to come over?"

She covers the phone or something, but it doesn't mute her voice. "Do you mind? This is private."

"One of your cunt lickers?" he says.

There's a crack and a squeal. Reeve yells, "Robbie, no!" She comes back on. "Don't call me here." The phone cuts out.

The horror of her life grows in my chest like cancer.

I head to my room, seething. I need to get her out of there. Take a drive. Pick her up and maybe drive to Fallon Falls. As I'm clomping down the stairs to leave, Tessa slides open the patio door and steps out. She has on shorts and a grungy tee of Martin's that reads: DINOSAURS DIED FOR OUR SINS.

"Are you leaving for school?" she says. "It's late." She checks her watch.

"School's over," I tell her.

"It is?" She blinks like she's been asleep, or out of it. "I guess it is that time already. Do you have a watch?"

"Yeah. Why?" Pretty cold. I want to ask how she is, but I can't get the words out.

We stand there. A cloud passes in front of the sun and the temperature drops ten degrees. Tessa clutches her coffee mug with both hands and drinks from it. She glances up and starts to cough. I want to pound her back, comfort her, tell her how much I love and miss her.

She chokes out, "What happened to you?"

The wound is scabbed over and the bruise is receding. Still yellow-gray around the edges.

"I fell down the . . ."

Tessa says, "Why didn't you—" at the same time I say, "It was the same night you—"

We both stop. "I'm so sorry about the baby," I say.

She says flatly, "Thank you. Isn't that what I'm supposed to say?"

I don't know. Is she asking me, or telling me. . . .

"Johanna, I—"

My key ring falls off my thumb and chinks on the flagstone. I bend to scoop up the keys. When I straighten, Tessa's looking at me, into me. "I can't believe you're not going to your own graduation. It's an accomplishment," she says. "It means something."

I shrug. "Not to me."

"Not to you," Tessa repeats. "What is significant and meaningful to you?"

"Besides being gay? Besides coming out to you and you not even caring enough to call me and talk about it?" My voice sounds shrill.

Tessa swallows hard. Her cheeks flush red, like mine always do when I'm embarrassed or mad.

My throat closes completely. I have to get out of here.

*   *   *

I veer into a 7-Eleven to use the pay phone. *This* is significant and meaningful in my life, Tessa. I dial Reeve's number. The mother answers and I hang up. Your love and acceptance. *That* would have been significant.

All you had to do was call. Say, Johanna, I got your letter.

I get in the car and drive. When someone writes, "I have something really important to tell you," you respond. When they write, "Last time you were home I wanted to talk to you about it, but I was too scared. I don't know why. I know you love me. You'll love me no matter what. Right?" You confirm, Tessa. I poured out my *heart* to you.

What was your reaction when you read, "Okay, here goes. I'm gay"? What did you think? For weeks, months, I sweated it. I still do, every day. Are you deliberately making me go through this hell? You've never once brought up the subject the whole time you've been home. Significant and meaningful? What's *your* definition, Tessa?

I look up and I'm sitting at the curb in front of Reeve's house. Consciously, I channel my anger into courage to get out and go up to Reeve's door. As I'm locking the car, Reeve storms out of the house, her mother on her heels. "I told you I need a fix *today*," she screeches.

"I heard you!" Reeve heads for the van. I wave to flag her down, but she shouts, "I'll follow you!" and jumps in the van.

I get back in the car and shift into gear. Reeve backs out the driveway and squeals a wide arc in the street, then waits for me to pass her. About half a mile down the road, right before the highway ramp, I pull into a Ramada Inn and Reeve drives up behind me. We both get out.

"What do you want?" she yells, stalking up to me and whacking my shoulder.

I take her hand. "You." I pull her to me, pressing her face to my shoulder. "It's okay," I say into her hair. "I'm here."

She doesn't struggle. "Why?" she asks.

"Why what?"

She smacks me again. "Stop saying that. Why?" she repeats. "That's what I want to know. Why do you care?"

I trace the side of her face with my knuckles. "Because I love you. And you need me."

"You're wrong. And you're stupid." But she snakes her arms around my neck.

"And you're warm," I say.

And you're mine.

Chapter 23

Reeve points across the street to a Village Inn. "Can we go there? I'm hungry."

"Have you ever been?"

She frowns. "No."

"Then, yeah. It'll be a first for both of us."

She smiles into my eyes.

I ache to hold her hand crossing the street, but if someone honks or hurls a slur . . . Reeve doesn't need that right now.

At VI the hostess shows us to a booth and we scoot in across from each other. I feel lighter, buoyant almost, like a boat. Reeve moors me.

"You have to get out of there," I tell her.

The waitress comes and Reeve orders coffee. Reeve opens the menu and says, "I don't have any money."

"I'm buying," I tell her. "Order whatever you want."

She studies the menu while I study her over it. She's not wearing makeup and her eyes seem smaller, more recessed. A carafe of coffee arrives and Reeve pours us both a cup. "Are you getting breakfast or lunch?" she asks.

I'd check my watch if I was wearing one. "Whatever you're getting."

Reeve drinks her coffee black and I make a mental note: Learn her habits. The waitress returns and Reeve orders French toast. "Same," I say.

I lean across the table and reach out my hands. "I'm serious about you moving in."

She pulls the rack of jellies over in front of her and sorts through them. "We haven't even had sex yet."

"We will."

She doesn't glance up, but her lips twist. Her face is kind of pale and splotchy. The few eyelashes she has left are white blond.

"I know what you're going to say," I continue. "Bring him. Robbie can move in too."

"Just move in." Reeve skids the jellies to the wall.

"I'll help you move."

She blows out a breath between her teeth.

"What?"

She sits back, crosses her arms, and steels her face. She looks so fierce and bold. I scoot out the end of the booth and around the table to slide in next to her, to put my arm around her, both arms. She lists, resting her head on my shoulder.

"You don't understand," she says quietly. "You don't know everything."

"I don't care." Only now matters. What we do with our life together.

Reeve doesn't speak, so I press my temple to her head to will her thoughts into my brain.

The waitress brings our food. She looks at me and says, "Are you sitting on that side?"

I go, "Is that okay?"

She sets our plates in front of us and replies, "I don't care, but it's a family restaurant."

Reeve and I look at each other and crack up. I'm staying put.

The French toast is awesome. I can't remember the last time I ate a real breakfast.

"Are you going to graduation?" Reeve asks, sawing off a corner of bread.

"I don't know. Are you?"

"Are you kidding?" She chews and swallows. "It's the biggest day of Robbie's life. The whole family's coming." She pours more hot syrup over her stack and adds, "Even my dad might show."

"I thought he was gone."

She eats in silence.

"You have to come," Reeve says in this pleading voice. "I want you to graduate with me."

"Then I will."

She freshens her coffee from the pot and says, "We have to go to Novak's party too."

"No."

"Yes." She whaps my arm. "We're both going. I want to see that bitch's face when I fuck you in her bed."

I hesitate . . . then laugh.

Reeve takes my face in her hands and kisses me. In broad daylight, in the Village Inn.

We drive back to my apartment to hang for a while. Get naked? Do it in *my* bed I hope I hope. Tessa and Martin are out back planting flowers or shrubs. Martin usually does the yard work, cleans the house, cooks. He's the total package.

Reeve says, "Is that your sister?"

I tighten my grip on her hand and tug her toward the stairs. "Do you know when we can pick up our caps and gowns? Like, how much time do we have?" I start up the stairs, but Reeve slips out of my grasp. She heads for Tessa.

Shit.

Tessa straightens, arms at her sides, digger pointed at the ground.

Reeve says, "I'm sorry about your baby."

Tessa's eyes fuse to mine. What is that expression? Horror? Outrage? She aims the sharp point of the digger at Reeve, or me.

Martin pops up from behind the forsythia bush. "Hey, Mojo." He looks at Reeve.

"This is Reeve," I say, threading my fingers between hers. "My girlfriend."

Martin's eyes bulge. He sticks out his hand and shakes Reeve's. "I'm Martin, the evil bro-in-law."

Reeve says, "I'm sorry about your baby."

Martin cuts to Tessa, then back to Reeve. "Thank you."

Tessa, with the digger.

Reeve adds, "I was in your house while it was happening."

"What?" Tessa says, sounding shocked.

"We're out of here." I go to grasp Reeve's hand, but she's way ahead of me. She's halfway up the stairs. On the landing, she crosses her arms and taps her foot. I reach around her to unlock the door.

Reeve charges inside and whirls on me. "They didn't even know who I was. Didn't you tell them about me?"

"No. I mean . . ." I expel a breath. "My sister knows I'm gay, but—"

She storms down the hall and slams into the bathroom. I say through the door, "Reeve, I'm sorry." I'm not sure what I'm apologizing for. "We don't talk that much. Not about significant things. Meaningful things."

The door swings open and Reeve lunges out at me. She smashes me against the wall, her face on fire. "Bye."

She heads out.

"Don't go!" I chase her down. "Reeve." I catch her as she grabs for the doorknob, flinging my arms around her waist from behind and pulling her into me.

We stand pressed together, front to back. She's trembling. "I'm sorry. I don't think about introducing my friends to Tessa anymore."

"Is that all I am? A friend?"

"Of course not," I say. "I love you."

"Am I the only one?" she asks.

"Yes. Completely." First, last, and always.

She turns and kisses me so hard she cuts my lip on her teeth, then pushes me back. I taste blood.

Her face disintegrates and she shrivels into herself. I hold her; kiss the top of her head gently. "I want us to be together. Always." She needs tenderness, reassurance. "I love you," I say softly.

"I don't trust Robbie to be alone with Anthony. I shouldn't have left him there. I have to bail," she says.

"It's okay." I rub her shoulders and gaze down into her eyes.

"Maybe I can get out later."

My hopes soar. "I'll be here." I smile and see her relax.

Hand in hand, we descend the stairs. I walk Reeve to the van and we linger on a goodbye kiss. When I return, Tessa is looming at the edge of the patio. "I want to talk to you," she says.

Well, finally. I cross my arms, bracing.

She says, "I can't believe you told a complete stranger about my personal life."

"She's not a complete stranger, obviously. Reeve Hartt, by the way. That's her name. She's my girlfriend."

Tessa saws her jaw until it pops. "The baby was our business. My private business, Johanna."

My arms uncross and dangle at my sides. "Sorry." It comes out a murmur.

Tessa's eyes pool with tears. She rushes to the sliding door, rolls it open then closed behind her.

I think, God. I'm the worst sister in the world. No wonder she's given up on me.

Chapter 24

Shondri calls the next morning and asks if I can come in to work. "Yes," I tell her. I need the money bad.

She adds, "My kid has a doctor's appointment at eleven. You think you can handle it alone for an hour?"

"Absolutely." I didn't know she had a kid. "I'm on my way."

There's a knock on my door as I'm slugging down my last Fresca for breakfast. I open the door cautiously, scared it might be Tessa ready to rip into me some more.

"Oh my God." I throw my arms around Reeve. "Hi." Robbie's with her.

"You should ask who it is," Reeve says.

"I knew it was you."

She kisses me. I pull her inside and the kiss prolongs.

Robbie makes a gagging sound in his throat, like paper tearing, and Reeve and I start laughing in our kiss.

"Yikes," I say. "I have to go to work."

Reeve undoes the top two buttons on my white shirt. "Better," she goes.

Damn. Dammit. I have to go; I need the money for my insurance. "If you guys want to hang here for a while, that's cool. I'll try to get off early."

"Can we watch porn?" Robbie asks.

I just look at him.

Reeve says, "We're going with you."

"What?"

She fists me in the arm.

"To work?"

"Is that a problem?"

"Um . . ."

"We'll help out, won't we?" She elbows Robbie.

Okay. Wow.

The phone rings as we're leaving and Reeve says, "Don't you want to get that?"

I shut the door behind us. The only person I want to talk to is here. Novak called last night and left a message. She needed to see me. She needed to talk. She needs, needs, needs.

In my peripheral vision, I see Tessa and Martin on the patio, sitting next to each other in new chairs. Adirondack chairs with footrests. There's a new gas grill too.

I'm only doing this for Reeve. I tell her, "I want to introduce you officially. And Robbie too."

"Robbie!" Reeve calls to him. He's plodded off in the direction of my car. "Stop." He obeys.

They're deep in conversation, or at least Martin is. He's reading to Tessa from the gas grill directions.

"Um, guys?"

He and Tessa swivel their heads.

"I want you to meet Reeve and Robbie. Well, you've already met Reeve. But officially, this is my girlfriend, Reeve Hartt. And her brother, Robbie Inouye."

Martin loops his legs off each side of the chair and stands.

"They're twins," I say. Don't ask me why I think that's significant and meaningful. Because it is to Reeve?

Martin balls a fist and holds it out to Robbie. "Word up, homie."

Robbie knuckles him back.

"Nice to see you again," he says to Reeve, smiling.

She blinks. "Yeah, you too."

Tessa forces a thin, unconvincing smile.

Martin says, "You guys want to stay for lunch? I'm going to fire up this puppy and barbecue ribs. If I can figure out how to get the propane tank attached."

"No, thanks," I reply. "I have to go to work."

Martin fakes a pout. "How about you two?"

Tessa lowers her head and looks away.

Robbie says, "Okay."

Reeve grabs his sleeve. "We're going to work with Johanna. But thanks."

"Rain check," Martin tells them. "You're welcome anytime." He engulfs me in a hug, and Reeve too.

It makes me think he and Tessa talked about it—about me. He's showing support and acceptance.

Robbie says, "Just screw on the tank, dude." He shows Martin where on the gas grill.

"Dude," Martin goes. "Any moron could've figured that 'un out, eh?"

Everyone laughs but Tessa.

"He's cool," Reeve says as we round the corner of the house.

"Yeah, he's a good guy." Tessa found her soul mate. I smile. So have I. "You want to ride with me?" I ask Reeve.

"Absolutely. Since we took the bus."

She rode the bus clear over here to see me? What if I wasn't here? I told her I'd always be here. And I was. Score one for me.

The mall echoes our footsteps as all the stores and stalls are being readied to open. At Bling's, the grate is halfway up, so I duck underneath and Reeve and Robbie trail behind.

Shondri is loading the register. "These are my friends, Reeve and Robbie," I tell her. "Reeve is my girlfriend." I toss Reeve a quick smile, thinking, I just came out to Shondri. "They're here to help."

Shondri says to me, "Can I talk to you?"

My heart drops. Reeve takes the hint and shoves Robbie down the aisle.

Shondri says, "They can't work without applying and getting hired and filling out W-2s."

"They're not *working* working. They're just helping out. They're not getting paid." Do they expect to be paid? I'll just pay them out of my check.

Shondri eyes me, then shifts her gaze to them. "Is he the one smacking you around?"

I huff in disgust.

"Today you got a fat lip."

Do I? I feel it with my tongue and it is swollen. Reeve kissed me hard.

"It's . . . herpes," I say. "It flares up."

Shondri's expression doesn't change.

I tell her, "You could try them out. See if you want to hire them. We need help, right?"

Shondri watches Robbie pick up a ponytail holder and stretch it as far as it'll go, then snap it at Reeve. She throws one at him.

Shondri cracks a roll of quarters over the cash drawer. "My kid's got the flu bad. I've got to leave."

"I can handle it," I say. "If you want to go now, we can hold down the fort."

Shondri says, "I just need to be out of here by ten-thirty for the doctor." She slips the register key into the secret drawer. "It's on your head."

What does that mean?

"Show them how to set up the displays."

"Okay." I walk to the back, feeling weird about this. Why? I say to Reeve, "You're in. If you do good, Shondri might hire you."

"Yeah?" Robbie perks up.

Reeve screws up her face, like, Who'd work here?

Exactly. "Do you want me to put your purse in the storeroom?"

"I'm fine." Reeve squeezes her purse to her side.

Robbie has his case. I look at it, then him. He clutches it to his chest.

I stash my stuff, then show them the drawers where the inventory is stored; I tell them to reload the hooks on the walls and the racks on the tables. Robbie props his case against the wall and begins arranging the fake fingernails and stick-on jewels.

Reeve fills a spinner of earrings, while I do watches and bracelets. She meets my eyes once and winks. God, could I do her in the storeroom?

Shondri bustles by. "That looks nice," she grumbles at Reeve.

Reeve smiles. "Thanks."

Shondri never told me my displays looked good. I take my promotion as a sign she's satisfied with my work, though.

As soon as we open, it's a mob scene. Tweeners everywhere. I home in on this suspicious-looking group of grungy guys, all wearing lowriders and chains. The girls are sneaky. They finger the necklaces and talk on their cells. They leave without buying anything. A second wave flows in. Were they summoned by the cells? Sometimes they work in teams.

A commotion out in the mall draws my attention.

Mall security is there and . . . Oh my God. Oh no. A security guard has Robbie by the arm.

I dash out.

"What else did you take?" the guard says. Robbie yanks two scrunchies off his wrist.

"What's going on?" I interrupt.

Over Robbie's shoulder, I see Reeve. She slips a pair of earrings from her purse into her back pocket. I try to get her to look at me, but she gazes off into the mall.

The security guard goes, "Follow me."

"No." I snag the guard's arm. "It's a mistake. They work here."

"Oh, really?" She arches her eyebrows. "Then why were they leaving?"

God. Oh God.

"Please," the guard insists. "Follow me."

Reeve fixes on me.

"You have it wrong," I say. "I made them do it."

My story is lame. I asked Reeve and Robbie to come in and steal for me because I worked at Bling's and I didn't want to lose my job. I'm a terrible liar.

There are two security guards in the office, a lady and a man. The lady says, "Jim, I can handle this. Why don't you go on back."

I feel like hurling.

She eyes each of us—me, Robbie, Reeve. Reeve's head is down. "What's in the case?" she asks Robbie.

"Nothing," I answer for him. "I mean, there's an instrument. Robbie has a lesson today. He didn't put anything in the case."

"Is that true?" she asks Robbie.

He's suddenly a deaf-mute.

"They're innocent," I say. "They only agreed to do it because they're my friends."

The guard twiddles a red pen between her first and second

fingers. She taps it on her paper. "You can go," she says. I get up and snag Reeve's arm.

"Not you." She points the pen at me.

I sit.

Reeve and Robbie stand and leave quickly.

The guard says to me, "This is really stupid."

Tears well in my eyes. "I know."

"I'm going to let you off this time."

"You are?"

"You need to leave the mall and never come back."

But my job . . .

"Did you hear me?"

A long moment passes.

"Now would be a good time."

I scramble to get up. My heart hammers in my chest and my stomach hurts. I need my keys, which are in my bag, in the storeroom at Bling's.

Shondri's on the phone when I reenter. She looks right through me and her eyes go vacant.

I let her down. God, punish me.

Outside, I drive around the mall twice, but there's no sign of Robbie or Reeve. A raindrop splatters on the windshield and a hot tear streaks down my cheek.

Damn. I needed that job.

Chapter 25

She calls just as I'm about to crash. "You're so stupid."

I take the phone into the hall, sit on the floor with my back to the wall, and flatten my feet against the opposite wall. Tessa used to shimmy up the wall by pushing with her feet and wriggling her back. She called it the spider. As a kid I was always too short, but Tessa would put me in her lap and we'd spider together.

"That was crazy," Reeve says. She lets out a small laugh. "What did your boss say?"

"Nothing."

"You didn't get busted, though, right?"

"Right," I lie. "I quit. I hated that job anyway."

"Did security give you her number?"

"What?"

Reeve goes, "She's a dyke. She had our backs, girl."

She did? I guess I was too freaked out to register her on my gaydar.

"She wanted you bad."

"Oh, sure."

Reeve laughs softly. The laugh fades and she says, "I want you bad."

I stutter a breath. "Can you come over?"

She doesn't answer. "What time tomorrow can we pick up our caps and gowns?" she says. "Do you know?"

"No." I tongue the blood blister under my lip.

"We have rehearsal in the morning, so maybe we pick them up afterwards?"

"We have rehearsal?" I say.

"Where do you live, girl?"

"Here. Come over."

"I can't," she says. "We got back late and Anthony . . ." Her voice lowers. "Never mind."

If he hurts her, I'll kill him. I will.

Reeve says, "I'll check the schedule, if I can find it. I can't believe we're graduating Saturday."

"I could pick you up tomorrow. At the 7-Eleven or something."

"No. I'll come to you."

We don't speak for a minute, just cling to our connection.

Reeve says, "I'm in the closet."

"Oh, right." She's the out-est person I know. People sometimes delude themselves into thinking they're safe, that they blend, or pass. Everyone knows. Even if they suspect, you're tagged. "Your secret's safe with me," I say.

Reeve exhales audibly. "Someday I'll show you my closet.

It's deep and dark and there are secrets nobody knows. Secrets no one will ever know."

"Keep your secrets," I tell her. "You're starting life over with me."

When Reeve breathes out, I breathe in. I close my eyes and will us together.

She says, "I can't use the phone after nine. What time is it?"

I don't know. I'm sitting in the dark so I'm guessing it's after nine. "What happens if you get caught?"

"You don't want to know."

My imagination fills the blank spaces. Don't hurt her. Please, God.

"I'm pushing my luck. Better fly."

"I love you," I say.

She doesn't say it back, but she's thinking it. I know she is.

I forget, or never knew, that you have to pay ninety dollars when you pick up your cap and gown. If you don't order early. If you forget to order, or if you live day to day, in Joyland, for Reeve, with no plans for the future.

Reeve says, "I didn't forget. I just wasn't sure we were graduating. I skipped a lot this year. And Robbie . . ." She glances over at him. "Can you cover us? I'll pay you back."

I have my checkbook in my purse, but I still need to pay my car insurance, and my final check from Bling's will be minuscule now. If I even get one. The guy taking money for grad gear doesn't call the bank to verify my balance, thank God.

The ladies who are fitting robes in the gym can't get Robbie to drop his case. He shifts it from hand to hand, holding tight. Now I imagine he has a shitload from Bling's in there.

We aren't the only people who waited until the last minute and have to settle for leftovers. Our gowns are faded and shabby; mine's too short; Robbie's is frayed. While Reeve's getting hers from a rack in the back, Britt appears.

"Is she making you pay yet?" Britt asks.

"Huh?"

"All she does is take and take and take."

I click my tongue at Britt.

She says, "Don't say I didn't warn you." She slings her robe hanger over her shoulder and exits.

I go find Reeve. "Can we leave these at your place?" She folds her gown over her arm.

"Do you plan to spend the night?" I ask.

She says, "If only."

Robbie sniffs his cap. What does he smell? Our school colors are jade and pewter. We're going to look like a sea of algae.

"I'm stoked," Reeve says as we meander down the main hall from the gym. "I never thought we'd make it." Her eyes glisten. "We'll never walk these halls again."

I snake an arm around her waist and she rests her head on my shoulder. "Are you going to miss it?" I ask.

"Yeah," she says. "Aren't you?"

"Seriously? No," I admit.

"Not the school part, yeah. But the rest of it . . ."

The rest is what I'm terrible at—feeling a part of anything.

In the quad, seniors mill around and some girl calls out to Reeve. Reeve takes my hand and heads in that direction. All the years I dreamed about this, being together with her. The reality is even better than the fantasy.

The girls are the LBDs. Reeve says, "You guys know Johanna."

They all look at me like, Who? Except Britt. The rest of them check me out, sort of undress me with their eyes—not an unpleasant feeling.

One of the girls asks Reeve, "Are you still going to Florida State?"

Reeve says, "Sure. How about you?"

The conversation dulls in my ears and I stare at Reeve. She didn't tell me about going to college out of state. We haven't talked about the future. Yet.

Britt studies my face, then smiles. It isn't a happy smile. More . . . sympathy, or pity?

Pity you, Britt.

Robbie's case bumps my leg and I turn. He bumps me again. I mouth, Quit it.

He bumps me again.

I fake-jab an elbow into his gut.

Reeve is talking to the LBDs about Pride Day. When is it? Where should they meet? This beam inside me lights. I've always wanted to go to Pride, and now my first time will be with my girlfriend.

On the way to the car, I ask her, "Are you really going to Florida State?"

She eyes Robbie ahead of us and her whole body seems to deflate. "What do you think?"

* * *

My arms are full of robes and I feel weighted down with the realization that Reeve feels trapped. Novak rushes out the sliding glass door and flings her arms around me, almost flattening me. "Oh my fucking God, we're graduating! Here, let me help you."

We get wrapped up together in the billowing plastic cleaner bags. "Thanks."

Novak stoops to pick up one of the caps. "I just talked to Tessa." She clomps behind me up the stairs. "She's having her tubes tied."

I stop dead on the landing. "When?"

Novak shrugs. "She didn't say."

All Tessa used to talk about with me and her friends was how she was getting married as soon as possible and having kids while she was young, not like our parents. Back when I worshipped her, when she considered me a friend. She'd spider up the wall, the phone cradled to her ear. "I want six kids, at least." She'd wink at me.

Martin made lists of baby names: Emanuel, Aidan, Jake—wait. That's what he was doing on the laptop the day Tessa—

They were having a boy.

"Let me get the door." Novak takes the keys from my hand.

Tessa is giving up on something she desperately wants.

Novak opens the apartment door and we step inside. I heap the robes on the divan while Novak removes my bag from my shoulder.

"Stop it." I snatch it out of her hands. "What do you want?"

"God. Why are you so pissed at me?"

"Why am I pissed? You kissed me." You used me, I think.

"Dante dumped me," she says. Immediately, she adds, "Don't look so shocked."

Do I?

"We both knew it was coming." She flips her hair over her shoulder. "He was just waiting for the right time and place, when it would hurt me the most." Her eyes are puffy and she looks demolished.

"I'm . . . sorry," I say. "What a jerk."

"I don't know what to do, Johanna." Tears film her red eyes. "He wants me out today. I know I can't live here. I just need someone to talk to." She blinks and a tear spills over the rim. "Just talk to me."

God. God, Novak.

She buries her face in her arms and bawls.

At the hardest time in my life, when I was coming out, she was there for me. The whole time Mom was dying. She was the only one. Novak.

"Novak," I say softly. "Come here."

Joyland: Take 13

Night descends and the dark is profound. I'm falling, falling down a canyon wall into a river of syrup. She flows around me, through me. Her lips on mine are sticky sweet and I melt into the riverbed.

We're dragonflies on lily pads, mermaids swimming free. Her body wraps around me and fills the emptiness inside until I'm full to bursting at the gills.

My fingers tangle hair; the long, golden, silky strands twist around my fingers, pulling tight, fingers turning purple. I close my eyes and dream. She takes me into Joyland.

• • •

Chapter 26

Reeve calls to tell me she and Robbie will be at my place by nine to pick up their caps and gowns. "I love you," I say.

It's *you* I love.

She wears short shorts and a tank. She smells like heavy perfume or incense, and I bury my face in her hair. She whispers, "Me too."

I knew it.

Robbie has on a dress shirt that's yellowed and wrinkled, like right off the rack at Goodwill. Reeve says, "I should've come earlier so we could celebrate in private."

God. I kiss her to delirium.

A knock sounds on the door and I panic.

Robbie says, "I'll get it."

"Don't—"

He opens it to Tessa.

She delays a smile before going, "Hi." She doesn't enter. She stands at the threshold and looks at her watch. "Graduation starts at eleven, right? Do we need tickets?"

I blink to Robbie, then Reeve.

"Because when I graduated, family members had to have tickets. It was limited seating."

I say, "It's outside on the football field."

Reeve adds, "If you want to be in the bleachers, you should get there early. Otherwise, people stand or sit on the grass."

Tessa stares at me. What?

"Here." She holds out an envelope.

More money? I never asked for money. All I wanted . . . On the front is printed: CANCELLATION NOTICE. Shit.

"You're not driving without insurance," Tessa says.

Watch me.

"There's usually a thirty-day grace period, so you should be okay. Where's the money I gave you?"

It takes every ounce of willpower not to glance over at the candleholders. I say, "I have it."

Tessa says sternly, "Pay the bill, Johanna."

I toss the envelope on the divan.

She goes, "Is that what you're wearing?"

I scan my outfit. I have on shorts too, a tee, and my Converses. "Yeah." *What do you care?*

Tessa's eyes infiltrate my brain, where a steel grate slams down. "Could we get some pictures of you in your cap and gown?" Her attention shifts to Reeve. "All of you?"

I turn away. "We weren't going to get dressed until we got to—"

"Pictures would be cool," Reeve cuts in. She heads toward the bedroom. "Where is everything, Johanna?"

"In here." I hung our gowns in the coat closet. Robbie wanders out of the kitchen with the bag of Doritos. "You want some?" He extends it to Tessa.

"No. Thanks." She presses a hand to her stomach.

I notice then she doesn't look well.

Reeve takes the bundle of robes from me and sorts through them. She hands me mine and Robbie his.

Tessa says, "Do you need any help?"

She looks so pale and sad. "No," I say. "But thanks."

Reeve asks her, "Which side does the tassel go on?"

"Left," Tessa answers. "Then you flip it to the right at the end of the ceremony."

"Cool." Reeve smiles at her.

Tessa says to me, "Come downstairs when you're dressed. We can take pictures in the backyard." She stalls in the doorway, like there's more. "Is your family coming?" she asks Reeve.

"Oh yeah. Try and stop them." Reeve removes her cap from the bag.

Tessa says, "Maybe we could all sit together."

Reeve shoots me a panicked look.

"There'll be too many of them for you all to sit together," I say.

"Right." Reeve doesn't take her eyes off me. "They won't even all fit in the bleachers."

Tessa's eyes pierce me. *What, Tessa? Say it.*

"How do you get this thing on?" Robbie garbles through a

mouthful of chips. He's gotten himself all twisted up in his robe.

Reeve drops her cap on the divan to shake him loose.

Tessa's footsteps sound on the stairs.

I say out of nowhere, "She's going to have her tubes tied."

Reeve says, "Really? Why?"

"She doesn't want to get pregnant again."

"Duh. I mean, why doesn't Martin get a vasectomy?"

Robbie goes, "Ow. You stuck me."

Reeve snaps, "Stand still or I will."

"They shouldn't give up yet," I say. "They're still young. They should keep trying."

Reeve locates a straight pin in Robbie's hem. "When's she having the operation? Maybe you can talk her out of it."

"I don't know. She didn't tell me. She told Novak."

Reeve says, "She told Novak before you?"

I remove the plastic bag from my robe and think aloud, "She likes Novak better."

Reeve turns and asks, "When did you see Novak?"

I unclip my cap from the hanger. I separate the little plastic bag with the tassel, wishing I hadn't brought up this subject.

Reeve waits for an answer.

"Yesterday."

"She came here?"

This conversation can't continue. "Do you tie the tassel onto this knobby thing?"

Robbie says, "My zipper's stuck."

"Stop pulling." Reeve slugs him. "You broke it." She fists him again and I feel it in my chest.

"Here, let me help him." I take Reeve's balled fist and squeeze it gently. "You get dressed."

"Congratulations." Martin hugs me, then Reeve. With Robbie, he goes, "Dude," and they strike knuckles.

Martin drops his gaze. "What do you have there?"

Oh God. The case. Is Robbie actually bringing it to graduation?

"Is that a sax?" Martin's eyes gleam. "I played the sax in band. Can I see it?" He holds out his hand.

Robbie gives him the case.

Just like that. Martin squats to open it. "I think I still have mine in the garage. Alto or tenor?" he asks. He snaps open the clasps.

Robbie crouches down beside him. "It's not a saxophone."

Tessa calls, "Hurry up. Martin, what are you doing?"

Robbie relatches the case, stands, and grasps the handle.

Martin goes, "Show me later."

Robbie nods.

Tessa lines us up by the forsythia bush, whose yellow flowers are in full blaze. She snaps two or three pictures, then rearranges us. She says, "Can I get a couple of each of you alone?"

I hate having my picture taken.

"Smile," Tessa says.

I look more natural when I don't smile.

Martin goes, "I want in." He runs behind us and snakes his arms across our shoulders.

Tessa centers a shot.

Martin says, "Let me get one with you and Johanna."

Reeve must feel my muscles tense, because she says, "We better go. What time is it?"

I say, "We're already late. You guys go ahead; I'll meet you at the car."

I rush upstairs for my bag and keys. As I lock the door, Martin calls up the steps, "We'll give you a shout-out when you're on stage. Wave so we can get a picture."

Tessa says, "Johanna?"

I launch off the last step and head for Reeve and Robbie, who are halfway across the yard.

"Johanna!"

Reeve flings out a stiff arm to block me. "Go see what she wants." Reeve widens her eyes at me.

Only for you.

"Congratulations," Tessa says.

"Thanks." We stand there awkwardly.

Tessa picks up a box off the gas grill and hands it to me. It's wrapped in our school colors. I glance over my shoulder at Reeve, who's waiting by my car. "Open it," Tessa says. "You have time."

Quickly, I rip off the wrapping to find a blue plastic case. It's hinged. I open it, and gasp.

"Oh my God." It's a gold watch with a diamond-studded crystal. Are they real diamonds? "You didn't have to do this."

"Put it on."

Now?

Tessa takes the case from me and unhooks the watch from the velveteen base. "This isn't the original case. I lost it in the move." Her nails are manicured and polished, which they never are. "Mom gave me this for my graduation."

A lump rises in my throat.

Tessa flips my wrist over and adds, "I know she'd want you to have it." She clasps the watch.

I can't even look at it or I'll start bawling.

"It's too big," Tessa says. "I can take it in and get the band adjusted."

"No." I back up a step. "It's fine. I like it loose." My arm drops and the watch is gobbled up by the sleeve of my robe.

Tessa hugs me. Not tight. She lets go. I try to say thank you or thanks or I love you or I'm sorry, I miss Mom, don't you, don't you wish she was here? Do you hate me, please don't hate me anymore. Please, Tessa, please?

Chapter 27

It's a hundred degrees and I'm sweating in my robe. Ahead of me, perspiration beads up on Robbie's neck. He has bare spots in his hair, like mange or something. Like cigarette burns?

I can't see Reeve. Novak passes at the head of her row during "Pomp and Circumstance," but she seems lost in her own little world. Where's Reeve?

The bleachers are packed. I search but don't see anyone I know, not that I expect to.

The speeches are endless. Mrs. Goins accepts an award for her years of service and she almost breaks down. At the end, she opens her arms and says, "I'll miss you most of all."

My throat catches. Mom said that to me. Tessa was moving her out of the house to the hospice and Mom was looking at her things, touching them for the last time. Mom clasped my hand and said, "I'll miss you most of all." I think it hurt Tessa's feelings. *But Mom meant both of us, Tessa.* She did.

The roster of names goes on. When I get my diploma, Mrs. Goins hugs me and says, "Johanna. I'll remember your kindness and generosity."

"You will?"

A flashbulb blinds me.

Then it's over. We stand as a class and flip our tassels. I look around at all the people I know, and don't know, and a wave of panic sweeps over me. Real life starts now.

"We have to get over there." Robbie points.

I can't see through the forest of robes. Robbie begins knocking people aside with his trusty case.

Reeve has already found her way to the family area, where her mom slumps next to her, looking strung out. Anthony's there, his slicked-back hair. He blows out a stream of cigarette smoke and says to Robbie, "The retardo graduates."

Anthony smiles at me and my skin crawls.

There's no one else in their family group. Anthony keeps smiling at me.

Reeve says to no one in particular, "We have to go turn in our robes."

Anthony flicks a long ash onto her cap.

Robbie yanks Anthony's wrist up so hard it makes him yelp. "Don't!" Reeve says. She chops down Robbie's arm. Robbie brushes the ashes off her cap.

Anthony stubs out his cigarette in the grass and says to me, "I hope you're coming to the party."

I look at Reeve, but she's gazing off into the distance.

"Reevie"—he fingers my tassel—"if she's too much woman for you, I'd be happy to share."

Reeve doesn't hit him or kick him or spit in his face. She's fixed on an object, a moving object, coming our way.

Something tickles my neck and I flinch. Anthony has lifted my hair and is blowing on my neck. Blech. Get away.

Reeve says, "He's here." She ducks her head and shoots past me.

"Who?"

People have spread blankets on the grass and kids are running around. The zipper on my robe scritches and I glance down to see Anthony pulling it.

I lurch away, then charge off in Reeve's direction, feeling violated. "Reeve!" At the end of the folding chairs, she stops.

"You okay?" I ask.

She wheezes. "I can't see him. I don't want to talk to him."

"Who?"

"My dad."

I check over my shoulder. A skinny guy in a skullcap gives Anthony a high-five handshake. Robbie is rubbernecking the crowd and I hold up a hand to signal him.

Reeve yanks down my sleeve. "I don't want him to see me. Get me out of here."

I take Reeve's hand and we jog to the main building. At the gym, Reeve falls back against the brick wall, breathing hard. "He's come for us. He'll take us. He said he'd come and he did."

She doubles over and dry-heaves.

"Baby." I rub her back. "No one's going to take you."

"Where's Robbie?" She straightens fast. "Oh my God. I left Robbie."

I snag the back of her robe as she tries to bolt. "Robbie saw us. He's coming."

Reeve raises her eyes to me. "You don't know what my father will do. What he did to us."

I know enough. I wish I didn't. "It's over, Reeve," I tell her. "No one's going to hurt you again."

"You don't know that." She pushes me. "You don't know anything. You can't just say that and it fixes us."

I grab her wrists and draw her to me. I hold her hard. She starts shaking and I tighten my grip. I hold her until the earthquake ends.

"Where's Robbie?" she asks again.

I peer around the corner and Robbie almost decapitates me. He swishes by me in his billowing robe and halts in front of Reeve. They don't say anything to each other. Robbie flattens his back against the wall beside her, crushing his case to his chest.

"I killed him," he says. "I killed them both."

Reeve goes, "Sure you did."

He could splinter their skulls with that case.

Reeve says, "It's so hot." The noonday sun is directly overhead. "Let's take these off." Reeve unzips her robe.

Robbie unzips his. Mine is halfway unzipped already and I finish the job. We step out of the robes and I begin to gather them. Reeve says, "He knows we have to turn these in at the gym. Just leave them here." She kicks them into a heap. "Someone will find them."

I'll lose the deposit. But I never really paid it.

"We can't go back out there." Reeve shudders.

"We won't," I say. "We'll figure out—"

"The party." Robbie fits his cap on the end of his case. "That rich bitch's party."

"No," I say. "We're not going to Novak's."

Reeve looks at me. "Why not?"

My eyes fall. "I just don't want to go."

He says, "I do. It's the best place. We'll be safe there."

Reeve knuckles Robbie on the head. "Smart thinking, brainiac. Sometimes your mental powers scare me."

Robbie says, "The retardo graduates."

She laughs. I love Robbie for making her laugh.

But I really don't want to go to the party.

Chapter 28

A hundred cars cram Novak's circular drive. We have to park in the cul-de-sac.

Reeve says to Robbie, "Leave your case here."

Robbie squashes it to his chest.

"No one's going to take it," I tell him.

His eyes bounce around the car.

"I'll lock the doors. It'll be safe."

Reluctantly, he sets the case on the floor by the backseat.

The patio is a feeding frenzy. You can't see the band, but you can hear the reverb. The three of us hang at the fringe for a minute and, surreptitiously, I seek out Novak.

Robbie splits off and Reeve calls, "Where are you going?"

"I smell meat." He sniffs the air, then raises both arms like a zombie.

Reeve says, "Get me something too."

He weaves through a clot of blue-hairs toward the food tents and we lose him. "The whole fucking school's here," Reeve mutters.

She slides her hand into mine and smiles up at me. Her eyes shine. She's gone heavy on the makeup, green and silver, our school colors. "I always feel safe with you," she says. "That worries me."

"Why?"

"It just does. You might be the first person I've ever trusted."

I wrap my arms around her and close my eyes. I will the sick feeling inside to go away.

"Lesbo!" Attacking from behind, Novak swings me around and smothers me in a hug.

I peel her off.

Novak thrusts her fist into the air and whoops, "We did it!" She laughs in my face. Her shoulder glances mine and she says in my ear, "Thanks for last night."

Warning flares go up. Where's Reeve?

Novak touches my hand. "Meet me at the greenhouse?"

I step away, and see Reeve glaring at Novak. I reach for her but can't grasp her hand.

"I'm hungry," Reeve announces. "I'm going to find Robbie."

Novak's arm hooks around my neck. "Kiss me."

"Stop it," I say between clenched teeth. "Please," I plead with her. *Please, Novak.* I run to catch up to Reeve.

She's found Robbie in a food tent, where he's bent over a steaming vat of Swedish meatballs. He plucks out a meatball with his fingers and goes, "Hot." He pops it into his mouth. He shakes the steaming gravy from his fingers back into the pot.

A caterer in a white shirt smirks. Reeve slams the metal lid on Robbie's fingers. "Get a plate," she orders. "Get a couple. And forks too."

"What's she on?" Reeve says to me.

"Who?"

"The love of your life."

I just look at Reeve. "I don't know. You name it. And she's not."

Reeve goes, "What's going on between you two?"

Heat rises up my neck. "Nothing. We're friends. I told you."

Reeve narrows her eyes like she doesn't believe me. Then they go imploring like she wants to—needs to. Robbie shoves a plate in her face and says, "The meatballs taste like caca."

That sort of breaks the tension. Reeve and I inch along the buffet line, filling our plates. We're so close, I think. She trusts me. Nothing, *no one*, can be allowed to jeopardize that.

The first wave of people have finished eating and Reeve leads us to an empty table out on the lawn. People drink or dance or lounge around the pool. Robbie wolfs down his food. We eat in silence, watching all the people. I wonder what Tessa and Martin are doing. Are they here?

Reeve says, out of the blue, "So, where's the greenhouse?"

"What?"

She balls a fist.

The greenhouse, relative to where we are . . . ? "Over there somewhere." I wave my fork.

Reeve pushes back from the table and stands. "I know we weren't invited, but you don't mind if we come along with you." She yanks Robbie up by his arm.

"I wasn't going . . . I'm not go—"

She takes off, with Robbie in tow.

Don't be here don't be here please don't be here— "Shut the door!" a voice calls. I wait until Reeve and Robbie are inside.

She slouches against the far wall, an open bottle of vodka clutched in her hand. Bottles are littered across the dirt floor. "Welcome to my grad bash." Novak hoists the bottle to her lips.

If she drank all of this by herself, I think, she could die of alcohol poisoning. God, Novak.

"What are these?" Reeve asks. Her fingertips graze a blossom.

"Orchids," I tell her. "Novak's mom raises orchids."

"As opposed to children," Novak says, and laughs hysterically.

Robbie coughs behind me. I look at him and he plugs his nose. Yeah, it's pungent in here. Fertilizer and mold and booze. Sweat is filming on my skin.

Reeve moseys down the aisle, touching each of the orchids. A rectangular table splits the greenhouse in two. There are pots of orchids arranged on the table.

I cross to the other aisle to get to Novak. "You've had enough." I wrestle the bottle out of her hand. She grabs a beer beside her and I take that too.

Novak says, "When is it ever enough?"

I scan for Reeve. She's picking a tall purple and white orchid. *No, don't pick them!*

"Come on. You need to get up and walk." I try to pull Novak up, but she's limp.

"Joho." She smiles up at me. "Johanna, Johanna, you are a banana." She cracks herself up.

I yank on her arm.

Novak says, "Can I stay over with you?"

Across the table, Reeve's eyes meet mine.

"I promise to be a goo' girl this time. You know I'm good."

I mental Novak: *Pleeease.*

"You slept with her?"

"No," I huff. "It wasn't like that. We talked. Dante dumped her and she needed to talk."

"She stayed overnight?" Reeve says.

Novak goes, "You kissed me first."

I whirl on her. "Stop. You promised."

Reeve makes a sound in her throat.

"It wasn't like that," I say.

"You did it, Joho. You finally got me."

"Shut up," I snap at Novak. I catch Reeve's eye again. "Nothing happened."

"You slept in the same bed?"

Novak goes, "Naked."

"Shut. Up. We were not naked." I need to get to Reeve. "Novak was upset and she didn't have anywhere to go." I gauge the distance. I'm closer to the door, so I veer in that direction, stiff-arming Robbie out of my way. "Her mother kicked her out."

Reeve moves in the opposite direction, toward Novak.

"Lesbo's *damn* good." Novak clunks her head against the glass of the greenhouse. "But you know that, huh, Reeve?"

Reeve stops. She kicks Novak in the stomach. Novak grunts and doubles over.

"Reeve!" I yelp.

Reeve kicks her again in the side.

"Stop it!"

Then in the face. "Reeve!" I charge and push her away.

Novak groans. She crumples over and curls into a ball. I'm grasping Reeve's arm, but she kicks Novak hard again.

"Goddammit." I spin Reeve around. She fists my face. I feel my neck snap and something come loose. She slams me again.

The Earth trembles and Robbie's there, clenching Reeve's wrist, then both of them, forcing her back.

Reeve lets out this keening wail and wrenches out of Robbie's grasp. I step over Novak to get to her, to Reeve.

Reeve starts trembling uncontrollably and I say, "It's okay." I draw her into me.

Behind me, Novak writhes on the floor, moaning. She could die. She could pass out and die.

"I'm here, baby." Blood drips off my arm, onto the floor. "I only love you." My blood, spurting from my nose, smearing in her hair. I hold her tighter, squashing my nose into her head. "I'm sorry. I should've told you." I sniff and blood runs down the back of my throat. "She doesn't mean anything to me." My eyes shift down to Novak. "She's nothing."

Novak hauls herself up to her hands and knees. Her hair covers her face and she pukes.

Robbie goes, "Dude." He staggers backward. I steer Reeve ahead of me, out the door. I hear Novak hurl again.

Reeve's focused on me, her eyes wild.

"It's okay," I tell her. There's blood all over her hair and in my mouth. "It'll be fine." I press my wrist to my nose to stanch the flow and a sharp object scratches my face. The gold watch. "Let's go," I say. I take Reeve's hand and tug her toward the car.

"Where's Robbie?" She stops.

Where'd he go?

"We have to find him," Reeve says.

"I will," I say.

She blocks me. "You can't go." Her eyes skim down my front, my face. She swallows hard. "I'll go," she says. "We'll meet you at the car."

With the bottom of my tee, I wipe off Reeve's arm where blood dripped. It soaked into her shirt, but only the side. I want to kiss her so bad.

She touches the watch.

"It's yours," I say. What's mine is yours. *Just love me.* I unlatch the wristband, or try to. It's stuck. Reeve backs away before I can get it off.

Joyland: Take 14

The dark is bitter, thick and viscous. The dark fills every crevice and crack in my nails as I scrape bottom. I'm alone in this bottle of ink, this bottomless well of sticky pitch. I open my mouth to cry out, "Where are you, Reeve?"

She answers, "I'm here."

Her voice is so faint.

I claw through the murky tar as it hardens.

"I'm here." Her voice sounds clearer.

"Here."

Closer.

I reach her. We clasp hands. She's clean and washed, the water-fall cleansing her skin pure and white. I swim up next to her and feel the release, the warm, sweet rush of water. The darkness falls away, the ink rinses clear and free. A diluted pool of grayish scum swirls at my feet and down the drain.

She plucks a rose petal from my hair.

The petal liquefies in her hand and drips blood off her fingers.

She cries.

. . .

Chapter 29

My nose is broken. Overnight the bridge swelled to a bulb and the bruise radiated out and under my eyes. I stare at myself in the medicine cabinet mirror for a long time.

I deserve this. For what I did. I'm so . . . so weak.

Reeve, I'm sorry. I'm so sorry.

I don't know how long I stood looking at the busted back window of my car. Apparently, Robbie got his case. He and Reeve disappeared and I drove home feeling lost.

Then I remembered—Novak. I left her dying there. She couldn't die, could she?

Even though she promised—she *promised* not to tell—she didn't know what she was saying. She was hammered.

Betrayal all around. From all of us.

I think about driving to Reeve's house and reassuring her. *I'll always be here for you, baby. I'll never leave.* I'll explain how

I really do understand her need to test me, to see how far I'll go with her.

All the way, Reeve. All the way.

I go back to my bed. But for the life of me, I can't conjure up Joyland.

By afternoon, the bruising has spread down my whole left cheek. It symbolizes something—trust? Intimacy? You can trust me to take what you dole out, Reeve. I gaze into the mirror and think, This is a phase of our love. We're taking it to the next level.

I'll give Reeve time to regroup, or whatever, then I'll go to her. I need to focus on the future, next year. If Reeve wants to go to Florida State, I'll find a way to make that happen. I'll go with her. Robbie can tag along and I'll watch out for him. Why hadn't Reeve and I talked about the future? Because she doesn't feel like she has one and my future is her, the only thing I want in life.

A knock sounds on the door. "Johanna?" Tessa calls.

I don't want to see her.

She pounds harder. "I know you're there."

I shouldn't have parked in the driveway.

Tessa's dressed in flimsy drawstrings and a tank. I have this flashback to her last night home before college, when we stayed up all night to talk. All those nights. She's not talking now; she's slack-jawed. "What in heaven's name . . . ?"

I shrink behind the door.

Tessa muscles it open. "What happened to you?"

I say, "I fell."

"No, you didn't."

I open my mouth, then shut it.

"Come out here in the light." She takes me by the wrist. Her eyes squinch and she winces. "Your nose." She reaches up to touch it, but I move away. "We need to get you X-rayed."

"No. It's fine."

"It's not remotely fine. You're hurt. Who did this to you?"

"That's none of your business," I say flatly.

"I'm making it my business," she says. "You're my sister. I love you."

"Oh, really? Could've fooled me."

Tessa looks crushed. Her eyes pool.

The sliding door opens and Novak emerges. She glances up, shielding her eyes against the sun.

"What's she doing here?" I say. She limps over to one of the Adirondacks and curls into it, hugging her knees to her chest.

Tessa says, "She called last night and said she was in trouble. I told her she could stay here."

"She can't." I go to close the door. "Tell her not to call me again."

"She didn't call you. She called me. Reeve was here too."

I pull the door open. "When?"

Tessa rubs her eyes and stretches the skin across her temples. "I don't know. Two. Two-thirty. She was standing at the bottom of the stairs. When I came out, she left."

How long was Reeve here? Why didn't she come up? "Did Reeve see Novak?"

Tessa expels a weary breath. "I don't know. What does it matter?"

"It matters because Reeve might believe I brought Novak home."

Tessa bites her bottom lip and says softly, "Oh, Johanna."

It rips me. But I shut the door on her, the way she shut me out.

The bruising seeps down my face like ink. Now the left side of my mouth is swelling and turning black. Maybe more than my nose is broken? Foundation or concealer is never going to cover this. I need a mask, like the Phantom of the Opera.

It's a random solution, but I wonder if any costume shops are open. Even if they are, I don't have the money.

My watch sits next to my purse, which means I took it off at some point and laid it on the table. There's still blood smeared on the crystal.

I could pawn it, or sell it on eBay.

No. It was Mom's watch.

Mom, can you see me from heaven? Please don't look.

I need to get away from here, get out of my head.

At the bottom of the stairs, a wave of dizziness slows me and I steady myself on the wooden railing. I feel something carved in the wood. I lift my hand. Two words: I CANT

Who did this?

"Johanna. Hey." Novak springs like a cat.

I launch off the bottom stair and race for my car, throwing my bag across the front seat and cranking the ignition. A whoosh of air draws my eyes to the busted-out window.

"Joho!"

I shift into Drive.

"Wait."

She limps around the garage, clutching her stomach. *My stomach hurts too, Novak.*

Reeve did it, the carving. I CANT.

She doesn't mean that. We have to talk.

The gas gauge wiggles on E, but I can make it to Reeve's. I exit at Vasquez and run a yellow light. The same thought keeps winding through my brain: "I can't" is different from "I won't." "I can't" is not a decision.

She's still scared.

I see them as I turn onto 68th. Two cop cars parked in front of Reeve's house. What's going on? I pull to the curb across the street and wrench open my door. As I charge toward the driveway, an officer steps out from between the cruisers.

"You can't go in there," he says. Another cop is stringing crime-scene tape.

"What happened?" I ask.

He eyes my face. "What happened to you?"

I touch my nose and feel the bulge. "Nothing."

"Right." He shakes his head. "Are you acquainted with the residents of this house?"

The picture window is shattered, shards dangling from the window frame. "Where's Reeve Hartt?" I ask.

"Who is this Reeve Hartt?" The cop takes out a little note-book.

"Reeve and Robbie. They live here with their mom and . . . Anthony."

He flips a page. "That's Anthony Inouye, the uncle? Is there anyone else?"

"Not that I know of. Where are they?"

"Did you know them?"

Did I? What does that mean, Did I?

A movement in one of the police cars snags my attention. Behind the metal grate separating the front and backseats is Anthony. He meets my eyes and a chill slithers up my spine. He does that nasty flicking with his tongue.

The officer says, "The detectives may want to question you. Wait here."

He turns to leave and I run to my car.

This is stupid, just driving around. I do a U-turn in the Ramada lot and retrace my route back to 68th. At the last second, I change my mind and steer into the alley between blocks. I drive slowly, counting houses.

The chain-link fence in back of Reeve's house is trashed. The kitchen window is broken too. There's that yellow and black crime-scene tape everywhere.

Next door, the neighbor is outside on a plastic chair, watching a kid scrape dirt with a spoon. I park in the alley and approach her.

"Do you know what happened next door?" I ask. "Why the cops are there?"

She's not much older than me, I think. She flips through a fashion magazine. "There was a party." She dog-ears a page. "I couldn't get my baby to sleep because the music was so loud. Then there was yelling and crashing around, which is nothing new with them."

The kid is filthy, like he's been eating dirt. The girl squints up at me. "You must've been at the party."

"Me? No." Why would she think . . . ? I cover my nose with a hand.

She pages through the magazine and says, "I come out for a smoke and see Robbie tearing out the door with this knife and he takes off running. He's got blood all over him."

"Robbie?" I glance over at the house to see a man with a camera exit the back door.

"The ambulance comes, then the cops. That's all I know." She slaps her magazine closed, scoops up the kid, and disappears inside.

My vision blurs as I stumble back to the car. I feel queasy. My chest constricts and I can't breathe, like a panic attack. I make it to the car, but my aim is off and I can't stick the key in the ignition. I lie on the seat, convulsing.

I close my eyes to visualize her. Her emotions pour into me and I shiver. Her terror, hopelessness.

I CANT.

Somebody died. No no no. Don't think that way.

A final spasm ripples through me, then calm. Control.

I push on the seat to right myself. Think, Johanna. Make calls. Find her.

Chapter 30

I slam into the curb and almost hit the mailbox. My eye is swelling shut.

"Hey." Novak jumps up from the bottom of the apartment stairs. "I want to apologize—" She stops. "Oh. My. God."

I flatten my hands over my face. Tears threaten.

Novak says, "Did she do that to you?"

My panic attack returns full force.

"What? What, sweetie?" Novak clenches my arms.

I steel myself because I need to be strong for Reeve. "I have to find her. I don't know where she is."

Novak says, "You're shivering. Sit down. Tell me what's going on."

My legs give out and I drop to the step. I press my fingers over my eyelids and they burn, my nose throbs. Think.

Tessa says, "North Suburban's closest." She punches numbers on her cell. "Turn on the TV news. Yes, hello. I'm looking for someone who might have been brought into Emergency this morning? Thank you." Tessa slides onto a barstool at the counter and looks at me. "What's their last name again?"

"Hartt. Reeve Hartt," I say. "And Robbie Inouye."

The TV blasts in the living room.

Tessa says into the phone, "Hartt. Or Inouye." She asks me, "How do you spell that?"

Martin staggers in from the back, yawning. "What's up?" He rakes a hand through his messy hair.

"Someone got stabbed," Novak says behind him.

"We don't know that," I snap.

Martin asks, "Who?"

Tessa holds up a finger for silence. Bookmarking a page with her finger, she flips through a section of laminated sheets in the notebook and I see they're children's services and halfway houses, shelters and abortion clinics.

I never really knew what Tessa did at the free clinic. Fed poor people and vaccinated children?

"Okay, thank you." Tessa presses a button on her cell. "They might've gone to St. Joseph's. Or Denver Health." She pages back to the hospitals.

Martin settles a hand on my shoulder and asks, "What happened to your face?"

Novak reaches for my hand, but I won't let her. "Don't worry, Joho. We'll find her."

There is no "we." There is only me. And only Reeve.

I lower my head and close my eyes. I send her a silent message. *I'm coming. Hold on.*

"They're at St. Joseph's." Tessa shuts her cell.

Novak says, "They took Dante there after he totaled his car." She heads for the door and I snag her arm.

"You're not coming," I tell her. "This is partly your fault." I say to Tessa, "Nobody's coming."

Tessa says, "Johanna—"

"Stay out of it."

I race upstairs for my keys and bag, feeling a little dizzy. My face and hair are wet by the time I reach the car. When did it start to rain?

Tessa's waiting by my car.

I shoulder her aside and lock myself in. Jamming the key into the ignition, I crank and nothing happens.

I try again.

"Damn. Dammit." I'm out of gas. Rain is pouring through the broken window in back. I ball my fists and punch my eyes. *Ow.*

Now what? Think. THINK. My head hurts so bad.

I open the door and Tessa says, "We'll take my car."

We park in the visitors' garage and follow the signs to Emergency. The receptionist tells us, "I'm not allowed to give out information on that party. If you'll wait in the lounge, a doctor will be in to speak with you."

"What does it mean when they aren't allowed to give out information?" I ask Tessa.

"We're not family. It's not our information."

The signs point toward a corridor and as we turn the corner, I see her. "Reeve!" She's at the drinking fountain. She raises her head, pivots, and hurries off the other way.

I chase her down. I spin her around and lift her off her feet. "Reeve. Oh my God." I hold her so tight.

She says in a raspy voice, "Go away. Get the fuck out of my life."

Her carving fills my brain. I CANT.

"No, Reeve. I can't."

Robbie said he'd kill her. In his essay, he wrote, "May 23 I kill my mother."

Tessa is talking to an older lady who seems to be with Reeve. I don't see Robbie or their mom. I hear a few details: A bunch of Anthony's friends showed up with drugs and booze. The party got out of hand. Someone had a knife.

Reeve seems dazed, so I clutch her hand and lead her outside. There's a covered gazebo in the visitors' area. As we sit on the pentagonal bench, she looks at me, at my face, and visibly shrinks.

I lift her onto my lap and wind her legs around my waist. "It's okay, baby," I say.

"No, it's not." Her voice is hollow. "It's never going to be okay."

I rub her thin arms. "I'm here. I'm never leaving you."

Her chest heaves. I just want to hold her until she stops fighting it. She doesn't speak, doesn't volunteer information, and I don't want to push her to the dark place. I ask, "Where's Robbie?"

She shakes her head. "He grabbed the knife from Anthony and I couldn't stop him. He's so stupid." She draws her knees to her chest and I wrap my arms around her to hold her on my lap.

"Start at the beginning. You left the party. . . ."

"My dad was there."

"At Novak's?"

"No. At our house. I didn't want him to see me or Robbie, so we snuck upstairs and covered ourselves with a blanket."

No cover . . .

She lolls her head back. "I heard this crash and Mom screamed. Then Anthony yelled, 'Shut up, bitch! Shut that whore up!' She was doing meth and heroin. There was so much noise and I thought I heard a gun go off." Reeve closes her eyes. "When I got to the kitchen, Anthony was smacking Mom around. It wasn't the first time, but it was the first time she fought back." Reeve blinks at me. "She always took it. She kept taking it. My dad hit her too."

I feel my jaw clench.

Her hair is wild and tangled. I go to smooth it down and snag my fingers. "Where's your dad now?"

"Robbie sleeps so hard, you know? I thought he'd sleep through it. I don't know what happened to Mom. It was like, finally, something snapped. She said, 'That's it, Anthony,' and she grabbed a knife. I think she really would've cut him."

She should have cut out his heart.

I rub her arms. "Where were you? What were you doing?"

"Staying out of the way. I used to try to stop it, you know? With Dad too. I'd call the cops or run to the neighbors and they'd call the cops. Mom would get pissed."

"Why?"

"She didn't want to go back to rehab."

Gently, I comb my fingers through Reeve's hair. "You were just trying to save her life," I say.

"She doesn't want her life saved. She thrives on the hurt, same as you."

That stops me. "What?"

Reeve scoots off my lap. "You let me hit you. You *enjoy* it."

"No, I don't." Heat rises up my neck.

"Really?" She cocks her head. "You keep coming back for more."

"It's not the same," I say.

"How is it different?"

My mind scatters. "I don't know. It just is."

"When you figure out the difference, let me know." She turns to leave.

"The difference is . . . the *difference*"—I stand and clamp her arm—"is that you don't *want* to hurt me."

Her head swivels.

"That's the difference, Reeve."

"I don't see it. All I see is . . ." Her eyes sweep across my face.

"My love for you."

She lets out a hiss of air. "You're sick."

I take her hand and she tries to pull away, but can't. At last she surrenders. "Tell me the rest," I say.

"Can we go back inside?"

The rain mists our faces as we stroll toward the building. "So your mom's in surgery?"

She looks at me. "My mom's dead."

"No. You don't know that."

"I was there. They took her out in the ambulance."

Is she serious?

"Robbie got the knife away from Anthony, but . . ." Reeve swallows hard.

"Robbie was all bloody," I finish. "Your neighbor saw them."

Reeve's eyes fuse to mine. "Did my neighbor see Anthony kill Robbie?"

A chill slithers up my spine. "What?" I whisper.

Reeve goes, "He stabbed my mom, then he slit Robbie's throat."

Chapter 31

Robbie is dead. I can't believe it.

The gray lady is Reeve's social services caseworker. She says to Reeve, "How do I get in touch with your father?"

"Why?" Reeve asks.

"He's your only living relative. He could take you in until—"

"She can't live there," I cut in.

Tessa goes, "Stay out of this, Johanna."

"He molested them," I tell the caseworker.

The caseworker says to Reeve, "I never heard about this."

The halls have cleared; all the doctors, nurses, police officers have gone. "He abused both of them," I say. "He beat their mother too."

Tessa fixes on Reeve.

"She's coming home with me," I tell Tessa and the gray lady.

The caseworker looks like she has a problem with it, but Tessa says to her, "Can I speak to you in private?"

They leave and I hold Reeve. Robbie's dead. He's dead. He can't be.

Tessa comes back alone. "Let's go," she says. I think she means the two of us, but she grasps Reeve's arm too.

I sit in the back and hold Reeve. She's cold and stiff.

When we get home, I steer Reeve toward my apartment, but Tessa blocks my path. "Where are you going?"

Reeve's fingers are icicles.

Tessa says, "Come in the house. Let's figure this out."

What's to figure out? Reeve is living with me. It's cold and wet and I don't want to argue.

Reeve breaks away and opens the patio door to the house.

Novak ambushes us inside. "Hey, you found her."

I shield Reeve from Novak.

Tessa sets down her carryall. "Reeve can have the sleeper sofa, since Novak's in the baby's—I mean, the blue room."

"No way!" My voice echoes through the house. No way is Reeve going to be near Novak.

Tessa eyes me. "Okay. Then Novak can stay with you and Reeve can have—"

"No."

"It's the only solution," Tessa says.

"Reeve is moving in with me."

"We're through discussing this." Tessa heads into the living room.

I shout at her, "We're not through! It's not a solution!" I

follow her to the back. "Why can't Reeve stay with me? Because you're afraid we'll have sex? I'm gay, okay? It's what we do."

Tessa turns slowly, her eyes rise to my face. "That's not what I'm concerned about."

"I think it is."

Behind me, I hear Reeve tell Novak, "My mother and brother are dead."

Novak goes, "Oh my God."

I say to Tessa, "You just want to keep us apart."

Tessa says, "Yes. I want her as far away from you as possible."

I knew it.

In a calmer voice, she adds, "Johanna, look at your face. Look what she did to you. I'm afraid to leave her alone with you."

"I can take care of myself. I love her."

Tessa's eyes soften. "You have strong feelings for this girl. You want to be her savior. But the way she treats you, that isn't love."

We look at each other intensely. I say, "She doesn't mean it. She can't help it."

Tessa gives me a slow shake of her head.

"You don't understand," I say.

Tessa opens the linen closet and hauls out an armload of sheets, towels, a pillow. "She's not staying with you." She walks past me. "Reeve, you're here on the sleeper sofa. Temporarily. I hope you don't mind."

I charge past Tessa and reach for Reeve's hand. "She's living with me."

Reeve pulls away.

What? Why, baby?

Tessa says, "Johanna, if you need sheets or blankets—"

"Fuck you," I say. I storm out, slamming the sliding door so hard the glass cracks.

Ramming my throbbing skull against my car's seat back, I squeeze my eyes shut and get sucked into the undertow. From some roiling sea inside me, an angry wave of tears swells to the surface.

Robbie's dead. Their mom is dead. Reeve saw it happen.

What does it do to a person to live with violence every day? With fear? In my entire life I never once woke up feeling afraid. Well, not of physical violence. My biggest fear was that I'd wake up every day alone, that I'd never find someone to love.

But I did. I found Reeve. We're going through a rough patch. I can smooth it out.

It's freaking Siberia in the car with the window broken. I curl up tight on the seat. I wonder if Reeve is crying, if there are enough tears in a person to cry that much out. I remember this one youth service project we did where we went to the inner city to work with kids. It was Martin Luther King Day or something, and we asked the kids to draw their dream. We told them, "If you can see it, you can be it."

What does Reeve see?

She just lost her brother and her mother.

I lost my father and mother, but it doesn't seem the same. They died in peace.

Tessa lost two babies. And her parents.

Reeve's pain can be my pain. I'll take it. I think about what Reeve said, that the reason I take it is because I don't value my life.

That's not true. I've never had anything to live for as important as her. If someone came at me with a knife and tried to hurt me, I'd defend myself. So why didn't I even try against Reeve?

Because I never felt in danger. I only felt . . . in love.

My legs cramp. I roll onto my back and stretch my legs to the window. My life isn't a constant struggle for survival. Occasionally I worry where my next meal will come from, but I know I won't starve. I never worry about having a warm place to sleep at night.

Except . . . Who's got a bed tonight? Everyone but me.

I have to pee. The security light under the house eave is burned out and I trip over an Adirondack footrest, scraping it across the flagstone. If that doesn't wake the devil . . . The sliding door is locked. Thanks, Tessa.

I creep up the apartment stairs quietly so Novak won't hear. *She* didn't lock me out, at least.

Objects in the room take shape. The divan, TV, hallway. I go to the bathroom. Novak isn't in the bed, or on the divan. I switch on the light in the kitchen and see my spiral, the one I wrote letters in, lying open on the table. Open to a page where I wrote out a scene from Joyland.

On the opposite page, Novak left a note:

Lesbo,

You're a horny bitch. There are lots of grlz who'd sleep with you. I'm going home to kiss my mother's ass. I'd like to remove the poker from it first, but she might bleed to death. Sorry. Inappropriate humor considering the circumstances. If I promise to be a good girl from now on, maybe she'll let me stay until I leave for college. How long do you think I can keep that promise?

About a minute, I think.

I know I don't deserve you. I took advantage of you and I'm sorry. Tell Tessa thank you, okay? Tell Reeve I'm so so sorry. OMG. I can't believe her mom's dead. And Robbie. OMG.

I have to be honest, Joho. I don't think she's good for you. She might feed your caring soul or your nymphomania, but she's damaged. I know love is blind and all, but not to everyone around you who loves you and doesn't want to see you get hurt. Like me. And Tessa.

She talked to Tessa about Reeve. She told her.

You've already ripped this up, so it's not going to matter if I say what I'm going to say next.

"I'm still reading, Novak," I say aloud.

I'm not sorry I kissed you. You can forget what happened, but I won't. I think we both wanted it. Maybe I'm bi, or maybe you're just so fucking irresistible you made me gay. Guys suck, okay? They're never there when you need them the most.

There's an arrow (over), and I can't help myself.

You were always there for me, Johanna. I needed you more than I should have. Sound familiar?

Chapter 32

Novak straightened my room. My shirts are hanging in the closet and my jeans are folded. She made the bed. Why couldn't she leave my place the way she found it? Why couldn't she leave me the way she found me?

I sit up all night, picking off the black tips from all the candles I lit the night Reeve came over. A tendril of desire tickles my belly.

Death drowns it. A familiar sense of loss seeps through my veins.

Reeve is close, right downstairs. All I have to do is go get her.

No. She needs space to grieve. I have to let her come to me. With time and trust, she can be healed.

When I raise my head from the table, I have a crick in my neck. It's morning.

The curtains on the sliding door are drawn, and Martin, most likely, has duct-taped the crack in the glass. That's going to cost me. Tessa's in the dining room, drinking coffee.

"I'll pay for the glass," I tell her, easing the door shut behind me.

She presses an index finger to her lips. The house is still.

"Does Novak want breakfast?" Tessa whispers. "Do you?"

I cross into the kitchen. "Novak went home."

There's a prolonged silence. "Look. I'm sorry," Tessa says. "Not for what you think. I'm doing what's right for you—for once."

"What does that mean?"

Tessa goes, "Shh. Come sit with me a minute." She motions to the chair beside her.

I open the fridge and grab the jug of milk. There's a clean glass in the dish drainer next to the sink.

Sliding into a chair across from Tessa, I sip my milk. She says, "I should've had this talk with you a while ago."

Blood rushes up my neck. Here it comes.

"I feel completely responsible for everything that happened. I should've stayed home to go to college. I knew how dependent Mom was after Dad died and I shouldn't have dumped that on you."

Does she think I did a crap job of it all?

"I just couldn't quit school so near the end—" Tessa pauses. "Yes, I could have. It's no excuse. And your letter—"

A shadow behind her snags my attention. Reeve. I get up to meet her under the archway. My momentum carries us both backward into the living room and I hold her. I kiss her gently on the mouth and she lets me.

I sense Tessa behind me. Always, I feel her judging me.

Reeve detaches and says, "I need to get my stuff from my house."

I say to Reeve, "Novak's gone. She said to say she's sorry about your mom and Robbie. She's gone, okay?"

"When did she leave?" Tessa asks, eavesdropping on my private conversation.

"I don't know." I smooth Reeve's hair. "I wasn't in the apartment."

Reeve says, "Where were you?"

"In my car."

A glint of emotion passes through Reeve's eyes and a tiny smile crooks her lips. An instant of relief, and trust?

Crime-scene tape is strung along the fence and crisscrossed on the doors and windows. Tessa says, "We should've gotten permission, or a police escort."

Reeve goes, "Fuck the police."

Tessa's eyes narrow at Reeve.

"We'll just get some clothes and leave," I say. "We won't destroy evidence or anything."

From the car, Tessa scans the area. "I don't know."

"You don't have to come inside," I tell her.

Reeve gets out and makes a beeline for the back. I'm on her heels. A basement window has been rigged and Reeve fits through easily, but it's a squeeze for me.

The first thing that hits me is the smell. Like vinegar.

Reeve says, "Mom cooks down here."

Cooks? Then I see it—drug paraphernalia. A thump behind me makes me yelp. Tessa. She claws a spiderweb off her face. Reeve pushes a trapdoor and light filters down a laddered shaft.

The air is a relief. I climb up after Reeve and we emerge in the kitchen, where jagged shapes cut eerie shadows. There are splatters of red on the wall. Is that blood? Oh my God. Reeve's breathing is stuttered and shallow.

"It's okay, baby."

Sidestepping a pile of rubble, she says, "Stay here."

Tessa breathes, "Oh, Johanna," as Reeve's footsteps pound on the stairs. "What are you into?"

Her, I answer silently. I leave Tessa behind and catch up to Reeve.

The second floor is destroyed. Doors are busted down or missing and there are gaping holes in the walls. It stinks like vomit. I flip on a light switch, but nothing happens.

Reeve goes, "I told you to stay downstairs." She comes out of nowhere, pushing me back.

"But I want to help."

"I can do it. Don't come any closer." She balls a fist in my face. "I mean it."

This has to be hard for her, returning to the scene where Robbie . . . her mom . . .

Reeve skitters to the end of the hall, crouches on the floor, and starts shoveling clothes into a pillowcase. I trip on a hunk of loose carpet.

"Damn you." She flies to her feet and charges me. She rams me into an exposed wall beam, gouging my spine.

"Let me help," I say.

"No!"

"Why?"

She sets her jaw.

"I . . ." What doesn't she want me to see? I've already seen it all. I glance over her shoulder. "Is that your room?" It's a closet, or used to be. There's no door. A small, square mirror hangs by a string on a nail. The clothes she hasn't shoved into the pillowcase are scant. She has, like, three shirts and a pair of jeans.

This is where she sleeps? In a closet?

"Don't." She squeezes my arms so hard it hurts. "Don't you fucking feel sorry for me."

I meet her eyes. Snatching the pillowcase from her hand, I edge past her to the closet and sink to my knees. I jam the rest of the clothes in as this fire burns in my belly. How unfair is this? How little she has, how she—how anybody—has to live this way.

Me thinking it's so cool, so vintage. This isn't vintage. It's poverty.

I storm to the stairs and throw the pillowcase down to Tessa. "We're taking everything!" I yell.

Robbie had a room—no door, no closet, no plaster on the walls. He slept on a crappy single mattress on the floor. Reeve slept right outside his door.

His case is sitting on the mattress. He's never coming back.

"That's it," Reeve says.

"Do you want Robbie's things?"

She avoids looking into his room. "No."

As we load up Tessa's Subaru, I think, Get the hell out of

here. Torch it. Demolish the whole block. Tessa pulls away from the curb and I yell, "Stop!"

She slams on the brakes.

"I forgot something," I tell Tessa. "Go back."

I don't wait for her. I fling open the door and sprint to the house.

The case, it could be empty. It could be full of—who cares? That case is all he had.

Chapter 33

Tessa calls this mortuary and schedules a service for Robbie and their mom on Wednesday. Tuesday she goes back to work at the clinic.

I gather up all the candles that still have wicks and wash the sheets and lower the miniblinds. The bedroom isn't pitch black, not at eight-thirty in the morning, but the gauzy natural light with the flickering candles feels dreamy and romantic.

I hear the apartment door open, close, and lock. I feel her coming down the hall. She lingers for a moment in the doorway. I've been waiting so long for her, for this, for the two of us to finally come together.

Reeve says, "Do you mind if I take a shower?"

"Do you want me to help?"

A smile tugs her lips. "I think I can handle it."

I listen to the water run and imagine her taking off her

cami, her shorts, her bra. Testing the water. Stepping into the spray.

I'm already naked under the sheets, and ready. Reeve comes in, clutching a towel to her front. She looks all pink and tingly. She drops her towel and slides in underneath.

I pull her into my arms.

"Johanna," she says, "I know what you want." She presses her forehead to mine. "I want it too, but . . ."

Her hair is damp and combed straight. I curl her hair over her ear so I can look at her face.

"What do you need, Reeve?" I ask.

Tears glisten in her eyes. "I need you to hold me."

I draw her in closer. Her stick-thin arms slide up between us, sharp elbows pressing into my breasts as her head burrows into my neck.

"I can't give you what you need," Reeve says in a small voice. "I'm sorry."

I close my eyes and fight down the disappointment. "It's okay. I understand." She needs time to heal. "You're all I need."

"Sure," she goes. "But you couldn't wait."

I bleed out internally.

She rolls over, away from me, and I release her from my needs. I'd never force her.

I've never wanted anything or anyone so much.

To cut the silence and tension, I say, "The rule is, after number ten you have to start counting over."

"At number two?"

I clench my throat to keep from crying.

We lie together in bed for a while.

"I want to take you somewhere," I say.

"I told you I'm not ready."

"Not there." I slide out from between the sheets. "Get dressed."

She twists her head to look at me.

"Please?"

"Where?"

"It's a surprise."

"I hate surprises."

So do I. We have that in common.

Memorial Hospice is a hodgepodge of structures—on one side, a cottage house converted to a café; on the other, the new addition, with a glassed-in entrance to hide the older building, the public ward.

"What is this?" Reeve asks.

"A hospice."

"What's a hospice?"

I take her hand. "It's a place where people come to die."

Reeve stops in her tracks.

"I come here when I need hope," I say.

She pulls her hand away.

"It's not like that. It isn't—"

"Why would you bring me here?"

"Reeve, no. It's a beautiful place. It's peaceful. I guess I wanted you to see that life doesn't always end the way you experienced."

"You don't know what I've experienced," she snaps.

"I know I don't. I just wanted you to see . . . the other side."

She stares ahead at the front door. "You come here to watch people die?"

"Yeah. Well, no. To share in their final days."

"You're so weird."

I let out a short laugh. "You like that in a girl, remember?"

She shakes her head, but a smile leaks out.

I take her hand again and she hangs on.

Jeannette stands at the welcome desk, talking to the receptionist. When she sees me, she says, "Johanna. I was about to call you."

"This is my girlfriend, Reeve." I get it out quickly, before I lose my nerve. There's an awkward moment as Jeannette's eyes dart from Reeve to me. To my bruised face. It's okay, I want to tell Jeannette. Everything's under control.

At last Jeannette smiles and extends a hand. "Hi."

Reeve shakes it.

Reeve is trembling. God, is it too soon?

"Johanna, let's . . . ," Jeannette says as she cups my elbow, "over here." She leads me to a sunny nook with chairs and a coffee table, and I tug Reeve along. A purple orchid snakes out of a crystal vase and I think of Novak. "Sit." Jeannette motions us down.

Reeve and I take chairs next to each other.

Jeannette says, "Mrs. Mockrie died early this morning."

"Oh no." I cover my mouth.

"An hour later, Mr. Mockrie passed."

Tears well in my eyes.

"She and her husband came in together," Jeannette explains to Reeve. "They absolutely adored Johanna." Jeannette smiles at me, then cringes like it hurts to look at me.

I shield my face with a hand.

"I'm sorry," Jeannette says, touching my knee. "I know you loved them too. We all did. They went peacefully in their sleep."

I try to mental Reeve: See? Death can be a beautiful thing. We could die together.

Jeannette gets up and presses a hand on my shoulder. She says, "Nice to meet you, Reeve."

Reeve just looks at the orchid.

A gurney rolls out from the corridor. ". . . not happy with her physical therapy regimen. Jeannette! I want to talk to you!"

Does Carrie's mother always have to shout?

"You want me to give you a tour?" I ask Reeve.

She turns to face me. "If that's what you want." Her voice is flat.

"Or we could go." I shouldn't have brought her here.

"What's down there?" She eyes the hall.

"The private suites. People with money. Or insurance."

Reeve stands. "Show me those people."

The first room is crammed for a birthday party, or something. The lady, I know, has terminal cancer. She's propped up in bed, surrounded by people and balloons. I turn to tell Reeve, but she's gone ahead. She's stalled outside the second door. "Who lives here?" she asks. "Or should I say, who dies here?"

I see Carrie's room through Reeve's eyes. The posters and

paintings on the walls, the pictures of Carrie. Her pink flow-ered comforter and frilly curtains. "Her name's Carrie. She was in a car accident that left her . . ." I don't finish because Reeve has entered Carrie's room.

I check the corridor and slip inside. "We shouldn't be in here," I say quietly.

"But this is where you come." Reeve wanders around, looking at everything. The ribbons, awards, certificates. She picks up a framed photo. "Is this her?"

"Yeah. She's pretty, huh?"

"She's hot," Reeve says.

"What?"

Reeve sets the picture down. "I'm kidding. Is she a rich bitch?"

I try to take Reeve's hand, but she slithers out. She yanks open the bedside drawer and selects a tube of lip gloss.

"Don't touch her personal things," I say. "Her mother's the rich bitch."

Reeve uncaps the tube and sniffs it. In Carrie's little vanity mirror, she glosses her lips.

She straightens slowly and crooks a finger at me, like, Come here.

I widen my eyes at her.

Reeve comes over, stands on tiptoe and kisses me. She touches my face and arm sensuously, sending tingles to my feet.

"Reeve, not here." I feel a tug on my bag and shift my gaze to see Reeve has opened it. She drops in the lip gloss.

"You can't—"

"She won't be needing it."

True. But . . .

Reeve shovels out a fistful of makeup and transfers it to my bag.

"Don't."

"Don't what?" She pulls me down to the bed and kisses me. Her lips are slick and hard. She parts my mouth with her tongue and sucks in my lower lip. The heat begins in my brain and smolders all the way down. Reeve's on top of me, her hand up my shirt, fingers crawling under my bra, over the flesh, touching my nipple.

"What the *hell* are you doing?"

I push up and Reeve goes flying.

Evelyn's face is so red I think she'll explode. "You." She points. "How dare you?"

I can't speak.

"Were you in there?" I follow her shaking finger to the bedside table. The drawer is open.

Evelyn rushes past me, stops at the drawer, and spins around. "Give me your purse."

Reeve hands over her purse. *Thank you, thank you. I love you.*

Carrie's mom empties the contents onto the bed. Cash, mascara, my gold watch.

It's okay. I was going to give it to her anyway.

"Now yours."

Reeve grabs her stuff and pushes me toward the door. "We're out of here."

"You have no right," Evelyn goes. "No right." Her voice breaks.

I claw all of Carrie's makeup out of my bag and wedge around Evelyn to replace it in the drawer. "I'm sorry." I fumble around, lining up the tubes. "I'm so, so sorry."

Evelyn hiccups a sob. "Jeannette's going to hear about this."

"I know. I'll tell her."

She makes this raw, retching sound in her throat, then rasps at my back, "Pervert."

Joyland: Take 15

The silhouette behind the scrim is angular and nude. The scrim rolls up and I see she's painted plaster. Blue stage lights illuminate the mannequin.

She wears a mask of wax; then, on cue, she comes to life. She strips off her mask to reveal round red cheeks and anime eyes. Dressers dance en pointe to clothe her, but she doesn't like the frilly collars and corseted gown, so she pulls a knife and cuts them.

I pass her on the right, according to script, to get her attention. I'm not the kind of person she'd notice, in my drab overcoat and checkered Converses. As I pass the huge snow globe, a girl steps out from behind it. "Fair warning," Britt whispers. "She's not your fairy princess."

I draw my sword and Britt retreats.

We're alone onstage. The lights have been extinguished. Reeve says, "Tell me what you see."

My mouth moves, but indistinguishable sounds come out.

"Tell me what you see," she demands.

I CANT

She peels away a second layer and the face is shapeless skin. No eyes, no nose, no mouth.

This can't be her, I think. Not the real Reeve.

• • •

Chapter 34

The organist is playing a dirge while a man in a gray suit sits on a high-back wing chair behind the pulpit. Tessa's crying.

Tessa cried more at Mom's funeral than I did.

Reeve and I slip into the row behind Tessa and Martin. There are two tall stands, like plant stands, supporting two square objects draped with cloths.

The ashes. Robbie's ashes and their mom's.

The minister gets up and says a prayer while I hold Reeve's hand. It's limp and cold. No one else is here. Wait. A person sneaks in on the other side. She kneels and steeples her hands. Novak.

The minister reads a passage from the Bible, then asks if anyone would like to come up and speak about the deceased. Reeve shrinks in her seat. I look to Novak, who is blowing

her nose. When I die, I want someone, anyone, to speak for me.

I stand and sidestep out of the pew. Everyone's eyes are on me. At the pulpit, I say, "Robbie didn't deserve to die. He never hurt a living soul in his life." Not on purpose. "He was a good friend and a great brother and he didn't deserve this." I feel my throat tighten and I stumble back to my place. I was mostly mean to him. Everyone was.

The organist plays a hymn and the minister hands the urns to Reeve. She won't take them. Tessa and I end up with one each.

When we get home, Martin leaves for work. Reeve heads for the blue room and I follow, but at the door she turns and pushes me back. An arm shoots out to clench Reeve's wrist. It's Tessa.

Reeve says, "I just want to be left alone."

Tessa says, "Then go. But don't ever push her."

Reeve shuts the door on us.

I'm up early to save Reeve. No, I don't mean save. I don't know what I mean.

"She's gone," Tessa says as I pass by the dining table, where she's casting on, beginning a new knitting project. The click-click of her needles takes me back. I used to sit at her feet and ball yarn while she told me about her date the night before.

"Where'd she go?"

"I don't know," Tessa says. She gets up and pours a cup of coffee.

"You're lying." She's *lying*. She lifts her cup to her lips and

I smack it out of her hand. It shatters against the wall and coffee splashes everywhere. Tessa looks at me, through me. Calmly, she crosses the room, but I beat her there and kick the pieces away.

Tessa squats to pick up a shard and I push her into the wall. She bangs her head.

"She's turned you into a monster."

"Where is she!" I screech.

Tessa stands. "Johanna, we need to talk about Reeve."

"Shut up." I tell Tessa, "Don't talk to me. Don't ever talk to me again."

The phone call comes while I'm sitting on the divan, fuming. Feeling wrecked and worried about Reeve. It has to be Reeve calling. I lunge for the phone.

"Hello, Johanna. This is Jeannette."

All the blood drains from my face.

"I've been waiting for you to call me to explain, but I guess that's not going to happen."

Words jam up in my throat.

"All I have is Evelyn's version. If you have a different story, I'm willing to listen."

The jam unclogs, but I can only manage one word: "No." Evelyn got it right.

Jeannette waits, then sighs and says, "You realize I'm going to have to ask you not to return to the hospice."

A candle inside me extinguishes.

*   *   *

Martin pounds on my door and when I answer, he says, "I'll collect this now." He shoves my IOU at me.

"I don't have it," I tell him. "I lost my job. But I'm looking for another one. I'm going to pay you back."

His eyes are black. As he clomps down the stairs, I call to him, "I promise."

He clomps back up. His vibe scares me. "For your information, your sister put you on our car insurance. I told her to take away your keys and make you ride the bus, but she's too nice for that. I expect you to pay *both* of us back."

"I will," I say. "Every penny. As soon as—"

He stomps down the stairs and I close the door behind him, sinking to the divan. All I want to do is crawl in a hole and die.

Day after day I drive by Reeve's house. The police tape is gone, but the windows are boarded up and the health department has posted a green notice on the door. Where is she?

I'm so desperate for human contact I actually call Novak. Her mother tells me she's gone; she moved to California to get ready for college.

She didn't even call to say goodbye.

Time is meaningless and insignificant. I need to look for a job, but it's so hard to get out of bed in the morning. One inconsequential day I'm jolted awake by shouting outside my window, and a door slamming.

I drag to my door and open it a crack. Martin's in the backyard, lighting up the grill. I squint at the TV clock. He's grilling at seven a.m.?

Tessa steps out and pulls the patio door shut. She looks worse than I feel. She's dressed for work, but her jacket is wrinkled and her hair isn't combed.

I glance back and see Martin looking straight at me. As I ease the door closed, I hear him snap at Tessa, "Get Johanna in therapy too. She needs it even more than you do."

Chapter 35

"Call me Mary-Dean," she says. I think it's a weird name for a therapist. I don't know why I come, because all I do is sit on this hard chair and cry. Mary-Dean says, "It's okay to get it out. We'll talk when you're ready."

I'll never be ready.

At our third session, Mary-Dean says, "Tell me about your girlfriend. Reeve. Is that her name?"

My brain instantly engages. Tessa's been talking to her about me. I should've known. "Whatever she told you is wrong," I say.

"Who?"

You know who. I blow my nose.

"The only thing Tessa told me is that you got hurt."

"By her," I mutter.

Mary-Dean says, "How did Tessa hurt you?"

A torrent of tears threatens.

Mary-Dean goes, "Then tell me about Reeve. She seems to be someone you care about very much."

I stammer out the words: "I-I loved her. I mean, I love her."

Mary-Dean leans forward. "What does love mean to you, Johanna?"

That's the question. "You know."

"I want to hear it from you."

"Reeve was—is—my girlfriend. I'm gay." I wonder if Tessa told her that.

Mary-Dean doesn't look shocked. In fact, she smiles. Not fake, not patronizing.

"I love Reeve with all my heart."

Mary-Dean says, "That's a good feeling, isn't it? Falling in love. Does Reeve love you?"

"Yes."

Mary-Dean nods and says, "How do you know? How does she show her love?"

I know where she's going with this. I won't go there. I can't. I stare over Mary-Dean's shoulder at the black-and-white photo on the wall of a mother holding a child. I have to get out of here.

Tessa's appointments with Mary-Dean are on different days than mine. I don't think it's right that she's talking about me when I'm not there, so I go down to the house to confront her. She isn't home. Neither is Martin. He's left her a note on the counter. "Sweetie. Your grief support group mtg is canceled today. Luv U."

Tessa's in a grief support group. Of course. She lost her baby. She lost two babies. And her parents. And me.

Mary-Dean tries again. "Tell me what love means, Johanna. I'd just like to hear your take on it."

I've been thinking a lot about it and I'm prepared. "Love is being there for someone no matter what."

"Even if they hurt you?"

"Yeah," I say. "Especially then."

Mary-Dean studies me. "Why?" She removes her glasses and sets them on the table between us. "Why does love have to hurt?"

"That's not what I said." Is it?

"Do you think love hurts?"

The people I know who've loved and been loved have all been hurt. Mom when Dad died. Novak every time she got dumped. Tessa.

"Yeah, I think there's an element of hurt."

"Physical?"

"Sometimes," I say. "Not all the time."

"But when?"

"When you let it."

"Did you let it?"

I say to her, "Sometimes you don't have a choice."

She says, "Don't you always have a choice? At least about your actions, how you respond?"

These questions make me anxious. Yes, I let Reeve hurt me. No, I don't believe that's showing love. But I love her. With all my heart, I still love her.

"I don't know how to explain it," I say to Mary-Dean.

She smiles and puts on her glasses. "You'll get there."

I land a job at the cineplex. I figure, hey, can't let that Film Studies class go to waste. Mostly, I'm proud of myself for finding the motivation. It's hard to get out of bed every day and face myself in the mirror. The bruises are gone, but I don't feel healed.

On my way out one day, I pass Tessa coming in. "I've got a job now," I tell her. "I'll pay you guys back soon."

Tessa raises her eyes to meet mine. She says, "It doesn't matter."

"Yes, it does." I say more insistently, "It matters to me. I need to pay you back."

"Okay." She nods. I think she understands.

The next session, Mary-Dean hands me a yellow tablet and says, "I want you to make two columns, or two separate lists. Label one 'Gains' and the other 'Losses.'" I must look confused, because she adds, "Write down all you gained and all you lost, with Reeve."

"Now?" I say.

"You can take it with you for homework," she adds. "Sometime soon I want to hear about your mother and father, and your sister leaving. It must've been extremely hard to lose them all so close together."

I break down, and Mary-Dean immediately passes me a giant box of Kleenex.

* * *

It's a slow night, Tuesday night, and the ten o'clock shows have all started. In the ticket booth, I take out the yellow tablet and begin with Gains. I think, This'll be easy.

Love. Knowing love. Loving and being loved.

Reeve did love me. She still does. *Where are you, baby?*

Nothing else comes to mind right away. But there's got to be more. I flip the page and write: "Losses. What I lost:"

Money
My job at Bling's
Mom's watch
The hospice where I love to volunteer

These are coming too fast.

I page back to the Gains list. Love. It outweighs everything. Back to Losses.

My car window. It's covered with plastic until I can afford a new one.

Martin's trust. He moved, or locked up, the loaded potato.

Novak.

But it's not really Reeve's fault I lost Novak. Is it?

I rip out the page. Look at what Reeve lost—her mother, her brother, her home. *You still have me, baby.*

At the next session, I tell Mary-Dean I forgot to do the assignment. She says, "That's okay. What I really wanted to know is where you would put self-respect."

"Self-respect?"

"Would you say your relationship with Reeve gained you self-respect or lost you self-respect?"

"Gained," I answer automatically.

"How?"

Why? When? How? Reeve would be slugging Mary-Dean continuously.

"I guess . . . I feel . . ."

"Did you respect yourself before you met Reeve?"

"Yeah. I mean, I think I'm a good person. My teacher Mrs. Goins said I was kind and generous."

"Of course you are, Johanna. You're a wonderful person."

"So is Reeve." She just didn't have a choice.

We always have a choice—about our actions.

She didn't have to hit me.

I let her do it.

It was wrong. I was wrong. We were . . .

Mary-Dean asks, "Do you respect yourself more now than you did before?"

This question makes me search my soul.

And I don't like the answer.

Joyland: Take 16

We dash behind the waterfall, holding hands. The rocks are slippery. We balance for a moment, making sure everyone's secure. I'm awed by the power, the majesty, the roar of water rushing off the cliff.

Robbie sits on the shore. We've just been to his funeral. He removes his shoes and socks, stuffs the socks inside the shoes, and ties the laces together. Reeve says, "Don't lose those, asstard."

Robbie says, "The retardo is a high school graduate."

Reeve turns to me. "Scary, but true."

Novak takes my arm. "Remember when we used to come up here?" She has to yell to be heard over the falls.

"No!" I yell back. I say to Reeve, "She never came here with me."

Novak leans around me. "We came here when Tessa lost her first baby."

"No, we didn't."

Teetering on the rock, she goes, "Yes, we did. We made a little boat and put a pink Care Bear in it. A heart bear. We set it in the river, right here." Novak indicates a spot in front of us where water is pooling between the rocks. It forms an eddy, then swirls off toward the falls. "Tessa said, 'My sweet baby girl. Have a safe trip home. I'll see you when you get there.'"

Reeve stares at the box in her hands. Her mother's ashes.

Robbie is wearing his shabby graduation robe. He's holding the other box.

Mom's an angel in heaven. She says, "You're such a comfort to me."

Novak screams, "Oh my God, Robbie! You're alive!" She hurdles rocks to get to him. He stumbles backward but catches her in his arms. Without warning, he kisses her.

Novak looks stunned.

Reeve says, "You're just so damn irresistible."

That cracks us all up.

"You really know how to pick 'em," Reeve says.

"Yeah, I do," I say.

Reeve's eyes fall to the ashes. She looks up at me. "Should I just dump them?"

Robbie is climbing on the boulders behind Fallon Falls and Reeve hollers, "Get back down here! You have to do this with me!"

Novak says, "He kissed me."

Reeve goes in my ear, "Tell her he has herpes."

I laugh. Reeve bumps my shoulder. I lose my footing and splash into the river. The current is strong and Novak jumps in and saves me while Reeve just stands there.

Reeve opens the box and says, "How do you want to do it,

Robbie?" The ashes are in a plastic bag inside the box. "You just want to pitch the bag?"

Robbie lifts out his bag and hauls back his arm.

Novak bounds back from the river, cries, "No! You have to scatter them. You can't just throw the bag in the river. God." She rolls her eyes at me. "That's littering."

"You do it." Reeve snatches the bag from Robbie and slams it into Novak's chest.

Novak arches her eyebrows at me.

Do it, I shrug.

She removes the twist tie from the bag and, reaching in, grabs a fistful of ash. It's gray and sort of greasy looking. She holds the ashes out in front of her. She shouts at Reeve, "What was your mom's name?"

"Gladys," Reeve says.

Novak widens her eyes.

"Not really."

"Consuela Meaty Loins," Robbie says.

We all look at him. He grins.

Reeve tells Novak, "It's Jaclyn."

Novak extends her arm over the water. "Ashes to ashes. Dust to dust. Go home to Jesus, Jaclyn."

Reeve mutters "Bye" under her breath.

Novak opens her fist and the ashes fly back in our faces. We spit and swipe our eyes.

Robbie snatches the other bag from Novak and raises it high in the air. The ashes stream out and spread over the rocks and water and river grass.

They leave a film. It's gross.

I look over to Robbie, but he's gone.
Reeve's gone.
Novak.
Mom.
All gone.

. . .

It isn't Joyland; it's just a dream. I wake up crying, feeling inconsolable. I stumble to the kitchen and almost trip over it—again.

Robbie's case. I keep moving it from the front closet to the storage room to my bedroom. I don't know why I haven't opened it.

It's time. I thumb up the latches and flip the cover.

There's a threadbare baby blanket rolled up and paper-clipped. I pull the clip, find the edge, and unroll the blanket. Inside is . . . junk.

A magpie feather, an avocado peel, a hunk of bubble wrap, two golf balls, a syringe, a rusty razor blade, string tied to string tied to string . . .

Carefully, gently, leaving everything exactly the way he saved it, I reroll the blanket and shut the case lid.

When I get home from work, there's a box at my door. I know the handwriting and my heart leaps. The first item is a picture postcard. This fat, hairy guy in a Speedo at the beach, snarfing a hot dog. A voice bubble is drawn in: "Eat my wiener."

I crack up. Classic Novak.

On the back, her note says: "Banana, I met someone. Her name's Cate. She's a lez and she's into me. What's her damage?"

She met someone already?

"Miss u, you crazy bitch. Come to CA. grlz, grlz, grlz. U'll never go hungry here ☺. U R 4 Evah my BFF. I wanted to give you this for grad, but I didn't get it done in time ☹."

It's wrapped in tissue. I lift out the bundle and open it carefully. Oh my God. It's a jacket, all different colors, soft as cashmere. I put it on and feel Novak next to my skin. A pang of loneliness stabs at my heart.

Miss you, Novak.

A quiet knock sounds on the open door. I turn and see Tessa.

"Oh wow. She finished it." Tessa walks in and runs her hand down the sleeve of the jacket. She steps behind me. "She picked the hardest thing to knit, this Meg Swansen Round-the-Bend. When she said she was going to modify the pattern to make it a hoodie jacket, I thought she was insane."

I twist and our eyes meet. "I wanted to say—"

"Johanna, I—"

"Tell Martin I have your IOU money, with interest, and I'll have your insurance money to you by the end of the month."

Tessa nods and smiles. "Thank you. May I?" She indicates the divan.

I slip off the jacket and fold it tenderly, feel the love Novak put into it.

"Johanna, I wanted to talk to you about your, um, revelation. Long before now. But I just didn't know how. That's not true. Well, it's sort of true." What's Tessa talking about? She pats the place next to her and I go sit. She says, "When I got your letter, honestly, I was shocked. I've always considered myself open-minded; I've had gay friends. But when it's your own sister? When it hits so close to home?" She looks at me and I see the lost look in her eyes.

"It's okay."

"No, it's not. I'm ashamed of myself. I should've accepted it immediately and embraced it and been happy about you finding yourself and having the courage to come out."

"Yeah. You should've."

"You'll laugh"—she shakes her head—"but I thought it was just a phase."

I'm not laughing.

"I did write you back, but I didn't know what to say. If I didn't mention it, it'd seem like I was avoiding the subject. Which, I guess, I was. And I knew how important this was to you. I ripped up so many letters. I could never find the right words."

I know how that feels. "I'm sorry."

"What do you have to be sorry about? You should be mad as hell. Here I am, your sister, your only family, and I'd already deserted you once. I know you needed me. And before, with Mom. I'm sorry. I'm the one who's sorry." Her eyes pool. "I just want you to be happy, Johanna. It's all I ever want for you."

I tell her, just so she knows, "It's not a phase."

She lets out a short laugh and sniffles. "I got that." She swipes her nose. "I love you no matter what. I want you to know I'll always be here for you. From now on."

Finally, at last, we hug. We rock each other for the longest time and this huge sense of joyfulness infuses my whole entire being. I have my sister back.

Tessa says, "I want to ask you something. You can say no." She leans away from me so she can look me in the eyes. "I want to sell the house and move back to Minnesota. I want to finish my master's in social work and get certified there. And I want to try to have a baby."

My heart soars. "Tessa, that's great."

She drops her head. "I don't know. Martin's settled here now."

"He'll do whatever you need to make you happy. You know that."

"You'd come with us." Tessa looks at me. "I wouldn't go without you. You'll love Martin's family; they're insane. The university's right there and you could go to college, live with us, or in the dorm. There's a large gay and lesbian population in Minneapolis."

This tiny trickle of excitement burbles inside me.

"Think about it." Tessa lifts a hank of my hair over my shoulder. "We'll make a fresh start." She holds my eyes. "Johanna, can you ever forgive me?"

I just hug her again. She hugs me right back. I feel this weight lift from my shoulders. Then Tessa says, "Why don't you ever wear the watch?"

I let her go fast and push to my feet. "I lost it," I lie. "I'm sorry." I head for the kitchen.

"You lost it?"

"It was loose," I say over my shoulder. "It fell off."

Tessa sighs. "I should've taken it in to get it adjusted."

That stops me in my tracks. "It's not your fault, okay? It's mine. I let it happen. We're both on these major guilt trips. We need to get off this stupid treadmill and move on."

Tessa stands. "You're right. We do. But that's not the only reason I came up here." She approaches from behind and touches my hand. She turns it palm up and sets something in it. A folded piece of notepaper.

"To be honest, Johanna, I'm against this. Every fiber of my being says I shouldn't do it, I should keep you safe, but Mary-Dean insists this is something you need to do for yourself."

What could it be? I unfold the paper and see it's an address.

"She's living there," Tessa says. "At least, she was."

Chapter 36

The sign in front of the building reads: SAMARITAN HOUSE. Is this a homeless shelter? *Oh, Reeve.* It looks nice, though, like an old converted Victorian, with three floors and balconies.

The door has a double lock and security cameras. I ring the buzzer and a woman says, "May I help you?"

I don't see a microphone to speak into. "I'm looking for Reeve Hartt?"

"What's your name?"

"Johanna Lynch," I tell her.

"And you are . . . ?"

What am I? "A . . . friend."

"Please wait."

I wait an eternity, standing there feeling like I'm being scanned with metal detectors. I check my watch. Ten to ten. Cheap watch from Target. I have to be at the cineplex by eleven.

An older couple across the street are out pruning hedges. They remind me of Mr. and Mrs. Mockrie and my heart aches for that loss.

The front door whooshes open.

My stomach catches.

Reeve flies out the door and throws herself into my arms. "She told me not to call you or see you ever again. She said if I loved you, I'd leave you alone." Reeve crushes me so hard I can't breathe.

Or maybe I can't breathe because she's in my arms, stealing my breath away. Reeve kisses me and the world spins out of control.

Behind us the door opens wider and this formidable woman steps onto the porch. She says, "Honey, are you okay?"

Reeve goes, "Yeah. This is my girlfriend, Johanna." Reeve smiles at me as she intertwines our fingers. The woman gives me a visual shakedown.

Reeve says to her, "Would you sign me out?"

She asks, "Where are you going?"

Reeve looks at me.

Fallon Falls, I think.

"To the park," Reeve says. "I'll be back in an hour."

The woman folds her arms.

"If I'm not, call the cops. God." Reeve rolls her eyes at me.

"One hour." The woman steps back inside.

Reeve pushes me down the steps. "Fucking warden."

"What is this place?" I glance up to see eyes watching us through the front security screen.

Reeve hops on me piggyback, wrapping her legs around my

waist. "A women's shelter. Tessa got me in." Reeve bites my ear and nuzzles into my neck.

At the car, I let her down and go to unlock the door, but Reeve pulls my hand away. "I can't," she says. "I'm not allowed to get in anyone's car. House rules."

I arch my eyebrows. "Since when do you play by the rules?"

A grin sneaks across her face. "Really." Then her eyes get serious.

"It's okay," I say quickly. "How far's the park?"

"We can walk." She loops both arms around my waist and my arm naturally crosses her shoulders. She smells like Ivory soap. Her hair's been cut recently and I can actually feel meat on her bones. Her eyes are beautiful, of course. Blue mascara, three shades of eye shadow.

"I've missed you so much," she says.

I rest my head on hers. "Me too." All the nights I lay awake worrying, wondering about her.

Behind the trees at the end of the block is a sculpture garden. Reeve leads me to a concrete hexagon, which is smeared with pigeon poop. We don't sit on it. We stretch out on the cool grass, facing each other.

"I've been seeing someone," Reeve says.

My heart explodes.

She jabs my shoulder. "You didn't say 'what?'"

I don't want to know who either.

She pinches my arm playfully. "Not like that. A counselor. Or psychologist, I guess she is."

"You have? Me too."

Reeve frowns. "Why?"

I can't look at her without wanting to kiss and touch her, run my hand up her hip and under her shirt. But we *need* to have this conversation.

I roll onto my back. "You know. Abandonment issues. Self-worth stuff, blah blah." I gaze into the sky.

Reeve's eyes graze the side of my face, then she rolls over onto her back too. "Abuse. Repressed anger. My mother and brother getting murdered in front of me."

She makes it sound like a competition. You win, Reeve. Hands down.

A puffy cloud floats in front of the sun and I shiver. "Are you okay?" Reeve asks.

The word "yes" sticks in my throat. "Are you?" I twist my head and look at her.

"Oh yeah. I'm fly."

Her pain is palpable.

"I don't miss her," Reeve says. "She was sick and twisted. Her whole fucking life was using. I don't even know if I ever loved her. That's so wrong, not to love your own mother."

Reeve . . .

"But damn. What did he do? All he ever wanted was to be left alone. Stupid asstard." She balls her fists at her sides.

I push up to an elbow and pull her into me.

"I don't cry," she says in a hiccup.

"I know."

She holds me hard. She kisses my neck, my jawbone, my face. She's soft and sweet in my arms. She kisses my lips.

God, help me.

She stops and says, "Let's get a place together. I have a job now, at Chili's. Where are you working? I assume you are."

Yeah, and I need my job. "I'm still looking."

"You could work with me. Think of it, Johanna. Living together, being together all the time. We could make it; I know we could. We'd get married and have kids. Since they run in my family, maybe we'd have twins." She grins. "Doublemint gum."

"I'm moving to Minnesota," I say.

At the sudden shift in mood, a chill fills the air.

"When?" Reeve asks.

"Soon."

She climbs off me.

"Tessa and I are selling the house. She wants me to go to college in Minnesota and she's going to have a baby. I want to be there for her. You know?"

"What about me?" Reeve's voice is flat. "Were you going to ask me to come?"

My silence is my answer. She scrambles to stand and I clench her wrist. The rage inside her still surges; I can feel it in her muscles and bones. "I just don't think we're ready."

She slit-eyes me. "*You're* not. Speak for yourself."

"Okay, I will. I'm not."

She goes limp and her head drops back. I stand, still holding on to her wrist. "I love you. I do. But we both need to be in a better place, Reeve."

She raises her face to the sky. Oh, Reeve. *I want you so much. But it's not a good love. It's cruel.*

She says, "What time is it?"

I look at my watch. Shit. I'm going to be late for work. "Ten fifty-five."

"We should get back," she says.

"Reeve—"

She presses a finger to my lips. "You're smart, Johanna."

Am I? I want to ask. Or just scared.

"I like that in a girl." Her finger trails down my front.

I take her hand and kiss it. "Are you going to be all right?"

"Me?" Reeve points to herself. "You talkin' about me? Shit, I'm a survivor."

She's stronger than anyone I know. In some ways.

We walk back to Samaritan House together, yet apart. At the curb by the gate, Reeve turns and says, "I have something for you. Wait here." She sprints to the porch and disappears inside.

I unlock the car door and lean against it, waiting. Thinking how I'm going to drive away from here and probably never see her again. Wondering if I have the strength to leave.

She hurries back, out of breath, and hands me an object. My gold watch.

"I took it," Reeve says. "I'm not a nice person."

I click my tongue. "Yes, you are." Sometimes.

"I can't give you back everything I took."

Our eyes meet and hold. She understands.

"It doesn't matter," I say. Some things I have to take back for myself. "I have something for you too." I open the car door and reach into the back.

"No." Reeve steps away.

"You're going to want it."

Reeve pushes out with both arms.

I extend the case. "It's all he had."

"No," she says. "Get rid of it."

"He'd want you to have it, Reeve," I say softly. "To keep it safe for him."

She loosely hugs herself. "You know what it was? His safe place. That's what he called it."

"Maybe it can be yours too."

She just looks at me. "That'd be retarded."

I crack up. So does she. But she reaches across and takes the case. "He didn't bust your window. I did. He'd never hurt you."

"It's okay. I won't be taking my car to Minnesota," I say. We both hold our breath, like we can't say goodbye to him or each other.

"Johanna." Her eyes sweep up to my face. "I'm sorry."

"I'm not," I say. Not for knowing love, loving her.

She backs up, away, hugging the case to her, walking, trotting toward the porch. Through the door, into the building. I look at the watch in my hand and latch it onto my left wrist. Two watches, too heavy, as if I'm weighted down by time. I remove the cheap watch.

"Hey! Johanna."

I glance up. On the third-floor balcony, Reeve leans over the railing. "I forgot to tell you something."

"What?"

She smiles. "Firsts are overrated."

Thank you, Reeve. Thank you for that.

I get into my car and crank the ignition. Another place, Reeve, another time. I pull away from the curb and say softly, "See you in Joyland."

Resources

The Web site links and organizations listed below can provide information and help to those experiencing violence in dating and relationships. In addition, many local resources can be found through schools, police precincts, social services, hospitals, and community support groups.

Choose Respect: Preventing Dating Abuse
www.ChooseRespect.org

National Coalition of Anti-Violence Programs
www.NCAVP.org: 1-212-714-1184

National Domestic Violence Hotline
www.NDVH.org: 1-800-799-SAFE (7233); 1-800-787-3224 TTY

National Teen Dating Abuse Helpline
www.LoveIsRespect.org: 1-866-331-9474; 1-866-331-8453 TTY

The Network/La Red: Ending Abuse in Lesbian, Bisexual Women's & Transgender Communities
www.thenetworklared.org: 1-617-742-4911; 1-617-227-4911 TTY

Acknowledgments

Long, long overdue acknowledgment of my cherished critique group, the Wildfolk, who, for twenty-five years and counting, have nurtured and grown writers and illustrators for young readers. When I dumped this mess of a manuscript on them and wailed, "Help! What does this story say to you?" they weren't afraid to tell me it was a beautiful disaster. Emphasis on "disaster." Eternal, heartfelt gratitude to Hilari Bell, Jane Bigelow, Lisa Brown-Roberts, Meridee Cecil, Carol Crowley, Anna-Maria Crum, Laura Deal, Coleen DeGroff, Wick Downing, Amy Efaw, Randy Fraser, Claudia McAdam, Sean McCollum, Pam Mingle, Christine Liu Perkins, Cheryl M. Reifsnyder, Shawn Shea, Bobbi Shupe, Caroline Stutson, and Denise Vega. I love you guys.

it painful to immerse herself in the psyche of *Rage*'s narrator, Johanna, who allows herself to be assaulted and controlled. And while she guesses that we all put on some blinders about the shortcomings of those we love, especially when we love in a head-over-heels way, she feels that Johanna's sexuality probably makes her more inclined to defend the damaged girl she's in love with—perhaps because she feels she has fewer opportunities to find love, or more to prove.

Julie's own relationship with her partner, Sherri Leggett, poses no such trauma, as they recently celebrated their thirty-fifth anniversary. Julie and Sherri share their Colorado home with a never-ending stream of rescued homeless cats and foster kittens.

You can visit Julie Anne Peters on the Web at www.julieanne peters.com.

About the Author

Julie Anne Peters grew up in Colorado in a lively, noisy household where she was a regular kid who tormented her older brother and harassed her younger sisters. Past employment stints include teaching and several left-brain ventures involving computers, statistical research, and systems engineering.

But then . . . writing beckoned. Not easily, not instantly, but the voices, the situations, the details began to come, and to insist themselves upon her pages. Julie's books have received young reader awards, critical acclaim, and literary recognition. Even though her first love has always been young adult literature, her early books were easy readers and middle-grade novels. Then came *Define "Normal,"* *Keeping You a Secret,* and the National Book Award finalist *Luna.* Her young adult novels feature the universal truths and particular challenges of gay, lesbian, bisexual, and transgender teens. She wrote *Rage* at the behest of a young friend who was entrenched in an abusive relationship, but only after many months of her friend's persistent encouragement, and after the relationship had ended. Julie says her aim was to portray teen-dating violence where neither victim nor villain is painted in broad strokes and where redemption is authentic.

Julie has often explored the question of how much we're willing to sacrifice for love, in its many guises and disguises. She found

THE
NIGHT BUS

THE
NIGHT BUS

JANICE LAW

A TOM DOHERTY ASSOCIATES BOOK
NEW YORK

THE NIGHT BUS

Copyright © 2000 by Janice Law

This book is printed on acid-free paper.

A Forge Book
Published by Tom Doherty Associates, LLC
175 Fifth Avenue
New York, NY 10010

www.tor.com

Forge® is a registered trademark of Tom Doherty Associates, LLC.

Design by Lisa Pifher

Library of Congress Cataloging-in-Publication Data

Law, Janice.
    The night bus / Janice Law.
      p. cm.
    "A Tom Doherty Associates book."
    ISBN 0-312-84882-X
    1. Married women—Fiction. 2. Runaway wives—Fiction. 3. Connecticut—Fiction. 4. Amnesia—Fiction. I. Title.

PS3562.A86 N54 2000
813'.54—dc21

                               00-023938

First Edition: June 2000

Printed in the United States of America

0 9 8 7 6 5 4 3 2 1

for Genevieve and Jamie Trecker, with love

THE
NIGHT BUS

1

THE WOMAN WAS RELIEVED WHEN it got late and the lights were dimmed. She liked leaning against the bus window, where the interior reflections and tinted glass narrowed the landscape to faint, fugitive images. By night, the interstate was reduced to the streaming lights of the traffic, the tall beacon lamps of the exits, the illuminated posts of periodic call boxes labeled For Emergency Use Only. She imagined herself on the roadside, outside the air-conditioned cocoon of the bus, hearing the traffic and the sound of her feet walking toward the call box, the call box where she'd lift the receiver and say, "I need help."

Better not. Better stay in the bus where night was closing down the world. That's what she'd like to do. She wanted to close down the past like the iris of a camera shutting up tight. The bus was good, a good escape, but oblivion would be even better, so she mustn't think of help or of call boxes, real or symbolic. She had to think, instead, of shutting down, erasing, fading to black like the ending of a film without credits, where all the actors were unknown.

And that's where the night bus came in, the night bus where the lights were hypnotic, and the soft drone of the passengers, the bluesy tunes on the driver's radio, and the whoosh of passing cars made a soothing white noise. She could feel herself forgetting with every mile, slipping away into limbo, escaping. She'd fall asleep soon and wake up in another town, another state, another state of mind. She just had to sleep. She just had to fall asleep and everything would be all right. If she could only sleep.

She looked at her watch: five hours. Five hours away. She had dozed briefl/ when the sun came out north of New York, awaking dry-mouthed and stiff-necked when they slowed for the city traffic. Now in the semidarkness of the night bus, she was wide awake and getting used to the rhythm of the trip: hypnotic stretches of super-highway with greenish-purple blacks, round white lights, and a steady seventy mph, interrupted occasionally, as now, by sudden clots of traffic and lighted apartment windows and corporate logos blazing against the sky. Then came the wheeze of hydraulic brakes as the blocky vehicle swung off the highway and eased onto a city street. Against the black night, ramp lights flared orange, and blue-white cones shone down from the heavens, illuminating the McDonald's, the Burger Kings, the Chilis, the Arby's, all the sacred places of refuge and re-freshment. The night bus, leviathan of the city streets, ignored them, huffing on with puffs of exhaust, cruising past gas stations and empty lots, bars and 7-Elevens, idle men and working women, to reach the terminal. The brakes sighed like lost souls, the driver spun the great wheel, and they dropped down a steep and narrow ramp, down, down, to maneuver with many a gasp and grunt between the cement pylons to their appointed bay.

As the greenish interior lights flooded on, disembarking passengers jumped to wrestle their bags from the overhead racks and eased parcels from the spaces between the seats. The door clanked open and the driver got out to throw up the luggage bays before returning to collect his little case and exchange jaunty greetings with the relief driver. She bent down to touch her own bag, a navy blue carry-on stuck protec-tively under the seat in front of her. Yes, it was still there. She'd thought she'd need a bag to look right, although there was nothing she'd wanted to bring away with her. Nothing at all. Still, she'd put in some underwear and some clothes, a comb, a toothbrush, a second pair of shoes, a swimsuit. She wanted to look natural, ordinary, like someone going on vacation.

New passengers clomped up the steps, their shoulder bags and knapsacks bumping against the poles, the seats, the seated passengers. She never got out in the terminals, not even when they had ten or fifteen minutes. She'd found just the right seat, second row on the right, at the window, and she didn't want to lose it. As far as New York City, a middle-aged woman off to visit her grandchildren sat in the adjacent seat. With her smooth, dark skin, the woman had looked too young to have grandchildren, though her thin hands were wrinkled and her black, hooded eyes were tired and sad as if she'd seen some long days. They talked in a friendly way about the grandchildren, who were cute but full of mischief and running wild. Their neighborhood was no good; here their grandmother compressed her lips and shook her head, "no good at all." Their mother, the woman's daughter, was not as strong as she might be, either. The woman tapped her own chest and shook her head and suddenly looked old enough to be a grandmother, after all.

She'd nodded at the woman sympathetically, although, of course, she had no troubles of her own, none at all. She was going on vacation, to Florida, to the sun. She could feel it already, warm and bright, where she'd throw away her parka, damp from the sleety March rain, put on her swimsuit, and walk along white sand in the sun. Perhaps she'd told the grandmother that—or other things—maybe she'd told her other things, for when she helped the woman with her bundles as far as the door of the bus, the older woman had said, "You take care, now," in a soft voice as if she knew everything. Everything.

Back in her seat, she'd worried about that and felt an irrational anger with the woman's kindly phrase. She felt that she was becoming transparent, her whole life evident, and she had to grip the back of the seat in front of her and fight the fear that she'd be found out. Through the tinted glass, she watched the grandmother walking away, weighted down with her cases and her bags, gifts for the children, a cake, some homemade bread, tokens against a neighborhood that was "no good at all," children who were "full of mischief and running wild," and a daughter with a bad heart—physically or metaphorically. Now she wondered which and, distracted, ran over their conversation, pondering the meaning of each word, as though it mattered terribly to her, as though she could flow out of the seat and lose her body and all her mental baggage and feel, instead, the pull of heavy suitcases and plastic carry bags filled with cake, surely squashed now, and bread, turning to crumbs from friction, and see in front of her the stairs up to the terminal and to New York and to that "not good" neighborhood where different problems awaited her.

She'd managed the stair and pictured herself on the street looking out for a cab or a bus, when the seat next to her depressed and a man with a handful of newspapers switched on the overhead reading light. They talked briefly. He was in sales, personalized computer mouse pads—"a great reminder for your business. The client sees your name every time he clicks." The salesman hated trains and planes, couldn't work in his car: the bus was his preferred mode of transport. She didn't have to say much in reply, which was good. She could hardly have told him the truth: that this bus was her one chance, her one chance to get away, and she'd taken it, no questions asked, buying a ticket for the furthest city she could afford, almost to the penny.

When he started on his papers, he offered her the *Washington Post,* an early edition which he'd picked up in New York, and she was grateful. She could hide behind the paper, lose her transparency, become someone else. Someone from Washington, DC, perhaps. Someone who would have bought this paper at home to read on the bus and who was off for a holiday. A holiday from what? One of the big government agencies, maybe. By the time she switched off her light, she'd decided she worked for the Environmental Protection Agency. She knew where she was renting, too: an apartment in a new complex near the Pentagon City stop on the Metro. All that was left was to select a name.

"Is this seat taken?"

She must have dozed off: they were in another terminal, awash in the orange garage glare, the acid-tinged bus lights.

"No, not at all," she said and looked at her watch. It was past midnight and she felt a sudden panic. "Where are we?"

"Fayetteville," he said, sticking his backpack between the seats. "It loses something at this hour."

"I have to change in Savannah."

"Long way yet." He had a light drawl. With the backpack and the longish hair, she'd pegged him as a college boy. Now that her eyes were adjusted, she revised his age upward. As old as she was, older, she guessed, maybe much older: a lean, bony face, a stubble of beard, light eyes, red-rimmed from the hour. He smelled of cigarettes, and, as he sat down, he touched the pack in his shirt pocket and smiled regretfully. "Give my lungs a rest," he said without pleasure or conviction. He fidgeted in his seat for a moment, arranging and rearranging his long legs, then reached back into his pack and produced a couple of candy bars.

"Keep me company," he said, handing her one. "I'm supposed to be quitting smoking. Substitute, they tell me, substitute one vice for another. What is the world coming to!"

"It's not making you fat, anyway," she said. She hadn't eaten since—when? Breakfast? A cup of coffee was all. By lunchtime she'd been on her way; by dinnertime, cruising on the bus.

He said that he was on his way to Savannah to stay with his sister for a while. Had she been to Savannah? "This is sure a nice time of year to see the city."

She was going to Florida, she said, unwrapping the candy bar. It had a rippled coat of chocolate the color of dried mud over a sugar-charged interior. A brief holiday. "Sun," she said.

"We all need some sun," he agreed. "But remember, 'We also ascend dazzling and tremendous as the sun.' "

"That's nice," she said, though she was skeptical; ascending "dazzling and tremendous" did not seem to be on her personal agenda at the moment.

" 'Dazzling and tremendous how quick the sun-rise would kill me,/ if I could not now and always send sun-rise out of me!' That's Whitman. Old Walt knew a thing or two." His hand scrabbled for the cigarette pack and then dropped back into his lap. She could not see his eyes. The bus lights had dimmed again and they hadn't bothered to put on their reading lights. "Old Walt knew something about the sun."

"Yes," she agreed. She understood that she needed to be polite and careful with him. They were fellow travelers.

"You don't believe me," he said.

"I believe you," she said, "I just don't believe it's true for me."

"Ahh." He nodded rapidly. He had a professorial air, as if he'd been a teacher or maybe a doctor, someone used to making a diagnosis and providing an answer, someone who gave out marks and orders. Or *had* given; she felt inclined to put his professional life in the past— though you never could tell. That was where she was an expert: on knowing how you could be fooled; on understanding that you never could tell. "But you're going to the sun. Old Walt would have liked that: 'the office worker, with her long, shining hair, off for her holiday, off to Florida, land of sun and oranges'. He'd have put you in his great poem, his great poem of everything."

"A nice thought," she agreed. "And you, too?"

"I already have the sunrise," he said, though he looked so gloomy and uncertain, that as soon as she could, she thanked him for the candy bar and said, "I'm going to try to sleep a while." For a long time, she heard him folding and refolding the paper, rustling the cellophane jacket of his cigarette pack, switching the reading light on, then off, then on again, and finally settling down with her discarded paper, the discarded paper of Lauren Randall, who worked at the EPA and had a nice sixteenth-floor apartment, two rooms plus kitchenette and bath. Who was going to Florida for a few days for a quick holiday. Who was a happy, normal person with no worries at all.

They reached Savannah before dawn and disembarked to the eternal fluorescent glare. The candy bar had left her unbearably thirsty, and the cold, metallic-tasting water from the fountain rushed a heavy chill straight into her stomach. For the first time, it struck her that cash would have been advisable, that spending every penny on her ticket had been imprudent, that she should eat. She opened her wallet, shivering a little in the air-conditioned dampness: she had only enough for a cup of coffee.

The bus station's tiny, stuffy lunchroom offered a few soiled chairs and tables, a counter, a board listing coffee, doughnuts, bottled water, soft drinks. She recognized a few people from their bus waiting to be served. The Whitman fancier was already seated with a cigarette and a cup of coffee. He had his back to her but she recognized the jacket, the backpack, the longish, untidy hair, and hesitated a moment. Should she buy a coffee and go over and sit down and keep him company? Was this far enough? Was there enough sun in Savannah? As she was hesitating, he suddenly dropped his head, covered his eyes with one hand, and began to weep, a loud, harsh sound that made the nearby patrons turn nervously away, while the folks standing in line refocused on the counter with its petrified doughnuts and big polished cylinders of coffee and hot water.

She felt that she should go over and say something, maybe remind him of the sun ascending, but she was no longer the person who understood what made people weep in bus stations. She was Lauren Randall now, a normal woman with plans of her own, who fled with her bag before he could draw her into his trouble and misery. She had to hurry, she had to get on the bus and find a seat where she could put out the light and sleep until they got to heat and white beaches, until they got to where everything would be all right.

Towards seven A.M. a raspberry-colored ball crawled up out of the horizon clouds, hesitated at pale lemon, then opened itself into a white Florida sun that burned off the mist and cloud and flashed the bus windows with a sheen of glare. Lauren Randall woke out of a fitful sleep to see palms and palmettos and groves of scraggly pines thinned out by the heat. She let her head loll against the window. The roadside was crowded with billboards offering fast food, motels, golf communities, retirement complexes, entertainments, and theme parks. A line from the Thanksgiving hymn started up in her mind, "all our wants to be supplied," but surely that was from another time, another life, not from this time, this life, where herds of humpbacked cows wandered ocher pastures under billboards offering "contemporary lifestyles" instead of whatever the Lord of Harvest has in mind for us.

But now, perversely, although she couldn't get the hymn out of her mind, it refused to come in any logical order: "Wheat and tares together sown," "All the world is God's own field," "Lord of Harvest, grant that we..." That we what? May flee to sun and sea? Adopt a "contemporary lifestyle" at the Egret Bay Townhouses, where we will have a "private golf course, gated security and free tennis courts"? Or at its rival, Pelican Cove, where we can pay more for two golf courses and a health club and avail ourselves of "optional assisted living"?

Once she had needed "assisted living," but not now. Not Lauren Randall, who worked in Washington somewhere and lived near... near... She couldn't remember. But something about the Pentagon. Or maybe she worked at the Pentagon and lived at...Crystal City. That was it. Near the Crystal City Metro stop. She'd been in the Metro. Of course, Lauren Randall *would* be in the Metro every day; she commuted. But *she* had seen the spare, surreal, coffered tunnels where everything was gray cement like a petrified brain. *She'd* been there and understood those tunnels bored deep into the brain of the 21st Century Ltd.

The next time she woke up, the window was warm and a gleaming white eye had burned through the tinting. The bus was sliding down the peninsula at seventy-plus and Lauren—was that really her name? She thought not: Laura, maybe; Laura had a nice ring, like Petrarch's sweetie whom he'd loved from afar with poetry. Though what good that would have done her—Petrarch's Laura—she wasn't sure. And all the time he was living with another woman and having kids. And what did she—the woman doing the cooking and cleaning and the having of the kids—think about the poems? Best, maybe, if she'd been illiterate. It was maybe best not to know some things or to forget them if you could.

She was getting good at that. Maybe too good. She liked *Laura,* but it was not what she'd initially chosen and even Washington was slipping away, dissolving into its brainlike tunnels, folding in on itself and disappearing. No wonder, the way her head hurt over her eyes and above her ears as if memory itself were imploding. Yes, the pain must come from the effort of forgetting, of closing down the iris and blacking out the past, and from the bus, too, for on longer acquaintance, the bus had a disagreeable sway, despite its size and weight, and a closed-up smell like a sleeper's mouth, and AC too feeble to thwart the sun hammering against the glass. Once she got off the bus, things would be different. She'd be all right then. She'd walk on white sand beside the sea, and the waves would fill up the tunnels and doors of memory. Everything would be all right once she got off the bus.

But though her destination sat smack on the bay, the water wasn't visible from the highway. Only a certain emptiness on the horizon indicated that somewhere soon the land ended, and she was disconcerted. She'd imagined the bus pulling up right along the shore. She'd imagined stepping onto the sand and seeing green water stretched out under a sea breeze. Imagination deceives us, as her husband always said. The bus doors opened, instead, to an airless, sauna heat that staggered her, and a few steps later, dizzy with surprise, stiff with sitting, and quite unprepared, she found herself on city pavement with the sun blazing and people pushing past with luggage and briefcases.

She was standing indecisively, her purse slung over her shoulder and her case at her feet, when a voice asked, "Waiting for someone?"

He was a little taller than she was, a handsome brown-skinned man with a jacket and bow tie and two-toned shoes; he was very sharp, very polite. Very casual, too, with his hands in his pockets.

"I'm trying to get to the beach," she said.

"A hot day," he agreed, smooth and friendly. "A good day for the beach—or maybe for a drink?" His voice held the ghost of an accent and his eyes were speculative. He had a lot of well-styled black hair and a neatly trimmed mustache.

She realized that she was thirsty, dying of thirst. "I don't know the city," she said vaguely.

He took his hands out of his pockets to gesture up the street. His hands were well kept, elegant almost. "No problem," he said. "I know everywhere worth going. All the hot spots." He smiled and put one hand out to her, but just then the sky grew dark as if he'd blocked the sun. His face turned blue from the shadow, and she saw, just for an instant, as if he'd become a mirror, how she appeared to him: a thin blond woman, no girl, but still attractive, with a troubled, vulnerable expression.

"No," she said sharply, then amended that to "No, thank you," because imagination can deceive you and and she meant no harm. "I'm on my way to the beach." She tried to sound definite, as if she knew where she was going and had the money to take herself there.

He did not seem offended, though it seemed to her that his face grew tight and closed. "Very nice beaches here. World-famous beaches."

"Yes," she said.

"I have a car." He indicated further down the street. "I could drive you to the beach in my car."

The heat from the asphalt and the pavement pressed against her like an unwelcome companion, making her feel dizzy, dislocated.

"It's very nice at the beach," he said. "Cool. It's always a bit cooler on the shore."

"It will be out of your way," she said, but she was already forgetting the warning, ignoring her instincts, letting herself drift on the heat, on the idea of the beach. Under the circumstances, timidity was foolish, maybe offensive. He would think her prejudiced.

"Nonsense," he said. "I've nothing to do this afternoon. So any direction's fine with me."

"But weren't you meeting someone?" she asked.

"She's come," he said with a gallant little bow and his face

18

smoothed out. He had eyes the color of amber, and she expected the irises to slit up like a cat's. But though he seemed amused when she insisted on carrying her own case, he was as good as his word: the car was parked two blocks away, a fine old Cadillac convertible as big as a houseboat. This disarming vehicle had sky-blue leather seats and a white exterior. She thought it amazing.

"A modern engine," he said. "But I like the old cars. They have—*presence*—is that the word?"

"This one has presence," she agreed.

"Yes. And people, too, sometimes, they have *presence?*"

"Oh, yes," she said. "Of one sort or another."

He smiled, opened the door, and took the club off the steering wheel. "This is modern, too, of course. And the seat belts." He made a face. "I had to have holes drilled in the frame for them."

"Well, it is safer."

"Beauty," he said almost angrily. "We must have beauty in life. Right? No one lives for safety!"

She got in beside him and sat down. Although hot, the seats were soft and comfortable. He started the engine and wheeled out into the traffic, where the car floated on its own immense weight, the big fins clearing a space around them. A breeze rushed over the windshield to ruffle her hair, while he talked about the car, about cars, about restoring what he called "beautiful works of art."

"This is my Havana car," he said. "For tropical nights and evening dress. Perhaps a gown of chartreuse silk for you? You'd be beautiful in chartreuse."

She didn't think she'd ever owned anything in chartreuse, never mind chartreuse silk. Her imagination was of another sort altogether. But that is one of the sorrows of the world; it is not ourselves that are incompatible, necessarily, but our imaginations.

The beach where they were going, he told her, was really lovely at night. You could walk in evening clothes beside the pale gulf and see the stars. But at this time of day, he thought it might be too hot for her at the beach.

"I want to go to the water," she said and automatically touched the handle of the door.

"We could get a drink," he said.

"At the beach," she replied.

"Good food, good wine—you don't find them at the beach. Ybor City—the little Havana section—there's where you find real food."

She could feel the car hesitate, tempted to swing east, away from the bay and open water. "I'm not hungry," she lied.

He smiled and did not seem annoyed. Perhaps he, too, was a fellow traveler, a slave to imagination, an escapee. He took an interstate that strode on pylons toward the bay, where, leaving hotels, condos, apartments, offices, and stores behind, the highway stretched itself into a pale thin line. There was nothing on either side but water and sky, a few bird-circled islands overgrown with mangroves, some fishermen's boats, and a freighter on the horizon.

"This is wonderful," she said.

He glanced at her, regretfully, as if he realized how far her desires diverged from his. "There's nothing here," he said.

She would have liked to step right out, but they were running along at fifty-five, the breeze from the bay swirling her hair around her face.

"The beach," he said again. "The beach is world famous."

They crossed another causeway to reach the barrier island: hot and bright with fifty yards of surf at the edge, children shrieking in the shallows, and red-shouldered vacationers speaking a dozen languages on the shore. They parked off the main street and walked on sand as dazzling as midwinter snow. Everything felt unreal, anticlimactic. The man told her his name was Raoul; he did "this and that" in the "entertainment business." When the sun flared behind his head, she saw darkness; the sea turned green and purple, and white foam swirled around her ankles.

"You're not used to the sun," he said. "You need a drink."

There was a bar near the beach, where he had a beer and she drank orange juice and ate nachos with cheese and salsa. "Beach food," he said. She should go to Ybor City for real cuisine. Perhaps she would like to go there now?

"In a chartreuse gown?" she asked.

"Ah, well," he said and spread his elegant fingers. "There's a problem with that. You have no money."

She did not reply. She understood that she had become transparent again.

"It is not an impossible problem. I myself arrived with nothing. *Nada*. There are ways." He nodded rapidly.

She could feel her head beginning to pound.

"You must use your assets," he said. "Survival is a matter of matching your assets with your circumstances. You understand what I'm saying?"

"But I'm afraid you're right," she said. "I don't have any assets."

"Assets for your circumstances," he said. "Now, I'm an educated man. I have a university degree. My specialty was literature. Yes." He nodded again. "But when I came here—well, there was no market for Spanish literature. I had no role. I didn't know the language—in more ways than one. You follow me?"

"Different places have different languages," she agreed.

"Precisely. I learned English, of course. I also learned another new and useful language. So you see me now: adapted."

"To the entertainment business."

"To the entertainment business, which sometimes enables me to help others arriving as I arrived, without resources."

The gluey cheese on the nachos made her feel queasy. There was a greasy undertone to everything.

"You could work for me," he suggested when she did not respond.

She looked at him. She had not thought of work or of a means of living; in retrospect, the absence of those considerations frightened her. "Doing what?" she asked.

"I run an escort service—for very nice polite gentlemen who are lonely and don't want to go to dinner by themselves. They need someone to make conversation, to be pleasant, to decorate the occasion."

She saw herself in a chartreuse gown rolling through pink Florida sunsets in his immense white Cadillac. Being pleasant, decorative, making polite conversation. She couldn't help laughing.

"You see," he said, "you are more cheerful already."

She shook her head. "You're very foolish," she said, "to hire people from the bus station. I might be anyone. I might have done anything. You wouldn't know."

Now it was his turn to laugh. He began to discuss his business with her, to tell her about rates and regulations—he made it all sound very proper, hedged by rules and customs like an old-fashioned finishing school. A finishing school for refugees and runaways and prisoners of the imagination. He was very strict, he said, with both customers and escorts.

She nodded her head; in some ways, severity would be a relief, a comfort, but she kept her own counsel about that.

"So you meet people at the bus station," she said. They were in the car by this time, heading east to the bay, the city, and the city within the city where penniless arrivals were outfitted with chartreuse gowns and became useful, working citizens. "You haven't thought of the dangers."

He looked at her curiously. He'd thought the first time that she was joking—or hopelessly naive. Now he was curious; he understood that she was an oddity. "What could be dangerous about you?" he asked.

They'd reached the causeway. Suspended between sapphire water and azure sky, the road ahead was like the straight and narrow path to the Heavenly City. Sun skidded over the surface of the bay and glimmered off his glasses, hiding darkness. She said, "I tried to kill my husband."

As soon as the words were out of her mouth, she knew that everything—Ybor City, chartreuse gowns, a regulated existence—was impossible. "You must let me out right away," she said. "You should think twice. You should be more careful."

They were coming into a toll plaza, and, although he tried to stop her, she opened the door. He jammed on the brakes and reached to grab her, but she slipped out, stumbling into the roadway, numbing one knee. A passing car braked and swerved, then she lunged through a gap in the slowing traffic and wound up clutching the rail that separated the road from the pedestrian walkway. She heard him call once before she was over the rail and scrambling toward the water.

The thin, elderly black man who was fishing a few yards away was too polite to take notice of her unconventional arrival. He had a bait bucket, a cooler, and a little folding canvas stool. She thought how fortunate he was to have everything organized, to have useful possessions. Unlike her. Her case was in the trunk of Raoul's white Cadillac; her purse, still suspended from her shoulder, contained an empty wallet and a comb. She'd embarked without necessities.

She watched the man fish for a little while before walking off along the sand. She passed a few more anglers stationed on the rocks and a man and a boy floating just offshore in a flat-bottomed boat; then, abruptly, she was alone with the steady traffic humming behind her, the city in the distance, the bay and sky one gorgeous emptiness before her.

This was what she had needed. This had been her destination all along: not the beach crowded with vacationers, but this spare ambiguity where water blended into sky and sky was mirrored in water. Overhead, the sun flared out pure whiteness, and a little breeze turned ripples in the flat liquid sheet. She sat down on a worn patch of grass, took off her shoes, rolled up her pants, and waded into the shallow water, where small silver fish took fright at her every move, and the universe turned fluid and benign.

She'd been right. This was the place she had to come, and after a while, she got out of the water and lay down with her head on her purse under one of the scrubby, big-leaved bushes. She'd been dozing there, emptying her mind and working on forgetting, when she realized that the sky had gone slate-colored to the south and west, and the breeze which had tamed the heat was now slopping water against the causeway and whirling gulls and terns over the gray water. She sat up, uncertainly. Her head hurt a great deal, and, considering everything, she felt it would be best to sleep for a while. But when she lay down again, she heard the water sloshing against sand and stone and splashing up into the bushes. There would be a storm.

She rose to find herself unsteady and had a moment to wonder at her own folly, before she remembered the fishermen and the pathway. She could walk into the city. Overhead, the sky grew alarmingly dark; just for a second, the slate gray turned navy blue, the clouds, black with curious purple halos. Realizing that she had to get off the causeway, she set out unsteadily to cross the water on the thin gray steel pedestrian bridge.

The shore was further than she'd imagined, or perhaps she was sicker than she'd realized. Wading in the bay, she'd noticed the big red scuff mark on her knee slowly turning dark underneath, and now her leg was stiffening up. When the causeway rose into a bridge, the wind turned cold, and she felt herself buffeted by the gusts that whipped off the surface. By the time she reached the tangle of highway ramps and streets, the maze of condos and apartment houses, of offices and garages along the shore, she was exhausted. Shivering, her head on fire, she walked east, away from the water. A truck honked at her so that she pulled back from a street just in time, and she got caught momentarily in a crosswalk and had to stand, as thin as a matador, while the traffic rushed by.

Over the bay, the clouds were streaked with lightning, and she knew that she had to find shelter. She was looking for a sandwich shop or some fast-food place where she could buy a cup of coffee and sit out the storm, when she saw two boys on bikes. "Choppers," she thought they were called, with high handlebars, so that the children sat far back on them like motorcyclists.

The boys looked at each other, and began pedaling hard along the sidewalk toward her. Darkness flared behind them, but though she started to move toward the street, they'd already split apart, one on either side, and the boy on her right reached out as he passed to grab the strap on her purse. Only reflex made her hold on, so that she fell, sideways and backward, hitting the sidewalk before the strap broke and the wheels and laughing children dropped her into darkness.

2

BENEATH THE BED, SHE COULD feel the rolling wheels, the sway, the springs and shocks of the night bus, now accelerating, so that the round white lights of oncoming traffic were stretched to comets' tails, and the billboards, ramp lights, roadside attractions, and rest stops were squares of blue and orange and green, no sooner glimpsed than vanished. Her head hurt a great deal, a very great deal, but she knew that was because she was preparing to ascend, to be splendid, to send sunrise out over the bay in a silver, pink, and turquoise dawn. She was in a chartreuse gown that flowed across a thin ribbon of asphalt like solar wind. The city had vanished with the night, and as far as she could see there was nothing but endless water and the pale road stretching forever onward.

She pointed out the absence of the city, the unreality of the road, the implausibility of their vehicle, which was sometimes the night bus and sometimes an antique Cadillac, but the faces that looked down on her from great and hazy heights were unperturbed. As the bay dissolved into the darkness of the night journey and the bus became Raoul's white car, she found herself unable to explain why any of this should be significant. Then the beach, blindingly bright and smelling of salt, turned into a large, darkened room, where someone was weeping and quoting Whitman, and passengers fell against her seat, crying out for succor or salvation.

She was in some sort of anteroom; she had reached the city after all and awaited welcome, papers, something official. But she felt she must sleep for a while longer and dropped back into the night bus, which rattled her bones hour after hour until the sun rose, burning off all lesser lights, evaporating the bay, and reducing the splendor of the city to a single room.

She opened her eyes and saw the white walls, the bars and curtains, heard the rattle of carts and equipment, and knew, even before she understood where she was or what had happened, that she had to be careful. Everything she noticed subsequently confirmed that first impression. There was a tube in her arm and a bag of clear liquid hanging overhead on a wire rack. She was wearing a paper and plastic bracelet and lying in a hospital bed with the tubular sides raised. She couldn't see beyond the curtains, even when she sat up, but she could hear rattling food trays and the sounds of other patients, and one high, querulous voice repeating over and over again, "I need to go to the toilet." Although she knew that she should be making plans and explanations, she lay down again to doze and watch the curtains.

"Ah, you're awake." The nurse was compact and efficient-looking, with curly hair, round glasses, and a faint accent that suggested Raoul and beaches and useful employment. "Feeling better?"

"A little."

The nurse stuck a thermometer in her mouth and put cool fingers on her pulse. She removed the IV tube and took her blood pressure. After reading the thermometer and entering the data on her clipboard, the nurse asked, "Want to tell me your name? You were unconscious when you arrived."

She hesitated. For a second or two, she truly didn't know; then she remembered the night bus and Whitman. "Laura," she said.

The nurse started writing. "Last name?"

She understood how much better she might have prepared and began to shiver.

"You've still got a touch of fever," said the nurse.

"Whitman. Laura Whitman. I work in Washington, DC. I came here for a vacation."

"Not much of a vacation," the nurse said sympathetically. "The business office will send someone to get your insurance information a bit later. You had no identification on you. Did you lose credit cards? A license? You might want to notify the companies . . ."

Laura Whitman shook her head.

"Is there someone you want us to contact?"

"No," she said, too quickly, "there's no need."

The nurse raised her eyebrows and frowned slightly. "I'll have some breakfast sent up for you. You're lucky: Sunday breakfasts are late."

"It's Sunday?"

"You've been out a day and a half. You take it easy now."

Laura Whitman took this advice. She slept all day, her roommates providing a disturbing obbligato that never quite succeeded in waking her fully. There was a teenaged girl who'd been in an auto accident. Her head was bandaged and one arm splinted, and she moaned monotonously, as if still under anesthesia. Opposite was a tiny old woman with skin the color of wax paper. Frail and birdlike, she was constantly climbing out of bed, ringing for the nurse, or crying, in a high, desperate voice, that she needed to go to the toilet.

In late afternoon that day—or it might even have been the next day—a clerk arrived from the business office for a short and unsatisfactory interview. Laura Whitman had no documents, no insurance cards; she couldn't remember her social security number or any other identifying digits. She was hazy about her address and vague about her work. The only things Laura Whitman remembered clearly were the causeway into the city, children on odd bicycles, and a darkness descending over water.

"The police will have been notified," the clerk said. Her mouse-colored hair was done up in a tight permanent and her thin face was shielded by big octagonal glasses. "What they'll do for a stolen

28

purse . . ." An eloquent shrug covered the deficiencies of the city police. "Maybe since you were injured. Since you were injured, they might try harder. But you've got to call your boss; get some information for us, all right?"

Laura Whitman said that she thought she might be able to call the next day. She'd been told that she had pneumonia and a slight concussion; she found it hard to concentrate on numbers.

"We get a lot of head injuries here," the clerk said.

Laura Whitman tried to take that as a recommendation for the facility, but when she lay down, she was worried. She hadn't anticipated injuries when she'd set out to lose herself. She hadn't realized paper would be so important. She'd acted on impulse and desperation, and now she was caught between who she'd been and who she'd intended to become. Hazy with sleep and fever, she began to wonder how long it would be before they realized that Laura Whitman was a replacement for the woman, vaguely familiar but thoroughly unreal, who had been lost to her in the middle of the bay.

The doctor appeared every morning around ten. The new doctor, that is. The pulmonary specialist made his rounds earlier, always by eight-thirty or so, entering with a barrage of pronouncements and orders. He liked to come in at high volume, shake up the ward, and set the nurses running. One of the long-suffering LPNs said that he was just newly out of the army, and although his name was Collins, Laura thought of him as "the colonel."

The colonel had arrived immediately after breakfast. He listened to her chest while she contemplated his receding, sunburned hairline and inhaled hospital disinfectant and aftershave; he scowled at her temperature chart and declared loudly that she could go home, if they could find out where her home was. "No way, otherwise." He pulled a regretful face that made Laura feel like a malingerer and said, "Dehydration's the enemy." That was his way: brisk pronouncements full of military metaphors. But though the pulmonary specialist was brusque, he was not unperceptive, and he handed her over to the neurologist.

Laura much preferred the neurologist, who was soft-spoken and calm, without the noise and bustle of his colleague. Dr. Arce had the long, sad face of a Mayan prince and came accompanied by a retinue of students. He looked at her eyes and checked the pupils, while the two interns of the day, a man and a woman, leaned over her bed to watch.

"You see, no longer any sign of concussion, despite the nasty contusions." His long fingers probed the side and back of her head. The students were invited to feel the still-tender lumps.

"All in all, a mild trauma for the brain, and yet, memory loss lingers. Am I right, Ms. Laura?"

The neurologist had been called in because the hospital had discovered that there was no Laura Whitman, or, rather, that the four Laura Whitmans living and working in the Washington, DC, area were all present and accounted for. Two were black; the one white woman was in her late fifties; the fourth was an adopted Korean. Nonetheless, she persisted in thinking that her name was Laura.

"I remember the bus and walking on the beach and along the causeway."

"And before that?"

"I remember some things. There's a big yellow house and a garden with delphiniums and what seems to be a church interior. I don't remember any names or addresses."

"The big house. Is it in the Washington, DC, area?"

"I don't know. I thought I worked in Washington. At some government agency."

"Yet we can find no record of such a person. You see how the mind fills in," Dr. Arce told the interns. "The mind cannot bear gaps in its history, so it invents a plausible story to hold the personality together."

"Could this damage have been caused by fever instead of the head injury?" This question was from the female doctor, a pretty cinnamon-colored woman with a long, thick braid. As the object in question, Laura waited for the answer with some interest.

"No, her fever was never in the danger range. This shows you the sensitivity of the brain. Although mild concussion is often considered trivial, all head injuries are serious to some extent, and even fairly minor injuries can produce subtle, temporary damage. The most likely scenario for you," he told Laura kindly, "is that one day soon you will wake up and remember everything. If just the brain is involved, that is most likely."

The students looked at him curiously, and Laura wondered what he was suggesting, as well.

"Do not forget the mind," Dr. Arce said. "While it is affected by the physical brain, the mind has its own logic. Ms. Laura's mind may have its own reasons for retreating, reasons it doesn't choose to let her remember." He gave Laura a close, astute glance, and she let her eyes half close as if she was ready to fall back to sleep.

"Time," he said to her gently. "It's still true that time is the great healer. We like to think that we can control diseases and injuries, but in reality, we must always wait for bodies and minds to heal."

He patted Laura on the shoulder and for just an instant, she felt that she remembered everything and could tell him. If there were no students, no patients, no hospital ward; if only they were walking on the causeway with the water and sky and sun, she would remember, and he would give her good advice. That conviction passed as quickly as it had come, leaving her with a familiar sense of mild dread, overlaid with the torpor of serious illness.

"Rest," said Dr. Arce.

Out in the hall, beyond earshot of the enigmatic Laura X, Dr. Arce questioned his students. "What do you think?" he asked. "Is our patient truly amnesiac, is she confused, or is she faking? Those are our possibilities, are they not?"

"There's something not right," said Dr. Byron. He had a thin, intense face, accentuated by the pallor of long nights on call and a painstaking temperament that constantly put him at odds with his overloaded schedule. Though he was intelligent and hardworking, Dr. Arce sometimes wondered if this intern's talents were not for study and research rather than for healing. Nonetheless, on physical symptoms, Dr. Byron was the most astute of his pupils.

"She has no identification. Okay, that was presumably stolen with her purse, but she seems totally unconcerned about it. She has no luggage, either. No cash and, again, no concern for whatever money she might have had. Or for her credit cards. You get robbed, your first concern is to cancel your credit cards and get a copy of your driver's license."

"Not everyone has credit cards," Dr. Rahman said.

"This woman is middle class," Dr. Bryon said. "Poor teeth but good dentistry. No drugs or alcohol in the body. No sign of addiction or of injuries indicating abuse. Her hands are in good shape, and her general physical condition, aside from dehydration and bruises from the mugging, is good."

"What were her clothes like?" Dr. Rahman asked.

"I asked the nursing staff that," Dr. Arce said. He opened his little notebook. "A pair of J. Crew slacks and a cotton polo shirt."

"Irreproachably preppy, middle class," said Dr. Bryon.

Dr. Arce nodded. "She is lying, then, do you think?"

"No," Dr. Rahman interrupted. "She seems genuinely anxious and confused."

"She could be lying," Dr. Byron said. "But—no," he corrected himself and rose in Dr. Arce's estimation. "No, I can't say I think she's lying exactly."

"I think she maybe was lying and then got hurt," said Dr. Rahman.

"Ah," said Dr. Arce. Dr. Rahman showed almost too much imagination sometimes, but this new idea struck him as accounting for the sadness that he sensed in his patient, the sadness which he felt was more dangerous for her than either concussion or pneumonia. "That would be a truly terrible situation. To lie and get caught in it permanently."

"That is a matter for a police investigation," Dr. Bryon said.

Dr. Arce's smile was resigned. Americans had remarkable faith in police and in what they called "law and order," but Dr. Byron was correct, nonetheless. A Sergeant Torres had visited, interviewed, and photographed their patient; a bulletin was to be sent out nationwide. It was strange, though, if Dr. Bryon was correct about the woman's social class, why no one had reported her missing. That detail continued to trouble Dr. Arce, and when, three nights later, he heard from the night nursing supervisor that a relative had been located, he called and talked to the police and then went to see Ms. Laura.

It was after nine o'clock. Surrounded by Mylar balloons and clutching a stuffed toy, the auto accident case was watching TV with rapt attention. The old woman slept noisily, snuffling and twitching. Automatically, Dr. Arce listened to the sounds of her breathing and frowned: he did not like an irregularity that he detected. His own patient was sitting up reading one of the brown Gideon Bibles found in every bedside cabinet.

"I'm interrupting you," Dr. Arce said.

"Not at all. It is always nice to have a visit from you." Ms. Laura had what Dr. Arce thought of as a genuine smile, not a matter of muscular adjustments, but a spontaneous illumination of the features. Although they could not have been more unlike physically, Ms. Laura reminded him strongly of his wife, and that was perhaps why he was disregarding a police request and the considered opinion of his respected colleagues, Dr. Collins and the night nursing supervisor, to pay her this visit.

"This is a book I know very well," Ms. Laura continued. "Very, very well. And that is unusual, isn't it, today?"

"Perhaps you belong to a fundamentalist church," Dr. Arce said. The quirks and passions of this group had become well known to him during his practice in Florida.

"I'm not churchy religious," Ms. Laura said very definitely. "Though I don't know how I know that."

"Patients sometimes recall skills or bodies of knowledge without any context for them. Or they can lose skills and forget facts yet keep a sense of where they are." He lifted his long, elegant hands, and Laura smiled again, because, although what he said was sad, he moved so gracefully.

"You comfort your patients with grace," she said without thinking, and Dr. Arce realized that he must tell her straight out.

"They've found someone who has identified you," he said.

In the flaring darkness, she felt the sway of the night bus and said nothing.

"A woman is arriving tomorrow or the next day."

"A woman," she exclaimed, the way she might have said "an angel" or "a monster." "They did not tell me." She caught her breath. "When did they find out?"

"I don't know. I just learned an hour ago."

"They weren't going to tell me," Ms. Laura concluded.

"They thought," Dr. Arce said delicately, "that you might be anxious, and also that the sudden shock might be beneficial. That it might jog your memory."

"You felt otherwise?"

"I don't believe in routine shock therapy."

"If I could, I would tell you everything," she said suddenly. "I could tell you if I could tell anyone."

Dr. Arce was touched by that confession and troubled, too: trust brings a weight of obligation. "You must not force yourself. You must wait for your mind to be ready."

"I believe that, but now there isn't time. Tomorrow or the next day, someone will come—with proofs and documents, I suppose—and I'll have to go home with a stranger."

"Don't you want to go home?" he asked.

"I don't know. I don't know where or what home is. As for finding out about it, I'll have to think that over."

"Once you have documents, you do not have to leave. If you have a social security number and proof of citizenship, you can live and work wherever you want. You are an intelligent, employable person."

She smiled sadly. "Perhaps I'll remember some valuable skill," she said, "but I sense that I was not a useful person."

When Dr. Arce started to ask what usefulness was, she shook her head. Although he was kind, she was in no shape to think of practical things or to make plans, and she was afraid of disturbing the tenuous balance of her indifference. "Just the same, you were right to tell me, and I am very grateful," she said with a formal and dignified manner that told Dr. Arce there was no more he could do.

He stood up and shook her hand. He wished he had some words of wisdom for her, but all he could do was to wish her luck.

And that, perhaps, was what Laura needed more than wisdom, because, around midnight, she woke out of an exhausted, drugged-up hospital sleep with a sense of dread and desperation, all the more potent for lacking any clear focus. She lay in bed for a while, listening to the old woman's breathing, footsteps passing in the corridor, the beep, somewhere close, of a monitor. The shift was changing and the nurses would be busy. With no more thought than that realization, Laura slipped out of bed, struggled into her street clothes, and went to the partially open door of her room. She watched the hall until she saw an orderly arrive with a gurney, provoking a flutter of activity at the main desk. Laura walked quickly down the hall, opened the door to the stairwell, and left the deceptive cool of the air-conditioned ward for the stuffy dampness of the tropical night.

By the third flight down, she felt dizzy and clutched the rail, but she didn't dare go out onto the floor to take the elevator. And that was silly, really, because she wasn't a prisoner; she could leave when she liked, although they'd want to know who she was and whether she had health insurance, and, if not, who was going to pay her bill. No doubt whoever was coming would give them the answers. She herself preferred to decline revelation, and so the only thing to do was to clear out, get away, take herself off to the beach or the bus or the causeway, where she might be able to retrieve the self she'd discarded so carelessly.

After another flight, Laura sat on the steps for a moment before she descended one more. She was extraordinarily weak. Restricted to the ward, cossetted by the nurses, she hadn't realized her own condition, but she was determined to manage. One more flight and she'd be on the lobby floor. Then out to the night bus which would rescue her from both knowledge and decision.

She pushed the heavy door and stepped into the lobby with its hard, shining floor and pastel chairs. The glass walls of the gift shop displayed hopeful stuffed toys and pretty nightgowns. The flower shop, smelling of pollen and fertilizer, blazed with mums and daisies, lilies and azaleas that made her think of a garden, a garden with darkness all round, a garden, as Dr. Arce said, "without context." She paused a moment, crafty, to study the flowers, as if she were a visitor detained on some desperate vigil, before she crossed to the automatic doors and stepped into the neon-washed night and her own private darkness.

3

"I CAN'T BELIEVE YOU WERE so thoughtless," Yvonne said. Yvonne was sitting with her back to the window, and Florida light was pouring in around her. So it was Florida, and a big window with institutional venetian blinds meant the hospital again. Probably. But she knew for sure it was Yvonne. The woman had been introducing herself over and over, and by now she recognized the thick, well-groomed dark hair, the long, handsome face, the large eyes and mouth, the aquiline nose, the white, aggressive teeth. This was Yvonne, all right, dressed very neatly in a short-sleeved white suit. With gloves. Laura was quite taken with the gloves, which showed smartness and discipline and which, now that she'd had a good look, must have been custom made, for the right hand had only four fingers.

". . . sue the hospital and that damn Mexican doctor. I was explicit with them, although, God knows, I never thought you'd pull this sort of stunt."

She, Laura, was supposed to know Yvonne, and, in a way, she did. Now that the fever was gone, she no longer perceived danger as a darkness pouring toward her. That had been some sort of hallucination, she supposed, or maybe a trick of the unfamiliar brilliance of

Florida light. Instead, Yvonne triggered uneasiness, which might mean unpleasant, if presently irretrievable, memories or just discomfort with this forceful and outspoken personality.

At the moment, Yvonne was describing the inconveniences of her stay: the work piling up at home, the deals missed, the noise in her motel, the stupidity of the hospital staff, the cholesterol-heavy menus at nearby restaurants. Yvonne made it very clear that all these griefs were Laura's fault, but instead of being apologetic, Laura felt indifferent. She hadn't asked for this person she was supposed to remember; she hadn't asked for her at all.

"We'd have been back a week ago," Yvonne said, "if this bunch of crackers had followed instructions."

A week! Laura thought. A week lost! The tenuousness of reality would have shocked her, if she hadn't remembered something more frightening. She wasn't Laura. Not Whitman, and not Laura, either. She was Catherine. Cath. And her last name was Tolland. So Yvonne said.

Now Yvonne was describing how she—Cath, that is—had wound up in the emergency room. She'd collapsed near the waterfront, and, thinking she was drunk or on drugs, the police had picked her up. "Right off the street," Yvonne said with a certain relish. Cath had actually been taken to the county lockup before they realized that she was seriously ill. "Who knows what would have happened to you if you'd been put in a cell!"

Yvonne kept trying to impress Cath with the extreme danger she'd been in; Yvonne called this "being realistic and facing the facts." She was also eager to stress the good fortune of Cath's deliverance, as if she thought her insufficiently grateful. "You don't know how lucky you were!" Yvonne exclaimed for the second or third time.

Cath couldn't remember enough to judge how grateful she ought to be, but she did remember Dr. Arce wishing her luck. Although she'd finally given up trying to defend him to Yvonne, she'd appreciated his good thoughts on the night she'd stepped off into oblivion. Otherwise, her adventures had been reduced to a confusion of lights against darkness, strangers' voices, warm pavements, sea winds, and the velvet freedom of a tropical night where she had learned detachment. Detachment, she recalled, was a Buddhist virtue; perhaps she had had a religious experience. Perhaps she had become enlightened.

"You've no idea," said Yvonne.

And perhaps she *had* been lucky. Here she was safe back at the hospital. She had a private room, this time, with pretty wallpaper and a large bunch of flowers, for whoever Yvonne was, she seemed to have gone to quite a bit of trouble. Maybe that represented luck.

"We still don't know where you were or who you were with!" Yvonne said with a probing glance that Cath found distasteful. She had a dazed memory of questions, of medical personnel, of a variety of humiliating examinations. It drifted into her mind that they thought she might have been raped. Yes, that was certainly what they'd thought. Or, perhaps, what Yvonne had suggested to them. Cath suddenly had no doubt as to the source of the idea. And that reminded her of something about Yvonne—whom she must remember on some level—namely, an avidity for scandal, for gossip, for knowledge of the sort that gives one leverage and power. Cath knew that, not through any rational thought process, but by the return of a familiar but inexplicable sense of dread which told her that Yvonne was not to be trusted.

"You can't imagine what we've been through the last few days with you," Yvonne was saying. "Thank God, Derek didn't come. He'd have been frantic."

"Who's Derek?" she asked.

That was the first thing Cath had said which stopped Yvonne and made her think. Her face took on a shrewd and concentrated expression. Cath realized that Yvonne was intelligent as well as curious. "Derek's my brother." Another sharp glance. "Your husband."

Cath said that she didn't believe it, and she didn't—not entirely. Now that she was definitely feeling better, Cath was able to see from one moment to the next, to connect ideas, to be prudent. And what could be more prudent, when her head was still spinning and days had been lost and her mind had shed its skin, than to stall for time? To refuse conventional wisdom. To await what might happen without preconceptions, except for the notion that Yvonne was not to be trusted.

Yvonne opened her purse and produced a Connecticut driver's license belonging to Catherine Tolland. In the photo ID, Catherine Tolland looked thin, blond, and startled, but that might have been the effect of the DMV camera. Her face was pale and definitely lacking in radiance. She didn't look to be acquainted with chartreuse gowns or solar winds or detachment, either. Cath shrugged noncommittally.

"This doesn't prove I'm married," she said stubbornly.

Yvonne glared at her as if trying to see beneath her skin. Then she produced another photograph, showing a young man and woman standing companionably arm in arm. Cath recognized Yvonne, a younger Yvonne.

"It was taken a couple of years ago."

"More than a couple," Cath suggested. She examined Yvonne's image with exaggerated care as if the man meant nothing to her.

"Around the time you met Derek."

At the mention of his name, Cath's eyes slid irresistibly toward the man in the photo. Tall, with a lean face and dark eyebrows, Derek looked a great deal like his sister, but the bold features were even more satisfactory in masculine form. Although his high, prominent forehead and deep-set eyes kept him from being conventionally handsome, he was still an exceptionally attractive man. Cath admitted that. At the same time, she felt her mouth go dry and her body turn heavy, as if the fatigue that had settled into her bones was pulling her right down through the bed and the floor into some subterranean psychic chamber.

"You recognize him, don't you?" Yvonne asked in an angry voice, as if annoyed by the success of this ploy. "Don't tell me you don't recognize him. I can see it in your face."

"He looks like you," said Cath. More than that she couldn't, wouldn't say. All she felt was exhaustion. She slid her hand down to the call button and pushed it surreptitiously.

"Don't try to fool me," said Yvonne. "Fever, I could understand. Disorientation even. You were never too well oriented, were you, Cath?

40

I knew that from the start, and I warned Derek." She gave a tight, bitter smile. "This is something else, isn't it? The doctors have been giving me a line, but no matter what that idiot Mexican thinks, you know perfectly well who we are. So you'd better straighten up. I won't have you hurting Derek with this nonsense. You don't know how lucky you are to have such a wonderful husband."

"Why didn't he come?" Cath asked. It seemed to her that a "wonderful husband" came when his wife was in the hospital, even if she'd been plucked off the street or decamped on the night bus. "If he's such a wonderful husband, why did he send you?"

Yvonne looked at her as if the question were incomprehensible, and Cath felt her head beginning to hurt. There were things she'd wanted to forget; she understood that now. But there were also some important things that she had lost in transit or mislaid along the causeway or discarded out on the warm pavements.

"It's difficult for him to take time off!" Yvonne said at last. "It's hard enough for me, but my hours are flexible. With his schedule, it's just impossible."

"Not even for his wife?"

"We hardly expected there'd be all this trouble, all these delays," Yvonne said. "I've had to cancel I don't know how many appointments. And Derek had his services, important duties."

Ah, duties, duty. As in *a sense of.* As in *do your duty,* Cath thought. "What does he do?" she asked.

"He's a minister," Yvonne said. "You know that. He handles all the music. You should know. The only thing you were ever willing to do about the church was to play with the choir."

"The choir?" Cath asked.

"You sang," Yvonne said grudgingly. "And played the violin— when necessary."

"I can play the violin," Cath said. That was a pleasing thought. And true. She felt it was true; the information felt different from some of Yvonne's other statements.

"Don't get carried away," Yvonne said. "You were no Midori. But Derek was always indulgent about your music."

"He's a musician." "Musician" had a nice sound. A reliable sound. "He's a musician" was a statement that could be tested; it had a certain empirical reality. Whereas "He's a wonderful husband" might be a matter of opinion or perspective.

"He's music minister," Yvonne said. "He's not an ordinary musician. He has a very important position in the community."

Cath had frankly disbelieved the business about the church, but the words "music minister" brought up a startlingly clear image of a dark, old-fashioned sanctuary. "Is the church dark wood?" she asked with sudden anxiety. Rising in her mind's eyes were heavy pews, stained glass, and stone pillars, all drenched in the lingering scent of incense, dusty carpet, gladiolus, and chrysanthemums.

"Dark walnut and oak," Yvonne said. "Wonderful acoustics from the vaulting and bric-a-brac and all that old wood." She hesitated a moment, before speaking in a rush, as if talking to herself or thinking aloud: "I'm not sure Derek would have accepted the position if it hadn't been for those acoustics. A man of his talent—you and I know that he could have gone anywhere. Any of the really big congregations, one of the cathedrals. And, of course, in the secular world—but that was never his ambition. Sacred music, sacred choruses and masses. The heart of music, as Derek always says."

The nurse came in before Cath had to answer, and she was glad, because she felt that she needed time to digest this information. Music, a music minister, a wonderful husband; Yvonne, a sister-in-law, a messenger, a danger.

"How are you doing, Mrs. Tolland?" The RN was one Cath liked: she had short gray hair, a pleasantly brisk manner, and what Raoul would have called "presence."

So it was official; not just some idea of Yvonne's. She was Catherine Tolland, married to Derek Tolland, who was some sort of minister.

"I'm getting quite a headache," she said.

The nurse looked swiftly at Yvonne, whom she'd sized up early on. "Maybe enough visiting for today," she told Cath.

Yvonne started to describe all that still had to be settled, but the RN cut her off. "Mrs. Tolland must rest. If you expect her to be able to travel."

Yvonne made a face but stood up. Cath handed her the photo. "The license, too," Yvonne said, holding out her hand, the left hand. Cath noticed that she kept the one with the four fingers half hidden behind her back. "I'll keep it for you."

"I should have a purse or a wallet of my own to keep it in."

"You lost everything," Yvonne said. "Incredibly careless. Thank God you'd left all your credit cards at home or we could have been out hundreds, thousands of dollars."

"Perhaps you could get me a wallet. There must be a store."

"Gift shop has them," the nurse said briskly. "We can put the license in your cabinet for now."

"Thank you," said Cath, understanding that the nurse was on her side. But it was obvious that Yvonne believed she was lying and did not want her to have any kind of identification. As Cath slipped into sleep, she realized that, in her present weakness, retaining her license was the most temporary of victories.

4

LOST IN EXHAUSTION, CATH WAS dozing with her head against the car door when Yvonne said, "Here we are. We're home." Cath opened her eyes to the first solid things of the journey: a big colonial house with a shabby picket fence, two maple trees, an old covered well in the front yard. A green work van was parked in the drive. The low sun intensified the yellow paint on the clapboards, and the late-afternoon shadows darkened the grass, bringing the house and yard to the unnatural vividness of a doctored photograph. Or maybe it was just that, as recognition rose out of the swamp of fatigue, everything she'd seen for the past weeks paled in comparison. Cath pushed open the car door and stepped out, greedy for the cold air that carried a smell of dried leaves, turned earth, and, somewhere close by, running water.

This was her great-grandmother's house. Passed down through the generations of Pierces, Stotts, and Mackeys, who'd left their trunks and boxes in the attic, their handiwork, in gleaming chestnut and oak floor-boards and in patched plaster walls smoothed by layers of paint. Any one of them would remember the seasonal rustle of mice in the cellar, the lingering spoor of wood ashes in the fireplaces, the chilly toilets, the drafty kitchen. Even in the dark, even blindfolded, even blind, she'd have known where she was instantly by the smell of woodsmoke, age, and vegetation, by the dampness in the air, by the creak of the gate, by the starlings in the locust trees across the road. In spring, daffodils would run down the field toward the water, lilacs bloom around the barn, and roses stretch themselves along the peeling picket fence. Out of so much unreality, she remembered this; for better or worse, she was home, and nothing else really registered, not even the stranger climbing out of his van, waving to Yvonne, crossing the grass.

"You see," said Yvonne, her voice gentle, not at all unkind. "You just needed to get back to your own surroundings." Cath wondered if she had misjudged Yvonne, who had been quite pleasant once she was discharged. Perhaps the really sinister feature of her illness had been those curious insights and warnings, those umbrae of darkness and disaster. So maybe Yvonne was right that she'd had some sort of breakdown; that she had left, inexplicably, a happy marriage, a pleasant situation, this beloved house; that Yvonne had seemed cross only because they had all been frantic with worry. Leaning on the fence, looking at the house, Cath considered that possibility and hoped it was the right one.

"Do you need some help?" the man asked, and Cath looked at him. But though he was tall, he was not the man in the photograph. He was not Derek. This man carried no umbra of memory, no shadows. She noticed he had kind eyes.

"No, we're all right," Yvonne said to him. "My sister-in-law's just tired from the trip."

He opened the gate for them nonetheless, and took Cath's arm. "You've been sick," he said.

"Yes, but now I'm home." She looked around greedily. This tall man and Yvonne and the mysterious Derek were all opaque, distant, mysterious. The cracked flagstones, the ivy on the well, the tangle of shrubs around the building, the one broken shutter—they were not only vivid but convincing. Even the shifting golden light in the west and the robin's-egg sky behind the tall chimneys carried a conviction her companions could only approximate.

"You'd better go in," Yvonne said. "This is pretty chilly after Florida. She's had pneumonia."

"Oh, I'm sorry. Should I come back another day?" the man asked.

"No, no, I'll just get Cath inside. You must go in," she said to Cath, who agreed out of politeness, though Yvonne seemed even more of a stranger here than she had in Florida. And Derek, who should have been, must be, must once have been, closer to her than anyone on earth, was imaginable only as a kind of ghost. Cath wasn't sure she believed in him at all.

Thank you," Yvonne said to the man as she unlocked the door. "I'll only be a minute. Can you make the stairs?" she asked Cath. "We can fix a bed for you downstairs after dinner."

"I don't want dinner," Cath said, for the world was contracting around the edges as her exhaustion rebounded. She could still feel the motion of the car, the noisy vibration of the plane, the dislocations of the journey. She was chilled to the bone, too, for the old house was always cold and she had lost her parka. "I want to go right to bed."

The stair was a long straight run, so steep that Cath had to hold the rail as she struggled to the top. The sun had already dropped below the bare tree branches, and beyond the back window, the blue sky had begun to fade, but even in the dim light, every detail was sharp in Cath's mind. It was no mistake, but a deliberate choice, that she walked straight down the familiar, creaking hallway to a small back room with the sort of solid, mismatched furniture reserved for spare bedrooms before they were elevated to "guest rooms." Cath kicked off her shoes and flopped on the bed.

"It's not made up," Yvonne said. "I thought you'd want your and Derek's room." She stood in the doorway, a vividly healthy presence that persistently suggested unreliability.

"Derek's not here," said Cath. It was not a complaint, just a statement of fact. She'd had to take him on faith with just a photo to go on, and, until he appeared, she preferred not to think about him at all. She'd forgotten Derek, a state of affairs which seemed alternately to exasperate and please Yvonne.

"He had a rehearsal. I explained that to you."

"Then he'll probably be late. I've just got to sleep, Yvonne," Cath said, beginning to shiver. "If you could bring me a quilt, I'll be fine here."

Her face unreadable, Yvonne shrugged and went out to the hall. Cath heard her rummaging in the linen closet before she returned with sheets, a quilt, an extra blanket, and a towel.

"Get up," said Yvonne when Cath didn't move. "So I can make the bed."

Cath rose, uncertain on her feet, and took the towel into the adjoining bathroom. The seat was cold in the poorly insulated building and the hot tap produced ice water. Cath ran it to lukewarm, washed her hands, and splashed her flushed and feverish face before returning to the bedroom to grapple with reality. She was home, in her great-grandmother's house. Her husband was at his job, an hour away in a rich suburban town, rehearsing a chorus. And that was his sister, who, having made the bed and located a pair of pajamas, was descending the bare treads of the stair to talk to Vincent, the man with the kind eyes. He did furniture appraisals, Yvonne said, and could advise them on some of Aunt Elizabeth's antiques. Cath heard them talking down in the hall, then their footsteps, before a door opening and closing. Left alone in the still-light room like a child sent to bed on a summer evening, Cath lay down as if drugged and tumbled into sleep.

Voices downstairs brought an awareness that the night walls were washed with moonlight instead of the hospital ward's fluorescent glow. She must have gotten out; yes, she was home, back home, and that was Yvonne's voice and a man's, too, low and familiar, if presently unintelligible. Her heart began to race: Derek must be home. That must be him. And now that she'd heard him, she should get up and go downstairs. That would be the natural thing to do, Cath knew, for she retained a good theoretical grasp of marriage, even if her own was incomprehensible. But instead of feeling natural, she felt nervous, and embarrassed, too, by the stupid melodrama of her situation.

She lay in bed, trying to decide what to do. When she finally got up—the room drafty, the floorboards icy—instead of going to the door, she went to the back window and opened it slowly and gently. They, Yvonne and the man who must be Derek, were in the kitchen, for a trapezoid of light painted the grass. Cath imagined them sitting at the kitchen table, companionably talking. About his rehearsal, or about some newly chosen music, or about her? What were they saying? So much better? So much worse? Forgotten everything and everyone but the house? Or will be all right now that she's home?

Cath leaned on the sill and concentrated.

"... situation is completely different," said Yvonne.

"A fresh start. That would be best ... might still be possible."

Yvonne's voice was a murmur, a whisper. Cath strained her ears, but the only other thing she heard was the conclusion, as Yvonne's voice rose slightly in exasperation: "You're crazy. You're crazy to hope ..."

Shivering in the draft, Cath closed the window and fell back into a sleep broken by the sound of footsteps on the stairs. There was a pause, and after Cath heard them going into the front rooms on either side, she lay in bed waiting, listening for Derek's tread in the hall, hoping that he would come in and horrified that he might; excited, frightened, feverish, until her acute ears ceased to detect any sounds except the shrubbery's dry rustle and the house's arthritic sighs, which reemerged in her dreams as the wind off the great bay, the bay, not as she had seen it, glittering under the Florida sun, but a milky, moonlit sheet, luminous, ghostly, and troubling.

The next morning, Cath remembered pale water and a sense of unease, before the realization that she was home blotted out everything but the facts of the moment: the sun was up, and someone was making breakfast. Feeling exhausted, shaky, and desperately thirsty, she got out of bed, and, before she could lose herself in nerves, threw on yesterday's jeans and sweatshirt and went downstairs.

They were both at breakfast. Cath stepped from the hall into the awkward old farm kitchen to see Yvonne fixing a melon at the sink, while the man read something to her out of the morning paper. Yvonne wore an apron to protect her red blazer and dark slacks. She had rubber kitchen gloves on her hands. Cath had an instant to remember that Yvonne had wanted to modernize the kitchen, and that she, Cath, had refused, before Derek looked up and she lost herself in seeing him.

He was heavier than in the picture, older, but handsomer, too. He'd lost the lean intensity of what she understood now must have been a photo from his teens or early twenties. He'd filled out into a big, robust man with strong, regular features and a wonderful gap-toothed smile that sent a shock wave through her body. Derek, this was Derek, whom she'd known, loved, married; whom she didn't re-member except just the physical fact that here was the one man she'd ever wanted madly.

"Cath," he said. "Darling." He dropped the paper and came over to hug her, gently but cautiously, and kiss her cheek. She thought "cautiously," but her skin was gone, her nerves bare; she'd momentarily lost her mind.

"You're Derek," she said, clutching at last the notion that she had to be careful.

He hugged her again. "Great to have you home. Sit down, sit down. You need breakfast. Better get her some juice or coffee, Yvonne."

Lemon-colored morning light was rolling through the speckled glass of the back door and the square window over the sink. As time slowed unbearably, Yvonne went to the cupboard for another juice glass. Cath felt them waiting for her to speak but found nothing to say: they were strangers, and she had always been shy and awkward with new people.

"What time is it?" she asked in desperation.

"Usual breakfast time," said Derek. He nodded toward the clock over the stove. Of course there was a kitchen clock. It was a quarter of eight. "Practice at ten," he said briskly.

"At ten," she said, as if this meant something. She had learned how to operate with Yvonne. Repeat things knowledgeably, nod, pretend comprehension. People are reassured by speech, by agreement.

Yvonne gave her a glass of orange juice and a plate with a thick melon slice. "She hasn't eaten since yesterday lunch on the plane." This to Derek.

"I was too tired." Cath felt that she was defending herself against some charge of carelessness. "I was tired out from the trip."

"We wanted you home right away," Derek said, "but it was perhaps too soon for you to travel." He spoke as if he'd had nothing to do with the decision one way or another. But perhaps he hadn't; she didn't have any real idea of their relationship.

"Yvonne was worried about the bills," Cath said. Her voice, too, sounded neutral and detached. That was good. Neutrality and detachment are right in awkward situations.

"She wasn't getting better," Yvonne said quickly. She addressed all her remarks to Derek as if Cath were a child or an incompetent. "She didn't remember anything clearly until yesterday afternoon. As soon as we got here, she knew where she was."

"And us?" Derek asked, turning to look at her. He had amazing eyes, green rather than blue, bright and deep. Movie-idol, magazine-cover eyes. "Of course you remember us!" He spoke lightly, as if he thought she might be joking. "You can't have forgotten your dearly beloved."

Cath took a deep breath, tempted to lie, to see how far imagination and restoring wits would carry her. But he was her husband, her love; he deserved the truth. "I'm not sure," she said.

"She remembers me." There was an edge to Yvonne's voice; maybe it was her kindess, not her irritation, that was feigned.

"I learned who you were," Cath corrected. "You came every day and told me your name. I know you are Yvonne."

"But you know we're married," Derek said.

"Yvonne told me that. And I feel I knew you once, but that's all. It's dreadful, but I can't seem to remember people at all."

Derek drew in his breath and raised his eyebrows as if this were something he needed to think over. Beyond that, his handsome face was unreadable. Disconcerted? Offended? Indifferent? She hadn't any idea; he might have been a photo in a tabloid. "Well, we are ephemeral creatures, aren't we?" he said, as he picked up the paper again. "Houses are good for the ages. Semipermanent."

"*Permanent* is right with this one," said Yvonne. "A permanent money pit." *She doesn't like the house,* Cath realized, and that was why she, Cath, had resisted all improvements.

Derek resumed reading the paper. Was his calm exaggerated? He'd taken her reappearance very coolly. But maybe he'd been wounded by her abrupt departure. Or maybe, whatever Yvonne said, he was sorry she'd returned. That idea made Cath hate his good looks. The fact she found him attractive made her physically sick, and the melon was soft, too soft, almost mushy. "I can't eat any more," she said.

"Have some toast and tea. The water's ready." Yvonne jumped up, full of solicitude.

"I'd rather have coffee."

"Clear fluids," Yvonne corrected. "You're supposed to keep forcing clear fluids."

"If I'm well enough to travel, I'm well enough to have coffee," Cath said.

"How's your headache?" Yvonne countered.

"It's not too bad."

"But still there? That's dehydration." Yvonne had picked up the jargon and knew all the explanations.

"All right, don't make a big deal of it. Give me the tea." Cath knew that she sounded snappish and out of sorts. She could not have said why everything about Yvonne seemed to irritate her, but her sister-in-law had a way of bringing out her worst side, even now, when Cath wanted to make a good impression and hoped things would go well.

Really, she did, although that anxiety was humiliating, too, because they knew all the answers, and she was left to guess how things had stood and how they all felt about each other.

Derek was busy scanning the newspaper columns, reading or pretending to read, as if he didn't want to get between the two women. He read very rapidly, Cath suddenly remembered, and she giggled nervously. She might have been given something more useful, but for some reason her racing mind streaked toward irrelevancies as if there was safety in triviality. Yvonne and Derek exchanged glances over the remains of their breakfasts.

"I'm sorry, my mind's in bits and pieces," Cath said. "I'm overtired. Maybe I should lie down for a while." As soon as she spoke, she realized that she was exhausted. The dazzling morning light made her head hurt, and Yvonne and Derek, the focus of much interest and anxiety only a moment before, were fading into insignificance. She pushed herself back from the table and made her way down the bare, chilly hall to the stairs. By the time she reached her room, all she could do was brush her teeth and fall into bed.

At lunchtime, she stayed upstairs until she saw her sister-in-law walk over to the garage. Out to do the shopping, probably. Cath found a banana and an apple in the kitchen, and ate them along with a cream cheese and jelly sandwich. It was the first meal in a while when she hadn't had Yvonne giving her advice, and that made everything taste better; she couldn't stomach Yvonne's air of superiority and grievance. Cath wondered how she'd coped with a live-in sister-in-law, but perhaps Yvonne had only arrived after she got sick. She'd have to ask in some tactful way. Still, the idea that Yvonne might not be a permanent presence cheered Cath enough that she ventured outside.

The long winter freeze was over. The grass was still brown; the lawn, damp in spots, but slim fingers of crocuses and daffodils were poking through the leafy crusts of the flower beds. A dog, Cath thought. It would be nice to have a dog, a species possessing the gift of happiness. What fun it would be now to open a run or undo a chain and see the animal leaping with joy as it romped toward the river. Her mind presented her with a variety of breeds for inspection, but when she reached spaniels, she felt uneasy. She did not want to think about dogs, imagine dogs, remember dogs. She refocused her interest, instead, on the music that was drifting through the bare lilacs.

Derek was playing the studio piano in the professionally convenient "new" wing, added around the turn of the century when an enterprising and impoverished ancestor had started taking in summer "guests." Derek kept his beautiful Steinway grand on the lower floor of this addition, along with his harpsichord and a small pump organ. Her violin would be there, too, Cath thought.

When she opened the studio door, Derek was playing through the Schubert Mass. A cup of coffee sat on the top of the Steinway, along with a litter of parts and notes: preparations for the next big occasion. Derek was immensely thorough and painstaking. As minister of music, he had built a very good church choir, supplemented, whenever the budget allowed, by experienced professionals, usually tenors. That was always a delicate matter, Cath recalled, tenor stipends being particularly offensive to the unpaid sopranos and altos.

Then there was the perennial difficulty of the instrumentalists, who were, by and large, semiprofessionals or dedicated amateurs. What was good for the nonprofessional singers, namely quicker tempi and a good deal of accompanying pianissimo, often made problems for the hard-pressed string ensemble. Success required a sensitive balance and an accurate judgment of what could be expected from each musician. Derek was, Cath somehow knew, very good at knowing just how much he could get out of people. He was an excellent conductor.

"You're up," he said, turning from the piano.

"Something new?"

"Old and new. I've done the Schubert before. Not with this group, though." He closed the score and opened another volume that was sitting on the piano. "This is more your style."

She knew it right away, the little 'Pulchra es' section of the *Vespro della Beata Vergine*, which she had been learning before the night bus and the bay and the hospital. Monteverdi's music was exactly right for her voice, which was pure rather than powerful: a nice amateur instrument. She'd known fairly early on that she did not have a big enough sound for a professional career. Having been spared hopes of fame and fortune, she had found in music a deep pleasure, uncomplicated by anxiety or ambition.

Derek slowed, paused, and, with a nod, restarted the "Pulchra es," bringing in the second soprano part with his right hand: *"Pulchra es, amica mea, suavis et decora sicut Jerusalem . . .* Thou art beautiful, my love, Sweet and comely daughter of Jerusalem." Concentrated as she was on the music, Cath did not have time to consider the choice of this lyric, for her sound came as a surprise, like another dimension, the obverse of the dark waves and hallucinatory insights of her Florida trip. The voice was small, certainly, but Yvonne had been wrong; it was exceedingly sweet and flexible.

Derek was smiling, rumbling the continuo in his left hand, bringing in the second part with his right and humming an octave down. Their timing was exact, and from that perfect consonance, she felt a sense of harmony. For the first time, she believed that they were married, that they'd been happy, that things had been wonderful. "Thou art beautiful, my friend . . . *terribilis ut castrorum acies ordinata . . .* Terrible as an army / Drawn up for battle." Surely a curious simile for one's beloved. *"Averte oculos tuos a me quia ipsi me avolare fecerunt . . .* Turn away thine eyes from me / For they have made me fly away."

Her voice wove around the accompaniment with a joyous exuberance that didn't diminish until she began to feel light-headed. She managed to hold the last note, although by then the room was wavering and Derek's smiling face had darkened. She put her hand on the piano for support and coughed slightly.

"Perhaps not such a good idea," he said. She felt the absence of any real concern in his voice as a sudden jolt, as if she'd stepped in a hole. "We don't want you collapsing like Antonia in *The Tales of Hoffman.*" He stood up and brought over a chair.

"It's so annoying; everything's tiring," said Cath. "I really have no other symptoms. But that's such a lovely piece."

"You would have sung it well, too. We got lucky with a girl from the music school. Yvonne thinks we should use her from now on."

Cath felt him studying her face, waiting for her reaction. "College girls come and go," she said indifferently, although she was hurt, although this was the wrong note for a homecoming.

"Of course, I disagreed," Derek said quickly, having, perhaps, learned what he'd wanted. "You have a great talent for the sacred repertory. It may come with . . ." And he paused.

Averte oculos tuos a me, Cath thought, but she was brave enough to ask, "With what?"

"A touch of inspiration, a certain visionary quality." He started sorting his music. "We needn't discuss any of that now."

For some reason Cath was reminded very forcibly of Raoul. "I met someone with a visionary quality," she said, "who thought I should wear chartreuse." She could see that threw Derek off a bit.

"Now that you're home, you should try to forget whatever happened in Florida. None of that can do you any good. You want to start fresh, don't you?"

"I am starting fresh," Cath said. "I have no choice but to start fresh."

"Well," he said, "not quite. The 'Pulchra es' was word perfect."

"That's not the same thing. Dr. Arce said—"

"Arce's that shifty Mexican neurologist. Yvonne thought that—"

"Yvonne didn't like Dr. Arce, but he was very good, very kind." Cath heard the positive note in her voice and a touch of desperation, too. "He said that some patients remember skills and knowledge and lose their context. And with others, it's the reverse. I've apparently lost my context."

Derek looked as if he was thinking this over.

"I'm sorry," she said. "I know it's awkward for you, for us."

He smiled. "It presents certain novelties," he said.

Cath felt him appraising her, and she wasn't sure she liked that.

"But no," he said, "what bothers me is something else. Something I take quite seriously."

He waited. There was something—paternal? pedagogical? vaguely punitive?—in his tone, and Cath waited. One thing she'd learned from the night bus and Raoul and disorientation was the value of keeping her mouth shut.

"Apparently, you've been lying to Yvonne," Derek said.

Cath felt herself flush. He didn't believe she'd really forgotten. Now she knew for sure: he didn't believe her. His handsome face really was *"terribilis ut castorum acies ordinata,"* and there was something mysterious behind his eyes. Of course, she had been lying in one way, but concealing her dislike of her sister-in-law was surely just good manners. "How have I been lying to Yvonne?"

"And to me."

"How can I lie to you? I don't know you at all."

"Yet you recognize what I'm playing and sing it without hesitation. Maybe you see why I find it hard to credit the idea that you don't know who I am."

"You're my husband, Derek, although I didn't believe it at first. I know that you're responsible for all the music at a big suburban church, the name of which I've forgotten. I know that you read fast and that you always have trouble hiring tenor soloists. But I don't know who you are. I don't know what you're like. And I don't know how you feel about me. Were you in love with me?"

"Maybe more to the point after all that's happened, do you love me?" He seemed angry and puzzled, and Cath couldn't help noticing that he'd avoided her question.

So she hesitated, feeling, rather than seeing, a darkness at the edges of things, but that was surely because she was exhausted; the trip had been so tiring, and these were just the aftereffects. She had to remember that and resist irrationality, if she wanted to be well. If she wanted things to be all right. If she wanted this homecoming, her marriage, ordinary life to be a success. "I think you're very handsome," she said. "That's part of love, isn't it?"

He laughed softly, but his face cleared as if some anxiety had been lifted. "So you're still attracted to me, whoever I am. That's reassuring.

I was, you know, a very devoted husband. Very. A model, one might say."

That should have pleased her; made her glad. Instead, she heard herself say, "Yet you seem cautious. Emotionally cautious."

"You might remember that you gave me some reasons to be."

Cath shook her head. "Did I? Were things my fault? I don't know," she said. "All I remember is getting on the bus." She shook her head again and felt the room sway.

Derek grabbed her arm and kept her from falling. "You'd better go back to bed. Yvonne was sure you'd be in bed the whole day."

"Yvonne went out," Cath said as he helped her up the back stairs and along the corridor to the bedroom, not to their room, but to the one that she now thought of as hers, the little back guest room.

"Errands and things. I never cook when she's away."

Something about the way he said that struck Cath: "when she's away," rather than "when you're away," or "when you're both away." The questions that phrasing raised reminded her of what she wanted to know. She shook off lethargy to ask, "Is Yvonne living here permanently?"

"What a funny question," he said, sounding genuinely surprised. "You've forgotten. Yvonne and I were always very close. She's always lived near me."

"I mean, in our house. Did she come when I went away?"

"Before that," Derek said, and her heart sank. "Oh, she had to come before that."

"Why?" asked Cath.

"Well," he said, "you were sick, for one thing, and then you were never really interested in church work, were you? Yvonne's always been the greatest help to me. A really Christian woman."

"Oh," said Cath.

"Whereas you, my darling, were always a pagan at heart."

5

CATH SAT IN HER AUNT'S ancient chaise longue, an ideal convalescent furnishing, which Derek and Yvonne had fetched from the barn. Yvonne had fussed about the dust, the mouse droppings, the dirty, threadbare arms, but Cath had them leave the chaise out in the sun all one afternoon and air the cushions over the clothesline. With a couple of patches on the arms and an old sheet over the leaking feather pillows, it was perfectly comfortable, and its nostalgic old barn odor, an essence of long-disappeared hay and horses, discarded furniture and crumbling fabric, was very suitable for someone engaged, as she was, in recovering the past.

Cath had embarked on this project with the help of an ugly little spiral-bound notebook. Years ago, without ever wanting to record anything in particular, she had coveted a friend's schoolgirl diary, a burgundy leather item with gold-tipped pages and a neat little lock and key. Cath had almost asked her sister-in-law to buy a similar volume before deciding that a plain spiral notebook would be altogether less conspicuous. Unfortunately, it had also proved uninspiring. Cath had made little progress beyond recording the books she'd been reading and an alphabetical list of everything she disliked about her sister-in-law. Cath had allotted several more pages to this as yet unfinished, and probably unfair, indictment. Yvonne had been very helpful, Cath had to admit. And reasonably pleasant, *reasonably*, especially when Derek was home. Just the same, Cath didn't like her company and rejoiced to see her leave the house. If Cath put her mind to it, she could make a much longer list of things she disliked about Yvonne.

But lists and books were not the real enterprise, not the one she'd been postponing. That was *La Recherche du Temps Perdu,* as Proust puts it: the search for lost time, though his had, perhaps, been more mislaid than lost. Cath was well aware of the distinction. Some of her memories were lost, truly lost and irrecoverable, like the night she left the hospital, the morning before she was returned. Other memories drifted, elusive but extant, through her neural circuits. Those memories were retrievable, if she felt up to facing the underlying uneasiness of the remembrance of things past.

Shakespeare described "sessions of sweet silent thought," but Cath wondered. Personally, she found the process exhausting, especially when she had fresh and unpleasant discoveries like the state of her desk to think about. Shakespeare must have been different. Instead of mulling potentially disagreeable memories, he must have spent his time waiting for the next great line, the next great character, for Hamlet or Cleopatra or the Macbeths to arrive.

Still, she, Cath, was doing her best to ascend a dazzling rationality as tremendous as the sun. She would dress in chartreuse and learn a new lingo for this new place. At the same time, she'd better restrain her wayward imagination, which might, momentarily, sweep her away from the here and now. Such impulses to escape were dangerous.

Kind Dr. Arce, who understood in part, had suggested a diary, a record of thoughts and memories. Cath had agreed to try, although she had a skepticism amounting to distaste for all forms of therapy, self-helpism, and "recovery," a reaction, she supposed, to her parents, who'd been giddy, faddish people very taken with "self-realization." In childhood, Cath had accepted their eccentricities, although she'd been vaguely embarrassed by their hippie dress and slovenly housekeeping.

When she grew older, she'd become increasingly irritated by the odd mix of frivolity and earnestness with which they cherished their psychic energies and pursued a movable feast of enthusiasms, from locating the "inner child" to dancing naked in the woods, accompanied by the beat of badly made drums. Her friends alternately thought them "neat" and peculiar, but Cath had longed for normal parents, the sort who hold recognizable religious beliefs, run the household, and behave like grown-ups.

While her parents evaded conventional roles, Cath found the order she craved in music. She insisted on studying the violin and, later, singing. She loved the scales and exercises, the routine of practice, even the salutary terrors of recitals. Her taste ran to firm tempi and polyphonic complexity. Bach, Monteverdi, and Vivaldi became her gods, because she needed a structure for life, which, otherwise, bled off at the edges and became unmanageable, unintelligible. Here Cath stopped to open her notebook. *Why?* she wrote and stopped again. Why had she been so ill-adapted to her parents?

They were kind, if self-absorbed. Interesting people. Inclined, even overly inclined, to fun, to good times, to novelties and recreations: she could certainly have been born into much less agreeable circumstances. But the family hadn't worked, somehow, and she had to admit that the disenchantment had been mutual. Her parents'd had hopes, a sort of New Age millennialism, Cath decided, invested not in a new world, but in a new person. They'd expected her to be free of all the old baggage: a new child for a new age, preserved from all that had hitherto held back the human soul by their impeccable child rearing. When she turned out to be just another ordinary kid with more than the ordinary anxieties, they'd been disappointed.

The more so, she recalled now, because she'd had the appropriately New Age gift of genuine, nonpharmacologically produced visions: eyes in the sun, light streaming out of flowers, shadows uncoiling like snakes, and unfamiliar faces that peeked from the corners of mirrors. It was a sobering thought that the shadowy waves which warned her of Raoul were not unique. Florida had been not just a symptom of her illness but a continuation of something she thought she had left behind in childhood.

Oddly enough, with so much gone, discarded, ignored, Cath remembered the very last of those curious visionary moments. She had been here, in fact, visiting her great-aunt Elizabeth, her favorite relative, another refugee from eccentricity and disorder. It was late summer and Cath was on her way to pick the blackberries that grew in a field near the house. She'd crossed the blotchy green summer shade of the wood, climbed over the barway, and reached the sunny, undulating pasture that curved down toward the state road and the forest beyond. Something made her stop at the crest of the first hill just as a breeze ruffled the meadow. The grasses, consumed by their own vitality and glowing like the sun, turned the earth to fire, and the material world dissolved in waves around her.

Quite classic, Cath learned later. The mystical unity of all life was the bedrock experience; whether you called it God or the Oversoul or the Tao or the Spirit Vision, the psychological experience was identical. As a college student, she'd read William James and his scholarly descendants with interest, for, by that time, the pasture and all previous visitations were purely theoretical, objects for scholarship, phenomena safely in her past. She'd learned to lose herself in music—a safer and more predictable experience—and she had acquired a modern picture of the world in the energy webs of physics, themselves mystical, but domesticated, like music, by mathematics. Cath had held on to those abstractions, clung to the surface of things, and maintained all boundaries and categories—until Derek. She thought now that Derek might have marked the start, the resumption. Though she could not be sure, she sensed that Derek was somehow out of category, a creature beyond calibration.

She wrote, *Derek, the start. Out of category,* and stopped. She wasn't anxious to examine her feelings about him or to speculate on his for her. Fortunately, he had been working such long hours preparing for the big Easter services and for the spring sacred concert that they'd hardly had two words without Yvonne being there, which, to Cath's mind, was like not talking at all. They had been alone only once, that few minutes in the music room when she'd sung "Pulchra es" and nearly collapsed and he'd remarked that she'd always been a pagan. An odd thing for a music minister to say, Cath thought, but then she wasn't even sure that the conversation was real. She might have dreamed it, and Derek, unfailingly polite and thoughtful, might never have risked more than the superficial remarks he passed at dinner to her and Yvonne.

And yet, it was in character, now that she thought about it, for the Derek she did remember, not the husband or the music minister but the boy she'd met at school, the man, really: he'd been a graduate assistant at the start of her junior year. The school had expected great things of Derek Tolland; he was already semilegendary, in the way that certain students, outstanding or of outstanding personality, impose themselves, not just on their classmates but on the institution.

Derek was a dual major in conducting and piano, and he was a very impressive instrumentalist, particularly on bravura passages and big, showy pieces where a certain emptiness of heart—Cath winced as she saw what she'd written—could be concealed with flamboyance. Derek had real charisma; he came onstage like a panther and absolutely seized a hall. Without any obvious showmanship, he had the audience on the alert before the first note was struck.

And then, how he played! Big gestures, drama on every note, a way of shaking his thick hair and letting his eyes sweep over the audience before plunging back into the thickets of notes and bringing up a strong, clear, melodic line. While others, who were perhaps more technically perfect, more creative, or more subtle, shyly offered their interpretations, Derek overwhelmed an audience. He took them hostage to his personality; he dazzled and confounded. *Listen to this!* he seemed to be saying. *Watch my hands. Lose yourself in my music.* He was irresistible in person, and he should, by rights, have had a very good concert career.

The difficulty was that he never sounded quite as good in recordings as he did live, and tapes were essential for submission to the various competitions and to agents. Even she, who'd adored him, even she had had reservations, even about recital tapes where he had entranced the audience, where she'd been moved almost to tears. Those wonderful performances lost their luster on rehearing: the dazzling crescendos seemed bombastic; the rippling arpeggios, a little too schmaltzy; the shape of the whole, clear, indeed, but lacking in subtlety. It was baffling and distressing, but like certain wines, Derek's riveting performances didn't travel well. They required the darkened concert hall, the torpor of Sunday afternoons, the rustle of programs, broken suddenly by the thin, handsome magician who swept onstage and bowed, his teeth gleaming in a smile, his eyes intense and predatory. When he shot his long white wrists and hands free of his cuffs and poised his fingers over the keys, you felt anything was possible. He created that aura of possibility and drama—and maybe danger, too, though that was ridiculous at a concert, at an entertainment, unless you thought of rock concerts, where a certain ersatz danger is the stock-in-trade. Yet Derek produced that rare, energizing frisson; he created suspense.

She remembered him walking off at a year-end recital. A group of high school students who were considering the school had been brought to the auditorium. Only a couple of them were music majors, and some of the rest became noisy. Derek stopped dead in the middle of the Chopin F Minor Fantasie, said he wouldn't tolerate discourtesy, and walked off. Everyone was stunned and embarrassed, but when he came out five minutes later and restarted the movement, the auditorium was dead quiet. Although the incident had distressed her, Cath had admired him; she'd thought she would never have been able to pull off anything like that herself.

Recalling that day, she laughed uneasily. She had done all sorts of surprising things since, including the night bus, and something else, which was teasing at the back of her mind, that she was sure put interrupting a concert quite in the shade.

But Derek was truly a fine performer, and only his absolute dependence on a live audience had steered him to conducting, where he was good with the orchestra and absolutely brilliant with the chorus. On the podium, Derek was genial, dogmatic, scathing, and inspiring by turn. Singing her first big aria in the Mozart B Minor, Cath had been both terrified and enchanted by him.

He was delightful with her right from the start, patient, gentle, encouraging. She had a vivid memory of a practice room in the old music building, now supplanted, she understood, by a modern facility. The practice spaces were all much the same, hot and cramped with upright pianos, a music stand or two, sometimes an extra straight chair. The ceilings were acoustic tiles darkened with age and stained by furtive drips from leaky plumbing; the walls, cream paint; the floors, green and brown squares. She remembered the snatches of sound in the hallways: a woodwind, vocal scales, Bach unaccompanied from a violinist, the scherzo of one of the big piano concertos. In the particular room of her memory, there was always the sound of a metronome and of her own voice, sweet but dwarfed by the cramped space and heavy insulation. On the day in question, she was having difficulties with one of the intervals in the "Incarnatus est."

"You're straining," Derek said. His eyes were brilliant as he glanced up from the score. It was curious how clearly she remembered his eyes, his glance; just that. His face, now that she saw him every day, had the mobility and indefiniteness of daily life. In memory, the glance was sharp, finished; she could remember exactly how he looked up, how he took in her difficulties, how, it seemed to her, he had registered her whole personality. He played the figure on the piano. "You're going to find the note just fine; your pitch is perfect, and you'll have enough breath if you relax."

Yes, she'd felt that was true, but she'd needed to hear it, to be encouraged, to know she'd be fine. She needed his approval. At the same time, when she was trying to concentrate everything on the "Incarnatus," she was intensely aware of his eyes. They reminded her of some feral creature, their extraordinary vividness like eyeshine at night, like the sly glance of a wild animal on some errand of its own. Sitting on her aunt's old chaise, she asked herself if there had been darkness even then, but that was impossible; she was not ready to think that. What she remembered clearly was her heart beating, a dizziness of desire; then she straightened her back, took a deep breath, raised her chin, began again, for anything else was impossible. Derek was engaged, as everyone knew, to Esther Neilson, a terrific cellist, who had a debut coming up with the Hartford. Esther Neilson was a serious musician who planned a career, and who was, Cath thought in a moment of despair, every glamorous thing that she was not.

"Yes, yes," Derek said. "Don't rush, don't rush it, yes!" He stopped beating time with his hand, put in the bass line, and at that instant the music took off; Cath felt the change from concentrating, counting, struggling, thinking over every note, to sudden freedom and the mathematical magic of beauty.

When they finished, he smiled. "That will do very nicely," he said. And it had. Even the recordings of their performances together were excellent. Perhaps because her voice was small, Derek constrained his flamboyance; perhaps it was something, after all, in her interpretation, not his, but their work together was charming. Cath might not have remembered that if she hadn't found a couple of tapes in the bookcase: the junior year concert with the B Minor Mass, the big senior year concert, and her senior recital. She remembered what Derek had said about the latter: "Magic, just magic. It's a damn shame you didn't get a bigger voice."

She'd been delighted, nonetheless.

"A bigger voice," said Derek, "a bigger chest. Inside that little frame, there's a one-thousand-pound soprano trying to get out." He'd kissed her when he said that and she'd laughed. They were on different terms by then. March or April of senior year? Yes, they'd started going out together by then. That was after the inexplicable horror of Esther Neilson's suicide. Derek had been devastated, as all Esther's friends had been, by surprise, by helplessness, by the guilt of as yet undetermined omissions and failures. Everyone who knew her asked, *Could I have stopped this terrible thing? Should I have known? What did I do?*

Of course, it was worse for Derek, her lover, who had known her best, who had been engaged to her, who had seen all his assumptions overturned. The pagans and primitives, Cath thought, were right: death, especially violent death, is polluting, and Derek was the proof, for from that time he lost the golden glow of promise, the general assumption of celebrity and greatness. He did not get, as they'd all expected, the summer internship at Tanglewood or the grant he'd hoped for his doctorate. In taking her life, Esther had somehow darkened his spirit, so that his intensity and magnetism took on another, less attractive coloration, and the inevitability of his success was somehow lost. He became like the rest of them, doomed to struggle with the appalling odds of their difficult profession.

Cath hadn't thought about that. She had felt the emptiness in his life, not just the romantic emptiness, the grief, but something else, a terrible void of meaning that reminded her irresistibly of her parents. But while they had been frivolous, playful to the end, Derek had a deep and troubling anger. He was a more forceful, passionate, and dramatic personality, and the emptiness in him exerted an almost gravitational psychic attraction. Foolish and infatuated, Cath had rushed to fill it. She had not listened to the gossip, the hints; she had closed her eyes to the ferocity of his desire, to the warnings of his despair. She had even ignored Yvonne, his alter ego, his double, the uncharmed shadow at the edge of his once charmed life.

In retrospect, Cath was surprised that she had overlooked Yvonne, but she had. And then, Derek had needed Cath; she was the one person, the one person alive, who was supremely necessary for him, and Cath was not used to being either important or necessary. His need gave a shape to her life, so she had offered up her small voice, her competence on the violin, her pliant personality, her not unpleasing person, her absolute faith in him, and he had accepted.

Cath made a question mark in her notebook and drew a series of boxes around it. What should she have asked? What should she have known? What did she ignore that evening, that evening in the auditorium as they were finishing up practice? The house lights were down, and they were alone in the white cone cast by the stage lights above the piano. He had switched on the recorder, and they sat together, companionably, on the piano bench as they listened. He made a few notes—stronger attack on one phrase, more color on another—but Cath could tell that he was pleased. She had chosen a Bach aria in addition to some lieder and several American songs.

"You have a talent for sacred music," he said.

She shrugged; this was a topic that skirted difficult things, troubling memories, the essential shapelessness of the universe. Religion, mysticism, all spiritual things were slightly awkward, and Cath wondered if she had incautiously mentioned some of her childhood experiences, if she had confided in Derek, if she had trusted him too much. And yet what he said was true: the compensation for her rather small, rather "white" sound was a corresponding intensity and purity of tone that lent itself to certain pieces of high spiritual yearning.

But she had not needed to discuss these things, for he took her hand, suddenly, impulsively, the way he did all important things. It was hard, after all these years and the night bus and everything that had happened, to recapture the force and power of his concentration or the hypnotic intensity of his eyes. Familiarity breeds a certain domestication of sensation, even with powerful personalities; at the time, she'd felt her will shriveling like a leaf in a flame. "You can save me," he had said. "You're the only one in the world who can save me."

Sitting in her aunt's chaise, Cath shivered. The irrationality of his demand, when she had been hypnotized by him, fascinated by him, overpowered spiritually and intellectually, staggered her, yet it seemed that she *had* saved him, at least temporarily. From what and for just how long were the questions, but before she could consider them, she heard a door bang downstairs and Yvonne's footsteps in the hall. Cath stuck her notebook under the cushion of the chaise, where it fit much better than any deluxe, leather-bound volume. She was reading a Ruth Rendall novel by the time Yvonne appeared upstairs.

"I bought a lot of canned goods. Stop and Shop had a two-for-one special," her sister-in-law said. "Want to give me a hand?" Yvonne was trying to get Cath to do "a little more each day," as she put it.

"Sure," Cath said, although she didn't feel like moving, and going downstairs seemed like an excursion, if not a journey.

Two paper grocery bags sat on the kitchen table. While Yvonne went back out to the car for more, Cath carried the bags to the pantry and started unloading an assortment of spaghetti sauces and canned vegetables. She was busy arranging these on the shelves when Yvonne struggled in with two more paper bags and a bulging plastic carrier dangling off her wrist like an oversized jellyfish. "I got some really good buys today. It pays to shop, to watch the specials." She put the plastic bags down in the pantry. "More canned goods. They're not too heavy for you?"

"No," said Cath. Yvonne was being thoughtful and pleasant; she was in one of the up moods that always made Cath suspicious. Yvonne, after all, had tried to convince Derek that she was lying.

"Leave out a can of spaghetti sauce."

Cath set one on the table.

"With mushrooms. You know that Derek likes mushrooms in his spaghetti sauce."

That culinary detail had slipped Cath's mind. She replaced the plain sauce on the shelf and brought out one with mushrooms. "You might have bought them all with mushrooms."

"They're for other casseroles. Busy-day food."

Casseroles, especially spaghetti-sauce-based casseroles, had a depressing ring, reminding Cath of church suppers and cafeteria food. "I don't know where your office is. Where are you working now?" Cath hadn't bothered to ask before. Surely that was rude.

"The local office in Putnam. *Selling* is hardly the word; the market out here is so flat. But it's the only solution when I'm trying to do everything around the house and take care of you, too."

"I'm feeling quite a bit better," Cath said, starting on another bag of cans and bottles.

"Well, the realty company will certainly be delighted to hear that. They told me I could go back to the suburban office anytime. I was top of the sales chart, Gold Key Club, before I moved out here. Of course, I'm one of the best out this way."

"Of course," Cath said. It went without saying that Yvonne was terrific at whatever she attempted. Absolutely terrific.

"If you get back on your feet, I'll need to do a little more parish work." Yvonne always referred to Saint Martin's as "the parish," like something out of Jane Austen. "Things have gotten behind since you took off." That was also Yvonne: a certain inconsistency of tone. "Since you took off" was not, Cath would bet, how real "parish ladies" talked. There was something faintly bogus about Yvonne, which intrigued Cath at the same time that it worried her.

"I could fix dinner," Cath suggested. She'd tasted Yvonne's spaghetti sauce, and, without having any real evidence, Cath was confident that she could cook up something better. With or without mushrooms.

"A new interest! You were never terribly domestic. You were always scheduled right through—" Yvonne broke off abruptly.

"Scheduled?"

"Rehearsals and things. You always needed a lot of rehearsals and practice time."

"I imagined I had a job," said Cath. She must have. The last few days, she'd been checking the bills that came in the mail, and during an extensive rummage through her desk that afternoon, she'd found one of Derek's pay stubs. Even considering that the house was hers free and clear, she must have had to work.

"You have a small income," Yvonne said reluctantly. "Some sort of trust, nothing very much. That's been your contribution." She assumed a martyred and vaguely disapproving expression.

"I see," said Cath, who felt a trust was plausible, although there had been no records, no check receipts. But then, her desk had been virtually emptied, and the one thing she'd known as soon as she sat down at it was that this was where she used to pay the bills. "How often do the checks come?"

"The lawyer sends them through monthly," Yvonne said.

"Does this lawyer have a name?"

"I hope you don't think we're stealing your money," Yvonne said with a show of indignation. "Everything goes into the household budget. And for extras for you—Saint Martin's benefit package isn't that generous when it comes to mental illness."

The pantry was the cave of the winds, a howling abyss of darkness and hot air, but Cath pulled herself back from temper and said, "As you advise, I'm trying to 'do a little more each day.' I just want to know what our finances are like—after all the costs of my illness."

"We're managing," Yvonne said, more cheerfully. "I sold a house last month in spite of everything. Persistence, persistence, that's the key to sales; in early, home late." When she talked about work, Yvonne looked almost unnaturally bright and determined, like someone in an infomercial. Cath thought that her sister-in-law would be a terrifying person to buy a house from.

"The parish made a contribution," Yvonne added. "A special appeal; everyone was very kind; of course, they all think the world of Derek. And I believe I've done my share, too."

How humiliating, Cath thought. "I must thank them," she said, pleased with her self-control, although she felt like temper or even tears. She felt she could weep in an instant out of frustration, fear, and irritation. She could, if she weren't careful.

"Oh, I've done that already. We couldn't rely on you to do that."

Horrid plural! *What sort of marriage have I had,* Cath wondered, *with Yvonne and Derek in such solidarity?* "Perhaps some flowers for the sanctuary," she suggested.

"It's not necessary. Everyone understands your situation. And under the circumstances, I think they'd just as soon forget the matter."

Cath's heart sank. She could imagine the detailed and dramatic story Yvonne had put round. Yvonne with her smarmy ideas, her resentment, her anger about being detained in Florida. Cath wondered how she'd face the people in the choir and the friendly string and woodwinds players.

"Just the same, I was the one they helped," Cath said stubbornly.

"I'll call the florist this week. But I want to talk to the lawyer, too. If you'll tell me his name, I won't have to go through the phone books." As soon as she spoke, Cath realized that her address book had also been missing from the desk.

"If you've got to know, if you don't trust us to handle your affairs a moment longer after all the time we've taken care of you, it's Beausoleil."

"Luc Beausoleil? Right here in the village?"

Yvonne looked satisfied, as if she'd caught Cath at something. "That's right."

"The money came from my aunt Elizabeth, then? With the house?" Clever Aunt Elizabeth with her stock market "hobby" and her modest land purchases, all paid for by her appetite for hard work. Cath remembered being told as a child how Aunt Elizabeth had started an elegant little bed-and-breakfast for parents visiting the private school just up the road. This was long before B and B's became one of the chief cottage industries in the region. Aunt Elizabeth had parlayed the success of that establishment into a top-paying job running the region's only big, expensive inn.

"I don't know why you had to ask if you remembered all that," said Yvonne.

"It's the way the mind works," Cath said. "I've tried to explain that to you. Everything comes in pieces."

"The way *your* mind works, anyway."

Cath ignored this. There was something else she needed to know. "So with this trust fund—I never had to work, is that right?"

Yvonne did not reply instantly, and, in her caution, Cath sensed a lie. Well, she was alert for that, because she knew Aunt Elizabeth had died only seven years ago. Just before Cath had married Derek.

"Well, not recently," Yvonne said. "Your health has been unreliable for some time."

"Some time," Cath repeated.

"More or less as long as I've know you."

"So I was sick even when Derek and I were married?"

71

"Derek's got the patience of a saint," Yvonne said.

Cath was willing to consider that proposition, for their marriage, even at best, could not have been unalloyed happiness, but she was already feeling tired. As small a task as putting away the groceries had exhausted her. Did seeing Luc Beausoleil really matter? Did looking over the expenditures? She'd be better advised to trust her husband and avoid worry.

"Nobody knows what you've put him through," Yvonne added.

Cath retaliated by saying, "Someone's cleared out my desk."

"Your desk? That was never much more than an ornament," Yvonne said. "I've kept it dusted and so on."

"Including the checkbook," Cath said.

"We had to take that from you a while ago. When you began to get really bad. Back and forth, three of us writing checks, everything was getting mixed up. So now Derek writes the checks. He has for ages."

"That's kind of him, when he's so busy," Cath said, but she felt a deep uneasiness. She had been sick, she knew that: the night bus and the bay and Raoul and the hospital were all arrayed in evidence. But that she'd been so sick as to be irrational, incapable of simple trans-actions, and for an extended period of time, was frightening. She could feel her heart fluttering and the sweat breaking out on her forehead. But maybe it wasn't true. She had to keep that possibility open, for Yvonne lied. Cath had to remember that, and to be careful, even when she was dropping with weariness. "But of course, Derek has the pa-tience of a saint," she said and left the kitchen.

6

THEY HAD AN EARLY SUPPER, and Cath went for a walk afterwards. She put on an old pair of garden boots for the ticks and took the wagon track across the pasture to the river, flowing swift and spring full, the ripples glazed pink from the warm light in the west. Recently, Yvonne had started hovering whenever Cath showed signs of leaving the house, so tonight she said she was just going out to look at the garden. She fiddled around a few minutes weeding the lettuce seedlings until she saw the kitchen was empty, then walked down the slope toward the water.

Don't do too much, you've got to get built up, mustn't overdo. Cath could have taken this for concern, but she was skeptical; she knew Yvonne wanted to keep an eye on her. One day in exasperation, Cath said, "I'm hardly going to throw myself in the river," and saw Yvonne's face flush with anger before settling into an unconvincing anxiety.

"You can't afford to get tired out," her sister-in-law said. "Not in your present emotional state."

"My present emotional state is that I'm bored being indoors," Cath said, and she went out to the yard. Yvonne appeared half an hour later to persuade her to come back inside.

Tonight, though, Yvonne had *let down her guard, been caught napping,* perhaps, or *hadn't been focused,* as the sports announcers like to say, so Cath was free to wander along the marshy side of the river. As she walked, she thought again that she'd like a dog, perhaps a boat, too. Rowing might be good for her. She'd have to see if there was money for a boat; a canoe or a kayak, they weren't too expensive, nor too heavy to paddle. Of course, Derek and Yvonne might discourage such a purchase, for, increasingly, Cath had the feeling that she was expected to stay in a kind of purdah as punishment for the night bus and for other unspecified, but serious, failings. These were never discussed. Instead, her health did duty for all sorts of things. After being exhorted to "do a little more every day" when she was totally exhausted, Cath was now cautioned against exertion. There had been real consternation when she suggested having an elderly bike repaired; both Yvonne and Derek had brought up the hills and the traffic, as well as the cost of repairing what was very nearly an antique.

"We'll take a ride to the state forest at the end of the week if you need to get out. You used to like the state forest," Derek said, while Yvonne noted that Cath was still not "doing much around the house" and not "showing much energy." The bike would be too tiring, a bad idea.

Cath picked up a stone and skimmed it over the water, which looked as smooth and tight as the sheets on a well-made bed. She remembered swimming in a pond—where had that been? At school perhaps? Or here? Or somewhere else now forgotten? What she remembered was how a breeze had come up, making her aware of a ripple in the water, as if liquid were a kind of tissue, a sheet with mysterious connections and tensions. Watching the river fade into darkness, Cath thought that she believed in mysterious connections, in sudden jumps of energy and enlightenment, in the surface tension that preserved reality.

After she startled a pair of mallards and a big heron that squawked away on slow, heavy wings, Cath walked home. She returned to luck: except for the new wing, the house was dark. Only a few stray notes came from the studio, where Derek must be reading through his scores, but Cath could hear that Yvonne had one of the Chopin nocturnes on the living room stereo.

Musically, Yvonne concerned herself solely with Derek's career, with what selections would be suitable for the choirs, with scheduling recitals that would be prestigious. But though she only went to concerts if her brother was performing, she sometimes shut herself away with the stereo, always alone, always in the dark, to listen to the big classics of the piano repertory. She might listen for two or three hours at a stretch, and that solitary communion was one of the few things Cath liked about her sister-in-law. Cath found it hard to imagine the joys of a life in real estate, promoting the *fixer-upper,* the *executive property,* or the *starter home.* And she found it impossible to imagine Yvonne's curious, obsessive role as Derek's sister. But Cath could imagine sitting in the darkened living room with the pink light behind the trees, saturated squares of color on the bare boards, a liquid flash of lavender and gold in the big circular mirror, and, in the shadows of the bookcase, the key thing, the stereo with its glowing lights and softly reverberant voice.

She and Derek had invested in a good system that put out a remarkably crisp, realistic sound. If she closed her eyes, the big amps took Cath straight to a perfected concert hall where she could hear every note without any of the distractions, the stray coughs, the muffed notes, the little imperfections, which, to her mind, made for the excitement of a live performance and which she, being a fallible performer herself, easily forgave.

Yvonne, conversely, preferred the stereo, craved perfection, liked a known commodity, a famous name. Chopin tonight, perhaps that new young pianist Anawagan Pratt. Yvonne would listen to a performance over and over until she knew every nuance, then she would put the CD away, and there would be days or weeks of silence before she would again take over the living room for long, seancelike sessions with the stereo. Sometimes, if Cath or Derek had already staked out the territory, Yvonne would descend late, after everyone else was in bed, to listen on her earphones. Cath could understand that, too. She could understand a craving for music, for distraction, for an entry to another, private world.

Cath went around the side of the house and opened the studio door.

"You must have gone for a walk," Derek said by way of greeting. So he had noticed her absence.

"It's a beautiful evening," Cath said. She stepped out of her garden boots and put them on the stoop. "I saw a great blue heron down along the river."

"Must be wet down there," her husband said. "Full of ticks. Watch you don't get bitten."

Cath dutifully checked the legs of her slacks for dog ticks and for the tiny, but dangerous, deer ticks.

"Where's Yvonne? Didn't she go with you?"

"Yvonne's listening to the stereo," Cath said. "I didn't want to disturb her."

Derek sighed and played a few bars of the *Moonlight Sonata* with a soft and yearning melancholy. "You know Yvonne was truly gifted. She had the most beautiful hands, the most wonderful rhythmic sense."

"That's doubtless why she's never been enthusiastic about my playing."

"More talent than either one of us," Derek said, and Cath knew, somehow, that this was a rare admission. "She should have been the performer, not me."

"Her hand," said Cath, who realized that she hadn't thought about the subject at all. She had noticed Yvonne's hand, observed the gloves, registered the fact but no more: Cath had had problems of her own.

"Yes, her hand."

"Was it an accident?"

"Of course it was an accident," Derek said angrily. "No one ever suggested anything else. A totally freakish accident."

"I didn't mean it wasn't. I just don't remember what you told me."

"It was an accident, that's what I told you." He was tense with a contained, half-suppressed anger Cath found familiar.

"We don't need to talk about it," she said. "Not if it upsets you." She had wanted a quiet, pleasant talk with Derek. Perhaps some music, perhaps the "Pulchra es" again. She wanted to look well and normal, ready to get off the night bus and face the world.

"We do if you have any questions," Derek said. "If you have questions and doubts."

"I don't have questions or doubts," Cath said. "I've simply forgotten. I don't remember whether I ever had doubts." As soon as she said that, she knew that once she would have reassured him. Once she would not have hesitated at all.

"Of course," said Derek, "it's very awkward when you remember some things and forget others."

Cath shrugged. There was really nothing to say to that.

"The accident was partly my fault," he said. "But you can be at fault in an accident, a pure accident."

Perhaps it didn't matter whether she remembered or not, Cath thought. Perhaps he needed to tell her again, perhaps he needed to remember—or to convince—himself.

"We were at the lake when it happened. My parents had a cabin on Schroon Lake in the Adirondacks. We rent it now." He played another few bars of the sonata, but his touch was heavier, the notes sounded harsher; it really wasn't his sort of piece, and Derek seemed nervous.

Odd, Cath thought, how clearly nervousness comes through in music. Other emotions are hit and miss: great passion and deep feeling sometimes fall flat, but nerves have a way of proclaiming themselves.

"You never had a boat, did you?"

"No," said Cath. "We never had boats."

Derek smiled then. "Poor Cath," he said. He had always liked to be the one to introduce her to new things; he enjoyed a superiority of knowledge.

"I was thinking tonight I'd like a boat," she said, in part to shift the conversation away from what she could sense was *deep water, shoals and reefs.* She searched for but did not find another pertinent nautical cliché, another neat phrase to encapsulate the situation. "A canoe or a kayak for the river would be fun."

"Boats are dangerous," Derek said, but without the sort of heavy certainty that meant he would oppose one.

"Life is dangerous," Cath said. "Buses, bikes, what isn't?"

Instead of answering, Derek resumed the first movement of the *Moonlight,* and Cath sat down in the straight chair near the piano. Although normally she liked few things better than sitting listening to Derek play, she was waiting, not for the familiar chords and melodies but for the rest of the story. "You never know what will change your life," he said, dropping the volume without immediately ceasing to play. "We took the boat out one afternoon when Mom and Dad were away getting groceries with the car. It was just a little rowboat with a kicker on it. We'd been allowed to use it for years. Years and years. We were thirteen and fifteen then. Experienced boaters."

The running line in the right hand reminded Cath of drops of water falling, drops of water like rain, like tears, very soft, final, and inevitable.

"You'd think experienced boaters would be all right, wouldn't you, Cath?"

"You never know," she said. It seemed to her sometimes that she was still on a metaphoric night bus, a refugee from some other life. Time is an illusion, physicists said, but if there is only the present, her sense of being caught between past and future was an illusion, and she was permanently trapped. Cath realized that Derek had stopped playing and was speaking in a quiet, strained voice, telling her, as he had indeed told her before, the story of the lake, the boat, the kicker, his sister's terrible mutilation. Curious how memory comes back. Cath could see the lake's weedy brown bottom, the way the surface turned from blue to green to steel gray as afternoon clouds boiled up over the humid forest. She could see Derek and Yvonne, thirteen and fifteen, the gifted, handsome Tolland children, heading off in the boat, gliding into the shadows of big boulders and ledges and trolling for sunfish, bass, and perch along a marshy stretch. Was that the problem? Weeds, reeds, some old line tangled in the kicker? Was that the reason their motor seized up? And what was *their* context? Had they brought oars they could have used? Or just some strange emotional baggage? She couldn't remember, but she could see the boat.

"It looked like a storm," he said. "We thought we should get back. Otherwise we could have rowed."

Isn't that the way, Cath thought. There are always reasons, contingencies, little details that push toward one decision or another. What had pushed her toward the night bus? That was probably more important for her to remember than how Yvonne lost her right thumb and part of her forefinger, but what Cath saw in her mind's eye was the boat rocking gently on a sheet of water turning silver with the coming storm, and Yvonne, the older, dominant sibling, impatiently pulling out the weeds or old fish line or whatever the propeller blades had picked up.

"The motor was dead. I never touched the starter, everything was off, completely stalled," Derek said. "Then the engine jumped to life and she screamed."

"She might have been killed," Cath said quickly. "You saved her life."

"The kicker stopped again right away. She was making the most terrible sounds. Can you ruin vocal cords that way, I wonder? Yvonne used to sing quite well. She might have concentrated on her voice and had a career in music, after all, but she never sang again. Her voice died right there on the lake. That's what sticks in my mind, her screaming and the blood, just like fish blood, staining the water and pooling in the bottom of the boat." He hit the keys in a violent dissonance. "But you're right, of course, I saved her life. I have to remember that. You know I married you, Cath, for your timely reminders of the better side of my personality. That's true. Don't you believe me?"

"I suppose I'd hoped for something more romantic."

Derek gave a weak smile. "There was that, too. But timely reminders are not to be undervalued. Yvonne is inclined to undervalue—though she has a reason, you see: that blood in the water. I did what was necessary. I had my T-shirt and an old rag: pressure to stop the bleeding, a simple tourniquet. We were lucky that the engine started up again right away—she must have cleared just enough from the blades, just enough to ruin her and save her—so that we could run across the lake to the general store for help and adult supervision. Our generation never had quite enough adult supervision, did it, Cath?"

"I don't think our generation knew enough adults," Cath agreed.

"So we had to improvise. I must remember that. You're not the only one who's forgotten important things. Yvonne and I, especially Yvonne—she was two years older—we had to improvise and make up adult life as we went along. She was white as a sheet when they lifted her out of the boat. She hadn't looked; she didn't know. She just knew her hand hurt. But I knew everything, and I had to tell our parents."

"Oh, yes," said Cath, "parents are the hardest people of all to tell." She thought momentarily of her own parents, of their undying hopes for themselves, of their extravagant, pathetic ambitions for enlightenment and self-development which had led them to the ashram and disaster. She remembered *that* very well.

"They'd expected great things from Yvonne. They'd seen her talent right from the start. Did you know she'd played with the local symphony when she was twelve?"

"Yes," said Cath, though that was something else she'd forgotten.

"Very well, too. My talent was slower to develop. I began to be serious about music only after Yvonne's accident."

"Boys mature more slowly," said Cath.

"Do they? I always thought of my musical seriousness as an exchange for Yvonne's, a direct exchange in one sense, because the focus of parental interest turned my way. That's when I was sent to boarding school. Tuition was a financial strain, but a change was considered best after everything that had happened. I'm afraid Yvonne did without so that I could get a superior education. That was really not fair, was it?"

Cath wanted to say that she thought Yvonne had made up for it since, but that would have been cruel. Instead she said, "You've been a devoted brother."

"Yes, I've been that. And a devoted husband. Don't you think I've been a devoted husband? I wanted to be, please believe that I wanted to be, Cath."

His voice was penetrating, and its particular timbre reverberated in her bones. "Yes," said Cath. She could believe that, the wanting to be, that is.

"We can fail," he said sadly, "even when we are trying our best."

Cath wanted to ask if that was why he had not come to Florida, but she had become cautious; she was living with *be careful* and *keep alert,* the lessons she had learned down south. "I wanted to ask you something," she said, "since you're a devoted husband."

Derek began the sonata again, and this time Cath thought the *Moonlight* a good choice for him: it spoke of memory and longing.

"I'm feeling so much better I'd like to go to church with you this Sunday. Not for the choir," she added quickly. "But I would like to see some of the people I know. I think it would help to bring everything back. I've lost my context, Dr. Arce said, and I need to start making connections." Cath realized that she was speaking far too fast, that for some reason this whole topic made her nervous.

"Surely for the service, too," Derek said.

Cath smiled; he was the one who had called her a pagan. "We are all in need of grace," she said.

"The church in town is supposed to be nice. The Congregationalist. The Catholic church, too. Since you are hardly doctrinaire, either one would be less effort."

"It would be good for me to see the people I know in the choir. And to hear them sing, too. You'd like me to come, wouldn't you?" Cath asked.

She felt she had him there, and he said, "Of course. The choir hasn't been the same without you. Especially the soprano section. But it's a long morning when you've been so tired and . . ."

There was something else, Cath could tell.

"And?"

"Nothing, just we don't want to wear you out when you are finally starting to seem like your self. Like our old Cath." He slid over and patted the piano bench. "What shall we sing?" he asked.

Cath came and sat down beside him. "Your pleasure," she said, but added, "I could take the second car"—she didn't like to say "Yvonne's car"—"and come home early."

"No, no, we'll work something out. Yvonne can bring you home if you get tired. We'll talk about it later with her."

Cath wanted to object to this, but he was already into the introduction of the Steven Foster ballad, "Jeanie with the Light Brown Hair." He'd transposed it for her, and she let herself be beguiled by the sweet melody, which floated her voice effortlessly around the lyrics. Derek smiled at her, not the smile she thought of as his captivating smile, all teeth and flashing eyes and a calculated charm that got you to accept things you might not want, but the real expression of pleasure and happiness, the happiness which she felt came for him only from music, perhaps only from music with her. That thought brought Cath a mixture of joy and sorrow, which wove its way into the song.

"Lovely," said Derek when the song was finished. "I've found another score for you." He took out a photocopy of a soprano solo and started the accompaniment.

"Oh," said Cath. "That's from the Gorecki, isn't it? The *Symphony of Sorrowful Songs?*"

"This was made for you," Derek said. "Just vocalize. We'll get the Polish written out phonetically later."

Cath tried a little, and yes, it was doable, though she had Dawn Upshaw in her ear, though she'd never reach those empyrean heights. Still, the line was beautiful, and, working on the piece together, she and Derek were happy. She was happy, at least, and maybe he was happy, too, for Derek, unlike Cath, was a master of living in the present. Maybe he could be happy sitting playing the piano, listening to his wife, who—in the ironic jest of his fate—brought out the best in him musically, and then, when she had gone up to bed, exhilarated but noticeably exhausted, he could go into the living room in a very different mood to talk to his sister.

Yvonne was still sitting in the dark with the stereo. Chopin, again. Lately, she had played nothing but Chopin, especially the nocturnes, moody, introspective music of endless subtleties. What did that mean? Derek stood in the dark hallway, half his mind on the clean passage work, the beautiful balance between the treble and the bass lines, the other half on Yvonne, on their situation, on what Cath had taken to calling their *context*. He felt, sometimes, between the two women, that he was suffocating, that he'd complicated his life to the breaking point, that he would have to escape. More carefully, this time.

The Opus 9, no. 1 in B-flat minor: reflective, melancholy; Chopin wrote music that breathed. There was space between the chords and phrases that provided time to reflect, time to wonder, time for God knows what to whisper suggestions to your mind. While seeing the genius of them, Derek was not terribly fond of Chopin's nocturnes. He wondered now about those pauses, the inspiration of a man dying of tuberculosis, of lung disease, of lack of breath. Our dying begins at birth, thought Derek, whose second degree, in theology, had been undertaken, like so much in his life, impulsively, almost reflexively. He had tried, he told Cath, and that, of all the things he'd told her, then and earlier, was the truest.

Fortunately, Derek thought, he had chosen a denomination which values intentionality. His intentions, he thought he could say, had mostly been good. That did not mean, however, that he wanted to listen to more Chopin, or to fill in the blanks, or to see what might stir in those brief, pregnant silences. He tapped on the door to alert Yvonne and then stepped inside and found the lamp switch. As his sister sat up on the couch, a wing of her dark hair fell over one eye, and, with a graceful, languorous gesture, she pushed it back with her left hand, the left hand that had the long, polished nails, the silver link bracelets. There was still something heart-tuggingly glamorous about Yvonne. When he was twelve and thirteen, he had been dazzled, quite overwhelmed. He'd had to escape any way he could. That memory made him abrupt. "Cath wants to go to church on Sunday," he said and watched his sister's face change.

"Really?" she said. She listened to his explanations, his arrangements, but what she heard in his voice was something else. Yvonne realized that he was still susceptible to his wife; she realized that he was thinking of sleeping with Cath again.

They were all three very quiet on the ride into town on Sunday morning. Derek was always preoccupied before a performance, even before church services, which really shouldn't, Cath thought, be considered a performance by a music *minister,* and Yvonne seemed tense and irritable, too. That was nothing unusual, but today, Cath sensed that there was tension between Yvonne and Derek. They hadn't wanted her to come, that was it, or he'd thought it a good idea and Yvonne, a bad. Something like that. Cath had a disagreeable sense of being between the two of them, not a mediator, exactly, more like a physical, or perhaps psychic, barrier. As she watched the green woodlands shrinking into shopping centers and highway ramps, she realized that this had been one of her important roles over the last few years: she'd marked off some division between Derek and Yvonne. Exactly what this division was, she had forgotten, or never known, or maybe learned suddenly and taken the night bus to forget, though she would rather not believe that.

Saint Martin's Church was in the oldest part of town, right over the Hartford border, a section of mansion-sized homes: Queen Annes, Victorians, Four Squares, and Italian Revivals—Yvonne knew all the styles and values to the penny. Some had gone two-and three-family or student rental; some had been restored, gentrified. This was a *transition neighborhood,* Yvonne liked to say, with *fluid property values* that would depend on area crime rates and on whether the schools stayed sound. The area around Saint Martin's was, Cath thought, a nice illustration of the limits of materialism. All this brick and wood, slate and lath and plaster really depended on intangibles, on the suburban state of mind.

One of the more tangible intangibles was Saint Martin's itself. Not just the dark, angular, imposing building, but the congregation's reputation for supporting good music and liberal ideas. There really wasn't a more prestigious church in the area, and along with the gospel of salvation, the parishioners had the satisfaction of picking up a bonus in worldly reputation. Cath suspected that Yvonne saw her efforts on the church's behalf as part and parcel of her real estate endeavors. Certainly, being in the forefront of Saint Martin's fund-raising efforts, doing yeoman work with the music library, serving on this committee and that task force had not hurt her suburban sales at all, and the great grief of the move to the country had been that Yvonne lost the contacts she had built up within the parish.

Derek turned into the narrow drive and snagged the last reserved space behind the church. He immediately hurried into the vestry to put on his robe and see about the choir. Yvonne, who had made a deal about leaving late so that Cath wouldn't have to hang around and get tired, now made as big a production about how much she had to do and how quickly she had to do it. Unwilling to watch her sister-in-law's exertions, Cath said she would go sit in the sanctuary. She knew the choir would be getting into their robes and collars, collecting their music, checking on the order of the hymns; the little string and wood-wind group would already be tuning up and running over difficult passages. This was not a good time to visit.

Thankful for the brilliantly sunny morning, Cath walked around to the front entrance. Two late dogwoods, resplendent as brides, bloomed in big square beds cut in the paving. Their attendants, two smaller borders along the front of the building, had already been filled with pink and white begonias, the whole horticultural ensemble lending a soft prettiness to what was otherwise a rather dark and assertive brownstone edifice capped with a big Victorian tower and a steeply angled roof. As Cath climbed the wide stone steps, she smiled at the elderly man on the door. "Good morning," she said, pleased that she recognized him, glad she did not need to remember his name.

There was a pause, a hesitation; she could see his eyes flicker behind his round bifocals, and, though this tiny interaction took only a second, she felt the radiance drain away from the cloudless blue sky, from the intense green and white of the dogwoods.

"Mrs. Tolland," he said. Cath felt the weight of courtesy on his tongue.

"A lovely morning," she said, her own voice neutral.

He nodded and turned, too quickly, to wave toward someone else arriving from the parking lot.

Cath stepped past him into the foyer. Notice board, extra chairs, door to the tower steps, then the double doors into the sanctuary, which was just as she had remembered it: dark wood, high ceiling, a small fortune in stained and painted glass interspersed with plain windows of a sour yellow—a curious choice, she'd always thought—marking the end point of donor money. The pews already held a sprinkling of parishioners, mostly the stiff-jointed and slow-footed who feared being late and maneuvering in a crush. Recognizing several of them, Cath waved. She was about to start down the aisle when they turned away without acknowledgment, and Cath felt her stomach drop.

She stood toward the back, looking around. There was pretty, smartly dressed Mrs. Wilde of the music committee, a fund-raising heavyweight. Cath had once sung at a party she'd given, the Rachmaninov "Vocalise" and some show tunes, "If I Loved You" from *Carousel* included by special request. She remembered the music and Mrs. Wilde's low-cut black dress and a disagreeable sense of being subtly patronized. But Mrs. Wilde was the only one Cath recognized, so she asked, "How are you? Isn't this a lovely day."

Mrs. Wilde stopped a few feet away without putting out her hand, which would have been the friendly thing to do. "You're back," she said without warmth.

"Yes," Cath said eagerly. She hated herself for being nervous, for being eager to talk to the snobbish Jackie Wilde. "Pneumonia in Florida, of all places. It's taken me a while . . ."

"I'm sure it has," Jackie Wilde said, and she moved away toward the center of the church. Cath, still talking, followed her.

"I'm sorry, but we usually sit as a family," Mrs. Wilde said when she stopped by her pew. "I always save seats for my sister-in-law's children." She managed this with a straight face, though the church was still half empty, though such a pleasant morning would tempt the golfers and tennis players, though there was no chance whatsoever of the sister-in-law or her children going without seats.

"Of course," said Cath. "Charity begins at home." She stepped back and looked around, disguising the fact she had been snubbed, searching the congregation for some friendly face. She did not want to sit alone as a curiosity and an occasion for comment, but, with a growing sense of alarm and disorientation, Cath saw that she knew no one else. As in some uneasy dream, the faces, anonymous, unfamiliar, all looked indifferent at best, hostile at worst.

All this time, she had been thinking of Saint Martin's as a place where she was known and liked. She had believed that. She had possessed, not exactly an image, but an emotional conviction which had turned out to be false. In truth, she was virtually a stranger here, a newcomer dubious in some way. For a moment she felt the sway of the night bus; then, with her heart hammering, she took an inconspicuous seat toward the back on the side aisle. Surely there were some things she needed to remember right away.

One was that Derek had not worked for Saint Martin's terribly long. She had known that without taking in the implications. They had left Boston, abruptly, and when they came to Hartford, Cath had not involved herself much with the church except for the music. She had probably not done as much as was expected, as was desired. That might be the reason for her chilly and awkward reception; people are not always charitable when work has to be divvied up. Cath told herself that had to be the reason; she was foolish to feel so nervous, and spineless to think that Yvonne might have been right, that this visit might be too much, that there was some reason, some shameful reason, to avoid her husband's church.

There now, there was the prelude. Bach. She loved Bach, although at this moment she'd have appreciated something lighter. Derek had found some very nice little Venetian pieces from the eighteenth and early nineteenth centuries: cheerful things that raised the proverbial "joyful noise unto the Lord." Cath remembered that they had been well received in concert but not as preludes to the service. Saint Martin's preferred its preludes slow, minor, and penitential.

But Derek did play well, and the choir sounded good. The choir was real, and Derek and the sound of the organ; everything else existed at one remove, on the margins. Cath hardly heard the readings and drifted away during the sermon to a detailed examination of the big window next to her seat: Saint Martin dividing his cloak with a beggar. Saint Martin was on a gray horse done in milky white glass. The animal had large, mulish ears and big shod hooves. The saint himself looked grand but noncommittal, rather like Yvonne when she was being important and managing. His sword was impressive, and the scarlet cloak, beautifully done. Cath thought that the beggar did well to look uneasy and propitiatory when confronted with that blank expression and massive weapon.

Of course, serenity is for saints—and certain psychopaths. Which, she wondered, was Saint Martin? There he was with his horse, his sword; a professional soldier, as she recalled, a killer by trade. But cutting up his uniform to help the poor was extremely unmilitary, the result, surely, of some basic alteration in reality. Such changes were dangerous. Cath understood that.

"Go in peace," said the priest, and the choir sang a Benedictus and a particularly beautiful amen. She always liked the end of services, not just because she sometimes found church boring, but because she liked the idea of benediction and enjoyed the long-drawn, peaceful phrases of assent and completion. The choir sounded very nice, if maybe a tiny bit weak in the soprano section; maybe she was missed after all. Maybe, but with people standing up, talking to their neighbors, returning, in her eyes, to strangeness, Cath did not feel up to visiting anyone. What she wanted to do was to get out as quickly as possible, to pass the dark, dusty space between the doors and reach the sunny sky and the dogwoods.

"You're back, Mrs. Tolland," someone said. "Jason's missed you."

The woman who spoke was large, heavy almost, with a fine, full face, a lot of sandy hair, and freckles.

"I've missed him," Cath blurted out, though she didn't recognize the woman, couldn't recall any Jason, and the idea that she had known this person, had known a Jason, filled her with panic. She clutched her purse and managed to ask, "How is he doing?"

"Very well. He's at the conservatory now. He was so fortunate," the woman said, smiling like one of the blessed. "They've put him with Dr. Bernard in the advanced section. That's Dr. Thomas Bernard, who soloed with the symphony. He told me himself that Jason had been awfully well prepared."

"I'm so pleased," said Cath, though she was choking, though the sanctuary was turning dark, though it seemed to her that the floor with its dark maroon carpet runner had begun rippling like the saint's cloak. "Please, you must excuse me. Please," she said and pushed her way back down the aisle toward the vestry, startling a row of departing parishioners and almost knocking over an elderly woman in a pastel print suit. Cath felt the collision as a distant event, a glimpse of pink and mint green, a wrinkled hand clutching the back of a pew. "Sorry," she said. "I'm so sorry." Then she pushed open the door to the hall, ran past the minister's room and the toilets to Derek's office, and shut the door behind her. She could feel the sweat running down her back; she could hear the wheels, the white noise of the highway, the murmur of fellow travelers, before she pulled herself back from the danger of escape, of an imagination unhooked—or was it *unhinged*—from the here and now, which was Derek's office. Not the big one in Boston, but the one in Saint Martin's with the little side windows that looked out through a screen of greenery to the parking lot. A gray metal desk sat in the middle of the room with a computer on it and a snake of cords running off under a plastic channel in the floor. A typewriter had been relegated to the top of a file cabinet next to open green metal shelves holding scores, additional maroon-bound hymnals, piles of photocopied program notes. These things had a reassuring solidity; these things were familiar, and so was the drawer that Cath opened, quite without thinking, and the next one and the next, until she found not just their current family checkbook, but several previous books of stubs. Feeling she needed something to hold on to, literally and metaphorically, Cath put the two most recent ones in her purse. She was still standing, frightened and half dizzy, holding the purse to her chest, when Yvonne came in.

"I thought you were going to visit with the choir. They're all changed and on their way."

Cath sat down heavily in the chair behind the desk. "You were right," she said. "This was a little too much. I suddenly felt I just had to get away from the crowd."

Yvonne gave her a close, shrewd look. "People will wonder why you came to hide in here," she said, looking round as if she thought Cath might have pilfered a hymnal.

"People won't wonder at all, because hardly anyone knows me," Cath said. "Now I want to go home."

7

LIGHTLY, EFFORTLESSLY, RUNS OF SIXTEENTHS spun off into the quiet morning. As Cath's bow bounced and skipped across the strings, the music of the little Mendelssohn sonata dropped around her. The sound reverberated off the wide chestnut boards and flew out the windows to soak into the green lawn and blend with the sparrows, wrens, and robins burbling in the overgrown shrubs. There was gaiety in the music, an unserious happiness which Cath, playing from memory in the empty music room, would have rated as very serious and very important indeed, if she had been thinking of anything besides the line, the timing, the buoyant, effervescent feel of the whole. If Cath had been stopped right then and asked, she would have said the creation of happiness was one of the most important things in the world and the preservation of that bubbling cheerfulness, one of the great and useful achievements of mankind.

She took the ending chords with big sweeps of her bow, paused, then lowered the instrument and stretched out her shoulders. She had only been playing for a couple of days and although there were some awkward passages and stiff muscles, she already felt better. It was amazing that she had hesitated, that the violin had aroused such mixed feelings, but she was *taking a new track, getting off on the right foot, making a fresh start.* Cath had gotten fond of making up strings of clichés, of thinking of one after another like protective pickets in a mental fence; it was a silly habit, but one conducive to cheerfulness. And she was feeling cheerful today. She had gotten organized on Monday and called the post office to ask them to send her mail to their RFD box. Yvonne picked up her own at the post office and Derek got most of his at Saint Martin's, so Cath rarely saw anything until evening. And though Yvonne thought it was ridiculous duplication for the post office, Cath had been rewarded this morning with a nice little get-well card from Edith, one of the sopranos in the choir.

> Sorry we missed you Sunday. Yvonne said you were tired out. Can't blame you! Bet our Mozart didn't help, either. Get well soon, we need you back. Particularly on the high fast stuff!!!

Cath had already called to thank her, and though her hands had been shaking when she picked up the phone, they'd had a good chat. What an idiot she'd been to take such a panic in church. She'd nearly run over that old lady on her way out. Disgraceful! Cath felt she owed some flowers for that if for nothing else. She would send some, really nice ones, though that horrid Jackie Wilde was probably on the flower committee, too. The main thing was to fight worry and confusion and keep cheerful. That was the key. What was that other old cliché—*Let a smile be your umbrella?* Could that be the right phrase? She'd have to try that one on Yvonne.

Cath put down the violin and wandered over to the deep bookcases that held their music. The collection seemed smaller, though she could not say precisely what was missing, and idly, resting her arm, she began to flip through the sheet music and the bound volumes: *Schirmer's Complete Beethoven Sonatas,* almost crumbling with use; her beloved *Bach for Unaccompanied Violin.* She studied the famous chaconne for several minutes, thinking soon she'd tackle that again. She had new ideas, curious new insights; she felt she understood the musical architecture better. Maybe you appreciated architecture more after chaos, after chartreuse gowns and white convertibles and the gaping darkness at the end of the causeway.

Then sonatas, Brahms to Vivaldi, for one, two, and three violins, and several exercise books with lists of names and dates on the inside cover, which one part of her brain recognized as student assignments and another part ignored. Concertos, too, Mendelssohn through Beethoven and Tchaikovsky, and a newly published collection of pieces for violin and piano by Amy Beach. She hummed the melody of the Romance in A and smiled at the dense, chromatic piano line. Derek could have made much of that. Cath remembered pushing him to learn these salon pieces for a recital. Had they agreed on that? She'd have to ask him. Perhaps they could perform together again; she was getting better and music would keep her well.

She was thinking about playing with Derek, about the delicious tension of performance, when she saw, stuck between the Hindemith and the Copland sonatas, a little beginner's book, easy pieces for the violin, including the famous variations on "Twinkle, Twinkle, Little Star."

Cath stopped, feeling the good and happy mood, which had been sustained by Mendelssohn, the sunlight, the note from Edith, draining away like an unplugged sink. It was hers, of course, from years back, though the cover looked shiny and new, though she did not test her assumptions against the copyright date. But while she had ignored the earlier evidence of the Kreisler exercises, her mind was capricious: the "Twinkle, Twinkle" variations returned her to a winter morning, a child's slim arms and soft fingers, her own hands straightening a bow, the sound of her voice counting, and, outside, light snow falling, whitening the air and casting a veil before the brownstones. Why that day, why that pupil? Perhaps because that had been the last day she was really happy.

Cath straightened her back and set the book down on the pile. Her student music books were what was missing, her teaching materials, the books of scales and exercises, the scores, packed away when she and Derek left Hartford, along with her hopes for a series of earnest and not so earnest pupils. Her career was gone as if it had never existed. But that was her fault, she knew that, though she'd been happier not knowing, though she'd ignored the facts as long as possible, though she'd "forgotten" and become Laura and gone south to be in the sun and safety. Cath turned away from the bookcase and admitted that in some ways Yvonne was correct: she had been lying, but to herself.

Cath picked up the violin, carefully wiped off the rosin, and, after loosening her bow, placed both in the case. Then she pushed open the heavy screen door to the garden. Her first idea was that she had to think through everything, that she had to make herself remember so that she could start acting on her knowledge. The second was that she ought to stake the neglected peonies, which were budding heavily. The old border was such a mess that Yvonne had recommended taking everything out and putting in shrubs and woodchips to make a suburban garden.

Cath found a bundle of bamboo stakes in the barn and a big hank of raffia. She took the hoe, too, and loaded everything in the wheelbarrow and pushed it down to the border. After she took a good look at the plants, she went back for the fork and shovel to start digging out the weeds. The peonies would need feeding, too; she should get fertilizer, dig in some compost if there was any left in the old pile, maybe get some mulch to keep down the weeds. The place was a mess. For a moment Cath felt the nervousness of too much to do and not enough energy to do any of it well; then she decided to tackle one or two bushes a day and got to work pulling the grasses and dandelions, leathery long-rooted weeds that needed the shovel to shift and thin sprawling ground covers that came apart at the slightest tug, leaving daughter plants behind. Two strategies for survival: hang on for dear life or fall apart and hope some fragments remain. Cath had the sense she'd tried both and that neither was quite satisfactory.

She'd cleaned out around two of the peonies, staked one, and was busy setting the stakes for the second plant when she heard someone approaching. When she turned, Cath saw a woman, short, quite stout, with thick glasses and a tall walking stick coming along the old wagon road from the river. Their elderly neighbor, Stel Pye, stopped a dozen feet away to peer at Cath with a concentration that would have been rude if Cath had not known that Stel was terminally nearsighted.

"How are you, Mrs. Pye?" When the woman seemed uncertain, she added, "It's Cath Tolland."

"You're back home!" said Mrs. Pye. "I thought it might be Yvonne, but she doesn't like to work in the garden, does she?"

"Not that I've noticed," Cath said, nodding toward the wheelbarrow heaped with weeds and debris.

"Your aunt Elizabeth would be turning in her grave if she could see those peonies gone to weeds." She stepped closer and noticed the stakes. "That's going to help. Oh, I think these are the nicest peonies in town; they just need so much work."

"I'm trying," said Cath.

"And are you feeling better?" Mrs. Pye asked cautiously. She had very white, colorless skin and pale, clouded gray eyes. With her large, soft nose, Stel Pye reminded Cath irresistibly of a big albino mole.

"Yes, thank you. They got the pneumonia early."

"Oh, that's a blessing, though they can do such wonderful things. I remember when pneumonia was fatal: it was called the 'old man's friend.'"

"A somewhat sinister friend," Cath observed.

"Well, dear, better than all those machines and tubes. That's what I worry about: not dying, exactly, but getting kept alive beyond my time. That's what worries me."

"I hope you won't have to worry about that for a while," Cath said politely.

Mrs. Pye looked back over to the house and barn. "Is it to be painted?" she asked.

"Not for a while, I'm afraid."

"Though you're making a start on the yard. That's nice. We were all pleased when you moved back here. Some of us kind of hoped you might do a bed-and-breakfast, before we understood about your health, I mean." Mrs. Pye realized that she had gotten onto dangerous ground and added, "But you're busy in the garden. I'm supposed to be walking, you know. Good for my heart, but I don't really like walks."

"This would be an ideal place for a bed-and-breakfast," Cath said, "although maybe there's too much competition now. What do you think?"

Mrs. Pye looked uncomfortable. "Well," she said and paused.

Cath straightened up from her work and began unwinding the raffia to tie up the plant. "Is something wrong?"

"A B and B might put a lot of strain on you, that's all," Mrs. Pye said carefully. "After everything that's happened."

Cath took that under consideration.

"There are people in town—" Mrs. Pye began and stopped. "It's just that a bed-and-breakfast depends so much on word of mouth—if you're really thinking of opening one."

"I'm not," said Cath. "I just said the house would be ideal."

"But now that you're feeling better, you'll be thinking of what to do next, won't you? Have you gotten into the center yet?" Mrs. Pye asked in a careful tone. "To the post office or the general store?"

Cath shook her head. "Yvonne and Derek have been doing the errands. With Easter being so late, Derek just barely got finished with the music for services before concert rehearsals started. And Yvonne's out every day anyway." She heard herself rambling on, half apologizing. The fact was she hadn't wanted to see anyone and neither Derek nor Yvonne had made any effort to change her mind.

"I should perhaps warn you about something," said Mrs. Pye, "if you won't take it the wrong way."

"Warn me about what?"

"There's such a bunch of gossips in town."

"Town and country gossips," Cath said bleakly. Vague memories of before Laura and the night bus began to press against her temples like a physical weight. Mrs. Pye stood motionless in the brightness. She was wearing a long, lightweight coat somewhere between gray and brown and a pair of leather walking shoes and a dark skirt. The sun flashing from her thick glasses gave her face a surreal, oracular air. Impulsively, Cath said, "Tell me the truth."

"People say—" Stel Pye began and stopped. "Half the time you don't know what to believe."

"I'd better know just the same," Cath said. "I had a head injury in Florida. Everything will come back, the doctors say, but for a while I'd even forgotten Derek and Yvonne."

"Ah, Derek and Yvonne," said Mrs. Pye, and she shifted her walking stick. "Yvonne says that you weren't well at all before you moved back. That's what I was told. The strain, maybe, of all that teaching and performing had gotten you down, and then, after the accident, it was thought best to bring you back here."

Cath began to feel sick, as if her body knew what was coming before the mind could recollect. She sat down on the damp grass. From that angle, Stel Pye looked monolithic.

"I believe it was an accident myself," said Mrs. Pye. "I do believe that, but there are some that don't. Be careful of Faye Harris."

"Who's Faye Harris?"

"She works the register at the feed store. Gossip Central. Her cousin is a nurse in a doctor's office in Hartford."

Cath closed her eyes.

"That's apparently where he went the day it happened, not to the emergency room. Faye's cousin says he had a towel around his arm and there was a lot of blood."

"Derek had been taking glass out of a sash," Cath said. Amazing she remembered that; what a frightening illustration of the fact one can remember a lie and forget all sorts of things that are true.

"I believe that, dear," said Mrs. Pye, "but Faye Harris's cousin said it was a puncture, a stab wound, and not half an inch from a major artery. I wouldn't be surprised if Faye's added a little more detail since then."

"Why should she care?" Cath asked. "She doesn't know anything about us." She thought of kind Dr. Arce and of context. What was the context, the context for what had happened?

"There wasn't a word in the papers, you see, so no one knew the facts, not like what happened when Willie Harris set those Dumpster fires and got his name spread all over the *Bulletin*."

"I remember hearing about that," said Cath.

"Anyway, when Faye got hold of the story, she just ran with it. Kind of compensation, I suppose, for what happened to Willie. He's her youngest and she's been worked off her feet trying to provide for them ever since she and Herman divorced."

"Yes," said Cath, who felt she understood about compensation, about the balance of evil in the world, about trying to even things out.

"The people who knew you, of course, they didn't pay much attention," said Mrs. Pye. "Not at the time. But everyone noticed how you and Derek moved here right afterwards."

"With Yvonne," Cath said.

"That's right, Yvonne came pretty soon after you. It was from Yvonne that I got the story, the right story, I mean, about how you'd been sick." She let her voice trail off.

Cath could have eaten her heart on a plate: Yvonne's presence was her own fault; she herself had given Yvonne the foothold.

"Your sister-in-law's done her best, but still Faye feels, well, she feels you maybe got away with something. There are always people like that," Mrs. Pye said. "And she's talked it up, her and some others. Attempted murder, that's what they say, so you see it's going to be difficult for you here, even though your husband has been making himself popular."

"Yes," said Cath. "Yes, I see." That was all she could say. She had no defense, no answer. There was no way to change reality except the way she had already tried and failed: the night bus. The fact was that she *had* tried to kill Derek, her husband, the man she loved. She told Raoul the truth on their surreal ride across the causeway. She remembered the apartment kitchen, pale autumn light, a steak knife in the cutlery basket by the sink. Like watching a silent film, she could see herself screaming. She could see Derek's arm in his thick black sweater—Cath was sure it would never have happened if his arm had been bare. She saw him reaching toward her, then the knife again and the blood and his look of astonishment, before her hand set the knife down on the counter and reached for a kitchen towel as his blood dripped brightly onto the Formica and the black and white tiles of the floor.

What was wrong with this memory? There was definitely something wrong, something anomalous, curious, suggestive of warning, but Cath could not bring this thing to light, though she closed her eyes, though she saw the kitchen again and Derek and the hand that represented herself.

When she stood up and returned to the yard, Mrs. Pye, identifiable only by her stiff, slightly rolling gait, was a diminishing figure far down the wagon road. Cath walked toward the house, leaving her gardening equipment behind. Everything struck her as bright and distinct and as remote as a photo from Mars. The leaves of the lilacs, the peeling clapboards, the loose hinge on the shed door, the reflection of a branch in a window of the music studio: how strange that objects should have such supernatural clarity when the sum total of things was so elusive, so unpatterned, so without order or hierarchy. In her shock, Cath could no longer make sense of the world, and the only thing that her mind could grasp was the idea of sanctuary flowers. She had been planning to send flowers to Saint Martin's. That was something she'd wanted to do, must do, must set about doing. *A duty. A dutiful thing to do. Duty calls. Uncle Sam expects each man will do his duty.* Cath giggled slightly and picked up the phone book to find a florist.

She knew exactly what she wanted: pale, waxy spring lilies in pink, white, and yellow, those gorgeous trumpets of annunciation and resurrection, along with some pale blue and lavender Dutch irises. Hothouse daisies to cut the heavy scent of the lilies would be nice, too, pure white, and maybe anemones with ivy and ferns for greenery. She had in mind, not the usual churchy blossoms, stiff in the big vases that flanked the altar, but a resplendent, protective arrangement, a buoyant bouquet like the ones in Chagall's paintings, where flowers bear lovers through night skies or blossom with people and animals like living Trees of Jesse.

". . . for Saint Martin's Church," she told the florist. "Lilies. I want a lot of lilies."

"And your credit card number?" asked the woman, who, after all, was in commerce, not magic.

Cath caught her breath. "I don't have one," she said in a small voice. "I don't have one handy."

But the instant she spoke, she knew that she'd had one, several, in fact. Out of the chaos of objects, the phone, the table, the multicolored spines of the books lining the next room, the brown vinyl floor, the clock over the refrigerator, came the idea of ordering flowers and, then, the existence of her credit cards. As she put the receiver down with the florist still talking, Cath remembered how Yvonne had focused on the carelessness of losing her purse and on the inexplicable stupidity of going off in the first place without plastic. So, yes, there had been cards, but they were not in her desk, nor in her wallet, either. Her new, hospital gift-shop wallet, a sickly lavender imitation leather, held only her driver's license and the green plastic hospital ID that would, the business office lady had assured her, save a great deal of time if Cath were ever admitted again.

But she mustn't think about hospital IDs or about hospitals at all. It was the credit cards she had to focus on, for those credit cards, like Ariadne's string, formed a tenuous connection with the world of before, with rationality, with cause and effect, with an orderly, coherent universe that didn't collapse into meaningless objects and unfamiliar faces. Cath knew she must find the cards, and, though she had not entered their bedroom since before the night bus, she went straight upstairs and opened the door to the past.

The walls had a pretty red and cream paper in a small, old-fashioned flower print. The woodwork was cream and there was a fireplace with wooden cupboards around it. An impressive four-poster bed with an off-white afghan stood on the dark red floor. The heavy furniture and old New England decor suggested this must have been one of the B and B rooms from her great-aunt's time. Must have been, because Cath found the tasteful room almost completely without associations except for the photograph of two children: Derek and Yvonne, looking dark and preternaturally serious. There was also a well-framed shot of Cath herself, in her wedding gown, looking so radiantly happy that she might have been another person in another marriage altogether. There was no other trace of the present marriage except for Derek's electric razor on the dresser.

Cath stood in a square of sunlight, contemplating the chipped painted floor and the age-darkened woodwork. She had been ill, mentally ill, she might as well admit, and they had left Hartford after she stabbed Derek. They came to this house, which she had been renting to a woman who ran a B and B but who had subsequently moved on. The house was empty at the time they needed it, so they were able to move away from all the people who knew too much about them. They moved to the country with Yvonne, who sacrificed her position at a good suburban real estate office in order to help out. Now Yvonne worked out of the local branch office, assisted Derek at the parish, and looked after the housekeeping.

Of course, Cath had made certain sacrifices, too, although she did not want to think about them. There was a sort of symmetry: Yvonne's sacrifices were open, celebrated, "Christian" with the sort of obvious piety that Cath distrusted. Yvonne talked about what she had given up; her sacrifices were public knowledge. Cath's, on the other hand, were hidden, unmentioned, perhaps unmentionable. And, of course, she could hardly claim she'd sacrificed her music. She'd given up teaching music for stabbing Derek, for becoming unreliable, for becoming a person not to be entrusted with children.

After that happened, there was no reason to stay in the city and pay a big rent. Although it meant a commute for Derek, they pulled up stakes. Cath considered the phrase for a moment, *pulled up stakes*; it suggested camping or traveling with a nomadic band or maybe even freeing a vampire: *pulled up stakes*. And who was the vampire? That depended on your choice of scripture, on whether you wanted the standard text or the Apocrypha. In the Revised Standard, of course, Cath was the one who caused all the trouble and heartache.

Maybe that was right. Standing in the sunlight in Derek's room, a room where, she was suddenly sure, she had never slept with him, Cath wondered. Deep in the back of her mind was an apocryphal text which she had tried to forget, but which she might eventually have to recover. But not yet. She was already overwhelmed by the past, which had come up behind her like a big beach roller and tipped her into some psychic surf. At the moment, it was enough to remember that they'd moved in hastily and done nothing with the house beyond a little rewiring. She remembered the electrician had come. They'd left everything else alone, because they'd been unhappy and demoralized, and Cath hadn't cared whether the paint was fresh or the paper was to their taste.

In fact, the only one who had cared about the state of the place was Yvonne, who saw the house, in real estate lingo, as a *fixer-upper,* needing *TLC.* Not quite a *handyman special,* but a *wonderful opportunity for the right family.* Yvonne also had her eye on the pasture. There were still fifteen acres left, and Yvonne envisioned a subdivision, seven houses on two acres each with the old house either demolished or anchoring the development as a B and B. Alternately, they could leave quite a bit of land open and take the old farmhouse completely *upscale,* making it a *prestige property.* Yvonne was full of ideas for getting cash out of the old place, and Cath remembered telling her sister-in-law that any changes would be made *over her dead body.*

And what had Derek's opinion been about that? Cath had no idea, but they were still living in the old house, so either he had agreed with her or the property was in her name only. Perhaps she should think about that, about all the implications, but her only idea was to follow the trail of her credit cards. And where might they be? Like a sleep-walker, Cath opened the two small drawers of the dresser to see ties and socks and little dark leather boxes of dress cuff links and shirt studs for the big winter concerts. Cath ran her hand over them with wistful sadness. Derek had such talent, such potential, and with all that, the priceless gift of personal magnetism. Yet here he was, living on the cheap in her great-aunt's house with her and his sister, conducting what was, after all, only an ambitious suburban church choir.

She closed the drawers and opened each of the others in turn: underwear, dress shirts fresh from the laundry, summer-knit shirts, shorts, sweaters, and sweatshirts. She remembered him wearing some: memory produced a winter day skating at the lake, Derek flushed with the wind and cold, looking young and happy; a concert in the rose garden, Vivaldi and a golden sunset and summer ease on a picnic blanket; repair work on one of the rain gutters, the feel of the heavy wooden ladder and the sight of Derek's dark leather work boots balanced on a rung just over her head. The last two drawers held her winter clothes, but no context—no emotional context, that is—and no cards.

That left Yvonne's room, because Cath already knew there was nothing in the music studio. Though she hated to sneak around and feared being caught, she crossed the hall and opened her sister-in-law's door. Cath had not been inside this room since the move. It was square like the master bedroom, but slightly smaller and more personal in decor; Yvonne evidently had not been as disheartened as the rest of them. There were some Chinese jars on the nice marble mantle, and the floor had been refinished. Cath looked around the room: blue paper, some contemporary prints, her great-aunt's walnut sleigh bed, and a nice little Victorian writing desk with a key in the lock and a pretty striped ribbon ornamenting the handle. Cath went over, pulled out the slides, and dropped the writing surface to reveal a bank of drawers and pigeonholes. She flipped through bills, envelopes with letters, a couple of receipts for bank CDs, a passbook, and canceled checks: paper that might have been informative if she had been calculating and thinking instead of blindly seeking for the cards, which were not so much money as a talisman. The little inside drawers came next: the first had postage, an address stamp, a cheap ring, and thirty-five cents in change. The second had some old leather corners for a blotter, a fountain pen, and a little pile of plastic with an elastic band around it. Cath smiled when she saw her library card on top. Underneath was her Visa card, her ATM card, store cards from Filene's, Jordan Marsh, and Penney's, and several supermarket IDs. Here were places where she was known, where she had appropriate numbers, identifying digits, an exemplary credit record. She put the cards in her pocket and closed up the desk. She was turning the key in the lock when she heard footsteps downstairs and woke to the fact that time stops for no one, not even sleepwalkers and shock victims: Yvonne was home. Before Cath could get out of the room, her sister-in-law was standing in the lower hallway.

"What are you doing?" Yvonne demanded. She was dressed in her real estate kit: red blazer with the company logo on the pocket, dark slacks, a striped blouse, dark gloves. She had her briefcase in one hand, and her face was flushed and angry. "What the hell were you doing?"

She did not sound at all like a parish lady. Without answering, Cath held up her credit cards.

"As if there's anything you needed," Yvonne said. She came up the stairs fast, her heels making a heavy staccato on the bare treads. "I'd have gotten anything you needed." In her dress shoes, she was half a head taller than Cath; she looked big and official, certifiably sane, normal, and righteous, a star salesperson of terrifying competence.

"I told you, I wanted to order some thank-you flowers for Saint Martin's," Cath said apologetically. "The cards weren't in Derek's dresser or in the music room desk, so I thought of yours. I must have left them in mine," she added, as her dislike of her sister-in-law began to overcome her embarrassment and nervousness. *Tit for tat, one good turn deserves another, what's good for the goose, etc.* What those old clichés told Cath was that people like Yvonne are with us always.

"I'm trying to move property in the back of beyond and run everything and hold things together for Derek," Yvonne said, working herself up. "And what the hell are you doing? Snooping around in my room the minute I turn my back." She reached suddenly behind Cath and jerked the door shut with a bang. "You are never to go in my room again. Do you understand that?"

Her adult, schoolmarmy tone made Cath angry. "What I understand is that you're living in my house," she said. "I suppose I can go where I want in my own house."

"Your house! You're lucky you're home at all and not in some institution."

"Yet you wanted me to come back. You went all the way to Florida to find me. Just what was in it for you, Yvonne?"

"I did it for Derek, of course."

"I guess I knew it wasn't for me."

"No, you're right about that. Now give me those cards." She grabbed hold of Cath's arm.

"Don't touch me," Cath said, jerking away and putting the cards into her jeans pocket. The mix of fear and anger in her own voice surprised her. "Don't touch me."

Yvonne picked up her head. "Then give me the cards," she said, blocking the hallway.

Cath saw that there was no way to get past, and her heart began to hammer. She was a little bit afraid of Yvonne, with her self-confidence and her closeness to Derek. She was afraid, too, of physical violence, which, she knew, could break out suddenly and irrationally in otherwise safe places, in a city kitchen, in the upper hallway of her old house. "There's no reason for you to have them. I expect you have your own; you seem to have your own accounts and everything else."

"I knew you were snooping," said Yvonne. "I know what Derek will say about that."

"I was looking for what was mine," Cath said. "What right had you to put my cards in your room, anyway?"

"We can't trust you with credit cards. That's why they were locked in my room. And you're not to have them. Now hand them back."

Cath didn't move, and when Yvonne stepped forward and tried physically to take the cards, Cath shoved her away. Yvonne grabbed Cath's arm, slamming her up against the bedroom door. Twisting Cath's wrist with her good hand, Yvonne tried to fish up the cards with her right, while Cath attempted to shake herself free. They struggled in the narrow space, banging against the door and the outer wall, a matter of a few seconds only, but a few seconds elongated by the fear of struggle and a frustration verging on hysteria; for, even while they were wrestling over the cards, Cath had a sense of the ridiculousness of it, the stupidity.

It was only when a sharp pain shot through her wrist that Cath lost her perspective and, with unexpected force, thrust Yvonne away. As she broke free, her sister-in-law brought down one of her sharp heels on Cath's right instep, and, in a desperate reflex, Cath swung her fist in an arc that caught Yvonne on the shoulder. Unstable in her high heels, she fell against the rail as Cath rushed past her into the open hallway. Yvonne was halfway over the banister, the slightest touch from falling to the foyer below, before she grabbed the newel post with her damaged hand and pulled herself back from the stairwell.

She faced Cath in the hallway. "I could have fallen," Yvonne said, breathing hard. Her perfect hair was askew, one shoe was off, her face was white and sick looking.

Breathing hard with nerves and exertion, Cath leaned against the far wall by Derek's room and rubbed her sore right wrist; her bowing wrist had been wrenched, probably sprained. She was still too angry to be frightened. Her imagination had not yet kicked in, the imagination that would later suggest the catastrophe of Yvonne tumbling over the rail and plunging down the steep stairs. "I warned you not to touch me."

"I don't think you realize what you've done," Yvonne said, gathering her forces as she spotted an advantage. "I don't think you see the danger you're in with your past record. I could have been hurt just now, killed even. I have almost no strength in my right hand. You wouldn't get off a second time, no matter how foolish my brother is."

Cath said nothing; she was still in the grip of intense and complicated emotions.

Yvonne straightened her blazer, brushed some dust from her slacks, put herself back together as *she who knows best*. She did not realize that she might have betrayed herself to Cath, for she did not consider her brother's wife particularly intelligent. "There's no need to panic," she said. "Give me those cards and we'll forget about this. You won't need to worry that I'll tell Derek."

Cath could almost see the emotional gears working. A certain mechanical quality, an obviousness of calculation, was Yvonne's weakness.

"I'll tell Derek about my wrist," Cath said. It was marked red from Yvonne's long fingers and already swelling. "I'll tell him you attacked me."

"Do you think he'll believe you?" asked Yvonne. "Do you think anyone will believe you?"

"You're not hurt," said Cath, though now she could see her own danger, the danger of precedents, of a track record, of town and country gossip.

"Other than the fact that my hand's in agony and I could have broken my neck, you mean? You lucked out, so I don't think we need to worry Derek about this," Yvonne said.

Cath pounced on that concession. "We wouldn't need to worry Derek at all, if you'd stop trying to run our lives and mind your own business."

"You ungrateful bitch," Yvonne said. She had been edging closer to Cath as they spoke and now she slapped Cath very hard, driving the tears into her eyes. "There are plenty other places I could be."

"If you don't like living here," Cath shouted, throwing up her arms so violently that Yvonne stepped back out of reach, "why don't you move to the city?"

"You won't suggest that in front of Derek."

"The hell I won't! I want you out of my house! I want you out of my house now." Cath whirled around and ran down the stairs.

"You're just saying that because I caught you in my room," Yvonne said, leaning over the banister. "You're afraid of what Derek will say." Nonetheless, she started after Cath.

"Don't come near me. I'm surprised you're not afraid to come near me," Cath said. She was beginning to weep with rage, though that was a mistake, though that strengthened Yvonne, who was pulling herself together, putting on her smooth, adult face, dropping her voice, her voice which had risen, Cath thought, *like a fishwife's*. That was a phrase of her great-aunt's: *a voice like a fishwife*.

"And what about Derek? Who'd make the meals and run the errands? Do all the housekeeping you're too good to touch?"

"You've been very careful never to leave me a car," Cath said, backing toward the kitchen. "It's funny with all this 'a little more every day' that you never suggest a run into town."

"You don't want to show your face around there anyway," Yvonne said abruptly. "Any more than you'll want to go back to Saint Martin's. I know how you ran out of the church. And I know why."

"I wouldn't have had to run out of church if you hadn't been going around telling everyone I'm mentally ill. Explaining my symptoms and spreading gossip, while pretending to set the record straight."

"People were talking," Yvonne said. "As well they might."

"People would talk a lot less if you kept your damn mouth shut."

"You might remember," Yvonne shouted, "that you stabbed my brother. If we hadn't protected you, you'd have gone to jail for assault, even for attempted murder. Or is that something else you've conveniently forgotten?"

Cath looked away and didn't say anything for a few seconds. It was fortunate that she'd been warned, that she'd seen Mrs. Pye, that she'd already absorbed this news. When she spoke again, her voice was low, neutral, a good tone for serious danger. "And why did I stab him, Yvonne?"

She glanced at Yvonne quickly enough to see that she was disconcerted.

"You stabbed him because you're crazy, you always have been," said Yvonne.

"But he's stayed with me," Cath cried. "When he had good reason to leave."

"He feels sorry for you. You amuse him; he thinks he plays better with you. How the hell do I know!" Yvonne exclaimed suddenly. To

Cath's astonishment, her sister-in-law seemed on the verge of tears. "He doesn't think about anyone but himself and what he wants. His whole life is selfishness." Yvonne grabbed her briefcase, stamped back upstairs, then jerked open the door of her room and slammed it shut behind her so hard that Cath felt the tremor in the hallway.

8

ROUND ABOUT FIVE O'CLOCK, WHEN she expected Derek momentarily, Cath went into the kitchen and started rattling around with the pots. A big one for pasta, a small one to heat tomato sauce, a fry pan for browning the mushrooms and the Italian sausages she'd found in the freezer. There was some lettuce in the crisper and a round, red, handsome-looking tomato with the disappointing, whitish interior of the long-distance shipper. Cath cut it up anyway and added a few olives, a handful of croutons, a little grating of Parmesan: your basic gourmet touches to indicate what—sanity, self-possession, a generalized critique of earlier meals and salads?

At five-thirty, she heard Yvonne come downstairs and go into the living room. Cath knew exactly what Yvonne was doing. She was standing at one of the big windows looking down the road. At quarter to six, when Cath had turned on the heat under the pasta pot and turned off the fire under the sauce and the sausage-mushroom mixture, Yvonne came into the kitchen. She was wearing jeans, a sweatshirt, and sneakers; her seriously styled real estate hair had been pulled back, and her face seemed to have been wiped clear of all anger and emotion, a process no doubt helped by the consumption of the painkillers she took for her damaged hand. There was something permanently wrong with the nerves in the hand. Yvonne took codeine and, in the winter, when the pain was worse, Darvon. She made no reference to their quarrel, to slapping Cath, to that undignified, potentially dangerous struggle in the hallway.

"He's late" was all she said.

Cath shrugged. She could not have explained right then why she was nervous. "Of course, there's always a lot of traffic on Route Six."

"There's some construction near Willimantic, too," Yvonne added. "You won't have noticed that. And there's always construction and one thing and another in Hartford."

"Yes," said Cath. She found a box of pasta and opened it, but did not put the fettuccine into the water. "I think he would have called if it had been something at work."

"There was no reason for him to be late at work this week," Yvonne said.

Cath thought that it was not so much what Yvonne said that was annoying as her air of certainty; she was an illogical positivist. "I just meant that probably he's been delayed on the road where he can't call conveniently."

Yvonne pivoted on one foot and began to pick nervously at the lettuce in the salad bowl.

"He's a good driver," Cath said after a moment.

"I don't worry about his driving," Yvonne snapped. She gave Cath a close, sharp look, opened her mouth, and then thought better of whatever she'd had in mind to say. "But with all those trucks..."

"Should I put in the pasta, do you think?" Cath asked. "Are you hungry?"

"No," said Yvonne. "I'm not particularly hungry. I'll just have my salad."

"All right." Cath sat down at the table, poured out two glasses of wine, and served the salad. The two women sat across from each other and ate in an uncomfortable silence. A wind had gotten up, bringing intermittent gusts of rain that rattled against the windows and drummed on the metal propane tank outside the kitchen door.

"Slow going in the rain," observed Yvonne.

"The storm's probably coming from the west," Cath agreed. "Slow going through the city." She put down her fork and flexed her stiff wrist. She was going to have trouble bowing. Her practicing would be set back for sure.

Yvonne ignored this. "It's amazing," she said, "how a little rain disrupts traffic." She had opinions on driving, on rain, on Connecticut drivers.

What are we worried about? Cath wondered while her sister-in-law talked. *Derek's only an hour or so late. What is it that is making us nervous?* "We could call Saint Martin's if you're concerned," she suggested finally.

"There'll be no one at Saint Martin's now," Yvonne said, and that was true, because it was very nearly six-thirty.

"Perhaps the custodian," said Cath.

"Derek won't be at Saint Martin's at this time," Yvonne said. There was an edge to her certainty, and she gave Cath another one of her secretive and appraising looks.

"I think I'll put the sauce in the fridge," Cath said. "We can reheat everything when Derek comes home. Unless you want to go ahead now."

Yvonne set her face. "No, I'll wait. You eat if you want."

Cath could not help a half smile. She was not about to be outdone in devotion by Yvonne. "I'm not hungry, either," she said. "I'll be in the music room. There's some new songs I want to look at." She had reached the hallway before Yvonne spoke again.

"We shouldn't worry Derek when he comes in tonight," she said. Yvonne *ought* to have been a singer; her voice had a thousand shadings.

"Derek will be tired," Cath agreed.

"There is a lot of strain at work. You've never involved yourself in parish politics, but there's no way he can avoid them. It's hardly worthwhile for all they pay him."

"Do you think that's why he's late? The strain of parish politics?"

"I think he's been held up on the road," Yvonne said with a note of dull finality.

Cath went along to the music room. She found the Gorecki and began picking her way through the intervals, checking her pitch against the piano, getting the sound in her ear. She put the recording on Derek's small studio CD player and listened to the sound of the Polish words in the *Symphony of Sorrowful Songs*. Outside the rain had intensified, flowing seamlessly into the soft chords of the opening of the symphony and forming a natural, liquid obbligato to the soft, pure tones of the soloist's prayers and lamentations.

Not perhaps the sort of cheerful music that she should be singing, but Derek was right, as he was always right about her voice: the *Sorrowful Songs* were a perfect fit. She could feel how the musical line unfolded and the emotional line, too, a curve of grief that held her like a perfectly banked roadway. Because she had felt the centripetal forces of chaos on the night bus, Cath could imagine the intensity of prayers from dark cells, prayers opening against moral and physical blackness like the soundless trumpets of lilies. Pagan that she was, Cath understood how such prayers would sound.

She was still absorbed in the *Songs* at eight-thirty when car lights swept across the studio. Derek was home. Cath hurried into the kitchen to turn on the burner under the pasta water and to pull the pans of sauce out of the fridge. She could hear Yvonne's voice in the hallway, then Derek's. "... worried. With all the accidents on Route Six!" "Couldn't be helped." "... have called us at least." "... make a fuss ... You might have confidence ..." "How can I have ..."

Cath thought that she should be the one at the door, greeting and scolding. Instead, she put the sauce on the stove.

"Ten minutes," she said when Derek looked in at the doorway. "We'll be ready in ten minutes."

"You shouldn't have waited." He came over and kissed her cheek. There was something different about him, Cath noticed, a certain— what? Self-satisfaction? Was that it? She thought that he might have been drinking, too. She could smell alcohol, but just a trace.

"I was late at the church. I should have called. Rehearsal ran late, but I still expected to be home for dinner. Then there was an accident: Route Six as usual. We had to detour through Coventry."

A laundry list of excuses. Cath asked, "A bad accident?"

"Truck jackknifed. Nobody hurt, but the road was closed. By then I was so late I didn't want to stop."

"I didn't think you had a rehearsal scheduled for this afternoon," Yvonne said.

"Unexpected," Derek said. He seemed to have lost bits of his syntax. Was that how men reacted to stress, dropping articles and nouns and verbs, *cutting to the chase,* was that what the British said, or was it *cutting to the heart?* Cath could tell that Yvonne was upset. She had the odd sense that she and Yvonne, who had been, quite literally, at each other's throats, were now on the same side. But what side was that? There was something else, Cath felt, that she still didn't know.

"That soprano from the college—who filled in for you, Cath. She's having her big student recital. Quite a nice program, including the 'Pulchra es.' Not as quick a study as you, I'm afraid."

"You said she sang very well. I thought I was to lose my place in the choir to her," Cath said, not quite joking.

"That was strictly because of your health," Yvonne said so quickly that Cath wondered to what extent she was ready for Yvonne as ally.

"Let's say there's no real comparison." Derek seemed very gallant, very up, somehow. "Do I have time for a shower? I'm pretty wet. I didn't have a raincoat with me."

"A quick one," said Cath. "The sauce is getting warm."

"Pasta with mushrooms and sausage: my favorite. Happy memories of student life."

Derek breezed upstairs, humming an aria from *La Bohème* as he went, so that Cath couldn't help smiling. Yvonne cut herself the end of the Italian bread and began nibbling at the crust.

"What's she like?" Cath said without planning, or really meaning to ask.

Yvonne seemed startled. "Who? Who are you talking about?"

" 'Pulchra es,' my replacement, the music school recital?"

"Oh, Jane Henkel. Jane's all right. Not a bad voice, a little thin, kind of like yours. Or did you mean what's *she* like?"

"I was just making conversation," Cath said. "I feel out of touch. So what is she like?"

"Nineteen," said Yvonne sourly, "or maybe twenty. Red hair, plump, kind of a fat nose. Pleasant enough."

"If you like fat noses," Cath suggested, but Yvonne, who never had much of a sense of humor, was in no mood for jokes.

"Is that pasta ready yet?" she asked.

"Almost," said Cath. "How did she turn up in the choir?"

"One of Derek's contacts at the college. She's actually quite talented." Yvonne ran through Jane's whole résumé, local gigs, favorite repertory, vocal range. This was not exactly what Cath felt she wanted to know, but then it was all irrelevant, because there was no need to be interested in Jane Henkel at all.

They heard Derek's feet clattering back down the stair, so brisk, so breezy, "L'Allegro" to the women's "Il Penseroso." He came in with smiles and high spirits and put his arm around Cath. "So what were you up to today?"

"I worked on that little Mendelssohn sonata for a while, and then I was trying to make my way through the Gorecki songs. They're quite marvelous."

"Just don't learn the words until we get the pronunciation sorted out. We don't want faux Polish."

"There must be some Polish speakers in the area."

"We'll find them. In the meantime, the violin for you." Derek liked giving orders, aesthetic advice, program suggestions.

"I'm afraid I won't be playing for a week or so," Cath said. "Yvonne, would you drain the pasta for me?"

Yvonne gave her a warning look, which Cath ignored. She held up her wrist, which was slightly swollen and starting to bruise.

"How'd you do that?" Derek asked, as Yvonne carried the pot over to the colander Cath had left in the sink.

115

"Stupidest thing imaginable. I must have twisted it while I was out in the garden. I worked on the peonies today. Weeding around them and staking them up."

"I thought we were going to take those out," Derek said. "Didn't you think lawn and shrubs would be best, Yvonne?"

Yvonne swallowed her opinion and relieved her feelings by plopping the fettuccine violently onto the colander, spattering hot water over the sink. "The peonies are nice enough in bloom if Cath wants a garden." She gave a little sour smile and added, "Something constructive for her to do."

"Cath will have plenty of music to keep her busy," Derek said.

"Yes, between that and the cooking and the garden," Cath said. But though she could feel her face flush with nervousness, she pressed on. "I've been thinking that now I am feeling so much better, it's rather a waste for Yvonne to be working out of the local office. I didn't realize until we went into Saint Martin's last Sunday, but she lost all her good Hartford contacts when she moved out here. It's really not fair to expect her to stay with us."

"We don't want to put Yvonne out the door," Derek said in a jovial tone that told Cath he didn't take her suggestion seriously, that he'd rather not discuss this. "Picture my only sister cast out into the storm."

"Yvonne could do what you do: commute to work if she wants to keep living here. I just wanted to say I don't want to impose on her."

"She's not imposing, she's my sister," Derek joked. "Or rather, she is imposing, but not imposing on us. *Imposing*." He sang the word, placing a percussive emphasis on the second syllable. "How strange more songs haven't been built around *imposing*."

Yvonne said nothing to all this persiflage and seemed, amazingly, to be considering the suggestion. Cath thought this must be what high-stakes poker was like, when two players held good cards. She flexed her wrist deliberately and helped herself to more bread.

"I might talk to the district manager," Yvonne said. "The difficulty is that you show houses at odd hours."

"There's a motel in town, isn't there?" Cath asked. "That would be cheaper than an apartment but still convenient if you had to be in late."

Derek looked at her with surprise. He was, like most people, prone to cherish particular images of those nearest him. After all Cath's troubles, he'd almost forgotten that she had considerable practical capability.

"The Town Motor Inn's a thought," Yvonne said. "But maybe we should wait a while. Maybe we ought to think about a holiday, about getting away, instead. Maybe you and Derek could take a weekend or a few days on your own. Or maybe I could run out west to visit our cousins. With such a small family, we should keep in touch."

When Yvonne said that, Cath thought she had perhaps underplayed her hand. She should have demanded more, maybe even told the truth. But it was too late for that; she was committed to lies, had been for some time, perhaps for longer than she remembered. She could see that her husband was frowning slightly. He liked to be the one making plans and arrangements and rather expected that such plans and arrangements would be focused on him. Also, though Cath could not see this, Derek was not quite sure what to make of the unexpected amity between his sister and his wife. Although he would have described their friendship as vital to his happiness, the fact that the two women were divided by a deep, almost instinctive antipathy actually suited him better. "We could go to the lake," he said with a glance at his sister. "The Adirondacks are very nice this time of year."

Derek's story about the lake, about Yvonne's hand, about the terrible accident was still so vivid in her mind that Cath was appalled by this suggestion.

"We always rent the cabin," Yvonne said; her face had become somber, thoughtful.

"We could rent at the lake. People rent camps and cabins there all the time. It's no innovation to rent a place in the Adirondacks!" Derek said, as if the lake, the Adirondacks, the camp had never held ancient miseries, as if he had not been near tears while telling Cath the story, as if he had not spoken in anguish.

But Cath had noticed Yvonne's expression. "What about the shore?" she asked.

"The Sound will still be too cold, and there's nothing to do at the shore if you can't swim. Whereas the lake," Derek said, turning to his sister, "the lake would be ideal. Symmetrical, don't you think, Yvonne?"

"I'd rather go West. If I sell that raised ranch, I think I'll go. There's a Rhode Island couple seriously interested as long as the septic system tests out okay. Then I might consider Cath's idea about the town office. I've got to think of my own future." She avoided Cath's eyes and looked at her brother very deliberately, so that Cath had the familiar sensation of observing a conversation in an unknown language.

"I'm to be deserted, I see," Derek said, his tone mock tragic, "at the very moment when I desire the woods, when I need to escape from civilization and parish committees."

"And long rehearsals?" Cath asked, though she could have bitten her tongue as soon as she said it.

"And long commutes," he said, "and squabbling women." The touch of acid in his voice killed Cath's appetite. She stopped pushing the pasta around her plate.

"You and Cath might go alone to the lake." Yvonne's voice was angry. "You might take Cath for her birthday."

"We never bother much about birthdays," Cath said quickly. "July's always nice right here."

"But this is a special birthday, isn't it?" Yvonne said, though her brother was glaring furiously at her. "You'll be thirty."

"Thirty is a big number," Cath said. "The end of youth and promise." For a horrible moment, she felt she might weep. A year ago, she had been happy; she knew she had.

"Your trustees in their wisdom thought it the right time."

"Oh, that." Cath remembered something about a trust fund, about her "contributions" to the household, but in the present heavy and poisonous atmosphere, she was indifferent to small fund checks. "I think you said Luc Beausoleil handles my trust fund. Otherwise I don't remember anything about it."

"You won't have to worry." Derek's voice went soft and affectionate again with a suddenness that alarmed Cath almost more than his anger. "Yvonne and I can manage that for you. After your birthday."

"We were happy once," Cath burst out suddenly, as the pressure of the day, of Mrs. Pye's revelations, of the quarrel with Yvonne, of Derek's mysterious lateness folded in on her. "I know we were happy once."

Derek and Yvonne exchanged glances. "Of course," said Derek. "Of course we were, and we will be again."

His voice was so smooth, so reassuring, that Cath, unaccountably, knew it was false. Tears streaming uncontrollably down her face, she jumped up from the table and ran out of the kitchen.

They could hear her footsteps in the hall, up the stair, along to her room. "You are a fool," said Yvonne to her brother.

"And what about you? *A special birthday, your trustees,* Christ! Yvonne!"

His sister gave a bitter smile. "How little you know her. She doesn't care about money. The money means nothing to her."

"That doesn't mean she's stupid."

"Not as stupid as you," his sister agreed. "Coming home over three hours late with lame excuses and bourbon on your breath after rehearsing some young soprano."

"I stopped for a drink after rehearsal. No big deal."

"Drink at home," said Yvonne furiously, "and don't even think of threatening me."

"Was I threatening you?" Now that his sister was angry, Derek felt himself relax.

"Even Cath noticed."

"You know I love Cath, and maybe I don't care about money either," Derek suggested. He helped himself to more sausages. "She really does cook a great deal better than you do."

"You want to ruin everything," said Yvonne. "You ruined my life, you ruined Cath's, now you want to ruin whatever's left."

"I had some help. You might remember, I had some help."

Yvonne shrugged. "We were children."

"Yes, we were children, and I've never been able to escape."

"Poor Derek," Yvonne said in a dry, mocking voice. "So pathetic and now so idealistic. How will you be able to afford your little habits? Jane Henkel! At least she's of age. You've learned your lesson there, at least."

"Shut up," said Derek without real anger.

"Cath is unstable," Yvonne said. "Don't push her."

"I know all about Cath's instabilities. She could have severed an artery. I could be learning the left-hand repertory."

"You could be dead," said Yvonne.

"So could we all: the common fate of mankind. I use the term generically, including women."

"That *is* nice of you," said Yvonne.

"In deference to your sense of feminist sisterhood, which is particularly evident tonight. You seem to have reached a modus vivendi with Cath. How did that happen? Or is she just the lesser of two evils?"

"She is your only hope for when Saint Martin's decides genius doesn't excuse everything. That will be sooner rather than later, I'd guess, with Ms. Henkel getting private lessons."

"Absolutely nothing happened with Jane. Nothing. Why do you think I stopped for a drink? Pure frustration. You should be pleased. You've always been afraid of Cath, worried about Cath, afraid—"

"Cath has always been the danger," Yvonne said. "But for you, not for me. I'm amazed you don't see that. Cath is no real danger to me at all."

"She's forgotten," said Derek. "I'm convinced she has, so she's no danger to anyone—except maybe herself. Poor Cath was born too late to make use of her unique spiritual gifts."

"Saving her from being hanged as a witch," said Yvonne.

"How can you be so cynical! Spiritual gifts are appropriate in a churchman's wife."

"The church is not interested in the more eccentric varieties of spirituality. Or physicality, either."

"She's forgotten," said Derek.

"Yet she's getting better. Surely you see that." Her face intent, Yvonne leaned forward and tapped softly on the table. "And as she gets better, she remembers. For one thing, she knows she stabbed you. She remembered that today."

"Most likely you told her," Derek said, unperturbed. He'd been bored, and he couldn't tolerate boredom. But now that there were interesting complications, now that Yvonne had given him a weapon against her self-righteousness, he felt alert and relaxed. "Just the way you told her about her trust fund. You've got things the wrong way round. You're the one who's been trying to sabotage me. Maybe you should take Cath's suggestion. Maybe you should go back into Hartford and rent an apartment. You can afford it. You haven't spent a dime here."

"Sure," said Yvonne. "Suppose I do that. What will happen to you?"

Derek pushed himself away from the table. "I think I'll settle down to be happy with my wife."

He *had* been intending to play a little Schubert and so discreetly prolong the exhilaration of a satisfactory afternoon that had ended in Jane's little studio apartment. Jane had been his spring project, winter-spring, really. He had invested a lot of time and effort, endless hours of rehearsal, phone conferences about this song or that, intense discussions of German lieder. And then, quite suddenly, this afternoon, working with her in one of the cramped practice rooms at the college, he'd felt the certainty of success. Rain was coming, the first drops pattering on the glass. Jane was singing a pretty Mozart aria, her voice young and ardent, with a delicacy now and again in the high notes that reminded him of Cath. Those high notes, that purity of tone made him say, "Lovely, that's lovely," and cover her hand with his own. She leaned over and kissed him, and he'd pulled her down onto his lap on the piano bench and rumpled all her clothes so that they felt drunk and were actually staggering as they left the music building.

Jane lived in Hartford, on the fourth floor of a big, anonymous building just off Farmington Avenue. The elevator was ancient and slow, and he'd slipped off her panties before they reached her floor. He remembered her laugh, giddy and nervous, and a smell of sweat and perfume that set his head whirling. Her apartment was neat, homey, even, with a paisley spread and gingham curtains and a vast brown and white plush menagerie of stuffed animals, one of which somehow got entangled in their bedclothes. Afterwards they drank bourbon with Sprite, and he fondled her fine breasts. Enough, really, for any afternoon; he should play the piano and rest on his laurels.

But into this happy mood came the shadow of his sister; Yvonne was always maneuvering and trying to gain control. Look at the way she'd tried calling in old debts and obligations at dinnertime. She'd met him at the door, worse than his wife, and it was just to spite Yvonne that Derek clattered up the stair and went straight to Cath's room. Amazing, he thought, as he tapped on her door. Amazing that he'd put up with this separation.

There was a pause, then Cath said, "Yes?"

"It's me."

"Come in."

She was sitting on the bed with her feet up, the Gorecki score in her hand. He'd imagined her weeping and distraught, had pictured the subtle pleasures of comforting her. But though her eyes were red, she seemed quite calm. There was, he supposed, just a chance Yvonne was right.

"I'm so sorry about dinner," Cath said. "This wasn't the best of days."

"I know." He sat down on the edge of the bed. His handsome face was rueful, a little rumpled looking, with all the quick bitterness gone—or hidden. Cath felt her caution evaporating, her heart melting. "You have to expect a few of those," Derek said.

"Yes." Cath nodded with a sad little smile. She was not thinking of the seesaw progress of convalescence but of the first faint age lines around his eyes, of the line of his jaw, of the sudden, logic-defying power of his charm.

"You are getting better, you know that."

She gave him a long look before she said, "I found out today."

Derek's mind jumped several gears before Cath reached over to touch the scar on his bare forearm. "I'm so sorry."

"Yvonne—" Derek started to say, but Cath shook her head.

"Yvonne didn't tell me."

Derek wanted to ask who, who had she been seeing, who had she talked to, but stopped himself in time.

"But I did ask her why," Cath added. "I asked her why, but she wouldn't tell me."

"No one knows," Derek said, recovering himself. "You'd been kind of depressed and then all of a sudden you just weren't yourself. You had a moment of madness. That's the only way I can describe what happened."

"It's a frightening thing not to be oneself."

"You mustn't think about it. There was no real damage done, and I put it right out of my mind—once the bleeding stopped, that is." She laughed with him, then bit her lip as if she might weep. Derek reached out to stroke her hair, which had a soft, silky texture he had always loved. He had not touched her since she'd come back, not like this. Her illness and her mysterious amnesia had separated them so completely that now she was like a stranger, like a new and different woman. "You know that's why I sent Yvonne to Florida."

Cath turned to look at him, curiously.

"I was afraid of bad memories for you. Maybe I was wrong, now I think I was wrong, but I—well, when I heard you had lost parts of your memory, I thought we could start over fresh. I knew how you'd feel, and I hoped you would just forget entirely."

That was certainly a possibility, a solution, but she could not think rationally about anything. She took his hand and kissed it. "I never meant to hurt you," she said.

"I know that. I know that," he said and hugged her. And the odd thing, Derek thought, was that he did. He did know that. She had loved him. She had trusted him and for a time that had been enough.

"Of course, I was sick," she said in a slow, careful voice, "but I remember thinking that there are two Dereks. The Derek I loved and another man, a stranger. Could that be true?"

She was offering to go back and wrestle with his demons, but though he felt the excitement of the enterprise, such bravery was impossible and the attempt, undesirable. "There's only me," he said. "I suppose one's enough." He squeezed her shoulder, urging her to laugh, to make a joke, to return to the surface of life where she must learn to swim again.

"Yes," said Cath without complete conviction. "Yes, of course, I've been sick. I know that now, because in Florida, I had visions."

"What sort of visions?" Derek asked, half fascinated and half uneasy.

"I had the perception of evil. I saw evil intent as rolling clouds of darkness. I had warnings and saw the world in a different light."

"You could see evil?" Derek asked. "As a sort of entity?"

"Of course, it was just my fever. The manifestations more or less disappeared when my temperature went down."

"But warnings," he persisted, though he realized that this was a topic better avoided. "Was there some reality to them?"

"I think so," she said. "You meet dubious people at big bus stations. Predators of one sort or another."

She seemed curiously calm and unfrightened. Derek wasn't sure what to make of that. His wife was vulnerable and unstable but also gifted with curious talents that must complicate any calculations.

"Of course, I suppose you could say that I was dubious, too, when I landed in Florida." She remembered Raoul's carelessness with something approaching affection. She had had certain advantages despite her despair.

"That's all over now. You're really getting well," Derek said. "And looking very pretty and singing beautifully and getting better every day."

Cath took this as flattery, but she was still pleased. "I have some ideas for the Gorecki," she admitted.

"It's too bad it's so late," he said. "It's really a bit late to start work on the score now." He shifted to sit next to her, looked over her shoulder at the music, and began stroking her arm. There were other ways to prolong the pleasures of the afternoon, for it was a curious fact of his erotic life that he was only interested in musicians, in singers.

Cath flushed and moved the merest fraction of an inch: she felt the difference in his touch, heard the slight change in his breathing. Her body remembered, though her mind had forgotten. She gave him a weak, nervous smile.

Of course, Derek thought, if she really had forgotten he was even more of a stranger to her than she was to him. But he couldn't resist. He'd always wanted her most when there was someone else. Infidelity accelerated the universe for him. "Do you remember loving me?" he asked. "Do you remember how I loved you?"

"We were sitting on a piano bench," Cath said, and Derek felt a twinge when he remembered his afternoon with Jane. It is disagreeable to be reminded that even the most spontaneous gestures have a pattern. "You told me I was the only person in the world who could save you. I took it that you loved me." Her look was both searching and dreamy, as if she were intent on two things at once. With his wife, Derek thought, there was often a curious sense of events happening on several different levels.

"You did save me," he said. "You saved me at a very bad time."

"Esther's suicide. That was a terrible, mysterious thing. That was the forces of evil."

He started a little in spite of himself. "Why do you say that? What an odd expression."

"I'm sorry," Cath said. "I shouldn't have mentioned it."

"No, no, of course you should mention it. We must talk, we mustn't have secrets and things left unsaid. What I meant was that the phrasing was odd."

"I believe in evil forces," Cath said. "Don't you? Or do you just believe in good forces? I thought the church believed in both."

"Evil forces aren't fashionable just now," Derek said. "Not in our church."

"But fashion has nothing to do with belief, with what one believes, with what is true."

"You'd be surprised," Derek said with dry cynicism. "You, for one, might be happier in another denomination."

"You think I'm a pagan," Cath observed, "but I believe in evil forces. We have to be careful how we act, because we can attract either good or evil. I think that's true no matter what denomination one is."

"And you blame Esther's death on evil forces?"

"We never talked about Esther's death," Cath said.

Derek started to disagree, although he knew she was right.

"I loved you too much," Cath said. "I loved you too much to upset you, to risk having you think about her and compare . . ." Her voice trailed off.

"You are nothing like Esther," Derek said gently.

"Esther was every glamorous thing I could never be."

"Yet she couldn't save herself," Derek said. "And she couldn't save me. Only you could do that."

"Did I?"

"Yes," he said, "yes, I wouldn't be here without you. I wouldn't have survived."

"What would have happened to you?" Cath asked.

How like her that she should ask straight out. "I don't know, but nothing good. I need you with me." He leaned his head against hers, and for a moment, it was true.

"And did you love me?" she asked.

"I couldn't live without you," Derek said.

Cath bit her lip and looked at him, at his dark hair and eyes, at his smile, at the shadows gathering behind his white shirt and blue vest sweater. There was no one else like him for her, ever, and her heart was jumping in her ears, in the vein of her throat. "And now?" she asked.

"Now," he said, "I think we should go to bed."

"Tell me that you love me," Cath said, as if words could make a difference. Later, perhaps, she would look back on this moment and notice all she should have seen.

"I do, I do love you," Derek said, drawn by her large, mild, oddly focused eyes and her soft prettiness—and her perception of evil. She would understand, she would save him, yes, he could be saved. "Stay with me," he said. "I love you."

"Enough to live with me alone?" Cath asked, though she was falling into his eyes as into the void, as into oblivion. "Do you trust me enough to live alone with me?"

"Alone?" His thoughts had run ahead to pleasure, to rumpled sheets, and memories of white legs amidst plush bears and dynelle dogs.

"Without Yvonne," she said. "We never did get along well, did we?"

"Yvonne's been very good," Derek said, stroking Cath's hair.

"Very good, but we don't like each other. I must know if you trust me. If you really think I'm well."

"I think you're well," he said, though at that moment he did not know what to think. *The perception of evil.* She was both unstable and unsafe, and he found her irresistible. "Yes," he said in answer to her question. "Yes, Yvonne can take a holiday, move into town, whatever you want." He began kissing her.

"Yes," said Cath, because she loved him more than anyone, because she could save him, because she had been given a second chance. She put her arms around him, though his face was dark, and the room was darkening around them and a shadow was stirring behind her eyes. She didn't need to remember, not at this moment, maybe not ever, and if she wanted, she could close her eyes and not see the darkness.

9

————

CATH PUT DOWN THE PAINT roller and surveyed the pale grayish umber on the living room walls. She'd selected an unusual color, neither really gray nor brown, pale as beige but with a purply undertone that had taken three different trips to the paint store and numerous consultations with the saleswoman to achieve. The paint looked a little dark and shiny when wet, but on the south wall, finished first, the color was perfect, and once she freshened up the white woodwork, which was original and abundant, she thought the effect would be very nice, even elegant. Cath felt a sense of satisfaction. She was feeling normal and well and painting her house in the precise colors she liked. She was *getting on with her life, making a fresh start, taking hold.* And these were all good things. This was, she supposed, a happy ending. Indeed, if she had been keeping up with her writing, she could have closed her memory book a couple of weeks ago with the words *We lived happily ever after.*

The key, Cath thought, in happy endings, was knowing when to close the book. *She married the prince, he finds the treasure, they kill the witch:* the old storytellers knew when to make an end. Moderns tend to ask the awkward question *And then what?*, as if moments of hope

and happiness weren't enough, as if the old stories hadn't been set in hard times, as if *They lived happily ever after* hadn't been the really fantastic part of the story, while the witches and goblins, magic beans, talking horses, and clever cats were only reflections of reality. Which they were. Just this past week, Cath had become acquainted, not with a talking dog but with an eloquent dog collar: a heavy round green leather collar jingling with old rabies tags and bearing a metal plate engraved *Danny* and a previous phone number.

She had found the collar while working around the house, her daily occupation ever since Yvonne sold the split-level on the Canterbury Road—*nice family home, move-in condition*—and taken herself off for a two-week vacation in Colorado. When she returned, Yvonne had decided to spend five days a week in Hartford and resume work out of the suburban office. This was *a happy ending* by anyone's standards. Although her sister-in-law arrived every weekend, Cath finally felt that the house was hers, and she'd gotten busy with the barn and the yard and with redecorating. When she got stronger, she intended to paint the exterior, and she'd been pricing extension ladders and also scaffolding, which would be more expense and trouble in the short run but safer and easier to use. Cath thought that she'd go with scaffolding, though Derek said he'd help her with the ladder and seemed a bit dismayed at the size of the project.

Derek thought that she should rest and leave the house alone. He worried about her, brought her books and new sheet music, and picked up the groceries on his way back from the city. On the weekends they went for short hikes and often took a picnic supper Sunday evenings. She saw no one else, except Mrs. Pye, who often came over when Cath was working in the yard, and the neat-suited Jehovah's Witness and Mormon missionaries who arrived in pairs all through that summer, bearing leaflets and magazines and mysterious briefcases. Cath would have liked to ask about the contents of those briefcases, about what they considered essential baggage, but such curiosity opened possibilities best left unexplored. "My husband is music minister at Saint Martin's Church," she would say, and they would wish her a good day, not wanting, she supposed, to poach. *My father's house has many mansions.*

Still, she might have talked to them out of boredom—or interest, for some, despite their tidy suits and clean white shirts, had the hungry, fanatical faces and dreamy eyes of sailors on turbulent inner seas. Cath recognized them; she had herself seen the roadway open to the Heavenly City and the shadows of evil clouding the surface of the bay. But despite her semicloistered situation, she resisted the strange pilgrims who turned up, uninvited and unexpected. She was determined to be well and normal and living in a happy ending.

So instead of listening to their solutions and trading pregnant texts, Cath would pick some peonies, roses, or early daylilies for Mrs. Pye, who would sniff them appreciatively and turn to her fine collection of vases. Though the old lady had a real flair for flower arrangements, she always asked Cath's advice in order to be sociable, and they could spend a good half hour, if they liked, on picking out a vase that would suit and arranging the blossoms just so. They always did this pleasant work in Mrs. Pye's cool pantry, a little stone-floored room with a scarred wooden countertop and a deep galvanized sink. The vases, along with several fine French metal flower buckets, were kept in glass-fronted cabinets. The flower scissors and a more substantial pair of nippers hung from hooks near the sink, and the whole room smelled of old fieldstone and flowers and of the earth that lay just under the massive floor.

There was something feminine and old-fashioned about the pantry. Snipping the ends of the rose stems or checking the peonies for ants, Cath sometimes imagined herself transported back to another era, when one could spend a guilt-free morning arranging flowers and exchanging gossip. This sense of the antique was accentuated by the fact that the old lady spoke often of Cath's aunt Elizabeth, who had been one of her dear friends, and of other departed townsfolk, so that Cath was up to date on local gossip from the eighties and before. On contemporary events, Mrs. Pye preserved a charitable silence, and Cath, surely one beneficiary of that discretion, did not feel able to raise too many questions.

Nor was there anyone else to ask, for visiting was difficult; a second car was financially impossible, Derek said. Without giving any details, he often spoke of their precarious finances. *I don't want to worry you,* he'd say, *but money is very tight.* She agreed, of course, but while Cath could now walk or cycle into the village, she felt uncomfortable at the general store, where she was certain to be an object of curiosity. She had no excuse to go to the post office, not since she'd had their mail delivery restarted, and she felt shy about calling people whom she'd known only casually and through her great-aunt. Especially when she came with such awkward baggage, Cath did not feel able to put herself forward.

"*Don't do too much,*" Derek told her. "*Rest and work on the Gorecki, the violin.*" So she did. She had him bring home the new choir music, and they spent a pleasant evening running through the soprano parts, with Derek playing the piano and singing the baritone line. She could feel his concentration on the music, on her, on her voice. Now and again he smiled, to himself or to her, and she felt that he was happy, which made her try harder. She always sang her best for him, her very best, ever since the first day when he came to rehearse the college choir.

"That's nice," she said when they finished the soprano part from a Bach cantata, "but difficult."

"It's making for some problems," Derek admitted. "We only have two more weeks to get ready."

"I'll have it ready before then," Cath said, because she knew her husband had been pleased. He always made her feel confident about her voice.

His face changed as she spoke, and that was maybe the first thing, the first slight cloud on their happiness, on their *happy ending,* on *they lived happily ever after.* He shook his head. "You won't be ready, I'm afraid, not without straining your voice."

"The Bach lies very well for my voice," Cath protested. Derek was being too careful, overprotective; she wanted to rejoin the choir.

"Not enough volume," Derek said, turning back to the music. "It breaks my heart," he said coolly, "but there's just not quite enough strength and volume yet. Nice enough here—these lovely old chestnut floors, the real plaster walls, they're all flattering for the voice."

"But Saint Martin's acoustics," Cath said. She could hear Yvonne's voice with perfect clarity: *I don't think Derek would have taken the job without those acoustics. He could have gone anywhere, to one of the big urban congregations . . .* "Saint Martin's acoustics are very good."

The brilliant green eyes gave her a sidelong glance. "I suppose I can decide that, being the director."

"Of course," she said, wounded. "I just want to help."

"In this case, you can help by staying home."

"You seemed to feel you needed another voice," Cath protested.

"I've found a solution. A *temporary* solution."

"Jane Henkel," Cath said.

If Derek was surprised, he concealed it. "She needs the exposure, and the work will look good on her résumé. She's trying for a scholarship for next year, a full scholarship. Appearances with the choir, working with me—you understand, don't you?"

"I never thought you could have too many good sopranos."

"Give me a wealth of sopranos," Derek said, in the bright, opera buffa voice he reserved for evasion. He had a number of voices, Cath thought, not all of them sincere. "But I don't want to strain your vocal cords when we don't absolutely need you. And there's something else, too."

"What's that?"

"Well, you're my wife. Any hint of favoritism would be awkward. Especially now—when there are other factors. You understand."

Cath did understand, but she said, "I want to go back to the choir. I want to go back as soon as possible. I need to get out, to see people, to make music again."

"And you will." He took her hand.

"When?" she asked, half stubborn, half desperate.

Derek smiled. "Shall we say after your birthday?"

"My birthday?" Cath asked, surprised. Yvonne had said something about her birthday, too,

"Four, five weeks? That's reasonable, isn't it? Your voice should be in really good shape by then. A birthday celebration. A new debut. Better than ever." He patted the bench beside him and put his arm around her when Cath sat down.

"I still get a little tired," she admitted, because she loved him and wanted a happy ending. And if she sometimes felt isolated, virtually marooned, she knew that was unfair: poor Derek was commuting almost an hour each way so that she could live in the country house she loved and escape all the unhappy memories of the city.

Besides, she had every reason to be optimistic. She had fallen into love as into a bottomless well, a quick, ecstatic trip back to the delirious territory she had last visited in her final year in college, the year when Derek had loved her, when they had been giddy with happiness, when she had put rationality on the shelf, and dreamed, like Floria Tosca, of living for art and love.

She remembered that time, not just as a series of separate incidents, but as an overall haze of emotion and sensation: languid afternoons in his apartment before he went to his evening job with a church choir. *Do they know what you're up to in the afternoon?* she asked, and he laughed. She remembered that laugh, because for a long time, he had no laughter. (Cath gave mirth back to him, a gift that must count for something on their list of credits and debits.) Her senior recital with Derek accompanying, a full house, a wonderful success, their friends cheering and applauding when they sang a duet from *Don Giovanni* as an encore. Snacks at the pizza shop late at night, a score between them, bed ahead, the last flare of acid rock on the sound system. Outlining some new theory or interpretation, Derek would stab impatiently at the score, his hair flopping into his eyes as he spoke.

He'd seemed to live, Cath thought, on a different plane, in the realm of serious people and art and ideas. In this realm, life was lived more intensely; music sounded sweeter and more seductive; emotions were stronger, personalities more powerful. Derek carried with him an air of consequence and excitement, shaded, ever so delicately, by tragedy, by danger. After Esther's death, he told Cath that he thought he would be destroyed. *I loved her more than anyone in the world,* he said. Her family, grief stricken, blamed him: there were obscure charges and vague, malicious rumors, painful to hear, impossible to answer. *He broke her heart,* Esther's mother said. *She was always such a happy girl.*

Cath told him that grief made people irrational, that there was no reason for him to feel guilty. *I don't,* he said. *I really don't.* But he suffered, he said; he would be destroyed by suffering without Cath, because she, Cath, was his light in the darkness. Thank God he had found her. This had made her heart leap, though now, spreading pale umber paint along the ceiling line, she added a reservation, something she had not noticed or had ignored at the time: Derek had started paying attention to her a couple of months before Esther died.

But that was music, school, business, a different sort of relationship. *But had she had hopes?* Impossible. Esther had been one of the goddesses of the campus, and the scuttlebutt—bulimia, some said, or anorexia nervosa, or maybe just the strains of senior year, starting a career, preparing to marry Derek—if you could consider *that* a strain—had been envy and gossip. Just the same, Cath momentarily wished that she had paid more attention to Mrs. Neilson, who grieved in the press and started a suicide prevention foundation and, without a scrap of evidence, blamed Derek. Perhaps Cath should have listened to Mrs. Neilson, whose words had been annihilated when Derek told her, *You're the only one who can save me.*

He'd meant this sincerely; Cath hadn't doubted it then and didn't doubt it now. For whatever reason, he was powerfully drawn to her, and the idea that she would be his salvation was not entirely hyperbole, not even entirely impractical. Given the rumors emanating from the Neilson family, a blameless young woman like Cath was his best defense. Had Derek thought about that? Or had his feelings been purely romantic and Wagnerian? Had he seen himself as a latter-day Flying Dutchman, a Dutchman saved by love, not in extremis, but in his youth, so that he could go on as brilliantly and effortlessly as he always had? Sitting beside her in the stacks examining scores, necking under the shadow of her dorm, leading a choir through the tricky repetitions of a Glass song, Derek did not know that his charmed life was already over, that he must leave the higher realm, that the grinders of the ordinary were ravenous for him.

Cath had lived in ignorance, too, the ignorance of a bliss so complete that now, years later, she could still forget everything, possibly forgive everything—that was a possibility—in the green splendor of his eyes, in the sight of his tanned arms and back wrapped in her sheets, in their musical harmony, in the edge of excitement that love gave the commonplace. She had been sleepwalking, under anesthesia, oppressed by mysterious clouds; then, suddenly, she had indeed *risen tremendous like the sun.* Old Whitman, beloved of her acquaintance on the night bus, had been right after all: it was possible to send out sunrise, and the old house, the yard, the music studio were filled by light as rosy and dramatic as any dawn over the great bay.

In these circumstances, her mind had drifted over the hidden snags of practicalities and anomalies; later, when she had other emotions, when she saw that sun makes for shadows, she found it best to work on the house, to putter, selecting paint chips, to move pictures around, to prowl, with Derek, or occasionally with Yvonne, the cheaper antique and secondhand stores in search of intesting old prints, a nice mirror, an inexpensive chest of drawers. She called rental companies about scaffolding and started refurbishing the interior.

On the weekends, Yvonne would scan the results with her sharp, critical eye, pointing out skips in the paint or spots on the floor. But whenever Derek complained that painting was too much for Cath, too smelly, too disruptive, Yvonne would point out that a fresh coat of paint was one of a property's *best selling points,* provided that the colors weren't too eccentric. *Neutrals,* Yvonne would say, neutrals were good, *and white, but not a cold white.* Yvonne had a high opinion of her own good taste, which was, unsurprisingly, identical to the demands of the real estate market. Cath paid little attention. She intended to put white gloss enamel on the living room woodwork and to close her ears to her sister-in-law's mantra that semigloss in cream was the trim color of the moment. Since Cath had no intention of selling her house, there was no reason to please anyone except herself and Derek, who ignored decorating decisions as long as the music studio met his specifications. In this aesthetic harmony, Yvonne was a minor nuisance.

And yet, Cath thought, as she started cutting in along the ceiling of the last wall, she had perhaps underestimated her sister-in-law. She was coming to understand, not so much Yvonne, who was, in Cath's opinion, incomprehensible, as the function of Yvonne. *Function*, as in *mathematical function,* a formula or recipe into which numbers are placed to arrive at a result, at a reality. *Function,* as in form follows function. *Function,* as in I can't function or *functional,* one of Yvonne's pet phrases for any kitchen not absolutely unmarketable. The *function* of Yvonne was to be a counterbalance for Derek. Cath had sometimes seen herself as a division between Derek and his sister, as a separation between two powerful, opposing forces, but she had misread the terms of the equation, failed to understand the operation of the *function.* Theirs was a more complex relationship, and when Cath succeeded in eliminating Yvonne on a daily basis, when she reached, that is, for *a happy ending,* she had upset a delicate equilibrium.

The question was, what to do? Go back or go forward? When she'd found her spaniel's collar, her hands had trembled so that the old tags rattled; then she'd brushed away foolish tears and stuck the painful memento back inside her desk. At that moment, Cath had decided to go forward, to leave the past, to forget the day—recovered with a sharp, immediate certainty—when she'd returned east after wrapping up her parents' affairs. She'd arrived on the red-eye and, dislocated by morning, had been disgorged in front of their building from an airport cab. She remembered running up the four flights to the apartment, her backpack banging against her leg all the way. Derek opened the door; he was smiling, beautiful, saying *You're home!* so that she almost wept for joy. She remembered kissing Derek out there in the hallway and clutching him so that love could fill up the caverns of regret and grief. It was a few moments before an unfamiliar silence made her ask, *Where's Danny?* and her heart jumped, because she couldn't hear the joyous scramble of his feet on the wood floors, the jingle of his tags, the one short bark that always announced her arrival.

"Oh, Danny," Derek said. "I had to have him put down. He was just too much work while you were away. He was messing the floor and chewing things. An old dog, anyway." He spoke quickly, without a hint of remorse, as if he could brush over this betrayal.

Cath had been sick right there in the foyer. "I guess I'll be next, then," she'd said, and they'd had an awful fight.

As she ran the pale umber paint along the molding line—good work to make you concentrate, to keep your nerves under control—Cath thought that she might have stabbed Derek right then. Had they been in the kitchen she might have, though that was a painful idea, dangerous even to contemplate, suggesting, as it did, a darkly impulsive and violent side to her personality. But she had already been distraught that day, and the loss of her old companion, coming on top of her parents' disaster, had pushed her emotions over the top. *Over the top,* another pregnant phrase. Derived from *going over the top* of World War I vintage, going, that is, over the edge of one's own trenches and barbed wire and sandbags to mud and slop and poison gas and hideous death. A pregnant phrase, indeed.

Cath climbed down from the stepladder to get the paint tray and roller. As she began covering the wall with big wet stripes, another idea came to her as unbidden and persistent as the pilgrims of spirituality: what had Derek done that she should try to kill him? For what could be worse than that destruction of her old dog, that carelessness at an already terrible and vunerable time? Why *had* she stabbed Derek? *You had a moment of madness,* he'd told her. *You're crazy,* was Yvonne's more direct assessment. But though Cath wondered, she might have put the question back in the drawer with the eloquent dog collar if it had not been for something indeterminate in the mass of daily trifles that made her nervous and had made Yvonne nervous, too, for Yvonne had surely been jumpy that rainy night when Derek arrived home so late.

He hadn't done that again. He was scrupulously punctual, or if he was going to be late, he phoned, explained; Cath could rely on Derek to call, absolutely. No, it was trifles, all trifles that drove her to home decoration, to cleaning up and cleaning out. There was the phone call, first. She remembered the night, remembered waking up as Derek got out of bed, probably to go to the toilet, and she would have gone back to sleep automatically if she had not had the curious feeling that he was looking at her, watching her. Would things have been different if she had sat up, spoken, or really been asleep? She opened one eye and, in the faint light from the open windows, saw him pick up his robe. Instead of going into the bathroom, he went out, soft-footed, to the hall. She could feel that he was moving carefully, but the old house's dry, creaking floors betrayed the slightest step, and Cath heard him descend the stair and walk along the lower hallway to the kitchen, where he seemed to talk on the phone for a very long time.

The next morning she asked, "Did I hear you up at the phone last night?" There was a pause in which he was tempted to lie. She saw that so clearly.

Instead, he said, "I'm sorry I waked you up. You know that awful feeling when you wake up in the middle of the night and remember something you should have done? I was afraid I'd left the side door unlocked. I had to call the custodian. At home. But I couldn't take a chance, not with the church's insurance."

"Oh, no, you couldn't," said Cath. "It's breaking and entering if a door is locked and simple trespassing if it isn't."

"You know the strangest things," said Derek, and he looked at her, as he sometimes did, as if she surprised him, as if she had escaped from his idea of her, the idea that was all-important to him.

After he left for work, Cath warmed up with scales on her violin and with double-stops, good for the concentration. Just the same, she made such a hash of an unaccompanied Bach sonata that she put the instrument away and went into the kitchen to call Saint Martin's. Without having any idea of what she was going to say, she asked to speak to Eric, the custodian.

"Oh, I'm sorry, he's away on vacation," the church secretary said. "He'll be back next week, but I'd be glad to take a message."

"That's all right," Cath said hastily. "I'll contact him next week." *Contact,* as in cement, or as in *to make contact,* with worlds beyond or with useful people, as in *a business contact. Contact* was a word Cath liked: it sounded official, in control, ordinary. *Contact* was a good word for when she was standing in the middle of the kitchen with her heart hammering and a sick, fluttery feeling in her stomach. But, of course, Eric might be home. Not everyone went away on vacation. Not everyone could afford to go away on vacation. Like Eric. He couldn't earn very much. If Derek's salary was any indication, Saint Martin's did not believe that charity began at home. And they'd surely pay their music minister more than their custodian. So Eric might have been at home last night, having a suburban vacation of day trips and sleeping in, a budget vacation disturbed in the middle of the night by the choir director and music minister who wanted him to check the status of the side door.

This scenario was plausible, but having gone that far, Cath went a step further and dialed Eric Hobshaw's home number. When Valerie Hobshaw answered, Cath almost hung up in relief: they were home. "Hello?" Mrs. Hobshaw repeated.

"I'm sorry to trouble you. It's Cath Tolland. Could I speak to your husband?"

The merest hesitation. This call was unusual, and Cath herself, irregular.

"But maybe my husband already contacted Eric," she said quickly. "Derek left me a confusing note. Something about the side door of the church?"

"I don't know," Valerie Hobshaw said. "But Eric's away for a couple of days fishing. I said to him, camping's no holiday for me, so he's to have a few days and then we'll go to the shore with the children."

"A good idea," Cath said, though her mouth felt numb.

"I can take a message," said Valerie Hobshaw.

"Oh, Derek will speak to him when he gets back. I don't know, it was just something about a lock."

"I'll see it's checked. Eric's very careful with anything about the doors and locks. He's probably noticed it himself."

"Oh, he probably has," said Cath. "It might even have been an old note."

"Do you remember what door?" the relentless Mrs. Hobshaw asked.

"I think it was the side door," said Cath. "Round by the choir."

"Eric will take care of it when he comes home, if he hasn't done so already. Just have your husband double-check that it's locked at night. If something's loose in the mechanism, the latch may not be engaging."

"Yes," said Cath, "thank you. I'm sorry to disturb you during Eric's holiday."

"You're not the first," said Mrs. Hobshaw, who added, because she was kindly at heart, "I hope that you are keeping well now."

"Very well," said Cath and she hung up, feeling sick. Just the same, she got a great many weeds cleared out around the garage and had pretty well rationalized the call by the end of the day. Of course, Derek had called Jane Henkel. She knew his habits, his way of coming up with ideas at night, of suddenly solving tempo or interpretation problems, of being full of a new idea. He'd suddenly seen a solution to a difficulty she'd been having and had called her up. And then lied to save Cath anxiety and jealousy. If she hadn't been quite so suspicious, so nosy, she could have spared herself grief. She could have; she wanted to believe that.

And she might have if something else hadn't happened just the other evening. Derek was getting set to mail off a score to a friend when he discovered a tear in the envelope. "Do we have some tape down here?" he asked, and Cath, busy in the kitchen, said, "I think there's some in my desk."

A moment later, she heard his voice raised in exasperation. "I can't find anything in this muddle." At that precise moment, she had an image of herself hiding in the music office in Saint Martin's and going through desk drawers and picking up books of check stubs, which she'd hidden without examining. Another *moment of madness,* she supposed. Cath hurried into the living room, opened the correct drawer, and handed him the tape. Her eyes fell on Danny's collar, and Derek saw it, too.

"That's what smells," he said. "That old leather. I wondered why your whole desk smells like dog. I'm surprised you kept that collar—under the circumstances."

Cath looked at him, surprised. "What do you mean?"

"You don't remember?" His eyes were shrewd and bright. "Maybe just as well."

"No, what do you mean?" Cath repeated.

"Well, the accident was sort of your fault," Derek said. "Though, of course, nothing deliberate, just your usual overindulgence. You'd gotten back from California—I think it was when you came back from California. He got all excited and you insisted on taking him right out and didn't bother with his leash."

Cath shook her head. She felt the approach of panic.

"I remember calling after you as you went downstairs," Derek said. "He was a bit blind and he ran into the street and was hit. There was nothing the vet could do. We had to have him put down. Poor old Danny."

Cath picked up the collar—round, heavy, the green on the leather worn away in patches with use and age. The collar was real, and she needed to hold on to something real. Danny had been real, and his death, too.

"What's the matter?" Derek asked. Again, there was something sharp and interested in his glance.

Cath shook her head. She wanted to argue, to explain, but Florida whispered *Be careful,* because either alternative was terrible. It would be terrible if her memory had been damaged beyond reliable recovery; it would be equally terrible if her husband was taking the opportunity to rewrite their past. Cath took a deep breath. "I've been thinking about another dog," she said. "A pet would be company when I'm alone so much."

"Dogs are expensive," Derek said, and she could hear the distaste in his voice. He'd never liked animals, never liked Danny. "Pets are too much work for you when you've been so ill."

"I suppose," said Cath.

"You need to rest up," Derek said. "All this work on the house is an awful lot for you."

"Paint is expensive, too," Cath said dryly.

Perhaps he suspected that he'd gone too far, because he said, "It's not the money, it's your health." Jovial now, all darkness expunged. "We need you in the choir."

"After my birthday," Cath said mechanically. He hugged her, but he couldn't bring her back from doubt, so that with these and other trifling lies and omissions, joy drained out of life, and Cath awoke to her situation: she was married to a charming, talented, handsome man, a veritable prince, whom she loved but didn't trust.

And so she faced a decision, a decision made possible by her illness, by her real moment of madness: the decision to remember or to forget. She was in the curious position of being able to do either, and one reason she was painting her living room walls and cleaning out old bureau drawers and weeding the yard was because she wasn't able to decide which she wanted to do.

In the end, Derek decided for her on the very day that she finished the trim in the living room. The white gleam of mantel, bookcases, cornice, and molding against the satiny, pale purplish umber of the walls filled her with satisfaction. She'd accomplished something solid, concrete. Cleaning, repainting, repairing: these produced unequivocal results; they had a pleasant factuality. *Factuality*: was that a word? Cath wondered. She hoped so, because she needed a word that suggested the reasonable certainty of things being in their expected and habitual places.

She went out to the barn to clean up her brushes and rollers and to put away the leftover cans of paint. She folded up the drop cloths and hung the brushes up to dry. She washed her hands well and then took a shower and got changed and went back into the living room to admire her handiwork again. She needed to have the floors done, but the effect was lovely even so, and she looked at her watch, because she wanted Derek to be home to see the woodwork, to admire the room, to admit that she was well and normal and making their house look very nice.

The phone rang as she was considering where to hang a faded old map of the county that she'd dug out of the barn loft. Cath put down the map and ran through to the kitchen.

"I'm going to be a bit late tonight," Derek said.

"Oh, that's too bad. I can't wait for you to see how the living room looks. What time for dinner?"

"Go ahead and eat. I'll probably grab a burger on the way home."

"I don't mind waiting," said Cath. He always called, she realized, but never explained, never elaborated. That had been their tacit agreement. Tonight she asked, "Rehearsal running late?"

"Starting early," he said. "I knew I'd have to remind you: the choir's in early tonight. There's no point in my coming home and turning around for a seven o'clock rehearsal."

"Oh, I had forgotten," Cath said, though she was sure he hadn't mentioned any schedule change, though he certainly might have called earlier. "I finished painting the living room. I think you're going to like it."

"I'll see it at its best in the morning light." Which was his way of telling her he would be late.

"Yes. Good night, then," Cath said, to let him know she understood. She hung up the phone and went straight to her desk. Now that she had stopped working with the paint, she was aware of the keen chemical odor. She opened the lower drawer, lifted some family pictures—she and Derek at their wedding, a snap of her with Danny, a handful of very old pictures of her parents—and found the books of check stubs. She closed the drawer, pulled down the work surface, and began reading through the stubs, working from the most recent payments back: light and electric and gas and oil. Telephone, dentist— dentist? Yes, Derek had broken a tooth and had needed it capped. The university music store, car payments, the annual septic tank pump. These were all in Derek's hand. These were all recent.

Then late winter. Some in her hand. Rather shaky, she had to admit. Were graphologists right? Was one's script diagnostic? But late February, early March: she was still writing checks right up to the night bus. And what had she written them for? Gas, light, electric, phone, oil. Dr. Friedland, their local GP. A mysterious gentleman who turned out to be a CPA. Tax preparation, surely. And that was odd; she couldn't think they needed help with their income taxes. She'd sent for some goods from a mail order clothing company. She'd written small checks to a variety of charities and worthy causes, and to several booksellers and quite a number of music publishers. There was nothing revealing, nothing at all mysterious except for the fact that Yvonne had lied to her about the checkbook and that Derek had thought it worthwhile to take this and the current checks into Saint Martin's and keep them in his office.

Cath had been concentrating completely on disbursements, on handwriting—hers or Derek's—but when she turned to the left-hand side of the checkbook and looked at deposits, she began to understand. There were large, regular, probably automatic deposits. She first took these to be Derek's salary from Saint Martin's, but they were too large, and while he was paid weekly, these deposits, several thousand dollars at a time, were monthly. Nor could they be Yvonne's. Yvonne's chief source of income was her commissions, which came in large, irregular spurts. Cath went quickly through both sets of check stubs. The money rolled in, month after month, to be spent some months and in others to be transferred to their savings account or to cash or to a mutual fund. She was almost at the end of the book when she found stuck, forgotten in the back, a bank statement with their account number and identification number and every numeral she needed to access the bank's automated twenty-four-hour information line.

Ten minutes later, having been assured that the bank was monitoring her call in the interests of quality control and staff training, and having survived the automatic system's unsettling combination of elec-

144

tronic good cheer and technological efficiency, Cath sat down in shock at the kitchen table. *A small trust fund,* Yvonne had said. Cath had envisioned a few thousand dollars a year. Instead, her trust fund churned out a few thousand dollars a month. Cath was, in a modest way, a wealthy woman. She could afford a dog, a car, a hired painter, and, presumably, a psychiatrist if she wanted one. And maybe she needed one, because, instead of celebrating like a lottery winner, like the recipient of the grand prize, an all-American dream ticket, she was sitting at her kitchen table thinking about the night bus and escape and the falsity of all her hopes.

10

CATH RECOGNIZED LUC BEAUSOLEIL'S DARK and ugly office as soon as she stepped in the door: fake wood paneling, green industrial carpet, dark vinyl blinds. The windows were narrow, the exterior plantings overgrown; the once well-proportioned dwelling had been partitioned so that no one room had enough light. In compensation, ceiling fixtures like giant egg crates flung a sickly greenish fluorescence over gray metal desks, scratched file cabinets, crammed bookcases, and a sad collection of calendars from such Beausoleil clients as the lumberyard, the mortuary, the hospital, and the local Grange. The net effect was depressing in an almost Dickensian manner, but when Cath had mentioned that one day to Luc, he'd laughed with delight.

"So who's the most trusted lawyer in town?" he demanded. "Who did your canny Aunt Elizabeth trust? Even fresh out of law school?"

"Everyone knows you're honest."

"Ah, that's right. And I am honest. But how do they know it?" He waved one of his neat square hands. "Voilà! I'm not wasting my clients' money on decor. Not one penny. No yuppie refurbishing, no fancy prints, no ferns, no designer furniture. Eat where the truckers eat and do your legal business where old Yankee farmers go to law."

She'd teased him just the same, and it had become a joke between them. She remembered that, standing in the reception area, easily the most hideous room of the whole suite. The receptionist was new, a woman in her fifties or sixties, plumply attractive and businesslike with pure white hair, smart makeup, and long red nails. The nameplate on her desk read *Pat DeRoche*. Ms. DeRoche looked up as the bell jangled and gave her visitor a thorough once-over. *I should have called,* Cath thought. *This is a mistake.*

"Yes?"

"I'm Cath Tolland. I wonder if I could see Luc this afternoon?"

"Do you have an appointment?"

"No, I'm sorry. I wasn't sure of the weather. I have to cycle into town." Cath gestured awkwardly. Her old bicycle, chained up to the metal post holding the LUC BEAUSOLEIL, ATTORNEY-AT-LAW sign, did not look like an upscale mode of conveyance. And she didn't look particularly prosperous, either. She had come impulsively, straight from readying the dining room for painting. She'd moved out the chairs and covered the table and washed down the walls and the woodwork. And then, without stopping to change, just in her old jeans and T-shirt, she'd gotten out the bike and ridden straight into town. "If it's not convenient . . ."

"He has a three o'clock appointment," the receptionist said in a doubtful voice. "You've dealt with Attorney Beausoleil before?"

"Oh, yes. We're old friends. He handles a trust fund for me."

"Oh. *That* Tolland." The receptionist took another look, committing Cath's image to her memory and doubtless labeling it unfavorably. "Just have a seat. I'll check with Attorney Beausoleil."

"Thank you," Cath said. "Tell him I only need a minute."

Ms. DeRoche walked across the hall and vanished into the dark warren of rooms. She reappeared almost instantly, accompanied by her boss, a trim, animated man with neat features in a square, bony face.

"Well, Cath," he said. She stood up with a smile, glad to see him in spite of everything, and he came over to give her a hug. "You're looking well! Come in, come in."

"I came on the spur of the moment," Cath said. Her gesture encompassed her untidy, paint-spattered clothes, the disruption of his schedule. "But it was a nice day to cycle, and I don't have a car."

"Healthy exercise," Luc said. "I've got a little time. My next appointment's at three, isn't it, Pat? Come this way. I've allotted myself a bigger office."

"With a fireplace! Very grand."

"Inoperable," Luc said happily. "Keeps down the insurance rate. Sit, sit, the chairs are functional."

Cath sat down and Luc perched on the edge of his large desk, as if this was a semiformal visit. *Semiformal*, as in dance, a *semiformal dance,* where, once upon a time when such things were important, women wore short, strapless dresses and men wore dinner jackets with boutonnieres and cummerbunds. Although she and Luc had never managed a formal or even a *semiformal,* they had gone dancing more than once during a not-too-serious romance one summer while she was staying with Aunt Elizabeth. Who knows what might have developed if she had not met Derek at school and had her life altered completely?

"You had a question about your trust?" Luc asked.

Cath realized that he had been waiting for her to speak.

"With your illness, I've been sending the reports to your husband . . . I'll see that's changed—"

"Don't bother," Cath said. She gave a soft, nervous laugh. "I'd forgotten about the money. I've had a quite serious head injury, and the money just slipped my mind."

"Your funds have done very well," Luc said.

He was, Cath thought, pleasingly earnest and boyish looking, though he was her age, exactly, and so only a few years younger than Derek. But though Luc still looked youthful and uncomplicated, she must remember that appearance is deceiving. After a certain age, no one is young and everyone is complicated.

"Of course, you mustn't think this market will go on forever. Now, I've asked Philip, the broker who handles my accounts, to be very conservative. When you take over, you can fly a bit higher if you want, but—"

"You've made me a rich woman," Cath said. "I never asked for you to do that."

"*Rich* is a relative term," Luc said, "but yes, I think we've done well for you. You certainly can afford a better set of wheels than that antique Schwinn." He smiled, pleased with his own competence and the success of a variety of mutuals and bonds which had grown Cath's trust fund nicely. At the same time, Cath's reaction, half friendly, half resentful, was not what he'd have expected from a client on the eve of assuming control over a tidy accumulation of wealth.

"Where did that money come from?" Cath demanded.

Luc felt his uneasiness increase. Cath Mackey had always been a sweet girl. Even his mother, who had been alarmed at the obvious— Cath's Protestant, eccentric connections—had agreed Cath Mackey was a sweet girl. *I wouldn't worry if she wasn't. She's a darling, but they're all nuts except the old aunt. Every one of them. And her parents are the worst ever. Don't break my heart!* At the time, he'd been sure Cath had escaped her heritage with nothing more than a few oddities. Then came news of the stabbing and of her breakdown. She'd run away to Florida and lost her memory and become a recluse. Luc had heard all about it, including the thematic variations offered at the general store, the feed shop, the church. Under the circumstances, he really should have gone to visit Cath, should have called up, dropped by. He hadn't realized that she couldn't drive, that she was cycling, that she was stuck out at the old house.

"Well, the original fund was started by your aunt Elizabeth. You remember Aunt Elizabeth."

"Of course," Cath said impatiently. "I remember the distant past quite well." She put emphasis on *distant* in a way that made Luc feel unjustly rebuked.

"That original investment's had quite some time to build up," Luc continued.

"My fund," Cath said, "is churning out several thousand dollars in interest a month. Is that correct?"

"The markets have been especially strong. You mustn't count on quite so much as a permanent thing. We're overdue for a correction."

Correction as in *department of corrections*, as in *being corrected*. Cath had a disturbing vision of a woman in black leather with a long whip and a professional frown. The woman looked rather like Yvonne, and Cath gave another smothered giggle.

"You understand," said Luc.

"There's still too much money," Cath said stubbornly.

"All right!" He stood up and walked around the desk to barricade himself behind formality. This was no longer a *semiformal* visit. "After your parents' deaths, when the ashram settled—"

"I told you I didn't want their money. I told you to give it to charity, the hospital, the animal shelter. I didn't want the money."

"The money arrived, and it was thought that you were not in a state of mind to make a decision."

"*Who* thought?" Cath asked, raising her voice at that impersonal, imperial passive. "Who thought? *I* knew what I wanted, and I didn't want a cent of it."

"Your husband and I discussed it," Luc said. His mother had been right. He hated to admit it, but his mother with her old country caution had been right: *The only one safe to marry would have been old Elizabeth Mackey.* Well, Mom needn't have worried. He didn't marry Cath Mackey, not even close. Instead, he'd fallen madly for Renee Courtemanche, a distant, distant cousin, who was providing him with a life of stimulating dissension.

"You and I discussed it, too," said Cath angrily. "I made my wishes very clear, but you disregarded them."

"Cath, if you can remember—cast your mind back, please—you sat right in my office, my old office, and told me I could steal every cent. Do you remember that? You can't ask me to believe that you were serious."

"You were already married then," Cath said. "And now you have young children. You could have put it all in trust for them, for their schooling."

"I am *your* trustee. I had a moral and legal obligation to protect *your* interests. And it was clearly in your interest to take a settlement in excess of two hundred thousand dollars and invest it wisely! You were under extreme emotional duress at the time. You'd had a terrible tragedy; you weren't—"

"I wasn't in my right mind," said Cath.

"You were under stress," Luc repeated. He rose from behind his desk and stole a quick glance at his watch. It was only twenty to three. Another five minutes. Then he would tell her that he had to prepare for his next appointment. "And lately you've been ill. Please, Cath, don't be precipitous about this."

"How can I be anything else?" she asked, standing up in turn, as memory, which had been building in her brain all spring like a thunderhead, suddenly burst upon her. "You've ruined my life," she cried. To their mutual surprise and distress, Cath burst into tears as she spoke.

Without saying good-bye, she ran from his office, through the foyer, and down the steps to her bike, where she struggled with the combination lock, tears dripping over the dial, hands shaking, her whole personality dissolving into rage and regret. The lock disengaged; she wrenched off the chain, swung her leg over the bike, and rolled down the drive, indifferent to everything, even to the green van turning in from the road, even to the angry burst of his horn. Cath saw the vehicle too late to stop. She wrenched her handlebars as the driver's brakes screeched. The bike slewed across the driveway but not fast enough, for the front bumper of the van caught her rear wheel, thrusting the bike toward the grass and throwing her onto the gravel.

The metallic sound of the van door opening, an anxious voice. "Are you all right?"

He seemed young to Cath, and pale. He'd gotten a fright. She herself was stunned, still beyond fear.

151

"Here, I'll get that." He took hold of her bike and lifted it from her legs.

She scrambled up, shivering all over.

"Are you sure you're all right?" He was tall and fair, with a drooping reddish mustache, dark eyes, a nice, open, worried face. "I'm Vincent Courtemanche. I met you one day just after you'd come home. With Yvonne."

Cath had a vague memory of a van, of Yvonne talking about furniture. "A difficult day," she said.

"This isn't much better." He was still nervous. "I was just coming in to see my brother-in-law. I sure don't want to lose him a client."

He was trying to make her laugh, Cath realized. She tried to say everything was okay, for really she wasn't badly hurt; she'd been lucky; she could have been under the wheels. Instead, she opened her mouth and said, "Luc's ruined my life," so that they looked at each other in surprise for a peculiar, charged moment.

"He's made me rich," she exclaimed, as if that were an explanation. "I never asked him to do that. People shouldn't change your life without asking you, should they?" Then she wrenched the bicycle from Vincent's grasp and turned it toward the road.

"Wait," he called. "Wait, just a minute! Your knee's cut!"

Cath looked down. Both knees were scuffed and abraded, the raw red patches speckled black with bits of dirt and gravel. A fat trickle of blood flowed from one deeper scratch.

"Hold on," he said. "I've got a Band-Aid in the truck."

Cath's side burned, too, and her knee began throbbing. She felt that she had to escape, that she couldn't bear this kind, nervous stranger, but blood was pooling at the top of her sock, and she took a deep breath. He banged open the rear door of his van, reached in, and pulled out a square plastic box, white with a red cross on the top, dusty but official. "Don't leave home without it," he said.

That little, lame joke brought Cath back far enough to say, "That's what I need. A first aid kit. For cuts and scrapes and other things."

"We should wash this," he said when he got eye level with her knee. "We can go in and get this washed."

"No," she said. "No, I can't go in. Luc thinks he's done such a good job for me, he can't possibly understand why I'm upset. Please tell him it's nothing to do with him. Nothing at all. Please tell him that."

"Yes, I'll do that." Vincent put on some antiseptic that burned. "Wash this well when you get home."

"Yes," she said.

He put on the bandage. "Your knees are going to hurt. Let me drive you home. I think the bike will fit in the van."

"No, no don't bother. It was all my fault."

"Please. I've heard you sing," he said, as if that explained everything. As if, Cath thought, it was all right for him to knock her over and help her up and involve himself. "You have such a beautiful voice."

She didn't answer. Her heart was beginning to hammer again, for she'd already delayed too long. She felt she had to get away before her mind broke into pieces, before she revealed herself.

"Just let me move a couple of boards," Vincent said, walking back to the van. "I'm sure we can get the bike in."

Cath threw her leg over the bar as soon as his back was turned and pushed off down the drive, her knees on fire. Behind her, Vincent was shouting something, but she ignored every sound: his voice and the rattle of her torn fenders and the rolling hum of heavy wheels on the state road. She had to get away. She forced her legs up and down, her side aching, her knees burning, her only thought to get down the road and out of town and home. Standing up to pedal, trying to get some speed, Cath let the bike wobble out from the rough and uneven shoulder, before a shock wave from a big log truck set her wheels trembling and told her how close she'd come. Cath didn't care. She put her head down, ignored the pain, and dug into the pedals as if she could regain enough momentum to overtake the night bus.

*　　　*　　　*

Cath considered herself a thoughtful person. She certainly spent a good deal of time listening to that inner monologue which accompanies the human animal. But when it came to important decisions, she rarely trusted to rationality. By the time she reached home, shielded, no doubt, as Aunt Elizabeth used to say, *by the Providence that protects bairns and drunkards,* Cath had recovered her equilibrium and made her mind a blank. She pushed everything that bothered her, prosperity, deception, the horrors of memory, back into her unconscious and waited to see what the dark circuits of survival and imagination might suggest. Over the weekend, she was very careful, very quiet, very self-contained. *Emotion is dangerous,* Florida cautioned. *Be careful,* and she was. She spent most of her time painting the dining room, keeping herself incommunicado amid the fumes, the rollers, the paint trays, and the drop cloths. She did not go to services at Saint Martin's, which seemed to please Derek, and she accepted Yvonne's advice on the color of the front hallway, which put her sister-in-law in a good mood.

Sunday night, Cath baked two loaves of gingerbread and a big batch of oatmeal cookies. Monday morning, she worked on her music and returned the chairs to the now aired and dried dining room. She picked a large bunch of Shasta daisies and early lilies and divided them with Mrs. Pye, who helped her make a nice arrangement. Cath had just returned home with her flowers when a car pulled into the yard. Luc Beausoleil had one indulgence, after all, a beautiful, dark green Saab.

He got out and looked at her over the top of the car. "I was just passing," he called.

Cath smiled, and Luc crossed the lawn to the house. "With your birthday coming up and all, I should really have stopped by before this to talk to you and Derek."

"Derek's at work." Cath held the front door open. "And you've neglected me shamefully."

"Ah, that smells like your aunt Elizabeth's gingerbread!" Luc exclaimed. "She made the greatest gingerbread."

"I made some for you. It's her recipe."

"And how were you going to get it to me, if I can ask?"

"I knew you were coming," Cath said.

"I didn't know I was coming myself until I was on the state road."

"I have a telephone. I was going to call if you didn't come by today."

Luc gave a rueful smile. He mustn't give their last, uncomfortable meeting too much weight.

"I made you some of her oatmeal cookies, too," Cath said. "I hate making cookies, but I behaved very badly the other day, so I thought I should make the cookies as well."

"I suppose the money came as a shock," Luc said, as he followed her into the dining room.

"We'll have some gingerbread, shall we? And talk business afterwards."

"I don't know what my wife will say if I come home with gingerbread on my breath."

"Is Renee jealous?" Cath asked. "I hope you don't give her reasons."

"My wife is jealous," Luc said, "but I haven't given her any reasons yet."

"A dramatic marriage," Cath guessed.

"Yes, I suppose so."

"I have a different sort of marriage altogether." Cath went back into the kitchen for some aluminum foil, and after she had cut some slices of cake, she wrapped the rest up. "For Renee and the children. Tell her it is a thank-you cake."

"It's very good," said Luc.

"The tea will be ready in a minute," said Cath. "You like coffee, but Aunt Elizabeth always served tea."

"That's right, she did! And butter for the gingerbread." He helped himself to some and spread it on the rich, dark bread. Cath had plates out and flowers on the table, and he believed she really had known he was coming. For all that, she seemed perfectly calm and ordinary, an old friend who was a reasonable sort of client.

155

"You've been getting the place fixed up, I see."

"Do you like the colors?"

"Very much. You're doing it yourselves?"

"Oh, yes. The reason I was all paint the other day. I didn't know then that I was rich and could hire someone. I don't know how it was, but I'd gotten the room ready to paint and then it was suddenly the right time to see you, though I handled it badly."

"You've been ill."

"Yes, I've not been really well since—since I lost a baby last year." Cath frowned and blushed the way she always did when she lied. Whatever had made her say that? She heard herself mentioning something about a miscarriage and knew that she was committed to the story now. What stupidity to say such a thing to a sensible old friend like Luc. She would have been better to tell one of the nice Florida doctors, who were looking for reasons, explanations, who wanted to help, who might just have understood.

"Oh, I'm very sorry," said Luc.

"And then I remembered at a bad time," Cath said, almost stumbling over the words in her haste to change the subject, to bury the topic. *Nothing is more humiliating than lying,* she thought, and yet Freud was right when he said that some lies are more revealing than the truth. Cath was sure he was right about that. "Perhaps you can have memory fits like epileptic fits. Mine are getting more intense, though my memory is still incomplete."

"Was that what happened in my office? A 'memory fit'?"

"Yes."

There was a pause in which each digested the implications of such an event, before Luc said, "The reason I wanted to talk to you is because you haven't a will. And with the trust funds coming to you—"

"I might die intestate," Cath said promptly. "*Intestate* is a curious word."

"A Latin word," Luc said. He'd forgotten her fascination with words, with individual words and phrases. He'd forgotten the way she could take refuge in odd, unusual words and in the connotations and suggestions of ordinary language. "It simply means that you die without a will."

"It reminds me of *interstate*," said Cath. "Of being between one place and another. Of course, in my case, I might be considered *intestable*. Lunatics are not considered eligible to make wills, are they?"

"You are very far from being a lunatic."

"I'm glad to hear you say that," said Cath, suddenly confident and businesslike. "Because that is the first thing I want from you. I want you to consider the idea that I may be quite sane and normal and have good reasons for everything I do. Will you consider that?"

Even allowing for the exaggerations of his neighbors, Luc felt uncomfortable. "Everything?" he asked. As her lawyer, he would have to be blunt. As her friend, a certain delicacy was allowed.

"You are thinking about the night bus," she said, nodding her head.

"The night bus?" Perhaps, Luc thought, she was not as entirely rational as she seemed on the surface.

"My departure to Florida, to madness, pneumonia, and disaster. A trip for which I may have had reasons or I may not. That's the second thing I want you to do for me. Do you have a piece of paper handy?"

Luc pulled out his pocket planner.

"Please write this name down: Esther Nielson."

Luc printed the name neatly. "Who is Esther Nielson?"

"Was. She has been dead for over seven years. I want you to find out everything you possibly can about her death."

"She wasn't a local person?"

"She was a music student in Syracuse while Derek and I were studying there. She committed suicide."

"The death was investigated, then? The coroner ruled it suicide?"

"Yes. There was quite an extensive investigation."

"And you remember the details of the case? Cath, please enlighten me, because I don't see the point of this."

"At the time, we—those of us who were her friends—were terribly upset. I think we may have closed our minds to—certain possibilities."

Luc raised his eyebrows and sat heavily back in his chair. He knew she was speaking about herself. "And something since has made you"— he coughed slightly—"revisit these ideas?"

"I have been caught in a storm of memory."

"There are people who specialize in investigations," Luc said after a moment.

"If detective novels are to be believed, they are around every corner. As a practical matter, I thought an attorney might know someone discreet."

"I don't handle criminal cases," Luc said. "I do wills and property and divorces and disputes between tenants and landlords."

"But you could find me an investigator? And pay him or her out of the trust and keep all the bills and records to yourself?"

"That might be expensive."

"You've ensured I have the money," Cath said briskly. "The main thing is that you handle everything. I'll come by now and again and get the results. Or you can stop by, but call first. Send me nothing."

Luc realized that he should have asked about her marriage, about her situation, before getting involved in a way he disliked, in a matter that would be hard to keep secret, in procuring revelations that might prove awkward. "Want to tell me some more about"—he glanced down at his notebook—"Esther Nielson?"

"No," said Cath, "I don't want you to have any preconceptions. I just want you to gather everything you can."

"All right," said Luc, though the project seemed dubious, unwisely undertaken, possibly destructive. "And the will," he said. "What about letting me do something I'm competent to do? How about letting me draw up a will for you?"

"If I should die intestate, everything goes to Derek. Is that correct?"

"That's correct, provided you have assumed control of the trust and have no other living relatives. I've forgotten, is there anyone else?"

"Very distant cousins is all."

"Then I think you need a will to be absolutely sure there is no claim. If you want everything to go to Derek, that is."

"Who else would I want to have the money?" Cath asked.

Luc nodded. "Very well. Though we hope it's a long way away, a will would still simplify matters for him."

Cath smiled. "I'll certainly do that, after you find out about Esther for me. But you said everything would go to Derek provided I have received the money from the trust. Suppose I die before my birthday?" She remembered the shock wave from the log truck. "Suppose I get hit by a car or something?"

"God forbid," said Luc. "Then the situation is completely different. I checked your aunt's will after I spoke to you the other day. If you die before assuming control of the trust funds, the money goes back into her estate and is distributed to a variety of charities, the Heifer Project, the Audubon Society, the local animal shelter, the Salvation Army. They all got small bequests when she died."

"I'd better live to be thirty," Cath said lightly, but Luc noticed that she had gone pale.

"You are quite well now, aren't you? You've recovered from your illness?"

"Oh, yes. It's just—what was that old phrase, 'someone walked over my grave'? It's an odd thing to know the value of your life almost to the penny."

Derek set his briefcase down on the oak chest in the hallway and ran his hand across his forehead. A dull pain pulsed monotonously over his right eye; sinus trouble, his quack said: the Connecticut Valley was notorious for allergies and sinus infections. Dr. Friedland had discussed the geographical and horticultural particulars with the smug enthusiasm of a man with a well-situated practice. Derek gave the pretty bunch of yellow lilies on the chest a baleful glance. Pollen was bad, so was perfume, and paint was even worse. He could still smell the dining room and the living room, though Cath had been finished in there for almost a week, though the weather had been perfect, warm and dry, though every window in the house stood open and the screen doors permitted a constant cross breeze. The smell still lingered like a romance gone sour, a tormenting physical embodiment of present irritations and problems.

He'd been fine until she started painting. Perfectly fine. The painting was the start of everything, Derek thought. At the moment Cath was outside scraping away at the kitchen clapboards. She'd waved to him from her perch on the old wooden ladder, calling down to tell him that she'd moved outside because the smell had been bothering him. There was so much prep to do that it would be a while before she could start painting again. She had it all figured out. She'd do the music studio last and he could maybe stay over with Yvonne a couple of nights until it was dry.

Derek couldn't see her eyes, just the smile from under her straw hat and the shadow line breaking over her nose. She seemed—what? *Happy* was too strong a word; so was *contented*. Self-contained, maybe; maybe that was it. He had the feeling that, like him, she was waiting, cautious and watchful. In the meantime, she was busy working on the old house, learning the Gorecki, keeping cheerful.

Derek rubbed his head again and went into the bathroom for some aspirin. The paint was giving him headaches, and Cath was making him nervous, though that was ridiculous. She adored him, and he had always trusted her simplicity, her willingness to see the world as he presented it; he had nothing to fear from Cath. Nothing at all, yet the sound of her work, a steady *scritch, scritch* like the claws of a giant cat, ratcheted up his headache. For all that, she'd smiled at him, though he hadn't seen her eyes.

Just as well. She'd had the perception of evil. She'd told him that outright, though, if true, didn't that mean she'd been deceived? She'd sat on her bed, smiling into his eyes, ready for his arms, and talked about clouds of darkness and the forces of evil. *I need another aspirin,* Derek thought. *Two at least.* Yvonne couldn't smell the paint. *The house has a* new *smell,* she said, her face like a cash register, toting up the possibilities. Yvonne wouldn't hear the cat claws, either; she'd hear profits, and she'd talk of charm and restoration. So perhaps his headache really wasn't from the paint or the Connecticut Valley pollens, either. Perhaps he was suffering from the pressure of his situation, caught as he was in a pack of women, all stupid and demanding.

He went back out to the hall, collected his briefcase, and took it through to the music studio. The piano would drown out the sound of the scraper and of Cath's ladder thumping against the side of the house as she moved from one section to another. Of course, he should change and go out to help, but he'd seen enough women for one day. Derek loved the female voice and, on too many occasions, the female body, but in most ways, he didn't like women. Didn't like them at all. And, except musically, he couldn't much respect creatures who didn't seem to know who liked them and who didn't.

Unlike animals. Derek disliked them, too, but animals know what's what. Cath's old dog had known its fate the moment she left for California. Derek respected that instinctive knowledge; it made sense to know your enemies. But that idea, too, made his head pound, because he had perhaps fallen into a similar trap with Cath. No, he denied that idea. Cath was the exception, which was why he'd married her, why he'd stayed with her, protected her, loved her—albeit in his own fashion. The others were on a different trajectory. He pursued them until lust turned to possession and then—Derek's face took on an expression of distaste. Women had two lusts, while men had only one. Men wanted the body and pleasure. Pleasures, in the case of singers and musicians.

Women wanted all that and permanence, control, especially control. All his life, his adult, sexual life, Derek had fought the stifling possessiveness which emerged out of sexual attraction like some rampant vine. Controlling females were the bane of his existence, though, of course, all their efforts had proved futile, because he was too clever, far too clever. Not even Esther had managed to rein him in. But, ultimately, the effort to remain free ended desire. Again and again, he'd turned from love and passion filled with revulsion and bent only on escape. Even if escape meant hurt feelings, even actual hurt: he had to get away.

So maybe the problem wasn't the paint, but Jane, who'd begun as a challenge and become a pleasure and who should now, by rights, have disappeared. Gone, graduated, died, even. Even died. Sometimes people died, even young people, even young women. Perhaps Jane, too, would disappear, though it was wisest not to think of that. But even if she did, his problems would remain, for there was always Cath, who possessed the antidote, who'd saved him once or twice already, who was a permanent fixture. Cath was painting the old house as if she intended to live in it forever, even though Yvonne, his other constant, had already sold the place in imagination half a dozen times already.

Derek sat down at the piano, his head hurting too much to concentrate. Weeks, he thought. Weeks ahead of him, weeks in which he had to plan, initiate a plan. The plan. The lake was the plan. Yvonne had insisted that the lake was a solution. And with Cath's mental state, everything had seemed straightforward, though now Derek wasn't so sure. But that was just his headache, his headache and his rage at Jane, who had turned demanding, manipulative, whiny. She'd mentioned the department chair at the college. Just dropped the name like a stone down a well, and like the vicious bitch she was, the next name would be the minister of Saint Martin's. Derek knew that. He could not afford a scandal, not even an indiscretion, not after Cath's disaster. It was Cath's fault, really. That day in the kitchen. She'd had her eyes closed, and when she opened them, she couldn't face reality. That was her trouble. Really, she deserved everything she got.

So in some ways, it would be simple. Disagreeable, but simple, and then his problems would be solved. He'd be independent of Saint Martin's and its prissy minister and of the college, too. He'd be able to travel, to build a national, even an international, reputation. Europe would be nice; Asia, too. If he were careful, he could live independently for a long time. But there was something—the real source of his headache, along with the paint—that suggested Cath was slipping away from his vigilance. She'd done it first with madness, flight, amnesia. How could anyone have stopped that descent into oblivion? Yvonne was asking too much to expect him to have managed that! The situation now was different. Except for the treacherous blanks in her memory, Cath seemed almost normal. She was losing her shyness and talking with nosy Mrs. Pye, for one. And maybe with others, too, because she'd stopped asking about the choir, about going in to Saint Martin's, about *regaining her context*. She'd gotten the old bike fixed, as well. What for, if not to go into town, to visit, to confront old rumors? She had gone ahead and ordered paint supplies, too, though he'd reminded her about money, about the need to be cautious. *Paint's expensive,* she'd admitted, but her voice was dry, as if she knew everything, as if she could read his mind, as if she'd had some perception of evil.

He personally wouldn't have risked this business. They could have worked something out, left Cath in the south, sent her money, even. But Yvonne had insisted, and he'd given in to her, as he always had. He'd agreed to this crazy scheme at his cost. He'd never felt this bad before. Never. And that was because of Cath, scraping the house, scraping off the coat of the house, rooting down under the surface and making everything new.

At six o'clock, his wife came in to get cleaned up, apologetic because she hadn't started dinner. "You must be hungry," Cath said. "I didn't realize how late it was." She was tanned from the sun, her arms glinting copper, as she stood at the sink and gulped down a big glass of water.

"Why don't I get a pizza?" asked Derek. "You've been working hard all day."

"All right," she said, smiling, happy. She had the capacity to be happy over trifles. She had distractions from the horrors of life. "We're saving a fair bit on the paint prep," she said.

"Yes, indeed," he said. "So long as you don't work too hard."

Solicitous. He knew when to be solicitous, even though his head was pounding, even though he doubted he could eat anything, far less a pizza.

"You're sure you want a pizza? You're having some trouble with your headaches again, aren't you? Or you call, and I'll pick it up," she offered.

"No, no," he said. "By the time you get a shower, the pizza will be ready." He went right to the phone and called. He could hear the water running overhead, running down the cast-iron pipes in the walls. He felt surrounded by noise, surrounded by Cath, and, as quickly as he could, Derek went out to the car and drove toward the village.

There were steep, even dangerous hills both coming and going, yet Cath had fixed the bike—Mrs. Pye, of all people, had brought her the parts! Who would have thought that Mrs. Pye with her thick glasses even possessed a license? There were, Derek thought, far too many old people driving, creeping up and down the roads, struggling to hardware and bike shops to buy parts for mad wives who would otherwise be safe at home. Whom had Cath been going to see? What was she up to? No one rode these hills for fun; Derek was certain of that, but when he'd asked her why she bothered with the bike, she'd spoken of exercise, of a backup in case of emergency. She never mentioned visiting anyone, but then she'd never had much gossip or small talk. Her silence on such topics meant nothing.

The parking lot of the general store was full, and the building was crowded with craftsmen picking up beer and cigarettes, and harried working moms juggling last-minute groceries, tired children, and packaged dinners. Reluctant to go home, retired farmers gossiped on the front porch, while kids rented videos and bought sodas or hung out by the pay phone, their skateboards tucked under their arms. Derek collected his order and stood in line for the register, the pizza box warm in his hands, his head throbbing, his nerves jangling with the noise, the shouted greetings, the easy laughter. A woman brushed by him with a toddler, who, seeing a stiff old dog waddle in the door, broke away to pet the animal.

"Come back here, Jeffrey!" She bumped into another customer as she turned, and, as he stepped back, he jostled Derek. The man was compact, slight, dressed in a well-cut business suit that stood out against the paint- and grease-spattered overalls, the jeans and shorts of the rest of the crowd. They exchanged apologies, laughing at the child, who stood blissfully grasping handfuls of the dog's thick blond coat. "He just loves that dog!" the mother said, her annoyance turning to the most irritating sort of maternal indulgence.

Derek managed to smile anyway. "A fine little fellow," he said and watched Mama beam.

"He'll be ready for the Little League, next thing you know," the other customer teased, and when the woman said, "I hope you're still coaching then, Luc," Derek realized who he was.

"You're Luc Beausoleil."

"That's right." The man turned. His face was blandly pleasant, the features of a man without headaches, without the corrosive odor of paint, without a mad wife.

"Derek Tolland. We met a few years ago, when my wife rented out the old Mackey house for that bed-and-breakfast."

"Of course," said Luc. "Sorry, I must have been a million miles away. Of course I remember you."

"You were a tremendous help to Cath at that time." Derek's voice was genial now. He'd caught the right tone for Cath's lawyer. Neighborly, friendly. Too bad he couldn't risk inviting Luc over, but that would be going too far. But friendly was important. It was important to be friendly with Cath's lawyer.

"Yes, I think we worked out a good deal. Maybe too good. The Urfelds couldn't really make a go of it. That's too strong. They decided to bed-and-breakfast elsewhere, that's all."

"The building needs quite a bit," Derek admitted. "We didn't realize how much until we moved in ourselves."

"The story of old houses in this town. You're eternally fixing them up. I should have known better, but I bought one myself." Luc Beausoleil smiled, tolerant of his own foibles, then waved past Derek to a

165

thin, sunburned man in brown overalls and a trucker's cap. "You get that tractor out of the field?" he called.

The man held up three fingers. "Three hours."

"No! You're kidding!"

The fellow took this for encouragement to bore all and sundry with the various ailments of his John Deere. Derek set his pizza down on the counter and took out his wallet. "We'll hope to see you," he told Luc as he settled up with the clerk.

"Right, sure. My best to Cath." A smile, a nod, then back into the tractor saga. "You check the carburetor? I don't know how that antique runs in the first place."

Derek walked back to his car, pizza in hand and one more thing on his mind: Luc Beausoleil should have asked about Cath. After everything that had happened, it would have been natural for him to ask. Nothing nosy—lawyers were paid to be discreet—but a quiet *How's Cath?* Or *I hope Cath's keeping well now?* That's what you'd expect. *My best to Cath,* Luc Beausoleil had said, *My best to Cath,* as if he already knew how she was, as if he'd already been in touch.

I'll ask her, Derek thought. *I'll ask if she's seen Luc lately. And if she has, she'll say yes, and it will all come out. Or else she'll say no, and I'll know she's lying.* He thought about that all the way home, how he'd phrase the question, how he'd trap her with her honesty or her lies, one way or the other, because he was sure she'd cycled into town to see the lawyer. But by the time he reached their drive and pulled into the old garage, he'd had another thought: he was already one step ahead of her. He already knew she'd seen Luc Beausoleil. Derek was sure of that. And why should he warn her and let her know that he knew? He could be cautious, too. Derek got out of the car feeling better, in control. Cath was deceiving him, so it was going to be her fault after all, and there was no reason for him to have regrets. None whatsoever. He just had to watch his step.

11

~ ~ ~ ~ ~ ~ ~

CATH SAT IN A LITTLE dark room at Luc Beausoleil's office. She was reading through a pile of photocopied newspaper clippings and interview transcripts procured from Confidential Reports, an investigation firm specializing in divorce cases and in background checks for businesses.

"If there's dirt, they'll find it," Luc had said. He'd been parked safely and officially behind his desk at the time, while Cath sat in the visitor's chair, thinking over the firm and deciding whether or not Confidential Reports sounded like what she really wanted.

"So," said Luc after a minute. "You want to go ahead with this?" He was rather hoping she would say no. He sensed this business could be disagreeable. Either it was preliminary to a matrimonial mess of the sort he detested, or his old friend, who had *memory fits* and moments of irrationality, was out prospecting for trouble. Either way, Luc felt, he didn't need business that badly.

"They're discreet?" she asked.

"Safe as an undertaker."

"Undertaker," Cath said. She turned the word over in her mind— *undertaker, one who put you underground, a conduit to the netherworld—*

before giving a wan smile. "We'll give it a try. I'll come by a couple times a week. Or call me during the day if there's anything really important."

That's how they'd left it, and she'd stopped in twice before anything arrived. Luc wondered why she didn't phone first, but he supposed she wanted the exercise—and maybe to avoid having calls to his office show up on her phone statement. Although such circumspection was typical of domestic disputes, Cath seemed so calm and matter-of-fact that he put her caution down to eccentricity.

The correctness of this diagnosis was confirmed by her reaction to the report, which she insisted on reading at his office. Whenever Luc glanced in to see how she was getting on, he found her gazing into space, obviously far away. In spite of Cath's charm and wit, it seemed to him that her mind had been subtly disturbed. This impression was strengthened by the fact that, as far as Luc could tell, there was much that was sad but little that was suspicious about the death of Esther Nielson. On Cath's insistence, he read everything Confidential Reports turned up. But aside from the fact that the young woman had been engaged to Derek Tolland, Luc could see no cause for concern. He decided he would let things ride for a while, but before Cath ran up too big a bill, he'd have a talk with her.

And perhaps with her husband as well. Derek Tolland had seemed a pleasant fellow on the few occasions they'd met, and Luc wondered if he'd been wrong to be so discreet and lawyerly at the general store. He probably should have asked about Cath and gotten Derek's read on her condition. Maybe asked if he could stop by to talk about the trust and about drawing up wills for both of them. That would have been a good idea, for if Derek had hesitated, Luc would have been on guard. And if he hadn't, if he'd said, *Come by anytime, we'd love to see you,* well, then, Luc could be pretty sure things were all right. In the meantime, though he had the feeling that he was helping Cath waste money, he dutifully read Confidential's reports, summarized his reactions, and left everything for his client, who would sit dreaming over the materials for a hour or two before leaving without comment.

What Luc could not know was how powerfully those dull, sad pages stimulated Cath's memory. Reading them, she was no longer upstairs in what, from its yellowed, figured wallpaper, had surely been a child's room, but back at the college, back in the cold, black winter nights with slushy streets and gutters ankle-deep in icy water. She remembered fierce winters in which she'd been warmed with the exhilaration of music and performance and of falling in love with Derek. *Falling in love,* an odd phrase, really, but apt. She'd fallen under his spell, under his influence; she had been *operating under the influence.* And like someone driving *while impaired,* she might well have ignored a warning and gone off the road. That warning was what she was really looking for, but if there was such a thing, it was destined for her alone. Luc regarded Esther's death as a sad business and advised Cath not to let it *prey on her mind,* another phrase she found apt if subtly unsettling.

Esther had died on a Friday night, the week before the big winter concert when the whole school was in rehearsal. Between the orchestra and the choir, Cath had virtually lived at the music building, but that was all right, because Derek was there. She'd had the pleasures of working with Derek and talking to him and relaxing with him during their hasty coffee breaks.

And where was Esther? She'd had strep throat; that was in one of the stories. " *'She missed a couple of practices because of strep throat. Usually she called, but we weren't too worried, because we all knew she'd been sick,' said Melaney Roberts a junior."* Cath remembered nothing about Melaney Roberts, who'd concluded, " *'We just never thought there was anything wrong. Nothing serious.' "* How focused they'd all been on their own concerns; Cath, too. At the time, Esther's presence or absence had been important only for the program, because Cath had a purely musical interest in Derek Tolland, who was a prince, out of her sphere, in love with a fine musician and a beautiful woman. At least, that's what Cath had told herself, which was as good a sign as any that she'd been *DWI, driving under the influence,* her scruples dissolved by love.

Ensconced at LUC BEAUSOLEIL, ATTORNEY-AT-LAW, she had a

169

different perspective and remembered how, not too long before Esther's death, Derek had started to confide in her, confirming her status as a professional, musical colleague. He always spoke as if she was someone he trusted, a valued friend rather than a romantic interest. *I can talk to you,* Derek told her. They were in the Garden Café at the time, a student hangout, crowded, humid, noisy, cheap, full of potted plants and posters. She and Derek sat at a round metal table, their thick sweaters slung over their shoulders, their coats steaming on the big iron radiators, their boots leaving puddles of dirty water on the dark wooden floor. They cradled cups of coffee, letting the warm china mugs gradually loosen their stiff fingers. Steam rose from the liquid, and, as they leaned toward each other, he said, *I can talk to you.*

What he talked about was Esther. Cath had forgotten that until she read the clipping containing his statement to the press. Derek had been anxious about Esther, he'd told the reporter. She had recently become nervous and uncharacteristically touchy. In the Garden Café, he'd told Cath that Esther's jealous suspicions were driving him wild, particularly now when she'd been sick and had to stay in, when she couldn't get out to rehearsals and classes. Cath had forgotten all that, though she'd remembered the flakes of snow caught in his dark hair and how his green eyes had looked almost black in his pale face.

"You will be married soon, then things will be different."

"Do you think people change when they marry?" he asked her. "Do you think you can change the person you marry?"

She'd had to say, *Not very much.* How had she forgotten that? But later when he told her she could save him, she'd forgotten everything, even those ambiguous meetings, even their rapt, intense conversations, his attention to her music, his attentiveness to her. The fact was, Esther had had reason to be jealous, to be concerned. But not to kill herself, not that. Esther was beautiful and talented; she had an engagement with the Hartford and one with the Syracuse Symphony. The whole music school assumed she would enter the big competitions, perhaps win one. They knew that she would look lovely on advertisements and record and CD jackets, that she would have a glamorous career.

Instead, her friends, rivals, and colleagues woke up on Saturday morning, late and exhausted after a rehearsal that had run into the wee hours, stumbled out for bagels and coffee or bought doughnuts at the convenience store—and saw the headline through the glass of the newspaper boxes: "Music Student Found Dead." Unbelievable. Holding the photocopy, Cath remembered buying a paper and standing, cold and still breakfastless, the thin pages rustling in the stiff December wind. Esther, beautiful, talented, destined, had been found by a neighboring tenant who, aware she'd been sick, became alarmed when she answered neither the door nor her phone. And then, worse news, if there could be worse news yet: Esther had apparently died of an overdose of sleeping pills, combined with blood loss from a wrist so deeply slashed her right hand was nearly severed. She left no note, no explanation, just a wide, dark pool of dried blood and several empty bottles of sleeping pills and patent pain medicines.

Cath had put the morning paper down on top of the box and started to walk away before she realized that Derek would never believe the story without it. She ran back and collected the pages, already separating in the wind, and set out for his apartment in a big multi-family shingled pile with snow blowing along the wraparound porches, and green and pink plastic-wrapped advertising circulars scattered around the door like oversized leaves. Cath rang the bell, and saw, as soon as he appeared, that Derek already knew. His face was chalk white and his eyes clouded, as if the intense life behind them had been turned down like a gas flame. "Oh, I'm so sorry," Cath said. She dropped the paper. She'd taken her mittens off to read it, and had forgotten to put them back on. Her hands were frozen. "I didn't know you already knew. I wouldn't have come..."

"They called me," Derek said. "They called me just after we got back from rehearsal." He stood with the door wide open, oblivious to the cold wind sweeping off the porch and up the main stair of the house.

"You'll get cold," said Cath, after a moment. "I'll go."

"No," he said with a kind of desperation. "Come in. Make me some coffee. I can't seem to face doing anything."

She went inside. The hallway held rows of drying winter boots, damp parkas, umbrellas, two badly bent snow shovels, a small trash can full of sand for the walk, and several mailboxes with the tenants' names pinned up beside them. Chipped white-painted doors on either side led into the two first-floor apartments, but Derek and his sister had the entire upper story, which was entered through a chilly but spacious living room with a bright window bay. There was an upright piano, a dusty green velvet couch facing the fireplace, a couple of wicker chairs, and a great litter of books and scores. The kitchen beyond was typical, old and not too clean, with a bulging trash can, two woks, and a general air of improvisation. Cath found the kettle and a jar of instant coffee.

"Have you any food?" she asked. She remembered that you were supposed to feed people in shock. "Bread for toast? Muffins?"

Derek cleared his throat, and Cath expected him to be angry, to ask how he was supposed to think of food at such a terrible time. Instead, he went to one of the cupboards and began searching listlessly, until Cath took over and told him to sit down. Eventually she found a container of frozen juice in the freezer compartment and a half loaf of bread in the icebox. There were some eggs, as well, and she fried up two of them. Neither she nor Derek said a thing until they heard a door opening.

"We have company, Yvonne," he called.

When she came in a few minutes later, Cath got a shock. Her mind was full of Esther and of her tragedy, and there, at the kitchen door, was a tall woman with dark hair and a long, handsome face; nothing like Esther, not really, not on reflection, but creating the same impression of forceful beauty. Yvonne was wearing corduroy slacks tucked into the thick gray and white socks that could serve for slippers indoors and for boot socks out. A heavy, black, oversized sweater covered her hands, so that Cath did not notice the gloves immediately.

She had not met Yvonne before, though she had heard, early in the fall, that Derek's older sister, business degree in hand, had arrived to take up residence.

"My sister, Yvonne," Derek said. "This is Cath Mackey. She saw the paper and came to tell us the news."

Yvonne cast a cold, dark eye on Cath and on the remains of the breakfast. "I smelled the eggs," she said, "and I woke up."

Cath felt acutely uncomfortable. "Would you like me to fix another egg?" she asked, though as soon as she spoke, she was sure this was the wrong thing to say, the wrong approach.

Yvonne did not choose to answer. She put on some more water for coffee and then asked, "You have a morning paper?"

"Oh, yes. Or I had it. I dropped it on the porch." Yvonne said nothing, and Cath added, "I can go get it. I'm sure no one will have taken it." She started to get up, but Yvonne turned and went out through the living room, leaving Cath feeling more awkward than ever.

"Shock," said Derek. "Yvonne was very fond of Esther. Very fond. They were like sisters." He gave a strange, nervous smile that tightened over his high cheekbones without changing his blank and somber expression.

Yvonne returned with the paper, dark-spotted from the damp. Her face had been, Cath thought, concentrated rather than shocked, but after so long, *after so much water over the dam,* as Aunt Elizabeth had liked to say, it was hard to be sure.

Cath picked up the photocopy from Confidential Reports and looked at what Yvonne had seen that Saturday morning: "Music Student Found Dead." Cath had reread all the stories, and three things stood out, three things that were messages for her alone. One was that Esther had had codeine in her blood, although she had not had any prescriptions for that particular painkiller. A grieving friend admitted she'd given Esther some prescription aspirin with codeine for menstrual cramps, but that had been only a few pills. Of course, Esther could have been stockpiling such medicines. She could have collected a few pills here and a few there, for she'd had sorrows like the rest of them. Even talent, looks, and charm had not been sufficient against the malignancy of the universe. Still, the codeine was an anomaly, and of all the people who had waked up that morning to shock and grief, probably only Cath and Derek recalled that Yvonne always kept a large supply of codeine-based painkillers for the damaged nerves of her mangled hand.

Yvonne was very fond of Esther, Derek had said. *They were like sisters.* Whatever Cath had thought at the time, she did not think she believed that now. The scuttlebutt had been that Esther had been unpleasantly surprised by Yvonne's arrival at the apartment. Cath remembered the couch, the piano, the piles of scores, the sound of wind rattling the loose sash in the bay windows, the hiss of scavenged wood burning in the fireplace. Later those features and all the rest of the apartment became familiar to her, for Derek, notwithstanding her awkward shyness, began to call her, to ask her over. *Bring your books, if you want. The apartment's quiet. Or your violin. We could work on that Hindemith sonata.* When she protested that she was taking up too much of his time, he said, *I find it hard to be alone. I can't stand the silence.*

During that winter, when his sister worked nine to five for a commercial realtor, Cath would arrive in the early afternoons, bringing her schoolbooks and a loaf of Italian bread from the neighborhood bakery. She and Derek made hero sandwiches and ate them with potato chips. Sometimes they worked on songs she was learning; other times Derek studied his scores, and Cath made her way through the novels of her nineteenth-century lit course. She read *Wuthering Heights* and *Middlemarch* and *Great Expectations* while sitting on the green velvet couch, her feet tucked up under her to keep them from the chilly wood floors. If it was snowing, as it often was that long, dark winter, they would build a fire in the fireplace and Cath would make cups of hot chocolate: innocent pleasures. Derek would sit on the floor with his back to the fire, talking and dreaming—he did not yet know that the gods had withdrawn their favor. Cath sat with her feet up on the sofa, her books willingly interrupted to listen to him.

She became essential to him; talking to her, he was again the man he wanted to be. In her eyes, he was still the gifted, promising music student, though maybe a less ambitious one, because Esther, a serious, even a brilliant musician, had been replaced by Cath with her small, sweet voice, her modest violin technique, her marked lack of drive. But their relationship was completely different: she was Derek's friend, the confidante who could convince him that the world still belonged to him; his real attraction remained to quite different women, to women like Esther.

Nonetheless, that spring, Derek and Cath fell in love, or rather, she fell in love, and he realized that she could save him. Cath started leaving her books behind, and they spent the cold, gray afternoons riotously in Derek's bed. One thing did not change: she was careful to be gone before the Wolf Street bus brought Yvonne home. Derek never had to say anything; that was just understood from their very first visit together, an awkward *pins and needles* sort of meeting during which he either talked nervously or lapsed into morose silence, while Cath tiptoed around his grief and threaded her way through a field of sharp, treacherous ideas, the sharpest and most treacherous being the idea of avoiding Yvonne. Had Esther understood that, Cath wondered, or had her predecessor been spoiled by pre-Yvonne romantic evenings?

Certainly romantic evenings would not have been the same *with* Yvonne, who could be relentlessly intrusive. How she had haunted the hospital in Florida, alternately bullying and cajoling, insisting all the while that she had Cath's best interests at heart. Putting those two memories together produced an unpleasant feeling, which Cath might have suppressed if it had not been for two other details: the injury to Esther's wrist, an injury of incredible force and brutality, the razor blade broken off in the wound, and the feature article of the following Monday, which Cath lifted from the pile and reluctantly unfolded. She already knew that the story contained several pictures of Esther, including one fine yearbook shot. Cath had postponed really looking at them, without being completely conscious of her evasion. Now the images had to be faced. She smoothed the photocopy out on the desk and looked at Esther Nielson.

Since the casket had been closed at the funeral service, the last time Cath saw Esther had been the week before her death, when she performed a movement of the Dvorak cello concerto. Esther had looked slightly flushed and had complained of a scratchy throat, but none of that had shown in her big robust tone, her incredible steadiness of pitch and rhythm, her obvious joy in the music. Sitting with the first violins, Cath caught glimpses of Esther's smile and of the shining length of her dark hair flung backwards whenever she drew a particularly long, fine tone from her instrument. Oh, yes, appearance is deceiving, but Esther had looked satisfied, confident. The thought passed through Cath's mind that had Esther disliked Yvonne or found Derek difficult, she would have had plenty of other choices. She'd had no need for despair, and even if, under the influence of viruses and disappointments, she had swallowed some pills, even a lot of pills, there was no need to go the step further and cut her wrist. And even if she *had* done that, as in moments of madness one may do unimaginable things, to nearly sever her hand, her bowing hand, to make disaster irrevocable, to end forever that glorious music—no, Cath balked at that. She could not imagine it, though she could imagine other things.

She ran her hands over the photographs as if reading them like a strip of braille or playing them like musical glasses. Just enough time had passed so that Esther's long, glamorous hair now seemed unruly, and her eye makeup, artificial and heavy. Cath wanted to focus on such trifles, on the inessentials, on the details, because the photograph confirmed her shocked perception of that first morning in Derek's apartment: Esther Nielson bore a very marked resemblance to Yvonne. But why should that be upsetting? Wasn't it a cliché that men marry women who resemble their mothers, who probably resemble their sisters, as well? Surely something more than a passing resemblance lay behind Cath's sense of creeping, inescapable panic.

When she'd told Luc she'd had a memory fit, Cath had not really been accurate. What she'd felt was the emotional storm heralding the approach of real memory, which now arrived. Cath saw very clearly—so clearly that the familiar phrase *the mind's eye* took on a sharp newness—a young woman in a red jacket and a rakish black beret coming out of the New England Conservatory into bright autumn sunshine. She had beautiful dark hair and moved with a brisk, confident stride. Cath did not remember her name, maybe had not known it, but on the day in question, Cath had known that the young woman possessed an alto voice of high quality. The woman's image was interrupted by a memory of Boston traffic, of sunstruck glass and bright metallic colors; then the young singer smiled and waved across the street, mouthing a greeting to Cath, or, more likely, to Derek.

This memory was perfectly clear and immensely frightening. Cath felt a queer, hollow sensation around her heart and a sudden, inexplicable anxiety. Her hands were actually shaking, the thin photocopy paper rustling under her fingers. She didn't know the woman's name, but the memory of her face stirred an awareness of something sad and scary and mysterious, something Cath had not wanted to confront, something she had not wanted to know or to remember. *Sins of omission:* that was the operative concept, one that might stretch to cover forgetting, ignoring, not seeing.

A Boston street in autumn. A few years after she and Derek had married—happily, on the whole. They had been happy, she could say that, though Yvonne had recently followed them to Massachusetts, transferring to the main New England office of her realty company. That autumn Cath saw a singer with long dark hair, a pretty face, a brisk, confident manner. Was it a sin to have forgotten her name, to never have learned it? Was it a sin to have ignored—what? What sad, mysterious event? Sad enough and frightening enough so that Cath's head was beginning to pound. She vaguely remembered someone making a comment: *Oh, you do know her. She sang—*something Cath had forgotten—*I just can't get over it, a terrible tragedy, wasn't it?*

Yes, terrible, she remembered that, though the precise nature of the horror escaped her. The urban landscape is full of terrors, and each day's media provide small icons of suffering and cruelty. *Yes, awful,* Cath had agreed. *And so young. Who would want—?* Cath had agreed, again, that the death, yes, it was a death, had been inexplicable. Bizarre. There had been a touch of the bizarre, but she had forgotten quite what that was. Something shocking enough, outrageous enough, that Cath might have made certain crucial connections. Instead, she committed a sin of omission and put her imagination to sleep. That was in the autumn. At the end of the college semester, Derek abruptly accepted another position, no better, and worse paid, at Saint Martin's Church in a Hartford suburb.

Cath had been working part-time with a Suzuki class to get teaching experience, and she had been taken aback when Derek announced *out of the blue* that they were moving. Something *out of the blue* comes at you from the reaches of the sky, as unexpected as the hand of God, and upsets your plans. To be strictly accurate, Derek's announcement came, not from a blue, but from a stormy, sky. He had been sulky and nervous for some time, snapping at Cath, quarreling with Yvonne— Cath always knew when they had quarreled. *I need a change,* he said. *I'm sure you can see that.* She could, sort of, but she had committed to the full year at the Suzuki school, and *chopping and changing,* another phrase Aunt Elizabeth had favored, looks bad. *Chop:* that was it: the pretty alto had been mutilated in some way. Cath felt sick; she had known; the woman's hand had been damaged, crushed—and there were other injuries. Perhaps that was it; among the other injuries, a crushed, a *chopped,* hand was not significant, was not *diagnostic,* did not enable one to predict or to conclude. So perhaps she couldn't have known, perhaps she could not, and yet she must have suspected. She must have, or her heart would not be pounding against her ribs, she would not feel sick, she would not have become prey to memory fits and willful amnesia; she would not have gotten on the night bus.

But memory can be deceitful, and her own mind had thrown up much that was wild and fanciful, like the road to the Heavenly City and roiling clouds of evil intent. Fortunately, Cath would not have to rely on her memory. There would be stories, information; the murder of the pretty alto—even the existence of such a woman—could be proved or disproved. Perhaps disproved, for, after all, Derek had said, *You saved me. Did I?* she had asked. *Yes, you saved me.* She must remember that. *But from what?* He had not answered, for they had always left the precise danger undefined, leaving them free to argue about the move and to be miserable together until Cath gave in. She made her apologies to Madame Kurasawa, the Suzuki teacher, and packed their belongings. Perhaps Cath had consoled herself with the thought that they were escaping Yvonne, for *everything was fine before Yvonne came.* In her anger, had Cath told Derek that, or had she not dared? There are taboos in every relationship. That was one for her. He broke the one for him when he had her old dog put down. Did he know that? Maybe not; Derek did not seem as sensitive to taboos as most people.

"How are you getting on, Cath?" Luc stood at the office door. He was wearing a handsome blue-striped shirt with a white collar that set off his dark complexion and black hair, for Luc's second indulgence was a certain smartness of taste. He looked pleasant and normal, not a man in need of immediate salvation, and his voice pulled Cath back from a long way away. "Shall I ask Confidential for a final bill?" he asked.

He has a kind face, Cath thought, tempted to confide in him. But she hesitated precisely because he was so rational, so settled in the here and now, so anxious to save her money and protect what he thought of as her best interests; he'd made her rich, unnecessarily. And though he was certainly clever, she doubted that Luc understood the forces of evil or even, though he was a Catholic, *sins of omission* in quite the same way she did.

Cath shook her head. "I wish I could speak to one of their investigators."

Luc's face clouded subtly. He'd hoped to wrap up the business, and he'd expected her to trust him to conduct it. "I'll get you their number," he said. "If you want to call."

"It's just that what I want is hard to explain. It would be so much easier if I could talk to someone in person."

"Confidential's based in Providence."

"A little far for the bike," she admitted.

"Why don't you get a car?" Luc asked. "Now, there's an expenditure that your trustee could approve."

Cath hesitated a moment, the truth heavy on her tongue, *on the tip of her tongue,* a phrase she found slightly inaccurate; she herself felt words as a distinct mental pressure, as a temptation. "I can't drive at the moment," she said. "So there's no point in a car. My medication . . ." She smiled; she knew people accepted the idea of *medication,* a power word, so much more efficacious than *pills* or *prescription.* Luc was not apt to question *medication.*

"I'm surprised you're on the bike, then," he said. "I'd think a bike would be just as dangerous, especially on these narrow roads."

She hadn't thought of that. She was not, when it came right down to it, much good at deception. That was something she kept forgetting. "Well," she said, "everything's slower on a bike. And I'm very careful."

"I see that," said Luc, giving her what Cath thought of as his shrewd lawyer look. "I'll get you that number."

A few minutes later, the door of the little office was closed, and she was standing holding the receiver. Her stomach was aflutter by the time she got past the automated phone system and the secretary. Investigator Perez was out, but Investigator Lamson was in. A woman's voice came on the line and Cath was relieved. A woman would understand, would read between the lines, would not need everything spelled out.

"Were our previous reports satisfactory?" Ms. Lamson asked. She had a cool, professional voice and sounded slightly bored.

"Oh, yes," said Cath. "I just wanted to thank you. I won't take up your time." She reached over and cut off the line, so that the dial tone jeered her cowardice. *Stupid, stupid, stupid,* thought Cath, but her tongue had frozen. She had tried to say what year, Boston, a musician who died, but none of the words had come, none. She hung up the receiver and sat down at the desk, then folded her hands and tried to imagine herself as someone official, someone trained in things serious and useful: a legal aide, maybe, or maybe a lawyer like Luc. Such a person would take out one of Luc's yellow legal pads and write down the particulars: approximate dates—between September and the middle of December. The place, Boston. The subject—ah, there was the problem, *the rub*, as Hamlet says—what was the subject? A young woman's death. Young women die every day, every year. Say, a young musician's death, then, a young musician's *suggestive* death: suggesting what? Suggestive, why? The musician had long dark hair, great talent, a certain style of beauty, a certain confident presence, a certain force of character. And this young, beautiful musician, who died, tragically, miserably, had been, very likely—and here Cath felt the whole office darken, felt her head begin to throb, felt clouds of evil intent rise from some exterior or interior locale—Derek's lover.

No, that wasn't true. Cath shook her head back and forth. That wasn't true. She was confusing something else, something else entirely, something terrible and frightening, probably, but this was a transposition, an invention; she was making this all up. Dr. Arce, standing by her bed when she thought she was Laura Whitman, had turned to the student doctors, the interns, and said, *The mind cannot bear gaps in its history, so it invents a plausible story to hold the personality together.* That's what she was doing. This could be fiction, not memory, and even the woman with the long dark hair, the black beret, the red jacket, even the front entrance of the New England Conservatory on a bright fall day, even those might be her imagination, images transposed from God knows where, from another life.

Yes, most likely that was the case, yet she'd felt so frightened that she'd hung up on Ms. Lamson. Cath felt she'd acted stupidly. A sensible, lawyerly sort of person would forget the matter entirely, or, if she could not, would leave a short note for Luc. And ask him to pass it on to Ms. Lamson, just so that she, Cath, could set her mind at rest. For most likely there was no musician with long dark hair who'd disappeared—died—been killed—been mutilated shortly before the

Tollands left Boston. Most likely. Just the same, Cath wrote everything down, putting the disturbing ideas outside of herself and getting them on paper and under control. And then she thought that since she'd gone so far—*in for a penny, in for a pound,* as Aunt Elizabeth liked to say, or, more ominously, *as well be hanged for a sheep as a lamb*—she might as well request a photograph of Jane Henkel, too. Cath had barely finished writing the name when she realized that she already knew where she could find a photo. She drew a line through the postscript, scrawled, *"Never mind about this last,"* and signed the note, *"Thanks, Cath."*

Her handwriting was perfectly firm and normal, but when she stood up, Cath felt as weak as when she first got out of the hospital and had to clutch the desk for support. *I'm not going to put up with any nonsense,* she told herself, but though she managed to get out of the office and down the stair, she arrived in the reception area looking so white-faced that the rarely solicitous Ms. DeRoche jumped up from her desk and caught Cath's arm.

"Are you all right?"

"I'm fine," said Cath, but even as she spoke, she began swaying, and Pat DeRoche helped her to a chair.

"Put your head down."

"I feel fine, really," Cath said, but she dropped into the chair as into an elevator shaft. The ceiling had stretched to double height and the ugly vinyl floor seemed only inches from her nose.

"There's one of those twenty-four-hour bugs going around. Both my boys had it."

"Maybe that's it," said Cath, "but I'm sure I'll be all right in a minute."

Pat DeRoche's response was to lean across her desk and push the intercom button for Luc. "Mrs. Tolland's taken ill," she said.

"I'll be all right, really," said Cath when he appeared. "It was the stupidest thing. I'll be fine."

"Not on that bike, you won't," said Pat DeRoche, who fixed her boss with a look.

"No, no, certainly not," Luc said. "Listen, Pat, call Martin and tell him he needn't come in. I'll drop off those papers when I run Cath home."

Cath protested this while Luc sorted out his schedule and Pat DeRoche went to the phone. The two of them ignored her, and ten minutes later Cath had gotten her bike's front wheel off and Luc had managed to cram the rest of the vehicle in the trunk of the Saab. She stood up, still a little unsteady, and wiped her dirty hands on her jeans. "I really could have managed to get home, you know. If I could get that wheel off, I can cycle home."

"You look very unsteady. Maybe your medication isn't quite right."

Was it her imagination or did he put a sarcastic stress on *medication*? Cath shrugged.

"I don't know why you ride that thing anyway. Even cheap bikes come with better gearing than that."

"Poorer gears, more exercise," said Cath.

Luc gave a put-upon sigh and got into the car.

"I'm sorry. I know this is a lot of bother for you."

"Gets me out of the office. And I do have some papers that need to be delivered today." His smile was kindly and concerned.

"Oh, papers," said Cath, struggling around the bike's front wheel, which she'd insisted on holding to keep the Saab's back seat clean. "I left you a note. I think I did. No, wait, it's in my pocket." She put the folded sheet of paper on the dashboard. "To pass on to Ms. Lamson at Confidential."

"I thought you were going to call."

"I was, but I felt woozy suddenly. It was the silliest thing."

Luc reached over and put the paper in his jacket pocket. "Cath," he said after a moment, "this whole business is maybe not so good for you. When you've been sick."

"I think Pat's right," Cath said. "It's just some twenty-four-hour bug."

"You're not hearing me," said Luc. "What's the point of all this? Are you and Derek having problems?"

"No," said Cath. "Not at all."

"People," Luc began carefully, "only hire detectives for a couple of reasons, the most common being matrimonial discord."

"I wish I'd studied law," said Cath. *"Matrimonial discord:* that has an almost musical sound, like something quite insulated from the real world."

"You don't want to talk about it," Luc said.

"I don't need to talk about it," Cath corrected. He was, after all, her lawyer.

Luc raised his fine dark eyebrows. He felt anxiety with an edge of annoyance, or maybe annoyance with an edge of anxiety that would have been increased had he known that his wife had pulled into the office lot just in time to see him drive off with Cath Tolland. He would find out about that later. At the moment, he was complaining mentally that Cath could well become a high-maintenance client, that she took all sorts of little extras for granted, that she was going to buy herself grief.

"What are you looking for in all this, Cath?"

"I'm looking for peace of mind," she said.

12

THE JUNE SUN BRIGHTENED THE pale pink roses straggling along the fence and softened the house's cracked and peeling paint and the bare gray-brown patches where Cath had been scraping. The maples and oaks were fully leafed out, shadowing the shabby lawn with a lacy pattern of dark green. The late spring day was even kind to the old barn, which might have passed for picturesque with its big cupola and dusty windows. Pulling into the drive with Luc, Cath would have felt the familiar satisfaction in her old house if it had not been for the fact that the barn door stood open and Derek's car was parked inside. Instead of pleasure, she felt a queer, stomach-dropping jolt, like missing a step on a stair. *He's come home,* she thought, *to see what I'm up to,* but that was just her own guilty conscience speaking. Really, she'd known this had to happen sooner or later. Luc gave her a quick glance, as if trying to read the situation, and Cath said, "Of course, Derek doesn't know anything about Confidential Reports."

"He needn't," said Luc. "Though I'm just as glad he's home. I've been meaning to speak to Derek. You'll both need to think about new wills after your birthday."

"But not today," Cath said. "I don't want to talk about money at all." As Derek appeared in the house doorway, she added, "He doesn't realize that I know how much money is in the trust or that I've been talking to you, either."

"No?" asked Luc, surprised.

She shook her head, then pushed open the door of the car. "Hello, dear," she called to her husband. "You remember Luc Beausoleil, my lawyer? Our lawyer," she corrected herself as Derek came over. Cath handed him the bicycle wheel.

"Yes, of course. We met just recently in the general store." Derek looked at Cath as if to say, *You didn't know about that, did you,* before shaking hands with Luc. "I see Cath's saddled you with the bike monster." Derek's voice was genial; he was home early and in his charming mode. *What does that mean,* Cath wondered, then rebuked herself: there was no proof of anything; no reason for her doubts and anxieties; she herself might well be the source of those clouds of ill intent.

Luc opened the Saab's trunk and began explaining how Cath and her bike had wound up as his cargo. She listened with a sense of detachment. She needn't attend to the meaning of the words, for she understood just from his low, somber tone that he was warning Derek that she was unwell, that she needed looking after. ". . . gave us a fright . . . She was dead white. Glad she thought to come in."

Cath looked at Luc, who was lying to her husband, and felt her heart change its rhythm, adding an off beat, a little warning from her physiology.

"Must have been tough to get this thing in your trunk," Derek remarked. "No, I can manage. Don't get your hands dirty. Are your bike tools in the case?" he asked Cath.

"Yes, we used them to take off the wheel. Derek's so good with machines," she told Luc. "I always have trouble getting the nuts on tight enough. Or I get the handlebars twisted while I'm working on the rest of the machine. It never fails." She knew that she was rattling on and thought, *He'll know I'm nervous.* With an effort, she managed to smile at Luc and say, "Thank you so much. The whole thing was silly. I feel fine now."

Derek slid the bike wheel between the forks. "What I can't see is the pleasure of riding around here at all. With these hills." His long fingers were busy with the bolt but Cath felt that his attention was on Luc. On Luc's response, on the whole situation. She felt that her husband's suspicion was ironic, considering the reasons she'd been in Luc's office.

"Perhaps Cath will be able to drive soon," the lawyer said. "With the hot weather coming, cycling might be too much for her."

"Cath won't need to drive at all. The concert season's over now, so I'll be home early. I can take Cath out. That's what she needs. Less home renovation and more getting out."

"Home renovation," Luc exclaimed. "Good luck. How long have Renee and I been at work on ours? It's got to be six years. Not to mention the office."

"You've never done anything with the office," Cath teased.

"Seriously. These old houses are never done."

They stood for a few minutes by the car, the two men leaning on the chassis, Cath holding her reassembled bike, and talked about old houses. The town was famous for them, for their quirks and peculiarities, for the eccentricities of their builders, for the persistence of their mice, for the frequency of their carpenter ants, termites, and wasps. An old house was always a good topic in town, lending itself to concision or elaboration as desired. "You know old houses" or "I've got an old house myself"—those summed up a wealth of shared experience, while, in other moods, the swapping of old house stories created common ground in surprising, even uncomfortable, company. As proof of that, Derek shortly insisted on taking Luc around back to see Cath's handiwork.

"... been doing such a lot," she heard Derek say, as she wheeled her bike into the barn. Cath knew that he was explaining her, excusing her, fitting her into the picture that, she suspected, he and Luc shared, of a recovering invalid who had *memory fits* and assorted foibles, of a convalescent who need not, and indeed should not, be taken too seriously. Irked, Cath considered truth and taking the consequences, but only momentarily. Instead, she parked the bike in the barn and joined the men at the kitchen door, where Derek was pointing out her paint preparations and the cleaned-up garden.

"I feel a bit guilty," he said as she walked up. "Cath's been doing all the heavy lifting, haven't you?" He put his arm around her shoulders and gave her an affectionate hug.

He has the most beautiful eyes, Cath thought, and yet she felt there was something artificial in his gesture. "Not literally," she said. "I'm going to rent scaffolding. I think it's much safer than a ladder. Do you agree, Luc? You've painted your house."

"A job I hope never to do again," Luc said. "Get scaffolding. I wish I had. Those big ladders tear up your shoulders."

"Cath's done a marvelous job on the inside, too," Derek said. "I'm not surprised she's a bit tired out. She'd have had the whole house done over, I think, if I hadn't started complaining about the paint smell. I thought she'd take a break, but she just went and started outside."

"You weren't using oil base, were you?"

"No, latex. The damp weather made the smell linger," Cath said.

"The paint really wasn't that bad, but raising a row was the only way to keep you from overdoing it." Derek squeezed her shoulder again and smiled at Luc. "Come in for a minute. You won't know the old place." Derek was quite the house-proud owner, praising her redecoration to the skies—while keeping a sharp eye on the lawyer's reactions.

"I used to come here to see Cath's old aunt Elizabeth," Luc remarked as they went in the kitchen door.

"Don't look at the kitchen," said Cath.

"Now, I like the kitchen. It reminds me of your aunt."

"Hasn't been changed much since."

They laughed, even though they were all lying in one way or another, reading a little script, a script they might have agreed on beforehand, they read it so perfectly. Cath felt that she was watching a little play with a cast of proud husband, devoted wife, friendly lawyer. As usual, Derek assumed the major role, pointing out the new paint job, the nice prints. Luc admired everything with just the right degree of enthusiasm, so that Cath felt, for the first time, that her old friend would be a formidable opponent; she felt she understood the devious prudence that had enabled him to make her rich.

"Well, I can see how you've been spending your time, Cath," he told her. "I'm impressed."

"A long way to go yet," she said.

"Listen, ours is still a work in progress. You must come by, you and Derek. Our house is a little later—1850s. Not so solidly built as this one, I'm afraid. Do come. I'd like you to meet Renee."

"We'd love that," she said. "Now that Derek's not so busy with the church music." They escorted Luc to the door with pleasantries and vague promises of invitations they all felt confident of avoiding. Then she and Derek stood on the steps and watched Luc get into his beautiful little Saab.

"Nice car," Derek remarked. His arm was still draped across her shoulders. "For a country lawyer."

"He makes up for the car with his horror of an office. And that building used to be the Fullers' place, a nice old Victorian."

"You got a good look at it, did you?"

"Yes, of course," Cath said, slipping from under his arm and walking over to close the garage door. "They had me sit down, brought me water. The whole scene was quite ridiculous. I don't know what was wrong."

"I'll get the door." Derek caught up with her and reached for the overhead. "Better yet," he said, hesitating with the door down halfway, "don't bother with dinner. We'll go out to eat. Somewhere nice. How about that? Unless you're really not feeling well."

Cath studied his bright, sharp eyes and handsome closed face. He was more clever than she was. He was good at putting her in a false position, at making her confront false alternatives.

"I'm all right now. I just felt unsteady for a moment in the street. I probably shouldn't have skipped lunch, but I wanted to get out for a ride."

"Lucky you were near Beausoleil's office," Derek said.

He *is* suspicious, Cath thought. Would he be as suspicious if he had nothing on *his* conscience? "Yes," she said. "And it was good to see Luc again. He's such a nice fellow."

"An ex-boyfriend, I think. I think you once told me that. In one of your less guarded moments." Derek smiled to show that he was teasing.

"I haven't had too many guarded moments with you, have I?" Cath asked and felt a pang, because what was this, what was their life ever since she'd come home but *guarded moments*?

"I used to think you had none," he said, and he looked at her differently, the way he'd looked in the Garden Café, the way he'd looked in the college practice room, the way he'd looked when he'd said, *You can save me.*

"And that was true." She teetered on the abyss of candor and revelation and self-sacrifice: she *could* save him if she tried. "There was a time—"

"And now things are different." He spoke quickly, as if he'd sprung a trap, as if even his expression of desolate yearning had just been a gambit. "Now you don't confide in me. Now you don't tell me anything," he complained.

Cath drew back and smiled sadly; she might have said the same of him. "We must do some more duets; I must get back to the choir. Music demands sincerity, and we need music, Derek."

But he didn't really want to talk—except maybe about her always dubious health. "What you need is more fun. A bit less work. We'll go out, shall we? Have ourselves a romantic evening. What about that?" He reached over and nuzzled her hair, and Cath found herself agreeing. She had, in some ways, a susceptible nature. When he seemed happy, when he seemed to want to try to be happy, she was only too willing to go along.

*   *   *

Renee Beausoleil was a different type altogether. Luc's wife was tall and as fair as her husband was dark: that whole, distant side of the Beausoleil clan were big-boned people, pale and freckled and sandy-haired. Renee's short, straight, chin-length hair was red, and she had a cast in one of her light eyes that gave her a sensual, and deceptively sleepy, air. In fact, she was an extremely active person, volatile, jealous, and determined. From the day Luc met her at his oldest sister's wedding, he had found Renee an interesting, even an exciting, companion, and every time he grew restive under her hot temper he was drawn back by her passionate and fundamentally good-hearted nature. If his old friend, Cath Tolland, was still, but very deep, water, his wife was a racing, turbulent stream.

The boys were a curious mixture of their two opposing temperaments. They had black hair and light eyes. Henry, the elder, was quiet, humorous, slight of build, but reedy and promising to be tall. At six, he was curiously independent and emotionally self-contained. Jack, two years younger, already as heavy as his brother, was a rowdy, active, ceaselessly demanding, but desperately affectionate child: his mother's boy. The two of them had titanic quarrels over bedtime and scattered toys, yet Jack was jealous of his mother's attention, angling for her favor with almost comic persistence. Luc would sometimes observe Henry's amused reactions and recognize himself, a personality analytical and observant, a personality that, though clever and active intellectually, needed the emotional stimulation of a more aggressive nature. This Renee supplied.

"I saw Catherine Tolland today," she remarked after dinner as they were loading the dishwasher. The boys were upstairs in their room playing a complicated game with trucks and a ziggurat of toy blocks. Luc could hear Henry's voice raised with directions and commands and Jack's wailing imitation of a siren.

"She often rides into town on her bicycle. I don't think she's able to drive yet," said Luc, opting for an answer that was strictly true but scarcely comprehensive. His skill in this art was admired by everyone except his wife, who frowned and considered her next move. Renee genuinely hated being jealous, hated jealousy itself. It was the one thing that separated her from her younger son, whose temperament so closely mirrored her own. And, she'd have to say, Luc did not give her too many reasons. Not too many, though today she had seen him leaving his office with Cath Tolland. That thought twisted her heart like a wet dish towel. There he stood, neat and handsome and not a hair out of place, wearing the bland expression he put on with clients, with the importunities of the children, with all that he considered unreasonable or excessive. His hypocritical composure was unendurable and she told him so. And the reasons, too.

"You came by today?" he asked. "You didn't stop in."

"You wouldn't have been there," she said, aware that he had not answered her concern and that her anger was slipping slowly but surely beyond her grasp.

"Pat's always asking for you," he said, maddeningly calm.

To be honest, Renee didn't mind a scrap. She blew up in a moment and was reconciled just as quickly. In contrast, Luc's angers were rare, cold, and memorable.

"I should have gone in," Renee said, "and asked how often you're out driving with Cath Tolland."

"Pat's too good a secretary to tell you," Luc said, teasing. Then he saw that his wife was in earnest and added, "Today is the first time in a dozen years that I've been in a car with Cath. She took sick, actually. She walked in from the street looking very white."

Renee gave him a mean and chilly smile: how dare he lie to her so transparently? "Her bike's been out front of your office half a dozen times in the last few weeks."

Luc sighed and put down the dish towel. He might have known. There were folk in town who existed only to pass on news of their livelier brethren, yet evidence of their busyness never failed to annoy him. Cath annoyed him, too. This was what came of having friends as clients: they made irregular arrangements, expected special privileges, caused trouble. He should have told Cath to make her own contacts with Confidential—or better yet, with someone else of her own choosing—and spared himself this trouble on the home front. "You're serious," he said now to his wife with as great an expression of surprise as he could manage. "You're serious."

"Of course I'm serious." And she rattled the pots and slammed the washer door shut and vented her feelings to show him just how serious. She couldn't help it: with his discretion and self-control, there was something exasperatingly elusive about her husband.

"You know I manage her trust, don't you?" Luc began in his *lawyer knows best* voice. "I'm her trustee. She has quite a lot of money. It needs to be looked after."

"Don't talk to me in simple sentences," Renee said. "I'm not one of your moron clients. And don't tell me Cath's affairs are so complicated that she needs to stop by one and two times a week."

"Not her affairs," he said soberly. "Cath herself is." Luc considered his wife's flushed, angry face and estimated how much he would have to tell her. "They lost a child," he said after a moment. "She had a miscarriage last year—before all their troubles."

"Oh," said Renee, who'd worked full-time as an RN until Jack was born. "Oh, dear." She felt bad for the Tollands but also sulky that her husband had put her in the wrong. He might have mentioned all this weeks ago and shared some interesting news and spared her anxiety. With a mixture of irritation and regret, Renee took refuge in her medical knowledge. "That explains a lot. A miscarriage, especially a late miscarriage—there are certain biological changes."

"I wouldn't be surprised," said Luc. *Biological changes.* He should have thought of that. That might explain Cath's suspicion and paranoia, her dreamy absorption in Confidential's reports, the disjunction between her air of apparent calm and her willingness to hire detectives. "Anyway, she comes by wanting this done or that checked—all charged to her trust. It's really rather sad. She's all alone most days out at that big house. I think she stops by just for something to do."

"Is she still as pretty?" Renee asked, but Luc was good at recognizing loaded questions.

"She's been seriously ill. And there's something not quite right with her yet. Emotionally, that is. I wish I'd thought to ask you about her a couple of weeks ago." That was the truth, but he also thought it might further serve to mollify Renee, who tended to interpret professional discretion as a lack of trust. "Though she's out and around and working on their house. When I got her home, her husband insisted I have a look around the place. Otherwise, I'd have been back in ten minutes. You should have waited for me."

"But her husband *was* home," Renee pointed out. "What's he like, anyway?"

"Overly tall," Luc said, drawing himself up. He liked to think of himself as five-eight or five-nine—and five-ten in his winter work boots.

Renee gave a sly smile; fortunately, she had a sense of humor. "I've heard he's handsome. Someone said he was the best-looking man in town."

"You've got to like his type," Luc said.

"Tall, dark, and handsome?" she guessed.

"Saturnine and troublesome and probably a Scorpio. A man with a past," Luc said and stopped himself. He had been inventing, showing off for Renee's amusement, joking her out of the bad temper and suspicion which periodically darkened their marriage. He hadn't really meant to say that about Derek Tolland, for the idea of his sinister past was nonsense. Luc had read all the stuff Cath had wanted him to read, and there was nothing in it. He'd pointed that out to her as tactfully as he could: anyone could see that the time of death on the Neilson woman let Derek Tolland out absolutely. Had to. Yet instead of being delighted that her husband's old fiancée had been an open-and-shut suicide and nothing to do with him at all, Cath hadn't been satisfied. If anything, she'd seemed even more nervous and upset, and she was clearly ready to rush off on another tangent. The whole business was a ridiculous waste of time and money, yet somehow it had deposited the idea in his mind that *Derek Tolland was a man with a past.*

"Really," said Renee, who hadn't picked up on Luc's hesitation. "When can we see this handsome, dangerous man?"

"I've half invited them to dinner," Luc said. "But I don't think now that I'd better."

Renee caught her full lower lip in her small even teeth and smiled. Her husband was an amusing man and she forgave him almost everything when he made her laugh, when he made life interesting by putting aside his lawyer's discretion. She winked at him, and he came over and kissed her with enough enthusiasm that she had to remind him the children were still awake.

"What's the show they're always wanting to watch?" Luc asked, forgetting that they'd been insisting on no TV after supper. "Let them turn on the tube for half an hour."

Renee laughed and agreed they might do that just once, though, of course, it set a bad precedent and the kids would tease for the same privilege another night. "Yes," she agreed, though that didn't mean she had forgotten about Cath Tolland and her bike and her visits to Luc's office. No, indeed. There were still things Renee wanted to ask, needed to know, and intended to find out.

Cath turned her head on the pillow and looked out the window into the thick green screen of leaves. The light had already changed subtly, and from somewhere back in the trees came the seductive, liquid warble of a thrush: evening. She looked down at her bare legs, the rumpled sheets, Derek's hastily discarded shirt, and smiled. The water stopped running in the bathroom, and Cath stretched and reluctantly decided that it was time to rejoin the world.

"Hey," said Derek, opening the bathroom door. He had a towel around his waist, and his wet hair was dripping onto his shoulders. "You getting up?"

"I don't know."

He laughed and came over and kissed her and then began to tickle her.

"Only if we're going out to dinner," Cath said between giggles.

"Lazy woman! Hand me the phone book. It's on your side."

Cath swung her legs over the edge, found the book, then collected her underclothes and padded into the big, square, unimproved bathroom. Although the small window was open, there was steam on the mirror, and she thought, *We need a fan, maybe a tile floor. The old clawfoot tub could do with new fittings, too. Why not get them?*

She ran her bath and lay in the water, listening to the familiar sounds of Derek dressing, the rattle of the bureau drawers, the closet opening and closing, the bed creaking—perhaps something might be done about those springs—the sound of his shoes on the floor. Then the electronic chirp of the phone, as he dialed the inn to make a reservation.

"Seven-thirty all right?" he called.

"We can make that."

Cath stepped out of the tub and stood naked on the bath mat to fix her hair. To exist in the *here and now,* that was the thing. She hadn't done enough of that lately. She'd been worrying about the future and interrogating the past, when what one needed to live well was the present, the present moment when Derek was calling the restaurant and she was standing, pleased in her own body, happily considering what to wear.

Her silk dress, she decided. People turned up at the inn in a wide range of attire, but she thought her silk dress—if it still fit her; she'd lost a bit of weight—and her brown suede heels. She'd bought both for a concert or perhaps for one of her students' recitals, but she did not want to think about students, student recitals, anything but the present in which Derek was taking her to dinner, encouraging her to get out, to be well, to meet people, some of whom might be friends. *Actions speak louder than words,* louder, too, than suspicions and dubious memories. At the moment, Cath regretted Confidential Reports, regretted confiding even as much as she had to Luc, regretted, especially, her last scribbled request for information. Perhaps she should call and cancel that.

"You about ready?"

"I just need to put on my dress."

"I'll get the car," Derek said.

As she came out of the bathroom, she heard him clattering down the stairs. Light of foot. Light of heart? Yes, she thought so.

Cath found her brown dress a bit wrinkled—the closets of the old house were all narrow, shallow, quite inadequate for the expanded, wardrobes of the late twentieth century. But the cream flower print disguised the worst of the creases and the dress was wearable, even attractive. Cath found some nylons and put on her brown suede heels. Sandals would have been preferable for summer. She needed a pair of sling-back sandals in bone or a tobacco brown. And beads. Something for her neck. Cath poked around in her jewel box and found a topaz pendant on a chain. Yes, that was very nice.

"I am well," she told her image in the mirror. "I've come out of *the winter of my discontent*, gotten off the night bus, become normal, and now my husband and I, having spent a pleasant hour in bed, are going out to a dinner we can certainly afford." She looked at herself in the mirror: an attractive blond woman with large eyes. Darker, maybe, than they used to be. Cath raised an eyebrow, aware of subtle differences. Somewhere between the night bus and home, she had lost some of her soft prettiness; she seemed older, more severe, perhaps more interesting. She smiled at that idea, and the figure behind her in the mirror nodded. She started to say Derek's name, but he was downstairs, for she could hear the car starting up in the garage. Derek was pulling out the Subaru, and the mirror was empty.

Cath took a deep breath: just a shadow, such as she often saw. And to which, in childhood and in illness, she gave credence, labels. Her mind was porous; her imagination seeped into her perceptions. She understood that now; even her musical imagination was wayward, for there had been a time when she'd heard faint, whispery notes as evocative as the thrush. Cath had a moment's nostalgia for that past when the whole world was alive. Then she smoothed her dress, feeling dainty and elegant after so many weeks in jeans, and walked with quick eagerness out of the room and down the stairs.

The Drover's Inn occupied a big wood-frame colonial, heavier on atmosphere than comfort. The pricey menu was good, with vaguely French pretensions, and, as the only significant restaurant near the university campus, the inn did a fine business. When Cath and Derek arrived, they found the low-beamed lounge and bar annex crowded with patrons waiting for their tables. Derek ordered a whiskey and soda, and Cath drank some mineral water, for her throat had gone dry as soon as she saw the crowd, the festive lights of the restaurant, some familiar faces. One belonged to a music professor who'd enjoyed Saint Martin's spring concert. As they started to talk shop, Cath relaxed.

Around her, academic types were exchanging gossip and ideas with equal relish, while four men who looked to have come straight from the golf course leaned against the small bar to rehash their games. In the air was competition and camaraderie, in roughly equal proportions. Cath surveyed the room, admiring one woman's pretty knit dress, another's handsome blazer, while half listening to a conversation about Whitman and whether or not Queer Theory shed much light on *Leaves of Grass*. She'd felt a strong impulse to break in and ask, like her friend on the night bus, if they intended to *rise tremendous like the sun*. Then she thought she heard Jane Henkel's name, but she must have shifted her attention too late, for now the professor was boasting about a young tenor who'd enrolled the previous fall. "At the audition, he took the high B on the 'Ave Maria'—not the slightest effort. I can tell you I jumped right out of my seat and said 'That one's mine!' He's only seventeen, too. A jewel!"

"I'd be thankful for any tenors at all," Derek said, genuinely envious. He must find out where this prodigy sang and whether he would be open to other gigs.

"But you were given a lovely soprano," Professor Daniels said, bowing toward Cath, who had been left somewhat on the edge their conversation. The professor was a short, black man with a round cheerful face, a mobile little mustache, and very gallant manners. "No, no," he said when she demurred, "I heard you sing the Brahms Mass a couple of years ago. Beautiful. And I'm told you're a very fine teacher. Tom Bernard at the conservatory was telling me about one of your violin students. Rock-solid technique, he said. Now that you're living out this way, I hope you'll consider working with us at the music school."

"Well," said Cath, surprised and pleased but unsure of how to respond.

"We've got all levels of students, you know. Oh, yes. We have a community school division and music education, too. Not that we pay particularly well." He gave a robust, apologetic laugh.

"Oh, but that's not so important," Cath said, as the idea of students, of teaching again—the idea that had seemed so remote, so impossible— suddenly leapt to a dazzling, radiant possibility.

"My wife has the true artist's indifference to money," Derek observed. There was a sour note in his voice which Cath heard, though the professor did not.

"Your wife's a realist. In today's market, you've got to love music to make it your career," the professor said. "I don't need to tell you that."

"No, indeed. Unfortunately, teaching's quite impossible for Cath at the moment. She's had some very serious health problems since you heard her sing. In fact, she had a bad spell today, while she was out cycling. Isn't that right, dear?" He gave her a sharp glance, and Cath realized she was caught.

"I had pneumonia in the spring," she told Professor Daniels. "I'm taking an appalling time getting better."

"Oh, don't rush it. Take your time! But was your voice damaged?" he asked, as if he really did remember her singing, as if he really did care.

What a nice, kind man, Cath thought. "My voice is fine, but Derek thinks it's still too weak for me to return to Saint Martin's choir. I'm promised after my birthday," she told the professor with a shy smile. "That's in a couple of weeks."

"Felicitations and good luck," he said.

Just then the hostess, very young and elegant in a long dark knit dress and platform heels, tottered over with her clipboard. The professor's table was ready and the Tolland party's, too. They picked up their drinks, the professor waving to a friend at the bar before collecting his wife and their dinner guest. After he introduced Cath and Derek, they followed the hostess through the crush into the big open dining room. The professor's party were seated by one of the unlit fireplaces set into the massive central chimney. A not unpleasing whiff of woodsmoke and ash lingered in the restaurant, mingling with the aroma of garlicky salads and grilling steaks.

"We're getting center stage," the professor said cheerfully. "I don't think we'll need the fire tonight."

His wife, short graying hair, a stout physique in a beautiful African shawl, a square, intelligent face, shook her head. "Though we needed it one night last winter," she said. They all agreed the previous winter had been brutal, Cath, too, though she could scarcely remember it, except for snow and moving and the knowledge that she'd never be quite happy again.

"It looks like we're to be by the windows," Derek said as the hostess headed toward a set of French doors. "How nice to have seen you again." The men shook hands, and Cath and the women exchanged a few words before the professor turned to her and touched her arm. "Call me when you feel better."

"How nice Morgan Daniels is," Cath said when they were settled at their table. "I think I've met him once before, but that was just congratulations after some university concert."

"He is nice," said Derek, concentrating on his menu. "That's why you shouldn't take what he said too seriously."

"About contacting him for some teaching, you mean?" Cath was surprised and a little disappointed. The professor had seemed so genuine, so pleasant.

"Hmmm."

"I don't see why not," Cath said, but even as she spoke she began to feel strange again, isolated and self-conscious. She knew why not: she'd become unreliable in some fundamental way, she'd tried to stab Derek, she *had* stabbed Derek. Yet was that to be a life sentence? "I don't see why not," she repeated defiantly.

Derek lowered his menu. He seemed calm, rather bored. "For one thing, you don't have an advanced degree. The only place they could use you would be in the community division."

"What's wrong with that?"

"You wouldn't get the good students. And I doubt you'd get many younger students at all." His lips twitched in what might have been a smile. "Parents, you know. You know how parents are," he remarked, as if it were all a matter of indifference to him.

"Nothing—about what happened, I mean—nothing was ever in the papers, was it?"

"Certainly not. If it had been in the papers, if it had been that public, you would have been charged."

"But I wasn't. You know, some people do terrible things and go on as usual; even some who do get in the papers go on with their lives." She did not look at him as she spoke, but at the elegant script of the menu, which was twisting itself into meaningless swirls. She glanced up to see Derek watching her with a kind of shadow in his expression. "What I mean is, why should I be the only one? You've forgiven me, haven't you?"

"Of course, dear. But people, parents, they become nervous with—episodes."

"Episodes?" Like a serial, Cath thought. *Tune in next week for the next episode.*

"Of madness," said her husband, but he did not meet her eyes. Rather his gaze had slid away to the busy room around them, to the waiters and waitresses struggling with their heavy trays, to the handsome nappery, the bare wood floors, the mellow plaster walls, the old New England prints and paintings, the convivial diners.

How awkward a restaurant table can be, Cath thought. *How congenial if you are happy, how awkward and uncomfortable if you have nothing to say to the person across from you or if what you must say is painful. Short of making a scene, there really is no escape at a restaurant table.*

"An episode of madness," she said.

"Yes."

"But I never had a doctor, did I?" she asked, for she was getting better and could make shrewd deductions. "I don't remember a doctor at all—until Dr. Arce. Did I have a doctor, a psychiatrist?"

"You know you didn't," Derek said. "You wouldn't hear of one."

"Mad people don't always have a choice, though, do they? So perhaps, like Lord Byron, I was bad, instead. I'm finding it hard to decide." Cath's voice trembled on the verge of tears. Why had he raised the topic, anyway? Why did he have to discourage her?

"This is really not the place to discuss all this," Derek said coolly. He glanced around the restaurant to remind her that they were out in public, that she should behave herself.

"What is the place?" Cath demanded. "When is the time? There never seems to be a time to talk about important things."

"Now that the concert season is over, we'll have time. We'll make time."

"We didn't make time before, though, did we? I mean before I got sick. Before I took the night bus."

Derek reached across the table to take her hand. "We didn't come out to argue, did we?"

His silky voice, his confidence in his own attractions, infuriated her. "I didn't come out to be told I'll never work again, either."

"I didn't say you'd never work again." He raised his voice enough so that two older women in dark skirts and baggy sweaters interrupted an intense conversation about grant strategies to look their way.

"No, but you tell me I'm not well enough for everything I start to do."

"I'm concerned about your health, which, you'll maybe remember, has been a source of anxiety for months." Across the room, the waitress who had started in their direction doubled back toward the kitchen.

"I am perfectly capable of teaching again, and I intend to call Morgan Daniels."

"And what about today?"

"What about today? I got overtired cycling. You're always telling me the hills are brutal. I got tired and felt dizzy. It doesn't mean there's anything wrong with me."

"I'm glad to hear that. You just like to cycle yourself into the ground for no reason. You run into town half a dozen times a week just for exercise. Not to visit anyone, not to talk to anyone, just for the joy of humping that piece of junk over half the hills in Connecticut."

"You should hear yourself. Anyone would think you were suspicious of me. Or maybe of Luc. You went on long enough about my 'old boyfriend,' didn't you? For someone who's out as often as you are—"

"We're not talking about me, we're talking about you. I don't have to get driven home in a state of collapse."

"You have the car, after all," Cath said. "I think you're just annoyed because I cycle into town. Because I'm getting out. You'd be just as happy if I was a real invalid." She jumped up as she spoke, pushing her chair abruptly away from the table. As she did so, Cath was aware, even through the red lens of her anger, of the painful, focused quiet at the tables near them, of eyes turned in her direction, of intimations of social disaster.

"I'm not going to put up with this," Derek said, throwing his napkin down onto the table.

"And I'm not going to put up with being kept under lock and key. I intend to call the university music department this week."

"Go ahead," Derek said. "See if they hire you after this display."

Cath stumbled against the table. The dining room before her was enormous, a cavernous hall. The floors resounded with the bustle of the servers, but the murmuring obbligato of conversation had momentarily stopped. Cath was aware of a smear of faces, a blur of eyes and mouths, and knew she could not cross that expanse; it would kill her to pass the Danielses, to push her way through the bar. She turned to the French doors, twisted the handle of the nearest one, and lunged out onto the narrow stone terrace.

The sun was down, the air cool; Cath stepped from noisy brightness into summer twilight where the thickly leaved trees rose dark as thunderheads. Beyond the band of shrubbery and the parking lot, peepers were calling, loud, fresh sounds, but her own breath was louder yet; she was gasping like a drowning woman, fresh pulled from the sea. And she was nearly as wet, too, for sweat was coursing down her arms and running between her breasts.

Cath leaned on the stone wall edging the terrace and tried to control her breathing. *What's wrong with me,* she thought. She felt the same way she'd felt in Luc's office, when she'd remembered, imagined, decided that Derek had had a lover, a lover in Boston, a lover who died. A lover who had been killed. Who had been chopped. All this without proof, without the slightest reason except the pounding of her heart. She had been infected with the idea, so here she was, on their first evening out since her illness, shouting at her husband in the only good restaurant in the area. Cath wiped her face; for a moment, she thought she would throw up; the whole of her, body and soul, felt out of control; then she began to weep softly, the tears dripping between her fingers, as if her moment of horror and terror in Luc's office had been a live thing that she'd caught and put in a box and believed she had locked up and under control. But it wasn't locked up at all. It was crafty and sly; it had waited until she was happy, until she let her guard down, until she stupidly thought that she was well and normal and that her life could be happy. And then it leapt out to show her that all her assumptions were fallacious.

"Cath."

Derek stepped out onto the terrace. He had already apologized to the hostess and to the two nearest tables, murmuring, "She's recovering from a long illness ... first time we've been out ... an episode earlier in the day ... very difficult ..." and so reaped the sympathy and concern of the two old academics and the family party behind them. He had waved off Morgan Daniels, who had half risen from his chair. Derek thought that he had behaved as perfectly as a husband could under the circumstances, and more than one person remarked, "Poor man," before he opened the terrace door—a good deal more carefully than Cath had—and closed it softly behind him.

He could not see her for a moment, not against the darkness and the leaf-filtered glare of the parking lot. Then he saw her standing at the far corner of the terrace, one hand on the stone wall. The peepers were singing, a steady Glassian chorus, and pale moths fluttered in the air. Derek took a deep breath. What was it she knew? And what was it about her that moved him at unexpected moments, like now? With everything in his control, with events moving according to plan, why should he feel this sudden, irrational pain?

"Cath," he said again. "It's all right."

She half turned, but did not speak. When he came up beside her, he saw she was trembling, and when he put his arm around her shoulders, she felt hot and damp.

"You must come inside," he said. "You'll get pneumonia again."

"You don't get pneumonia from a chill," she said in a soft, strangled voice that told him she'd been crying.

"Chills weaken your resistance," Derek said.

"I don't have enough resistance," Cath agreed. She began to think of resistance, as in *French Resistance,* heart's blood once, now a matter of old movies. "I can't go back inside."

"You think in two hundred and fifty years, that's the first-ever argument in the inn?"

"It wasn't really an argument," she said. "More like an episode."

"We didn't intend to have either one," Derek said. "Did we?" No matter how well he knew her, he found it hard to credit the idea that she did little by calculation, that she did not have to plan her life, that her joys and sorrows were spontaneous.

"We'd intended to be happy," Cath said, and that intention seemed almost unbearably poignant.

"We are happy," said Derek. "We will be happy. You just have to be patient. You want to do everything right away."

"I feel a sense of time," Cath said. "Of time running out, of opportunity slipping away."

Derek hesitated. What did she mean by that? She'd said, in anger, a number of things that, on reflection, should make him uneasy; just the same, some concession was required. "But every day's closer to your birthday. We agreed that you'd start back with the choir on your birthday, didn't we?"

"Yes, that's what we agreed," Cath said, calmly now, for the strange, live thing was back in its box. "I can't tell you how I'm looking forward to that."

"So you mustn't push yourself," he said. "Even exercise, though good, though very good, can be overdone." He thought he could risk that much.

"I'm sorry," Cath said. "About dinner."

"We'll have dinner. No, no, we must. You've got to fight through these episodes. We'll start again," he said, concerned and gallant. He stepped back and offered her his arm. "You can do it," he said, just as if they were ready to step onto the stage, just as if she was ready to tackle some difficult music, and, for a moment, Cath thought she would break down entirely. "Yes, you can," he said, and she straightened her shoulders and lifted her head with a brave gesture that gave Derek a little pang. Then he led her back inside and smiled anxiously at her and pulled out her chair, so that everyone could see what a good husband he was.

13

"WE DON'T ALWAYS DRAW THE right lessons from what we learn," Cath remarked one day to Stel Pye.

"That's certainly true," the old lady agreed. "Sometimes you wonder what we do learn from life."

"I meant school things; you know, facts and theories. Like I remember learning about the plague, the Black Death of the Middle Ages."

"Terrible times," said Stel Pye. Cath had recently discovered that Mrs. Pye had taught in a one-room schoolhouse. The old lady knew, as she put it, "little bits about everything." "Of course," Stel added after a moment, "no one can really imagine something like the Black Death."

"History's a terrible subject. It has no meaning if you can't imagine the past, and what you can imagine is dreadful."

Mrs. Pye picked up her secateurs and trimmed a few inches off the stem of a particularly nice Queen of Denmark blossom. The antique shrub roses were doing so well this year. She really thought her Queen of Denmark, grown from a cutting, was superior to anything her friend, Lois Fletcher, had bought from the catalogue. But then Lois relied far too much on commercial fertilizers; she really ought to see a couple of these nice Queen of Denmarks.

The old pink roses were the backbone of the present arrangement, their ruffled heads like so many frilly spring hats. While Mrs. Pye did the honors with the roses, Cath was adding handfuls of an early white campanula and sprays of deep blue veronica. At the same time, she was playing with Belle, who kept lunging at the moving stems with her long white paws. Mrs. Pye would have scolded the cat and put her outside, but she knew Cath liked the animal, enjoyed its antics, needed, in some ill-defined way, its company. As Stel added another rose, she thought that Cath provoked all sorts of odd ideas. Something strange there.

"The thing about the Black Death," Cath resumed, "is that it recurred."

There's an example, Mrs. Pye thought. "Well, dear, it did kill a great many people."

"A third of the population of Europe. That's what you learn in school. The thing you forget is that it recurred."

Mrs. Pye admitted she had probably forgotten that. In seventy years you forget a lot, including the recurrence of the Black Death. Plus, she didn't think she had ever taught about the plague, not at the elementary, surely. The Black Death would never have been a suitable topic for the elementary. Cath was saying something about mathematics, about resonance, about the recurrence of plagues and illnesses. Mrs. Pye nodded, deciding that she had perhaps cut the last rose a bit short. "We'll have to bury this one in the front," she said.

Across from her, Cath smiled. She could say all sorts of things to Mrs. Pye, who absorbed ideas with a minimum of surprise and curiosity. Sometimes you need to say things out loud and to another person, because spoken words are different, and ideas change when they're told to someone else. Even ideas like the *plague.* What she was trying to tell Mrs. Pye and, indirectly, herself, was that disasters, infections, plagues recurred, returned: you were not free of them until every susceptible soul was dead. That was the lesson of the Black Death, a lesson which, she ought to have seen, could be applied to the human psyche, as well. You think you're cured of some affliction—say, of what passes as love, of desire, of lust—and then it recurs, because whatever is susceptible in your heart is still alive. They didn't teach her that lesson in college. They'd taught her about depopulation and religious hysteria and the rise in the value of labor, but they didn't teach her about the resonance of the human heart. "Maybe we each have to learn that for ourselves," she said aloud.

"There's no end to what we have to learn," observed Mrs. Pye.

Cath nodded so soberly that Stel said, "And you, my dear. Is everything all right with you?" Without really intending to, she added, "With you and your husband?"

"Yes. Yes, I think so." But just then, she picked up the cat, cuddling it in her arms, so that, despite her words, Mrs. Pye felt Cath had some hidden trouble.

Purring ecstatically, Belle began rubbing her mouse-colored head against Cath's shoulder. "I don't know," she said, tempted to confide. "I think—" and then she stopped. What did she think? She thought that her husband was unfaithful, although she had no proof. She was haunted by memories of two doomed young musicians with beautiful faces and long dark hair, one of whom was real, documented, indubitable. The other might exist only in her memory, or even in her imagination, a concept that would be difficult to convey to Mrs. Pye. And how would Cath explain that she herself had episodes of madness, at least one of which was certifiable, chargeable, homicidal? For that she had stabbed Derek was the only sure thing; she was the only one demonstrably guilty, and everything else comprised a Scotch verdict: *not proven.* Maybe not provable. Maybe not.

"I think it's difficult to adjust," Cath said, feeling she should somehow complete the sentence. "After being so sick."

"A big adjustment." Mrs. Pye understood that Cath did not really want to discuss the subject. Still, it would be too bad if they were having difficulties. She liked Cath and having a neighbor and seeing Elizabeth's nice old house reopened. "For your husband, too," she said, for she thought, somehow, that the trouble, if there was trouble, lay with Derek.

Cath nodded, but the moment had passed. She put Belle down and looked at the flowers, tipping her head slightly to one side. "A little ivy, do you think?"

Mrs. Pye stumped around the table to look at the arrangement from Cath's point of view. "Needs some foliage, yes. Do you want to take some ivy?"

"It will root in the vase, maybe. We could root some that way."

"If we change the water. We'll have to watch the water like a hawk."

They discussed the best way to root ivy, where to take the cuttings from, and where Cath should dig the plants in once they were rooted: that is the pleasure of gardening. There was always something to do, something to discuss, plans to be made, work to be done. It was nearly noon before Cath and Mrs. Pye had finished the flowers to their satisfaction. The tall Japanese vase with the Queen of Denmark roses, the campanula, veronica, and ivy, stood in its own reflection on the well-polished walnut table in Stel Pye's living room. Cath had a smaller ceramic with some of her own pink ramblers and a few of Stel's white Madame Hardys—roses with small chartreuse eyes and white petals touched by the faintest green imaginable. When they decided that ivy wasn't quite right with the smaller vase, Cath had added a couple of large peony leaves, instead.

"Quite nice," proclaimed Mrs. Pye, who was thinking that they might offer to do flowers for her church. Cath had such a nice touch with flowers, and volunteering would get her out of the house. She didn't go into the city with her husband on Sundays; Stel always checked the window when she heard their car and she knew that Cath was staying home. Still, would it be wise to suggest a connection with the local church when he was employed by Saint Martin's? Mrs. Pye decided she'd have to think the matter over; she didn't want to complicate matters or to put Cath in an awkward spot. Just the same, these were very nice arrangements, and if Cath wasn't going into town, it wouldn't hurt for her to attend services at the Congregational.

"Lovely," said Cath. "You have the most beautiful roses."

Mrs. Pye's face lit up: roses were her chief vanity. "Next year, we'll prune your old ramblers properly," she said. "You'll be surprised how nicely they'll come along."

"Yes," said Cath, though she hesitated, so that Mrs. Pye thought to herself, *I hope they will stay. I hope they aren't thinking of moving away just yet.* "I'm sure they'll be beautiful," Cath said then. "I was thinking I might get some more, another color, maybe."

They stood on Mrs. Pye's front step for a few minutes, talking about roses, before Cath walked across the lawns to her own house. She'd gotten the primer on the kitchen wing, but, as so often, the real magnitude of the job had only become evident once she was well started. There were acres more paint to be scraped and primed, and at the rate she was going, it would take her the whole summer to repaint the house. And then what?

When Stel had mentioned the roses, Cath had felt a momentary discomfort, almost a fear: next year and the next: roses, painting, renovation, filling up time, concealing the essential uselessness of her existence. A summer to do the painting, a decade for renovations, a lifetime for a garden. *Be careful what you wish for:* that was the old saying. She'd wanted this house, loved it, remembered it, yearned for it as for a beloved companion. In both Boston and Hartford, she'd awakened some mornings with the memory of her old room upstairs, the memory of starlings calling in the locust trees, the shudder of strong winds against the storm sash, and, most evocative of all, the compound of old timbers and dogs and lavender and gas stove that was the smell of Aunt Elizabeth's time, the smell of refuge, of order, of vacations. Now the house was hers; Cath was living where she'd always wanted to live, and she was wondering how she would put in the years which stretched ahead of her. Even half blind as she was, Mrs. Pye had noticed.

But what was there to say: *My husband keeps me off balance.* How about that? He was kind, affectionate, solicitous; they would play duets and spend early evenings in bed. Then, in a moment, he would grow irritable, or, worse yet, would calmly dismiss all her plans as impossible, the way he had that disastrous night in the restaurant. He had forgiven her, she perceived, in a very specific and particular way, conditional on her serving a life sentence. Though legally free and living in her own house, Cath was destined to be *a lifer,* her *episodes,* her *moments of madness,* hanging over her head like—what was that old phrase? Something classical: *the sword of Damocles.* Cath had entirely forgotten who Damocles was or why his sword was threatening, but the image was right: a large, shiny, lethal weapon poised at any minute to cut you off from all your hopes. Yes.

One night they'd argued about her teaching. She'd pointed out that the house was large enough for students. That with Yvonne in town and him out during the day, her pupils would bother no one. That even if he didn't want her to use the music studio, she could get another piano for the living room, that there was no reason—

Wham: it came down, the *sword of Damocles,* her *life sentence,* impelled by the incident which she had come to think of as the great *unmentionable,* like Victorian underwear. Underwear, underworld, *unmentionable.* He couldn't imagine her teaching again, couldn't imagine how she could make such plans. *Unimaginable.* With her illness. The strain alone. Et cetera.

"I must be better," she'd cried, her voice rising, sounding, she admitted herself, *unreliable.* "I must be better or I couldn't put up with this." *This* being his moods, his alternate tenderness and coldness, his lack of confidence in her, his memory of her misdeed. Sometimes she became skeptical, the plague receded, his charm failed. That was when she went out and planned a new garden, scraped a few more boards on the house, thought how she would advertise as a music teacher. In this mood, she was angry; she saw that he was keeping her off balance, perhaps deliberately; she understood he was manipulative and resolved to save herself.

And then, with a sudden and mysterious shift in the wind, with a sailor taking ill, with a strange ship drifting into port, the plague *recurred,* and she thought her heart would break. In these moods, she knew ecstasy and despair, and grew fatalistic. Like a gambler very deep in the hole, Cath was tempted to risk everything, to offer all she had, to see if she couldn't save them both. One night, lying in Derek's arms, she said, "I must see Luc Beausoleil." This was a test, and she thought she felt Derek stiffen slightly. "I need to sign my will; otherwise, should anything happen to me, there might be difficulties for you."

"Difficulties! I should think there would be difficulties," Derek said. "I'd be heartbroken."

"All the wills in the world couldn't change that, could they?" In the moonlight, his face was somber and he shook his head. The songs of insects filled the thick summer darkness and a wandering firefly glowed off and on, around the ceiling.

"I have some distant cousins. Apparently, they could make a claim. I don't believe they would win, but why have loose ends?"

"That sounds like your lawyer talking."

"I called him last week," Cath said. That was true. If Derek should check their phone statement, he would see that was the only call to Luc Beausoleil, attorney-at-law, in the past three months. "He was fussed about the trust funds coming to me. He wanted me to make a will and I said to go ahead."

"Can you make a will on the phone?" Derek asked. He sounded interested, concerned, but that was natural. Wills are a serious matter, the sort of matter men take seriously, or pretend to.

"Mine is easy. I told him everything goes to you, absolutely."

"My dear!" She could tell he was moved. And surprised? She thought he was maybe surprised, too.

"Who else?" Cath asked. "Who else would I want to benefit?"

He gave her a hug instead of answering.

"So it was very simple. And if you *predecease* me"—another of those precise, Latinate, lawyer words—"I told him to stay with Aunt Elizabeth's wishes: the animal shelter, the Salvation Army, the Heifer Project—the whole charitable lot."

"Ah," he said, hesitation, disapproval. *How well,* Cath thought, *I can read his moods.* She wondered if he knew that he was no longer opaque to her, if he knew that, though his motives, and perhaps his morals, were hidden, his moods were transparent.

"Hmmm? Is something wrong?"

"I was thinking of Yvonne."

"You need a will as well, Luc says. You can make yours in her favor."

"We're married. I would make a will leaving everything to you."

"If you wish. I mention this only so you'll know. Leave what you please to your sister, but I'm leaving her nothing. You know I don't like her."

"She thinks highly of you," Derek tried, though his voice sounded flat.

"It's not what she thinks of me, but what I think of her. Besides, I hope you'll live a good long time—longer than me. Anyway, you should speak to Luc Beausoleil."

"He's *your* lawyer," said Derek.

Did she detect a sulky tone? Was he really jealous of Luc? In another mood, she might find the idea of Cath Tolland, *rural femme fatale*, amusing, even cheering, but not now. "It might be easier for you to find someone in Hartford." She spoke indifferently. There were moments when she dropped into indifference, when nothing, least of all money, mattered. The day she called Luc, she had been tempted to tell him to send it all to Aunt Elizabeth's bequests, but she had been afraid of angering Derek, of being dependent, of having no means of support. She'd been afraid, momentarily, that it was true she could not work again, that she was, indeed, a *lifer*. Now she'd promised Derek and cut off that option. Had that been wise? She did not like to ask herself if it were safe.

"Well, what do you think?" Renee Beausoleil asked her brother. They were standing in the dusty, cluttered Attic Shop, contemplating a squat oak commode with an alligatored finish and missing knobs. They'd already looked at a little cherry chest and another walnut commode of considerably higher price. "It's just for Henry's room. He needs something beside his bed."

"But not a chamber pot," Vincent teased. He was tall like Renee, but more robust. Her little brother had grown up big and husky, with thick muscled forearms, broad shoulders, and large, strong hands: a physically powerful and impressive man. Only his round, unlined face seemed to Renee to belong to the younger brother she remembered as a child. His expression was still somehow boyish despite his red mustache, and he wore scholarly little gold-rimmed glasses that made his dark, untroubled eyes seem even younger and more innocent. People impressed with Vincent's expression of sweetness and content were sometimes taken aback by his quick, droll sense of humor.

"I was thinking shelves," Renee said, putting on patience. If there were to be shelves, Vincent would have to fit them, for Luc was quite hopeless with anything more mechanical than a paintbrush.

"Sure," said her brother. He squatted down next to the chest and, opening the doors, checked the interior. His inspection was slow and meticulous; Vincent never hurried, especially not with cabinetwork. Renee watched him run his hands over the wood, tapping the sides, checking the joints on what was, after all, only a very ordinary piece of secondhand furniture. He examined the back, too, not because he had any doubts about his ability to fit up a set of shelves for his nephew, but for the pleasure of handling old craftsmanship. She saw how he stroked the wood like a favorite animal. He sometimes said that wood spoke to him, that it told him what ought be made. Despite such eccentricities and his air of unhurried calm, Vincent turned out a steady stream of beautiful pieces. He made fine tables and chairs, breathtaking reproductions of eighteenth-century highboys and secretaries, as well as lovely chests and cabinets of his own design.

His talent had surprised them all. Her parents had been disappointed when Vincent, who showed every indication of intelligence, refused to consider college. He did a technical course at the local trade school and then, on the strength of a little tiger maple end table he'd made in the school shop, got himself apprenticed to a noted furniture conservator and restorer. He labored for five years in a shop north of Boston, *living on nothing*, their mother used to complain, before he struck out on his own, setting up a business with the same imperturbable confidence as he tackled fine antiques. Now he was becoming known; his own pieces brought amazing prices, and rich people brought him museum-quality furniture and waited until it pleased him to make the repairs. In retrospect, Vincent had known all along what he had wanted, and although Renee felt entitled to all the superior airs of a big sister, she admired her brother deeply, less for his prodigious skill than for his accurate and confident assessment of his talents and desires. She hoped her children would be so fortunate.

"The cherry's a better piece," he said now, "but this little oak commode will stand up to the boys."

"What about the finish?"

"Strip it if you want. Polyurethane." He made a face, but bowed to the realities of sticky snacks, milk, soda, Henry's beloved tank of guppies. "Poly the surface and you'll have no worries."

"All right," said Renee. "I'll take it." She wrote a check for the Attic Shop and exchanged enough pleasantries with the proprietor, a dubious, sallow-faced man in a dusty blue cardigan and filthy jeans, that he helped Vincent muscle the commode into the van. "Maybe I should send it to the stripper," she suggested, as they negotiated the dealer's narrow drive.

Vincent shook his head, although he had work piled up in the barn, although his shop was wall to wall, and he'd just gotten in some chestnut planks, a foot wide, an inch thick, with a lovely patina under the dirt and grime. He was thinking about using them for an armoire, a free translation of an old French piece he'd recently had a chance to study. "Loosen all the joints if you dip it," he told his sister. "I've got some new paste remover. Come by and I'll show you how to do it. Bring Henry along. This new stuff's not too toxic."

"All right," she said. She'd known he'd do it all along. "Put it in your barn, and then you come over to dinner. I've made lasagna."

"So you were prepared," he teased.

"I'm always prepared," she said. "Just drop me at the store, so I can pick up my car and get the dinner in the oven. You can bring Nancy, too, if you want. I've got plenty."

Vincent didn't say yes and didn't say no, which informed his sister that Nancy, another in a long line of nice women, was a nonstarter. Renee sometimes felt she would be perfectly happy with her brother if he would only get married, live with someone, even. Nancy had been rather nice, but though Vincent was enthusiastic about her for a time, Renee could see that phase had passed. He was too fussy. Or else he thought he'd know with a woman the same way he'd known with his profession. He expected a blinding flash of revelation or a sudden calm, unswervable conviction. Every time she thought along those lines, Renee became impatient with her brother, who was so contained and confident. It was to conceal this irritation, since he had, after all, taken much of the afternoon off and picked her up with his work van and promised to refinish Henry's new chest, that she cast around to change the subject.

Vincent was slowing down for the general store when Renee saw the bicycle—not parked at the law office, not there; Luc would know better than that now, but next door in front of the Paulsons'. Renee felt the hot beginnings of jealousy and indignation before she noticed the pink plastic basket with the perky artificial roses and realized that it was not Cath Tolland's bike. Not her style at all and much newer. Just the same, Renee mentioned her name.

"Funny, I thought that was Cath Tolland's bike," she said as they pulled into the lot next to her own car. "You don't know her, but Luc handles a trust fund for her. She and her husband own Elizabeth Mackey's old place. There was that awful—"

"I know who she is," Vincent said, as if he didn't care to hear the story.

"Do you? They haven't been in town that long. And she's been sick. Deathly."

"I heard her sing once," Vincent said quietly. "And I ran into her coming out of the law office a while ago."

"You hadn't mentioned meeting her. When was that?"

He shrugged. "I don't know. Month or so ago, maybe. I didn't really meet her; I nearly hit her with the van. But I knew who it was; I'd heard her sing."

"I didn't think she'd sung in town. They belong to a fancy suburban church in the city." Although Renee prided herself on a certain sophistication, she had gradually acquired a small-town taste for completeness of knowledge. Without ever thinking of herself as nosy, she would have been grieved not to know where Vincent had heard Cath Tolland sing and just how she had sounded.

"She sang at the college while I was doing that workshop on faux finishes. She has the most angelic sound imaginable."

"Really?" Renee felt she would rather her brother had picked a less laudatory adjective.

"Too small a voice, apparently, for a professional career, but beautiful. I've never heard a more beautiful singer," Vincent said.

If he'd just said, *She has a nice voice* or *Not bad, not a bad voice,* Renee probably wouldn't have spoken to Yvonne Tolland. Probably not. She hardly knew her, for one thing, and for another, Renee was in a rush to get home: she took pride in putting on a good dinner. But they'd met at one event or another, and Yvonne had sold Sarah and Bob Layton's house and gotten them a good price, plus, of course, Luc handled Cath's business. That meant it was only polite for Renee to wave to Yvonne Tolland, who was coming out of the general store carrying a *New York Times*. When Yvonne said, "Mrs. Beausoleil. Renee, right?" for she had a very good memory for names, contacts, useful people of all sorts, Renee closed her car door and asked how Yvonne was doing and whether the rest of the Tolland family were keeping well.

"Yes, we're all fine. Cath's as usual, of course."

"I'd heard she'd been sick. I'm very sorry. But a reaction's to be expected."

Yvonne looked nonplussed. "Reaction?"

"Luc finally mentioned it to me. I'd noticed her bike at the office, two three times a week. I couldn't help wondering . . ."

"Such a lot of legal business!" Yvonne exclaimed. "I hadn't realized."

"Oh, I don't think too much of it was legal business. She's alone all day, of course, and then when Luc said she'd had a miscarriage, everything was clear. I used to work in the OB-GYN section at the hospital . . ."

Yvonne flushed. "A miscarriage! Is that what Cath told your husband?"

Renee realized that she'd blundered into some private minefield. Well, she'd see about that! She was the innocent party in all this! "That's what Luc said. And there's no reason for him—"

"Not at all. I didn't mean to doubt your husband." Yvonne's voice was crisp and definite. Sarah Layton had said that Yvonne Tolland was an absolute bulldog in negotiations.

"I'm afraid I've upset you," said Renee.

"Yes, you have. We thought she was getting better, you see. She'd seemed—well, more rational, more cheerful in every way."

"A miscarriage is a more profound event than most people realize," Renee said, prepared to enlighten Yvonne on some of the finer points of gynecology and hormone imbalance.

"Cath was never pregnant," Yvonne exclaimed. She seemed to the embarrassed Renee both annoyed and alarmed. "Pregnancy, miscarriage—that's all pure fantasy. Poor Derek! She'll say or do just anything. But you say she's been visiting your husband?"

"She's been to the office frequently, yes," Renee said, not liking this turn in the conversation. She had a few things to ask Luc, and a few to tell him, as well.

"I'm glad you told me! No doubt she was trying to get his sympathy with that ridiculous story. She has such a tenuous grasp of reality, we never know what she'll make up. Warn your husband about that.

In fact, I'd better stop by and see him. His first name is Luc, it's Luc Beausoleil, right?"

"Yes. His office is right down the street."

"Of course. I know it: Victorian two-and-a-half-story with original gingerbread. Yes, I'd better talk to him. Everything falls to me, but rather than worry Derek . . . My brother has been half out of his mind with anxiety. First, she's, well, seriously unstable—and then she gets on a bus and leaves. Yes! Not a note, not a phone call. You can imagine how we felt! And then she loses her memory—or so she claims—and the police have to send out a bulletin. I went down to Florida to bring her back. Do you know," Yvonne said in a tone at once confidential and hectoring, "for days she actually kept up the farce of not knowing me. Days! She had the neurologist and the psychiatrist half buffaloed. It's a good thing I got there when I did."

"I can imagine," said Renee, for while the news about Catherine Tolland was alarming, Yvonne reminded her very strongly of certain difficult patients and "patient advocates" she'd come across in her nursing career.

"I'll stop by next week," Yvonne said, "and get things straightened out with your husband."

"Yes, do that. But be sure to call first," Renee added, for something about Yvonne's air of pressured importance irked her. "Luc's awfully busy."

14

- - - - - - -

CATH PICKED LETTUCE, ARUGULA, AND young spinach for the salad, then got her clippers to cut a few more roses: they were having a semifancy dinner for her birthday. Yvonne had not only insisted they eat in the newly redecorated dining room but had found an old white linen tablecloth and ironed it herself. Yvonne wanted candles, two centerpieces, and Aunt Elizabeth's sterling, even though the silver seemed a lot of work to Cath and the elaborate ceremonial preparations depressed her just a little. She didn't feel as excited about turning thirty as her sister-in-law did.

"It's your birthday, after all," Yvonne kept saying, "and a special one!"

Cath felt that twenty-nine birthday celebrations were plenty, but Yvonne was excited by the whole idea. "You're coming of age. Don't look so grim and spoil things for Derek."

Cath was tempted to say that Derek had been very subdued and out of sorts lately, anyway.

"We'll have a really nice dinner. Maybe that fish thing you do— you know, poached in wine. I'll get the fish and a decent wine. And dessert. I'll stop at the Italian bakery, so all you'll have to do is the fish and the vegetable. They sell very good bread at the bakery, too."

"All right," said Cath. "But if we're to have a little party, I'd like to invite Mrs. Pye. She's been awfully nice."

"Mmm," said Yvonne, noncommittally. With a certain chagrin, Cath realized that there was really no one else she *could* invite. Certainly not Luc and Renee Beausoleil, not after all the business with Confidential Reports. Strange, she hadn't heard back from them, but maybe that was for the best. She really should have thought how awkward the whole business might be.

"Stel evens out the table," she said, and Yvonne had nodded and conceded that, as their nearest neighbor, Mrs. Pye was entitled to an invitation.

As Cath reached around the thorny canes for the rose blossoms, she rehearsed her preparations. The fish was ready for the oven, the table set, everything cut for the salad except the lettuces. The bread Yvonne had bought could get warmed with the fish; the ice cream and cake were in the fridge. When Stel came, the fish would go into the oven while they drank sherry in the living room, and the sauce could get made while the others started their salads. Even with just Mrs. Pye and Derek and Yvonne, Cath felt nervous about this first special dinner, and she tried to convince herself that everything would go well. Yvonne had gotten some fine, fresh sole that would make an elegant entrée. The newly painted dining room looked pretty and bright, and the flowers were at their peak. All these things, dinner and redecoration and flowers, were signs of Cath's recovery, and coming back with the roses, she pushed herself to feel festive.

She was passing the overgrown yews at the corner of the living room when she heard the murmur of voices. She'd thought Derek and Yvonne were upstairs, getting changed.

". . . have to do it," said Yvonne. "You can see that now."

Cath had really not intended to listen, but something in Yvonne's tone, rather than her words, commanded attention.

". . . assured me . . ." Derek's voice, lower, was lost in the breeze and in the chattering of the sparrows.

"That's today." Yvonne's voice was sharp, a voice that carried. Or perhaps a voice that did not care whether or not it was overheard. "That's today. If she lied about one thing, there's no guarantee that tomorrow—"

"*Tomorrow, and tomorrow, and tomorrow, creeps in this petty pace*..." said Derek, projecting now in a loud, clear voice. He'd insisted on testing the sherry which Cath had ordered for Mrs. Pye.

"Don't play the fool, and no more sherry," Yvonne said.

"You're a real killjoy, Yvonne. And then you wonder why..."

"As long as you see it's inevitable. She must know..."

"Not everything, surely," said Derek.

Cath opened the screen door, and their conversation stopped like a car in the wrong gear, then restarted with a jolt. By the time she was in the front hall with her basket of lettuces and the bunch of roses, Yvonne was talking about birthday preparations. "You know about the cake, don't you?" she called through from the living room. Cath stopped in the doorway.

Yvonne was sitting on the couch, with one arm stretched along the back. With her long, dark green knit dress, silver necklace, and dangling earrings, she looked like an advertisement for something expensive and desirable. Of course, she didn't touch the cooking. Derek, still in his chinos and a sport shirt, was slouched in Aunt Elizabeth's leather easy chair. His face looked very thin, and, with the knowledge that he was unhappy, Cath felt her heart contract.

"Derek still believes in surprises," Yvonne said in the arch and playful tone she saved for social occasions. What control she had over her voice and her expression! "But I know you peeked at the cake."

"I saw the box in the fridge. I haven't opened it." Cath did not have such good vocal or emotional control. Even to herself, her voice sounded flat, wary.

"See, what did I tell you? You can believe Cath, who's always Girl Scout straight and truthful. Almost always. Isn't that right, Cath?"

"Don't start. I'm going to make the salad." Cath walked into the kitchen wishing that dinner was finished, that the weekend was over, that Yvonne had already departed for home. Although things did not necessarily go better without Yvonne, Cath always felt her presence as a strain. She hoped Stel Pye would be able to neutralize an atmosphere that, for all the celebratory touches and her sister-in-law's present vivacity, felt both heavy and unstable.

Cath washed the greens, mixed up the salad dressing, and carried the whole ensemble to the dining room in a nice wooden salad bowl. Punctual, Stel rang the bell a few minutes later. She parked her cane in the hall and maneuvered into the living room with the help of the doorjamb and the back of the couch. "Well, doesn't this look lovely!" she said. "Oh, Elizabeth would be so pleased to see this!" She beamed shortsightedly at them.

"It's a marvelous old building," Yvonne said. "Professionally speaking, I'd like to get my hands on it."

Mrs. Pye frowned slightly. "Professionally?"

"I'm in real estate. This could be a very special property."

"It has always been special to me," said Mrs. Pye. "Elizabeth Mackey was my dearest friend. Did you ever meet her?"

"No, though I think my brother did, didn't you Derek?"

When he didn't answer, Cath said, "Derek and I visited around the time of our marriage. Aunt Elizabeth wasn't able to travel by then."

Anxious for a topic, they settled on Aunt Elizabeth before branching out to the history of the house, its additions and renovations and owners over the years. Mrs. Pye's dwelling was another source of interest, at least to Yvonne, who did, Cath had to admit, know how to keep up her end of a conversation. Yvonne had settled into her hostess mode for the evening, a mode so glamorous and animated that real estate, Saint Martin's church, and country weekends seemed too dull and confining for her vivid personality. Derek, in contrast, remained quiet to the verge of rudeness during their discussion of Victorian farmhouse styles over sherry and of miscellaneous village gossip at dinner.

"That was delicious," said Mrs. Pye, when the poached sole and its julienne vegetables had been quite demolished.

"Yvonne got the fish," Cath said. "It wasn't hard to make a good dinner with such beautiful fish."

"Cath's too modest. She's a better cook than I ever realized. Of course, when I first came, I did all the cooking. When Cath was sick, I mean."

"What about finishing the salad?" Cath asked. She did not want to discuss past history, and Yvonne was fond of raising incidents best forgotten.

"I'm saving room for dessert," Derek said.

At this hint, Cath started to get up, but Yvonne exclaimed, "I'll take care of the cake. No, no, you did the dinner. Wasn't that awful," (this to Mrs. Pye) "to have to make her own birthday dinner? But you wouldn't want to eat my cooking!" Yvonne swept out carrying a handful of dishes, then returned with a tray balanced on the crook of her arm to collect the rest. "I'll just fix the candles."

"Can't have a birthday cake without candles," Stel Pye agreed.

"No, indeed," said Derek, belatedly making an effort at cheerfulness. But when Cath tried to catch his eye, to ask, *What's wrong*, he evaded her glance, and the anxiety she had caught from Yvonne's few overheard words returned.

"Derek, come help me with this," Yvonne called from the kitchen. He pushed back his chair. "Duty calls." A few moments later, there was a bustle in the hall. Yvonne switched off the chandelier, leaving the dining room lit only by the low evening light streaming through the southwest windows. As Derek stepped from the darkness of the hallway, the candles blazing on the cake washed his face with gold. The little bright flames threw shadows onto the ceiling and filled the dining room with the evocative smell of burning wax, creating a brilliant moment like a party scene in a film. "Music!" Yvonne commanded, and she, Derek, and Mrs. Pye struck up "Happy Birthday."

"What a beautiful cake!" Cath was unexpectedly touched. "Thank you, Yvonne. You remembered that mocha's my favorite."

"The Italian bakery on the bypass," Yvonne told Mrs. Pye. "Really good. They used to be in Hartford."

"Hartford has some good bakeries," Mrs. Pye agreed.

"This birthday's quite a milestone for Cath," Yvonne said with a glance at Derek. When he didn't respond, she smiled and added, "A milestone on her recovery." Then to Cath, "You'd better blow them out before everything melts."

"I hate to," Cath said. "They're so pretty." Yvonne had somehow crammed thirty-one candles on top of the cake, and the dense array of glowing lights reminded Cath of the votive candles in French cathedrals. On their trip to France, she'd wanted to light a candle for her parents but, out of a foolish shyness, had not.

As if he could read her mind, Derek said, "Candles have a certain sacramental appeal." He gave Cath a cryptic and not entirely pleasant smile.

"I like candles," she said. "They make you remember."

"Cath's half Catholic," her husband said.

"I thought you told me I was a pagan?"

"Pagan or Papist, some such."

"Look out!" Yvonne exclaimed. "The icing's melting."

"Make a wish, dear," said Mrs. Pye.

Cath took in her breath and thought, *Let Derek be happy,* then blew out all the flames on the first try, prompting applause.

Yvonne picked the smoking candles off the thick mocha frosting as quickly as possible. "Oh, get the ice cream, would you, Derek? You'll have some ice cream, won't you, Mrs. Pye?"

"I will, indeed. This is such a treat." Her face, as round and wrinkled as an old apple, was alight. Despite the undercurrents Cath sensed around the table, she was suddenly glad they'd had the party, and especially glad she'd included Stel. She reached over to touch the old lady's arm.

"I'm so glad you could come."

"Yes, indeed," Yvonne said, "and it needed to be tonight, too, because Cath and Derek are going to be on vacation for a while. I can tell you, Mrs. Pye, the only way my brother gets any time off is to go away. Church people assume your time is their time."

Mrs. Pye nodded sympathetically: her Congregational Ladies Guild suffered from the same assumption. Derek kept his eyes on his plate, and Cath gave Yvonne an irritated look that said, *No such thing has been decided.*

"Fortunately, our family has a camp on Schroon Lake. Nothing very elaborate, but quiet. I love the lake and the woods. Do you know the Adirondacks, Mrs. Pye?"

"We used to go to the Catskills when I was a girl, but never further up. Though I got to the White Mountains once. Those were in my hiking days."

"I like the seashore, personally," Cath said. "Cape Cod, the Connecticut shore. I like the ocean."

"Cath finds it hard to operate on a budget," Yvonne said, turning to Mrs. Pye. "You know what shore places cost today! While our camp in the woods is free! It needs a bit of work, but camps should be *camps*. You go to the Adirondacks to get away from civilization for a while, after all. To get in touch with the *primitive*." Again, there was something in her voice that disturbed Cath, a sense of excitement and anticipation.

"You don't often go to the Adirondacks yourself," Cath observed.

"Well," still addressing herself to Mrs. Pye, "so many of the things I liked to do in the woods are difficult now. Canoeing really needs two hands, and even fishing is awkward." She glanced at Derek, who was staring into his coffee cup as into a crystal ball. "But the woods are so soothing, so almost meditative. Going into the woods changes your whole attitude. You see things differently. New perspectives." Yvonne half closed her magnificent dark eyes as she spoke, revealing the green-tinged eye shadow that smudged her upper lids.

I must have the most glamorous sister-in-law in the world, Cath thought, as she watched Yvonne give Stel Pye a high dose of charm and fascination. What would Mrs. Pye think? What did people in general think about Yvonne? Was there some agreed-upon opinion? Or was that just another way of asking whether Cath was the only one to be reminded of a cat or a cobra?

"Well," said Mrs. Pye briskly, "the woods are nice and the shore, too, but for my money, summer right here is about perfect. There's nowhere else I'd rather be when my roses are out."

"But you have special roses," said Cath, grateful for a change of topic. "I'm not sure Yvonne's seen your roses. Paradise in the backyard."

"Now you are teasing," said Mrs. Pye, "though my Queen of Denmark is outstanding this year, and so is my Othello."

"Your Madame Hardy is pretty nice, too," Cath said, touching one of the roses on the table, so that Yvonne had to bring her formidable approval to bear on the flowers. She had questions for Stel, observations about horticulture. Yvonne had a listing for a fine house near Elizabeth Park in Hartford. This brought them to her work, her assortment of *prestige properties*, and the opportunities of a new development, before Mrs. Pye, seeing it was full dark or perhaps surfeited with real estate, said she ought to be going. The dinner was now admired again; the roses, ditto. Cath said she would walk Stel home, and Yvonne said she and Derek would do the dishes.

"Don't worry about the dishes," Cath said. "You'll want to get on the road for home, won't you?"

"You're not doing your birthday dishes," Yvonne exclaimed, "even if I am a little late. But Derek's going to wash and I'll dry and we'll be done before you get back. It was so clever of Cath to invite you," Yvonne told Mrs. Pye. "It's been such a pleasure meeting you."

Derek stirred himself to confirm this, and after Cath collected a flashlight and Mrs. Pye's cane, they set out across the lawn. The house lights thrust back the darkness for a few yards, then the clotted shadows of the maples rose against the stars and dark, furred shapes of brush and trees emerged from the deep grays of the meadow. Frogs were calling; bats fluttered in the air; the longer grass between the two lawns was already quite damp.

"Don't slip," said Cath. "It's so dark! I should have taken you in the car."

"I'm supposed to walk," Mrs. Pye reminded her. "And, do you

know, the only time I really like walking is at night. Norman and I used to go down the meadow just about every moonlit summer night. You didn't have to worry about ticks in those days—or neighbors, either." She stopped to look up at the night sky, the faint lights swimming like fish in her thick glasses. Cath found it hard to imagine squat, nearsighted Mrs. Pye on romantic evening walks, but she, too, had once been young and in love. *I'll be old like that,* Cath thought, *and people will think the same of me. They won't imagine that I was once pretty; they'll be amazed at what I did for love.*

"I never could live in the city," Mrs. Pye continued. "I couldn't stand all that city shine at night. I'm so glad you haven't put in one of those dreadful security lights. People who want that much security should live in town." She started forward again, poking her cane aggressively into the grass as if it, too, lusted after spotlights and other urban contrivances. Cath was relieved when they left the little strip of meadow for the smoother lawn. There, the yellow light from Mrs. Pye's porch and kitchen lit their way and she didn't have to worry about the old lady falling.

"That was a really nice dinner, dear," Mrs. Pye said when they reached the porch. "Many, many happy returns."

"Thank you," said Cath. "You were kind to come. I've felt"—and she paused again, uncertain what to say, uncertain how loyal she needed to be—"I've felt rather isolated with being sick. I know I've taken up a good deal of your time."

"Nonsense," said Mrs. Pye. "Your company has been a pleasure. I hope you won't forget me now you're back on your feet."

"We've got a lot of gardening and flowers to do yet," said Cath.

"When you get back from your holiday," suggested Mrs. Pye.

"If we go. I don't know whether we'll go. I'm not sure I want to go to the Adirondacks."

"Very beautiful, I'm sure," said Mrs. Pye reflectively, "but I never liked being in the really deep woods. You're too closed in, somehow. I like to see what's coming around me." She turned and unlocked her front door, then added, "I wouldn't go anywhere you don't want to.

Holidays are supposed to be fun. Even family holidays."

Cath thought about that adjective as she started back through the field: *family* holidays. *Family*, in this case, meant Yvonne, but since she had a lot of new *prestige properties* to unload during the prime selling season, Yvonne was planning to visit Colorado in the fall. So this wouldn't be a *family* holiday at all, and there was no reason for Yvonne to interfere with their vacation plans. No need for thrift, either. They could afford to go to the shore; they could afford to go to France, too, if they wanted, where they could see the cathedrals again and Monet's garden and walk along the Seine. They could go to concerts and hear music at night in the Tuilleries Gardens. They had possibilities, so many possibilities, if they were only willing to recognize the fact that she had money, money she had neither asked for nor wanted. Money they might as well spend. What could be the harm in that?

At the head of the track down to the river, Cath stopped to listen to the frogs, hoped for a woodcock, heard a dog—or was it a coyote?— far off in the woods. She would have liked to walk down to the water, though that was foolish without boots and long pants, though the grass was wet, and the track full of ruts and rocks. She lingered in the cool summer night anyway, until a cone of light swept over the lawn and striped the field and the path white and black, then resolved itself into round headlights turning onto the road: Yvonne was on her way into Hartford. Cath smiled and relaxed; the weekend was over.

"You were gone long enough," Derek said when she opened the front door. He was standing in the hallway, and, after the dark field, the overhead light was dazzling. She could not see his eyes.

"It's such a nice night, I was tempted to walk to the river."

"We thought Mrs. Pye had fallen or something. Why didn't you take the car?"

"I probably should have, but Stel likes to walk at night. She told me that she and Norman—that was her late husband—used to walk through the fields every nice moonlight night. She says there weren't so many neighbors then!" Cath wondered if Derek would take the hint, if he would be inspired by visions of bucolic love. "Old-time rural life clearly had its moments," she said.

"Moments." His voice was sour, and she changed the subject. "Yvonne's on her way?"

"Yes, as soon as we finished up the dishes. She wanted me to walk over and see if you two were all right."

"Yvonne worries too much," Cath said. She closed the inner door and turned the lock. Her eyes had adjusted to the light, and, belatedly, she had picked up his mood. She knew she would have to make an effort. "I'm glad she insisted on the party, though. It was fun. Thank you."

"Yvonne did most of the work," he said, meaning *You should have been back to thank her.*

"Stel really enjoyed the dinner," Cath said, ignoring this.

He turned away into the living room. "Though it would be nice if there were some other people we *could* ask." He sat down on the couch and rested one arm along the back, the very same pose Yvonne had taken when Cath had come in and interrupted their conversation. But with his sister, Derek had seemed nervous, unhappy. Now he was confident again and decisive.

"The choir," she suggested. "We should ask the members of the choir out in the fall. The house is in pretty good order now."

"In the fall?"

"Earlier, if you want. Right away."

"I thought we were going on vacation. I thought that was decided." He spoke quickly, as if it were a fait accompli. She'd once thought that phrase meant a fat accomplice; now it sounded like *fate*, like *one's fate accomplished.*

"A vacation would be nice," Cath said, "but nothing's been decided. The only one who's discussed a vacation is Yvonne."

"It's still a good idea. The church is always calling for this or that."

"And you've been working late nights," Cath said. "All spring." She could see from his expression that he didn't want to discuss late nights or his spring schedule.

"Time to get away," he said, and Cath thought of Boston, of his need to *get away,* to be somewhere else, to start fresh. Had it been partly for him that they'd left Hartford? She was surprised she'd never considered that before. "A little birthday gift for you," Derek added.

"All right. Where shall we go?" She sat down across from him in the armchair and put her feet up on the ottoman to show that she wasn't afraid to talk about vacations. And she wasn't, not really, though she had a strange, congested sensation in her chest, as if all her emotions had gathered there together. Still, she wanted to hear what he would say; she felt she needed to know.

"I think Yvonne's right. The lake is the cheapest place, and I've always liked it."

"I thought you had bad memories of the lake. I thought that's why you haven't gone back."

"I haven't gone back for a long time, it's true, but I'd like to see the camp again. I'm mature and adjusted now."

Cath did not say anything. She remembered his tears, his remorse and anguish when he'd spoken about the lake and Yvonne's accident. Then he'd been a man that Cath felt she understood, a man who'd held his own ticket for the night bus. But the Derek sitting across from her was different; he had a smooth, impermeable surface like Yvonne. Yes, in some ways Derek was very like Yvonne. He could put on Yvonne, as it were, with a change in posture, with this sophisticated calm.

"Now that Uncle Will's getting too old to rent it for hunting seasons, we'll probably have to sell the place," Derek continued. "For old times' sake, I'd like to go up. Maybe bring some of the furniture and the other stuff home—now that we have a house. Yvonne says there are some twig chairs that might be valuable. Next week, maybe?"

Cath leaned back in her chair and studied him for a minute. She had been tense and anxious all weekend. She was never completely easy with Yvonne, and the prospect of the dinner had made her nervous. But now that she faced a serious decision, Cath found she'd somehow stepped sideways from herself. She felt distracted, half anesthetized, as if she'd worn out her nervousness on trifles. Keeping alert was going to be difficult. "I think it's the sort of trip you might want to make alone."

"I don't see why," he said.

"Memory trips are best alone. I assume this is a memory trip."

"Sorry to be so unfashionable, but I have no secret psychic agenda," he said, his good humor ruffling like a pond under wind. "I don't have time for those things. I just thought you might want to see the old camp."

"I've spent all spring cleaning up elderly buildings. Besides, I've been alone so much lately that I don't think the Adirondacks would be much of a change."

"It's a little late to be craving bright lights. You weren't happy until we moved back here. We could have stayed in Hartford."

"Could we?"

"Whose fault was that?" Derek asked, his voice angry.

Cath was silent. She felt she really didn't know whose fault it was.

"The camp is free; we can manage it financially. Suppose we take a week. If you like it, we stay longer. If you don't, we come home."

She smiled sadly, as if she'd half expected to be disappointed. Though she'd given him his chance, Derek was set to maintain the charade a while longer. Cath suddenly felt sick of deception, of suspense, even of being careful. "We don't need to go to the camp to save money," she said. "There's absolutely no need for that at all. Not now. Not as of today."

He came alert all at once, ostentatiously alert, as if to signify a surprise he did not really feel. Derek's emotional control, like his sister's, was remarkable but somewhat mechanical. "What do you mean?" he asked.

"I should ask you the same thing." Cath took a deep breath. "Luc Beausoleil—and you—have made me *very comfortable,* as Aunt Elizabeth used to say. My trust funds spin off several thousand dollars a month. With your salary and this house, we don't have any money worries." This was a statement of fact, and Cath and Derek let it lie between them. Then he jumped up: no more Yvonne with glamorous gestures. This was Derek, tense, forceful, energy to spare, and for just an instant, Cath was nineteen again and he was the most amazing man in the world. He walked over to the fireplace and glanced at her in the mirror above the mantel. The reflection subtly distorted his features, giving him, Cath thought, a sly, fugitive expression.

"I suppose you wonder why we didn't tell you," he said. "I suppose you think there was some plot, some intention to keep things from you."

Cath shrugged. "I supposed it was because of my illness."

"You're damn right," he exclaimed, as irritable as if she *had* suspected him. Aunt Elizabeth was right: sometimes you are *as well to be hanged for a sheep as a lamb*. "You might have done anything. And your medical bills in Florida!" He went on about this for a few minutes. Yvonne had been heroic; he himself had been forbearing; they both had been frantic.

"I still don't know why I left," Cath said. "Or why you brought me back."

"Don't be so childish. What would have happened to you? You went off without anything! How would you have lived?"

"By honest work, like most people." She thought of Raoul and added, "Or by not so honest work."

"You certainly wouldn't have had time to play about with the violin and a garden in Florida," Derek said. "But it's ridiculous for you to talk this way. I can't make any sense of your behavior. And why you should lie about all these things is beyond me."

"What have I lied about?" Cath asked. "We've neither of us talked about the money. When did you ever bring up my trust fund?"

Instead of answering her question, he demanded, "Just how long have you 'remembered' about your income?"

"I think Yvonne mentioned the trust a few weeks ago." As Cath spoke, she seemed to remember that Derek had not been pleased when his sister raised the subject.

"You've been talking to Luc Beausoleil, too."

"I told you about that," Cath said. Her nervousness returned like a sudden electrical discharge, but Derek couldn't know about Confidential Reports. He couldn't. "Luc's been after me to make a will. He wants both of us to have new wills, so, of course, he's talked about the trust fund." Did that sound convincing? Although she'd wanted to be candid, certain things were impossible. How would she explain why she'd hired Confidential Reports, why she'd wanted to know about Esther and about Boston, why she'd had terrors and suspicions? Perhaps Derek sensed her reserve, for he was suddenly gripped by anger and by another emotion Cath could not quite identify.

"Your fund's needed intensive consultations, apparently." He left the fireplace and began pacing back and forth. "Ever since you got that damn bike fixed you've been up there." He turned to look at Cath, daring her to deny this, and she realized that she must have been seen at Luc's office.

"Luc's spent a good deal of time going over the trust. And persuading me to accept it."

Derek's face grew harder, but he did not speak.

"You know I didn't want that insurance settlement." In spite of herself, Cath felt her voice getting tight and thin. Fear is the enemy of the voice. Was it possibly fear that had kept her voice small? Was it?

"You'd have been a fool to turn it down." Derek was angry but in control. He was in control, Cath thought, because he'd been making the decisions, having his own way. Under the circumstances, reining in his emotions was easy for him.

"Nonetheless, I didn't want the settlement," she said. She heard the red edge of anger and recklessness in her voice: she'd been careful so long, ever since that day in the kitchen when her temper had burst out like an animal from a cage. "No amount of money could bring my poor parents back."

Now it was his turn to make an effort, to be careful. Why did they always feel they had to be so careful? Almost the first thing she remembered in Florida was *be careful*. And Derek, who was not by nature cautious, not a person to weigh and consider, Derek, too, was being careful. She could see him putting aside his anger and that other, more exotic emotion that she sensed but did not recognize, or maybe recognized but could not name. She could see Derek making an effort and wondered what he was afraid of. Was there really a cage in their marriage, a cage with the animals that were their respective tempers?

"Listen, having to cough up the settlement put that phony guru and his crackpot ashram out of business." Derek sounded encouraging, hearty and confident. "They'd ignored every fire regulation on the books."

"I know that!" Irritated. "I did try to warn Mom and Dad!" She felt as if he were accusing her of carelessness, of some neglect of duty. "I had such bad feelings when I saw the place, but there was no talking to them!" For a moment, Cath could think of nothing else, not the argument of the moment, not the questions about Luc, not the vacation, not her own precarious position. She saw the old California mansion with its big shedlike assembly hall topped with fashionable wood shingles, the worst possible choice in a canyon full of tinder-dry brush. As usual, her parents had no eyes for the mundane. All they saw was the guru, a stout, hairy man in saffron robes, and the magnificent sea view to the west. They'd been as happy as children at summer camp, transparently happy, such funds as they still had, well lost. Cath had seen that in an instant, literally at a glance. And at a glance, too, she'd detested the guru and his lieutenant, Brother Hari, with his thin, cold face.

"And you had such gifts as a child!" her mother exclaimed. "How you can close yourself off to all this!" She raised her arms as she spoke and gestured toward the Pacific with its big blue water rollers and smog-smudged LA. It was useless for Cath to respond, to say that the ashram gave her the creeps, that for so many residents the building was totally inadequate, that Brother Hari struck her as having the soul of a calculator. Useless, but perhaps she should have tried harder, even called the fire marshal: it was obvious the place was a fire trap. She just hadn't thought of fire really happening; she hadn't imagined a sudden late-night conflagration that would roar out of the kitchen to envelop the ashram and incinerate the hopeful pilgrims setting out on the guru's *Higher Path*. "I couldn't save them," she repeated. That failure was the yawning horror of her life; it was the reason she was susceptible to appeals for salvation.

"Think of the settlement as the cost of shutting down that operation," Derek said. To him it was simply dollars and cents.

"I have thought of it that way," Cath said angrily. "But my intention was to send the money to charity. To Aunt Elizabeth's charities with the rest of her money. You knew that, Luc knew that, I suppose Yvonne knew that, too."

"That decision was the first sign of your illness," Derek said in a superior way. "You don't remember the state you were in when you came back from California. We had to think of your best interests. We had to consider that you might not be able to work. We had to weigh a lot of things in order to do what was best for you."

"I assume that's what Luc thought, too: that he was serving my best interests."

"And now you can't work," Derek said. "So it's a very good thing you have the funds. But we'll have to be careful with them."

"We don't have to go to extremes," Cath said. "I'm going to get a car. And I think we can take a nice holiday. I think we can do that."

"Oh, I see," Derek said in a nasty voice. "You've come into money, so now you make the decisions."

Since the last important decision she'd gotten to make was buying her ticket to Florida, Cath thought that was unfair. What right had he to be so superior, so certain? She distrusted certainty now. "I don't think it's unreasonable to have a second car. What would you do with the money?" she asked. And then, because she was angry, she was careless, and added, "What have you been doing with it?"

"Taking care of you," he said, his voice raised, furious. "Do you have any idea of your bills in Florida?"

Cath did not. "But we have health insurance. Through Saint Martin's."

"You don't get complete coverage for mental illnesses," Derek said. "I had pneumonia and a head injury," Cath corrected.

"You left home with nothing but the money in your pocket. You traveled under an assumed name and wound up on the street in Florida. Tell me that wasn't mental illness."

"Yet I don't remember any doctor, any treatment. How was that?"

He hesitated, even in anger—his face flushed, the strong cords of his neck taut—he hesitated, and with deep pain, Cath knew he was going to lie. "You resisted all treatment," he said. "We couldn't get you to see anyone."

"I'm surprised you stayed with me," she said. "I tried to kill you. I attacked you without warning or provocation, didn't I? I could have gone to jail." The words sounded unreal, like the score of a badly understood song.

"I stayed because I knew you needed help," Derek said. Again, the superior tone that drove caution from her brain.

Cath stood up. "You should have said, because you loved me."

"Of course I loved you. It goes without saying that I loved you."

"And what about this spring?" Cath asked. "Have you still loved me this spring?"

"This spring you forgot me," Derek said, and there was some justice in that.

"So you forgot me, in turn," Cath said. "With Jane Henkel."

He went white. She remembered that later, how his skin lost its color as if she'd opened a vein. How the flesh at the corners of his mouth and nose took a bluish tinge, how a change in expression altered his face almost beyond recognition. Maybe that was it: for a moment he ceased to be Derek, so that she was released to be candid.

"There's nothing," he said. "Nothing. Don't you dare accuse me!"

Cath found herself in the kitchen again, with the tiled floor, the autumn light, the sharp weight of opportunity lying in the cutlery basket; she was in the apartment kitchen with Derek, the knife, and knowledge, knowledge she couldn't bear, wouldn't recognize. "It wouldn't be the first time," she screamed as the room darkened around her. "It wouldn't be the first time."

His hand lashed out and everything collapsed, the room, the house, the night with its sounds of insects and peepers, their life as it had been, their life of lies and evasions. Pain astonished and frightened her; a line of fire ran across her cheek and her ears started ringing.

"You never loved me," she said and started from the room. He caught her arm. "Don't touch me. Don't ever touch me!" They struggled in the hallway, and when she broke free and ran up the stairs, he followed her. He was speaking, yelling, explaining, but Cath heard nothing except the roar of anger and grief within her own head: a moment of madness. That's what lies do, that's what a refusal to see the world does; evasion protects you for only so long and then reality breaks in and the world shatters and you feel the wheels of the night bus under your feet.

At the top of the stairs, Cath ran into the bedroom and tried to close the door behind her, but Derek was too quick and too strong.

"Listen to me," he kept saying, but she did not hear him. *Listen to me! Listen to me!* He said he loved her, but that was a lie, Cath knew it was a lie. She told him so and they struggled again. He wanted her to believe him, he wanted her to believe what he was saying, to trust him.

"You know I love you," he said. They were on the bed now. She wanted to get up, to get away from the sound of his voice, from his rough, caressing hands, from violent emotions that ignited her own. No one in the world had ever made her feel the way he did, and yet it was lies, all lies. She insisted that with increasing desperation, because he was kissing her now, caressing her, pleading and threatening at once. And he was strong; she had not realized that; his gentleness with her had concealed the fact, so fundamental, so basic, that he was very much stronger than she was.

15

CATH FELT AS IF SHE'D been drugged. The shades were up and the summer night was a lighter darkness beyond the window frame. Window frames. Three windows. Their room, then, their room in the old house late at night. Sunday night, the night of her birthday, the night she'd felt the return of madness and knowledge and understood the value of forgetfulness. Cath closed her eyes again, only to come really awake with a heart-jolting start. Derek was asleep next to her. She could hear him breathing in a summer darkness made porous by the small, familiar sounds of the rural night. She sat up, all her senses alert, and pushed down the sheet. The springs complained as she stepped out onto the wide oak boards. If she moved with great care the floor would be silent. Great care. Her life depended on it. Remember the sidewalk game? *Step on a crack, break your mother's back.* Cath and her friends used to walk faster and faster, courting disaster at every step until someone stumbled onto the fatal line. Then laughter, teasing, a release from purely imaginary terrors.

Just at the door, a loose board and a hand-cut nail chirped in the darkness like an early cricket. Cath froze; her eyes had adjusted enough to make out the lighter rectangles of the windows, the posts of the bed, the looming shapes of Aunt Elizabeth's big oak dressers and bureaus, even Derek's dark head against the pillow. Silence and her heartbeat, before the insects, the peepers, a car passing on the main road. How long did she stand there? Long enough.

She went into the hall and down the stairs that they'd come running up last night. She wasn't sure how to define last night. A moment of brutality on his part? Not quite, although she'd been frightened. A moment of crazy love on her part? That was closer, but, still, she shook her head in the darkness: not quite true. Last night, she'd succumbed to an emotion that was not love, or not entirely love, including, as it did, the fear of madness and of memory. For an instant in the hallway, she'd remembered their Hartford kitchen, and the image still lingered: autumn light through the window over the sink, some dirty dishes waiting to be washed, a ceramic chicken on the sill, one cracked pane the landlord had not repaired. She'd been washing dishes, and she had just rinsed the steak knives and placed them in the cutlery basket. When her mind went, her hand had reached out of its own accord and picked up the knife. Oh, yes, she remembered that, and that, like last night, she had been split in two: the Cath who watched and remembered without fear or visible emotion and the Cath who fell into passion, as into an irresistible torrent, and was carried away. *Carried away;* strange, the truth in old clichés. *It wasn't my fault, I was carried away.* Away from what? No one ever asked, but now it was obvious to Cath that you were carried away from yourself.

Along the downstairs hall, past the kitchen, where there were other steak knives. Singers used knives: Don Jose, Rigoletto, Lucia, Tosca. *Vissi d'arte, vissi d'amore,* then straight to the heart. Singers were old-fashioned; they killed for love, a dubious concept, or cut their wrists. For love, too? At the door of the studio, she stopped, realizing the track lights would throw their brightness on the lawn, and went to fumble amidst the garden boots and the recyling for a flashlight. Back again to the studio: the piano, lid open, swam in the half light like some monster of the deep, and two stands rose, spiky as trees, against bookshelves crammed with scores, programs, reference works, albums.

Quick, on with the flashlight. 1993, 1994, all in order; Derek was so organized. Light off. Minimize the risk. Oh, madness is crafty. Would this year's be up to date? Find out. Put the album on the table, but quick, catch at the unstable pile of scores that tilts toward the floor. Carefully clear a space, open the album. Light on: a blindness of glare reflecting off the glossies: the black and white code of tuxedos and formal dresses, the maroon robes of the choirs, and Derek, looking like a stranger, a celebrity of sorts, someone safely removed from reality. Is that how she'd look, too? She would be in the previous album, in another life, *another universe,* as the mathematicians say. But no time, no delays. Spring concert: the whole ensemble against the pipes of the organ. Then the orchestra, the choir, the soloists, faces easily distinguishable now, even with the glare. And labeled, too. Derek always has the church secretary type up the identifications. First row to the right, second from the center. *Jane Henkel.* Red hair, a fat nose, a thin voice?

Cath had never quite believed that description, but still reality came with a shock, a terrible jolt of recognition, of realization. Jane was tall, even *statuesque,* that old-fashioned word, with black hair, certainly black or very, very dark brown, a prominent nose, right enough, but not fat, not fat at all. Was *aquiline* the word? Cath thought so. And magnificent eyes: Esther at twenty-one, Yvonne at twenty-three. There was a street in Boston, too, where a woman was trying to cross against the traffic, a woman who stopped, waved, a pretty woman with dark hair, a young woman such as Derek liked. A very young woman? Cath could go that far, but no farther.

She could hear her own heart beating, the sound of blood. Strange, how we talk about *the sight of blood,* how terrible it is, and neglect to mention *the sound of blood.* That's what your heartbeat is: *the sound of blood.* Down the hall again. The possibilities of the Touch-Tone phone with its lighted dial. In the dark kitchen the little buttons lead her to directory assistance, to Jane Henkel's phone number, to the sound of a phone ringing, ringing in the early-morning darkness. Jane Henkel sleeps soundly. Or, citywise, knows enough to ignore early-morning calls. But does she have no friends, no family? Is there no call she fears? *Dad's taken worse, Mom's had a stroke, your brother's been in an accident.* Everyone fears some call, because death doesn't meet you in Samarkand anymore, but calls you up, instead, and freezes your heart via a Baby Bell. And what of Jane Henkel? Had the call already come for her? There was a thought that wouldn't bear examining.

Cath stood trembling in the kitchen and wondered, *Why hasn't Luc called? Or Confidential Reports?* Hadn't she involved them precisely to avoid this moment of doubt and indecision? She thought she would call Luc, and she had the first digits punched up before caution saved her. It was three A.M. and, being so close to madness, she had to be careful; she would call Luc in the morning. During *business hours.* She would pretend that everything was *strictly business*; she would pretend that everything was all right. And maybe everything *was* all right. Maybe it was; God, it had to be: she could not bear to fail again.

A shift in the geography of their mattress: Derek getting up in the morning. Cath heard him cross the floor and close the bathroom door, initiating the familiar sequence: the toilet flushing, water running, the click of a belt, the rattle of the brass pulls on the bureau drawers. She gave no sign she heard; she was still asleep. A pause and a silence in which she knew he was looking at her.

"Cath?" His voice was soft, tentative; he wanted to talk, to explain, perhaps, to tell her how she should interpret recent events. She didn't breathe. Then his footsteps in the hallway, descending the stairs. A few moments later, she smelled coffee brewing. But though sleep had deserted her, Cath did not get up until she heard Derek go out to the car, and even then she waited just to be sure that he was on his way, that he hadn't forgotten something. Cath didn't want to see Derek, not this morning.

Cars passed on the road without slowing; a courting robin sang with sweet monotony, and the young crows, noisy, demanding avian adolescents, called and squawked after their parents. Cath rolled over on her back, stretched her legs, and tried to think out the day: what she would do, when she would do it, and what she would be like when her husband returned. So many decisions and not one of them spontaneous. She'd been spontaneous last night; she'd said what was on her mind, attempted honesty: fantasy stuff. She'd known that as soon as his hand shot out. Well, she could not say too much; she understood how such things could happen, how one's body contains memories and impulses beyond the knowledge of one's mind. But somewhere there is always a reason, unexamined, perhaps; disagreeable, certainly; suppressible, probably. She herself had had reasons for everything, and Derek must, too. So now things were different; she had to be careful of him as well as of herself. Cath got out of bed with that in mind. She washed her face, surprised that she looked exactly the same, with just a little redness over her left cheekbone, nothing more, no trace of fury and fear and being carried away by treacherous desire, by love, by desperate hopes. None whatsoever.

She'd make breakfast, she decided, then try Jane Henkel again. It made sense to have breakfast. To call Jane. In that order. But as soon as she got into the kitchen, she lifted the receiver. Jane Henkel's phone rang unanswered. It was only eight-thirty. An early lesson? Time in the practice room?

Cath had cold cereal, orange juice, a piece of toast. Most summer mornings she liked to carry her breakfast outside and sit on the bench overlooking the garden and the field. Today, she sat at the kitchen table and interrupted her meal to try Jane Henkel's number again.

At nine, having had no answer in Hartford, Cath phoned Luc Beausoleil.

"Report?" he asked. In his bland tone, she heard disinterest and guessed that he'd forgotten about Confidential, about her desperate concern, about her precarious future. But if he'd been remiss, he covered it well. He put on his lawyer voice and spoke of delays, noted that it was early, said that the mail hadn't come yet.

Cath realized that she should have waited, should have called later. Nine o'clock on the dot suggests urgency—or anxiety. "It's been a couple of weeks," she said, and Luc assured her that he'd get right on the matter.

"Good," she said. "Because I think we may be going on vacation."

"Well, there's no hurry at all, then, is there?"

How did he know whether there was a hurry or not? "I'd like it before I go," she said, like an efficient person; *crisp* was the sound she wanted, but she thought that her voice had the exact timbre of thin, brittle crackers.

"I thought," Luc said in a careful tone, "that you'd been satisfied with what you'd already learned." This wasn't true and he must know it: he was just being discreet and lawerly. "I thought that things were going better for you."

"Things are going fine," Cath said. "Just please get me that information."

"Are you sure?" he asked. What had he detected in her voice? It was wearying to have to be so alert, so careful. Life was full of details, and every one was important.

"Yes, of course, I'm sure."

"Because, Cath, I've become a bit concerned," he started, but she hung up the phone and didn't answer when it rang immediately. She didn't want to talk to Luc; she wanted to talk to Jane Henkel. That was still the first order of business. Cath punched up the numbers and listened to the phone ringing, ringing in Hartford.

Nearly nine-thirty on a Monday morning. Jane had been out all night with a boyfriend. She'd draped her magnificent hair across his futon and wrapped him in her long limbs, and cried out to the gods of ecstasy and despair. Cath hoped that was true. There were other, less pleasant scenarios, but she wasn't going to think about those. She couldn't. Instead, she was *hedging her bets,* calling Luc, on the one hand, and imagining a boyfriend for Jane, on the other. And what might that boyfriend look like? Surely handsome, perhaps dark. Musically talented, maybe? Cath felt her stomach turn over.

At ten-thirty, she phoned the music school at the university. She was calling from Saint Martin's, Cath said. They were making plans for the fall season and wanted to get in touch with Jane Henkel, who'd sung so charmingly at the spring concert. Just charming, especially since she'd been a last-minute substitution. Was that too much? Cath wondered. Was that *laying it on too thick?* Or was flattery like butter and more always better?

The secretary agreed Jane Henkel was exceptional, so exceptional, in fact, that she'd gotten a summer engagement at Aspen.

"That's terrific!" Cath exclaimed, and she really meant it. She had a genuine interest in Jane Henkel's success. "So—she's already gone?"

"Last week, I believe."

"A wonderful opportunity for her."

"Yes, it is. I'll take a message and have her call you when she gets back."

"That's all right," Cath said. "We'll call again in late summer." She put down the receiver and let out her breath. Jane Henkel was safe in Aspen. Derek's moods and upsets were suddenly comprehensible, and there was nothing to worry about. Nothing. Her fears had all been nonsense and hysteria. She hadn't failed after all, and if she'd made mistakes (which she had; of course she had) she'd been given a second chance.

Cath kicked off her loafers and put on the old sneakers she kept for the garden. She'd sow some more lettuce and put in the first beans, maybe turn over another few feet of the garden for squash—the soil was getting warm enough. She'd work in the garden today, serious work, and when Derek came home—but there her imagination stopped. She wasn't sure what happened when Derek came home. She couldn't plan that out the way she could plan the garden. She would have to wait and see about Derek.

Cath got the beans in, then lugged compost and manure to make hills for the squash; the entire pumpkin family are heavy feeders. She decided she might as well mulch right away, which meant getting the Sunday papers and spreading them around the hills and begging another bale of hay from Mrs. Pye, so that the paper could be covered up. She watered the whole thing to get the seeds started and to pack down the mulch, then went on to the beans. She mulched them, too, folding the sports and arts and business sections in half and laying them between the newly sown rows, before bundling clumps of hay over the top. When she was finished, the garden had a tidy geometry, the pale biscuit-colored hay striped bright against the good dark earth and circling the mounds for the squashes and pumpkins like the white on a fried egg.

This neatness was pleasing, suggestive of control and of good prospects for success. *If my garden is tidy, my life must be all right:* the psychology, Cath supposed, that led people to buy books by Martha Stewart, and gourmet guides, and all the rest. Cath's own marriage was all right. There had been mistakes and accidents and misunderstandings, but, fundamentally, the project in which she had invested her life, her heart—perhaps even her integrity—was all right. Jane Henkel was alive and well and singing in Aspen. Lucky girl! Jane was a sensible woman who'd been attracted to Derek, but not attracted enough. *Enough* was the key. Cath was the only one attracted enough *to stay the course.* She wondered where that phrase came from, which sport. But it was applicable, because Jane had gone to Aspen, leaving Derek temporarily depressed and irritable. Temporarily. That could be, would be, made right. And then everything would be okay. Had to be, Cath thought, and she was beginning to be convinced, for one of the values of gardening is the time it gives to think things out, or, alternately, to think things in, that is, to firm up certain desirable ideas like the concept of things being okay, and to repeat them until they seem right.

"Cath!" Derek called from the front hall. "Cath!"

She was sitting at the kitchen table studying the score from the *Sorrowful Songs* and keeping an eye on a pot of beans that kept threatening to boil over. Cath was clean and tidy, hair washed and dried, her garden clothes replaced by a T-shirt and a long print skirt. She looked, and felt, sane and domestic: the rewards of *being careful.*

"I'm in the kitchen," she called.

"Come see this!"

She heard the front screen close again and went through to the hall. Her husband was standing on the step holding a big potted nursery plant, a hydrangea with glossy chartreuse leaves and pinkish stems. "The nurseryman said it wouldn't be too late to transplant. I'll dig it in," he added, with a shy, tentative smile. "You'd mentioned you thought we needed something by the barn."

"Yes." Cath bent to check the tab. "Oh, this is the tree variety. Yes, that would look good. They're white, you know."

"Is that the right color? We can exchange it. The nurseryman said if you didn't like it, we could exchange it."

"The blues are lovely but not by a red barn. I don't think we want to repaint the barn just yet."

"Life's too short to be painting barns." His dark eyes were anxious, despite his jocular tone. "So, we'll put it in?" he asked.

"Let's give it a drink and pick a spot. I can dig it in tomorrow."

"No, no, my treat," he said. "I'll just change my pants."

"I spent the day in the garden," Cath said.

"So, my turn, then. Do you like it? Really?" Eager as a small boy with a birthday gift.

"Yes, I do. Thank you so much."

He put his arm around her. "I really wanted roses, but they said it was getting late for them."

"We can get roses in the fall."

"I'd like that. Lots of roses for you." And he leaned his forehead against hers. "Oh, Cathy," he said. "I'm so sorry about last night. I'm so damn sorry."

"You've been very unhappy," she said, instead of what she'd thought she might say, namely that Jane Henkel had gone to Aspen.

"Not your fault," he said. "It's been a bad spring. A lot of stress." He squeezed her shoulder. His brilliant eyes were close to hers, and Cath wondered if eyes could be *magnetic,* if light could have a certain force of its own. "Things have just seemed out of control."

"It's been difficult," Cath agreed. "For everybody."

"For you, especially, but you've been tough." He squeezed her shoulder again. "You've hung in there. Though twice I thought I'd lost you. When you went away. And again when you came back."

"I truly did not remember anyone. Not anyone. Not right away."

"I couldn't believe that," Derek said. "I couldn't believe that at first."

"I know it was unbelievable, but it was true."

"I know that now," Derek said, "but in the meantime, I thought I'd lost you."

Cath hugged him. "Never," she said.

"I can't lose you," Derek said, and the desperate unhappiness in his eyes lent his words conviction. "I cannot lose you. It would be a dangerous thing for me if I lost you. You know that, don't you?"

"I'm not going anywhere," said Cath. "I'm well now and perfectly normal. Don't you think I'm well?"

"Better all the time," he said, and Cath heard a breeziness in his voice that hadn't been there an instant before; her husband's emotional gears had shifted. "Let's dig in your new plant." Derek was suddenly eager and cheerful; he put a bounce in his step, held the door for her, ran upstairs, whistling. From their room, he began calling down suggestions and directions. "Get me the shovel, would you?" "What about right beside the barn door?" "Do you know where my khaki shorts are?"

Cath changed into her garden sneakers and went to the shed. She got out the wheelbarrow as well as the shovel, because they'd need some compost and manure, and dragged the hose from the vegetable garden over to the barn. After Derek dug a load of compost, they took the wheelbarrow around to select their spot. Too near the drive was bad, because the snowplow took everything in its path. The corner of the barn momentarily looked promising, but no more than eight inches down Derek hit a mix of stone and concrete, the footing of some forgotten outbuilding. Further from the barn might be better, anyway, Cath decided, so they tackled the scrap of lawn in front. The first hole hit a large rock; the second was not too bad, just the usual potato-to bowling-ball-sized stones.

"This is why they left, you know," Derek said, as he levered out a rock the size of a cantaloupe.

"Who?"

"The old New Englanders. That's why they went to the Midwest. They got sick of humping these stones. What's the occasional tornado compared to an eternity of rock?"

"They come up from the earth. You can never get them all out." The image of stones migrating, churning up from an unquiet earth, was an idea that she found curious and subtly disturbing. "It's a geological process."

"A damn inconvenient one." He stepped back from his work. "Think that's deep enough?"

"Yes, but a little wider. We want the roots to be able to spread."

He widened the hole, and they dumped in some compost and set the plant. "We'll need to stake it," Cath said. By the time she found a couple of stakes and some string, Derek had the hole filled and the plant watered. They put in the stakes and tied the hydrangea, then put away their tools and watered the young plant once again. Cath stood to one side, watching the soil darken and little rivulets flow across the muddy and trampled lawn. Although the sun was still high, the light had made an unmistakable tilt toward the rosy gold of late afternoon. The planes of Derek's face were shadowed, his hair, darkened, and his tanned arms, suffused with sienna. She had such a strong sense of him, of his appearance, of his physical body, and, yet, something whispered in the back of her mind that this was all a trick of the light. "Jane Henkel has gone to Aspen for the summer," she said.

Derek let up on the nozzle trigger, and the stream of water stopped with a plastic click. In another mood, he'd have been angry or demanded to know how she knew this, but he really was sorry, Cath saw, for he simply nodded. "Jane has a good opportunity."

"Is she coming back to school?" Cath asked. What she really meant was, *Is she coming back to you?*

"She graduated," Derek said. "If Jane finds work out west, I'm sure she'll move."

So she'd left him, broken off the affair. "You've missed her," Cath said.

"A moment or two." He put down the hose. "Jane wasn't important. Jane would never have happened if it hadn't been for your illness. It was the strain." He spoke nervously, and suddenly there were tears in his eyes. "Don't leave me because of Jane. Please, don't leave me because of her."

Cath shook her head. It should be obvious to him now that she wouldn't leave. "But no more Janes," she said. "Ever."

"Never, ever. She came at a bad moment. I couldn't bear to be without you. And when you came back, it wasn't you. Not right away. You know that."

Cath did know that, and so when he reached out and stroked her hair, she kissed him and told him everything was all right. And when he said that he needed to get away, that there had been so much stress, that they needed to go somewhere, just the two of them, somewhere quiet, somewhere for *him,* Cath found herself considering a short visit to the camp.

"I really think I have to go there," Derek said. "I really think I do. I've realized that there is a lot of unfinished business in my life. I feel I've got to confront that. For us. For our future. I really do. And then we'll go to the shore. How about that? We could do the Great Northern Tour. Go up to the old camp and then across by ferry to Burlington and on to the shore. We're in no hurry to get back, are we?"

"No, though there's the garden. Our new hydrangea." Once in the ground, the plant looked slight and vulnerable, the broad, bright leaves as transparent as a kitten's ear. Cath thought it would be a bad omen if this gift were to wither.

"Stel Pye would do the garden, wouldn't she? Ask her, see if she'd do the watering. And there will be rain. There's always some rain in June. But not at the camp," he added quickly. "It never rains when you're at the camp." Teasing now and kissing her forehead. "It'll be fun. We can leave tomorrow. Or Wednesday. Better say Wednesday. All right?"

"Yes," she said, for it sounded like fun. It did. It would be fun. And he'd made the first step, hadn't he, in admitting Jane? Looked at in that light, even the lake was a good sign, his talking about the lake, *confronting* the lake, though she wasn't sure how that was done, something like King Canute, maybe. But yes, his *confronting* the lake was good and she had every reason to be hopeful. "Yes," she said again, looking at his eyes, trying to judge her fate. But she was sane now, and the gods no longer spoke; shadows no longer materialized; as far as truth and safety went, she was on her own.

"You're the only one in the world for me," he said. "The only one who ever mattered."

In that moment, she thought he was worth every risk, or maybe, having taken so many risks, made so many compromises, gambled so much, she thought that she had no other choice, but only this last chance against madness and despair.

"I love you more than anything," she said, ready to lose the world for him. Then there was his arms, his hands on her shoulders, exploring her hips, and the taste of his mouth, the slight roughness of his cheek, the strong line of his thigh against her legs. They stood kissing in the middle of the lawn, locked in each other's arms, until a car passed on the road, and he said, "Let's go inside." Cath swayed dizzy in the sun, drunk on the bright surfaces of things.

"Wednesday," he said as they entered the hall. "Wednesday, all right?"

"I'll speak to Stel," Cath promised.

He had the softest hands when he wanted, and he kissed her and caressed her until Cath thought that her bones would melt. Beside them in the hallway, Aunt Elizabeth's long gilt-framed mirror reflected their interlaced images, and after several long moments, Derek paused to consider their shadows, dark speckled where the silvering had worn away. "What a handsome couple," he joked, "though you're kind of a mess." It was only then that she noticed the muddy handprints on her T-shirt and along the top of her skirt.

Pat put the report on Luc's desk with the other mail, and when he saw the return address, he made a mental note that it was there. Cath would call, he figured. Or ride up on her bike, though she hadn't made a nuisance of herself lately. Not lately. In fact, now that he thought about it, she'd not been up to sign her will. Not that there was anything very complex about her legal status, but he liked everything tidy. He should call to remind her about the will, but then, of course, she'd ask about Confidential again and expect his opinion on this latest report. Unless she was on vacation. She'd said something about a vacation. Maybe he could assume that she was away and he could put off reading yet another expensive, useless report. He had deeds to check and a trust to draw up, papers an inch thick in his in box; he could put off Cath Tolland's troubles for a little while.

Luc was about ready to go home when he saw the Confidential Reports return address again and, impelled by one of those subterranean veins of duty, opened the envelope and began skimming the contents: all the usual sorts of dates and names. Nothing new, nothing surprising, nothing—then he stopped, uneasy. Luc Beausoleil was not a criminal lawyer. So far as criminal law went, his practice was pretty much confined to the occasional case of juvenile delinquency or the defense of a DWI charge. Those he found disagreeable enough: sad, sordid matters he took on as favors to the unlucky families. He didn't consider himself an expert in criminal investigation or forensics, certainly not in homicide or suicide. And yet he knew enough to feel uneasy. Sitting in his office with the windows open and the smell of fresh-cut grass, he caught a whiff of the jail, the morgue, the holding pen at the county court—the spoor, that is, of trouble.

The folder with the other Confidential Reports was in the file, and when Luc began looking from one case to another, he found a number of things that disturbed him, as they had undoubtedly disturbed his old friend. Two young singers, two possible suicides, two mutilated hands; two young women, exceptionally good-looking, with long dark hair. Probably coincidence, but, just the same, Luc set the photocopies of their pictures side by side on his desk. He was troubled by the pictures, and the descriptions of the deaths were not very reassuring, either. Derek Tolland's former fiancée had had her wrist slashed; Kimberly Delane had had her wrist slashed but also "extensive mutilation of the face and body." So Kimberly Delane had been a murder victim, and, since Esther Nielson had been a suicide, any similarities were surely coincidence. Surely. That's what he could tell Cath with pretty good conscience: coincidence with a hint of doubt.

But as Luc was closing the file, he saw Cath's scribbled request for information on the Boston-area singer who'd turned out to be Kimberly Delane, age twenty-three, a murdered mezzo-soprano of genuine talent. And, yes, he'd remembered correctly that Cath had originally wanted information about someone else, too. Just indecision, he'd thought at the time, for she'd written something, then crossed it out. The words were still legible under the hastily scratched lines. *Jane Henkel. Kenyon Street in Hartford.* Luc went to his shelf of phone directories and checked. Yes, there was a Jane Henkel on Kenyon. And he guessed she was a musician or a music student. Maybe at the university. He tried them first. "Attorney Beausoleil calling. I'm trying to locate a music student named Jane Henkel. K-E-L, that's right. No? Sorry to trouble you."

The conservatory next. Then, third time lucky, the music school in Hartford. World famous. He should have tried them first. He remembered that Esther Nielson had been on the verge of a big career; Kimberly Delane had been making a name for herself in Boston. And Jane Henkel? Graduated. And now off on a fellowship. Away for the summer. Luc could not have said quite why he felt such relief, except that he was getting as crazy as his client. He should close up, get home on time, maybe take Renee and the boys out for dinner. They hadn't done that for a while. There was a new Italian place that was supposed to be nice; the kids always liked to eat Italian. In the middle of this thought, he called through to Pat.

She stuck her head in the door. She was getting ready to leave, he saw, for she'd already put on her smart linen jacket. Chartreuse today. Very bright, cheerful, and professional. He was lucky to have Pat, who was a terrific receptionist and a pretty good secretary. "Pat, what did you tell me the other day about Web pages?"

"Johnny's, you mean?"

"Yeah. He's got his through the college, right?" It came back to Luc as he spoke. Johnny was Pat's youngest, her pride and joy. A sophomore at the university, doing well in engineering.

"That's right. Animation, even. The stuff that kid can do with a computer." She seemed set to enlarge on this congenial theme, but Luc cut her off.

"A lot of colleges do that, right? Give kids their own pages?"

"I think so. Yes, it's common. Not all are as elaborate as Johnny's."

"Hooked in through the main college page?" Luc asked.

"I can show you," she said. And this was generous, because it was now a few minutes past five.

"I want to look up someone at the music school in Hartford."

"Oh, well, that may be different, but try the name dot edu."

"Right," said Luc. "See you tomorrow."

Pat said good night. Luc heard her closing up the office, shutting the windows and putting the phone onto the answering machine. She called good-night again as Luc watched the school's brilliant red logo blossom across the top of his screen. Click on "Music." Courses, schedules, faculty. Students? Yes, e-mail addresses, and yes, some had pages. Who more likely than a talented singer looking for gigs? Jane Henkel's name appeared in a fluorescent green, indicating a link, and Luc clicked onto the "Jane Henkel Homepage." The type loaded first: her résumé, roles performed, musical interests, courses, instructors. She'd "worked intensively on sacred music with Derek Tolland." Was that a reason to feel uneasy? Luc wondered. After all, Derek Tolland was a distinguished choral conductor who must work with a lot of young musicians. Or was that in itself a reason for worry? Above the text, an image was starting to load. There was a kind of fascination in watching the bands of color move down the screen. Long hair, dark. High, smooth forehead, large, dark eyes, a shapely mouth: a beautiful woman, whose image should be recorded. The big laser printer hummed in the next room as Luc quit the Net and switched off his screen. He laid the printout on the desk next to the pictures of Esther Nielson and Kimberly Delane, then sat and thought things over until five-thirty, too late, he realized with a pang, to see more than the last few minutes of Henry's soccer game. He had to go; he really had to go. And, Luc thought as he replaced the file and locked his windows, he really would have to talk with Cath Tolland.

16

THE LAKE HAD A GRAVITATIONAL force, a certain psychic mass capable, like other force fields, of distortion. Cath felt the first intimations of its power in Derek's growing silence as they drove north.

But, at first, the trip was perfect. All the way up to the Mass Pike they smelled cut grass and early hay, and the happiness ignited when he bought the hydrangea and she agreed to visit the camp continued. Cath drove for a while through the Berkshires, the first time she'd driven since before the night bus, and decided that she ought to stop marking time by her illness. She'd pick a new event, and what better than this trip? From now on, she'd remember that she first drove again *on the trip to the lake*. She'd remember that they went to the shore *the year they visited the cabin*, and that she painted the house the same summer.

In Albany, they picked up the Northway, stopping for a late lunch at a pretty café in Saratoga. They sat outside under a green and white umbrella and admired the town. Cath had never been in the area; her whole knowledge of Saratoga life was derived from Doctorow's *Billy Bathgate* and Dobyns's Charlie Bradshaw mysteries. Derek preferred his fiction from the wild, early days of the area. He had a vivid recollection of an old *Drums along the Mohawk* movie, and the recent Daniel Day-Lewis film had revived his college memories of the *Leatherstocking Tales*. Derek said he rather fancied himself the Deerslayer type, until Cath pointed out that Natty Bumppo was only sexy in the film.

"You know such unromantic things," Derek said, for he could be funny when he wanted to be.

"A man named Natty Bumppo is almost unromantic by definition."

"Fortunately, I know about things more elevating to the spirit than the sexual habits of Natty Bumppo," Derek said, and he switched the subject to colonial choral music. He thought the choir should do an early American music concert instead of yet another Bach, Vivaldi, Handel, and Monteverdi gig. Cath agreed that an early American program would be a fun challenge, a concert that would be noticed, and sitting unhurried in the sun, they discussed this project. At one point, Derek began singing the anthem, fortunately sotto voce, with the original tavern lyrics, making Cath laugh out loud. She'd have to say that the trip went well to Saratoga, and if Derek seemed newly quiet when they got back in the car, he was driving by then and the summer vacation traffic between Saratoga and Lake George was already pretty heavy.

Lake George village was small and touristy, shadowed by big conifers, the lake a silver presence in the low afternoon light. The air felt cool and Cath could smell the pines. They laid in their provisions at the local supermarket, its aisles full of campers and visitors. Derek said that their cabin had been retrofitted for electricity twenty years before so there was a small refrigerator, electric lights, running water. "Careful on the toilet, though," he added. "It's an artesian well. We only flush when we must." They joked about that as they organized their menus, adding pasta, beans, cheese, and other things that would keep, because, as he kept reminding her, it was a very small fridge.

When they were ready for the Northway again, she offered to drive, but Derek said he knew the road, and Cath understood that he wanted to be busy. He seemed to have left his morning cheerfulness behind in Lake George, for he grew quiet, monosyllabic. He was anxious now to get to the cabin and regretted their pleasant lunch in Saratoga and their few minutes looking around Lake George. "You don't realize the time it will take to get the water line hooked," he said, as if the delays had been Cath's idea entirely. The cabin was boarded up, too, and taking the plywood off the windows was always a pain. In short, getting the place livable was a project which they should have started hours ago. Having laid out these difficulties, Derek fiddled with the radio until he found Tchaikovsky's *Pathetique*, a symphony which Cath always found beautiful but depressing. Her husband hummed quietly to the melody for a few minutes, then lapsed into silence.

By this time, they were well inside the enormous park, New York State's big half-wild, half-touristy wilderness. The Northway with its light pylons, rest stops, and commercial fringe was a homogenized corridor beyond which the rough, forested landscape unspooled like a film panorama. *There is a sort of unreality to car travel,* Cath thought. *You don't get the taste and smell of a place until you are outside, on the ground, moving under your own power. To know where you are, you need to leave the carefully contrived sameness of the interstates, carefully contrived,* she suspected, *to lure you on, to keep you from realizing how far you've gone from home.*

Outside, the green monotony of the forest; inside, string-propelled Slavic melancholy: Cath was dozing when Derek woke her with the remark that Schroon Lake had been named for a Frenchwoman; the spelling was a corruption of the original name of the famous Madame de Maintenon, the morganatic wife of Louis XIV.

"Ah," said Cath, who appreciated the curious etymology of a name she'd assumed was Dutch. "Not Madame's sort of place, probably." But who knew what people really liked? Perhaps Madame de Maintenon had grown bored with the French court. Perhaps she'd have liked nothing better than to live in the woods with a *courrier de bois* or to push off in a canoe with some *voyageurs* or to return now, when the *bois* was threaded by roads, and parasails, speedboats, and cross-country skis offered diversions. And was this Cath's sort of place? It had certainly been in the back of her mind that she might not care for the camp, but she liked the smell of the pines.

"We're the next exit," Derek said. "Our cabin's on the eastern shore."

Instantly, she felt the atmosphere shift, the tedium of motion exchanged for the eagerness of arrival, for the interest sparked by any new, even if temporary, home. The wide concrete ramp of the interstate dwindled abruptly to a narrow paved road where the relative silence seemed anticlimactic after the steady roar of wind and engines. A few houses, signs for cabins, bait, ice, boat rentals. Another narrower road, lapsing to dirt, the trees closer, the lake lost in the woods, then a deeply grooved track with grass struggling along the center.

"We've got to stop at Walt's," Derek said, pulling up at a little, low shingled cabin that rambled back from a narrow front porch. "Let him know we're here and pick up the keys."

An RV was parked in the long grass beside the house, a little oblong satellite disk scanned the heavens, and a huge red-brown coonhound rested atop a doghouse. When the dog gave a long, low-toned bark and jumped down, Derek tooted the horn for Walt. The dog strode back and forth before the car—*baying* was the word, Cath thought. Wolves howl, dogs bark, and hounds, which have gotten stuck between the two, *bay*. Derek muttered something about *The Hound of the Baskervilles*, but guessing that the dog was without any real malice, Cath opened her door and stepped out.

"Hey, Rex! All right, boy." Walt appeared at the door of the screen porch. His age was not easily determined. He was tall, stooped, and bespectacled, but he came smartly down the steps to collect his dog, and his red, weatherbeaten face was shaded with a Yankee baseball cap stuck back at a jaunty angle. He waved a large wrinkled hand to them and caught Rex's collar.

"A beautiful dog," Cath said.

"That's a working dog," Walt said with a nod that might have passed for a greeting. "Derek! Good to see you. You made pretty good time."

"Pretty good," he agreed. They talked about driving times and the summer traffic on the Northway, about how long it had been since Derek had been up, about how glad Walt had been to hear from him—and Yvonne, too—before Cath broke in to introduce herself. Walt touched his hat, the ghost of old custom, but did not shake her hand. Cath thought his cool manner odd, given his obvious delight in seeing Derek, but perhaps Walt's mind was still on driving times and traffic patterns, for he was clearly a great one for travel. He liked, he said, "to crank up the RV and head out with Rex." He did some coon hunting in the Midwest, took Rex to some of the competitions, kept the dog in trim. "You might not guess that's one of the best redbone hounds in the East," he said.

Derek looked as bored as he undoubtedly felt, but Cath said the dog was magnificent, and Walt, who had been giving her suspicious, sidelong glances, thawed a little.

"So," he said, "it's your first time at the lake?"

"First time in the Adirondacks."

"Hope you'll enjoy yourself. Nice and quiet here. They haven't spoiled this side yet, have they, Derek? This is an ideal place for you to get feeling better."

"I'm feeling fine already," Cath said in a definite tone. "I'm hoping to do a lot of swimming and hiking."

"Lake's still cold," said Walk. "You want to be careful swimming in that cold water. Especially since—"

"We'd better get to the cabin," Derek interrupted. "We need to hook up the water, get the windows open. Cath isn't for living in a cave, are you, dear?"

"My husband lured me up here without telling me how much work a summer cabin can be."

Cath was joking, but Walt said, "Oh, don't tell your sister, but the cabin's already open. Your uncle Will was up for the trout season. He said once he got them boards off, he didn't have the energy to get them back up."

The mention of Uncle Will was good for extended considerations of his passion for fishing and of his increasing age; Walt raised the prospect that Uncle Will might have to give up his winter visits. "He always has trouble with the windows. You know, I'd of given him a hand, but I figured with you coming there was no need to worry. I've been taking Rex for a run down that way near every day. Keeps kids out of there."

They thanked Walt for this favor, which required a discussion of youthful vandalism, the newcomers at the condos, and the changes on the lake, before Derek could hint again for the keys. This time, Walt decided that courtesy had been served, for he went into the cabin. Derek checked his watch as soon as the door closed and rolled his eyes in exasperation. "He hasn't seen me in years and he still wants to talk my ear off. Yvonne was his real pal. He used to play country fiddle and she'd play piano for the square dances. Semimandatory recreation."

"Yvonne called him," Cath said, understanding Walt's curious reception. "He's already had a chance to talk to Yvonne."

"Of course," Derek said quickly. "She handles the cabin. She rents it occasionally, too, not just to Uncle Will. She pays Walt to keep an eye on it, but I leave all that to her."

"She didn't have to tell him I have three heads or whatever she said."

"Don't be paranoid," Derek began, but just as he spoke, the screen door opened and Walt came down the steps carrying a heavy ring with four keys on it.

"Keys to the castle," Cath said.

"You want the second back-door key?" Walt asked Derek. "Or will you always be out together?"

"Let's have the second key," Cath said.

He glanced first at Derek, which annoyed Cath, and only produced the second key after her husband nodded. "Rentals only get the cabin key," Walt explained. "I usually come down and get out the boat and start the water for them myself. Best way to do it. You need the water started or do you remember how it's done?"

"I remember," said Derek. "You use a siphon to get it started."

"Right. There's a piece of hose in the well house. Come get me if you need help—I'll be in tonight."

"We'll manage."

"No trick if you know how to do it. Now, if I'm away when you leave, just put the keys in at the bait shop as usual," Walt concluded. "That's what I do with your uncle. He's always at that bait shop, anyway. Feeds half the fish in the lake."

This was clearly an opening for gossip about the semilegendary Uncle Will, but Cath mentioned that they had groceries in the car.

"Icebox isn't on," Walt said. "You remember, Derek, that you've got to plug everything in."

"We'll do that first thing," Derek said, opening the car door. "Thanks, Walt."

Rex barked, heralding their escape, as they backed the car out of Walt's drive and started down the track.

"How far is the cabin?"

"Quarter mile, half mile. Little more than a half mile, maybe. It used to seem like a long way when we walked up to Walt's and on to the baitshop for ice cream."

A warm, forest smell of humus and bark and resin blew through the car windows; a brief clearing showed the lake, silvery blue against the conifers along the shore, and the lighter green of the mixed woodlands rising up the hills behind.

Then trees again, the track dark ahead with their shadows, every little dip and rise mysterious as the road wound farther and farther back into the woods.

"Here we are," said Derek. He abruptly put on the brakes, reversing the car so that he could make a sharp left turn down another shallow grade. A roof appeared out of the trees and beyond it, the light-saturated surface of the water. Derek stopped in a little open area behind the house and turned off the motor.

"Oh, it's pretty. Right on the water."

"I told you the cabin was on the shore."

"I didn't imagine stepping from the porch into the lake."

"Not exactly. The lot slopes pretty sharply. There's a twelve-foot drop and quite a few rocks. The view on the porch side is nice, but we have to go in through the back."

He opened the trunk, and Cath went to unlock the door of the cabin. "I had the distinct feeling Walt didn't want to give me a key," she remarked.

"No, so if you got locked out, he could escort you back and deafen you about Rex and his RV. Here, this has the eggs, I think. Why don't you unload while I take a look at the water line."

Cath took the bag of groceries and stepped into the entryway, dark and none too clean, the boards of the sheathing hung with old snow-shoes, a fishing net, several rods of different vintages, a pair of cracked waders, and several ancient windbreakers. The back of a fieldstone chimney almost filled the end wall. Cath opened the inner door to a dazzle of lake-reflected light that silhouetted a dining table, couches, the famous twig chairs. Behind her was the massive fireplace and its stone hearth. Ahead was the water, the feathery tops of hemlocks, the distant hills. Cath stood for a moment, the long trip, Walt's reluctance, even her husband's moody silences forgotten: she was prepared to enjoy the lake. Then, remembering the chicken parts and the milk, she went into the kitchen—small, a bit greasy, not nearly so inspiring as the main room—to plug in the fridge and the stove and to start sorting out their groceries.

She put the food away and went outside. Derek had the door of the little springhouse open and one panel of the lattice under the cabin removed, as well. Cath fetched the sheets and towels from the car and had a look around the cabin. There was a small bathroom, a narrow south-side bedroom with bunk beds, and on the north side, another bedroom, little more than an alcove, with a double bed. Cath made this up and put towels in the bathroom. She wanted to use the toilet, but there was no water yet. She went outside and called, "How're you doing?"

He was doing his best, Derek replied crossly, and needed to concentrate on the task at hand. He did not need Walt's help, and did not much appreciate the suggestion that he would, either. Cath took their bags inside and got out a sweater to put on over her T-shirt. Out on the porch, she leaned on the railing and spotted a path winding to the shore between colossal boulders. She went down the porch steps and checked again at the springhouse, where Derek said he could get the water line working just fine if he had another pair of hands. Cath asked what she could do to help and got high speed and confusing directions.

"You need a clamp, don't you? To hold the hose on? Once you've gotten the siphon started?"

"I know that," he said with a show of irritation, but Cath guessed that, in fact, he hadn't known, because the clamp was nowhere in sight and should have been on the hose already. They had a fine rummage around looking for a clamp, and when they found one, they discovered they had no pliers, either.

"Godammit, Uncle Will's taken the pliers for his fishing kit," Derek exclaimed. "Why the hell couldn't he have left them in the springhouse?"

"Well, they'd probably have rusted," Cath said, but common sense was not in such demand as shared aggravation. He stamped over to the house, and they checked the entryway and then the kitchen. It was just by luck that Derek finally found the pliers in a pile of oddments on the mantelpiece. Back out to the springhouse, deep in shadows now. Derek thought a flashlight would help and Cath said she would try to find one. Derek said, "You don't need to *try*, there's always one in the glove compartment." But the light wasn't there, and obviously he'd moved it because she hadn't driven in months. Finally, the flashlight turned up in the toolkit under the mat in the trunk, and, by the time

Cath found it, got the batteries lined up and the contact working, she felt as irritable as her husband. As her feet grew wet in the puddle around the siphon and her hands froze in the chilly spring water, Cath recognized the curious dominance of domestic annoyances, which are capable of overshadowing any number of more serious problems. There is, indeed, something uniquely irritating about the errors of our nearest and dearest, and Cath had not been on the job more than a few minutes before she concluded that this was about the stupidest water system in the world and the whole idea of coping with it, pretty dumb as well. But just as she was ready to risk wrath and suggest Walt again, Derek exclaimed, "There we go. There we go! Tighten it up, tighten it up, don't let it slip now."

Cath dropped the flashlight and twisted the clamp. "That's on, but you'd better give it another turn." She had no feeling in her fingers, and there was still a bit of water leaking from the connection.

Derek took the pliers and gave the clamp a decisive pinch. "There," he said, leaning back on his heels. "What a bitch of a job."

"Now do we have water?" Cath asked. Really she did want to use the john.

"There's a valve by the house that I need to open. Then we can turn on the taps and the toilet."

"I'll do that," said Cath.

"You seem a bit anxious," Derek teased. Now that the water line was connected and running, he was feeling triumphant.

Cath nipped into the house, turned the valve under the tank, and heard the gratifying sound of the toilet filling. She got the bathroom taps on, too, all cold, of course, and heard Derek in the kitchen bringing the water into the sink.

"Not too bad?" Derek asked. He'd switched on the wrought-iron chandelier in the main room. "Cozy at night."

"*Cozy*'s not the first word that comes to mind. What do you think the temperature is? Fifty degrees, maybe?"

"You're soft," said Derek. "But I'll make a fire. I'm good at that—

way better at fire making than plumbing. I'll just make sure there's nothing in the chimney." He got down on the hearth. "Ah, yes, raccoons, owls, mice. Begone! Begone!" As Cath went into the kitchen to start dinner, she heard him hammering and banging, opening the flue and loading in wood, while singing snatches from *Dido and Aeneas* and inviting the assorted chimney fauna "to share the fame of a mischief."

"Cath, any newspaper in there?"

"No."

"Uncle Will strikes again!" he cried, but without anger, for this was the Derek who was charismatic and amusing. He'd somehow recaptured cheerfulness and high spirits. Perhaps their struggle with the water line had brought them both back to normalcy, or perhaps he'd just been nervous, wondering if he'd made the right decision, wondering if it was really right to come back. "I'll be collecting twigs in the woods," he called, "lost in the wilderness with a flashlight."

"Would a paper bag do?"

"Brilliant idea. My salvation."

"There's the wrapper from the chicken, too."

"A woman of infinite resource! Or was it variety? Cleopatra? A woman of 'infinite variety'! Give me a woman who starts fires with poultry papers."

"I don't think Cleopatra had to start fires at all," Cath said, dropping the chicken into the pan. "We'll have potatoes and a salad, all right?"

"Chicken tonight; tomorrow we'll have fish. I'll catch you some fish. I will perform prodigies with reel and line."

"What about the fire?" Cath asked.

"You wait and see." He carried the papers back to the hearth, where Cath heard him singing, ebullient, mercurial, entertaining. *Unreliable,* a little voice whispered, but she shut her ears. And she was right to do that, because when she carried through the skillet, sautéed chicken with the boiled potatoes added to brown in the fat, the fire was burning brightly. Derek had set the table and cut up the bread.

He'd also opened a surprise bottle of wine, the pale liquid like early sunlight in the old jelly glasses. "To our holiday at the lake," he said. "And to you."

"To us, rather," she said, and like an echo he repeated, "To us."

After supper, they went out on the porch and watched the western sky darken and the lights of Schroon Lake village come up on the far shore. Something rustled down along the rocks and Cath caught a flash of green eyeshine.

"Raccoons, probably. We used to like to put out the lights and wait for them to come up on the porch. Yvonne liked to put out bits of bread and things so that they'd come."

"Your folks must have loved that," Cath said, thinking scattered garbage and rabies.

Derek gave her a quick, sidelong glance. "My folks were always off somewhere, playing bridge or going to dances. Yvonne and I were alone a lot. We had a thoroughly unsupervised childhood."

His tone was so ambiguous that Cath couldn't decide how he'd felt about his parents.

"Of course, there was less for them here so we did more as a family. And Yvonne didn't have to practice, which was nice." He turned and opened the glass door to the living room. "Some of my happiest memories are here. I wonder now how we managed that when there really wasn't all that much to do."

"I think children like not having too many things to do."

"You're right. Too much organized fun is bad for the soul. Or the digestion." Derek dropped into one of the twig chairs and examined his fire with a critical eye. "Warm enough?"

"Yes, the fire's lovely."

"We used to sit around and watch the fire and play board games. We should still have some board games and cards, if Uncle Will hasn't lost them."

"This cabin would be perfect with music," Cath said. "I'm sorry I didn't think to bring my violin."

"Next time, perhaps," Derek said. He leaned back in the chair and was silent. "We could have artistic evenings."

Cath detected a satiric note in his voice and said, "Unless that's too much like work."

"No, no. It would be delightful. The wilderness civilized." Then a bitter note like a sudden surprise dissonance: "Maybe we should have brought music with us when I was a child."

In the morning, they drove to the bait shop for the newspapers and assorted staples they'd forgotten to purchase and some big kitchen matches for the fireplace. They stood outside the shop in the morning sunshine, scanning disaster headlines that had no relevance for them, safe as they were in routine, in nonthreatening ordinary life. *How heartless we are,* Cath thought, flipping from a murdered child to starving Somalis to a new Algerian massacre, yet to think of all these things, to feel each one, would be to go mad. Normal life required a selective blindness, and the reward was that she could stand in the early sunlight and smell the pines and listen tranquilly to Derek calling his sister on the pay phone.

"No, no trouble. Walt was asking for you. Talkative as ever!" Gossip about the town. What had changed. What had not. The cabin. Good repair but not too clean. Uncle Will's advancing age. The business of the windows.

Cath turned to the comics; the local paper's selection was poor, and she was folding it up when she heard Derek saying, "Sure, sure. Boat's in the water. No problem." She glanced round. They hadn't even looked at the boat, never mind launched it. And that bothered her, for it reminded her that Derek lied very easily. Of course, Yvonne was persnickety about property. Cath could almost hear her saying, "And the boat? What kind of shape is the boat in? Did Uncle Will leave it out? The tenants won't like it if it's gotten too beat up," etc., etc. And yet, Cath would rather he hadn't lied about the boat.

"No problem. There won't be any problem," Derek was saying, and when Cath turned around and started walking toward the phone booth, he added, "Cath's getting impatient. We're going for a hike. See you next week. All right. Bye."

"I was going to ask her to call Stel Pye if she's going to be at the house. That way Stel won't have to water."

"Sorry. We'll be calling Yvonne again, though. She'll have some other questions for me. For sure," he added, but the prospect didn't seem to discourage him, for he was in an enthusiastic, energetic mood. He wanted Cath to see the area, to admire the woods, to enjoy herself. There were some nice trails near Paradox Lake, he said, that were easily reached. For some others, you needed a canoe; you portaged between the lakes; you did serious Natty Bumppo stuff. Where they were going was a piece of cake.

A few miles from the bait shop, he stopped at the head of a trail leading into deep forest. As they moved through the woods, the solid wall of trees became a shifting, diaphanous pattern; each turn of the trail, a green surprise. In damp places, there were deer tracks and the little anthropomorphic handprints of raccoons; occasional clearings were thick with chartreuse ferns and bracken. Wild geraniums bloomed among the thin, dew-spangled forest grasses that edged the trail, and anemones and pale wood violets, in the deeper shade, while brilliant patches of skunk cabbage lightened the marshy edges of the woodland streams. Whenever Cath and Derek stopped, they could hear small birds singing high up in the canopy or whistling from the dark curtains of the hemlocks and pines. As the morning advanced, the cool shadows shrank and lifted. The grass along the track dried, and the damp, humusy smell gave way to the scent of resin and of sun on leaves. "We should have brought a picnic," Cath said.

"We'll do that tomorrow. We could come to the lake here and rent a canoe, then go across to the trail for Peaked Hill."

"An adventure," Cath joked.

"One of the treats of my childhood." Derek was talking about this route, about their day trips in the wilderness, sometimes with the family, sometimes just with his sister, out all day by themselves, when Cath caught the primordial odor of decay.

"There's something dead nearby," she said.

"Pretty strong, too. Maybe a dog or a deer."

A sound from the trees ahead made them start, as one, two, three vultures launched their heavy bodies into the air and flapped across the trail. More were visible through the trees and brush. They hopped slowly away from where they had congregated, their bright eyes baleful in their red, naked heads, their gait at once awkward and menacing, like dragons with feathers. Curious, Derek left the trail and Cath followed.

"It's a doe," he said, startling the remaining vultures, which flew up into a dead oak nearby. "And her new fawn."

The deer fur looked like an old doormat, and one of the doe's thin, delicate legs had been dragged several yards from her body. Cath did not look at the fawn. The smell and the broken-up, disemboweled carcasses made her feel sick. "Who'd be hunting this time of year?"

"Dogs maybe, but coyotes are more likely. I don't know if there are wolves here now. The doe looks too big for a bobcat."

The infinite variety of violent death, Cath thought.

"That's your balance of nature. The Darwinian survival of the fittest."

"Yes," said Cath, but the lingering smell of decay made death real in a way this morning's news headlines had not. Even the grimmest of reports couldn't evoke the smell and mess and ugliness of death as forcefully as two dead deer. This might be Darwinian, but it was everything she'd come on holiday to evade, everything she'd left the city—no, she would not finish that thought. She would not. But though Derek wanted to push on further around the lake, Cath used the excuse of the ever increasing deerflies to turn back, and she walked fast enough that they arrived at the cabin in time for a late lunch. Afterward, they sat out on the porch, read the papers, and wished they'd brought books. Around three o'clock, when the sun had become hot, Cath asked Derek if he thought the lake might be warm enough for a swim.

"A bit early in the season, and the lake's never really warm."

"I thought I might give it a try."

"What about if we take the boat out? I'll see if I can catch a few fish, and if the water's too cold, you can row for a while and I'll troll. See if I can tempt a lake trout."

"If you want to," Cath said. She'd been hesitant to bring up anything to do with the boat.

"If we're going to fish, we'll need it," he said and got up and went down the porch steps. He unlocked a panel in the lattice under the porch. The fiberglass rowboat, faded to gray and worn along the gunnels, was up on a couple of cement blocks. There was a pair of oars, some rope, and, sitting on a plank atop a couple more blocks, a small kicker.

Derek gave the boat a quick examination and lifted one side off the blocks. "You can get mice nesting under the seats," he said.

This time the boat was unoccupied, and they carried it down to the shore. Derek kicked off his shoes and, with reflections about the temperature of the water, guided the craft into the lake and tied the rope to a piling that served for a mooring. Cath went in to get changed. Derek fetched the oars and a bucket for a bailer and for fish, then went to assemble his kit. When Cath came out of the bedroom with her swimsuit and a sweatshirt, Derek was swearing at Uncle Will again.

"No rod? I thought I saw some in the hall."

"Plenty of rods. No reel. And I hate to have to borrow one from Walt. If we go down there, it'll be dark before we're on the lake."

"Oh, that's too bad. Would your uncle have locked up his equipment?" she asked, looking around. Cath already knew that the closets were empty; the covered bin by the fire held wood. "What's in this?" The tall cabinet, built of what looked to be unnecessarily substantial oak boards, was mounted on the wall.

"Oh, that. That's the gun case. My dad was safety conscious. And I think he liked the idea of a gun case, you know, English-country-house-type furniture." Derek took out the ring of keys Walt had given him and used the smallest to unlock the cabinet. "Ha! You are psychic! Here we go." He reached in and took out a spinning reel which had been left beside two rifles. "I bet you Uncle Will didn't want me using this."

"Did your dad hunt?" Cath asked, surprised at the guns. She really knew very little about Derek's parents, who seemed to have been important chiefly for their absence in his life.

"Hmmm. He did and Will does. This is a twenty-two for small game. And this is a shotgun. Quite lethal. You load it with buckshot for deer." There was a clip of bullets for the twenty-two and several cardboard boxes of cartridges for the shotgun. Derek showed Cath how to put the clip in the rifle and then broke open the shotgun. "Drop the cartridges in here, so; close it up and always, always put the safety on. My first lesson in firearms."

"You learn something every day," said Cath. "But you surely won't leave them loaded?"

"Not a bad idea, actually, when we're in such a remote place. Loaded, safety on, case locked. No accidents possible," he said, giving her a look. "With proper precautions, there are no firearms accidents."

"Which must mean that there are a lot of careless people," Cath said.

"Or more deliberate shootings than coronors bring in," Derek replied, but he was feeling nostalgic rather than sardonic. "When we were alone at night, Yvonne and I used to keep the twenty-two in the corner and the clip on the table." He gave a little chuckle. "We used to frighten ourselves, thinking we heard something—or saying we did. We had a drill. Hear a noise: I went for the gun, she went for the clip, we met in the middle of the room to load. One night she shot a possum."

That sounded to Cath more like the Yvonne she knew. "I thought she fed the wildlife."

"She did, but we thought we heard someone out on the porch in the dark—and she didn't like possums, anyway. We got in trouble for that, because Walt heard the shot and told our parents. Afterwards, we had to go to the dances and Yvonne started to play the piano with Walt."

"I should have thought they'd have taken you with them in the first place," Cath said, and wished she hadn't, because she knew it sounded prissy.

"I don't know that they were wrong. I got an appreciation for fear," Derek said. "I learned that fear's erotic—in small doses. You could say it made me what I am—the irresistible lover of a beautiful musician."

17

THE WATER WAS ICE COLD. That was the key detail, Cath thought. If the water hadn't been cold, there would have been nothing to think about and the incident, the moment, would have passed unnoticed and certainly unreflected. But the water was cold, ice to the veins and an ache to the bones that ran from the toes to the knees and from the fingers to the shoulders. The cold gripped the stomach and contracted the chest so that the lungs took fright. The cold was the detail, tiny in itself, which would amplify other effects to produce a still uncertain outcome.

So the water was cold; she had to start there. Cath leaned back in the twig chair and looked at the glowing log, alligatored red and black in the darkness. They had not bothered to put on the light. Though Derek rarely smoked, he was lying on the couch with a cigarette, and that was detail number two, if she was counting. He smoked once in a while after a concert—usually a celebratory cigar—and sometimes when he was under stress, he had a cigarette. In either case, smoking was a ritual for him. First, there was purchasing a cigar or finding a cigarette. He usually had an open, half-smoked, squashed-up cigarette pack stuck in a coat pocket or in his desk drawer. He'd have to shake out a cigarette, smooth it and straighten it, tap it on some hard surface. Then another search for matches, because he never carried them, either. Finally, all ingredients assembled and a saucer ready to serve as ashtray, Derek would light up, draw in a mouthful of smoke, exhale with a sigh, and lie back to study the thin blue plume rising toward the ceiling.

Cath smelled the cigarette smoke mingling with the faint, pleasingly sour fume of the wood fire. She had left the front windows half open, and the cool night air came in to keep the room fresh. Over on the couch, Derek lay silent; neither of them had spoken in a long time, Cath had been waiting for him to speak; if he spoke she would not have to think, but since he was silent, had been silent, showed every sign of continuing to be silent, she thought that the water had been ice cold.

They'd gotten in the rowboat, and Derek pushed off with the oars. A few strokes and they were away from the stones, a few more and they were in deep water. A sailboat drifted mothlike along the opposite shore, and a passing powerboat left a wake that set their boat rocking. Further down the lake, a water skier cut a curving white plume, and little yellow-and-red-sailed Sunfish clustered near the town dock. Derek pulled steadily on the oars. He'd gotten his old Walkman from the car before they left, and he wore a distant, meditative expression as he listened to music that reached Cath only as a faint hum. She pulled off her sweatshirt and trailed her hand in the water, testing the temperature. "It doesn't feel too bad," she said.

Derek removed the earpiece.

"I said that the water doesn't feel too bad."

"My ankles are still thawing from putting the boat in."

"I want to say I've been in the lake." Though just why Cath should care and just whom she would tell were good questions.

"We'll go a bit further along. Water skiers are a menace for swimmers."

"If you're worried about the powerboats, wouldn't we have been better to stay inshore?"

"The shallows are full of rocks and pond weeds," Derek said.

He put the earpiece back and began humming along with the music, his handsome dark face remote in the sunlight. *In another world.* Beethoven's, she guessed, perhaps the *Pastoral Symphony,* a good choice for a day in the country, for an afternoon on a lake. As he listened, Derek pulled a strong, economical stroke, the powerful muscles of his arms tensing and stretching, his head and shoulders moving rhythmically, forward, back, forward, back, using the lake's elusive substance to propel them. Cath always found something pleasingly improbable about rowing, and something satisfying about watching an oarsman.

They traveled to the gentle plash of the strokes, to Derek's humming, to an occasional burble as her hand disturbed the water flowing back across the bow. They'd reached a deserted stretch, where a small island cut off their view of the village, when Derek asked, "How's this? Private enough to change? You won't want to sit about in your wet suit. This should be a good place to fish, too."

Cath took off her shorts and sandals. Derek shipped the oars, and she clambered gingerly over the stern. Entered that way, the lake was cold enough to take her breath away.

"How is it?" Derek called. He lifted out his earpiece to hear her answer, but Cath couldn't speak. Then she managed a big gasp of air and said, "Freezing."

He laughed. "Told you so. Want to get back in?"

"I'll warm up swimming," Cath said, although the water was so cold she hated to get her face wet. She struck out parallel to the shore anyway, hoping to find the rhythm, to get her lungs calm, but very soon her ankles and knees started to ache, making her think that she could wait until July to swim. She stopped and turned, but instead of seeing Derek nearby, she saw a long stretch of blue-gray water with the rowboat at the end of it. Not possible! She couldn't have been in the water five minutes! Cath lifted her head and thought she saw the splash of Derek's oars. With her heart fluttering on the outskirts of panic, she raised one arm, waved and shouted, before striking out after him; then, as she felt the cold seeping into her chest, toward her heart, she faltered and looked toward shore. A hundred yards, maybe more.

Though distances on water are hard to estimate, Cath decided for the shore.

Sitting in the twig chair, of primitive but surprisingly comfortable construction, she wondered about that decision. Whatever had she been thinking? She'd thought that she could not swim much longer and figured that the lakeshore was closer than the boat. The proximity of cold water, pond weeds, and the murky bottom of the lake had shut out other, wilder ideas, and Cath had set off with a steady crawl toward the dark, serrated woods and pale rocks. She heard Derek calling when she was maybe twenty, thirty yards from shore. By then, she could see the small leaves of the birches, the tracery of young trees struggling up out of stony crevices, the outlet of a tiny stream. She'd gotten into a rhythm by that time. Stroke, stroke, breathe, stroke, stroke, breathe, over and over again. Her legs were numb, and though she thought she was still doing a steady flutter kick, one, two, one two, she couldn't be sure of any motion beyond the roll of her hips.

"Cath! Cath!" Derek's words had a fuzzy, remote quality. She might have been within a feverish dream, for the cold had slid into an overall ache, and her situation—water, air, a certain dread of heart—no longer felt like ordinary life.

"Cath! Cath!"

She stopped when she heard the steady splash and pull of the oars, only to find that her legs had failed her. Instead of treading water, she slid under and had to haul herself to the surface. She began struggling toward Derek, pulling herself over the water as across sand, and then, as she neared the boat, a shadow moved upon the surface, and she dived.

That dive was what had occupied her mind ever since. College swim class in the Women's Building on a dark winter day: steamy chlorinated air within, sleety snow falling outside. The lesson was the basic surface dive. Tuck and pike, or the art of disappearing from the surface quickly. A gulp of air, a sudden shift in bodily alignment, then the blue-green bottom of the pool coming up fast amid streams of bubbles from other learners. The memory of that sequence had lain in her muscles until, half unconscious from the cold, a darkness advanced toward her head and she dived.

A sudden shock spread numbness; cold pounded along the bones of her face and folded the back of her skull into a darkness rising from the depths. She might have gone all the way down, but she hadn't had enough time to breathe properly. Her legs uncertain, the shallow breath finished, Cath raised her arms and propelled herself toward the blue water and the fat bullet shadow of the rowboat. She clawed again toward the light before breaking through into the glitter dazzle of the sun, Derek's silhouette, and the sound of his voice, "Cath! This way. Catch the oar!"

She splashed up out of the water, catching a mouthful of lake, but seizing the oar. When he drew it in, she clutched the boat, hooking one arm over the side. She thought that she would just climb over, a misjudgment, Derek said later, that would have capsized them for sure and which was most certainly a sign of hypothermia.

"Shock and cold cause errors in judgment. That's how skiers and climbers die," he said. But that was later, when she'd caught her breath and he'd calmed down. At the moment, the moment when she hooked her arm over the side and thought to come aboard, he'd yelled, "The back of the boat," and grabbed her arm and steered her around. He was crouching between the oars, trying to keep the boat stable, holding on to her, his fingers slipping on her wet flesh. She must think of that. If she thought of the shadow, it was only fair to think of his struggle to get her out of the water when her legs were lead, her arms jelly. A sharp jerk set the universe rocking, water fell away into space, and Derek yelled, "Grab the seat, grab the seat!" Which she did. Violinist's hands are strong, the only strength she had left. Then Derek edged back to the center bench and pulled her the rest of the way into the boat.

Cath lay exhausted between the seats, her cheek against the boards, her hair in muddy water, until Derek got her sweatshirt and her towel. He rubbed her face and her back. He pulled down her wet suit, forced the sweatshirt over her head, and fought to get her arms, quite absent from her control, into the sleeves. Another struggle with the bottom of her suit, tight and refractory, spilling blue-white flesh, then her shorts. He wrapped her legs in the damp towel, jammed his cap on her head, and began rubbing her back.

"Better?" he asked. "Better?"

There was a frantic edge to his voice, and she made the effort to say, "I'm all right," although she felt nothing in some places and as though her bones were broken in others.

"Christ, you gave me a fright! Didn't you hear me calling?"

When Cath did not answer, Derek spoke of hypothermia, the malady of mountain climbers, the death of Arctic and Antarctic explorers. "You could have died!" he cried. "Surely you know I love you now!" before he took up the oars and rowed for the cabin like a madman, tears and sweat running down his face. When they got back, he helped Cath change into her wool sweater and jeans. He had her put on thick socks, wrapped her in a blanket, and poured her hot tea with lots of sugar.

"What a stupid thing to do," Cath admitted.

"It's too early for the lake. I thought you'd be in and out."

Cath saw the boat, a darker rectangle against blue-gray water, saw the motion of the oars, saw distance as a sweep of sunstruck wavelets. "I didn't intend to go so far."

"As I say, hypothermia distorts the judgment."

"Yes," Cath said, as she must if they were to arrive at normalcy. The shadow had been a misapprehension, a misjudgment, a product of incipient hypothermia. "And I was already tired. We walked a long way this morning."

"But mainly it's the cold. Drink up your tea." They had some cookies in the kitchen, and Cath dutifully ate one. Her skin felt as if it was covered with ants, as if she'd been frozen and was now thawing into pieces.

"You frightened me," Derek said. "You could have gone into shock, into cardiac arrest."

"I'm tough," said Cath.

He was sitting on the couch beside her, watchful and anxious, and, in response, he buried his face against her neck. "Yes," he said, "yes, you are, my darling. I couldn't bear to lose you." There was an edge of desperation in his voice, as if he might really have lost her—or himself. Maybe himself, for Cath saw the shadow that had hovered over the water fluttering in his eyes. "You know I love you," he said. "Tell me that you believe I love you."

It seemed to be terribly important that he be believed, that he be *trusted,* and she said yes, because she loved him, and because she had promised to save him, and now, at last, she had a sense of what it was he feared. "Yes," she said, "yes, I know you do."

"But you're still shivering!" He put his arms around her and kissed her face and then her throat.

Cath said, "You saved my life."

Derek drew back from her, his eyes troubled, although he was the one who had spoken of Arctic disasters and lost climbers and the perils of cold water. "Oh, you're a strong swimmer. You'd have made the shore all right."

"Maybe."

"You would," he insisted, alarmed, Cath sensed, genuinely alarmed. "Don't even suggest you wouldn't have. There was only a moment when things looked dangerous. Only a moment."

"A moment of hypothermia," Cath said. She seemed destined to queer moments of madness—or of hypothermia—which certainly sounded better, more scientific, possibly verifiable. But the lake remained, a difficulty and a puzzle, a glittering sheet of water with a boat in the distance. "I still think you saved my life."

This time he stroked her face and, as if she had been in doubt, he told her again that she must believe he loved her. She must remember that, he said, as he slid his hands under her wool sweater. "God! You're still cold!" Which she was. Her hands and feet were still numb, her whole body, cool to the touch.

"I must feel like a corpse," Cath said, but Derek was pulling off his polo shirt. His body was radiant with heat and vitality; warmth raced from his skin to hers, half pleasantly, half painfully. Transported with violent pleasures, he told her that he loved her, and later, struggling ecstatically, tangled in the sheets, he whispered, "Your hair was so dark in the water, it looked black." But maybe she just imagined that, because there was a phantasmal edge to everything, like the line of fire along his body, not quite real, yet infinitely suggestive.

From these hallucinatory moments, Cath dropped into sleep, profound, dreamless, until Derek woke her, his legs and feet moving so violently that she got out of bed. It made her momentarily sad that he had bad dreams, too. Cath stood looking at the lake, silver edged with the blackness of the pines, until he stopped mumbling and stirring. As she lay back down beside him, Derek woke up smiling and kissed her face, so that Cath was reminded of afternoon love in his college room. He asked the time and when she said it was past seven, he suggested that they drive into the village for dinner.

"A date," Cath said. "Remember how we used to go to the pizzeria?"

And he smiled again, recalling, as she did, the start of their love and how it felt to emerge from passion to the cold, shadowed afternoons, the first streetlights, the clear, empty, pink northern sky; how it felt to have the secret of love, of energy, of the world transformed.

"We'll get Italian," he said, and they drove around to a pizza and spaghetti place near the town beach. The sun had dropped behind the hills, but there was plenty of light reflecting off the water. People were sitting at the picnic tables near the dock, while their children raced excitedly between the daylight shore and the night already held under the pines and hemlocks. Still disoriented by the strangeness of awakening to twilight, Cath and Derek went to look at the boats and shivered in the breeze to watch the day colors sink into the indeterminate grays of evening. Inside, the warm, bright restaurant had an eclectic decor of deer antlers and stuffed animals, checked vinyl tablecloths, Chianti bottles, and strings of red peppers.

After they ordered, Cath visited the washroom, and passing the pay phones on her way back, she remembered her garden. "Hi," she said, when Yvonne answered her call. "How are things?"

There was a moment; even down the line, Cath felt it: a little jolt, an almost physical surprise. "Cath? Is that you?" Surprise, certainly. Something more? Or just a poor connection?

"Yes, can you hear me? We're out for dinner and it's pretty noisy."

"Where's Derek?" Definitely an edge of alarm, though Yvonne never wasted much formality on Cath.

"He's at the salad bar under the moose head." It was one of Cath's weaknesses that she could not resist humor with her humorless sister-in-law. "I'm at the pay phone. Next to an entire black bear, poor thing."

"I want to speak to Derek," Yvonne said.

"I'll give him a wave. What I called about is, are you going to be at the house tomorrow? I don't want Stel to have to bother watering if—"

"I'm staying in town," Yvonne said. "There's a house I think I can close on."

"Oh, good luck. There was just no point in duplicating—"

"Would you put Derek on, please, Cath?"

"I told you he's at the salad bar. We're in a restaurant. I can't just yell." She waved in her husband's direction, but he seemed absorbed in the iced bank of greens, cut veggies, assorted toppings. "Just give me the message," Cath said. When that was unsatisfactory, she said she'd have Derek call back.

Her husband was tucking into his salad when Cath returned to her seat. "Thought I'd lost you in the ladies' room," he said.

"I remembered we hadn't called Yvonne. I wanted to see if she was going to be at the house."

His expression changed. "You called Yvonne? Just now?"

"For all the good it did me. She's hoping to sell a house, so she's staying in town. She really wanted to talk to you, but I couldn't get your attention. How's the salad?"

"I wish you hadn't done that," Derek said.

"Done what? Call your sister?"

"I'll be right back." He went quickly to the phone.

Cath raised her eyebrows in exasperation but said nothing. At the salad bar, she collected an assortment of greens, some hard cherry tomatoes, and grayish chickpeas from under the gaze of the depressed-looking moose. At the back of the restaurant, Derek stood with his head bent close to the phone as if in deep consultation with the black bear. Cath noticed the salad bar had soup, too, and returned for some chicken vegetable that was homemade and very much better than the salad. Derek talked on with his sister, and Cath felt the intensity and pleasure of the evening begin to dissipate; they were not on a date after all, and the time in Derek's room seemed increasingly distant.

She had almost finished both soup and salad before he came back to the table. "Well," she said.

Derek shrugged and sat down, looking tense and pale. "I don't know why you had to call her."

Cath hoped they weren't going to quarrel. "I told you. I wanted to have her do the watering if she was going to be at the house."

He started on his salad, then pushed it aside.

"Is something wrong?" Cath asked.

He looked away without answering. That might have been preliminary to an argument, a scene, even, but before Cath had a chance to say anything, the waiter arrived with the pizza, a big, round, festive bread, bubbling with tomato sauce and cheese, studded with sausages and onions, smelling wonderful. Derek pulled himself back from wherever he'd been with Yvonne and said, "Oh, you know her. Everything's a crisis."

"What is it this time?" Cath asked, although she could see he didn't want to talk about Yvonne, and she certainly didn't, either.

"She's nervous about this big house she's selling, that's all. The most important property she's handled since she switched offices again. You know how she is."

"Up to a point," said Cath, who tended to be precise, even literal-minded in all questions about her sister-in-law.

"Let's not talk about Yvonne tonight," Derek said. He gave a tight smile and dug into the pizza before looking around as if he had just noticed the Napoli-backwoods decor. "Nice pizza. Weird decorations."

"Ye olde Italian Adirondacks?"

"That moose head is old enough."

"It's losing its fur," Cath observed.

"The secret ingredient in the salad," said Derek, and they managed to laugh. After that, it was easy to talk about the restaurant, the food, about other restaurants, about pizza joints they had known at school, about such questions as, Was pizza good for the voice? Every couple has such a selection of topics, dependable even when there is trouble somewhere, even when nightmares and hallucinations hang on events like cobwebs. Dinner was fine, the evening pleasant on the whole, and it was only when they came back to the cabin, to the woods and the isolation, back, in short, to themselves, that they ran out of things to say.

Shifting in the creaking twig chair, artisan made, probably valuable, Cath looked from the fire to Derek and said, "I think we should go home."

He took another drag on his cigarette before answering. Derek smoked his rare cigarettes very slowly, as if smoking were a discipline like scales or school figures in skating. "I thought you liked the place," he said.

"I do. I do like the place. I just think it's maybe not the right place for us at the moment."

"How tactful you are, Cath. Almost always tactful. And thoughtful. You've been sitting thinking for"—here he turned his wrist and checked his watch—"over an hour."

Cath did not like that touch of condescension, but she didn't want to argue. She felt it would be bad to argue now, even—but she would not think that. "I've had the sense you might be thinking, too," she said.

"And now you've come to the decision that we should go home early."

Riddled with fire, a big piece of the log had separated from the heartwood and dropped onto the hearth, throwing up a cloud of golden sparks. "I think there are bad memories here for you," she said.

"I thought we were supposed to confront bad memories," he said.

Cath shrugged. "We live as best we can."

"We aim to make life supportable? Is that the best we can do?"

"You're the theologian. For more abundant life we need grace. We need some supernatural intervention."

"Do you believe that?"

"I did feel for a while that less supernatural intervention might be better for me."

"You were gifted with the perception of evil," Derek said slowly. He might have been savoring the words.

"A strange gift," Cath replied.

"You don't take it seriously enough. Think of the implications. One being that evil implies good, a kind of proof—"

"It almost drove me mad," she said flatly.

He hesitated before asking, "And then you lost it? The perception of evil?"

Cath looked away from his shadowed eyes. What was the truth in this matter? What was the right answer? The right answer to give him, that is. *More or less? More or less* might open up undesirable topics. Or could she safely confess madness and put everything in the past? *Behind me,* as they said. As in, *I've put all that behind me. I've gotten on with my life, gotten a grip, gotten things under control.* The manifold possibilities of the verb *to get.*

"You still have moments," he concluded from her silence. "Moments when you can sense—"

"It's brain chemistry," she said briskly, for she did not want to discuss the shadow on the water, the shadow moving toward her head, the impulse for tuck and pike, or the art of disappearing from the surface. "You were explaining hypothermia to me. How it leads to bad judgment. I suppose that something similar was at work earlier."

When she met his eyes again, she saw he was sad, and Cath had a terrible moment of doubt about her own perceptions, about her own grip on the world.

"We can't leave tomorrow," Derek said after a pause. "There's something I need to do tomorrow."

"We don't need to leave tomorrow," Cath said, for she felt he had conceded. "I just think we should go home soon."

"Day after tomorrow," Derek said. "Tomorrow we want to go for a hike. Right? I want you to see a little more of the area. And then I want to take the boat out with the kicker. I'll have to do that alone, you understand."

He was up early, took a quick breakfast, and then carried the motor down to the boat. Cath went with him to buy gas and the morning papers, but he would not let her help with the boat. She sat on the porch, reading the news—international, national, local—while he tinkered with the engine, adjusting the carburetor and sending a column of blue exhaust into the cool, clear air. After some time, the engine started with a sudden roar that dropped back to a hum, and Cath saw the boat pull away from the mooring, swing out onto the lake, then circle back to idle. She stood up at the rail and waved. "Success," she called, and he echoed, "Success."

They made sandwiches and went for a hike to Crane Pond: vultures riding the mountain thermals, bullfrogs and peepers in marshy ecstasy, warblers and flycatchers flitting between the branches, towhees and sparrows rustling in the leaves. Derek, changeable as the weather, whistled as they walked and sang arias from *Don Giovanni,* so that Cath felt his morning experiments with the boat had settled something for him, had calmed his mind, had lifted the sadness she'd sensed the previous night. She began to think that they might stay a couple of days after all, that she had been foolish to worry, that the woods, if not the lake, were good for Derek. She was surprised when, cleaned up from the hike and sitting tired but relaxed on the porch, he said he wanted to take the boat over to Schroon Lake village.

"For dinner?" she asked, for they'd already bought a small steak and some baking potatoes.

"No, no. Just a run. I feel I should do that. You remember, you said this was a memory trip?"

"I thought this morning—" Cath began.

"I just wanted to be sure the engine would run this morning."

"Do you want me to come with you?" she asked, though a certain shadow lingered, though she disliked the idea of being on the water.

Derek smiled but she felt the sadness again, a kind of wistfulness quite foreign to him. "Not this time," he said. "You can't come this time, though it was kind to ask." He got up then, touched her shoulder, said, "You've always been kind," and went into the cabin. A few minutes later he called, "Do you have your key? I don't know what I've done with mine."

Cath took the key out of her pocket. "I won't have the door locked," she said.

"You should when you're alone." He went back inside for his sweater. When he returned, he had the ring of keys he'd gotten from Walt. Cath noticed he'd picked up his windbreaker, too, although it was mild in the sun. "I'd left the keys in my other pants. You take these: front door, back door, storage area, springhouse, gun case. You never know."

"I'm not sure that I'd know what to do about the water," Cath said, but she put the key ring in her pocket. "What time for dinner?"

"I won't be late. I have to be back before dark."

"There's hours before dark. You're only going across to the village, aren't you?"

"Around the island and then across. I'll bring back some ice cream, shall I? For dessert?"

"Peach," Cath said. "See if there's any peach."

He reached out and touched her hair, then hugged her with a sudden intensity of feeling that startled and worried her.

"You don't have to go alone," she said. "You don't have to go at all. I don't want you to go alone."

"It's best," said Derek. "We'll go home tomorrow. We'll go straight home and you can make reservations for the shore."

"But this was nice, too," she said. "The woods and hiking and everything."

"And you learned that I love you. Don't forget that. You won't forget that?"

Cath shook her head. Derek went quickly down the porch steps and along the path to the boat. Watching from the rail, Cath saw him untie the boat, push off, and start up the engine. He pulled away slowly in a curving wash, waving as he went, then disappeared into the white reflecting glare, to emerge, a small figure in a toy boat, heading north.

18

THE SHADOWS CAME DOWN OUT of the hemlocks, staining the porch with their cool darkness. The hills to the west faded; the sky overhead turned lavender; the lake was calm. The water-skiers and power-boaters had gone for supper, and only a few sailboats still ran before the breeze on the way to the marinas and the public dock. Cath looked at her watch. Derek had left before five; it was now a quarter to seven. Time enough, she thought, to have rowed to the village and back, never mind zipped over under power. Yet the lake was without a ripple, and Derek had newly filled the gas tank. There was no reason for him to be late.

No reason for her to worry, either. *I have to be back before dark*, he'd said. Darkness was still another two hours away. Maybe Derek had met Walt, and talking with Walt could surely fill an hour. The village had antique shops, too, though Derek would have been mean to leave her home if he'd intended to go shopping. But perhaps he'd planned a surprise, possibly a chest for their hall at home. Cath tried to envision a little bureau wrapped up in a tarp and balanced precariously between the seats of the rowboat. He'd need a couple of blocks to keep the legs out of the bilgewater, and the chest would have to be a small, low design. Or else he'd bought a print in a nice old frame. The restaurant the other night had some hunting prints in worn but attractive frames, the sort you find in less pretentious antique stores. So perhaps there was a brown paper package sitting in the bow with a piece of plastic over it to keep off the spray. Cath tried to see the package, tried to imagine the spray as the little boat shot across the purplish surface of the lake, but while she could imagine the package— or a little bureau—she somehow couldn't get the boat on the water; she couldn't envision Derek coming home. Nonsense. *I have to be back before dark,* he'd said, and there was lots of daylight left.

Cath went into the galley kitchen and scrubbed the potatoes and made a salad, nibbling on the carrots and celery as she worked. At seven-thirty she put the potatoes in to bake and went back out onto the porch to check the empty water. Thinking that Derek would surely show up if she went for a walk, Cath put a note on the door and started up the road toward Walt's. A veery called out of sight in the underbrush, producing beautiful descending runs, and, on the way back, a wood thrush, liquid and mysterious, sang like the most beautiful flutist ever, so that Cath lingered in the shadows, listening. Then she hurried back, because the sun was down, the sky turning rosy, the trees, black. She hoped Derek had thought to put on the broiler and start the steak.

Cath went around to the side so that she could make sure the boat was tied up where it belonged. But the mooring post remained empty, and even the birds, frogs, and insects could not fill up the evening. Cath felt reluctant to enter the cabin, which meant confronting absence and considering its implications. Instead, she unlocked the lattice door to the storage area. Inside were fish buckets, nets, old rope, and, half sunk in the dirt and dusty leaves, a plastic fire truck, the base and mast of a toy sailboat, various small vehicles, and plastic dolls with missing limbs: poignant reminders of vacations and of childhoods past, beloved companions abandoned along with the imagination of youth. Derek and Yvonne must have had to rely a great deal on their own resources, Cath thought, and she wondered what games they had played. What

had these dolls represented? And these other toys? Fire departments
and police, cowboys, families and spies? The musty storage area with
its lost, secret life seemed to Cath as intimate as an old photo album
and touched with the same melancholy.

She closed and locked the door. Inside the cabin, she tested the
potatoes and decided to eat her salad, because as soon as she started
eating, Derek would show up. She set the table in the main room and
wondered if she should attempt a fire. But though the hemlocks were
cutting off the last red glow in the west, she hesitated to switch on the
lights. *I have to be back before dark*, Derek had said, and turning on
the lights was a confirmation that he would not be back. Cath thought
she would leave the steak and take out the potatoes. She'd eat hers,
and then, if Derek wasn't back—for there was still light on the lake,
which glowed in the twilight as if powered from within—she'd drive
the car around to the village. How long could that take? Ten, fifteen
minutes? She could drive right to the dock and see if his boat was
there.

Before she had finished her baked potato, Cath had to put on the
chandelier. Instantly the lake and the cloudy filigree of the hemlocks
vanished, revealing her reflection, the table and the light against the
darkness of the bedrooms, the hearth, the gun cabinet: something was
wrong. Cath carried her plates through to the kitchen sink, rinsed them
hastily, and got her jacket from the hall. She put her hands in the
pockets, then remembered that Derek had driven to the gas station
that morning. She opened the drawers in the bedroom, looked on the
bedside table, and checked the narrow counter in the kitchen. She felt
along the mantelpiece and searched the spare bedroom before resigning
herself to the fact that Derek had pocketed the car keys.

Cath decided to walk to Walt's, instead, and use his telephone.
She'd found the flashlight and gone outside before she wondered whom
she could call. The police? The warden at the dock? *Have you seen a
tall, handsome man in a gray fiberglass rowboat with an old kicker?* How
far would that get her? Well, she could still go to Walt's. Even in the
dark, she could find the way. She'd need her flashlight for the drive,

but then she could follow the dirt road easily. And what to say to Walt, who was already suspicious of her? *Has Derek called you?* That would expose her to all sorts of doubts and unpleasantness. Besides, if Derek had called, if there had been news, wouldn't Walt have come down in his truck? Wouldn't he have pulled up with Rex alert on the front seat? It was easy to envision the toot of his horn, the headlights washing the back of the cabin, and her own self coming out, half relieved and half anxious, to get the news, whatever it might be.

No, Cath didn't think Walt had gotten a call. Inside the cabin, she took off her jacket, then checked the porch: only the village lights twinkling across the water, nothing more. No sound of an engine, nothing mechanical, nothing human. She was closing the glass door when headlights swept the feathery darkness of the trees. She heard a car, maybe a truck, maybe Walt, and ran down the steps and across the yard toward the drive. Then stopped, for there was nothing. No lights, no engine. She might have imagined the car, conjured a phantom light out of anxiety and expectation. Nothing. Were there houses further down on this road? Cath tried to remember what Derek had said when he'd been talking about the condos, that new development. Was it on this road? Yes, but she thought south of them, and that must be right, because they hadn't heard a single car. Not one.

Cath walked back to the porch, her feet noisy on the leaves and twigs. Just a camper, she thought. Someone with a small RV or, more likely, a four-wheel-drive with a tent in the back. But, nonetheless, Cath was infected with nervousness. She felt exposed and vulnerable in some way she had not been just moments before. She was sorry that there were no blinds on the windows, that there was no outside light, that she did not have the car keys. The car keys were a particular loss, because she would very much have liked to drive around to the village, to find Derek, to sit in the bright Italian restaurant and have coffee and a pizza and an ordinary evening.

After she'd locked the porch door, Cath went quickly through all the rooms in the cabin, making sure that nothing had come in out of the dark. Then, although she had lost her appetite, she decided she would fry part of the steak with onions and a couple of tomatoes. She told herself that cooking would be a good idea, that slicing vegetables and browning meat, washing up dishes and being busy would keep everything normal. Cath was something of an expert on normalcy. She felt she'd spent much of her marriage searching for the ordinary and keeping assorted shadows at bay.

As she carried the steak through to the table, the evening wind blew up; the hemlocks' soft branches were rubbing against the porch railing. Something was different; a change in atmospheric pressure, perhaps, or a new smell in the air: there was definitely something. Most likely stupidity, Cath told herself and began on her steak. She ate it with the onions and tomatoes and sopped up the mingled juices with a piece of bread. Everything was normal, but Derek was not back, and with darkness and silence, with no car keys and a curious light on the road, Cath could not help reviewing the afternoon, the night before, even incidents from the previous afternoon which she had preferred to put out of her mind.

I have to be back by dark. We'll go home tomorrow. Unambiguous statements. Statements of intentionality, if she remembered the terms correctly, statements carrying the inescapable implication that something had happened to Derek. Other phrases jostled in her mind for attention, and, more than phrases, his tone, the wistful finality she'd detected in his voice. *You've always been kind. You must know now that I love you.* Those words had an elegiac tone, *elegiac* from *elegy,* a remembrance, a lament, a poem for the dead. Cath thought that a literary education could be pernicious, making one oversubtle in interpretation and susceptible to melodrama and panic. But what of that sudden embrace before he left? No rhetoric there. Just the convulsive clasp of his arms before he left to take a short before-dinner run across the lake. What did that mean? And the other things: the shadow, her dive, their curious conversation in the firelight. *You had the perception of evil and then you lost it.*

Outside, a footstep, distinct, unmistakable. No doubt about it, she'd heard a footstep. Cath straightened her back and concentrated on a rustling in the brush to the north of the cabin. She got up, switched off the overhead light, and went into the dark bedroom to look out the window at stars caught in the screen of trees and a white, cloud-riding moon doubled in the sheen of the lake. Frogs in the marsh, insects trilling; otherwise, silence. A deer, Cath thought, but she did not switch on the chandelier again, and after she finished washing up the dishes, she put off the kitchen light, too.

She went onto the porch, waiting until her eyes had adjusted. She looked toward the village, checked the boat mooring, concentrated on the trees just beyond the cabin. She was ready to give up when she heard footsteps again. Not a deer, not that sound. Someone was walking through the dry leaves in the yard. Derek must have had trouble with the boat and gotten a lift back. Cath went to the south side of the porch and called. "Is that you, Derek?"

Silence, the profounder silence that follows sound. Not the explosive bound of a startled deer, nor the short-legged scramble of raccoons or possums, but silence. She called again, less confidently. "Derek?" Silence.

Cath went inside, closing and locking the porch door behind her. There was someone outside. She realized that and then that she was holding, not her single key, but Derek's key ring. She felt her way to the small table light by the fire, switched it on, and unlocked the gun case. The two long guns stood balanced on their polished stocks, their barrels gleaming in the lamplight. The twenty-two was for birds and small game, Cath remembered, the shotgun, for deer, for large game, for noises in the night. She set the shotgun carefully on the floor until she relocked the case. Then she picked up the gun again. Where to put it? To sit and hold the weapon was a ridiculous admission of seriousness, of danger. By the door? That seemed unwise. Leaning up against the chair? Unsafe. Behind the couch? Immediately visible from both doors. Cath checked that the weapon was, indeed, loaded and that the safety was on, then deposited it just inside the bedroom door, where it would be close at hand but out of sight. That seemed the right degree of precaution, because probably the footsteps she heard belonged to some tardy hiker, embarrassed to have blundered onto private land. Probably. She was in a popular resort area, safe, civilized, full of families with children, and the feel in the air, that nasty atmospheric shift, that *something* elusive and indefinable, was no more than imagination, a hangover, as it were, from the night bus. There was no need for her to think of Esther Nielson, nor the mezzo-soprano Kimberly Delane, nor . . . But here Cath stopped. She got the flashlight, sat down in the chair near the fireplace, and switched off the table lamp.

In the darkness, all her senses came alert and her heart, despite her best efforts, began racing. Cath held the flashlight in her lap and waited. Now the void was pierced by the gray rectangles of the windows and the glass door to the porch. Moonlight came in behind her and cast skewed rectangles on the floor, and out in the yard there was another sound, closer. Cath wanted to jump up and run to the window, to call out, "Who's there?" But she stopped herself. A hiker? A runaway? Someone without much luck looking for a place to stay? She knew what that was like.

Steps on the porch stair now. She would wait, Cath decided. Maybe whoever it was would try the door, find it locked, and go away. Best outcome. And if not, the flashlight's bright, accusing glare, four steps back to the bedroom, and the shotgun. A good plan.

A shadow moved on the porch with a step that was both familiar and unsettling. The rattle of the latch and then the shock of a key turning in the lock. Cath raised the flashlight and turned it on to see Derek standing in the doorway.

"Oh, God!" Cath exclaimed, jumping up. "Derek, you gave me such a fright! Didn't you hear me calling? Whatever happened to the boat? I've already had dinner." She reached back as she spoke and switched on the table lamp. Derek stepped into the room, and in that moment Cath's heart stopped. The same hair and eyebrows, one of his shirts, a pair of khakis, even the familiar Docksiders on his bare feet, an appearance so similar—there was where the horror lay—so similar, but not Derek, and Cath, who had left behind the night bus and visionary moments and the perception of evil, needed nothing beyond the common sense she was born with to recognize danger. Though she wanted to scream, she took a breath and closed her mouth. The person who was not Derek came closer, so that Cath saw the elegant, thin leather gloves, one specially made, and understood that she'd feared the wrong things entirely.

"Where's Derek?" she demanded, her voice rising in spite of her efforts. "What's happened to Derek?" She wanted him here, now. She did not want to be alone with Yvonne. Not now, not here.

Beneath the short, masculine wig, her sister-in-law's brow furrowed slightly. "You don't seem glad to see me."

Cath caught her breath and put her hand on her heart. "Of course I'm glad to see you," she said. That was what you said when people visited. That was the normal, sensible thing. And normal and sensible were important, because Derek was not there, because he might come home late, maybe even too late, but she mustn't think about that. "You might have driven up the regular way and knocked on the door. You just about scared the life out of me." Cath could hear that her voice was tight and strained.

"You seem a little nervous, Cath. Perhaps your vacation hasn't done you as much good as we'd hoped. You seem to have lost your sense of humor."

"I don't think this is a joke in very good taste." Cath felt exactly the way she'd felt as a child, alone at the playground with the school bully. Her mouth was dry and her legs had gone stiff. She seemed to have lost some vital link between thought and action.

"Maybe this isn't a joke at all," Yvonne said. "But you were fooled, weren't you? Admit it: Derek and I look alike at first glance. Of course, as children, we were virtually indistinguishable. And inseparable. One flesh, you might say."

Beware of Yvonne quoting scripture, Cath thought. She would have liked to say that, to make a joke, but she seemed to have misplaced humor. Instead, what came into her mind was the musty storage space under the cabin, something Derek had said about the erotic affects of fear, and a sudden awareness of the sort of games the Tolland children might have played. Cath pushed this unsettling revelation aside; Yvonne was always full of snide remarks and insinuations. Cath knew she must not be distracted; she had to concentrate, she had to keep her focus on Yvonne.

"I'm not sure you understand," Yvonne continued, dropping her voice into fake confidentiality, "how dangerous it would be for anyone to try to come between us."

Yvonne sounded very like Derek—how had Cath not noticed that before? At the same time, there was a strangeness about Yvonne, who gave the impression of moving mechanically, unspontaneously, as if gripped by some purpose or idea beyond her control. This was Yvonne and not Yvonne, too.

Outside, the hemlocks scratched against the porch, and a suicidal moth flapped inside the shade of the lamp. Cath wished desperately that Yvonne would leave; she wished that they had never come to the cabin; she wanted never to have to think of Yvonne or her unseemly hints again. Very aware of the cabin's isolation, Cath sat back down carefully and, instead of repeating her questions about her husband, asked, "Who'd ever want to come between you?" as if this were just an ordinary chat.

Yvonne gave her arch "social" smile and took the other twig chair. The lamplight was bright on her body and on her mouth and chin, but the upper part of her face was almost lost in the shadows. Cath could just barely see how restlessly her eyes moved. "I think you know who," Yvonne said.

"Yet you're pretty well established in our lives," Cath remarked. It took an effort to sound calm and controlled, when her arms were running with sweat. "We couldn't do without you."

"That's true." Her tone was judicious, almost detached, as if Cath and the cabin and the situation were not entirely real to her.

"Like now," said Cath. "Silly me, I can't find the car keys."

"You don't need the car," said Yvonne.

"I'm worried about Derek. He left in the boat just before five to run over to the village."

A pause. That was what was odd. Yvonne's speech was oddly paced, oddly punctuated, as if the normal nodes of conversation had been displaced. "The boat."

"Yes, he just got the motor running today. After a struggle." Cath described getting the boat down to the lake and starting up the motor. "Yesterday, we took the oars." She heard herself rattling on, filling up the silence, pushing back the darkness. Her arms trembled as if this were physical work with actual weight. "I went for a swim yesterday. The water was terribly cold."

"I know what happened yesterday," Yvonne said.

"Well, you can see why I'm worried."

"Derek has more sense than to swim this early. He's not fond of swimming at all." So flat, so positive. That habitual certainty was what Cath hated about Yvonne.

"You have your car. You could run around to the town. What is that—ten, fifteen minutes?"

"We could go together," Yvonne said.

Cath's heart jumped, confirming her apprehensions. Although she had to pretend this was just an ordinary visit, she did not want to leave the cabin—or the gun. "I'd better stay," she said. Her voice was higher; she could hear the nerves, and Yvonne would, too. "Derek might still come back. I just can't help thinking there's been some problem with the boat."

"The boat," Yvonne repeated again. "The boat is unlucky. But not for you. You were out in the boat yesterday. You were lucky in the boat."

"I should have listened to Derek. He said the water would be too cold."

"As if he cared," Yvonne said.

"Derek is my husband," Cath said. She spoke carefully, for she could feel anger creeping in under her anxiety.

"That's irrelevant. Your marriage has always been irrelevant. Now especially. You've never really been the right type at all."

"The right type?" Cath asked, though she wanted to ask, *Then why are you here?*

"The right type for Derek. But you know what I'm talking about. Don't pretend you don't."

"Like Jane Henkel."

Yvonne made a face. "Like Jane Henkel."

"Jane's gone to Aspen," Cath said.

"And you think she'll be the last?" Yvonne was scornful.

"I think so." Cath wondered if she believed that.

"But maybe she won't be. Is that why you've been spending so much time at the lawyer's?"

Cath did not answer.

"I know all about that," Yvonne said. "Running to your lawyer." She gave a deliberate, artificial laugh to indicate contempt rather than amusement. "You really are pathetic, telling him you'd lost a baby."

Cath's stomach clenched and her cheeks flushed, as fear fought with embarrassment. How did Yvonne know that? Who had told her? Was it Luc? And if that, what else? Cath knew she had to be careful; she had to think what to say, decide how to play her cards. Yet even now with darkness and danger all around, she had a sense that in some inexplicable way, her bizarre, humiliating story was true after all. She'd had a reason, she knew she had, a reason beyond the carelessness of a sunny day, of a happy day. She and Luc had been standing in the newly painted dining room, old friends talking about Aunt Elizabeth, when the words slipped out, escaped from her control and took on a life of their own. She'd gotten careless, that's all, and momentarily succumbed to the impulse to excuse herself, to reveal how the world looked to her. Maybe succumbed to the need for sympathy, too, though that idea disgusted Cath.

"I was able to straighten him out." Yvonne smiled, ignoring Cath's silence. "I assured him that any pregnancy of yours was pure fantasy. I don't think your attorney will take you seriously again. Or that anyone else will, either."

Feeling isolated and humiliated, Cath still did not answer.

"Everyone knows you're unstable," Yvonne continued. "You make up stories and lose your memory and you stabbed Derek. That was unforgivable. I trust you haven't forgotten that."

"I stabbed Derek," Cath admitted in a small voice. She felt at fault there and knew that weakened her case. She felt herself sliding toward a dangerous passivity. "I know I had a reason, but I can't remember what it was."

"Can't you?" Yvonne put on a thoughtful expression, and Cath noticed that adjustment, as if Yvonne realized this was a situation requiring the pretense of reflection. "I suppose it was that little music student. Stupid girl."

Anger surprised Cath. It boiled up like grease on an open flame, and she recognized the murderous fury that had flooded her mind one winter day, leaving devastation behind and memory-erasing madness. She had not remembered, not until now. She saw her Hartford studio with spring snow falling beyond the windows and Sarah, long black hair, dark eyes, rapt expression. They were working on the Franck sonata, preparing Sarah for an audition. *Beautiful, beautiful,* Cath had said, and, in the same moment, she noticed that Sarah was pale, that there were circles under her eyes. Cath hadn't thought to ask more. She had been so concentrated on the music, on the line. Or had she feared even then? Feared Derek's interest? Feared his offers to run Sarah home so that she wouldn't have to take the bus? Feared his willingness to accompany Sarah? Maybe Cath had known the day she came into the studio and found him already seated at the piano. Cath had seen his eyes and perceived his longing, a desire, she now realized, for something more subtle and complicated than sex, something strange and powerful and sinister, something inextricably connected with Yvonne. Cath wondered if she'd known that day in the studio and had unconsciously been afraid. She wondered if that refusal to see what was in front of her marked her real madness.

"Sarah was my student," Cath said, anger making her careless. "She bled to death in the girls' locker room at her high school."

"Girls that age have no sense."

"She was sixteen, pregnant, and frightened to death. She was my best student, so full of promise, such a lovely girl."

"Don't go on about her," Yvonne said impatiently, as if none of this were important. "She took some violin lessons from you, that's all. It was no business of yours."

"No business of mine! That pregnancy ended my career. And almost ended my marriage. You know it should have been my child. You know that. That's how I lost my baby." Cath heard her voice rising to a howl and didn't care. Anger makes everything unreal; it flattens the landscape and prepares you for madness so that you can forget. Forget the snow-lit studio and the kitchen with the knife on the counter. Forget Sarah, forget even her name, but not really. Oh, Cath had always known; she'd known everything—and nothing, as it turned out. She had not envisioned Yvonne—nor imagined this grotesque confrontation.

"Well, he preferred her," Yvonne was saying in a superior tone. "He's never been satisfied with you. You should have shown a little more self-respect and gotten out early on."

"He's promised," Cath said stubbornly.

"I'll bet he promised after Boston. I'll bet he did, just so that you'd go to Hartford with him. And perhaps he promised after Hartford, too. Face the facts: Derek is never going to be faithful, and it's driven you crazy."

"Derek's lovers die," Cath said, for she had access to anger now, and anger pushed her through fear to force the issue. "That's a fact, too."

"They see their situation," said Yvonne calmly.

"And you help them see it. You told Esther—"

Yvonne's lopsided smile was unconvincing. "I told her that no one could ever come between Derek and me. I told her why, and now I've told you."

"You did more than tell her. She died with your painkillers."

"Despair is evil," said Yvonne, and her voice turned complacent, though her mouth remained hard. "You should know all that—you, the music minister's wife. Despair is the ultimate sin."

"Then what is pushing people to despair?"

"She wanted me to go back west. She tried to put pressure on Derek by threatening to call off the engagement. He was still under the impression he wanted to marry her. I had no choice."

Cath took a minute to digest this, and in that moment, terror began to seep back into her consciousness. She took a deep breath and asked, "And Kimberly? Kimberly Delane. She lived in Boston. A mezzo with a beautiful voice who died violently."

"I know all about Kimberly." Yvonne sounded impatient.

"But Derek and I were married then. He was already married."

"Your marriage meant nothing," Yvonne said brutally. "I never worried about you. Kimberly was different. She thought Derek might leave us both for her."

Was that possible? Cath wondered before doubt made her cruel. "He certainly wanted to get away from Boston. Or was it from you? We were happy enough until you followed us to Boston. There was no Kimberly until you arrived. He used Kimberly to keep away from you." As she spoke, Cath realized that this might be true. And if it were, how blind she had been.

"That's nonsense." Yvonne leaned forward into the light, her eyes focused now and dangerous. "We've always lived near each other. We've always included each other in everything. In all our plans. All." Her voice had lost its detachment.

Cath heard resentment and, running underneath it, hysteria. *Be careful,* she told herself, but she couldn't stop trembling. *Besides, Yvonne has started this. If it's time for home truths, let's see how she would like some.* "Do you know what Derek said before we were married?" Cath asked. "He said that I could save him. What was I to save him from, Yvonne? Or was it who? Was it you?"

"Don't be misled by melodrama and flattery. Derek's always been good at both. Especially with singers like you who like their sex with mumbo jumbo. Derek thinks you have a certain 'spiritual dimension'— as if that was what he was after." Yvonne gave a short, bitter laugh.

She looked around the room, taking it all in after so many years: the heavy post-and-beam construction, the rustic paneling, the stone fireplace, the faded prints of bass and trout, the dusty sofa. The single lamp threw the shadows of the beams onto the ceiling, turned the trusses and braces and their multiple shadows into a mesh like a lobster trap. "You can't imagine how perfect this place was. The lake was a world of its own in those days. A world for the two of us. We had to find our own way into life, and no one else's rules made much sense to us."

"And Derek?" Cath asked, for the whole idea gave her claustrophobia. "Did Derek see things the same way?"

"There was no separation in our personalities. Never. How could there be, when we knew what each other was thinking? We were one person." Yvonne gave a smile that was sly and suggestive. "In every sense," she added, so that this time her meaning was unambiguous, and Cath was left in no doubt that the relationship had been sexual. Yvonne leaned back in the chair again so that her eyes sank into the shadows.

In the long silence that followed, Cath struggled with her breathing and understood that this time she could not forget. "And when you both grew up?" she demanded. "When Derek started to want girlfriends? And he did have girlfriends, didn't he, girlfriends who tended to look like you. What about that?" Cath's heart jumped with anxiety.

"Our life as children was perfect," Yvonne said, her determined, confident voice edged with anxiety. "Perfect. Nothing can change that. Or the fact that I had to make certain decisions, that I had to decide what was best for us both. You want to blame me," she said, flaring in anger. "Derek sometimes blames me, too, but it was not my fault that they left us alone so much." She began twisting her hands in her lap, the dark gloved fingers turning over and over. "There was no one else on earth for me," she said. "No one else could ever take Derek's place."

The anguish in her voice turned Cath's stomach. "So you had sex together as children." Emphasis on *children*. "Such things happen, but then he grew up and you didn't. He wanted a different life, and you couldn't accept that." Cath waited to see Yvonne's reaction, which might tell her when the affair ended. It must have been long over, Cath thought, it must have been. She felt that she could not endure to learn otherwise.

Yvonne laughed, a superior, carefree laugh. "There's no way you'd understand how I felt, how we felt, how Derek felt—and still feels. You wouldn't know anything about it. You're a very white-bread sort of person, Cath. That's the reason he's gotten bored with you. Life never would have been perfect with you."

This was an answer that told Cath nothing and only increased her anxiety. "Things were perfect, then?" she asked angrily. "Things were perfect and everyone was happy until the boating accident?"

"The accident ruined my chance for a career, but Derek took over our dream. The accident made Derek a musician."

Although her husband had told her virtually the same thing, Cath asked, "Was it really an accident?"

"Of course it was an accident. He was devastated. I should know."

Cath shrugged. "Derek seems very defensive about it."

"He feels guilty, horrified. The accident was the turning point of both our lives."

"I can believe that," Cath said, before nerves made her reckless. "But I've been wondering if he turned on that outboard motor deliberately. I've been wondering if he wanted to escape from your 'perfect' life."

"And Derek thinks you're so sweet." Yvonne shook her head violently. "He sobbed all the way across the lake. He was only fourteen. He didn't know that no matter what happened I was going to be with him. He didn't understand that he could never leave me."

So Derek periodically felt suffocated and needed to "get away." Cath understood that and that their marital failures might not be her fault after all. She might still salvage something, if she could keep calm, if she could be careful. "You might have built your own life," she said

305

after a moment. "It's not too late now, at least, not for Derek; it's not too late for him to have an ordinary life."

"What do you know about ordinary life?" Yvonne demanded. "You're certifiable. And a failure, while I've been a success. I am a success."

She switched back to her everyday personality, bossy and impatient, full of facts and figures, confident and aggressive. "Gold jacket four years in a row. Top twenty-five percent even in the boonies. Do you know what that took? And now that I'm back at the suburban office, I figure I'll be the top sales person in six months. Maybe I'll switch to commercial properties. You have no idea."

She sounded so normal, that was what was really frightening. She sounded the way she always had, and Cath found it hard to associate sales figures and gold jackets and Yvonne's bossy aggression with the ambiguous person sitting opposite, the person filled with violent longings and homicidal jealousies. "I meant a personal life," Cath said quietly, though she wanted to scream, though it was an effort to control her voice. "I meant a personal life of your own."

"But you see," Yvonne said in a serious tone as if she really did want Cath to understand, "there is no 'my own' at all. There's just Derek. We're inseparable, one person. You can't be expected to understand that or much of anything else about us, because you don't know him well enough. But I understand what Derek really, secretly wants." Yvonne's voice turned venomous. "You think that he wants to escape, to be *saved,* you presumptuous bitch. I know differently. I know what he needs, I see the hidden outline of his future, and I make sure everything happens just the way he wants it to."

"But where is he now?" asked Cath, for his absence suddenly suggested not just betrayal but disaster. Otherwise, why was Yvonne dressed the way she was? What else could her costume imply but that she had become Derek, that something terrible had happened? The blood beating in Cath's throat made her voice quaver. "What's happened to Derek?"

"Listen to you! You've heard nothing I've been saying. He'll be in the village, of course, being seen, establishing an alibi. He knows I'm here; we've planned everything."

"Everything?" Cath asked with a mixture of anguish and skepticism. "Esther and Kimberly, too? I'll never believe that."

"We're inseparable, indistinguishable," Yvonne insisted. She spoke hurriedly, insistently, as if she needed great speed to carry her from one idea to the next. "I've explained to you. Of course, he didn't need to say anything; he didn't need to do anything. I *knew* he wanted to be free. I knew he had to be released from distractions and temptations. Women know there's something special about Derek, that he's out of reach, and that makes him irresistible. But I'm speaking of tonight. We planned tonight. Now that you've come into your money, you're no longer necessary. I'm the only one necessary to Derek. The only one. Everyone else is expendable. You realize that, I know, and I think you're going to accept that you're unnecessary now. Fortunately, everyone knows you're unstable. No one will be surprised if you wind up in the lake."

Cath saw the shadow on the water and felt a terrible emptiness of heart. The world she thought she knew, the ordinary world, had lost its cohesion and ceased to support her. Daily life threatened to morph into the night bus, and Cath realized that though she had risked everything, she had failed. Failed to save Derek, failed to save herself, failed to keep hold of reality. This knowledge was so bitter that she might have given way to self-pity, if Yvonne, confident and on the offensive, had not resumed talking in her incongruously brisk and businesslike voice.

"The lake was the plan from the start. I made Derek see that and he agreed. Why else would I be here?"

Cath gave a little nervous laugh. "Last night I was standing by this stuffed bear," she said, "and you kept asking where Derek was. It's funny, isn't it, because now I have the same question: *Where's Derek?* When you asked, he was over by the moose head, and you were surprised and I didn't know why."

Yvonne made an impatient gesture, but Cath continued.

"I just now understand: he couldn't do it. He didn't want to do it. I know he didn't." Cath gained confidence as she spoke. Though she still had foolish hopes of reasoning with Yvonne, underneath everything, even under her fear, Cath wanted to be proved right; she wanted to know that Derek had chosen her. "You thought he would, you thought he already had, and that's why you were surprised when I called last night."

"Derek isn't always strong enough to do what needs to be done," Yvonne conceded.

"Derek was sorry he'd even thought about it. He saved my life."

"Now there you're wrong." Yvonne lost her detachment, sat forward, clenched her fingers.

"Why must you pretend you know everything! He did. Listen to me for once: Derek saved my life. The lake was terribly cold. We were quite a way from shore, and I could have died very easily. It could have been another boating accident."

"You're lying," said Yvonne. "You're an excellent swimmer. Better than he thought." She moved her head slightly, and Cath saw her eyes move in the darkness like fish in deep water. "He told me you're a better swimmer than he'd thought."

"Then he lied to you. Derek knew perfectly well I'm a good swimmer, and one thing more, he was sorry that I telephoned you. He said to me, 'I wish you hadn't done that.' Don't you realize that he's deceived you? You've said yourself Derek's selfish and self-centered. You can't trust him. You can't be so sure—"

Instead of answering, Yvonne jumped up abruptly. Cath again noticed a stiffness in her gestures, a certain mechanical quality.

"Derek doesn't know anything about this," Cath said, grasping for confidence and hoping to pull Yvonne back to her everyday self. "Even if he knows about this visit, he doesn't know about your ridiculous disguise. I know he doesn't; it's not Derek's style at all."

Yvonne gave a little start, but she was already moving back toward the gun cabinet, and Cath stood up as well.

"Luc Beausoleil has information," she said. "I got Luc to look into Esther's death. And to find Kimberly Delane's name. That's why I've been up at his office so much. We hired a detective, and if I tell them about this visit, about your threats—"

"No one will believe you. Everyone knows you're crazy." Yvonne tugged the handle on the gun case as she spoke, rattling it once, twice. She looked at the cabinet and tried the door again, then again, swearing violently, before shouting, "It should be open. We agreed it should be open. Why has he done this? Why has he done this to me?"

She wore such a terrible expression of loss and devastation that Cath almost pitied her. She remembered Derek leaving, the whole business of "mislaying" his keys—exchanging them, in effect, for her single key—before handing her the key ring and counting them off, *front door, back door, storage area, springhouse, gun case. You never know,* he'd said. And earlier, that demonstration with the guns. The type of shells, how to load, how to put on and off the safety. Even leaving both weapons loaded. Ready. *Just in case,* because *you never know.* Because when it came down to it, just as he'd told her years ago, she was the only one who could save him. And now she knew precisely what his danger was and had always been.

"He's betrayed us both," Cath said. Her voice shook, but that did not matter now. It was too late for deception and even self-control had become irrelevant, because Derek had chosen himself, first, as always, but to preserve her, second. "He left me to you, but he left the gun case keys with me."

Yvonne turned wildly around the room, a sleepwalker awakened too suddenly. Cath saw her eyes light on the table, where there was still a place set for Derek, glass, plate, spoon, fork, and steak knife. Cath backed toward the bedroom and reached around the doorjamb for the shotgun.

"Don't," she said. The shape of future events was revealed as madness and stupidity, and Cath was terrified of what might happen, of what Yvonne might attempt, of what she herself might have to do.

"Please! Don't! You don't understand, he left me the key. He intended to protect me. Please, Yvonne," Cath pleaded, "you must understand; I have the key to the gun cabinet."

"Give it to me," Yvonne demanded. She was perhaps misled by the tone of Cath's voice, by her sister-in-law's obvious terror. "Give it to me now," she repeated, the steak knife in her hand.

When she stepped forward around the table, Cath lifted the shotgun and flicked off the safety. Her arms trembled with the unexpected weight of the weapon. "Stay there and put down the knife."

"It's not even loaded," said Yvonne.

"Derek loaded it for me. He loaded it the first day we came."

"He wouldn't have done that." Yvonne shook her head, wildly, emphatically. "We planned everything. This is what Derek wanted."

With a kind of cold sickness, Cath wondered if some part of this were true, if tonight was to be Derek's escape, for, one way or the other, he could not come back, not now, not ever. "Please believe me, he loaded the gun and showed me how to use it."

"He can't have done that," Yvonne cried. "And that case should have been unlocked. I know he left the case unlocked."

"You saw yourself that he did not. He locked it and he left me the key. Yvonne, I don't want to hurt you. I don't like you, but I don't want to hurt you."

"You're lying," said Yvonne, in a voice neither her own nor Derek's. She lunged for the barrel, slashing out with the knife at the same time, so that Cath stumbled back and almost fell. But as Yvonne tried to wrench the gun free, Cath clasped the trigger and the shotgun discharged in a terrible wet explosion with a smell like firecrackers and another raw, primal smell that went with the spray of stickiness everywhere. In the roar of the shot, Yvonne fell silently and the shotgun dropped soundlessly after her. Deafened, Cath stood in the doorway of the bedroom and watched reality rearrange itself. There was smoke in the new reality and a dreadful smell and someone who was both Derek and not Derek, lying on the floor with a great red wound in the chest.

Cath knelt down after a moment and took Yvonne's wrist and

tried to feel a pulse but touched only the slippery stickiness of blood. She knew she should check the big artery in the neck, but she could not make herself reach across that dreadful wound. She could not; events had escaped her and the world was sliding hopelessly out of control, leaving her deathly sick. Cath straightened up. There was blood on her hands and she frantically wiped them on her jeans, staining them, too, with Yvonne's blood. Her face was wet and her legs. Yvonne seemed to have been reconfigured as a pollution Cath would never escape. She pulled up her shirt and wiped off her face, but everything she touched turned to blood. The smell was overwhelming; she was soaked to the skin in blood, sweat, and urine, and, seeing the mess on her clothing, Cath tore off her sweatshirt and pulled down her jeans. Her shoes were soaked, too, and as she tried to kick them free of her jeans, she slipped and fell against Yvonne, who was also somehow Derek, who was a sodden, disastrous ruin, who was her fault, her own doing.

Cath gave a cry of horror and thrust herself from the body. She struggled to her feet, her hands, arms, and torso smeared fresh with blood, her mind a jumble of images laced with the sound of the shotgun. She had to get away. She had to leave. If she stayed a moment more she would be lost, forever beyond rationality. She reached the door and began struggling with the knob, which slipped and slid under her wet hands. She twisted the knob with the front of her T-shirt and managed the door, then ran outside into the darkness and vomited over the porch rail. Cath could taste blood and bile. She pulled up her T-shirt and wiped her face, then, feeling the dampness against her chest, pulled off the shirt, too. She'd never get clean if she didn't get away.

Cath stumbled down the steps, slipping twice, her bare feet wet, too, then lunged across the yard, scraping against the trees, against the bushes, feeling nothing but the sour aftermath of nausea and the panicked throb of her blood. The long grass that lashed her legs kept her straight along the drive, though she fell in one of the ruts, and struggled up, aware of her arms, surprised by their curious white coldness in the moonlight, and by the strangeness of her bare legs, bleeding now from the branches and brambles. But the necessity of reaching the road, of escaping the cabin and gun smoke and the reeking stickiness of blood filled her whole mind, allowing nothing else, not even the events that had precipitated her flight. The clouds heaved the moon high into the silver sky and there was the dirt road, pale in the reflected light, cold and dusty underfoot. Cath followed it until she saw Walt's yellow windows and heard Rex barking, frantic with the smell of blood.

19

- - - - - - -

"THERE ARE ALTERNATE REALITIES," CATH remarked, and the large red-brown face near her made a sound between a grunt and a growl. A string of saliva glistened like an icicle from its mouth. "There are alternate realities," she repeated. "The trick is to remember that yours isn't the only one."

The face tipped to one side, quizzical, half sympathetic, then dropped down onto a large pair of paws. There it rested, level with her head, watchful but not unfriendly, not as long as she stayed where she was, which was wrapped in a blanket and shivering on the floor of Walt's cabin. She was not to get up. If she got up, moved around, showed evidence of violence or craziness, Rex was supposed to growl and threaten. Cath had no problem with that; she was not only lying down but lying low. With light and a friendly face, she had nothing to worry about except the notion of alternate realities. If Cath closed her eyes, she saw stars, nebulas, clouds of possibly malign intent. "The world is atoms and the void," she told Rex. "Darkness lit by electrical waves." Rex, smelling the excitement of the hunt but hearing the paradoxical calm of her musical voice, raised his muzzle and agreed life was mystery.

"You've got to know you're only partially right," Cath said and began to weep quietly, because though she'd escaped the worst, though she was alive and sane and back in the real world, she knew that Derek was gone forever. "Forever," she told Rex, who raised his head as if to ask how she could be so sure. "He'll never come back," she insisted and started to sob in earnest.

The troopers arrived with an ambulance and an emergency medical team. When Cath said that she was cold, they gave her another blanket, but she would not let go of Walt's, which was khaki and stained from Yvonne's blood. With Cath loaded on board, the ambulance roared for the Northway and headed south. "Where are we going?" she asked, but they would not tell her. "I'm not hurt," she said. "There's no need for all this." But they didn't answer that, either. Official personnel don't need to answer everything. Or anything, if they don't want to. Especially official medical personnel. Realizing that, Cath went to sleep, because they had given her something, something, they said, to make her feel better.

Cath knew she was under observation. She could feel it. Single room, barred window, closed door, toilet en suite. She still had the blanket, though, and when she got out of bed—hospital bed, high sides, a nuisance to get over—she wrapped the blanket around her shoulders and went to the window. Bars, a bad sign, and outside, a city. Recognizing a bad alternate reality, Cath felt a leap of fear, a sudden rattling of her heart. But there were no palm trees, no pastel high-rises, no hot, white southern sun. She was not back in Florida; she had avoided the night bus. Albany, maybe? Would Albany be the nearest big hospital? The nearest big psychiatric hospital, that is, because, of course, they thought she was crazy. It was crazy to shoot someone for wearing a wig; it was crazy to run naked down the road for help. She'd probably done other crazy things, too.

Breakfast came. Cath drank the juice and the coffee. The egg was repulsive; the toast stuck in her throat. Shortly afterwards, the troopers appeared, tall, rather good-looking, very neat and clean. She admired their grooming, their perfectly straight hairlines. The troopers brought a military sense of order that Cath found appealing under the circumstances. She wondered if their spiffy turnout was designed to comfort the distressed, but she knew better than to ask that question.

They had plenty of their own questions, in any case. Why had Yvonne come? Where was Derek? Had she, Cath, fired the gun? Why had she done that? Where were the car keys?

Cath clutched the blanket and tried to give them an account, but maintaining coherence was difficult when there were so many details, so many alternate realities. Her own reality had been shot full of holes. "I've been a great fool," she told them and watched them write that down. "I thought nothing could touch me. I felt some exception would be made for me."

The trooper looked up, blond, intelligent, alert. He was exceptionally alert, Cath noticed, watchful as a cat, waiting to pounce on the birds and mice of inconsistency and revelation.

"And your husband?"

She had already told them that Derek had taken the boat out on a memory trip. *At quarter to five.* They liked that and wrote the time in their little books. They liked precise times, forgetting time is relative. *He was going across to Schroon Lake village.* They liked that, too. A precise destination, though that might be relative, as well, for Cath remembered he'd headed north. *Around the island,* she said. They were puzzled by his detour, as quizzical as Rex. The blond one tipped his head in just the same way, so that Cath gripped Walt's blanket to keep from mentioning alternate realities. She shrugged. She had already tried to explain the memory trip. *Yvonne's hand,* she'd said. *You surely noticed her hand.*

They left after an hour or so when the RN on duty announced that a doctor had come to examine Mrs. Tolland. The medical staff treated her carefully, as if she was fragile—or dangerous. A physical exam first, the stethoscope cold as ice, then more questions. In the repetition of answers, reality began to congeal like fat, and what had been fluid and mysterious became banal. *I was frightened. Yvonne went to the gun case. When she found the case locked, she picked up a steak knife. It was on the table, because I'd left a place set for my husband. He'd expected to be back before dark.*

Afterwards, Cath slept. When she woke up again, she knew where she was. She was in the Psychiatric Center in Albany. Being evaluated. Being interrogated. Contemplating heartache. What she knew was this: Yvonne was dead and Derek would never come back. Never. He had *departed, decamped, absconded. Taken French leave.* Though she'd done her best. Though she'd ignored his failings and, despite a moral quea-siness, had let herself sink into his psyche until she'd come to see the world through his eyes. That had worked for a time, and, when it failed, she lost her memory and half her mind and prepared to sacrifice herself for him in a burst of folly. He'd taken her up on the offer, that was clear, and the only surprise was the completely unexpected price of his freedom and happiness. The cost was the deafening roar of a shotgun, the fleshy devastation of buckshot at close range, and a guilty regret for someone she had never liked. That was the cost, and paying the bill had drained half the life from Cath.

Renee took the boys to early Mass so that Henry could make the midday soccer game, and the house was unnaturally quiet without the children's rowdy exuberance. Luc sat in the kitchen with the paper and a cup of coffee, enjoying Sunday's dispensation of extra time, a late awakening, legitimate procrastination. He'd escaped Mass and the start of the soccer morning because he was expecting his brother-in-law, who was bringing over a newly refinished piece of furniture. As Luc waited, he worked the morning's crossword, penciling in the an-swers neatly and quickly. He found that the satisfaction of completing the morning's puzzle got his day off to a good start.

Renee had wanted him to come to Mass, but Luc said that they could hardly leave Vincent to bring in the new bureau alone. He would go later; perhaps he and Vincent would make the eleven o'clock service.

Renee had raised her eyebrows at this hope, but she'd loaded the boys into the station wagon, Henry with the big soccer gym bag, Jack still too young to play but entrusted with two of the game balls and full of importance. Luc would have to stop by the field later to cheer for Henry, and he smiled as he thought of his son, slight and eager, rushing from one side of the field to the other, flushed with exertion, enthusiastic rather than talented, but full of joy.

24 across: Silent star ZaSu. He tapped his pencil on the table impatiently. Of course, ZaSu PITTS. A neat row of letters, suggesting another deduction: 17 down must be TOUCAN. Luc was considering *25 across: Dark area on the moon,* when he heard the van outside and Vincent's cheerful double toot on his horn. Luc put down the paper and went to the door. "Time for a cup of coffee?" he asked.

"Always time for coffee," said Vincent. When he opened the back of the van, Luc saw a sturdy, honey-colored commode with handsome brass knobs on the doors.

"Hey, that's pretty nice. I'll bet it didn't come out of the junk shop looking like that."

Vincent smiled. "For my nephew," he said.

"We'll have to have the 'how to treat good furniture' lecture," Luc said.

"He'll take care of it," said Vincent. "Henry likes nice things."

"He will by the time you're done with him. You'll have him a cabinetmaker."

"He does like working with the tools." Vincent glanced at the house, clearly expecting Henry and Jack.

"They're at Mass at the moment. The before-soccer Mass. I said we might make the eleven A.M. service."

"Might," agreed Vincent, though they both knew that they would sit and talk in the kitchen, drinking coffee and finishing up the breakfast rolls. The brothers-in-law were simpatico; Luc had liked Vincent from the first, finding him a comfortable, relaxing personality, the eye of the storm among the volatile Courtemanches, a discreet person, a sensible man. For his part, Vincent had never forgotten that Luc was one of the few people who had encouraged his interest in building fine furniture. Luc was the only one in the family who hadn't thought that Vincent was crazy, feckless, deliberately difficult, and now Vincent never made any serious business decision without discussing it first with Luc. Vincent stopped by almost every Sunday, for dinner, of course, and to play with the boys, but also to chew over the events of the week and the Red Sox's prospects with Luc. If Luc had something on *his* mind, though, he saved it until the workweek, when he often found himself standing in Vincent's shop, leaning up against the bench, and talking about whatever was bothering him. That's how Vincent had gotten to know a bit about the Tollands' marriage and more than was quite proper for Luc to have disclosed from Confidential Reports.

The two men got on each side of the commode and slid the heavy oak piece from the van. They took the shelves out to make the commode lighter and easier to maneuver, then wrestled it up the steep, narrow stair to the boys' room.

"Looks great," Luc said, as Vincent replaced the shelves.

"Good solid construction, that's the main thing in kids' furniture." As Vincent spoke, something in his expression made Luc think that his brother-in-law ought to have children. He ought to get married and have children of his own. Of course, that's what Renee had been saying for years, but it was true, Luc could see that. The only problem was the girl. Vincent hadn't yet found The Girl, the one beyond doubt. Although Renee got exasperated by her brother's reluctance to commit himself, Luc understood that, despite Vincent's air of confidence, almost of complacency, his was an intensely idealistic and romantic temperament. As Luc saw it, most people go through life guided by that mediocre trio, the usual, the possible, and the sensible. Vincent had pursued his heart's desire, and, having found success once, saw no reason why lightning shouldn't strike again to produce The Girl.

Downstairs in the kitchen, they decided on second cups of coffee and heated up the Danish in the microwave so that the thick white sugary frosting turned translucent and the fruit got runny. Vincent hadn't had any breakfast, it turned out, and when he put on a couple eggs, Luc said he might as well have one, too. There was a melon in the icebox, and they had that and orange juice and figured they'd call it brunch, then catch the second half of the soccer game. They could trade cars with Renee and let her get a break. They'd gotten this planned and some trades settled for the Red Sox and exchanged sentiments on the selectmen's crackpot idea of taxing tools and home office equipment, when the phone rang. Vincent leaned back lazily and picked up the receiver. "It's your answer service," he said. He handed the phone to Luc, then watched his brother-in-law's face darken.

"I see. When did this call come in? Jesus Christ! That's why I have a service. I could have gone and checked the answer machine myself. Yeah, yes! Give me the number. That's his home? Just because he didn't say it was an emergency—probably didn't remember my home phone. Yeah. Right away. Any others, you call my cell phone. Got that? Anything like this, right to my cell phone. Right. Thanks." Luc hung up and took a breath.

It couldn't be the children, Vincent thought, or Renee. It couldn't be anything that had happened to the children.

"Cath Tolland shot her husband," Luc said. "Some guy in the Adirondacks called hours ago."

Vincent's stomach dropped and his chest clenched; he felt his forehead slick with dampness. "When?"

"Last night." Luc picked up the phone and dialed. "Mr. Swickley? Am I speaking to Walter Swickley? Luc Beausoleil. I'm Cath Tolland's lawyer. I just got your message."

He was on the phone for fifteen minutes, moving around the kitchen restlessly, stopping to scribble notes, gesturing for Vincent to hand him more paper. When the conversation was finished, Luc sat down heavily at the table. "What a fucking mess."

"What's happened?"

"Derek Tolland's sister was shot at close range with a double-barreled shotgun. Allegedly by Cath."

In the normal run of things, Vincent would have felt the shock of an acquaintance's tragedy: he'd done some work for Yvonne Tolland.

But this was not the normal run of things and he found that his whole focus was on Cath, who had entered his imagination in some subtle and mysterious way. The idea that that attractive and remarkable person had killed someone was inconceivable. Vincent remembered *allegedly,* and took comfort in the legal terminology. Luc knew what he was doing; he was the expert; he'd said Cath had "allegedly," not "certainly," shot Yvonne Tolland. "And the husband?"

"Nowhere in sight. The first reports were inaccurate, because his sister was wearing his clothes and a man's wig." Luc paused to let this sink in.

"What the hell was she up to?"

"Nobody knows, least of all Mr. Swickley, whose chief concern seems to be that he loaned Cath a blanket."

"A blanket?"

"She'd gotten blood on herself and ripped off all her clothes. Christ! I'll have to go to the office and try to contact a criminal lawyer in the jurisdiction. That's Essex County. I sure as hell don't know anyone in Essex county," Luc said, standing up. "I'll have to go into the office."

"You'll have to go north," Vincent said.

"I'm not a criminal lawyer, and it's out of my jurisdiction. Cath needs a good defense lawyer, someone who does trial work and can manage a homicide inquiry. I'm strictly property sales and legal documents, the occasional misdemeanor as a favor. Vin, I'm not competent to handle an alleged homicide. Probably a manslaughter," he corrected himself, "but still . . ."

Vincent did not budge. "You have those detectives' reports, haven't you? The ones you told me about? Won't they be important? You've got to go north with them, and I'll drive you. You can make your calls from the car."

"I can get her a lawyer just as easily from here. Fax his office everything that's needed or send it on by courier."

His brother-in-law set his face and shook his head. "She'll need friends. She'll need people who believe in her."

Luc hesitated. The papers were confidential, and he'd rather put the whole mess off until Monday. This was something best handled at a distance, best for all concerned, best for him, best for Renee, perhaps even best for Vincent, who was showing an unhealthy interest in a woman who was crazy and married and probably indictable.

At the same time, Luc did not feel completely easy with his own conduct. True, he had gone by the Tollands' house with copies of Cath's will, when he could have stayed in his office. And he had asked old Stel Pye about the Tollands' whereabouts, when he could have minded his own business. Luc done the normal things a lawyer could reasonably be expected to do. And yet, there were the detective agency's reports, and more than that, his own instincts, his observations—ignored, perhaps tragically ignored—of Cath's fatalism, her indifference to her wealth, her dislike of her sister-in-law.

"I didn't imagine anything was wrong," he protested to Vincent. "The Tollands were off on a holiday. I assumed domestic harmony was restored. There was nothing but coincidence against her husband, anyway."

Vincent didn't answer, and, as so often, Luc found himself moved to fill the silence. "If she'd had real doubts, I hardly think Cath would have gone away with him to the back of beyond."

"Have you ever heard her sing?" Vincent asked. "Something serious, a concert performance?"

Luc shook his head; what this had to do with the situation was beyond him. "Pop songs in the car, that's all."

"When she sings, you feel great things are possible from her. She has an extra dimension, as if she could do a great thing, take a great risk, make a great commitment. Maybe that's what she did."

"Maybe," said Luc. Despite his mother's warnings about generations of crazy Mackeys, he still felt a twinge of pity and regret: Vincent understood his old friend better than he did.

"So you'll go," Vincent said, "and I'll come with you."

*　　*　　*

Late afternoon: the rattle of trays in the hallway signaled an early dinner. Cath sat up in bed, the khaki blanket still around her shoulders. Whatever they had given her had worn off. The world was flat. She was indifferent to the rosy descending light on the buildings across the street, to the finned shadows, the unclouded sky. Although totally lacking the interest and energy to do so, she knew that she should make an effort. Demand a lawyer. Speak again to the troopers. Find an exit. She should be *charged or released,* as Amnesty International liked to phrase it. And what might the charge be? Murder? In the calculus of crime, there are several degrees of murder—all serious. Manslaughter? Man, of course, including woman. Assault with a deadly weapon? Closer, but *assault* didn't exactly describe the moment of confusion and terror that was dissolving, retrospectively, into ambiguity. Self-defense? Defense against what? What were you so afraid of? the troopers had asked. A wig? An unexpected visit? The sight of Derek's clothes? The answer to that, besides isolation and a change in the atmosphere, lay in Syracuse and Boston. The troopers would have to read those Confidential Reports and decide if she'd had reasons to be frightened and just how bad she ought to feel about having unlocked the gun case and taken out the shotgun.

Reasons, events, possibilities, and disasters tumbled in her mind, getting buffed up for presentation like stones in a polisher and giving her a thundering headache. Though she wanted to forget everything and go back to sleep, Cath could feel her mind running ceaselessly and slightly off kilter, as if some essential flywheel were missing. She walked around the room until, exhausted by indecision and uncertainty, she lay back down on her bed. A few moments later, there was a tap on the wide hospital door. Luc Beausoleil and another, taller man stepped into the room.

"Oh, Luc!" she said. Tears came into her eyes at the sight of his familiar face. How wonderfully ordinary he looked in his blue polo shirt and chinos. "How kind of you to come." She scrambled off the bed and put her arms around him. "How kind of you to come all this way."

Luc hugged her and kissed her on both cheeks; he had a tendency to turn courtly under pressure. "Three hours up the Pike is all." Luc was trim and smart in his weekend clothes; his face was composed, concerned but not alarmed. He managed to give the impression that he'd been just waiting to go lawyering. "Vincent drove me so that I could work the phone on the way up," Luc explained. "You've met Vincent, my brother-in-law?"

"Yes," Cath said, but she had to struggle to incorporate the second man, taller, younger, reddish hair and mustache, snub nose, round, bright eyes, into her present reality. She saw a green van parked in front of her old house and the way the ground rotates when a bike spins out on gravel. "You only appear when I am in trouble," she said.

"We met one day outside your office," Vincent told Luc. "When Cath took a nasty fall from her bike."

Cath felt a jolt, a sudden contraction of her muscles, a purely physical memory. "You hit my bike and almost ran over me," she corrected.

"I sure had to hit the brakes. My front bumper caught your wheel."

"I fell on the gravel."

"You got scuffed up pretty badly. I'm sorry."

"I wasn't looking where I was going," Cath said. "That was another bad time for me. You haven't exactly met me at my best."

"Oh, but I've heard you sing," Vincent said. "You didn't let me tell you that day." Cath took another look at him, at the smooth, open face, the wide cheekbones, the kind, anxious eyes. *You had the perception of evil and then you lost it,* her husband's voice said in her ear. Could you acquire the perception of good? she wondered, for she knew at a glance that this person was trustworthy, just as she'd known that she must avoid Raoul's chartreuse gown and beautiful car, just as she had known, always known, always denied, that there was a shadow behind Derek's eyes. But she must avoid thinking of unbearable things if she was to remain in control.

Vincent started talking nervously about a concert where she'd sung Monteverdi, and Cath thought of concerts and singing and a normal life, and managed to smile. Simultaneously, Luc, brisk and official, told her that he'd located a good firm, old and established, well connected, too, which might be important. He'd had a chance to talk to Tom Jenkins, senior partner at Jenkins, Rodriguez, and Reid, who'd recommended Michele Rodriguez. "Very experienced. Very tough."

"Yes," said Cath, though he might have been speaking Greek. "I'm so glad you've come."

"You need a specialized lawyer," Vincent said.

Cath looked from one to the other. She realized that she was not normal yet, that shock had affected her, that her train of thought had been derailed by emotion.

"A criminal lawyer," Luc said, clearing his throat slightly. "I don't handle felony cases."

Vincent glared at him, but Cath said, "I've been trying to figure out just what I've done. Legally, I mean. In actuality, I shot Yvonne."

Luc sat down in the visitor's chair. "You told the police that?"

"The state troopers," said Cath. "What else could I have told them? It was obvious I'd shot her. I told Walt I'd shot her. Derek betrayed us both, you see. He was intent on saving himself—whatever the cost."

Luc didn't appear very happy with this analysis. "Want to tell me what you told the police? You'll have to tell Attorney Rodriguez, too, but I need to get some idea—"

"You'll have to tell me how far back to go. That's the thing, knowing how far back to go." And then she shook her head, because the trick was managing alternate realities. But maybe survival required many skills. Virtuoso adjustments. An unending attentiveness to pitch and tone.

"Let's start with your decision to come north," said Luc. Then, to Vincent, "You've got those phone numbers? See when we can meet with Trooper Callihan, then call Attorney Rodriguez. Tell her we've arrived, that we have information for her. Here, wait. My phone card. Use this."

Vincent went out, reluctantly, Cath thought, and she was sorry to see him go, for there was something indefinably reassuring about him.

As soon as his brother-in-law was gone, Luc became both more businesslike and more confidential. "You know that attorney-client conversations are privileged?"

"Yes," said Cath.

"Now, while Vincent's out of the room: have you anything you want to tell me privately? He could be questioned, you understand. He could be asked to testify against you. Which I cannot be." Luc waited.

Cath was surprised. "There's nothing I can tell you that I haven't already told the troopers."

Luc studied her face for a few seconds, then sighed. "All right. This vacation trip. I was a bit surprised when Stel Pye told me."

"Well, the holiday was a gamble," Cath admitted. "I couldn't bear what I'd learned and I wanted to live as if the world were hopeful."

Luc raised one eyebrow. "Just the facts, Cath. Just the facts for now."

So she gave him times, times and dates, though the facts were shifty, though time is relative, though even destination can become uncertain. A hike, a swim; a shadow on the water, a rustle in the leaves, a peculiar heaviness in the air; the keys, the table set: insignificant things until the gun discharged and her life shattered.

"You're saying that Yvonne picked up a knife after she found the gun case locked? Is that right?"

"Yes. But there won't be prints. Yvonne was wearing gloves. She always wore gloves on her damaged hand, of course."

"But she had gloves on both hands last night?"

Cath nodded. How odd to be talking to Luc, her emissary from ordinary life. How strange to be putting all this into words, as if events could be caught, held, sanitized.

"Walt said that you left all your clothes in the cabin," Luc observed cautiously, after they'd gone over the events of Yvonne's visit in some detail. He forbore to mention that it was her lack of clothing which had landed Cath in the psychiatric ward.

"I was soaked in blood. The place smelled like a slaughterhouse.

At close range, a shotgun—" Cath saw the moment when the world was altered and covered her mouth with her hand. She couldn't speak for several minutes; Luc's pen scratched on softly, putting down facts, times, circumstances. Reining in chaos. "I had no idea what such a gun would do," Cath said when she regained control.

"And that was all you discussed with the troopers? Just what had happened between you and Yvonne?"

"Yes."

"You didn't mention any earlier incident?"

Cath shook her head.

"I'm not referring to the detectives' reports. I'm referring to whatever happened between you and Derek before you left the city."

"I stabbed Derek," Cath said. She thought Luc gave a little start at that. She thought that had gotten under the lawyerly calm which was both irritating and reassuring. "That's the truth. Yvonne helpfully reminded me of the reason: he'd slept with one of my students and caused a disaster."

Luc made rapid notes as he listened. When she was finished, he looked up from his yellow legal pad and said, "Do not volunteer that information."

"I'm occasionally crazy, but I'm not a fool."

"When people are in shock," Luc said patiently, "they are not always prudent."

"I'm afraid I've done a good many imprudent things."

"But stabbing your husband is not the one to mention," Luc said.

"None of this seems quite real. I keep thinking that Yvonne will show up the way she did in Florida, that Derek will call, that there's been some cosmic error. I could believe I'm asleep and just haven't waked up yet." Her voice dropped to a whisper. "You understand that I thought I could save him. That was pride and foolishness. I understand that, of course. But he made me believe it was possible. He made me think that I could save him."

"Save him from what?" Luc asked, frowning slightly.

"From himself, I supposed. But what he really wanted was for me to save him from Yvonne."

Luc didn't answer.

"You don't believe me, do you? But why else wouldn't he have come back? Why would he have given me those keys? That key ring was in his pocket the whole time, right up to when he left yesterday. And the car—he took the car keys, too, so that there was no way I could leave."

"We'll get another set of car keys made for you."

"I don't care about the keys," she said angrily. "It's what their absence means. You don't want to think about what I've said. You don't want to think that he planned this. You think I'm paranoid and off on the night bus again."

"I'm thinking as your legal counsel," Luc said. "And I'm thinking that I wouldn't care to defend the case on your theory."

"And yet it's the truth. Please believe me, it is the truth."

Luc signed and reached over to touch her hand sympathetically. "Remember, Cath, cases aren't necessarily defended on the truth but on plausibility. On what a jury will believe."

At that, emptiness opened within her like a sinkhole. "Belief has put me where I am," she said. "Now only the truth will do, and the truth is that Derek will never return. Never of his own free will."

"That's another thing," Luc said. "Has he access to your funds?"

"To our joint account and our checking account, certainly. To my trust fund?"

"No, that's safe. But we'll have to close both those accounts tomorrow. You can give me power of attorney and I'll get that done." He scribbled something in his notebook.

"He'll need some money," Cath said. "He can't have had much with him. And no car. Just his credit card. He'll need money to start again."

"It's in your interest, Cath, that he show up soonest. There will be awkward questions unless he returns. If cutting off your joint accounts brings him back, so much the better."

"You don't understand," Cath cried, for Luc was cruel to suggest this, to suggest hope, to suggest anything but the inevitable, irrevocable fact of Derek's absence. "It's impossible. Yvonne's dead; he's gone for good."

"You better hope he's not," Luc said. "There's going to be enough interest in the case as it is."

When Cath shook her head, Luc said, "Not too many people get shot in this area. Add Yvonne's curious disguise and your husband's absence, and, trust me, there will be interest. Especially until Derek is located. The press will be all over the story."

Cath's heart jumped at one bound from numbness to frenzy. She had not thought about reporters, about cameras and microphones. She might have to answer questions. She might have to explain her sorrows and failures to the world, her guilt, too, for there was guilt: she had closed her eyes, lost her memory, sacrificed reason itself to her love. And yet, what was exposure compared to the fact that Derek was gone and Yvonne was dead?

Luc was asking her questions again. He wondered how she could be so sure; perhaps he wondered if she had made away with her husband, too.

"Have they found the boat?" she asked. "Derek's boat. Gray fiberglass with an old outboard motor? He was on his way to the village."

"That's one of the first things we're going to ask the arresting officers." Luc got up and went to the hall door. Cath saw him wave, heard him speaking quickly to Vincent. "Everything set? Did you get hold of Attorney Rodriguez and the officers?"

"The lawyer's coming by as soon as she can get here. The troopers will wait for us."

"We've got to go," Luc said, turning back to Cath. "We can't do any more here right now."

"I want to go home." Luc and his friend had brought her a glimpse of the everyday world, and Cath was horrified at the thought of being left behind. "Can I go home? Or will they keep me here or in jail?"

"We have to see whether or not you're to be charged," Luc said. "They'll have to decide that soon. I figure maybe they'll go for another twenty-four hours of observation, but then they'll have to make a decision. If you are charged, that means us going before the judge and asking for a reasonable bail. I've already contacted a bail bondsman."

"I will feel better when I can get out of here," Cath said. She twisted her hands together, then, remembering Yvonne's dark gloves and long fingers, stopped abruptly.

"Of course," said Luc, "but you have to appreciate that the police want to hold you until they feel they know what happened. And, Cath, at the moment it won't hurt for you to be incommunicado. Believe me, there will be TV crews, reporters, all sorts of questions. I don't think you're ready to face that."

Cath bit her lip.

"Don't talk to anyone until Michele Rodriguez arrives. If the troopers come back: not a word."

Cath listened with only minimal comprehension as Luc repeated the plans. What they would do. The things that had to be checked. The people that had to be seen.

"I'm very grateful," she told him. "Very grateful."

"Just do what Attorney Rodriguez tells you to do," Luc said, giving her a close look. "You'll listen to her, won't you, Cath? This is a legal matter. What matters are the legal facts of the case. Be careful of discussing anything else, even intentions."

"Even good intentions?"

"Especially good intentions," Luc said, moving back his chair and picking up his notebook.

"I don't want to stay here," Cath said. She could feel the rumble of the wheels, the sway and lights of the night bus, panic at her back. "I don't want to stay here." There was a high, nervous note in her voice.

"There's nothing we can do about getting you released immediately. And believe me, you're best out of the way." He gave her a quick hug.

"I'm out of the way in a mental hospital," said Cath. She felt numbness beginning to give way to fear and to the threat of tears.

"It will be all right," his friend said. His voice was definite, confident, as if he really believed what he was saying. "We're here. You're with friends now; everything will be all right."

"How can you be so sure?" Cath asked. "The last time we had a smashup."

"But you were all right just the same," he said, and Cath recognized him as a kindred spirit, as one of those hopeful beings with the gift of happiness and the curse of sudden, unasked-for passion.

"An insignificant collision," she agreed.

"For you, perhaps." Vincent's eyes turned sad: he was one for leaps and chances, one who would take risks for love.

Cath saw this so clearly that, even sunk in misery and fear, she roused herself to warn him. "Oh, be careful," she exclaimed, for she wasn't her normal self and could speak from the heart. "Be careful. Don't repeat my mistakes."

"It's maybe too late," he said, meeting her eyes. "It's maybe already too late."

"And do you believe me?" Cath asked, for her old friend Luc was a sympathetic professional who was keeping an open mind; things would be more bearable if his friend, at least, believed in her. "Do you believe I had no choice?"

"Yes," Vincent said, though he hadn't heard the whole story, though he was uninformed, unprofessional, just an amateur of truth and falsehood, just someone else who recognized alternate realities and psychic collisions.

"I feel better now that you're here," she said, meaning not just here in the Albany Psychiatric Center but in a certain state of mind, and she reached out to shake his hand.

20

IT WAS A MINOR CONSOLATION for Cath to think that she need never
see the Adirondacks again. Despite the beauty of the mountains and
the forest, she had no desire to see any more lakes, rustic cabins, or
forest trails. Albany was included in her anathema, and she felt that
she could even pass on the thin, silver Hudson. She'd prefer never to
venture further west than Pittsfield, for she'd had a bad, difficult time
to get through in the Adirondacks. So bad and so difficult that it was
fortunate she'd hesitated to freeze their accounts. Cath hadn't given
Luc the authorization he needed until Tuesday. By that time, Derek
had made ATM withdrawals on Saturday night, Sunday, and Monday,
revealing his progress north from Schroon Lake to Plattsburg to Ot-
tawa. Subsequently, his credit card showed charges in Canada; Derek
was alive; her story, strange as it seemed, had corroborating evidence
and might, after all, be true.

Nonetheless, Cath had still faced questions, assumptions, revelations of things undone or ignored, tales of madness and inattention.
Whose life is blameless? Who couldn't provide a few inches of sensa-
tional prose? Cath had done bizarre, embarrassing things; she had
made mistakes; she had, intentionality aside, killed someone in a par-

ticularly brutal way. Nothing could change that, yet Vincent believed her. He drove Luc home and returned in the green van that had nearly run her over and had involved him in a collision of a different type. He went with her when she faced the grand jury and heard the coroner's report, and he helped her push through the crush of press and gawkers outside the courthouse. But anyone could have done those things; those were ordinary kindnesses. What was extraordinary was that he'd believed in her, in her truthfulness and her sanity. He took the leap of faith that no one else was quite willing to take, and Cath was very grateful.

After the grand jury decided that she had acted in self-defense, and after police from three states finished asking her questions about past history and moments of madness, Cath packed her bags and went to the shore. She needed silence and time and a place without memories; she needed human contacts without complications. On the Cape, she rented a room in a budget motel, walked the beach early in the morning and late in the afternoon, and swam farther out in the surf than was strictly advisable. She ate picnic suppers alone and acquired, impulsively from the local animal shelter, a boisterous spaniel cross that reminded her of her old dog. With this reinforcement, she returned home to clean her house and tidy her garden and see what sort of life might be constructed.

The first weekend she got back, Cath called Vincent to thank him again for all he'd done. He sounded different on the phone, a shy, pleasant stranger. In the Adirondacks, stress and fear and extraordinary leaps of faith had made them close; they'd had things to talk about; they'd felt they understood each other. Now they were back in ordinary life, and it was difficult to know what to say. He asked the conventional things about her trip and the fate of her young roses, and she told him about her new pet, whose name was Nancy. "Such a boring name," she said, "but that's all she'll answer to."

"A dog of character," Vincent suggested, and Cath agreed.

"And how are things with you?" she asked at last. "I know you must have gotten behind in your work."

"No," he said, "no problem there, though I've lost my lease."

"Oh, that's too bad! Nice apartments are so hard to find."

"Oh, not my apartment, my workshop," he said. "The Beamons have decided to raise llamas. They want the barn, so I've got to start looking for something to rent."

"A barn!" Cath exclaimed. She'd felt so one-sidedly in his debt that his need for a barn delighted her. "Don't worry for a minute about a barn." She described hers: big and solid, a full cement floor, electric service installed. Of course, it needed work—what barn didn't? But the roof was sound and the walls could be insulated. Cath was rattling on, and she pulled herself up short. "Would you like to take a look?"

Yes, he would, but she should know that there was smell and mess with a workshop. He ran through the drawbacks: solvents, strippers, lacquers, thinners, varnishes. Noisy power tools and dust. And the van. Clients sometimes came, too, and needed space to park their cars. Would the neighbors complain? The town might require a permit, too.

Despite this litany, Cath sensed that he was eager to come and willing to consider her offer. "Luc can apply for a permit for me. Luc knows all about those things."

Luc's legal knowledge was invaluable, Vincent agreed. Early that evening, he appeared, smelling faintly of cologne and sawdust, and looking neat, fresh, and happy, to pronounce the barn perfect.

"It needs a lot of work," said Cath, reluctant, in turn. Now that he was there, she could see all the defects and drawbacks of the building. She saw the implications of his presence, too, and asked herself if she was ready for even the modest complexity of a tenant to whom she was deeply in debt. "The walls would need to be insulated for you."

Vincent said that he could do that himself and asked about the rent.

"Oh, no rent," said Cath. "This is a thank-you. Please, no rent. Though," she added, suddenly realizing that he might want some guarantee after his troubles with the Beamons, "you certainly can have a lease. As long as you want. The barn is empty; it's going to waste."

The barn was valuable, Vincent insisted, and he refused to take the building for free. He'd been paying the Beamons four hundred dollars a month, after all.

"Fifty," Cath said at last, fearing that she might have offended him. "Pay me fifty a month, then. And you do the insulating."

"No less than a hundred," he said.

"A hundred, all right, but we'll put the money in the repair fund. We'll have the barn done up right."

They agreed to this, and he arrived the next week with big rolls of fiberglass batting. He brought his power tools over, too, and stored them in the garage. From her painting scaffold, Cath watched the trucks come in: Vincent's van and two pickups loaded with power saws and routers, with a planer, a joiner, a drill press, a big worktable, toolboxes full of drills and hammers and screwdrivers and chisels, cartons of clamps, assorted planks and bundles of lumber, and a variety of chests and highboys and desks in various stages of completion and repair. Cath thought that Vincent's friends looked very young, and though she waved and called down in a friendly way, she put Nancy in the house and kept on painting. Cath had not thought of Vincent as being young, but he was. He and his friends were young and happy, and it struck her that she might fit only awkwardly with them. Besides, she did not want to be a nuisance; she'd only wanted to do him a kindness, to help him out, to show her gratitude, nothing more.

Vincent cleaned the barn and framed out the interior walls. He called Cath in to show her how he was constructing a new frame inside the old post-and-beam construction to hold insulation and as a support for the projected wallboard. Cath said he should do whatever was necessary and returned to painting the house. But if she was out on the scaffold when he arrived in the morning, Vincent would stop to see how she was getting along. And if she made lemonade or iced tea at lunchtime, Cath would take him over a pitcher. With these little steps, their friendship progressed, reminding Cath of the old playground game, Simon says. For the longest time that summer and fall, parsimonious Simon dished out only baby steps.

Finally, Cath finished the front of the house, clapboards, trim, door, shutters. Everything. The north side was next, and she faced the difficulty of moving her scaffolding. She was struggling with the staging boards when Vincent came out of the workshop to move the heaviest planks and to help her disassemble and shift the frame. "Oh," said Cath, "that's very kind. You must let me help you inside."

He said that she had lots of painting to do.

Cath insisted there must be some jobs requiring two people, and Vincent admitted that he was about to start the wallboard. With that, Simon, ancient playground dictator and arbiter of the heart, gave them a giant step. When the weather turned too cold to paint the house exterior, Cath kept busy in the barn. Together, they finished off the wallboard, installed a tiled floor for the display area, ran a proper vent pipe for Vincent's woodstove, and put in new, insulated windows. The electrician replaced the old wiring and the plumber ran a water line from the main well.

By the time the workshop was shipshape, they'd developed other resources. Vincent revealed that he could play the acoustic guitar. He liked to cook, too, and appreciated good food—*like all Frenchmen,* he said. By winter, it was easy for Cath to walk over to the workshop and say, "I'm making this or that for dinner. Would you like to stay and eat?" And it was just as easy for Vincent to say, "I'll be done by five." He took to keeping his guitar in the workshop, and after dinner they often sat in her living room, picking out old pop songs and show tunes and folkie things that suited the acoustic guitar. Or else they went back to the music room and played simple duets with the piano or Cath's violin, uncomplicated, happy music, good for exorcising old ghosts. And if on some cold, icy nights Vincent's van remained in the garage, there was no one to know except Stel Pye, who had a very good reputation for minding her own business.

One day nearly a year later, Cath woke to the realization that she was happy. Though there were gaps in her life, though she had losses and regrets, she felt that this was a life she could live indefinitely. Standing by the workbench, watching Vincent make the decorative

335

cornice for a chestnut armoire, Cath felt that she was as close to contentment as she was likely to get. Vincent was carving a thistle with a double serpentine stem, and Cath enjoyed watching the razor-sharp chisel shave away the pinkish wood and unveil the contours of the flower and the jagged spines of its leaves. As Vincent bent over his work, his fine, strong hands steady, his wide, bony face intent, there was a pleasing contrast between his powerful, almost awkward frame and the delicate touch of his clever fingers.

His skill delighted Cath, and after practice or a lesson, she often went out to the barn and watched him work. If she was learning a new piece, she sometimes brought her practice tape with her. Vincent would pop it into his tape recorder and listen, silent but absorbed, for he was very fond of music and of her singing voice.

"The workshop is certainly nice and warm," Cath remarked. Outside, a blustery early fall day hurtled red and yellow leaves across the lawn. She could hear the low-toned hoot of the wind in the stovepipe.

"Those windows make the difference. I haven't had to crank up the woodstove yet," he said, and they smiled at each other. A year of effort had produced a serviceable wood shop, and both Cath and Vincent were happy with the results, not least because converting the barn had cemented their relationship. As she looked around the plain, solid room, Cath wondered if she would be there at all without his support. Vincent always said yes, but she wasn't convinced.

"I saw Professor Daniels yesterday," Vincent remarked after a time, for he had been thinking, too, considering the next step toward his heart's desire, the desire which had been with him almost since the day of the collision, the desire to marry Cath and start a family. "I went over to show him those hinges."

"Oh, did he like them?"

"Well, they're not perfect, but they will do for now. His wife wants to be able to use the piece sometime in this decade."

"It's a lovely sideboard." The caution in her voice told Vincent that she knew what was coming but hadn't made up her mind yet. "I don't blame Willa for wanting to use it right now."

The sideboard was a rare African-American piece from slavery days, purportedly made by one of the professor's ancestors. They'd seen it the previous spring at the Danielses' house. That was right around the time Cath had published her intention to divorce on grounds of "willful neglect and desertion." She felt the awkwardness and humiliation of a public legal notice, and she'd been nervous and unable to concentrate. Vincent had been half afraid Derek might show up, summoned by that legal incantation like an unquiet spirit. But though Cath said Derek would never come back, not without Yvonne, that conviction did not give her comfort. As a distraction, Vincent began encouraging her to get out with him when he visited unusual clients or people like the Danielses, whom she knew already.

In the professor's garage, they gathered around the sideboard, a beautifully proportioned mahogany piece, but dusty and rickety. "Very nice, very rare," Vincent said. "Top-quality work, too. And some really lovely and unusual details, but, as you already know, you've got some problems here. There's some worm damage. Finish is clouded. This tenon is cracked. That's structural; that has to be fixed."

"One of the legs is wobbly, too," Willa Daniels said.

"Probably all of them need regluing." Vincent ran his hands over the wood gently, examined the hinges and drawers, tested the legs. "But under the dirt and grime, you've got a lovely patina. Whatever we do, we've got to preserve that. And match it here on the side where we need to repair the cracked panel."

The Danielses, standing somber-faced beside their treasure, nodded as Vincent scribbled his preliminary notes. Finally, after a slow and painstaking examination, he completed his assessment and was ready to make his proposal. When he sat down at the kitchen table to write up the estimate, Morgan Daniels turned to Cath and said, "So what are you working on now?"

She flushed slightly, well aware that she was, basically and permanently, unemployed. "I've picked up a few music students," she said. "Ones with careless mamas." That was a bad joke and Morgan ignored it.

"And your singing?" he asked.

"Nothing serious except Gorecki's *Symphony of Sorrowful Songs.* Derek thought it might be right for my voice, but of course..." She shrugged to excuse Derek's partiality.

"I'd think it would be suitable. I'd love to hear your interpretation. Did you know that we're planning on doing the symphony with the student string orchestra? I've already started negotiating for a soloist."

"It's a very exciting piece," Cath agreed. "A tremendous challenge for the strings, too."

"It will be that. But I'm serious about hearing you sing. I'd still like to get you working at the college if you've resumed teaching again."

"I'm not doing much, that's the truth, though I'm teaching a few kids from that new experimental outfit in town."

"That's the Summerhill-type school?"

"Something like that. They're on a learn-what-you-please-plan, anyway." Cath thought the school peculiar, and she suspected that the students who'd straggled down almost as soon as the school year started were initially drawn by the spurious glamour of her disaster. Only a few had stuck with their lessons, but those students were doing quite well. They were the ones Cath recognized as like herself, disorganized mortals who craved the order and discipline of music. "I have a couple of vocal students and one on the violin."

Morgan smiled, but his eyes had never entirely left the table where his sideboard's treatment was being outlined on a yellow estimate form. "Ah, Vincent's ready to give me the bad news. You must call me," he added to Cath. "Don't forget."

She had called, finally, and while she hadn't found pupils, she had picked up a little work coaching violinists before recitals. She'd sung for the professor, too, the Gorecki songs, and despite her struggle with the Polish lyrics, Morgan had looked thoughtful and said kind things: even that he regretted they'd already engaged a soprano for the winter concert.

Vincent was still talking about the new hinges, specially ordered, handmade, frightfully expensive. He was going to go over and put them on, because Willa Daniels was refusing to let the piece go out of the house even for a day.

"She must know how much stuff is already piled up in your workshop," Cath teased.

"Morgan wondered if you'd come, too," Vincent said. "He wants to talk you into singing the Gorecki. They've apparently lost the soprano they thought they had lined up."

Cath knew that. Morgan Daniels had called her the previous day. She'd refused, then hesitated, then said she would think it over.

"They need someone to rehearse with the orchestra," Vincent said.

Cath knew she could do the rehearsals, but with Derek gone, that whole part of her life had been destroyed. She wasn't sure she wished to revisit the ruins. As for a public career, even on the most modest level, she was a woman who'd stabbed her husband and shot his sister. Cath feared she lacked either the voice or the temperament to turn such past history to legend instead of disgrace.

At the bench, Vincent had put down his chisel and was sanding the trim, rather perfunctorily, Cath thought.

"I think if you did go to help the orchestra, you might get some more students." Vincent gave her a quick glance. He knew how much she liked teaching. He remembered how excited she'd been to get pupils again, even those sulky, adolescent voyeurs. To his surprise and relief, they proved far nicer than he'd expected, and Cath was great with them; the few who'd stayed would do her credit. Vincent understood that she needed work and music for her happiness, but there was something else she needed, too, a mysterious something capable of lifting the subtle cloud that had descended around the time she filed her divorce petition. At first, Vincent had thought it was fear of Derek's return and then that it was fear of committing herself, as he wished she would, to marriage, to children, to a life with him. But recently he'd decided the cloud had another source and required a different cure. "Morgan Daniels is a great guy. You could just talk to him. Maybe help with the rehearsals until they can hire someone."

Cath sat without answering for several minutes, turning one of Vincent's carving mallets over and over. "You know," she said at last, "the Gorecki was the last thing I ever learned with Derek."

"Maybe that's why you need to sing it. Even just for the orchestra rehearsals. You know you sound beautiful."

Cath shrugged nervously. "It's one thing to sound nice in the living room and another to sing with full string orchestra."

"I'm no expert like your husband," said Vincent, a little stiffly, for he was sensitive to comparisons, "but you're able to put music over. Your singing has soul."

"It's funny, but Derek used to say the same thing. He thought I had a talent for sacred music. He also thought—" But here Cath stopped.

"What did he think?" Vincent asked. They'd talked about her husband in the Adirondacks when everything had seemed terrifying and mysterious. Back in ordinary life, they avoided the topic. Vincent wasn't sure he wanted to know about her married life, which he saw as a mystery and a darkness. He preferred not to explore her attraction to Derek—nor the suddenness of his own to her.

"He thought my illness gave me a certain mystical bent."

"But you weren't ill very long," Vincent said cautiously.

"Just long enough, apparently." Cath was ready to make a joke, to defuse the moment, to avoid the conclusion.

"If he gave you the piece, he must have thought you could sing it," Vincent said.

"Not in public."

She spoke quickly, and Vincent thought he understood how her husband had gained such an immense hold over her: Derek had told her what she could do, had convinced her of her capabilities—and her limits. Though it was maybe unwise, Vincent was suddenly determined to break that spell. "You're different now. You're perfectly well and living a different life. He didn't know everything. He didn't have all the answers."

"No."

She spoke so sadly that Vincent said, "Maybe you have regrets."

"Don't be jealous of him." She slid off the bench and put her arms around him. "Derek's life was terrible and sad; it was madness to love him so. And I did, you know. I really did love him, but it was crazy. I had to be crazy to live with him." Her face turned thoughtful. "I don't have regrets, not now. But the thing is, madness destroys your judgment and takes you over, so that when it's gone there's such a terrible gap. Derek was an immense influence in my life—not necessarily a good influence, not a good influence at all, I suppose, except musically. But when he left so suddenly, the whole world was disarranged."

"You can't give up your singing just because he's gone," Vincent said. "You need to show you're independent of him. To show you're going on and to mark—" But here he stopped. In truth, Vincent wasn't quite sure what such a performance would mean.

"My declaration of independence? More likely, Bon voyage," Cath said reflectively. "We never said good-bye. He gave me the keys and saved my life, but he never said good-bye. It was as if he'd vanished into thin air." She wondered momentarily if Derek and Yvonne had been related at such a fundamental level that there was no way either could survive alone.

"He vanished, all right," Vincent said, "when he should have stayed and made sure you were all right."

"No, I can't blame him for that. That would have been too terrible for him. He did as much as he possibly could," Cath said, "for when it came down to it, he never could have refused Yvonne face to face. He must have chosen her, and he didn't want to, he was afraid to. He didn't want to have to make that choice; he didn't want to have that knowledge. I wasn't the only one to close my eyes, you see."

"And now your eyes are open," Vincent said. "And you're ready to say good-bye."

*   *   *

The green room: nerves and tension; a smell of rosin and paper, old woodwork, musty linoleum floors, powder, deodorant, and perfume. In the big mirror by the door, Cath checked her hair and fixed the one strand that kept coming undone. Her face, unnaturally vivid with the performance makeup, seemed all right, but her inspection was cursory; she did not want to examine her eyes. She spent more time checking the dress, a floor-length black panne velvet, dark and rich with long sleeves and a scoop neckline. Singers still performed in the outfits of a century ago; why was that?

Out in the auditorium, the string players were tuning obsessively and running nervously over the tricky passages. Listening to that familiar, unstructured wash of sound, Cath wished that she was sitting securely in the first violins, notes in front of her, companions all round. What had persuaded her to attempt so much pianissimo, those long delayed entrances, those tremendous crescendos? And everything in Polish, a nightmare language. Cath had come to the college every week for two months, working alternately with Professor Bobrowicz in the Slavic Languages Department and with Ursula Jelonek, one of the school's talented mezzos, repeating the words of the songs until they came to her in dreams, until she woke in the mornings to their alien sounds. Just last week, her tutors finally pronounced her accent reasonable, but what else could they say? The concert was scheduled; everything was set.

And even if singers do get a little leeway on pronunciation, Derek would never have encouraged her to attempt the Gorecki with full string orchestra. For though the auditorium wasn't terribly big, it wasn't lively acoustically, either, and the music department had mustered every cello, bass, violin, and viola in the department for the performance. She was going to need all sorts of sound on the big cadences. There was no way Derek would ever have encouraged her to attempt this.

Even so, the moment Morgan Daniels said the concert would be broadcast, Cath had known that she would do it; she'd known what was missing, known what needed to be done. And more, she'd had a suspicion—which she must recover—that she would manage. Somehow the possibility of success intersected with an image of eternally radiating sound waves to create resolution. She would manage, and she must, for this was the door between her old life and a new one, a new life in more ways than one. Cath smoothed the dress down over her hips and abdomen. A little tight there already. Just a hair.

A knock on the door; it was time. The leggy blond stage manager with the gold stud in her nose appeared. "Ready, Cath?" she asked. A friendly smile. Despite an initial hesitation which Cath had found very understandable, the students had proved generous and agreeable colleagues.

Cath took a breath, raised her head. She was almost sick with nerves until a performance started, and, at the moment, she felt like collapsing on the floor or retreating to the women's lav and hiding under the sinks. Fortunately, she couldn't possibly behave that way in front of a student. "Yes, thanks, Kelly," she said, quite the professional, quite the faker.

"Good luck." Kelly held the door, and Cath, surprised her legs were still functioning, went into the corridor.

Ahead, the stage door opened on a rectangle of brilliant yellow light with a dusty brown darkness beyond it. Dick Fairbrother, the orchestra conductor, was waiting. A slight, stooped man with a shock of wild, electrified gray hair atop a thin, serious face, he was dressed in an extraordinarily ancient tailcoat and trousers, worn thin in the knees, shiny in the lapels, with a similarly ancient and yellowed pleated dress shirt, his lucky performance outfit. With a tight smile he gestured for Cath to precede him, and she stepped out past the basses and cellos to take her place left of the podium. The house lights were down; the auditorium fell away like a canyon from the bright glare of the stage apron. Applause and the rustle of programs, before one of the doors opened at the back, bringing the inevitable latecomers. The rush of natural light accompanying them showed the auditorium nearly full. Vincent's face emerged briefly from the gloom, and Stel Pye's, and there was Luc and his wife, Renee. Cath thought she saw some of her students, too, the big awkward boy with the dreadlocks, the little girl with the punkish dyed hair and the raw, hungry voice: the new people in her life.

"No matter what time we set concerts, someone's always late," Dick Fairbrother whispered ruefully. He smiled tight-mouthed and nodded encouragingly at the orchestra. The string players kept looking from him to their music and back again. In the excruciating moments before the house fell silent, the violinists wiped their sweaty hands and tightened their bows; the cellists checked their end pins, and the bassists tipped their big, boxy instruments back and forth like sailboats tacking on an elusive musical wind.

Then she saw Dick nod, saw the violinists and violists tuck their instruments under their chins, the bassists and cellists set their short thick bows on the strings. Dick Fairbrother raised his hands—large, too large, they seemed, for his slight frame, and white, almost transparent, except for the nicotine stains at the fingertips. His hands hovered in the air for an instant, then rose, softly as doves, to indicate the beat, and he nodded for the basses to begin the long, slow canon that rises in fifths from the acoustic depths. The cellos and the upper strings join in turn, strengthening and lightening the sound, preparing for the moment when the soprano bursts forth in a fifteenth-century lamentation for the passion of Christ, the suffering of Christ. *Passion* originally meant *suffering,* Cath thought, and passion brings suffering, passion *means* suffering, produces suffering. ". . . you are already leaving me," the Virgin complains, "my cherished hope."

The Polish words leapt into her brain, jumped and twisted and threatened to confuse her, before Cath made a conscious effort to put them out. Rehearsals were over. She must be confident in her preparation; she must think of nothing but the polyphonic orchestration, that regular advance through the octaves, that slow, steady tempo; Dick had it set perfectly, the symphony progressing like the quiet, steady breathing of a sleeper who would awaken with her first words: *Synuku mily I wybrany . . . My son, my chosen and beloved.* Cath straightened her shoulders, shifted her feet—a long time to wait yet—and glanced up at the microphones hanging in a line at the precise point the light of the stage met the darkness of the auditorium. Cath had not the slightest doubt that Derek would hear her. Some fluke atmospheric effect, some far-off electrical storm, some almost unimaginable train of coincidence, but he would hear her. She was singing this for him, because of him. And when she finished, he would have lost the reality that still possessed her imagination. He would have to save himself from now on; he would have to look for someone else who knew moments of madness and understood passion.

The strings crept further up the octaves, everything shining, glistening like braiding silk. Cath closed her eyes for a moment, opened them on the darkness before her, and felt her heart skip a beat in panic at the thought she'd missed her entrance. No, not yet, but soon. Ten bars, five bars. The alert calm of performance settled over Cath. She took a deep breath and glanced at Dick Fairbrother, who nodded. *Synuku mily I wybrany*, she began, and her voice, initially almost lost in the continuing murmur of the strings, emerged from the violin range like an instrument suddenly given words. Softly, at first, but steadily gaining strength and volume, Cath began to sing.

"You need to give this piece a sense of inevitability," Dick Fairbrother had said one day at rehearsals. "Of sound rising inevitably. In the strings, in the voice."

Behind her, the massed chords of the strings grew like a wave ready to break over the edge of the stage and splash into the darkness. Cath stretched herself in the knowledge that the words had a long way to go, such a long way, and then the wonderful thing happened, astonishing her and filling her with pleasure: the voice was there. Not her ordinary performance voice, but the one she sometimes heard when singing alone in her house, the voice that was her inner, aspiring sound, the voice she always hoped to reach, to capture, to set free. Not an enormous Verdian instrument, to be sure, but ample, soaring, filling the auditorium and flooding the microphones. The voice seeped out into the foyer, too, and turned itself over in the sunshine. Pulled into the electronic web, it radiated high into the thin, far cold of space.

Fearlessly, buoyantly, the voice escaped sorrow and passion even as it embodied the Virgin's lament, the little prayer from the Gestapo cell, and that sad folk tune, another mother weeping for another son lost in another war.

Between songs, the symphony provides long pauses for the soprano, when the busy strings, building, rising, falling, weave dense curtains of sound that Cath now knew would part for her, because she had survived moments of madness, because she had opened her eyes and awakened her voice. In that joy of discovery, she had no sense of the length and strenuousness of the piece until she came, almost with surprise, to the final stanza, and, singing pianissimo again, let her voice die away into the strings as into the indifferent murmur of the universe. Cath looked up again at the microphones, which she had forgotten along with Derek and Vincent and Yvonne and everyone and everything else except the steady heartbeat of the music, the dense tissue of sound, the unfolding crescendos, the shimmer of her own voice. The last vibrations of the strings faded into the darkness that hovered over the auditorium, into a momentary stillness before a rush of sound and emotion. People were standing up to applaud, startling Cath, who felt herself shiver to be back in awareness, in ordinary life, on stage. She bowed and shook hands with Dick Fairbrother and the concert mistress and applauded the orchestra, who, happy now, were tapping their bows against their metal music stands.

Dick Fairbrother led her out, his hand on her shoulder, whispering something incomprehensible, his bony, lined face flushed. They were called back again and again; someone handed her roses in a cellophane wrapper that crackled as she bowed and gave up a weak, hothouse scent. Cath found the supreme lightness of relief in that faint perfume.

Finally, house lights up and stage empty, the instrumentalists crowded the corridor, noisy and excited, fussing over muffed chords or delayed entrances and crowing over difficulties negotiated. "Tremendous," they exclaimed to Cath, to their professors, to each other.

Cath stood awkwardly in the hall, isolated by the great emotion of the occasion. There was a reception to follow, there would be small talk to make, people to greet. After the hot stage lights, the chilly corridor made her shiver, but she couldn't remember what she'd done with her coat. She was looking around ineffectually when Morgan Daniels bustled into the green room with Willa, Stel Pye, and Vincent, and threw his arms around her. "Magic!"

"It was wonderful," Vincent said, his eyes shining. "Better than the Monteverdi." Cath reached out and took his hand without speaking.

"A big sound," Morgan pronounced. "Bigger than I'd expected." His satisfaction was so apparent that Cath belatedly realized he'd taken a professional risk in pushing for her, in recommending her so strongly.

"You were right all along. You and Vincent."

"I had no idea," said Stel Pye. "I had no idea you could sing like that."

Cath leaned over and kissed her on the cheek. "I'm so glad you came."

Dick Fairbrother hustled in to round everyone up for the reception. "Lots of good things: catered brownies, not food service, and a fruit tray. The undergrads will have eaten everything if you don't get there soon. Punch, coffee, too!" He was as ebullient as Cath was silent. He came over and kissed her, shook hands with everyone in sight, implored them all to get to the reception, which was jammed, he said. "A wonderful crowd. We need to meet the parents. Good administrative turnout, too," he added in an undertone to Morgan Daniels. "We all look like geniuses today." They laughed, but Cath took Vincent's hand again and didn't let go.

At the reception, Cath went around congratulating the string players, who, noisy with excitement, damp with effort and adrenaline, were clustered with their parents and friends. *Such wonderful support,* Cath said as the parents beamed. *You'd have made anyone sound good.* As she moved around the room, people came and crowded around her, so many people who wanted to say *Hello, Thank you, Lovely concert, I especially liked the section where . . .* that it was nearly an hour after the performance before she and Vincent got out of the building. In the deserted parking lot, high blue lights shone against a rosy western sky, and dark webs of leafless trees closed off the campus. The air was cold, and the chill from patches of ice went through her thin dress shoes. Still buffeted by the emotions of the performance, Cath took Vincent's arm unsteadily and leaned her head on his shoulder.

"It was really very beautiful," he said.

Cath smiled. "That was the very best we could do. The absolute very best."

"And now?" he asked.

She knew he was referring to the question that had hung between them ever since her divorce had come through: the question of their future, of her intentions—she already knew his. He was asking if the spell was broken, if her marriage was finished, if Derek was gone and exorcised for good, if it was safe for them both to have hopes. "Now," Cath said, "I think you should propose to me."

"Do you?" Vincent asked, slipping into the banter which so often concealed his deepest emotions. "Any reason except for my undying love?"

"Well, that principally," said Cath, "and the fact I'm close to four months pregnant."

He gave such a whoop, such a loud joyous yelp, that she nearly lost her balance. "You're sure?"

"I saw Dr. Campbell yesterday."

Another whoop of joy. Propelled by an irresistible gaiety of heart, Vincent began a happy little dance on the asphalt, skipping from one foot to another and throwing his arms in the air like a sword dancer. Watching him, laughing, Cath found Derek in her mind one last, vivid time. What she thought was that he would never have danced in a parking lot, because, unlike Vincent, he lacked the gift of happiness. Even his great talent, charisma, beauty, and intelligence had not brought him joy. There was nothing she could ever have done about that; she would never have been able to save him from sorrow. Never. Nor from Yvonne, either, except through disaster.

But she was different and Vincent was different. He orbited a different star. She watched as he pranced giddily in a big circle, then, returning, held out his arms. Cath could see the ice, literally and meta-phorically, but she stepped forward, resolved to be brave. They swirled around the lot, her roses rustling in the shiny wrapper, her long black dress lapping his legs. Underfoot, patches of ice, blue like skim milk, caught the electronic glow of the lights and the pink glimmer in the west, while overhead, night came down, dark and cold and pregnant with stars.